Dangweth Pengolod
: the
Answer
of
· Pengolod ·
to Ælfwine who asked him how came
it that the tongues of the Elves changed
and were sundered

Now you question me, Ælfwine, concerning the tongues of the Elves, saying that you wonder much to discover that they are many, akin indeed and yet unalike; for seeing that they die not and their memories reach back into ages long past, you understand not why all the race of the Quendi have not maintained the language that they had of old in common still one and the same in all their kindreds. But behold! Ælfwine, within Eä all things change, even the Valar; for in Eä we perceive the unfolding of a History in the unfolding: as a man may read a great book, and when it is full-read it is rounded and complete in his mind, according to his measure. Then at last he perceives that some fair thing that long endured: as some mountain or river of renown, some realm, or some great city; or else some mighty being, as a king, or maker, or a woman of beauty and majesty, or even one, maybe, of the Lords of the West : that each of these is, if at all, all that is said of them from the beginning even to the end. From the spring in the mountains to the mouths of the sea, all is Sirion; and from its first upwelling even to its passing away when the land was broken in the great battle, that also is Sirion, and nothing less. Though we, who are set to behold the great History, reading line by line, may speak of the river changing as it flows and grows broad, or dying as it is spilled or devoured by the sea. Yea, even from his first coming into Eä from the side of Ilúvatar, and from the young lord of

ᵗᵉⁿᵍʷᵃʳ (Tengwar inscription)

Works by J.R.R. Tolkien

THE HOBBIT
LEAF BY NIGGLE
ON FAIRY-STORIES
FARMER GILES OF HAM
THE HOMECOMING OF BEORHTNOTH
THE LORD OF THE RINGS
THE ADVENTURES OF TOM BOMBADIL
THE ROAD GOES EVER ON (WITH DONALD SWANN)
SMITH OF WOOTTON MAJOR

Works published posthumously

SIR GAWAIN AND THE GREEN KNIGHT, PEARL AND SIR ORFEO*
THE FATHER CHRISTMAS LETTERS
THE SILMARILLION*
PICTURES BY J.R.R. TOLKIEN*
UNFINISHED TALES*
THE LETTERS OF J.R.R. TOLKIEN*
FINN AND HENGEST
MR BLISS
THE MONSTERS AND THE CRITICS & OTHER ESSAYS*
ROVERANDOM
THE CHILDREN OF HÚRIN*
THE LEGEND OF SIGURD AND GUDRÚN*
THE FALL OF ARTHUR*
BEOWULF: A TRANSLATION AND COMMENTARY*
THE STORY OF KULLERVO
THE LAY OF AOTROU AND ITROUN
BEREN AND LÚTHIEN*
THE FALL OF GONDOLIN*
THE NATURE OF MIDDLE-EARTH
THE FALL OF NÚMENOR

The History of Middle-earth – by Christopher Tolkien

I THE BOOK OF LOST TALES, PART ONE
II THE BOOK OF LOST TALES, PART TWO
III THE LAYS OF BELERIAND
IV THE SHAPING OF MIDDLE-EARTH
V THE LOST ROAD AND OTHER WRITINGS
VI THE RETURN OF THE SHADOW
VII THE TREASON OF ISENGARD
VIII THE WAR OF THE RING
IX SAURON DEFEATED
X MORGOTH'S RING
XI THE WAR OF THE JEWELS
XII THE PEOPLES OF MIDDLE-EARTH

* Edited by Christopher Tolkien

The Peoples of
Middle-earth

CHRISTOPHER TOLKIEN

HarperCollins*Publishers*

HarperCollins*Publishers* Ltd
1 London Bridge Street
London SE1 9GF

HarperCollins*Publishers*
Macken House, 39/40 Mayor Street Upper
Dublin 1, D01 C9W8 Ireland

www.tolkien.co.uk
www.tolkienestate.com

This paperback edition 2015
24

First published in Great Britain by
HarperCollins*Publishers* 1996

A CIP catalogue record for this book is available
from the British Library

ISBN 978-0-261-10348-1

Printed and bound in the UK using
100% renewable electricity at CPI Group (UK) Ltd

To Baillie Tolkien

CONTENTS

PART THREE

TEACHINGS OF PENGOLOÐ

PART FOUR

UNFINISHED TALES

FOREWORD

In my Foreword to *Sauron Defeated* I wrote that I would not attempt a study of the Appendices to *The Lord of the Rings* 'at this time'. That was an ambiguous remark, for I rather doubted that I would ever make the attempt; but I justified its postponement, at least, on the ground that 'my father soon turned again, when *The Lord of the Rings* was finished, to the myths and legends of the Elder Days', and so devoted the following volumes to the later history of 'The Silmarillion'. My intentions for the twelfth book were uncertain; but after the publication of *The War of the Jewels* I came to think that since (contrary to my original conception) I had included in *The History of Middle-earth* a lengthy account of the writing of *The Lord of the Rings* it would be a strange omission to say nothing whatever of the Appendices, in which the historical structure of the Second and Third Ages, based on a firm chronology, actually emerged.

Thus I embarked on the study of the history of these works, of which I had little precise knowledge. As with the narrative texts of *The Lord of the Rings*, those of the Appendices (and of the Prologue) became divided, in some cases in a bewildering fashion, at the time of the sale of the papers to Marquette University; but I received most generous help, prompt and meticulous, from Charles Elston, the Archivist of the Memorial Library at Marquette, which enabled me to determine the textual relations. It was only now that I came to understand that texts of supplementary essays to *The Lord of the Rings* had reached a remarkably finished form, though in many respects far different from the published Appendices, at a much earlier date than I had supposed: in the period (as I judge) immediately following my father's writing of the last chapter of *The Lord of the Rings* in 1948. There is indeed a total absence in these texts of indications of external date; but it can be seen from many points that when they were written the narrative was not yet in final form, and equally clearly that they in fact preceded my father's return to the First Age at the beginning of the 1950s, as described in the Foreword to *The War of the Jewels*. A major upheaval in the historical-linguistic structure was still to come:

the abandonment of their own tongue by the Noldor returning
out of the West and their adoption of the Sindarin of Middle-
earth.

In my account I have of course concentrated on these early
forms, which belong so evidently, in manner and air, with the
narrative itself. I have little doubt that my father had long con-
templated such a supplement and accompaniment to *The Lord
of the Rings*, regarding it as an essential element in the whole;
and I have found it impossible to show in any satisfactory way
how he conceived it at that time without setting out the early
texts in full, although this naturally entails the recital, especially
in the case of the history of Arnor and Gondor, of much that is
known from its survival in the published versions of the Appendices. I have excluded the Appendix E ('Writing and Spelling'),
but I have included the Prologue; and I have introduced into
this part of the book an account of the origin and development
of the *Akallabêth*, since the evolution of the chronological
structure of the Second Age was closely related to my father's
original formalised computation of the dates of the Númenórean kings.

Following this part I have given three essays written during
his last years; and also some brief writings that appear to derive
from the last years of his life, primarily concerned with or
arising from the question whether Glorfindel of Rivendell and
Glorfindel of Gondolin were one and the same. These late writings are notable for the many wholly new elements that entered
the 'legendarium'; and also for the number of departures from
earlier work on the Matter of the Elder Days. It may be suggested that whereas my father set great store by consistency at
all points with *The Lord of the Rings* and the Appendices, so
little concerning the First Age had appeared in print that he was
under far less constraint. I am inclined to think, however, that
the primary explanation of these differences lies rather in his
writing largely from memory. The histories of the First Age
would always remain in a somewhat fluid state so long as they
were not fixed in published work; and he certainly did not have
all the relevant manuscripts clearly arranged and set out before
him. But it remains in any case an open question, whether (to
give a single example) in the essay *Of Dwarves and Men* he had
definitively rejected the greatly elaborated account of the houses
of the Edain that had entered the *Quenta Silmarillion* in about
1958, or whether it had passed from his mind.

The book concludes with two pieces further illustrating the instruction that Ælfwine of England received from Pengoloð the Wise in Tol Eressëa, and the abandoned beginnings of two remarkable stories, *The New Shadow* and *Tal-elmar*.

With the picture of such clarity in the tale of Tal-elmar of the great ships of the Númenóreans drawing into the coast, and the fear among men of Middle-earth of the terrible 'Go-hilleg', this 'History' ends. It is a long time since I began the work of ordering and elucidating the vast collection of papers in which my father's conception of Arda, Aman, and Middle-earth was contained, making, not long after his death, some first transcriptions from *The Book of Lost Tales*, of which I knew virtually nothing, as a step towards the understanding of the origins of 'The Silmarillion'. I had little notion then of what lay before me, of all the unknown works crammed in disorder in that formidable array of battered box-files. Nearly a quarter of a century later the story, as I have been able to tell it, is at last concluded.

This is not to say that I have given an account of everything that my father wrote, even leaving aside the great body of his work on the languages of the Elves. My father's very late writings have been selectively presented, and much further detail, especially concerning names and the etymology of names, can be found in texts such as those that I excerpted in *Unfinished Tales*, notably in the part of that book entitled 'The History of Galadriel and Celeborn'. Other omissions have arisen almost one might say from inadvertence as the work and its publication proceeded.

It began indeed as an entirely 'private' study, without thought or purpose of publication: an exhaustive investigation and analysis of all the materials concerned with what came to be called the Elder Days, from the earliest beginnings, omitting no detail of name-form or textual variation. From that original work derives the respect for the precise wording of the texts, and the insistence that no stone (especially stones bearing names) be left unturned, that characterises, perhaps excessively, *The History of Middle-earth*. *Unfinished Tales*, on the other hand, was conceived entirely independently and in an essentially different mode, at a time when I had no notion of the publication of a massive and continuous history; and this constitutes an evident weakness in my presentation of the whole corpus, which could not be remedied. When Rayner Unwin, to whom I am greatly indebted, undertook the uncertain venture of publishing my work on the history of 'The Silmarillion' (in form necessarily much altered) I had no intention of entering into the history of the Later Ages: the inclusion of *The Lost Road*, *The Drowning of Anadûnê*, *The Notion Club Papers*, and above all the history of the writing of *The Lord of the Rings*, extending the work far beyond my original design, was entirely unforeseen.

Thus it came about that the later volumes were written and published under much greater pressure of time and with less idea of the overall structure than the earlier. Attempting to make each book an independent entity in some degree, within the constraints of length, I was often uncertain of what it would or could contain until it was done; and this lack of prevision led to some misjudgements of 'scale' – the degree of fulness or conciseness that would ultimately prove appropriate to the whole. Thus, for example, I should have returned at the end of my account of the writing of *The Lord of the Rings* to give some description, at least, of the later developments in the chapters *The Shadow of the Past* and *The Council of Elrond*, and the evolution in relation to these of the work *Of the Rings of Power and the Third Age*. However, all the stories and all the histories have now been told, and the 'legendarium' of the Elder Days has been very fully mined.

Since the ceaseless 'making' of his world extended from my father's youth into his old age, *The History of Middle-earth* is in some sense also a record of his life, a form of biography, if of a very unusual kind. He had travelled a long road. He bequeathed to me a massive legacy of writings that made possible the tracing of that road, in as I hope its true sequence, and the unearthing of the deep foundations that led ultimately to the true end of his great history, when the white ship departed from the Grey Havens.

> In the twilight of autumn it sailed out of Mithlond, until the seas of the Bent World fell away beneath it, and the winds of the round sky troubled it no more, and borne upon the high airs above the mists of the world it passed into the ancient West, and an end was come for the Eldar of story and of song.

It has been an absorbing and inspiring task, from the splendours of the *Ainulindalë* or the tragedy of the Children of Húrin down to the smallest detail of changing expression and shifting names. It has also of its nature been very laborious, and with times of doubt, when confidence faltered; and I owe a great deal to all those who have supported the work with generous encouragement in letters and reviews. Most of all do I owe to my wife Baillie, to whom I dedicate this last volume: but the dedication may stand for the whole. Without her understanding and encouragement over the years, making mutual the weight of such a long and demanding work, it would never have been achieved.

Note on the text

As a general rule I have preserved my father's often varying usage in the spelling of names (as e.g. *Baraddur* beside *Barad-dûr*), but in certain cases I have given a standard form (as *Adûnaic* where *Adunaic* is sometimes written, and *Gil-galad* rather than *Gilgalad*). In his late texts he seldom used the diaeresis (as in *Finwë*), but (in intention at least) always employed Ñ to represent initial *ng* sounded as in English *sing* (thus *Ñoldor*); in this book I have extended the diaeresis throughout (other than in Old English names, as *Ælfwine*), but restricted Ñ to the texts in which it occurs.

References to *The History of Middle-earth* are given as in previous volumes in Roman numerals (thus VI.314). For the necessarily abundant references to the published Appendices I have used the letters RK (*The Return of the King*), the page-numbers being those of the three-volume hardback edition; and occasionally FR and TT for *The Fellowship of the Ring* and *The Two Towers*.

To the removal of error (especially in the citation of texts) from *The Peoples of Middle-earth*, which was completed under great pressure of time, Mr Charles Noad has contributed more perhaps than to any of the previous volumes which he has read independently in proof; and with the conclusion of the work I must express again my gratitude to him for his meticulous, informed, and extraordinarily generous labour. I wish also to record my appreciation of the great skill and care which Mr Norman Tilley of Nene Phototypesetters has again brought to this particularly demanding text – including the 'invisible mending' of errors in my manuscript tables.

Mr Noad has also made a number of suggestions for the improvement of the text by clarification and additional reference which where possible I have adopted. There remain some points which would have required too much rewriting, or too much movement of text, to introduce, and two of these may be mentioned here.

One concerns the translation of the curse of the Orc from the Dark Tower given on p. 83. When writing this passage I had forgotten that Mr Carl Hostetter, editor of the periodical *Vinyar Tengwar*, had pointed out in the issue (no. 26) for November 1992 that there is

a translation of the words in a note to one of the typescripts of
Appendix E (he being unaware of the existence of the certainly earlier
version that I have printed); and I had also overlooked the fact that
a third version is found among notes on words and phrases 'in
alien speech' in *The Lord of the Rings*. All three differ significantly
(*bagronk*, for example, being rendered both as 'cesspool' and as 'tor-
ture (chamber)'); from which it seems clear that my father was at this
time devising interpretations of the words, whatever he may have
intended them to mean when he first wrote them.

I should also have noticed that the statement in the early texts of
Appendix D (The Calendars), pp. 124, 131, that the Red Book 'ends
before the Lithe of 1436' refers to the Epilogue to *The Lord of the
Rings*, in which Samwise, after reading aloud from the Book over
many months, finally reached its end on an evening late in March of
that year (IX.120–1).

Lastly, after the proofs of this book had been revised I received a
letter from Mr Christopher Gilson in which he referred to a brief
but remarkable text associated with Appendix A that he had seen at
Marquette. This was a curious chance, for he had no knowledge of the
book beyond the fact that it contained some account of the Appendices; while although I had received a copy of the text from Marquette
I had passed it over without observing its significance. Preserved with
other difficult and disjointed notes, it is very roughly written on a slip
of paper torn from a rejected manuscript. That manuscript can be
identified as the close predecessor of the Appendix A text concerning
the choice of the Half-elven which I have given on pp. 256–7. The
writing on the verso reads:

> and his father gave him the name Aragorn, a name used in the
> House of the Chieftains. But Ivorwen at his naming stood by, and
> said 'Kingly Valour' (for so that name is interpreted): 'that he shall
> have, but I see on his breast a green stone, and from that his true
> name shall come and his chief renown: for he shall be a healer and
> a renewer.'

Above this is written: 'and they did not know what she meant, for
there was no green stone to be seen by other eyes' (followed by
illegible words); and beneath it: 'for the green Elfstone was given to
him by Galadriel'. A large X is also written, but it is not clear whether
this relates to the whole page or only to a part of it.

Mr Gilson observes that this text, clearly to be associated with work
on the Tale of Aragorn and Arwen (see p. 263), seems to be the only
place where the name *Aragorn* is translated; and he mentions my
father's letter of 17 December 1972 to Mr Richard Jeffery (*Letters* no.
347), who had asked whether *Aragorn* could mean 'tree-king'. In his
reply my father said that it 'cannot contain a "tree" word', and that
'"Tree-King" would have no special fitness for him'. He continued:

The names in the line of Arthedain are peculiar in several ways; and several, though Sindarin in form, are not readily interpretable. But it would need more historical records and linguistic records of Sindarin than exist (sc. than I have found time or need to invent!) to explain them.

PART ONE

THE PROLOGUE AND APPENDICES TO THE LORD OF THE RINGS

I

THE PROLOGUE

It is remarkable that this celebrated account of Hobbits goes so far back in the history of the writing of *The Lord of the Rings*: its earliest form, entitled *Foreword: Concerning Hobbits*, dates from the period 1938–9, and it was printed in *The Return of the Shadow* (VI.310–14). This was a good 'fair copy' manuscript, for which there is no preparatory work extant; but I noticed in my very brief account of it that my father took up a passage concerning Hobbit architecture from the chapter *A Short Cut to Mushrooms* (see VI.92, 294–5).

Comparison with the published *Prologue* to *The Lord of the Rings* will show that while much of that original version survived, there was a great deal still to come: the entire account of the history of the Hobbits (FR pp. 11–15) in section 1 of the *Prologue*, the whole of section 2, *Concerning Pipe-weed*, and the whole of section 3, *Of the Ordering of the Shire*, apart from the opening paragraph; while corresponding to section 4, *Of the Finding of the Ring*, there was no more than a brief reference to the story of Bilbo and Gollum (VI.314).

In order to avoid confusion with another and wholly distinct 'Foreword', given in the next chapter, I shall use the letter P in reference to the texts that ultimately led to the published *Prologue*, although the title *Foreword: Concerning Hobbits* was used in the earlier versions. The original text given in *The Return of the Shadow* I shall call therefore **P 1**.

My father made a typescript of this, **P 2**, and judging from the typewriter used I think it probable that it belonged to much the same time as P 1 – at any rate, to a fairly early period in the writing of *The Lord of the Rings*. In my text of P 1 in *The Return of the Shadow* I ignored the changes made to the manuscript unless they seemed certainly to belong to the time of writing (VI.310), but all such changes were taken up into P 2, so that it was probably not necessary to make the distinction. The changes were not numerous and mostly minor,[1] but the whole of the conclusion of P 1, following the words 'his most mysterious treasure: a magic ring' (VI.314), was struck out and replaced by a much longer passage, in which my father recounted the actual story of Bilbo and Gollum, and slightly altered the final paragraph. This new conclusion I give here. A part of the story as told here survived into the published *Prologue*, but at this stage there was no suggestion of any other version than that in *The Hobbit*, until the chapter *Riddles in the Dark* was altered in the edition of 1951. With all these changes incorporated, the typescript P 2 was a precise copy of the original version (see note 7).

This ring was brought back by Bilbo from his memorable journey. He found it by what seemed like luck. He was lost for a while in the tunnels of the goblins under the Misty Mountains, and there he put his hand on it in the dark.

Trying to find his way out, he went on down to the roots of the mountains and came to a full stop. At the bottom of the tunnel was a cold lake far from the light. On an island of rock in the water lived Gollum. He was a loathsome little creature: he paddled a small boat with his large flat feet, and peered with pale luminous eyes, catching blind fish with his long fingers and eating them raw. He ate any living thing, even goblin, if he could catch and strangle it without a fight; and he would have eaten Bilbo, if Bilbo had not had in his hand an elvish knife to serve him as a sword. Gollum challenged the hobbit to a Riddle-game: if he asked a riddle that Bilbo could not guess, then he would eat him; but if Bilbo floored him, then he promised to give him a splendid gift. Since he was lost in the dark, and could not go on or back, Bilbo was obliged to accept the challenge; and in the end he won the game (as much by luck as by wits). It then turned out that Gollum had intended to give Bilbo a magic ring that made the wearer invisible. He said he had got it as a birthday present long ago; but when he looked for it in his hiding-place on the island, the ring had disappeared. Not even Gollum (a mean and malevolent creature) dared cheat at the Riddle-game, after a fair challenge, so in recompense for the missing ring he reluctantly agreed to Bilbo's demand that he should show him the way out of the labyrinth of tunnels. In this way the hobbit escaped and rejoined his companions: thirteen dwarves and the wizard Gandalf. Of course he had quickly guessed that Gollum's ring had somehow been dropped in the tunnels and that he himself had found it; but he had the sense to say nothing to Gollum. He used the ring several times later in his adventures, but nearly always to help other people. The ring had other powers besides that of making its wearer invisible. But these were not discovered, or even suspected, until long after Bilbo had returned home and settled down again. Consequently they are not spoken of in the story of his journey. This tale is chiefly concerned with the ring, its powers and history.

Bilbo, it is told, following his own account and the ending he himself devised for his memoirs (before he had written most of them), 'remained very happy to the end of his days, and those were extraordinarily long.' They were. How long, and why so long, will here be discovered. Bilbo returned to his home at Bag-End on June 22nd in his fifty-second year, having been away since April 30th[2] in the year before, and nothing very notable occurred in the Shire for another sixty years, when Mr. Baggins began to make preparations for the celebration of his hundred and eleventh birthday. At which point the tale of the Ring begins.

Years later my father took up the typescript P 2 again. He made a number of minor alterations in wording, replaced the opening paragraph, and rewrote a part of the story of Bilbo and Gollum (improving the presentation of the events, and elaborating a little Bilbo's escape from the tunnels); these need not be recorded. But he also introduced a lengthy new passage, following the words (VI.313) 'but that was not so true of other families, like the Bagginses or the Boffins' (FR p. 18). This begins 'The Hobbits of the Shire had hardly any "government" ...', and is the origin of most of section 3 (*Of the Ordering of the Shire*) in the published *Prologue*, extending as far as 'the first sign that everything was not quite as it should be, and always used to be' (cf. FR p. 19).

Much of the new passage survived into the final form, but there are some interesting differences. In the third paragraph of the section (as it stands in FR) the new text in P 2 reads:

There was, of course, the ancient tradition in their part of the world that there had once been a King at Fornost away north of the Shire (Northworthy the hobbits called it),[3] who had marked out the boundaries of the Shire and given it to the Hobbits; and they in turn had acknowledged his lordship. But there had been no King for many ages, and even the ruins of Northworthy were covered with grass ...

The name *Northworthy* (for later *Norbury*) is not found in the *Lord of the Rings* papers, where the earlier 'vernacular' names are the *Northburg, Northbury*. See p. 225, annal c.1600.

The fourth paragraph of the section reads thus in the P 2 text:

It is true that the Took family had once a certain eminence, quite apart from the fact that they were (and remained) numerous, wealthy, peculiar, and of great social importance. The head of the family had formerly borne the title of The Shirking. But that title was no longer in use in Bilbo's time: it had been killed by the endless and inevitable jokes that had been made about it,

in defiance of its obvious etymology. The habit went on, however, of referring to the head of the family as The Took, and of
adding (if required) a number: as Isengrim the First.

Shirking is of course a reduction of *Shire-king* with shortening (and
in this case subsequent alteration) of the vowel, in the same way as
Shirriff is derived from *Shire-reeve*; but this was a joke that my father
decided to remove – perhaps because the choice of the word 'king'
by the Hobbits seemed improbable (cf. p. 232 and note 25, and
Appendix A (I, iii), RK p. 323).[4]

The new passage in P 2 does not give the time of the year of the Free
Fair on the White Downs ('at the Lithe, that is at Midsummer', FR
p. 19), and nothing is said of the letter-writing proclivities of Hobbits.
To the mention of the name 'Bounders' my father added '(as they were
called unofficially)'; the word 'unofficially' he subsequently removed,
thus in this case retaining the joke but not drawing attention to it.

It seems to me all but certain that this new element in the text is to
be associated with the emergence of the Shirriffs in the chapter *The
Scouring of the Shire* – where the office is shown to have been long
established 'before any of this began', as the Shirriff Robin Small-
burrow said to Sam (RK p. 281). The fact that the term 'Thain' had
not yet emerged does not contradict this, for that came in very late (see
IX.99, 101, 103). I have concluded (IX.12–13) that Book Six of *The
Lord of the Rings* was written in 1948.

At the end of this passage on the ordering of the Shire, which as
already noted (p. 5) ends with the words 'the first sign that everything
was not quite as it should be, and always used to be', the addition to
P 2 continues (with a later pencilled heading 'Tobacco'):[5]

> There is one thing more about these hobbits of old that must be
> mentioned: they smoked tobacco through pipes of clay or wood. A
> great deal of mystery surrounds the origin of this peculiar custom ...

From this point the remainder of section 2 in the final form of the *Prologue* was achieved in P 2 with only a very few minor differences: 'Old
Toby' of Longbottom was Tobias (not Tobold) Hornblower (on which
see p. 69), and the date of his first growing of the pipe-weed was 1050
(not 1070), in the time of Isengrim the First (not the Second); the third
of the Longbottom varieties was 'Hornpipe Twist' (not 'Southern
Star'); and it is not said of *sweet galenas* that the Men of Gondor
'esteem it only for the fragrance of its flowers'. There is also a footnote
to the words 'about the year 1050 in Shire-reckoning':

> That is about 400 years before the events recorded in this book.
> Dates in the Shire were all reckoned from the legendary crossing of
> the Brandywine River by the brothers Marco and Cavallo.

Later changed to Marcho and Blanco, these names do not appear in
the narrative of *The Lord of the Rings*: they are found only in the

further long extension to the *Prologue* concerning Hobbit-history (FR p. 13) and in the introductory note to Appendix C, *Family Trees* (RK p. 379).

For the history of the passage on pipe-weed, which began as a lecture on the subject delivered by Merry to Théoden at the ruined gates of Isengard, see VIII.36–9. After much development my father marked it 'Put into Foreword' (VIII.38 and note 36).[6] – On Isengrim Took the First and the date 1050 see VIII.45, note 37. When this addition to P 2 was written the old genealogical tree of the Tooks (given and discussed in VI.316–18), found on the back of a page from the 'Third Phase' manuscript of *A Long-expected Party*, was still in being.[7]

As has been seen (p. 4), in P 2 as revised the story of Bilbo and Gollum was still that of the original edition of *The Hobbit*, in which Gollum fully intended to give Bilbo the Ring if he lost the riddle-contest (see VI.86). The curious story of how the rewritten narrative in the chapter *Riddles in the Dark* came to be published in the edition of 1951 is sufficiently indicated in *Letters* nos.111, 128–9. In September 1947 my father sent to Sir Stanley Unwin what he called a 'specimen' of such a rewriting, not intending it for publication, but seeking only Sir Stanley's comments on the idea. Believing that it had been rejected, he was greatly shocked and surprised when nearly three years later, in July 1950, he received the proofs of a new edition with the rewriting incorporated. But he accepted the *fait accompli*. Beyond remarking that the full correspondence makes it very clear how, and how naturally, the misunderstandings on both sides that led to this result arose, there is no need to say any more about it here: for the present purpose its significance lies in the conclusion that the revision of P 2 cannot have been carried out after July 1950. In fact, I believe it to belong to 1948 (see pp. 14–15).

From the revised and extended text P 2, now in need of a successor, my father made a new typescript (P 3). This was again an uncharacteristically exact copy. It received a good deal of correction, in the earlier part only, but these corrections were restricted to minor alterations of wording and a few other details, such as the change of 'Northworthy' to 'Norbury' and of the date of Bilbo's departure with Gandalf and the Dwarves to April 28th (note 2). From this in turn an amanuensis typescript was made (P 4), but this my father barely touched. These texts both bore the original title, *Foreword, Concerning Hobbits*.

The next stage was a very rough manuscript, P 5, without title (but with *Concerning Hobbits* added later), and without either the section on pipe-weed or that on the story of Bilbo and Gollum, which while constantly moving the detail of expression further towards the final form held still to the original structure, and retained such features as the Shirking.[8] To convey the way in which the text was developed (with minute attention to tone, precision of meaning, and the fall of sentences) in successive stages I give this single brief example.

P 1 (VI.311)

And yet plainly they must be relatives of ours: nearer to us than elves are, or even dwarves. For one thing, they spoke a very similar language (or languages), and liked or disliked much the same things as we used to. What exactly the relationship is would be difficult to say. To answer that question one would have to re-discover a great deal of the now wholly lost history and legends of the Earliest Days; and that is not likely to happen, for only the Elves preserve any traditions about the Earliest Days, and their traditions are mostly about themselves – not unnaturally: the Elves were much the most important people of those times.

P 2 (as revised)

And yet plainly they must be relatives of ours: nearer to us than Elves are, or even Dwarves. For one thing, they spoke a very similar language (or languages), and liked and disliked much the same things as we used to. What exactly the relationship is would be difficult to say. To answer that question one would have to re-discover much that is now lost and forgotten for ever. Only the Elves now preserve traditions of the Elder Days, and even their traditions are incomplete, being concerned chiefly with Elves.

P 5

Yet plainly they are relatives of ours: far nearer to us than are Elves, or even Dwarves. They spoke the languages of Men, and they liked and disliked much the same things as we once did. What exactly our relationship was in the beginning can, however, no longer be told. The answer to that question lies in the Elder Days that are now lost and forgotten for ever. Only the Elves preserve still any traditions of that vanished time, but these are concerned mostly with their own affairs.

To the manuscript P 5, however, my father added, at the time of writing, much new material. One of these passages was that concerning the martial qualities of the Hobbits, or lack of them, the existence of arms in the Shire (and here the word *mathom* first appears in the texts of the *Prologue*), and the 'curious toughness' of Hobbit character. This was already fairly close to the published form (FR pp. 14–15), and its most notable omission is the absence of the reference to the Battle of Greenfields; the text reads here:

The Hobbits were not warlike, though at times they had been obliged to fight to maintain themselves in a hard and wild world. But at this period there was no living memory of any serious assault on the borders of the Shire. Even the weathers were milder ...

The original text of the chapter *The Scouring of the Shire* had no reference to the Battle of Greenfields: 'So ended the fierce battle of Bywater, the only battle ever fought in the Shire' (IX.93). In the second text (IX.101) my father repeated this, but altered it as he wrote to 'the last battle fought in the Shire, and the only battle since the Greenfields, 1137, away up in the North Farthing'. It seems a good guess that (as with the passage concerning the Shirriffs, p. 6) the appearance of the Battle of Greenfields in the *Prologue* soon after this (see below) is to be associated with the writing of *The Scouring of the Shire*.

It is convenient here, before turning to the rest of the new material that came in with the manuscript P 5, to notice a text written on two small slips and attached to the amanuensis typescript P 4. This is the origin of the passage concerning the founding of the Shire in the published *Prologue* (FR pp. 13–14), but it is worth giving in full.

In the Year 1 (according to the reckoning of Shire-folk) and in the month of Luyde[9] (as they used to say) the brothers Marco and Cavallo, having obtained formal permission from the king Argeleb II in the waning city of Fornost, crossed the wide brown river Baranduin. They crossed by the great stone bridge that had been built in the days of the power of the realm of Arthedain; for they had no boats. After their own manner and language they later changed the name to Brandywine. All that was demanded of the 'Little People' was (1) to keep the laws of Arthedain; (2) to keep the Bridge (and all other bridges) in repair; (3) to allow the king to hunt still in the woods and moors thrice a year. For the country had once been a royal park and hunting ground.

After the crossing the L[ittle] P[eople] settled down and almost disappeared from history. They took some part as allies of the king in the wars of Angmar (sending bowmen to battle), but after the disappearance of the realm and of Angmar they lived mostly at peace. Their last battle was against Orcs (Greenfields S.R. 1347?). For the land into which they had come, though now long deserted, had been richly tilled in days of yore, and there the kings had once had many farms, cornlands, vineyards, and woods. This land they called the Shire [*struck out:* (as distinct from the Old Home at Bree)], which in their language meant an ordered district of government and business – the business of growing food and eating it and living in comparative peace and content. This name Shire served to distinguish it from the wilder lands eastward, which became more and more desolate, all the way back to the dreadful Mountains over which (according to their own tales) their people had long ago wandered westward; also from the smaller country, the Oldhome at Bree, where they first settled – but not by themselves: for Bree they shared with the Bree-men. Now these folk (of whom the brothers Marco and Cavallo were in their day the largest and boldest) were of a kind concerning which the records of ancient days have little to say – except of course their own records and legends. They called themselves *Hobbits*. Most other peoples called them *Halflings* (or words of similar meaning in various languages), when they knew of them or heard rumour of them. For they existed now only in the Shire, Bree, and [?lonely] here and there were a few wild Hobbits in Eriador. And it is said that there were still a few 'wild hobbits' in the eaves of Mirkwood west and east of the Forest. *Hobbit* appears to be a 'corruption' or shortening of older *holbytla* 'hole dweller'.[10] This was the name by which they were known (to legend) in Rohan, whose people still spoke a tongue very like the most ancient form of the Hobbit language. Both peoples originally came from the lands of the upper Anduin.[11]

The date '1347?' of the Battle of Greenfields[12] suggests that it was here that that event re-entered from *The Hobbit* (see IX.119); later my father changed it here to 1147, while in *The Scouring of the Shire* it was first given as 1137 (IX.101 and note 31).

Returning briefly to the manuscript P 5, I have not yet mentioned that in this text, as originally written, the old passage in P 1 concerning the Hobbits of the Marish ('the hobbit-breed was not quite pure', 'no pure-bred hobbit had a beard', VI.312), still preserved in the revision of P 2, was now altered:

The Hobbits of that quarter, the Eastfarthing, were rather large and heavy-legged; and they wore dwarf-boots in muddy weather. But they were Stoors in the most of their blood, as was shown by the down that some grew on their chins. However, the matter of these breeds and the Shire-lore about them we must leave aside for the moment.

In the published *Prologue* this passage (apart of course from the last sentence) comes after the account of the 'three breeds' (FR p. 12), in which the Stoors had been introduced. But a further new passage was added on a separate page of the P 5 manuscript, corresponding to that in FR pp. 11–13 from 'Of their original home the Hobbits in Bilbo's time preserved no knowledge' to '... such as the Tooks and the Masters of Buckland'; and the account here of the Harfoots, Stoors and Fallohides was derived with little change from the earliest version of Appendix F, in which (p. 55, note 10) the idea of the 'three breeds' is seen in its actual emergence. The text in P 5 is all but identical to that in the final form, lacking only the statement that many of the Stoors 'long dwelt between Tharbad and the borders of Dunland before they moved north again', and still placing the Stoors before the Harfoots (see *ibid.*).

The word *smial(s)* first occurs, in the texts of the *Prologue*, in P 5. Its first occurrence in the texts of *The Lord of the Rings* is in *The Scouring of the Shire*: see IX.87 and note 16 (where I omitted to mention that in Pippin's reference to 'the Great Place of the Tooks away back in the Smials at Tuckborough' in the chapter *Treebeard* (TT p. 64) the words 'the Smials at' were a late addition to the typescript of the chapter).

A further manuscript, **P 6**, brought the *Prologue* very close to the form that it had in the First Edition of *The Lord of the Rings*.[13] This was a clear and fluently written text bearing the title *Prologue: Concerning Hobbits*; and here entered the last 'missing passage', FR pp. 13–14, from 'In the westlands of Eriador ...' to 'They were, in fact, sheltered, but they had ceased to remember it.'

The text of P 6 differed still from the published form in a number of ways, mostly very minor (see note 14). The text was not yet divided into four numbered sections, though the final ordering and succession of the parts was now reached; and the concluding section, on the finding of the Ring, was still the original story (see p. 7): this was derived, with some rewriting, from the text of P 2, but with a notable addition. After the reference to Gollum's saying that he had got the Ring as a birthday present long ago there follows:

Bilbo might indeed have wondered how that could be, and still more why Gollum should be willing to give such a treasure away, if his case had been less desperate, and if in fact Gollum had ever given him the present. He did not, for when he returned to his island to fetch it the Ring was not to be found.

This part then concludes much as in P 2, with the addition of a passage about Bilbo's secrecy concerning the Ring, and his disposal of Sting and the coat of mail; ending 'And the years passed, while he wrote in his leisurely fashion the story of his journey.'

In P 6 the 'Shirking' had disappeared, and in its place stood at first the title 'Elder', though this was replaced by 'Thane' before the manuscript was completed, and the spelling 'Thain' was substituted later (see p. 6). In this text the Battle of Greenfields, with the date S.R. 1147, appears.[14]

The manuscript ends with a passage, subsequently struck out, that was preserved with little material change as the conclusion of the Foreword to the First Edition of 1954. This begins with the remarks about the map of the Shire (now with the addition 'besides other maps of wider and more distant countries') and the 'abridged family-trees' that go back to P 1 (VI.313–14), but then continues:

There is also an index of names [*struck out:* with explanations] and strange words; and a table of days and dates. For those who are curious and like such lore some account is given in an appendix of the languages, the alphabets, and the calendars that were used in the Westlands in the Third Age of Middle-earth. But such lore is not necessary, and those who do not need it, or desire it, may neglect it, and even the names they may pronounce as they will. Some care has been given to the translation of their spelling from the original alphabets, and some notes on the sounds that are intended are offered. But not all are interested in such matters, and many who are not may still find the account of these great and valiant deeds worth the reading. It was in that hope that this long labour was undertaken; for it has required several years to translate, select, and arrange the matter of the Red Book of Westmarch in the form in which it is now presented to Men of a later Age, one no less darkling and ominous than were the great years 1418 and 1419 of the Shire long ago.[15]

This text was followed by a typescript copy (P 7). To this my father made the corrections and additions that brought the *Prologue* to its final form (many being made to its exemplar P 6 as well); and it was on this typescript that he rejected the original tale of Bilbo's encounter with Gollum and introduced the 'true tale' (FR pp. 20–2). The story is told here on appended pages in exactly its form in the published *Prologue*, ending with Gollum's cry '*Thief, thief! Baggins! We hates it for ever!*'

From this point, however, there are two texts. In one of these the original story, now become Bilbo's untrue version, is not mentioned at all, and the text moves at once from Gollum's cry of hatred to 'Of Bilbo's later adventures little more need be said here'. But my father was in doubt, whether or not to say anything in the *Prologue* about Bilbo's doctored accounts of the events; for at the point where the actual story ends ('*We hates it for ever!*') he subsequently added in this text a direction to a 'Note' on a separate sheet, which was apparently written quite independently. In this 'Note' (which was the origin of the passage concerning the two versions in FR p. 22) the satisfying explanation of the difference in the story as told in the two editions of *The Hobbit* is probably seen at its emergence. He began: 'This is not the story as Bilbo first told it to his companions and to Gandalf, or indeed as he *first* set it down in his book' (my italics), but struck out the words following 'Gandalf'; he then went on to say that though Bilbo set down the false story in his memoirs, and 'so it probably appeared in the original Red Book', nonetheless 'many copies contain the true account (alone or as an alternative), derived, no doubt, from notes made by Frodo or Samwise, both of whom knew the truth.'

On this page he noted (later): 'Alternative, if the only reference to this is made in Chapter II (second fair copy).' This is a reference to the final typescript of the chapter *The Shadow of the Past*, that went to the printers. The explanation of this apparently very obscure comment is as follows. On the text preceding the one to which he referred, that is to say the penultimate typescript, he had introduced a long rider[16] after Gandalf's words (FR p. 66) 'I put the fear of fire on him, and wrung the true story out of him, bit by bit, with much snivelling and snarling.' In this rider Gandalf continued:

'... I already suspected much of it. Indeed I already suspected something that I am sure has never occurred to you: Bilbo's story was not true.'

'What do you mean?' cried Frodo. 'I can't believe it.'

'Well, this is Gollum's account. Bilbo's reward for winning was merely to be shown a way out of the tunnels. There was no question of a present, least of all of giving away his "precious". Gollum confesses that he went back to his island to get it, simply so as to kill Bilbo in safety, for he was hungry and angry. But as Bilbo had already picked up the ring, he escaped, and the last Gollum knew of him was when he crept up behind and jumped over him in the dark. That is much more like Gollum!'

'But it is quite unlike Bilbo, not to tell the true tale,' said Frodo. 'And what was the point of it?'

'Unlike Bilbo, yes. But unlike Bilbo with the ring? No, I am afraid not. You see, half-unknown to himself he was trying to strengthen his claim to be its rightful owner: it was a present, a prize he had won. Much like Gollum and his "birthday-present". The two were more alike than you will admit. And both their tales were improbable and hobbitlike. My dear Frodo, Elven-rings are never given away as presents, or prizes: *never*. You are a hobbit yourself or you would have doubted the tale, as I did at once.

'But as I have told you, I found it impossible to question Bilbo on the point without making him very angry. So I let it be, for our friendship's sake. His touchiness was proof enough for me. I guessed then that the ring had an unwholesome power over its keeper that set to work quickly. Yes, even on Bilbo the desire for ownership had gripped at once, and went on growing. But fortunately it stayed at that, and he took little other harm. For he got the ring blamelessly. He did not steal it; he found it, and it was quite impossible to give it back: Gollum would have killed him at once. He paid for it, you might say, with mercy, and gave

Gollum his life at great risk. And so in the end he got rid of the thing, just in time.

'But as for Gollum: he will never again be free of the desire for it, I fear. When I last saw him, he was still filled with it, whining that he was tricked and ill-used. [But when he had at last told me his history ...

In the following (final) typescript of the chapter the rider is not present; but my father added a note at this point 'Take in rider' – and then struck it out. It was clearly at this time that he wrote the note referred to above, 'Alternative, if the only reference to this is made in Chapter II': he meant, if no more was to be said of the matter in Chapter II than Gandalf's words 'I put the fear of fire on him, and wrung the true story out of him, bit by bit, with much snivelling and snarling' – i.e., *without* the rider just given. If that rider was to be rejected, then a passage on the subject must be given in the *Prologue*. This was ultimately his decision; and the second of the two texts appended to P 6 is exactly as it stands in the published *Prologue*, p. 22: 'Now it is a curious fact that this is not the story as Bilbo first told it to his companions ...'[17]

The *Note on the Shire Records* entered in the Second Edition. In one of his copies of the First Edition my father noted: 'Here should be inserted Note on the Shire Records'; but he wrote against this later: 'I have decided against this. It belongs to Preface to *The Silmarillion*.' With this compare my remarks in the Foreword to *The Book of Lost Tales Part One*, pp. 5–6.

I have given this rather long account of the history of the *Prologue*, because it is one of the best-known of my father's writings, the primary source for knowledge of the Hobbits, on which he expended much thought and care; and also because it seems of special interest to see how it evolved in relation to the narrative of *The Lord of the Rings*. I will here briefly recapitulate some elements that seem to me to emerge from this history.

While it is not strictly demonstrable, I think it extremely likely that my father returned after many years to the original form of the *Prologue* (or *Foreword* as he still called it) about the time, or soon after it, when he was writing the long first draft that went from *Many Partings* through *Homeward Bound* and *The Scouring of the Shire* to *The Grey Havens*, that is to say in the summer of 1948 (IX.12–13, 108). I have pointed to a number of indications that this was so. On the one hand, we see the appearance, at successive stages in the writing of the *Prologue*, of the Shirriffs in the revision of the old P 2 text (p. 6); of the word *smial* in P 5 (p. 11); of the Battle of Greenfields in P 6 (see pp. 9–11); of the title of Thane (Thain) in the same text (p. 11). On the other hand, all these first appear in *The Scouring of the*

Shire – and in two cases, the Battle of Greenfields and the title of Thain, they were absent from the original draft of that chapter. I believe that my father's return to the Shire at the end of *The Lord of the Rings* provided the impulse for his renewed work on the *Prologue* and its subsequent extension by stages. Moreover it is seen from the history of this text how much of the account of Hobbits and their origins actually emerged *after* the narrative of *The Lord of the Rings* was completed – most notably, perhaps, the idea of their division into Harfoots, Stoors, and Fallohides, which entered from the earliest version of the appendix on languages (p. 10). Some of these new elements were then introduced into the existing narrative, such as *smials* into the chapter *Treebeard* (p. 11), or Stoors into the chapter *The Shadow of the Past* (p. 66, §20).

Successive stages in the development of the *Prologue* were accompanied, of course, by development in the Appendices, as is seen from references to the languages and to dates, and from such points as the naming of Argeleb II as the king who granted possession of the Shire to the Hobbits (p. 9, and see p. 209). But the latest stage of the *Prologue* discussed here, the manuscript P 6 and its typescript copy P 7, which in all other respects closely approached the final form, still had the old story of the finding of the Ring, and can therefore be dated, at the latest, to before July 1950.

NOTES

1   *The Hobbit* was now said to have been 'based on [Bilbo's] own much longer memoirs'; 'Earliest Days' was changed to 'Elder Days', and 'Folco Took' (by way of 'Faramond Took' and 'Peregrin Boffin', see VII.31–2) to 'Peregrin Took'; 'the one really populous town of their Shire, Michel-Delving' became 'the only town of their Shire, the county-town, Michel-Delving'; and the boots of the hobbits of the Marish became 'dwarf-boots'. The Hobbits' antipathy to vessels and water, and to swimming in it, was the only actual addition.

In a letter to Sir Stanley Unwin of 21 September 1947 (*Letters* no.111) my father said that he was sending 'the preliminary chapter or Foreword to the whole: "Concerning Hobbits", which acts as a link to the earlier book and at the same time answers questions that have been asked.' From the date, this must have been a copy of the original version, as corrected.

2   The date April 30th was corrected to April 28th on the text P 3 (p. 7).

3   *Northworthy*: the Old English *worð*, *worðig* were common elements in place-names, with the same general meaning as *tūn* (*-ton*), an enclosed dwelling-place.

4   The fiction of 'translation' from the 'true' Hobbit language (the

Common Speech) was inimical to puns in any case, good though this one was.

5   The extension to P 2 on the ordering of the Shire was a typescript, but that on pipe-weed was a manuscript written on slips. My father inserted them into P 2 as a unit, but they clearly originated separately: see note 6.

6   In his letter to me of 6 May 1944 (cited in VIII.45, note 36) my father said that 'if [Faramir] goes on much more a lot of him will have to be removed to the appendices – where already some fascinating material on the hobbit Tobacco industry and the Languages of the West have gone.' I remarked (VIII.162) that Faramir's exposition of linguistic history 'survived into subsequent typescripts, and was only removed at a later time; thus the excluded material on "the Languages of the West" was not the account given by Faramir.' It is indeed difficult to say what it was. On the other hand, the 'pipe-weed' passage was removed from the chapter *The Road to Isengard* before the first completed manuscript was written (VIII.39). It is in fact quite possible that the account of 'pipe-weed' in the long addition to P 2 does go back so early, seeing that it was certainly written quite independently of the first part of the addition, on the ordering of the Shire (see note 5).

7   Similarly the statement in P 1 (VI.311) that Bandobras Took, the Bullroarer, was the son of Isengrim the First was retained in P 2 as revised: in the published genealogical tree he became the grandson of Isengrim II. – A curious exception to my statement (p. 4) that P 2 as typed was a precise copy of the original version is found in the name *Bandobras*, which in P 2 became *Barnabas*; but this was probably a mere slip. It was corrected back to *Bandobras* in the revision.

8   In P 5 the name *Lithe* entered as my father wrote, changing 'at Midsummer' to 'at the Lithe (that is Midsummer)'.

9   The name *Luyde* for the month of March is found once elsewhere, a comparative calendar of Hobbit and modern dates written on the back of a page of the earliest text of the Appendix on Calendars (see p. 136, note 3). Above *Luyde* here my father wrote a name beginning *Re* which is certainly not as it stands *Rethe*, the later Hobbit name of March, but must be taken as an ill-written form of that name.

10 On *holbytla* translated 'hole dweller' see p. 49, §48 and commentary (p. 69).

11 This is to be associated with the early version of Appendix F, §§22–3 (p. 38): '... before their crossing of the Mountains the Hobbits spoke the same language as Men in the higher vales of the Anduin ... Now that language was nearly the same as the language of the ancestors of the Rohirrim'.

12   The second figure of the date 1347 is slightly uncertain, but it looks much more like a '3' than a '1'.

13   The significant changes made in the Second Edition (1966) were few. On FR p. 14, where the later text has 'There for a thousand years they were little troubled by wars ...' to '... the Hobbits had again become accustomed to plenty', the First Edition had simply 'And thenceforward for a thousand years they lived in almost unbroken peace' (thus without the mention of the Dark Plague, the Long Winter, and the Days of Dearth). At the beginning of the next paragraph the reading of the Second Edition, 'Forty leagues it stretched from the Far Downs to the Brandywine Bridge, and fifty from the northern moors to the marshes in the south', was substituted for 'Fifty leagues it stretched from the West-march under the Tower Hills to the Brandywine Bridge, and nearly fifty from the northern moors ...'. My father noted that the word 'nearly' was (wrongly) omitted in the text of the Second Edition, 'so this must be accepted'.

On FR p. 16, in 'Three Elf-towers of immemorial age were still to be seen on the Tower Hills', the words 'on the Tower Hills' were an addition, and in a following sentence 'upon a green mound' was changed from 'upon a green hill'. At the end of this first section of the *Prologue* (FR p. 17) the sentence 'Hobbits delighted in such things ...' was in the First Edition put in the present tense throughout.

Lastly, in the first paragraph of the third section, FR p. 18, the sentence 'Outside the Farthings were the East and West Marches: the Buckland; and the Westmarch added to the Shire in S.R. 1462' was an addition.

14   A few further differences in P 6 from the published text may be recorded. In the paragraph concerning the script and language of the Hobbits (FR p. 13) P 6 had: 'And if ever Hobbits had a language of their own (which is debated) then in those days they forgot it and spoke ever after the Common Speech, the Westron as it was named', this being changed to the reading of FR, 'And in those days also they forgot whatever languages they had used before, and spoke ever after the Common Speech ...' And at the end of the paragraph the sentence 'Yet they kept a few words of their own, as well as their own names of months and days, and a great store of personal names out of the past' is lacking. Cf. the original version of Appendix F, pp. 37–8, §§21–3.

The founders of the Shire were still Marco and Cavallo (pp. 6, 9; later changed to Marcho and Blanco); and the second of the conditions imposed on the Hobbits of the Shire (cf. the text given on p. 9) was 'to foster the land' (changed later to 'speed the king's messengers'). The first grower of pipe-weed in the Shire was still Tobias Hornblower, and still in the time of Isengrim the First

(p. 6); the date was apparently first written 1050 as before, but changed to 1020. Later Isengrim the Second and the date 1070 were substituted, but Tobias remained. The footnote to this passage (p. 6) was retained, but 'about 400 years' was later altered to 'nearly 350'. The third of the Longbottom brands now became 'Hornpipe Cake', but was changed back to 'Hornpipe Twist'.

15 In the Foreword as published this concluding paragraph began:

> Much information, necessary and unnecessary, will be found in the Prologue. To complete it some maps are given, including one of the Shire that has been approved as reasonably correct by those Hobbits that still concern themselves with ancient history. At the end of the third volume will be found also some abridged family-trees ...

When P 6 was written, of course, the idea that *The Lord of the Rings* should be issued as a work in three volumes was not remotely envisaged. The published Foreword retained the reference to 'an index of names and strange words with some explanations', although in the event it was not provided.

16 I did not carry my account of the history of *The Shadow of the Past* so far as this: see VII.28–9.

17 In this connection it is interesting to see what my father said in his letter to Sir Stanley Unwin of 10 September 1950 (*Letters* no.129):

> I have now on my hands two printed versions of a crucial incident. Either the first must be regarded as washed out, a mere miswriting that ought never to have seen the light; or the story as a whole must take into account the existence of two versions and use it. The former was my original simpleminded intention, though it is a bit awkward (since the Hobbit is fairly widely known in its older form) if the literary pretence of historicity and dependence on record is to be maintained. The second can be done convincingly (I think), but not briefly explained in a note.

The last words refer to the note required for the new edition of *The Hobbit* explaining the difference in the narrative in *Riddles in the Dark*. Four days later he wrote again (*Letters* no.130):

> I have decided to accept the existence of both versions of Chapter Five, so far as the sequel goes – though I have no time at the moment to rewrite that at the required points.

II

THE APPENDIX ON LANGUAGES

Beside the *Foreword: Concerning Hobbits*, whose development, clear and coherent, into the *Prologue* has been described in the last chapter, there is another text of a prefatory or introductory nature; and it is not easy to see how my father designed it to relate to the *Foreword: Concerning Hobbits*. Indeed, except in one point, they have nothing in common; for this further text (which has no title) is scarcely concerned with Hobbits at all. For a reason that will soon be apparent I give it here in full.

It was typed on small scrap paper, and very obviously set down by my father very rapidly *ab initio* without any previous drafting, following his thoughts as they came: sentences were abandoned before complete and replaced by new phrasing, and so on. He corrected it here and there in pencil, either then or later, these corrections being very largely minor improvements or necessary 'editorial' clarifications of the very rough text; in most cases I have incorporated these (not all are legible). I have added paragraph numbers for subsequent reference. Notes to this section will be found on page 26.

§1　This tale is drawn from the memoirs of Bilbo and Frodo Baggins, preserved for the most part in the Great Red Book of Samwise. It has been written during many years for those who were interested in the account of the great Adventure of Bilbo, and especially for my friends, the Inklings (in whose veins, I suspect, a good deal of hobbit blood still runs), and for my sons and daughter.

§2　But since my children and others of their age, who first heard of the finding of the Ring, have grown older with the years, this tale speaks more clearly of those darker things which lurked only on the borders of the other tale, but which have troubled the world in all its history.

§3　To the Inklings I dedicate this book, since they have already endured it with patience – my only reason for supposing that they have a hobbit-strain in their venerable ancestry: otherwise it would be hard to account for their interest in the history and geography of those long-past days, between the end of the Dominion of the Elves and the beginning of the

Dominion of Men, when for a brief time the Hobbits played a supreme part in the movements of the world.

§4   For the Inklings I add this note, since they are men of lore, and curious in such matters. It is said that Hobbits spoke a language, or languages, very similar to ours. But that must not be misunderstood. Their language was like ours in manner and spirit; but if the face of the world has changed greatly since those days, so also has every detail of speech, and even the letters and scripts then used have long been forgotten, and new ones invented.[1]

§5   No doubt for the historians and philologists it would have been desirable to preserve the original tongues; and certainly something of the idiom and the humour of the hobbits is lost in translation, even into a language as similar in mood as is our own. But the study of the languages of those days requires time and labour, which no one but myself would, I think, be prepared to give to it. So I have except for a few phrases and inscriptions transferred the whole linguistic setting into the tongues of our own time.

§6   The Common Speech of the West in those days I have represented by English. This noble tongue had spread in the course of time from the kingdoms of Fornost and Gondor, and the hobbits preserved no memory of any other speech; but they used it in their own manner, in their daily affairs very much as we use English; though they had always at command a richer and more formal language when occasion required, or when they had dealings with other people. This more formal and archaic style was still the normal use in the realm of Gondor (as they discovered) and among the great in the world outside the Shire.

§7   But there were other languages in the lands. There were the tongues of the Elves. Three are here met with. The most ancient of all, the High-Elven, which they used in secret as their own common speech and as the language of lore and song. The Noldorin, which may be called Gnomish, the language of the Exiles from Elvenhome in the Far West, to which tongue belong most of the names in this history that have been preserved without translation. And the language of the woodland Elves, the Elves of Middle-earth. All these tongues were related, but those spoken in Middle-earth, whether by Exiles or by Elves that had remained here from the beginning, were much changed.[2] Only in Gondor was the Elvish speech known commonly to Men.

§8   There were also the languages of Men, when they did not speak the Common Tongue. Now those languages of Men that are here met with were related to the Common Speech; for the Men of the North and West were akin in the beginning to the Men of Westernesse that came back over the Sea; and the Common Speech was indeed made by the blending of the speech of Men of Middle-earth with the tongues of the kings from over the Sea.[3] But in the North old forms survived. The speech of the Men of Dale, therefore, to show its relationship has been cast in a Northern form related distantly to the English which has been taken to represent the Common Speech. While the speech of the Men of Rohan, who came out of the North, and still among themselves used their ancestral language (though all their greater folk spoke also the Common Speech after the manner of their allies in Gondor), I have represented by ancient English, such as it was a thousand years ago, or as far back from us about as was the day of Eorl the Young from Théoden of Rohan.[4]

§9   The orcs and goblins had languages of their own, as hideous as all things that they made or used; and since some remnant of good will, and true thought and perception, is required to keep even a base language alive and useful even for base purposes, their tongues were endlessly diversified in form, as they were deadly monotonous in purport, fluent only in the expression of abuse, of hatred and fear. For which reason they and their kind used (and still use) the languages of nobler creatures in such intercourse as they must have between tribe and tribe.[5]

§10   The dwarves are a different case. They are a hard thrawn folk for the most part, secretive, acquisitive, laborious, retentive of the memory of injuries (and of benefits), lovers of stone, of metals, of gems, of things that grow and take shape under the hands of craft rather than of things that live by their own life. But they are not and were not ever among the workers of wilful evil in the world nor servants of the Enemy, whatever the tales of Men may later have said of them; for Men have lusted after the works of their hands, and there has been enmity between the races. But it is according to the nature of the Dwarves that travelling, and labouring, and trading about the world they should use ever openly the languages of the Men among whom they dwell; and yet in secret (a secret which unlike the Elves they are unwilling to unlock even to those whom they know are friends and desire learning not power) they use a strange slow-changing tongue.[6] Little is known about it. So it is that here such Dwarves as appear have names of the same Northern kind as the Men of Dale that dwelt round about, and speak the Common Speech, now in this manner now in that; and only in a few names do we get any glimpse of their hidden tongue.

§11   And as for the scripts, something must be said of them, since in this history there are both inscriptions and old books, such as the torn remnants of the Book of Mazarbul,[7] that must be read. Enough of them will appear in this book to allow, maybe, the skilled in such matters to decipher both runes and running hands. But others may wish for a clearer key. For them the Elvish Script (in its more formal shape, as it was used in Gondor for the Common Speech) is set out in full; though its various modifications used in writing other tongues, especially the High-Elven or the Noldorin, must here be passed over. Another script plays a part both in the previous account and the present one: the Runes. These also, as most other things of the kind, were also an Elvish invention. But whereas the flowing scripts (of two kinds, the alphabet of Rúmil and the alphabet of Fëanor, only the later of which concerns this tale) were developed in Elvenhome far from Middle-earth, the Runes, or *cirth*, were devised by the Elves of the woods; and from that origin derive their peculiar character, similar to the Runes of the North in our days, though their detail is different and it is very doubtful if there is any lineal connexion between the two alphabets. The Elvish *cirth* are in any case more elaborate and numerous and systematic. The Dwarves devised no letters and though they used such writing as they found current for necessary purposes, they wrote few books, except brief chronicles (which they kept secret). In the North in those regions from which the Dwarves of this tale came they used the *cirth*, or Runes. Following the general lines of translation, to which these records have been submitted, as the names of the North have been given the forms of Northern tongues in our own time, so the Runes were represented by the runes of ancient England. But since the scripts and runes of that account interested many of its readers, older and younger, and many enquiries concerning them have been made, in this book it has been thought better to give any runic inscriptions or writings that occur in their truer form, and to add at the end a table of the *cirth*, with their names, according to the usage

of Dale, among both Dwarves and Men. A list of the names that
occur is also given, and where they are taken from the ancient
records the language to which they belong is stated and their
meaning, or the meaning of their component parts, is added.

§12   The word Gnomish is used above; and it would be an
apt name, since whatever Paracelsus may have thought (if
indeed he invented the word), to the learned it suggests knowledge. And their own true name in High-Elven is Noldor, Those
that Know; for of the Three Kindreds of the Elves in the beginning, ever the Noldor were distinguished both by their knowledge of things that are and were in this world, and by the desire
to know yet more. Yet they were not in fact in any way like to
the gnomes of our learned theory, and still less to the gnomes of
popular fancy in which they have been confused with dwarves
and goblins, and other small creatures of the earth. They
belonged to a race high and beautiful, the Elder Children of the
World, who now are gone. Tall they were, fairskinned and grey-
eyed, though their locks were dark, and their voices knew more
melodies than any mortal speech that now is heard. Valiant they
were and their history was lamentable, and though a little of it
was woven with the fates of the Fathers of Men in the Elder
Days, their fate is not our fate, and their lives and the lives of
Men cross seldom.[8]

§13   It will be noted also that in this book, as before,
Dwarves are spoken of, although dictionaries tell us that the
plural of *dwarf* is *dwarfs*. It should, of course, be *dwarrows*;
meaning that, if each, singular and plural, had gone its own
natural way down the years, unaffected by forgetfulness, as
Man and *Men* have, then *dwarf* and *dwarrows* we should have
said as surely as we say *goose* and *geese*. But we do not talk
about *dwarf* as often as we talk of *man*, or even *goose*, and
memories are not good enough among men to keep hold of a
special plural for a race now relegated (such is their fate and the
fall of their great pride) to folktales, where at least some shadow
of the truth is preserved, or at last to nonsense tales where they
have become mere figures of fun who do not wash their hands.
But here something of their old character and power (if already
diminished) is still glimpsed; these are the Nauglir[9] of old, in
whose hearts still smouldered the ancient fires and the embers
of their grudge against the Elves; and to mark this *dwarves* is
used, in defiance of correctness and the dictionaries – although
actually it is derived from no more learned source than child-

hood habit. I always had a love of the plurals that did not go according to the simplest rule: *loaves*, and *elves*, and *wolves*, and *leaves*; and *wreaths* and *houses* (which I should have liked better spelt *wreathes* and *houzes*); and I persist in *hooves* and *rooves* according to ancient authority. I said therefore *dwarves* however I might see it spelt, feeling that the good folk were a little dignified so; for I never believed the sillier things about them that were presented to my notice. I wish I had known of *dwarrows* in those days. I should have liked it better still. I have enshrined it now at any rate in my translation of the name of Moria in the Common Speech, which meant The Dwarf-delving, and that I have rendered by The Dwarrow-delf. But Moria itself is an Elvish name of Gnomish kind, and given without love, for the true Gnomes, though they might here and there in the bitter wars against the Enemy and his orc-servants make great fortresses beneath the Earth, were not dwellers in caves or tunnels of choice, but lovers of the green earth and of the lights of heaven; and Moria in their tongue means the Black Chasm. But the Dwarves themselves, and this name at any rate was never secret, called it simply *Khazad-dûm*, the Mansion of the Khazad, for such is their own name for their own race, and has been so, since their birth in the deeps of time.[10]

The opening remarks of this text certainly suggest that the narrative of *The Lord of the Rings* had been completed; and this in turn suggests that it was not far removed in time from the renewed work on the *Foreword: Concerning Hobbits* (i.e. the *Prologue*). Though it is not much more than a guess, I incline to think that when my father began it he intended it as a personal and dedicatory 'preface', entirely distinct in nature from the account of the Hobbits, which was a prologue expressly relating to the narrative; but that involuntarily he was soon swept into writing about those matters of languages and scripts that he felt needed some introduction and explanation at least as much as did the Hobbits. The result was, clearly, a combination wholly unsuitable to his purpose, and he put it aside. I would also guess that it was the writing of this text that gave rise to the idea of a special Appendix on languages and scripts (ultimately divided into two); and this is why I place it at the beginning of this account of the evolution of what came to be 'Appendix F', *The Languages and Peoples of the Third Age*. Since I shall number the texts of this Appendix from 'F 1', it is convenient to call this anomalous 'Foreword' F*.

My father did not lose sight of this text, however, and later used elements from it, both in Appendix F[11] and in the *Foreword* that accompanied the First Edition of *The Fellowship of the Ring*, published in 1954. Since copies of the First Edition may not be easy to come by, I print the greater part of it again here (for the concluding section see p. 12 with note 15).

This tale, which has grown to be almost a history of the great War of the Ring, is drawn for the most part from the memoirs of the renowned Hobbits, Bilbo and Frodo, as they are preserved in the Red Book of Westmarch. This chief monument of Hobbit-lore is so called because it was compiled, repeatedly copied, and enlarged and handed down in the family of the Fairbairns of Westmarch, descended from that Master Samwise of whom this tale has much to say.

I have supplemented the account of the Red Book, in places, with information derived from the surviving records of Gondor, notably the Book of the Kings; but in general, though I have omitted much, I have in this tale adhered more closely to the actual words and narrative of my original than in the previous selection from the Red Book, *The Hobbit*. That was drawn from the early chapters, composed originally by Bilbo himself. If 'composed' is a just word. Bilbo was not assiduous, nor an orderly narrator, and his account is involved and discursive, and sometimes confused: faults that still appear in the Red Book, since the copiers were pious and careful, and altered very little.

The tale has been put into its present form in response to the many requests that I have received for further information about the history of the Third Age, and about Hobbits in particular. But since my children and others of their age, who first heard of the finding of the Ring, have grown older with the years, this book speaks more plainly of those darker things which lurked only on the borders of the earlier tale, but which have troubled Middle-earth in all its history. It is, in fact, not a book written for children at all; though many children will, of course, be interested in it, or parts of it, as they still are in the histories and legends of other times (especially in those not specially written for them).

I dedicate the book to all admirers of Bilbo, but especially to my sons and my daughter, and to my friends the Inklings. To the Inklings, because they have already listened to it with a patience, and indeed with an interest, that almost leads me to suspect that they have hobbit-blood in their venerable ancestry. To my sons and my daughter for the same reason, and also because they have all helped me in the labours of composition. If 'composition' is a just word, and these pages do not deserve all that I have said about Bilbo's work.

For if the labour has been long (more than fourteen years), it has been neither orderly nor continuous. But I have not had Bilbo's leisure. Indeed much of that time has contained for me no leisure at all, and more than once for a whole year the dust has gathered on my unfinished pages. I only say this to explain to those who have waited for this book why they have had to wait so long. I have no reason to complain. I am surprised and delighted to find from numerous letters that so many people, both in England and across the Water, share my interest in this almost forgotten history; but it is not yet universally recognized as an important branch of study. It has indeed no obvious practical use, and those who go in for it can hardly expect to be assisted.

Much information, necessary and unnecessary, will be found in the Prologue. ...

In the Second Edition of 1966 this Foreword was rejected in its entirety. On one of his copies of the First Edition my father wrote beside it: 'This Foreword I should wish very much in any case to cancel. Confusing (as it does) real personal matters with the "machinery" of the Tale is a serious mistake.'[12]

NOTES

1   On this passage see note 11.
2   On my father's conception at this time of the use in Middle-earth in the Third Age of Noldorin on the one hand, and of 'the language of the woodland Elves' on the other, see p. 36, §18, and commentary (pp. 65–6).
3   On this passage concerning the origin of the Common Speech see p. 63, §9.
4   In Appendix A (RK pp. 349–50) the length of time between the birth-dates of Eorl the Young and Théoden was 463 years.
5   My father was asserting, I think, that a language so base and narrow in thought and expression cannot remain a common tongue of widespread use; for from its very inadequacy it cannot resist change of form, and must become a mass of closed jargons, incomprehensible even to others of the same kind.
6   This passage concerning the Dwarves, absent in the original version of Appendix F, reappeared subsequently (p. 75), and was retained, a good deal altered, in the final form of that Appendix (RK p. 410).
7   My father deeply regretted that in the event his 'facsimiles' of the torn and burned pages from the Book of Mazarbul were not reproduced in The Lord of the Rings (see Letters nos.137, 139–40; but also pp. 298–9 in this book). They were finally published in Pictures by J. R. R. Tolkien, 1979.
8   This is where the passage that concludes Appendix F in the published form first arose. See further pp. 76–7.
9   Nauglir: curiously, my father here returned to the form found in

the *Quenta* of 1930, rather than using *Naugrim*, found in the *Quenta Silmarillion* and later (see V.273, 277; XI.209). As with those referred to in notes 6 and 8, this passage, absent in the original version of Appendix F, was reinstated and appears with little change in the published form (where the name is *Naugrim*).

10   Years later my father called this text a 'fragment' (see note 12). It ends at the foot of a page, the last words typed being 'since their birth', with 'in the deeps of time' added in pencil.

11   For passages from F* that reappeared in the course of the development see notes 6, 8 and 9. In this connection there is a curious and puzzling point arising from F*. In this text my father showed his intention to say something in the published work about the fiction of translation: that he had converted the 'true' languages of Men (and Hobbits) in the Third Age of Middle-earth, wholly alien to us, into an analogical structure composed of English in modern and ancestral form, and Norse (§§5–6, 8). Introducing this subject, he wrote (§4): 'It is said that Hobbits spoke a language, or languages, very similar to ours. But that must not be misunderstood. Their language was like ours in manner and spirit; but if the face of the world has changed greatly since those days, so also has every detail of speech ...'

One might wonder for a moment who said this of Hobbits, and why my father should introduce it only to warn against taking it literally; but it was of course he himself who said it, in the original version P 1 of the *Foreword: Concerning Hobbits* (VI.311, cited on p. 8): 'And yet plainly they must be relatives of ours ... For one thing, they spoke a very similar language (or languages), and liked or disliked much the same things as we used to.' This was repeated years later in the revision of the second text P 2 (see the comparative passages given on p. 8), but here the qualifying statement, warning against misunderstanding, is not present.

I cannot explain why my father should have made this cross-reference to the *Foreword: Concerning Hobbits*, in order to point out that it is misleading, nor why he should have retained it – without this caveat – in his revision of P 2. What makes it still odder is that, whereas in the first versions of Appendix F (in which the 'theory and practice' of the translation of the true languages was greatly elaborated) the remark is absent, it reappears in the third version (F 3, p. 73), and here in a form almost identical to that in F*: it is given as a citation, 'It has been said that "the Hobbits spoke a language, or languages, very similar to ours"', and this is followed by the same qualification: 'But this must not be misunderstood. Their language was like ours in manner and tone ...' As a final curiosity, by the time the third version of Appendix F was written the remark had been removed from the *Prologue* (see the citation from the text P 5 on p. 8), and replaced by 'They spoke the languages of Men, and they liked and disliked much the same things as we once did', though still, as in the published *Prologue*, in the context of this being a sign of the close original relationship of Hobbits and Men.

12   Many years after the writing of F* my father noted on the type-script: 'Fragment of an original Foreword afterwards divided into Foreword and Prologue'. This was misleading, because F* played no part in the *Prologue*, but did contribute to the Foreword of the First Edition and to Appendix F.

The history of Appendix F, whose final title was *The Languages and Peoples of the Third Age* (while the discussion of alphabets and scripts, originally joined to that of the languages, became Appendix E, *Writing and Spelling*), undoubtedly began with the abortive but not unproductive text F*, but the first version of that Appendix is best taken to be constituted by two closely related manuscripts, since these were written as elaborate essays to stand independently of any 'Fore-word'.

Long afterwards my father wrote (p. 299) that 'the actual Common Speech was sketched in structure and phonetic elements, and a num-ber of words invented'; and in this work he is seen developing the true forms in the Westron tongue to underlie the translated (or substituted) names, especially of Hobbits. A great deal of this material was sub-sequently lost from the Appendix. This original version is also of great interest in documenting his conception of the languages of Middle-earth and their interrelations at the time when the narrative of *The Lord of the Rings* had recently been completed; and also in showing how substantially that conception was still to be developed before the publication of *The Lord of the Rings* in 1954–5.

To date this version precisely seems scarcely possible, but at least it can certainly be placed before the summer of 1950, and I think that it may well be earlier than that.[1]

The earlier of the two texts, which I will refer to as F 1, is a fairly rough and much emended, but entirely legible, manuscript entitled *Notes on the Languages at the end of the Third Age*. A second manu-script, F 2, succeeded it, as I think, very soon if not immediately, with the title *The Languages at the end of the Third Age*. Writing with great care and clarity, my father followed F 1 pretty closely: very often changing the expression or making additions, but for the most part in minor ways, and seldom departing from the previous text even in the succession of the sentences. The two texts are far too close to justify giving them both, and I print therefore F 2, recording in the primarily textual notes on pp. 54 ff. the relatively few cases where different read-ings in F 1 seem of some significance or interest (but in the section on

Hobbit names, where there was much development in F 2, all differences between the two texts are detailed).

F 2 was substantially corrected and added to (more especially in the earlier part of the essay), and some pages were rewritten. These alterations are not all of a kind, some being made with care and others more roughly, and I have found it extremely difficult to determine, in relative terms, when certain of them were made: the more especially since the development after F 2 was not a steady progression, my father evidently feeling that a different treatment of the subject was required. Some corrections undoubtedly belong to a time when the text as a whole had been supplanted. I have therefore included in the text that follows all alterations made to the manuscript, and in most cases I have shown them as such, though in order to reduce the clutter I have in some cases introduced them silently, when they do no more than improve the text (largely to increase its clarity) without in any way altering its purport.

In general I treat F 2 as the representative text of the original version, and only distinguish F 1 when necessary. The paragraph-numbers are of course added editorially. A commentary follows the notes on pp. 61 ff.

The Languages
at the end of the
Third Age

§1   I have written this note on the languages concerned in this book not only because this part of the lore of those days is of special interest to myself, but because I find that many would welcome some information of this kind. I have had many enquiries concerning such matters from readers of the earlier selections from the Red Book.*

§2   We have in these histories to deal with both Elvish and Mannish² tongues. The long history of Elvish speech I will not treat; but since three [> two] varieties of it are glimpsed in this book a little may be said about it.

§3   According to Elvish historians the Elven-folk, by themselves called the *Quendi*, and Elven-speech were originally one. The primary division was into *Eldar* and *Avari*. The Avari were those Elves who remained content with Middle-earth [*struck out:*] and refused the summons of the Powers; but they and their

---

* *The Hobbit*, drawn from the earlier chapters of the Red Book, those mainly composed by Bilbo and dealing only with the discovery of the Ring.

many secret tongues do not concern this book. The Eldar were those who set out and marched to the western shores of the Old World. Most of them then passed over the Sea and came to that land in the Ancient West which they called Valinor, a name that means the Land of the Powers or Rulers of the World. But some of the Eldar [added: of the kindred of the Teleri] remained behind in the north-west of Middle-earth, and these were called the *Lembi* or 'Lingerers'. It is with Eldarin tongues, Valinórean or Lemberin [> Telerian] that these tales are concerned.

§4   In Valinor, from the language of that Elvish kindred known as the Lindar, was made a High-Elven speech that, after the Elves had devised letters, was used not only for lore and formal writing, but also for high converse and for intercourse among Elves of different kindreds. This, which is indeed an 'Elven-latin' as it were, unchanging in time and place, the Elves themselves called *Quenya*: that is simply 'Elvish'.

§5   Now after long ages of peace it came to pass, as is related in the *Quenta Noldorion*, that the Noldor, who were of all the kindreds of the Eldar the most skilled in crafts and lore, departed as exiles from Valinor and returned to Middle-earth, seeking the Great Jewels, the *Silmarilli*, which Fëanor chief of all their craftsmen had made. Their language, Noldorin, that at first differed little from the Lindarin or Quenya, became on their return to Middle-earth subject to the change which even things devised by the Elves here suffer, and in the passing of time it grew wholly unlike to the Quenya of Valinor, which tongue the exiles nonetheless retained always in memory as a language of lore and song and courtesy.*

§6   According to the Elves Men shared, though in a lesser degree, many of the powers of the Elves, and they were capable of devising languages of a sort for themselves, as indeed they have done, it seems, in many remote lands. But in fact Men did not in all regions go through the slow and painful process of invention. In the North and West of the Old World they learned language direct and fully made from Elves who befriended them in their infancy and early wanderings; and the tongues of Men

---

* On the other hand the Noldorin and Lemberin tongues, that had long been sundered, being now spoken by peoples dwelling side by side, drew closer together; and though they remained wholly distinct they became similar in sound and style.

which are, however remotely, of this origin the Quendi have at
all times found the more pleasant to their own ears. Yet soon
even these western tongues of Men became estranged from the
speech of Elves, being changed by process of time, or by Men's
own inventions and additions, or by other influences, notably
that of the Dwarves from whom long ago some Men learned
much, especially of delving, building, and smithying.

§7   Now the Men who first came westward out of the heart
of Middle-earth to lands near the shores of the Sea were called
by the Elves Atani,[3] [added: or in Noldorin the Edain,] the
Fathers of Men, and there was great friendship between the two
races. For when the Fathers of Men came over the mountains
they met for the first time the Eldar, or High-elves; and the Eldar
were at that time engaged in a ceaseless war with the Dark Lord
of that Age, one greater far than Sauron, who was but one of his
minions. In that war three houses of the Fathers of Men aided
the Elves, especially the Noldor, and lived among them and
fought beside them; and the people [> lords] of these houses
learned the Noldorin speech [struck out:] and forsook their own
tongue.[4]

§8   When at last that war was ended, most of the exiled
Noldor returned over the Sea to Valinor or to the land of
Eressëa that lies / within sight of it [> near]. Then the people of
the Three Houses of Men were permitted as a reward to pass
also over the Sea, if they would, and to dwell in an isle set apart
for them. The name of that great isle was Númenor, which in
Quenya signifies Westernesse. Most of the Fathers of Men
departed and dwelt in Númenor and there became great and
powerful; and they were fair of face and tall, and masters of
craft and lore only less than the Eldar, and the span of their lives
was thrice that of men in Middle-earth, though they remained
mortal nonetheless, and were not permitted to set foot upon
the shores of the deathless land of Valinor. They were called
Kings of Men, the Númenóreans, or in Noldorin the Dúnedein
[> Dúnedain].[5]

§9   The language of the Dúnedain was thus the Elvish
Noldorin, though their high lords and men of wisdom knew
also the Quenya, [> Thus in Númenor two languages were
used: the Númenórean (or Adûnaic), and the Elvish Noldorin,
which all the lords of that people knew and spoke, for they had
many dealings with the Elves in the days ere their fall. But their
men of wisdom learned also the Quenya, and could read the

books of Elven lore;] and in that high tongue they gave names to many places of fame or reverence, and to men of royalty and great renown.* After the Downfall of Númenor (which was contrived by Sauron) Elendil and the fugitives from the West fled eastwards. But in the west-lands of Middle-earth, where they established their exiled realms, they found a common tongue in use along the coast-lands from the Mouths of Anduin to the icy Bay of Forochel in the North. This tongue was in Noldorin called *Falathren* or 'Shore-language', but by its users was called *Yandúnë* [> *Andúnar* > *Adúnar*] (that is Westron) or *Sôval Phárë* (that is Common Speech).[6]

§10   This Common Speech was [*struck out:*] in the beginning / a Mannish language, and was indeed only a later form of the native tongue of the Fathers of Men themselves before those of the Three Houses passed over the Sea. It was thus closely akin to other languages of Men that [> Other languages of Men, derived also from the tongues of the Edain or closely akin to them] were still spoken further inland, especially in the northern regions of the west-lands or about the upper waters of the Anduin. Its spread [> The spread of the Westron] had been at first due largely to the Dúnedain themselves; for in the Dark Years they had often visited again the shores of Middle-earth, and in the days of their great voyages before the Downfall they had made many fortresses and havens for the help of their ships. One of the greatest of these had been at Pelargir above the Mouths of Anduin, and it is said that it was the language of that region (which was afterwards called Gondor) that was the foundation of the Common Speech. But Sauron, who could turn all things devised by Elves or Men to his own evil purposes, had also favoured the spread of this Common Speech, for it was useful to him in the governing of his vast lordship in the Dark Years.

§11   Beside the Common or Westron Speech, and other kindred tongues of Men, there remained also in the days of Elendil the languages of the Eldar. Strange though it may seem,

---

*Of Quenya form, for instance, are the names *Elendil*, *Anárion*, *Isildur*, and all the royal names of Gondor, including *Elessar*; also the names of the kings of the Northern Line as far as the tenth, *Eärendil*. [*Added:* The names of other lords of the Dúnedain such as *Arathorn*, *Aragorn*, *Boromir*, *Denethor* are for the most part Noldorin; but *Imrahil* and *Adrahil* are Númenórean (Adûnaic) names.]

seeing that the Dúnedain had dwelt for long years apart in Númenor, the people of Elendil could still readily converse with the Eldar that spoke Noldorin. The reasons for this are various. First, the Númenóreans had never become wholly sundered from the Noldor; for while those who had returned into the West often came to Númenor in friendship, the Númenóreans, as has been said, often visited Middle-earth and had at times aided the Elves that remained there in their strife with Sauron.[7] Again, the change and decay of things, though not wholly removed, was yet much delayed in the land of the Dúnedain in the days of its blessedness; and the like may be said of the Eldar.[8]

[*This paragraph was rewritten thus:* Beside the Common or Westron Speech, and other kindred tongues of Men, there remained also in the days of Elendil the languages of the Eldar; for many still dwelt in Eriador. With those that spoke Noldorin the people of Elendil could still readily converse. For friendship had long endured between the Númenóreans and the Noldor, and the folk of Eressëa had often visited Númenor, while the Númenóreans had sailed often to Middle-earth and had at times aided the Elves in their strife with Sauron.]

§12 Moreover, those were the days of the Three Rings. Now, as is elsewhere told, these rings were hidden, and the Eldar did not use them for the making of any new thing while Sauron still reigned and wore the Ruling Ring; yet their chief virtue was ever secretly at work, and that virtue was to defend the Eldar who abode in Middle-earth [*added:* and all things pertaining to them] from change and withering and weariness. So it was that in all the long time from the forging of the Rings to their ending, when the Third Age was over, the Eldar even upon Middle-earth changed no more in a thousand years than do Men in ten; and their language likewise.

§13 Now the people of Elendil were not many, for only a few great ships had escaped the Downfall or survived the tumult of the Seas. They found, it is true, many dwellers upon the west-shores who came of their own blood, wholly or in part, being descended from mariners and from wardens of forts and havens that had been set there in days gone by; yet all told the Dúnedain were now only a small folk in the midst of strangers. They used, therefore, the Westron speech in all their dealings with other men, and in the governing of the realms of which they had become the rulers; and this Common Speech became now enlarged, and much enriched with words drawn from the

language of the Dúnedain, which was, as has been said, a form
of the Elvish Noldorin [> and much enriched with words
drawn from the Adûnaic language of the Dúnedain, and from
the Noldorin]. But among themselves the kings and high lords,
and indeed all those of Númenórean blood in any degree, for
long used the Noldorin speech; and in that tongue they gave
names to men and to places throughout the realms of the heirs
of Elendil.

§14   In this way it had come about that at the time when the
events recorded in this book began it might be said that nearly
all speaking-folk of any race west of the east-eaves of Mirkwood spoke after some fashion this Common Speech; while
Men who dwelt in Eriador, the wide land between the Misty
Mountains and Ered Lindon, or in the coast-lands south of the
White Mountains, used the Westron only and had long forgotten their own tongues. So it was with the folk of Gondor (other
than the lords) and of the Anfalas and beyond; and with the
Bree-folk / and the Dunlendings [> in the North]. East of the
Misty Mountains, even far to the north, the Common Speech
was known; though there, as in Esgaroth [> as beside the Long
Lake] or in Dale, or among the Beornings and the Woodmen of
the west-eaves of Mirkwood, Men also retained their own
tongues in daily use. The Eorlings, or the Rohirrim as they were
called in Gondor, still used their own northern tongue, yet all
but their humbler folk spoke also the Common Speech after
the manner of Gondor; for the Riders of Rohan had come out
of Éothéod near the sources of Anduin only some five hundred
years before the days here spoken of.

[*The conclusion of this paragraph was rewritten thus:* The
Eorlings, or the Rohirrim as they were called in Gondor, still
used their own northern tongue; for the Riders of Rohan had
come out of Éothéod near the sources of Anduin only some five
hundred years before the days here spoken of. Yet all but their
humbler folk spoke also the Common Speech after the manner
of Gondor. In the Dunland also the Dunlendings, a dwindling
people, remnant of those who had dwelt in western Rohan
before the coming of the Rohirrim, still clung to their own
speech. This was wholly unlike the Westron, and was descended, as it seems, from some other Mannish tongue, not akin
to that of the Atani, Fathers of Men. A similar and kindred
language was probably once spoken in Bree: see (the footnote to
§25).]

§15   More remarkable it may be thought that the Common Speech had also been learned by other races, Dwarves, Orcs, and even Trolls. The case of the Dwarves can, however, be easily understood. At this time they had no longer in the west-lands any great cities or delvings where many lived together. For the most part they were scattered, living in small groups among other folk, often wandering, seldom staying long in any place, until, as is told in the beginning of the Red Book, their old halls under the Lonely Mountain were regained and the Dragon was slain. They had therefore of necessity long used the Common Speech in their dealings with other folk, even with Elves.* Not that Dwarves were ever eager to teach their own tongue to others. They were a secretive people, and they kept their own speech to themselves, using it only when no strangers were near. Indeed they even gave themselves 'outer' names, either in the Westron or in the languages of Men among whom they dwelt, but had also 'inner' and secret names in their own tongue which they did not reveal. So it was that the northern Dwarves, the people of Thorin and Dáin, had names drawn from the northern language of the Men of Dale, and their secret names are not known to us. For that reason little is known of Dwarf-speech at this period, save for a few names of mines and meres and mountains.

§16   The Orcs had a language of their own, devised for them by the Dark Lord of old, but it was so full of harsh and hideous sounds and vile words that other mouths found it difficult to compass, and few indeed were willing to make the attempt. And these creatures, being filled with all malice and hatred, so that they did not love even their own kind, had soon diversified their barbarous and unwritten speech into as many jargons as there were groups or settlements of Orcs. Thus they were driven to use the language of their enemies even in conversing with other Orcs of different breed or distant dwellings. In the Misty Mountains, and in other lingering Orc-holds in the far North-west, they had indeed abandoned their native tongue and used the Common Speech, though in such a fashion as to make it scarcely less unlovely than the Orkish.

§17   Trolls, in their beginning creatures of lumpish and brutal nature, had nothing that could be called true language

---

*For there was an ancient enmity between Dwarf and Elf and neither would learn the other's tongue.

of their own; but the evil Power had at various times made use of them, teaching them what little they could learn, and even crossing their breed with that of the larger Orcs. Trolls thus took such language as they could from the Orcs, and in the west-lands the Trolls of the hills and mountains spoke a debased form of the Common Westron speech.

§18   Elves, it may be thought, had no need of other languages than their own. They did not, indeed, like the Dwarves hide their own language, and they were willing to teach the Elven-tongues to any who desired or were able to learn them. But these were few, apart from the lords of Númenórean descent. The Elves, therefore, who remained in the west-lands used the Common Speech in their dealings with Men or other speaking-folk; but they used it in an older and more gracious form, that of the lords of the Dúnedain rather than that of the Shire. Among themselves they spoke and sang in Elven-tongues, and throughout Eriador from Lindon to Imladrist [> Imladris] they used the Noldorin speech; for in those lands, especially in Rivendell and at the Grey Havens, but also elsewhere in other secret places, there were still many of the exiled Noldor abiding or wandering in the wild. Beyond the Misty Mountains there were still Eldar who used the Lemberin [> Telerian] tongue. Such were the people of the elf-kingdom in Northern Mirkwood, whence came Legolas. Lemberin [> Telerian] was the native tongue also of Celeborn and the Elves of the hidden land of Lórien. There the Common Speech was known only to a few, for that people strayed seldom from their borders.*

§19   The Elvish names that appear in this book are mainly of Noldorin form; but some are Lemberin [> Telerian], of which the chief are [added: Thranduil,] Legolas, Lórien, Caras Galadon, Nimrodel, Amroth; and also the names of the House of Dol Amroth: Finduilas, [added: Adrahil,] and Imrahil. The exiled Eldar still preserved in memory, as has been said, the High-elven Quenya; and it was from Noldorin visitants to the Shire that Bilbo (and from him Frodo) learned a little of that ancient speech. In Quenya is the polite greeting that Frodo addressed to Gildor (in Chapter III). The farewell song of Galadriel in Lórien (in Chapter   ) [sic] is also in Quenya. Tree-

----

* But the lady of that land, Galadriel, was of Noldorin race, and in her household that language was also spoken.

beard knew this tongue as the noblest of the 'hasty' languages, and frequently used it. His address to Galadriel and Celeborn is in Quenya; so are most of the words and names that he uses which are not in the Common Speech.[9]

§20 To speak last of Hobbits. According to accounts compiled in the Shire, the Hobbits, though in origin one race, became divided in remote antiquity into three somewhat different breeds: Stoors, Harfoots, and Fallohides, which have already been described. [*Struck out:*] No tradition, however, remains of any difference of speech between these three kinds.[10]

§21 Since Hobbits were a people more nearly akin to Men than any other of the speaking-folk of the ancient world, it might be supposed that they would possess a language of their own, different from the languages of Men but not unlike them. Yet of this there is no evidence in any record or tradition. Admittedly none of the legends of the Hobbits refer to times earlier than some centuries after the beginning of the Third Age, while their actual records did not begin until after the western Hobbits had settled down, somewhere about Third Age 1300; but it remains remarkable that all such traditions assume that the only language spoken by Hobbits of any kind was the Westron or Common Speech. They had, of course, many words and usages peculiar to themselves, but the same could be said of any other folk that used the Common Speech as a native tongue.

[*The latter part of this paragraph, following* any record or tradition, *was rewritten thus:* They had, of course, many words and usages peculiar to themselves, but the same could be said of any other folk that used the Westron as a native tongue. It is true that none of the legends of Hobbits refer to times earlier than some centuries after the beginning of the Third Age, while their actual records did not begin until after the western Hobbits had settled down, somewhere about Third Age 1300, and had then long adopted the Common Speech. Yet it remains remarkable that in all such traditions, if any tongue other than the Common Speech is mentioned, it is assumed that Hobbits spoke the language of Men among whom, or near whom, they dwelt.]

§22 Among Hobbits [*added:* now] there are two opinions. Some hold that originally they had a language peculiar to themselves. Others assert that from the beginning they spoke a Mannish tongue [> Mannish tongues], being in fact a branch of the race of Men. But in any case it is agreed that after migration to Eriador they soon adopted the Westron under the influence of the Dúnedain of the North-kingdom. The first opinion is now favoured by Hobbits [> is favoured by many Hobbits], because of their growing distaste for Men;* but there is in fact no trace to be discovered of any special Hobbit-language in antiquity. The second opinion is clearly the right one, and is held by those of most linguistic learning. Investigation not only of surviving Hobbit-lore but of the far more considerable records of Gondor supports it. All such enquiries show that before their crossing of the Mountains the Hobbits spoke the same language as Men in the higher vales of the Anduin, roughly between the Carrock and the Gladden Fields.†[11]

§23 Now that language was nearly the same as the language of the ancestors of the Rohirrim; and it was also allied, as has been said above, both to the languages of Men further north and east (as in Dale and Esgaroth), and to those further south from which the Westron itself was derived. It is thus possible to understand the rapidity with which evidently the Hobbits adopted the Common Speech as soon as they crossed into Eriador, where it had long been current. In this way, too, is explained the occurrence among the western and settled Hobbits of many peculiar words not found in the Common Speech but found in the tongues of Rohan and of Dale.‡[12]

---

* Supported, as it appears to them to be, by the fact that among themselves they speak now a private language, though this is probably only a descendant, the last to survive, of the old Common Speech.

† [*The following footnote was added*: Though the Stoors, especially the southern branch that long dwelt in the valley of the Loudwater, by Tharbad and on the borders of Dunland, appear to have acquired a language akin to Dunlandish, before they came north and adopted in their turn the Common Speech.]

‡ In Gandalf's view the people of 'Gollum' or Smeagol were of hobbit-kind. If so, their habits and dwelling-places mark them as Stoors. Yet it is plain that they spoke [> as Stoors; though they appear to have used] the Common Speech. Most probably they were a family or small clan that, owing to some quarrel or some sudden 'homesickness', turned back east and came down into Wilderland again beside the River Gladden. There are many references in Hobbit legend to families or small groups going off on their own 'into the wild', or returning 'home'. For eastern Eriador was less friendly and fertile than Wilderland and many of the tales speak of the hard times endured by the early emigrants. It may be noted, however, that the names *Deagol* and *Smeagol* [> *Déagol* and *Sméagol*] are both words belonging to the Mannish languages of the upper Anduin.

§24   An example of this is provided by the name *Stoor* itself. It seems originally to have meant 'big', and though no such word is found in the Common Speech, it is usual in the language of Dale. The curious Hobbit-word *mathom*, which has been mentioned, is clearly the same as the word *máthum* used in Rohan for a 'treasure' or a 'rich gift'. The horn given at parting to Meriadoc by the Lady Éowyn was precisely a *máthum*. Again, *smile* or *smial*, in Hobbit-language the word for an inhabited hole, especially one deep-dug and with a long, narrow, and often hidden entrance, seems related to the word *smygel* in Rohan meaning 'a burrow', and more remotely to the name *Smeagol* [> *Sméagol*] (cited [in the footnote to §23]), and to *Smaug* the name in [> among men of] the North for the Dragon of the Lonely Mountain.[13] But most remarkable of all are the Hobbit month-names, concerning which see the note on Calendar and Dates.[14]

§25   The Hobbits in the west-lands of Eriador became much mingled together, and eventually they began to settle down. Some of their lesser and earlier settlements had long disappeared and been forgotten in Bilbo's time; but one of the earliest to become important still endured, if much reduced in size. This was at Bree, and in the country round about. Long before the settlement at Bree Hobbits had adopted the Common Speech, and all the names of places that they gave were in that language; while the older names, of Elvish or forgotten Mannish origin,* they often translated (as *Fornost* to *Norbury*), or twisted into a familiar shape (as Elvish *Baranduin* 'brown river' to *Brandywine*).

[*The end of this paragraph was rewritten thus:* ... (as *Fornost* to *Norbury*). The Elvish names of hills and rivers often endured changed only to fit better into Hobbit speech. But the Brandywine is an exception. Its older name was the *Malvern*, derived from its Noldorin name *Malevarn*, but the new name appears in the earliest records. Both names refer to the river's colour, often in flood a golden brown, which is indeed the meaning of the

---

* The Men of Bree, who claimed, no doubt justly, to have dwelt in those regions from time out of mind, long before the coming of Elendil, had of course also adopted the Common Speech, but there were names in those parts that pointed to an older Mannish tongue, / only remotely connected if at all [> unconnected] with the language of the Fathers of Men, or Westron. *Bree* is said in that tongue to have signified 'hill', and *Chet* (as in *Chetwood*, *Archet*) 'forest'.

Elvish name. *This was further changed to read:* ... Of this the Brandywine is an example. Its Elvish name was the *Baranduin* 'brown river'. Both names refer to the river's colour, often in flood a golden brown, but the Hobbit name is historically only a picturesque alteration of the Noldorin name.]

§26 As soon as they had settled down the Hobbits took to letters. These they learned, with many other matters, from the Dúnedain; for the North-kingdom had not yet come to an end in Eriador at that time. The letters used by the Dúnedain, and learned and adopted by the Hobbits, were those of the Noldorin or Fëanorian alphabet (see below).[15] It was soon after their learning of letters, about Third Age 1300, that Hobbits began to set down and collect the considerable store of tales and legends and oral annals and genealogies that they already possessed. The lore-loving Fallohides played a chief part in this. The original documents had, of course, in Bilbo's time long been worn out or lost, but many of them had been much copied. When the Shire was colonized, about Third Age 1600, it is said that the leading families among the migrants took with them most of the writings then in existence.

§27 In the Shire, which proved a rich and comfortable country, the old lore was largely neglected; but there were always some Hobbits who studied it and kept it in memory; and copying and compilation, and even fictitious elaboration, still went on. In Bilbo's time there were in the book-hoards many manuscripts of lore more than 500 years old. The oldest known book, The Great Writ of Tuckborough, popularly called Yellowskin, was supposed to be nearly a thousand years old. It dealt in annalistic form with the deeds of Took notables from the foundation of the Shire, though its earliest hand belonged to a period at least four centuries later.

§28 In this way it came about that the Hobbits of the Shire, especially in the great families, such as Took, Oldbuck (later Brandybuck), and Bolger, developed the habit, strange and yet not unparalleled in our times, of giving names to their children derived not from their daily language nor from fresh invention, but from books and legends. These to the Hobbits high-sounding names were often in somewhat comic contrast with the more homely family names. Hobbits were, of course, fully aware of this contrast and amused by it.

[*The following passage was an addition:* The sections that follow are written mainly for those of linguistic curiosity.

Others may neglect them. For these histories are intelligible, if it is assumed that the Common Speech of the time was English, and that if any language of Men appears which is related to the Common Speech, though not the same, it will be represented by languages of our world that are related to English: as for example the archaic language of Rohan is represented by ancient English, or the related tongues of the far North (as in Dale) by names of a Norse character.

But this was not, of course, historically the case. None of the languages of the period were related discernibly to any now known or spoken. The substitution of English (or forms of speech related to modern English) for the Common Speech (and kindred tongues) of the day has involved a process of translation, not only of narrative and dialogue but also of nomenclature, which is described below, for the benefit of those interested in such matters.]

On Translation[16]

§29 The linguistic situation sketched above, simple* though it is compared with that observable in many European countries in our times, presents several problems to a translator who wishes to present a picture of Hobbit life and lore in those distant days; especially if he is more concerned to represent, as closely as he can, in terms now intelligible the actual feeling and associations of words and names than to preserve a mere phonetic accuracy.

§30 The Elven-tongues I have left untouched. I have in my selection and arrangement of matter from the once famous and much copied Red Book reduced the citations of these languages, apart from the unavoidable names of places and persons, to a minimum, keeping only enough to give some indication of their sound and style. That has not been altogether easy, since I have been obliged to transliterate the words and names from the rich and elegant Fëanorian alphabet, specially devised for them, into our own less adequate letters, and yet present forms that while reasonably close to the phonetic intentions of the originals are

---

*We are in fact in this book only primarily concerned with the Elvish Noldorin and the Mannish 'Common Speech' (with some local variations), while the Quenya or 'Elf-latin' and the archaic tongue of the Rohirrim and the Elvish Lemberin make an occasional appearance.

not (I hope) too strange or uncouth to modern eyes.*[17]

§31   My treatment of the Common Speech (and of languages connected with it) has, however, been quite different. It has been drastic, but I hope defensible. I have turned the Common Speech and all related things into the nearest English equivalents. First of all, the narrative and dialogue I have naturally been obliged to translate as closely as possible. The differences between the use of this speech in different places and by persons of higher and lower degree, e.g. by Frodo and by Sam, in the Shire and in Gondor, or among the Elves, I have tried to represent by variations in English of approximately the same kind. In the result these differences have, I fear, been somewhat obscured. The divergence of the vocabulary, idiom, and pronunciation in the free and easy talk of the Shire from the daily language of Gondor was really greater than is here represented, or could be represented without using a phonetic spelling for the Shire and an archaic diction for Gondor that would have puzzled or infuriated modern readers. The speech of Orcs was actually more filthy and degraded than I have shown it. If I had tried to use an 'English' more near to the reality it would have been intolerably disgusting and to many readers hardly intelligible.

§32   It will be observed that Hobbits such as Frodo, and other persons such as Aragorn and Gandalf, do not always use quite the same style throughout. This is intentional. Hobbits of birth and reading often knew much of higher and older forms of the Common Tongue than those of their colloquial Shire-usage, and they were in any case quick to observe and adopt a more archaic mode when conversing with Elves, or Men of high lineage. It was natural for much-travelled persons, especially for those who like Aragorn were often at pains to conceal their origin and business, to speak more or less according to the manner of the people among whom they found themselves.

Note

§33   I will here draw attention to a feature of the languages dealt with that has presented some difficulty. All these languages, Mannish and Elvish, had, or originally had, no distinction between the singular and plural of the second

---

*A note on my spelling and its intended values will be found below.

person pronouns; but they had a marked distinction between the *familiar* forms and the *courteous*.

§34 This distinction was fully maintained in all Elvish tongues, and also in the older and more elevated forms of the Common Speech, notably in the daily usage of Gondor. In Gondor the courteous forms were used by men to all women, irrespective of rank, other than their lovers, wives, sisters, and children. To their parents children used the courteous forms throughout their lives, as soon as they had learned to speak correctly. Among grown men the courteous form was used more sparingly, chiefly to those of superior rank and office, and then mainly on official or formal occasions, unless the superior was also of greater age. Old people were often addressed with the courteous form by much younger men or women, irrespective of all other considerations.

§35 It was one of the most notable features of Shire-speech that the courteous form had in Bilbo's time disappeared from the daily use, though its forms were not wholly forgotten: a reversal of the case of *thou* and *you* in English. It lingered still among the more rustic Hobbits, but then, curiously enough, only as an endearment. It was thus used both by and to parents and between dear friends.

§36 Most of these points cannot be represented in English; but it may be remembered by readers that this is one of the features referred to when people of Gondor speak of the strangeness of hobbit-language. Pippin, for instance, used the familiar form throughout his first interview with the Lord Denethor. This may have amused the aged Steward, but it must have astonished the servants that overheard him. No doubt this free use of the familiar form was one of the things that helped to spread the popular rumour in the City that Pippin was a person of very high rank in his own country.

§37 Only in a few places where it seemed specially important have I attempted to represent such distinctions in translation, though this cannot be done systematically. Thus *thou* and *thee* and *thy* have occasionally been used (as unusual and archaic in English) to represent a ceremonious use of the courteous form, as in the formal words spoken at the coronation of Aragorn. On the other hand the sudden use of *thou*, *thee* in the dialogue of Faramir and Éowyn is meant to represent (there being no other means of doing this in English) a significant change from the courteous to the familiar. The *thee* used by Sam

Gamgee to Rose at the end of the book is intentional, but corresponds there to his actual use of the old-fashioned courteous form as a sign of affection.

§38   Passing from the translation of narrative and dialogue to *names* I found yet greater difficulties. For it seemed to me that to preserve all names, Elvish and Westron alike, in their original forms would obscure an essential feature of the times, as observed by the ears and eyes of Hobbits, through whom for the most part we are ourselves observing them: the contrast between a wide-spread language, as ordinary and diurnal to the people of that day as is English now to English-speakers, and the remains of far older more reverend and more secret tongues. All names, if merely transliterated, would seem to modern readers equally strange and remote.

§39   For instance, if I had left unaltered not only the Elvish name *Imladrist* [> *Imladris*] but also the Westron name *Carbandur*, both would have appeared alien. But the contrast between *Imladrist* [> *Imladris*] and *Rivendell*, a translation of *Carbandur*[18] and like it having a plain meaning in everyday language, represents far more truly the actual feeling of the day, especially among Hobbits. To refer to Rivendell as Imladrist [> Imladris] was to Men and Hobbits as if one now was to speak of Winchester as Camelot. Save that the identity was certain, while in Rivendell there still dwelt a lord of renown older than Arthur would be, were he still living in Winchester today.

§40   To translate the names in the Common Speech into English in this way has the advantage also that it often, as in the case of Rivendell, provides the key to the meaning of the Elvish name as well; for the one was frequently a direct translation of the other. This is not, however, always so. Some place-names have no meaning now discernible and derive, no doubt, from still older and forgotten days. In some cases the names had different meanings in different tongues. Thus the C.S. *Dwarrowdelf*[*][19] was a translation of the Dwarvish name *Khazad-dûm*,

---

* That is 'Dwarves' mine'. I have translated the actual C.S. *Phûru-nargian* as *Dwarrowdelf*, since in Bilbo's time the word *phûru* (related to *phur-* 'to delve') was obsolete in ordinary speech, and *nargian* contained a derivative form of *narac* 'dwarf' that had long disappeared from use. *Dwarrow* is what the ancient English genitive plural *dwerga* 'of dwarves' would have become had it survived in use or in a place-name.

whereas the Elvish name *Moria* (older *Mornyā*) meant 'black pit'.

§41 The nomenclature of the Hobbits themselves and of the places in which they lived has, nonetheless, presented some obstacles to the satisfactory carrying out of this process of translation. Their place-names, being (in the Shire especially) almost all originally of C.S. form, have proved least difficult. I have converted them into as nearly similar English terms as I could find, using the elements found in English place-names that seemed suitable both in sense and in period: that is in being still current (like *hill*), or slightly altered or reduced from current words (like *ton* beside *town*), or no longer found outside place-names (like *wich*, *bold*, *bottle*). *The Shire* seems to me very adequately to translate the Hobbit *Sūza-t*, since this word was now only used by them with reference to their country, though originally it had meant 'a sphere of occupation (as of the land claimed by a family or clan), of office, or business'. In Gondor the word *sūza* was still applied to the divisions of the realm, such as Anórien, Ithilien, Lebennin, for which in Noldorin the word *lhann* was used. Similarly *farthing* has been used for the four divisions of the Shire, because the Hobbit word *tharni* was an old word for 'quarter' seldom used in ordinary language, where the word for 'quarter' was *tharantīn* 'fourth part'. In Gondor *tharni* was used for a silver coin, the fourth part of the *castar* (in Noldorin the *canath* or fourth part of the *mirian*).[20]

§42 The personal names of the Hobbits were, however, much more awkward to manage on this system. Rightly or wrongly, I have attempted to translate these also into English terms, or to substitute equivalents, wherever possible. Many of the family names have more or less obvious meanings in the Common Speech: such as *Goodenough*, *Bracegirdle*, *Proudfoot*, *Burrows*, and the like, and these can fairly be treated in the same way as the place-names.* In these cases translation will not, I think, be quarrelled with, and may even be allowed to be necessary. For if his name clearly meant to contemporaries 'horn-blower', it is truer to the facts to call a character Hornblower than *Raspūta*,[21] which though the actual Hobbit

---

* Some family-names, but fewer than in England, for the use of such names outside a few 'great families' was of more recent development, were actually place-names or derived from them. *Gamgee* is one (see below).

sound-form is now meaningless. But, of course, if a large part of the names are thus anglicized the rest must be made to fit; for a mixture of English and alien names would give a wholly false impression. It is thus with the less clearly interpretable names that difficulties arise. Some are border-line cases, such as *Baggins* itself, which because of its importance I have dealt with below more fully. Some defy translation, since they were to the Hobbits themselves just 'names', of forgotten origin and meaning. *Tūc*,[22] for instance, the name of the most eminent of the 'great families' of the Shire. According to their own tradition *tūca* was an old word meaning 'daring',[23] but this appears to be a wholly unfounded guess; and I have in this case been content with anglicization of the form to *Took*.

§43   More debatable, perhaps, has been my procedure with the many curious names that Shire-hobbits, as observed above, gave to their children. Here I long hesitated between leaving them alone, and finding equivalents for them. I have in the end compromised. I have left some unaltered. These are the not uncommon names which even to Hobbits had no 'meaning' or derivation or connexion with books or legends: names such as *Bilbo, Bungo, Bingo, Polo, Porro, Ponto*. Hobbits readily coined such names, and I do not think that the impression made by them in their day differed much from their effect today.*[24] But it would have given a very false impression of Hobbitry to the modern reader, if these personal names had in general been simply transliterated. All would then have today sounded equally outlandish, whereas to Hobbits personal names had many gradations of association and suggestion. Some derived from early history and ancient Hobbit-legend; some from stories about Elves and Men and even about dwarves and giants. Some were rare, others familiar; some comic in tone, others romantic or elevated; some were of high and some of lower social standing.

§44   It seemed to me that, once embarked on translation, even of dialogue, names of this sort would be best represented by drawing on the similar wealth of names that we find or could find in our own traditions, in Celtic, Frankish, Latin and Greek and other sources.

§45   This method entails, of course, far-reaching alteration

---

* In fact they ended as a rule in *a (Bunga)* not *o*, since an ending *a* was as a rule masculine. I have changed the *a* to *o*.

of the actual phonetic forms of such given-names; but I do not feel it more illegitimate than altering *Raspūta* to *Hornblower*, or indeed than translating the dialogue of the Red Book into English, whereby naturally its true sound is changed and many of its verbal points are obscured. I have, in any case, done the 'translation' with some care. The fondness of families for runs of similar names, or of fathers for giving to their sons names that either alliterated with their own or had a similar ending, has been duly represented.* The choice of equivalents has been directed partly by meaning (where this is discernible in the original names), partly by general tone, and partly by length and phonetic style. The heroic and romantic names, of Fallohide legend according to the Hobbits, specially but not solely affected by Tooks, have been represented by names of a Germanic or Frankish cast. 'Classical' names or ones of similar form on the other hand represent usually names derived by Hobbits from tales of ancient times and far kingdoms of Men.†[25]

§46   Hobbits very frequently gave their daughters flower-names. But even these are not so simple to deal with as might be expected. Where the flower is certainly to be identified I have naturally translated the name into English (or botanical Latin). But not all the wild flowers of the Shire, and certainly not all the flowers cultivated in its gardens can be identified with flowers that are now familiar. In cases of doubt I have done the best that I could. For instance: I have translated *Hamanullas*[26] by *Lobelia*, because although I do not know precisely what flower is intended, *hamanullas* appears to have been usually small and blue and cultivated in gardens, and the word seems to have been a gardener's rather than a popular name.

§47   For the benefit of the curious in such matters I add here a few notes in supplement of what has been said above to illustrate my procedure.

---

* The curious alternation between initial H and initial I in the names of the Old Took's many children represents an actual alternation between S and E.

† Thus the perhaps to us rather ridiculous subnames or titles of the Brandybucks adopted by the heads of the family, *Astyanax*, *Aureus*, *Magnificus*, were originally half-jesting and were in fact drawn from traditions about the Kings at Norbury. [This note was later struck out.]

Family names

Took   Hobbit *Tūc*, as noted above.[27]

Baggins   H. *Labingi*. It is by no means certain that this name is really connected with C.S. *labin* 'a bag'; but it was believed to be so, and one may compare *Labin-nec* 'Bag End' as the name of the residence of Bungo Baggins *(Bunga Labingi)*. I have accordingly rendered the name *Labingi* by *Baggins*, which gives, I think, a very close equivalent in readily appreciable modern terms.

Brandybuck   Earlier *Oldbuck*. These are direct translations of H. *Assargamba* [> *Brandugamba*] and *Zaragamba*.[28] [*Added*: *Zaragamba* is translated by sense, but since *Zaragamba* (Old-buck) was altered to *Brandugamba* by adoption of the first half of the river-name *(Branduhim)* I have used for it *Brandybuck*. For the treatment of the river-name *Branduhim* see (the note at the end of the text, §58).]

Bolger   Merely an anglicized form of H. *Bolgra*. By chance in C.S. *bolg-* has much the same significance as our 'bulge', so that if *Bolger* suggests to a modern reader a certain fatness and rotundity, so did *Bolgra* in its own time and place.

Boffin   Anglicized from H. *Bophan*. This was said (by members of the family) to mean 'one who laughs loud'. I thought at first, therefore, of rendering it by *Loffin*; but since, as in the case of *Took*, the family tradition is a mere guess, while in C.S. *Bophan* had in fact no suggestion of laughter, I have remained content with a slight anglicization.[29]

Gamgee   H. *Galbassi*. A difficult name. According to family tradition (in this case reliable) duly set out by Sam Gamgee at the end of the Red Book, this name was really derived from a place-name: *Galb(b)as*. That name I have closely rendered by Gamwich (to be pronounced *Gammidge*), comparing *galb-* = *Gam* with C.S. *galap*, *galab-* = 'game'; and the ending *bas* in place-names with our *-wick*, *-wich*. *Galbassi* may thus be fairly represented by *Gammidgee*. In adopting the spelling *Gamgee* I have been led astray by Sam Gamgee's connexion with the family of Cotton into a jest which though Hobbit-like enough does not really reside in the suggestions of the names *Galbassi* and *Lothran* to people of the Shire.[30]

Cotton   H. *Lothran*. A not uncommon village name in the Shire, corresponding closely to our *Cotton (cot-tūn)*, being derived from C.S. *hlotho* 'a two-roomed dwelling', and *rān* 'a village, a small group of dwellings on a hill-side'. But in this case the name may be an alteration of *hloth-ram(a)*, 'cotman, cottager'. *Lothram*, which I have rendered *Cotman*, was the name of Farmer Cotton's grandfather. It is notable that, though the resemblance is not so complete as between our *Cotton* and the noun *cotton*, in C.S. the words *luthur*, *luthran* meant 'down, fluff'. But unfortunately no such suggestions are associated with *Galbas*, and the village of that name was known only locally for rope-making, and no tissues were produced there of any fibre softer than hemp.

§48 *Hobbit*

Hobbit This, I confess, is my own invention; but not one devised at random. This is its origin. It is, for one thing, not wholly unlike the actual word in the Shire, which was *cūbuc* (plural *cūbugin*).* But this *cūbuc* was not a word of general use in the Common Speech and required an equivalent that though natural enough in an English context did not actually occur in standard English. Some Hobbit-historians have held that *cūbuc* was an ancient native word, perhaps the last survivor of their own forgotten language. I believe, however, that this is not the case. The word is, I think, a local reduction of an early C.S. name given to Hobbits, or adopted by them in self-description, when they came into contact with Men. It appears to be derived from an obsolete *cūbug* 'hole-dweller', which elsewhere fell out of use. In support of this I would point to the fact that Meriadoc himself actually records that the King of Rohan used the word *cūgbagu* 'hole-dweller' for *cūbuc* or 'Hobbit'. Now the Rohirrim spoke a language that was in effect an archaic form of the Common Speech.† The

---

*For another, I must admit that its faint suggestion of *rabbit* appealed to me. Not that hobbits at all resembled rabbits, unless it be in burrowing. Still, a jest is a jest as all *cūbugin* will allow, and after all it does so happen that the coney (well-known in the Shire if not in ancient England) was called *tapuc*, a name recalling *cūbuc*, if not so clearly as *hobbit* recalls *rabbit*. [This note was later struck out.]

† More accurately: the tongue of the Mark of Rohan was derived from a northern speech which, belonging at first to the Middle Anduin, had later moved north to the upper waters of that river,

continued on page 50

primitive form represented by Rohan *cūg-bagu* would in the
later C.S. have acquired the form *cūbug(u)*, and so Hobbit
cūbuc.[31] Since, as is explained below, I have represented C.S.
by modern English and have therefore turned the language of
Rohan into archaic English terms also, I have converted the
archaic *cūgbagu* of Rohan into an ancient English *hol-bytla*
'hole-dweller'. Of this *hol-bytla* (with the common loss of *l*
in English between *a*, *o*, *u*, and *b*, *m*, *v*) my fictitious *hobbit*
would be a not impossible local 'corruption'.

§49   *Personal names*

Bilbo   The actual H. name was *Bilba*, as explained above.[32]

Frodo   On the other hand the H. name was *Maura*.[33] This was
not a common name in the Shire, but I think it probably once
had a meaning, even if that had long been forgotten. No word
maur- can be found in the contemporary C.S., but again
recourse to comparison with the language of Rohan is
enlightening. In that language there was an adjective *maur-*,
no longer current at this time, but familiar in verse or higher
styles of speech; it meant 'wise, experienced'. I have, therefore, rendered *Maura* by *Frodo*, an old Germanic name, that
appears to contain the word *frōd* which in ancient English
corresponded closely in meaning to Rohan *maur*.

Meriadoc (Merry)   The real name was *Chilimanzar* [> *Cilimanzar*], a high-sounding and legendary name. I have chosen
Meriadoc for the following reasons. Buckland in many ways
occupied a position with regard to the Shire such as Wales
does to England; and it is not wholly inappropriate, therefore, to represent its many very peculiar names by names of
a Celtic or specifically Welsh character. Among such names
I chose *Meriadoc*, mainly because it gives naturally a
shortening 'Merry'; for the abbreviation of *Chilimanzar*
[> *Cilimanzar*] by which this character was usually known
was *Chilic* [> *Cilic*], a C.S. word meaning exactly 'gay or
merry'.[34]

before coming south in the days of Eorl. It was thus nearly akin to the
language of the lower Anduin, the basis of the C.S., but isolated in the
North it had changed far less and had remained little mingled with
alien words.

Peregrin (Pippin) The H. name was *Razanul* [> *Razanur*]. This was the name of a legendary traveller, and probably contains the C.S. elements *raza* 'stranger', *razan* 'foreign'. I therefore chose *Peregrin* to represent it, though it does not fit quite so well. Of *Peregrin*, *Pippin* is I suppose a not impossible 'pet-form'; but it is not so close to its original, as is *Razal* [> *Razar*] (a kind of small red apple) by which abbreviation *Razanul Tūca* [> *Razanur Tūc*] was almost inevitably known to his contemporaries.[35]

Sam His real name was *Ban*, short for *Banzīr*. In C.S. *ba-*, *ban-* occurred in many words with the meaning 'half-, almost', while *zīr(a)* meant 'wise'. I have therefore translated his name by ancient English *samwīs* of similar sense. This was convenient, since *Samwise* will yield an abbreviation *Sam*. Now *Ban* was a common short name in the Shire, but was usually then derived from the more elevated name *Bannātha*, as *Sam* is with us usually shortened from *Samuel*.[36]

The following passage (§§50–1) is a note (a part of the manuscript as originally written) to the name *Samuel*, but in appearance is a part of the main text, and is most conveniently given so.

§50 It will be observed that I have not [> rarely] used Scriptural names or names of Hebraic origin to represent Hobbit-names. There is nothing in Hobbit lore or history that corresponds [*added:* closely] to this element in our names. *Bildad*, a name occurring among the Bolgers, is an accidental resemblance; it is a genuine Hobbit name which I have left unaltered. Other abbreviations like *Tom* and *Mat* I have also often left unchanged. Many such monosyllables were current in the Shire, but were the shortenings of genuine Hobbit names. For instance *Tom* of *Tomacca*, *Tomburān*; *Mat* of *Mattalic*; *Bill (Bil)* of *Bildad (Bildat)*, *Bilcuzal*, or any of the numerous names ending in *-bil*, *-mil*, as *Arambil*. Farmer Cotton's full name was in fact *Tomacca Lothran*.[37] [*Added:* *Tobias* (Hornblower) is an exception. I have used this name because the resemblance of the real Hobbit-name *Tōbi* was so close, and it seemed inevitable to translate *Zāra-tōbi* by 'Old Toby'; no other name could be found to fit so well. *This was changed to:* *Tobias* (Hornblower) is not an exception. *Tobias* was his real name, though accented *Tóbias*. I have retained this name because the resemblance of the real Hobbit-name was so close, &c.]

§51 *Barnabas* is [*added:* not] an exception. Barnabas

Butterbur was a Man of Bree, not a hobbit. I gave him this name for various reasons. First of all a personal one. On an old grey stone in a quiet churchyard in southern England I once saw in large letters the name *Barnabas Butter*. That was long ago and before I had seen the Red Book, but the name came back to me when the character of the stout innkeeper of Bree was presented to me in Frodo's record. The more so because his name, in agreement with the generally botanical type of name favoured in Bree, was actually *Butterburr*, or in the C.S. *Zilbarápha* [> *Zilbirápha*]. *Barnabas* has unfortunately only a very slight phonetic similarity to the real first-name of the innkeeper: *Barabatta* (or *Batti*). This was the nickname of the landlord of 'The Pony' which he had borne so long that if he ever had another given-name it had been forgotten: it means 'quick-talker or babbler'. Still, in converting *Batti Zilbarápha* [> *Zilbirápha*] into *Barney Butterbur* I do not think I have been unjust.[38]

§52   A final consequence of the conversion of the Common Speech, and of all names formed in that language, into English terms has already been referred to above. It entailed translation of the related languages of Rohan and the North into terms that would correspond linguistically, as closely as possible, to the ancient situation.

§53   In the records of the Red Book there are in several places allusions to the fact that Hobbits hearing the tongue of the Riders of Rohan felt that it was akin to their own, and recognized some of the words used, though they could not understand the language as a whole. Since I had, necessarily, converted the C.S. of the Hobbits into English, it seemed to me that it would be absurd then to leave the related language of Rohan in its wholly alien form. Now the tongue of the Rohirrim was not only related to the C.S., but it had remained in a much more archaic state, and it was, even in its newer southern home, much less mingled with alien (Noldorin and Quenya) words; I therefore substituted for it a form of language resembling Old English, since this tongue, that was removed from its ancestral home to another, closely corresponds in its relation to modern English (especially in its freedom from accretions of French and Latin origin) with the relations of the tongues of the Shire and the Mark.

§54   This translation was not difficult, since the Rohirrim in fact used a very similar type of nomenclature to that of our own ancestors. I have usually considered the sense of their names rather than the form; except that I have chosen names in Old English of the same length, where possible, and have only used compound names, such as *Fréawine*, *Éomer*, *Éowyn*, *Hasufel*, *Halifirien*, when the originals were also compounded. The element *éo*-, which so often appears (not unnaturally, being an old word meaning 'horse', among a people devoted to horses), represents an element *loho*-, *lō*- of the same sense. Thus *Éothéod*, 'Horse-folk' or 'Horse-land', translates *Lohtūr*. *Théoden*, as are many of the other royal names, is an old word for 'king', corresponding to Rohan *tūrac*-.[39]

§55 *Note.* In a few cases I have, not quite consistently, modified the words and names of the Mark, making them more like modern English, especially in spelling. Examples of this process in varying degrees are: *Dunharrow* (= *Dūn-harug* 'hill-sanctuary'), *Starkhorn*, *Entwash*, *Helm's Deep*, *Combe* (= *Cumb*); *Halifirien* (= *Hálig-firgen* 'holy-mountain'); *Fenmarch* for *Fenmerce*; *Shadowfax* for *Scadufax*. In a similar way in 'The Hobbit' *Oakenshield* was anglicized from *Eikinskialdi*. The name *Rohan* itself is of Noldorin origin, a translation of the native *Lōgrad* (sc. *Éo-marc* 'the Horse-mark' or 'Borderland of the Horsemen'). Its strictly correct form was *Rochann*, but the form *Rohan* represents the actual pronunciation of Gondor, in which medial *ch* was colloquially weakened to *h*.

§56 This translation had a disadvantage which I did not foresee. The 'linguistic notes' on the origin of peculiar Hobbit words had also to be 'translated'. I have already alluded to the translation of the actual relation of Rohan *cūgbagu* and Shire *cūbuc* into an imagined one of *holbytla* and *hobbit*. Other examples are these (cf. [§24]): *Stoor* in relation to a Northern word meaning 'big' (cf. Scandinavian *stór*- 'big') is a translation of actual Hobbit *tung*[40] in relation to a similar word in Dale. Supposed Hobbit *mathom* in relation to Rohan (that is Old English) *māthum* is a translation of actual Hobbit *cast* (older *castu*) compared with Rohan *castu*.

§57 Similarly, Rohan *smygel*, actually an Old English word for a burrow, related to a Northern stem *smug* / *sméag* *(smaug)*,[41] here represents the genuine Rohan *trahan* related to Hobbit *trān*. From *smygel* I have derived an imaginary modern *smile* (or *smial*) having a similar relation to the older form. *Sméagol* and *Déagol* are thus Old English equivalents for actual

Trahand and *Nahand* 'apt to creep into a hole' and 'apt to hide, secretive' respectively. (*Smaug*, the Dragon's name, is a representation in similar terms, in this case of a more Scandinavian character, of the Dale name *Trāgu*, which was probably related to the *trah-* stem in the Mark and Shire.)

§58 *Note.* In cases where 'folk-etymology' has operated to alter older (Elvish) names into the appearance of names in the C.S. special difficulty may be met, since it is unlikely that suitable words will be found in modern English that will at once translate the C.S. name and yet also have some similarity in sound to the Elvish name. The chief example is that of the River *Baranduin*, the ancient boundary eastward of the Shire. This is an Elvish name composed of *baran* 'golden-brown' and *duin* '(large) river'. But it was by the Hobbits picturesquely perverted into *Branduhim*, signifying in their tongue 'foaming beer' (*brand(u)* 'foam'; *hīm(a)* 'beer'). I have imitated this by calling the river the *Brandywine*, similar in sound and a very possible 'corruption' of *Baranduin*, although the sense is not very closely similar. (There is, in fact, no evidence for the distillation of brandy in the Shire.)

§59 For the same reasons the Northern, or rather Northeasterly, 'outer' names of the Dwarves taken from the Mannish languages of that region have been all given a Scandinavian style: they are indeed all genuine Norse dwarf-names.[42]

NOTES

1 The idea of the three kinds of Hobbit, Harfoots, Stoors, and Fallohides, arose in the first of the two texts (F 1), and was then transferred (before the second text F 2 was written) to the *Prologue* (see note 10 below, and p. 10). But the text of the latter (P 5) in which it appeared gave only the old story of Bilbo and Gollum, and thus must have been earlier than July 1950: see p. 7.

2 F 1 as written had 'Human', subsequently changed to 'Mannish'; this term occurs later in F 1 as first written. See the commentary on §2.

3 *Atani*: in F 1 as written no Elvish name appears here, but *Atanatári* was added in the margin, then changed to *Atanni* (so spelt).

4 As originally written, F 1 had: 'In that war the Fathers of Men aided the Elves, and lived with them and fought beside them; and their chieftains learned the Noldorin speech, and some indeed forsook their own tongue, even in the daily use of their own

houses.' This was changed to: 'In that war three houses of the Fathers of Men aided the Elves, and lived with them and fought beside them; and the people of these houses learned the Noldorin speech, and forsook their own tongue.' On this see the commentary on §7.

The final reading in F 2, 'the lords of these houses learned the Noldorin speech', belongs with the changes made in §9 and §13 introducing Adûnaic, which were made after the third version of the text had been written, or was at any rate in progress (see pp. 74–5).

5 Throughout F 2 the name was written *Dúnedein*, subsequently corrected at all occurrences to *Dúnedain* (the spelling in F 1). This is not further indicated in the text printed, where I have spelt the name in the usual form.

6 At first F 1 read here: 'This tongue was in Noldorin called *Falathren* "Shore-language", but by its speakers Westnish or the Common Speech.' The name *Westnish* was used throughout F 1, changed everywhere to *Westron* (see the commentary on §9). The present sentence was altered to read: '... but by its speakers *Undúna* (that is Westron) or *Sôval Phârë* the Common Speech.'

7 F 1 has: 'First: the Númenóreans had not been wholly sundered from the Eldar that remained in Middle-earth, and there had been much coming and going between Númenor and the westlands.'

8 After 'in the days of its blessedness' F 1 has: 'and there the language of the Kings of Men had changed little and slowly. And the like may be said of the Eldar.'

9 For the passage in F 2 concerning Treebeard F 1 has: 'As was natural in one so ancient Treebeard also knew this tongue, and such words and names as he is here recorded to have used, other than those in the Common Speech, are Quenya.'

10 F 1 is here altogether different. Following the words 'To speak last of Hobbits' it continues:

> These were a people who, as has been said, were more nearly akin to Men than any other of the speaking-peoples of the ancient world. Their language must then be supposed to have been of similar kind and origin to the language of Men. But, owing to the absence of all records among the Hobbits before their settlement in the West, the remoter history of Hobbit-language is difficult and obscure. [*This passage was struck out.*]
>
> Among the Hobbits of the Shire, though a love of learning was far from general (unless it be of genealogical lore), there were always some few, especially in the greater families, who were lore-masters, and gathered information concerning older times and distant lands, either from their own traditions, or from Elves and Men and Dwarves. According to the accounts thus compiled in the Shire, Hobbits, though originally one

race, became divided in remote antiquity into three somewhat different kinds: Stoors, Harfoots, and Fallohides.

Here there follows in F 1 an account of the three kinds that is already very close to that in the *Prologue* (FR pp. 12–13); and it is clear that it was here that the conception of the three Hobbit-kinds first entered (see the commentary on §20). It is notable that while the actual wording of F 1 was little changed subsequently, the Stoors were at first placed before the Harfoots, and a part of the description of the Harfoots was at first applied to the Stoors and vice versa.

> The Stoors were broader, heavier in build, and had less hair on their feet and more on their chins, and preferred flat lands and riversides. [*Added:* Their feet and hands were large.] The Harfoots were browner of skin, smaller and shorter, and they were beardless and bootless; they preferred highlands and hill-sides. [*Added:* Their hands and feet were neat and nimble.] The Fallohides were fairer of skin and often of hair, and were taller than the others; they were lovers of trees and woodlands. [*Added:* All Hobbits were 'good shots' with stone, sling or bow, but the Fallohides were the surest on the mark.]
>
> The Stoors [> Harfoots] had much to do with Dwarves in ancient times, and long lived in the foothills of the Misty Mountains. They moved westward early, and crossed the Mountains and roamed over the land of Eriador beyond, as far as Weathertop or further, while the others were still in Wilder-land. [*Struck out:* The Harfoots lingered long by the Great River, and were friendly with Men. They came westward after the Stoors.] They were probably the most normal and rep-resentative variety of Hobbits and were certainly the most numerous. They were the most inclined to settle, and the most addicted to living in holes and tunnels. [*Added:* The Stoors lingered by the banks of the Great River, and were friendly with Men. They came westward after the Harfoots, owing to the great increase of Men in Anduin Vale according to the[ir] tales, and followed the course of the Bruinen (or Loudwater) southwards.] The Fallohides were the least numerous, a north-erly branch. ...

The text F 1 then proceeds in almost the same words as in the *Prologue*, as far as 'they were often found as leaders or chieftains among clans of Stoors or Harfoots' (FR p. 13). At this point there is a footnote:

> Thus it is said to have been clans of a still markedly Stoorish strain that first moved on west again from Bree and colonized the Shire, attracted originally to the riverbanks of the Baran-duin. In Bilbo's time the inhabitants of the Marish in the East

Farthing, and also of Buckland, still showed Stoorish characteristics. Yet even there the chief families, notably the Brandybucks, had a strong Fallohidish strain in their make-up.

(On this see the commentary on §20.)

Before F 2 was written the account of the Harfoots, Stoors, and Fallohides was removed to stand in the *Prologue*, where at its first appearance it had almost word for word its form in the published work (see p. 10).

From this point F 1 continues as the basis for the F 2 version from §§21 ff.

11 For this paragraph F 1 reads as follows:

> More recent enquiries have failed, it is true, to find any trace of a special Hobbit language, but they do suggest that Westnish [> Westron] was not in fact the oldest language spoken by this people. The very earliest glimpses of Hobbits to be caught, either in their own legends or those of their neighbours, show them rather to have at that time spoken the language of Men in the higher vale of Anduin, roughly between the Carrock and the Gladden Fields.

The footnote here in F 1 corresponds in subject to that in F 2 at the end of §23, and reads:

> If Gandalf's theory is correct the people of Gollum must have been a late-lingering group of Stoors in the neighbourhood of the Gladden. And it may be that the memories of Smeagol provide one of the earliest glimpses of Hobbitry that we have. It may be noted therefore that *Deagol* and *Smeagol* are both words in the languages of Anduin-vale.

12 The footnote here in F 1 (see note 11) reads:

> Of course, since the Common Speech was itself derived from a related speech, it may sometimes have happened that the Hobbits preserved in use a word that had once been more widely current in Westnish [> Westron].

13 F 1 has here: 'and to the name of the Dragon *Smaug* (if that is a name given to him by the northern men of Dale, as seems likely).'

14 F 1 does not have the reference to the Hobbit month-names, but introduces a paragraph that was not taken up here in F 2 (cf. §28, which appears also in F 1).

> Hobbits therefore appear from their linguistic history to have had in early times a special aptitude for adopting language from their neighbours, and in no other point is this better illustrated than in their giving of names. They had of course many names of their own invention – usually short and often comic in sound (to us and to Hobbits) – but from very

early times they had also in traditional use a wealth of other names drawn not from the language of daily use but from their legends and histories and fictitious tales which dealt by no means solely with their own heroes and adventures, but with Elves and Men and Dwarves and even giants.

15 This is a reference to the conclusion of the text, which is omitted in this book (see note 42).

16 The heading *On Translation* is absent in F 1.

17 For the reference of the footnote at this point see note 15. In F 1 the footnote reads: 'A note on the spelling and intended pronunciation of the Elvish words and names will be found at the beginning of the Index.'

18 In a draft of this passage in F 1 the Westron name of Imladris was *Karbandul.*

19 The footnote to the name *Dwarrowdelf* differs somewhat in F 1. The Common Speech name of Moria was *Kubalnarga* (changed to *Kubalnargia*), translated as *Dwarrowdelf* 'since in Bilbo's time the word *kubal* (related to *kubu* "delve") was obsolete in ordinary speech, and *narga* [> *nargia*] contained a plural [> derivative] form of *narag* "dwarf" that had long disappeared from use. *Dwarrows* is what our older *dwergas* would have become if the singular *dwarf* from older *dwerh* had not replaced it, long ago.' Subsequently the C.S. name was changed in F 1 to *Satun-nargia,* and finally to *Phurun-nargia* (with corresponding changes of *kubal, kubu* to *phurūn, phur-*).

20 The whole of the discussion in §41 of the name *Sūza* of the Shire and the reason for the use of 'Farthing' is lacking in F 1; but after the reference to English *wich, bold, bottle* there is a footnote which was not taken up in F 2:

In one case I have coined a word: *smial* (or *smile* if you prefer it so). The Hobbits used a peculiar word of their own, *gluva* [*written later nearby:* Rohan *glōba*], for 'an inhabited hole'. I would have left it unchanged but it would have looked outlandish in an English context. Accordingly I have used *smial,* since the ancient English *smygel* 'a hole to creep in' would, had it survived or been adopted by latterday Hobbits, have now had some such form.

21 In F 1 the Hobbit name for 'Hornblower' was *Rhaspûtal,* changed to *Raspûta* as in F 2.

22 In F 1 my father first wrote *Tûk* but emended it to *Tûca;* in F 2 he wrote *Tūca,* but then erased the final *-a.*

23 In F 1 the adjective *tûca* was described as 'a Fallohide word meaning "great"', corrected to the reading of F 2.

24 The footnote at this point concerning the masculine ending *-a* is absent in F 1.

25 The footnote concerning the 'to us rather ridiculous subnames or titles' of the heads of the Brandybuck clan is absent in F 1. See the commentary on §45.

26 *Hamanullas*: in F 1 the name was *Amanullith*, subsequently changed to *Hamanulli*.

27 In F 1 the name was *Tûk*, later corrected to *Tūca*, as previously (see note 22).

28 The names in F 1 were *Shûran-kaphir* and *Zarkaphir*, changed to *Assargamba* and *Zaragamba* as in F 2.

29 F 1 has the same note, but in addition it is said that *Bophan* was 'of Harfoot origin', and also that 'to Hobbits in general *Bophan* was as devoid of meaning as *Boffin* today.'

30 In F 1 the account of *Gamgee* was the same, but the underlying names were different: the Hobbit name was *Charbushi*, derived from the place-name *Charb(b)ash*; the Common Speech word meaning 'game' was *charab*; and the place-name ending was *-bash*, *-bas*. These forms were then corrected to those in F 2. *Charbash* appears again in the note on *Cotton* in F 1.

31 In F 1 the Shire word for 'Hobbit' was *kubud* and the obsolete Common Speech word from which it was derived was *kubud(u)r* 'hole-dweller'; Théoden's word was *kugbadru*. These forms were then changed: the Shire word became *cubut* (plural *cubudil*), derived from obsolete C.S. *cubadul*, and Théoden's word *cugbadul*.

   In F 2 *cúbuc* and the associated words and forms were all first written *cu-*, changed to *cū-*. The Common Speech and Rohan forms were a good deal altered in the text and I have given only those finally adopted: thus the plural of *cúbuc* was first *cúbuga* and then *cúbugen*, the obsolete C.S. word was *cúbugl(a)*, and the Rohan word was *cúgbagul* (again in §56).

32 In F 1 it is said that '*Bilbo* is the actual Hobbit name': see note 24.

33 In F 1 the name was written *Maurō* before being changed to *Maura*.

34 The note in F 1 on the true name of Meriadoc is the same, but with the spellings *Khilimanzar*, *Khilik*.

35 The note on *Peregrin (Pippin)* read in F 1, before emendation:

   The Hobbit name is *Rabanul*. This is not a name of C.S. form; it is said to be [Fallohide >] a Harfoot name; but since it is also said to mean 'traveller', and was in any case the name of a legendary rover and wanderer, I have chosen *Peregrin* to represent it. Of *Peregrin*, *Pippin* is I suppose a not impossible pet-form, though it is not so close to *Peregrin* as *Rubul* is to *Rubanul*. But *rubul* is in C.S. the name of a kind of small apple.

36 The original discussion of the name *Sam* in F 2 was rejected and

replaced. I give the second form, since it scarcely differs from the
first except in clarity. In F 1 the same statement was made, but the
linguistic elements were different. His real name was *Bolnōth*;
the common Shire-name (*Ban* in F 2) was *Bol*, held to be an
abbreviation of *Bolagar*; the prefix meaning 'half-, almost' was
bol-; and the word in the Common Speech meaning 'wise' (*zīr(a)*
in F 2) was *nōth*. These were changed to the forms in F 2, but
with *Bannātho* for *Bannātha* (see note 24).

37 For *Tomacca* F 1 has *Tōmak* (and *k* for *c* in other names in this
passage, as throughout), and for *Arambil* has *Shambil*; Farmer
Cotton's full name is *Tomakli Lothron*, changed subsequently to
Tomacci.

38 In F 1 Butterbur's real name was *Barabush Zilibraph*, the first
name meaning (like *Barabatta* in F 2) 'quick-talker, babbler',
shortened to *Barabli*, and the second a compound of *zilib* 'butter'
and *raph(a)* a 'burr'. This latter was changed to *Zilbarāpha*, the
form first written in F 2. At the end of the note F 1 has: 'the nickname which the landlord of "The Pony" had so long borne that
Frodo had never heard his true given-name'.

With the discussion of *Butterbur* the text F 1 ends, but my
father added the following in pencil later:

A final note on the other languages. Now since the language of
Rohann and of Dale were akin, that of Rohann closely akin in
origin to the Common Speech, it seemed plain that having
converted all C.S. into English the more northerly (archaic
and less blended) tongues must be represented in the same way.
The language of Men in Dale has thus been given (so far as its
names show) a Norse cast; and since as has been said the
Dwarves adapt their names and speech to those of Men among
whom they live, all the Dwarves of the North have names of
this Northern type (in fact the actual names of Dwarves in
Norse). The Rohirrim are therefore appropriately represented
by speaking a tongue resembling ancient English. It will thus
be noted that for the archaic Rohan *cugbadul* in relation to
Hobbit *cubut* [see note 31] I have ..... [?ancient] English
holbytla in relation to *hobbit*.

From here to the end of the text (so far as it is given here, see
note 42) F 2 exists in two forms, both consisting of two sides of
a single manuscript page: the second form is a fair copy of the
first, and follows it very closely, with for the most part only very
minor alterations of wording. I give here the second version, with
a couple of differences of form recorded in the following notes.

39 In the first form of the F 2 text the real word in Rohan
corresponding to Théoden is *tūran*, where the second form has
tūrac-.

40 The first form had *tunga* where the second has *tung*.
41 These are forms of the same prehistoric stem, with differing vowels (*sméag* being the ancient English form, *smaug* the Scandinavian, while *smygel* is an English development of the stem *smug*).
42 The remaining eight pages of the F 2 manuscript are taken up with an account of pronunciation, with sections on consonants, vowels, and accent, which was subsequently removed to become (in much developed form) the first part of Appendix E. I give here only the brief preface to this account.

> In transliterating words and names from the ancient languages that appear in the Red Book I have attempted to use modern letters in a way as agreeable to modern English eyes as could be combined with reasonable accuracy. Also I have used them as far as possible with the same value in all the languages concerned. Fortunately the languages of the Westlands of the period were fairly euphonious (by European standards) and simple in phonetic structure, and no very rare or difficult sounds appear to have occurred in them.
>
> Hobbit names, as has been explained, have all been converted into English forms and equivalents and can be pronounced accordingly. Thus *Celador Bolger* has *c* as in *cellar*, and *g* as in *bulge*. But in the alien languages the following points may be observed by those who are interested in such matters.

Noldorin appears, of course, for *Sindarin* throughout (see the commentary on §§5, 18). For Celador Bolger, who does not appear in *The Lord of the Rings*, see pp. 94, 96.

COMMENTARY

§2 So far as I have been able to discover, my father never used the adjective 'Mannish', whether of language or tradition, before its occurrence in this work. The change of 'Human' to 'Mannish' in F 1 (see note 2 above) therefore marks the entry of this term.

§3 The use of the term *Lembi* 'Lingerers', for those of the Eldar who 'remained behind in the north-west of Middle-earth', is a clear indication of date, substantiating the conclusion already reached that this earliest version of Appendix F was at any rate written before the middle of 1950 (see p. 28 and note 1). In the long and extremely complex history of the classification of the divisions of the Elvish peoples and their names, this represents the stage reached in the *Quenta Silmarillion* §29 (V.215), where by a change that can be dated to November 1937 the old term *Lembi* 'Lingerers' became the name for those of the Eldar who were 'lost upon the long road' and never crossed the Great Sea (V.215, 219). Thus while this earliest

version of Appendix F certainly belongs to the time when the end of
the actual narrative of *The Lord of the Rings* had been reached, it
equally clearly preceded the new work on the legends of the First
Age which included (as well as the *Annals of Aman*, the *Grey
Annals*, and many other works) the revision of the *Quenta
Silmarillion*: for in that revision the term *Lembi* was first changed to
Lemberi and then removed, and the name *Sindar* emerged (for a
detailed account see X.163–4, 169–71). As noted in X.91, the name
Sindar does not occur in *The Lord of the Rings* apart from the
Appendices.

§4   The name *Lindar* had been replaced by *Vanyar* when the *Annals
of Aman* and the *Grey Annals* were written.

The statement here concerning Quenya, the 'Elven-latin' originally deriving from the language of the Lindar, echoes that in the
Lhammas or 'Account of Tongues' of the 1930s (see V.172; 193,
195). It may be noted that the expression 'Elven-latin' survived in
the published form of Appendix F (RK p. 406): '[Quenya] was
no longer a birth-tongue, but had become, as it were, an "Elven-
latin" …'.

§5   The name *Quenta Noldorion*, for *Quenta Silmarillion*, seems to
be unique in this place (where it occurs in both texts). – Nothing is
said in this work of the adoption of Sindarin (or as it is called here,
Lemberin) by the Exiled Noldor: this fundamental development
(which first appears in the earliest version of the 'linguistic excursus'
in the *Grey Annals*, XI.20–1) had not yet emerged (see further under
§18 below). But the idea found in the earlier forms of that 'excursus' (XI.21, 25, 27) that the two languages, Noldorin and Sindarin,
changed in similar ways and 'drew together' appears in the footnote
to §5.

§7   In the list of *Alterations in last revision 1951* (see X.7), often
referred to, occurs '*Atani*   N[oldorin] *Edain* = Western Men or
Fathers of Men'. It is possible that the form in F 1, *Atanni*, replacing *Atanatári* (note 3 above), was the earliest occurrence of the
name.

In the sentence 'In that war three houses of the Fathers of Men
aided the Elves …' the word 'the' is not casually absent before 'three
houses': cf. §10, 'the native tongue of the Fathers of Men themselves
before those of the Three Houses passed over the Sea.'

The statement concerning the loss of the original language of the
Atani shows a curious uncertainty (see note 4 above): from the original version in F 1, 'their chieftains learned the Noldorin speech,
and some indeed forsook their own tongue', revised to the form in
F 2 'the people of these houses learned the Noldorin speech, and forsook their own tongue', which was then altered to 'the lords of these
houses learned the Noldorin speech'. That my father should have
entertained at all at this time the idea that the original language of

the Atani (of the Three Houses) was wholly lost is remarkable. In this connection it is interesting to compare what he wrote in drafting for the chapter *Faramir* (later *The Window on the West*), which can be dated precisely to May 1944 (VIII.144). Here, in a passage concerning the Common Speech which was only removed from the chapter at a late stage (see VIII.162), Faramir had said: 'Some there are of Gondor who have dealings with the Elves ... One great advantage we have: we speak an elvish speech, or one so near akin that we can in part understand them and they us.' At this Sam exclaimed: 'But you speak the ordinary language! Same as us, though a bit old-fashioned like, if you'll pardon my saying it.' Then Faramir replied (VIII.159–60):

'Of course we do. For that is our own tongue which we perhaps preserve better than you do far in the North. The Common Tongue, as some call it, is derived from the Númenóreans, being but a form changed by time of that speech which the Fathers of the Three Houses [*struck out*: Hador and Haleth and Beor] spoke of old. This language it is that has spread through the western world amongst all folk and creatures that use words, to some only a second tongue for use in intercourse with strangers, to some the only tongue they know. But this is not an Elvish speech in my meaning. All speech of men in this world is Elvish in descent; but only if one go back to the beginnings. What I meant was so: [the lords >] many men of the Three Houses long ago gave up man-speech and spoke the tongue of their friends the Noldor or Gnomes: a high-elvish tongue [*struck out*: akin to but changed from the Ancient Elvish of Elvenhome]. And always the lords of Númenor knew that tongue and used it among themselves. And so still do we among ourselves ...

See further under §9 below.

§9 It is an extraordinary feature of this account that there is no suggestion that the Númenóreans retained their own Mannish language, and it is indeed expressly stated here that 'The language of the Dúnedain was thus the Elvish Noldorin'. This is the explanation of the statement discussed under §7 that the Men of the Three Houses learned Noldorin and abandoned their ancestral tongue (as has been mentioned already in note 4 above, the emendation to F 2, whereby it was reduced to 'the *lords* of these houses learned the Noldorin speech', was made at the same time as the rough alterations of the text here and in §13 whereby Adûnaic was introduced as the language of Númenor).

I am altogether at a loss to account for this, in view of Faramir's disquisition to Sam cited under §7. Moreover, in the anomalous 'Foreword' that I have called F* my father had said (p. 21, §8): 'Now those languages of Men that are here met with were related to the Common Speech; for the Men of the North and West were akin in the beginning to the Men of Westernesse that came back over the Sea; and the Common Speech was indeed made by the blending of the speech of Men of Middle-earth with the tongues of the kings from over the Sea.' This is not very clearly expressed, but the implication seems clear that the Númenórean language that entered into the Common Speech was a Mannish and not an Elvish tongue. One seems to be driven to the explanation that my father when writing the present account had actually shifted away from his view that the Mannish language of the Three Houses was the common speech of Númenor; yet what does that imply of all his work on Adûnaic and *The Drowning of Anadûnê* in 1946?

In the footnote to §9 the tenth king of the Northern Line is named *Eärendil*, not as in Appendix A (RK pp. 318, 320) *Eärendur*; see p. 189.

It was undoubtedly here that the name *Westron* arose (apparently devised by my father on the analogy of the old form *southron*, itself an alteration of *southern*); the F 1 text as originally written had *Westnish* throughout (note 6 above). *Westron* occurs only once in the actual narrative of *The Lord of the Rings*, in the chapter *Lothlórien*, where Legolas says 'this is how it runs in the Westron Speech' (FR p. 353), and this was a late change from 'the Common Speech', made to the typescript following the fair copy manuscript: see VII.223 and 235 with note 48.

§10   In Faramir's account (see under §7) the Common Speech was expressly said to be 'derived from the Númenóreans': changed by time, it was nonetheless directly descended from 'that speech which the Fathers of the Three Houses spoke of old'. In fact, in corrections made to the completed manuscript of that chapter, the conception was changed to the extent that Faramir now says: 'The Common Tongue, as some call it, is derived from the Númenóreans; for the Númenóreans coming to the shores of these lands took the rude tongue of the men that they here found and whom they ruled, and they enriched it, and it spread hence through the Western world'; and he also says that 'in intercourse with other folk we use the Common Speech which we made for that purpose' (VIII.162). Of this I said (*ibid.*): 'Here the idea that the Common Speech was derived from "that speech which the Fathers of the Three Houses spoke of old" is denied'; but by 'the rude tongue of the men that they here found' Faramir may have meant language that in the course of millennia had become greatly altered and impoverished, not that it bore no ancestral kinship to that of the Númenóreans.

In Appendix F as published the section *Of Men* (RK p. 406) begins: 'The *Westron* was a Mannish speech, though enriched and softened under Elvish influence. It was in origin the language of those whom the Eldar called the *Atani* or *Edain*, "Fathers of

Men" ...' And further on in this section my father wrote of the great Númenórean haven of Pelargir: 'There Adûnaic was spoken, and mingled with many words of the languages of lesser men it became a Common Speech that spread thence along the coasts ...'

All these conceptions differ somewhat among themselves, but as is often the case when comparing varying texts of my father's one may feel unsure whether the differences do not lie more in differing emphasis than in real contradiction. In the present text, however, it is perfectly clear that the Common Speech was in origin one form of the skein of Mannish speech that extended from the North (Dale, Esgaroth, and the old lands of the Rohirrim) southward down the vales of Anduin (see §23); that this particular form was centred on the Númenórean haven of Pelargir (§10); and that it was for this reason much influenced by the Númenórean language – *but that language was the Elvish Noldorin* as it had evolved in Númenor.

§14 The statement (before revision) that the Dunlendings had forgotten their own tongue and used only the Westron conflicts with the passage in the chapter *Helm's Deep*, where the Men of Dunland cried out against the Rohirrim in their ancient speech, interpreted to Aragorn and Éomer by Gamling the Old (see VIII.21). In the revised form of the paragraph the Dunland tongue is said to have been 'wholly unlike the Westron, and was descended, as it seems, from some other Mannish tongue, not akin to that of the Atani, Fathers of Men'; cf. Appendix F (RK p. 407): 'Wholly alien was the speech of the Wild Men of Drúadan Forest. Alien, too, or only remotely akin, was the language of the Dunlendings.' In an earlier form of Faramir's exposition cited under §7 he said that there was a 'remote kinship' between the Common Speech and 'the tongues of Rohan and of Dale and of Westfold and Dunland and other places', VIII.159.

§16 'The Orcs had a language of their own, devised for them by the Dark Lord of old': in view of what is said in §7, 'the Eldar were at that time engaged in a ceaseless war with the Dark Lord of that Age, one greater far than Sauron', this may seem to refer to Morgoth; but cf. Appendix F (RK p. 409), 'It is said that the Black Speech was devised by Sauron in the Dark Years'.

§18 The entire conception of the relations of the Elvish languages in Middle-earth at the end of the Third Age as presented here was of course fundamentally altered by the emergence of the idea that the Exiled Noldor of the First Age adopted Sindarin, the (Telerian) language of the Eldar who remained in Middle-earth. Thus the language of the Elves dwelling west of the Misty Mountains is here Noldorin (see under §5 above), while the Lemberin (i.e. Sindarin) of Middle-earth is found among the Elves of Northern Mirkwood and Lórien. At the beginning of §19 names such as *Lórien, Caras Galadon, Amroth, Nimrodel* are cited as examples of Lemberin;

whereas in Appendix F (RK p. 405, footnote) they are cited as 'probably of Silvan origin', in contrast to Sindarin, the language spoken in Lórien at the end of the Third Age. – With the present passage cf. that in the text F*, p. 20, §7.

§20   It has been seen (note 10 above) that it was in the text F 1 that the threefold division of the Hobbits into Harfoots, Stoors, and Fallohides entered, whence it was removed, before F 2 was written, to stand in the *Prologue*. In the actual narrative of *The Lord of the Rings* there is no reference to Harfoots or Fallohides, but the Stoors are named once, in the chapter *The Shadow of the Past*, where Gandalf spoke of Gollum's family. The introduction of the name was made at a very late stage in the evolution of the chapter, when the passage read (cf. the oldest version of the text, VI.78): 'I guess they were of hobbit-kind; or akin to the fathers of the fathers of the hobbits, though they loved the River, and often swam in it, or made little boats of reeds'; this was altered to the final text (FR p. 62) by omitting the word 'or' in 'or akin', and by changing 'hobbits' to 'Stoors' and 'though they loved' to 'for they loved'.

§22   My father was writing of Hobbits as if they were still to be found, as he did in the published *Prologue* ('Hobbits are an unobtrusive but very ancient people, more numerous formerly than they are today', &c., though altering present tense to past tense in one passage in the Second Edition, p. 17, note 13). Here indeed he attributed at least to some of them a lively interest in linguistic history.

§§22–3   In the footnotes to these paragraphs the more complex history of the Stoors can be seen evolving. In the footnote in F 1 (note 11 above) corresponding to that to §23 in F 2, concerning Gandalf's opinion about Gollum's origin, it is said that his people 'must have been a late-lingering group of Stoors in the neighbourhood of the Gladden' (i.e. after the Stoors as a whole had crossed the Misty Mountains into Eriador). In the footnote in F 2 (belonging with the writing of the manuscript) my father suggested rather that they were 'a family or small clan' of Stoors who had gone back east over the Mountains, a return to Wilderland that (he said) was evidenced in Hobbit legends, on account of the hard life and hard lands that they found in eastern Eriador.

Later, there entered the story that many Stoors remained in the lands between Tharbad and the borders of Dunland: this was an addition to the *Prologue* (FR p. 12) made when the text was close to its final form (cf. p. 11), and no doubt the footnote to §22 was added at the same time.

In Appendix A (RK p. 321) the return to Wilderland by some of the Stoors is directly associated with the invasion of Arnor by Angmar in Third Age 1409:

It was at this time that the Stoors that had dwelt in the Angle (between Hoarwell and Loudwater) fled west and south, because of the wars, and the dread of Angmar, and because the land and clime of Eriador, especially in the east, worsened and became unfriendly. Some returned to Wilderland, and dwelt beside the Gladden, becoming a riverside people of fishers.

These Stoors of the Angle who returned to Wilderland are distinguished from those who dwelt further south and acquired a speech similar to that of the people of Dunland: see the section *Of Hobbits* in Appendix F, RK p. 408 and footnote.

§25   The name Brandywine emerged very early in the writing of *The Lord of the Rings* (VI.29–30 and note 5), but the Elvish name first appeared in the narrative in work on the chapter *Flight to the Ford* (VII.61; FR p. 222), where Glorfindel, in a rejected draft, spoke of 'the Branduin (which you have turned into Brandywine)' (the word 'have' was erroneously omitted in the text printed). In F 1, and again at first in F 2, my father repeated this: 'older names, of Elvish or forgotten Mannish origin, they often translated ... or twisted into a familiar shape (as Elvish *Baranduin* "brown river" to *Brandywine*).' But in revision to F 2 he rejected this explanation, saying that the Elvish name of the river was in fact *Malevarn* ('golden-brown'), transformed in the Hobbits' speech to *Malvern*, but that this was then replaced by *Brandywine* – this being exceptional, since it bore no relation in form to the Elvish name. This idea he also rejected, and in the final form of §25 went back to the original explanation of *Brandywine*, that it was a characteristic Hobbit alteration of Elvish *Baranduin*.

In the passage of *Flight to the Ford* referred to above the name of the river appears in the manuscript as *Branduin*, changed to *Baranduin*, and then to *Malevarn* (VII.66, note 36). It is surprising at first sight to see that *Malevarn* survived into the final typescript of the chapter, that sent to the printer, where my father corrected it to *Baranduin*; but the explanation is evidently that this typescript had been made a long time before. Glorfindel's use of *Baranduin* or *Malevarn* is in fact the only occurrence of the Elvish name of the river in the narrative of *The Lord of the Rings*.

§27   In Appendix D (RK p. 389) Yellowskin is called 'the Yearbook of Tuckborough'.

§37   It is often impossible to be sure of my father's intention in the usage of 'thou, thee' and 'you' forms of address: when writing rapidly he was very inconsistent, and in more careful manuscripts he often wavered in his decision on this insoluble question (if the distinction is to be represented at all). In the case of the chapter *The Steward and the King*, referred to here, the first manuscript (see IX.54) is a very rapidly written draft from which no conclusion can be drawn; while in the second manuscript, a good clear text, he decided while in the course of writing the dialogue between Faramir and Éowyn against showing the distinction at all. The 'sudden change' to which he referred here (but in F 1 he wrote only of 'the intrusion of *thou, thee* into the dialogue') is possibly to be seen in their first meeting in the garden of the Houses of Healing, where Faramir says (RK p. 238): 'Then, Éowyn of Rohan, I say to you that you are beautiful', but at the end of his speech changes to the 'familiar' form, 'But thou and I have both passed under the wings of the Shadow' (whereas Éowyn continues to use 'you'). In the following meetings, in this text, Faramir uses the 'familiar' forms, but Éowyn does not do so until the last ('Dost thou not know?', RK p. 242); and soon after this point my father went back over what he had written and changed every 'thou' and 'thee' to 'you'. In the third manuscript (preceding the final typescript) there is no trace of the 'familiar' form.

I record these details because they are significant of the (relative) date of the present text, showing very clearly that when he wrote this earliest form of what would become Appendix F he had not yet completed the second manuscript of this chapter.

'The *thee* used by Sam Gamgee to Rose at the end of the book' refers to the end of the *Epilogue* (IX.118): 'I did not think I should ever see thee again'. At this stage only the first version of the *Epilogue* was in being (though these words are used in both versions): see IX.129, 132.

On a loose page associated with my father's later work on this Appendix my father wrote very rapidly:

> Where *thou, thee, thy* appears it is used mainly to mark a use of the familiar form where that was not usual. For instance its use by Denethor in his last madness to Gandalf, and by the Messenger of Sauron, was in both cases intended to be contemptuous. But elsewhere it is occasionally used to indicate a deliberate change to a form of affection or endearment.

The passages referred to are RK pp. 128–30 and p. 165; in Denethor's speeches to Gandalf there are some occurrences of 'you' that were not corrected.

§39 For Westron *Carbandur* (F 1 at first *Karbandul*, note 18) Appendix F has *Karningul* (RK p. 412).

§41 With the Noldorin word *lhann*, said here to be the equivalent of Westron *sûza* as used in Gondor for the divisions of the realm, cf. the *Etymologies*, V.367, stem LAD, where Noldorin *lhand, lhann* 'wide' is cited, and also the region *Lhothland, Lhothlann*, east of Dorthonion (see XI.60, 128).

§42 The Westron name *Raspûta* 'Hornblower' is only recorded here (F 1 *Rhaspûtal*, note 21 above). Since it is said (§13) that the Common Speech was 'much enriched with words drawn from the language of the Dúnedain, which was ... a form of the Elvish Noldorin', it is perhaps worth noting that the stem RAS in the

Etymologies (V.383) yields Quenya *rassë*, Noldorin *rhaes* 'horn', with citation of *Caradras*. – In Appendix F (RK p. 413) the name *Tûk* is said to be an old name 'of forgotten meaning'.

§43   For the name *Porro*, not found in *The Lord of the Rings*, see pp. 87–8, 92.

§45   The 'classical' titles of the heads of the Brandybuck family given in the second footnote to this paragraph do not appear in *The Lord of the Rings*, but see pp. 102–3. Cf. Appendix F (RK p. 413): 'Names of classical origin have rarely been used; for the nearest equivalents to Latin and Greek in Shire-lore were the Elvish tongues, and these the Hobbits seldom used in nomenclature. Few of them at any time knew the "languages of the kings", as they called them.'

§46   Apart from the opening sentence nothing of this paragraph remained in Appendix F, and Lobelia Sackville-Baggins' true name *Hamanullas* was lost.

§47   Much information is given here on Hobbit family-names that was subsequently lost, notably the true Westron name of *Baggins* and its supposed etymology; other names (*Brandybuck*, *Cotton*, *Gamgee*), discussed in the notes that conclude Appendix F, differ in details of the forms. On the name *Gamgee* see the references in the index to *Letters*, and especially the letter to Naomi Mitchison of 25 April 1954 (no.144, near the end), which is closely related to what is said here and in Appendix F.

§48   In the note at the end of Appendix F it is said that the word for 'Hobbit' in use in the Shire was *kuduk*, and that Théoden used the form *kûd-dûkan* 'hole-dweller' when he met Merry and Pippin at Isengard, which in the narrative (TT p. 163) is 'translated' by *Holbytla(n)*, though no rendering of this given. In the present passage, both in F 1 (see note 31) and in F 2, the meaning 'hole-dweller' is given for *holbytla* and for the real Westron and Rohan words (cf. also p. 10). In view of the etymology of *bytla (bylta)*, for which see VII.424, VIII.44, one would expect 'hole-builder', but this only occurs in fact at an earlier point in Appendix F (RK p. 408): the word *hobbit* seems to be 'a worn-down form of a word preserved more fully in Rohan: *holbytla* "hole-builder"' (see further p. 83, note 7).

My father's remarks in the footnote to this paragraph on his asso-ciation of the words 'hobbit' and 'rabbit' are notable.

§49   In Appendix F (RK p. 414) Meriadoc's true name was *Kalimac*, shortened *Kali*; but nothing is said of the true names of Frodo or Peregrin.

§50   In the chapter *The Road to Isengard* the originator of pipe-weed in the Shire was first named Elias Tobiasson, and then Tobias Smygrave, before Tobias Hornblower emerged (VIII.36–7). Tobias remained to a late stage in the development of the chapter before he was renamed Tobold, though it is seen from the present text that my father for a time retained Tobias while asserting that the name (pronounced *Tóbias*) was not in fact a 'translation' of Hebraic origin at all.

Bildad (Bolger) is not found in *The Lord of the Rings* (but see pp. 94, 96); while the abbreviated names *Tom* and *Mat* are differently explained in Appendix F.

§51   As with Tobias Hornblower, my father retained Barnabas Butterbur, despite what he had written in §50, but accounted for it on the grounds that Butterbur was not a Hobbit but a Man of Bree. In Appendix F all discussion of the name of the landlord of *The Prancing Pony* was lost. The change of *Barnabas* to *Barliman* was made in very late revisions to the text of *The Lord of the Rings* (cf. IX.78).

§58   These remarks on the history of the Hobbits' name of the *Baranduin* (see also §§25, 47) were further altered in the final note at the end of Appendix F.

This is the most detailed account that my father wrote of his elaborate and distinctive fiction of translation, of transposition and substitution. One may wonder when or by what stages it emerged; but I think that this is probably unknowable: the evidences are very slight, and in such matters he left none of those discussions, records of internal debate, that sometimes greatly assisted in the understanding of the development of the narrative. It seems to me in any case most probable that the idea evolved gradually, as the history, linguistic and other, was consolidated and became increasingly coherent.

Central to the 'fiction of authenticity' is of course the Common Speech. I concluded that this was first named in the *Lord of the Rings* papers in the chapter *Lothlórien* (dating from the beginning of the 1940s): see VII.223, 239. In the second of these passages my father wrote that the speech of the wood-elves of Lórien was 'not that of the western elves which was in those days used as a common speech among many folk'. In a note of the same period (VII.277) he said that 'Since Aragorn is a *man* and the common speech (especially of mortals) is represented by English, then he must not have an Elvish name'; and in another note (VII.424), one of a collection of jottings on a page that bears the date 9 February 1942 (at which time he was working on the opening chapters of what became *The Two Towers*) he wrote:

Language of Shire = modern English
Language of Dale = Norse (used by Dwarves of that region)
Language of Rohan = Old English
'Modern English' is *lingua franca* spoken by all people (except a few secluded folk like Lórien) – but little and ill by orcs.

In this, 'Language of Dale = Norse (used by Dwarves of that region)' shows plainly that a major obstacle, perhaps the chief obstacle, to a coherent 'authentication' had by this time been resolved. When my father wrote *The Hobbit* he had of course no notion that the Old Norse names of the Dwarves required any explanation, within the terms of the story: those were their names, and that was all there was to it. As he said in a letter of December 1937, cited in the Foreword to *The Return of the Shadow* (p. 7): 'I don't much approve of *The Hobbit* myself, preferring my own mythology (which is just touched on) with its consistent nomenclature ... and organized history, to this rabble of Eddaic-named dwarves out of Völuspá ...' But now this inescapable Norse element had to be accounted for; and from that 'rabble of Eddaic-named dwarves out of Völuspá' the conception emerged that the Dwarves had 'outer names' derived from the tongues of Men with whom they had dealings, concealing their true names which they kept altogether secret. And this was very evidently an important component in the theory of the 'transposition of languages': for the Dwarves had *Norse* names because they lived among Men who *were represented* in *The Lord of the Rings* as speaking Norse. It may not be too far-fetched, I think, to suppose that (together with the idea of the Common Speech) those Dwarf-names in *The Hobbit* provided the starting-point for the whole structure of the Mannish languages in Middle-earth, as expounded in the present text.

My father asserted (§53) that he had represented the tongue of the Rohirrim as Old English because their real language stood in a relation to the Common Speech somewhat analogous to that of Old English and Modern English. This is perhaps difficult to accept: one may feel that the impulse that produced the Riders of Rohan and the Golden Hall was more profound, and that my father's statement should be viewed as an aspect of 'the fiction of authenticity'; for the idea of 'translation' had a further fictional dimension in its presentation as a conception established from the outset – which in the case of the Dwarf-names (and the Hobbit-names) it was most assuredly not.

On the other hand, he knew very soon that the Rohirrim were originally Men of the North: in a note made at the time when his work on the chapter *The Riders of Rohan* was scarcely begun (VII.390) he wrote:

> Rohiroth are relations of Woodmen and Beornings, old Men of the North. But they speak Gnomish – tongue of Númenor and Ondor, as well as [?common] tongue.

Taken with 'Language of Rohan = Old English' among the equations in the note cited above, from about the same time, it may be better not to force the distinction, but to say rather that the emergent 'transpositional' idea (Modern English – Old English – Old Norse) may well have played a part in my father's vision of Rohan.

In the present text it can be seen that as he penetrated more deeply into the logic of the theory he came up against complexities that were difficult to manage. For example, it seems clear that when he wrote in

§25 that the Hobbits had 'twisted into a familiar shape' the Elvish name *Baranduin*, making out of it *Brandywine*, he had not taken into account the fact that the Hobbits would have had no such word as 'Brandywine' (whether or not they knew of brandy, §58). This realisation led to his avowal in §56: 'This translation had a disadvantage which I did not foresee. The "linguistic notes" on the origin of peculiar Hobbit words had also to be "translated"'; and in §58 he is seen ingeniously introducing the necessary 'third term' into the history of *Brandywine*: the 'picturesque perversion' of the river-name *Baranduin* by the Hobbits was to their real word *Branduhim*, which meant in their Westron 'foaming beer'. He could still say that *Brandywine* was 'a very possible "corruption" of *Baranduin*', because *Baranduin* being an Elvish name was not translated; thus *Brandywine* must both 'imitate' the Hobbit word *Branduhim*, and at the same time stand in Modern English as a corruption of *Baranduin*.

It will be seen shortly that in the text of this Appendix next following my father moved sharply away from F 2, and removed almost all exemplification of true Westron names. It may be that at that stage he had come to think that the subtleties demanded by so close an examination of the 'theory' were unsuitable to the purpose; on the other hand it seems possible that mere considerations of length were the cause.

Note on an unpublished letter

A long letter of my father's was sent for sale at auction on 4 May 1995 at Sotheby's in London. This letter he wrote on 3 August 1943, during the long pause in the writing of *The Lord of the Rings* (between the end of Book Three and the beginning of Book Four) that lasted from about the end of 1942 to the beginning of April 1944 (VIII.77–8). It was addressed to two girls named Leila Keene and Pat Kirke, and was largely concerned to answer their questions about the runes in *The Hobbit*; but in the present connection it contains an interesting passage on the Common Speech. My father made some brief remarks on the problem of the representation of the languages actually spoken in those days, and continued:

In some ways it was not too difficult. In Bilbo's time there *was* a language very widely used all over the West (the Western parts of the Great Lands of those days). It was a sort of lingua-franca, made up of all sorts of languages, but the Elvish language (of the North West) for the most part. It was called the Western language or Common Speech; and in Bilbo's time had already passed eastward over the Misty Mountains and reached Lake Town, and Beorn, and even Smaug (dragons were ready linguists in all ages). ...

If hobbits ever had any special language of their own, they had given it up. They spoke the Common Speech only and every day (unless they learned other languages, which was very seldom).

The most notable point in this is the description of the composition of the Common Speech: 'a sort of lingua-franca, made up of all sorts of languages, but the Elvish language (of the North West) for the most part.' Allowance should perhaps be made for the nature of the letter (my father was not, obviously, writing a precise statement); but it certainly seems that as late as 1943, when half of *The Lord of the Rings* had been written, he had as yet no conception of the origin of the Common Speech in a form of Mannish language of the west of Middle-earth, and that Faramir's account of the matter (see p. 63), written nine months later, had not emerged. It may be that what he said in this letter ('the Elvish language (of the North West) for the most part') is to be associated with what he had written in the chapter *Lothlórien*, where he said (VII.239) that the language of 'the western elves' 'was in those days used as a common speech among many folk.'

He also referred in this letter to the adoption by the Dwarves of the Lonely Mountain of the language of the Men of Dale, in which they gave themselves names, keeping their true names in their own tongue entirely secret (see p. 71).

★

For the notes to this concluding section of the chapter see pp. 82 ff.

The third text ('F 3') was a typescript with the title *The Languages of the Third Age*, above which my father wrote 'Appendix I'. No other of the many texts that followed has any mention of its being an 'Appendix'.

This text F 3 represents in some degree a new departure. The first part of the work (that preceding the discussion of 'Translation') was reduced to not much more than a third of its length in F 2, and while my father had F 2 in front of him he turned also to the curious 'Foreword' F* that I have given on pp. 19 ff., and made a good deal of use of it, as has been mentioned already.

At this stage he had not changed his view that the Exiled Noldor retained their own language in Beleriand (see p. 62, §5), and the 'Telerian' speech (which in F 2 was originally called 'Lemberin') is confined to a few names. Thus the conception in F 2, §18, was in essentials preserved, although there entered here the more complex account of the Elvish peoples of Mirkwood and Lórien:

There were also Elves of other kind. The East-elves that being content with Middle-earth remained there, and remain even now; and the Teleri, kinsfolk of the High Elves who never went westward, but lingered on the shores of Middle-earth until the return of the Noldor.[1] In the Third Age few of the Teleri were left, and they for the most part dwelt as lords among the East-elves in woodland realms far from the Sea, which nonetheless they longed for in their hearts. Of this kind were the Elves of Mirkwood, and of Lórien; but Galadriel was a lady of the Noldor. In this book there are several names of Telerian form,[2] but little else appears of their language.

The extremely puzzling feature of the original version, that the language of the Númenóreans was Noldorin (for the Edain in Beleriand learned that tongue and abandoned their own) was at first retained in F 3; and thus the account of the Common Speech remained unchanged, becoming if anything more explicit (cf. F 2, §§9–10, 13):

The language of the Dúnedain in Númenor was thus the Elvish, or Gnomish speech ... After the Downfall of Númenor, which was brought about by Sauron, and the ending of the Second Age, Elendil and the survivors of Westernesse fled back eastward to Middle-earth. On the western shores in the days of their power the Númenóreans had maintained many forts and havens for the help of their ships in their great voyages; and the chief of these had been at Pelargir at the mouths of the Anduin in the land that was after called Gondor. *There the language of the Edain that had not passed over Sea was spoken,* and thence it spread along the coastlands, as a common speech of all who had dealings with Westernesse and opposed the power of Sauron. Now the people of Elendil were not many, for only a few great ships had escaped the Downfall. There were, it is true, many dwellers upon the west-shores who came in part of the blood of Westernesse, being descended from mariners and wardens of forts set there in the Dark Years; yet all told the Dúnedain were only a small people in the midst of lesser Men. They used therefore this Common Speech in all their dealings with other folk and in the government of the wide realms of which they became the rulers, and it was enriched with many words drawn from the tongues of the Elves and the Númenórean lords. Thus it was that the Common Speech spread far and wide in the days of the Kings, even among their enemies, and it became used more and more by the Númenóreans themselves; so that at the time of this history the Elvish speech was spoken by only a [*added:* small] part of the people of Minas Tirith, the city of Gondor, and outside that city only by the lords and princes of fiefs.

The account of the origin and spread of the Common Speech as it appears in Appendix F (RK p. 407) had, in point of actual wording, been quite largely attained – and yet still with the fundamental difference, that the Númenóreans themselves spoke an Elvish tongue, and Adûnaic does not exist.

Probably while this text was still in the making, my father retyped a portion of it, and it was only now that Adûnaic entered, or re-entered, the linguistic history. Making similar changes at the same time to the previous text F 2 (see p. 54, note 4), he wrote now that it was the lords of the Edain who learned the Noldorin tongue, and that 'in Númenor two speeches were used: the Númenórean (or Adûnaic); and the Elvish or Gnomish tongue of the Noldor, which all the lords of that people knew and spoke'. In the passage just given he altered the words that I italicised to: 'There [at Pelargir] the Adûnaic, the Man-nish language of the Edain, was spoken, and thence it spread along the coastlands...', the remainder of the passage being left unchanged. No further light is cast on this matter in the texts of 'Appendix F', and it remains to me inexplicable.

There is not a great deal more that need be said about the part of the text F 3 that deals with the languages. For the language of Orcs and Trolls my father followed F 2, §§16–17, but for that of the Dwarves he turned to F* (p. 21, §10), and repeated closely what he had said there. But at that point, still following this text (§11), he turned now to the subject of alphabets ('Of the alphabets of the Third Age something also must be said, since in this history there are both inscriptions and old writings ...'), and repeated what he had said in F* as far as 'the Runes, or *cirth*, were devised by the Elves of the woods'. Here he left the earlier text and continued as follows (the forerunner of the passage in Appendix E, RK pp. 395, 397):

... the Runes, or *Cirth* as they were called, were first devised by the Danians (far kin of the Noldor) in the woods of Beleriand, and were in the beginning used mainly for incising names and brief memorials upon wood, stone, or metal. From that begin-ning they derive their peculiar character, closely similar in many of their signs to the Runes of the North in our own times. But their detail, arrangement, and uses were different, and there is, it seems, no connexion of descent between the Runes and the Cirth. Many things were forgotten and found again in the ages of Middle-earth, and so it will be, doubtless, hereafter.

The Cirth in their older and simpler form spread far and wide, even into the East, and they became known to many races of Men, and developed many varieties and uses. One form of the old Cirth was used among Men of whom we have already spoken, the Rohirrim and their more northerly kindred in the vale of Anduin and in Dale. But the richest and most well-ordered alphabet of Cirth was called the Alphabet of Dairon, since in Elvish tradition it was said to have been arranged and enlarged from the older Cirth by Dairon, the minstrel of King Thingol in Doriath. This was preserved in use in Hollin and Moria, and there mostly by the Dwarves. For after the coming of the Noldor the Fëanorian script replaced the Cirth among the Elves and the Edain.

In this book we meet only the Short Cirth of Dale and the Mark; and the Long Cirth of Moria, as they were called at this time; for though the Dwarves, as with their speech, used in their dealings with other folk such scripts as were current among them, among themselves and in their secret memorials they still used the ancient Alphabet of Dairon. A table is given setting out the Short Cirth of Dale and the Mark; and the Long Cirth of Moria in the form and arrangement applied to the Common Speech. [*The following was subsequently struck out:* A list is also given of all the strange words and the names of persons and places that appear in the tale, in which it is shown from what language they are derived, and what is their meaning (where that is known);] and also the English Runes in the forms that were used for the translation of the Cirth in *The Hobbit*.

The first devising of the Runes by 'the Danians (far kin of the Noldor) in the woods of Beleriand' (where F* has 'the Elves of the woods') is found also in the two texts given in VII.453–5, where the origin is attributed to 'the Danian elves of Ossiriand (who were ultimately of Noldorin race)'. The old view that the Danas or Danians (Nandor) came from the host of the Noldor on the Great March was changed in the course of the revision of the *Quenta Silmarillion*, when they became Teleri from the host of Olwë (X.169–70; cf. the use of the old term *Lembi* in F 2, p. 61, §3).

The final section of F 3, *On Translation*, presents a very greatly reduced form of that in the original version, and loses virtually all of the exemplification and discussion of the 'true' names from which the 'translation' was made: the sole Westron names that survived were *Carbandur* (Rivendell) and *Phuru-nargian* (Moria). The new text had indeed the structure and much of the actual wording of Appendix F, but it was a good deal briefer; and the published text represents a re-expansion, in which some of the old material had been reinstated, if in altered form.[3] But since no new material was introduced in F 3, there is no need to give more account of this part of it.

The text ends with a return to the conclusion of F*, pp. 23–4, §§12–13:

In conclusion I will add a note on two important modern words used in translation. The name *Gnomes* is sometimes used for the Noldor, and *Gnomish* for Noldorin. This has been done, because whatever Paracelsus may have thought (if indeed he invented the name), to some *Gnome* will still suggest Knowledge. Now the High-elven name of this folk, Noldor, signifies Those who Know; for of the Three Kindreds of the Elves from their beginning the Noldor were ever distinguished both by their knowledge of things that are and were in this world and by their desire to know more. Yet they were not in any way like to the gnomes of learned theory, or of literary and popular fancy. They belonged to a race high and beautiful, the Elder Children of the world, who now are gone. Tall they were, fair-skinned and grey-eyed, though their locks were dark, save in the golden house of Finrod; and their voices knew more melodies than any mortal speech that now is heard. Valiant they were, but their history was grievous; and though it was in far-off days woven a little with the fates of the Fathers, their fate is not that of Men. Their dominion passed long ago, and they dwell now beyond the circles of the world, and do not return.

The naming of 'the golden house of Finrod' (later Finarfin) seems to have been the first mention of this character that marked out the third son of Finwë, and his children.

In a later (in fact the penultimate) text of the section *On Translation* my father still retained this passage, even though by that time he had decided against using *Gnome*, *Gnomish* at all in *The Lord of the Rings* (as being 'too misleading'), and introduced it with the words 'I have sometimes (not in this book) used Gnomes for *Noldor*, and Gnomish for *Noldorin*'. Perhaps because the passage now seemed otiose, in the final text he still retained a part of it but changed its application: the word to be justified was now *Elves*, used to translate *Quendi* and *Eldar*. In my discussion of this in I.43–4 I pointed out that the words 'They were tall, fair of skin and grey-eyed, though their locks were dark, save in the golden house of Finrod [Finarfin]' were originally written of the Noldor only, and not of all the Eldar, and I objected that 'the Vanyar had golden hair, and it was from Finarfin's Vanyarin mother Indis that he, and Finrod Felagund and Galadriel his children, had their golden hair', finding in the final use of this passage an 'extraordinary perversion of meaning'. But my father carefully remodelled the passage in order to apply it to the Eldar as a whole, and it does indeed seem 'extraordinary' that he should have failed to observe this point. It seems possible that when he re-used the passage in this way the conception of the golden hair of the Vanyar had not yet arisen.[4]

Despite the great contraction in F 3 of the original version, my father repeated the long last paragraph of F* concerning *dwarves* and *dwarrows* (pp. 23–4, §13) almost in its entirety, omitting only his remarks on his liking for irregular plurals, and introducing the

Westron name *Phurunargian* of Moria. With the words 'and has been so since their birth in the deeps of time' this text ends.

The next typescript, F 4, still called *The Languages of the Third Age* but changed to *The Languages and Peoples of the Third Age*, followed the major revision of 1951. My father's long experimentation with the structure and expression of this Appendix now issued in his most lucid account of the Elvish languages, in which the terms *Sindar* and *Sindarin* at last appeared, and the acquisition of the Grey-elven tongue by the exiled Noldor.

Besides this Common Speech there were, however, many other tongues still spoken in the West-lands. Noblest of these were the languages of the Western Elves (Eldar) of which two are met: the High-elven (Quenya) and the Grey-elven (Sindarin).

The Quenya was no longer a daily speech but a learned tongue, descended from ages past, though it was still used in courtesies, or for high matters of lore and song, by the High Elves, the Noldor whose language it had been in Eldamar beyond the Sea. But when the Noldor were exiled and returned to Middle-earth, seeking the Great Jewels which the Dark Power of the North had seized, they took for daily use the language of the lands in which they dwelt. Those were in the North-west, in the country of Beleriand, where Thingol Grey-cloak was king of the Sindar or Grey-elves.

The Sindar were also in origin Eldar, and kindred of the Noldor, yet they had never passed the Sea, but had lingered on the shores of Middle-earth. There their speech had changed much with the changefulness of mortal lands in the long Twilight, and it had become far estranged from the high and ancient Quenya. But it was a fair tongue still, well fitted to the forests, the hills, and the shores where it had taken shape.

In the fall of the Dark Power and the end of the First Age most of Beleriand was overwhelmed by the waters, or burned with fire. Then a great part of its folk went west over Sea, never to return. Yet many still lingered in Middle-earth, and the Grey-elven tongue in those days spread eastward; for some of the elven-peoples of Beleriand crossed the mountains of Lune (Ered Luin), and wherever they came they were received as kings and lords, because of their greater wisdom and majesty. These were for the most part Sindar; for the Exiles (such few as remained), highest and fairest of all speaking-peoples, held still to Lindon, the remnant of Beleriand west of the Ered Luin. There Gil-galad was their lord, until the Second Age drew to its end.

Nonetheless to Rivendell (Imladris) there went with Master Elrond many Noldorin lords; and in Hollin (Eregion) others of the Noldor established a realm near to the West-gate of Moria, and there forged the Rings of Power. Galadriel, too, was of the royal house of Finrod of the Noldor; though Celeborn, her spouse of Lórien, was a Grey-elf, and most of their people were of a woodland race.

For there were other Elves of various kind in the world; and many were Eastern Elves that had hearkened to no summons to the Sea, but being content with Middle-earth remained there, and remained long after, fading in fastnesses of the woods and hills, as Men usurped the lands. Of that kind were the Elves of Greenwood the Great; yet among them also were many lords of Sindarin race. Such were Thranduil and Legolas his son. In his realm and in Lórien both the Sindarin and the woodland tongues were heard; but of the latter nothing appears in this book, and of the many Elvish names of persons or of places that are used most are of Grey-elven form.

From the assured and perspicuous writing alone one might think that this belonged to the time of the *Grey Annals* and the *Annals of Aman*. But it was by no means the last in the series of texts that finally issued in the published form of Appendix F.

Of F 4 there are only a few other points to mention. The origin of the Common Speech is here formulated in these words:

There [at Pelargir] Adûnaic was spoken, to which language the tongues of Men that dwelt round about were closely akin, so that already a common speech had grown up in that region and had spread thence along the coasts among all those that had dealings with Westernesse.

After typing the text my father added this sentence:

Of the speech of Men of the East and allies of Sauron all that appears is *múmak*, a name of the great elephant of the Harad.

A carbon copy of F 4 is extant, and here my father in a similar addition named beside *múmak* also *Variag* and *Khand* (RK pp. 121, 123, 329).

Lastly, it was in F 4 that there entered the passage concerning the new race of Trolls that appeared at the end of the Third Age. Here the name was first *Horg-hai*, but changed as my father typed the text to *Olg-hai* (*Olog-hai* in RK, p. 410). The account of them did not differ from the final form except in the statement of their origin:

That Sauron bred them none doubted, though from what stock was not known. Some held that they were a cross-breed between trolls and the larger Orcs; others that they were indeed not trolls at all but giant Orcs. Yet there was no kinship from the beginning between the stone-trolls and the Orcs that they might breed together;[5] while the Olg-hai were in fashion of mind and body quite unlike even the largest of Orckind ...

With this text and its successors the section *On Translation* was typed and preserved separately, and it is not possible to relate these precisely to the texts of the first section. Of these latter there are four after F 4, textually complex and not all complete, and for the purposes of this account it is not necessary to describe them.[6] Even if my father had not said so very plainly himself in his letters, it would be very evident from these drafts that the writing of an account that would satisfy him was exceedingly tasking and frustrating, largely (I believe) because he found the constraint of space profoundly uncongenial. In March 1955 (*Letters* no.160) he wrote to Rayner Unwin: 'I now wish that no appendices had been promised! For I think their appearance in truncated and compressed form will satisfy nobody'; and in the same letter he said:

> In any case the 'background' matter is very intricate, useless unless exact, and compression within the limits available leaves it unsatisfactory. It needs great concentration (and leisure), and being completely interlocked cannot be dealt with piecemeal. I have found that out, since I let part of it go.

Even the final typescript of Appendix F was not a fair copy, but carried many emendations.

Two texts of the second section of Appendix F, *On Translation*, are extant, following the reduced version in F 3 (p. 76) and preceding the final typescript. They were evidently made at a late stage in the evolution of this appendix; and it was in the first of these, which may conveniently be called 'A', that my father reinstated a part of the detailed discussion of names in the original version that had been discarded in F 3. At this stage he very largely retained the name-forms found in F 2, in his discussion of *Baggins*, *Gamgee*, *Cotton*, *Brandywine*, *Brandybuck*; the word *hobbit*; the origin of Hobbit-names such as *Tom*, *Bill*, *Mat*; *Meriadoc*, *Samwise*. There are however some differences and additions,[7] notably in his account of the curious names found in Buckland (cf. RK pp. 413–14):

These I have often left unaltered, for if queer now, they were queer in their own day. Some I have given a Celtic cast, notably *Meriadoc* and *Gorhendad*. There is some reason for this. Many of the actual Buckland (and Bree) names had something of that style: such as *Marroc*, *Madoc*, *Seredic*; and they often ended in *ac*, *ic*, *oc*. Also the relation of, say, Welsh or British to English was somewhat similar to that of the older language of the Stoors and Bree-men to the Westron.

Thus Bree, Combe, Archet, and Chetwood are modelled on British relics in English place-names, chosen by sense: *bree* 'hill', *chet* 'wood'. Similarly *Gorhendad* represents a name *Ogforgad* which according to Stoor-tradition had once meant 'great-grandfather or ancestor'. While *Meriadoc* was chosen to fit the fact that this character's shortened name meant 'jolly, gay' in Westron *kili*, though it was actually an abbreviation of *Kilimanac* [> *kali*, *Kalamanac*].

The text A lacks the discussion (RK pp. 414–15) of the words *mathom* and *smial* and the names *Sméagol* and *Déagol*, and ends, at the bottom of a page, with this passage:

The yet more northerly tongue of Dale is here seen only in the names of the Dwarves that came from that region, and so used the language of Men there, and took their 'outer' names in that language. The Dwarvish names in this book and in *The Hobbit* are in fact all genuine Norse dwarf-names; though the title *Oakenshield* is a translation.

Thus the concluding passage in F 3 (see pp. 76–7) concerning the use of the word *Gnomes* and of the plural *Dwarves* is absent, but whether because my father had rejected it, or because the end of the A typescript is lost, is impossible to say.

In the second of these texts *On Translation*, which I will call 'B', he retained all this reinstated material from A, changing some of the name-forms,[8] and even extended it, going back to the original version F 2 again for a passage exemplifying his treatment of the true names in the language of the Mark. Here reappears material derived from F 2 §§54–5 concerning the real native name of Rohan *Lôgrad*, the translation of *Lohtûr* by *Éothéod* and of *tûrak* 'king' by Théoden; and this is followed by the discussion of *mathom*, *smial*, *Sméagol* and *Déagol* – the only portion of this passage retained in the final form of Appendix F.

In B my father followed the passage given above from A ('The yet more northerly language of Dale ...') with a statement on the different treatment of the 'true' Runes in *The Hobbit* and *The Lord of the Rings* that derives from that in F* (p. 22, §11):

In keeping with the general method of translation here outlined, as applied to the Common Speech and other languages akin to it, in *The Hobbit* the *Cirth* were turned into Runes, into forms and values, that is, practically the same as those once used in

England. But since the *Cirth* were actually of Elvish origin, and little used for writing the Common Speech (save by Dwarves), while many readers of *The Hobbit* found the matter of scripts of interest, in this larger history it seemed better to present the *Cirth* as well as the Fëanorian letters in their proper shapes and use. Though naturally an adaptation by the translator of these alphabets to fit modern English has had to replace their actual application to the Westron tongue, which was very different from ours.

This is followed by the conclusion concerning *Gnomes* and *Dwarves* which is lacking in A.

In the final typescript, that sent to the printer, many changes entered that were not, as was almost invariably my father's practice when proceeding from one draft to the next, anticipated by corrections made to the preceding text: they seem in fact to have entered as he typed.[9] There is no suggestion in text B, for instance, of the footnote to RK p. 414 warning against an assumption, based on the linguistic transposition, 'that the Rohirrim closely resembled the ancient English otherwise'; nor of the removal from the body of the text of the detailed discussion of the word *hobbit* and the names *Gamgee* and *Brandywine* to a note at its end;[10] nor yet of the alteration of the passage (discussed on p. 77) concerning the word *Gnomes* so that it should apply to the word *Elves*, and the placing of it at the end of the text instead of preceding the discussion of *Dwarves*. Nothing could show more clearly the extreme pressure my father was under when, after so much labour, he at last sent Appendix F to the publishers. It seems to me more than likely that had circumstances been otherwise the form of that appendix would have been markedly different.

NOTES

1 The apparent implication here that *Teleri* was the name exclusively of those of the Eldar who remained in Middle-earth was certainly unintentional.

2 A footnote at this point reads: 'Such as *Thranduil* and *Legolas* from Mirkwood; *Lórien, Galadriel, Caras Galadon, Nimrodel, Amroth* and others from Loth-lórien.'

3 For an account of this reinstatement of material from F 2 see pp. 80–1, with notes 7 and 8.

4 It must be admitted, however, that the statement in the chapter *Of Maeglin* in *The Silmarillion* (p. 136) that Idril Celebrindal 'was golden as the Vanyar, her mother's kindred' appears already in the original text (1951; see XI.316); and of course even if the re-use of the passage did precede the appearance of the idea of the 'golden Vanyar', it needed correction subsequently.

5   With this cf. the passage in F 2 concerning Trolls (p. 36, §17): 'the
     evil Power had at various times made use of them, teaching them
     what little they could learn, and even crossing their breed with
     that of the larger Orcs.'

6   There is scarcely anything in the last texts that calls for special
     notice, but it should be recorded that in the penultimate draft my
     father revealed the meaning of the sentence in the Black Speech
     uttered by one of the Orcs who was guarding Pippin in the
     chapter *The Uruk-hai* (TT p. 48): *Uglúk u bagronk sha pushdug
     Saruman-glob búbhosh skai*. At the end of the section *Orcs and
     the Black Speech* (RK p. 410) this text reads:

>   ... while the curse of the Mordor-orc in Chapter 3 of Book
>   Three is in the more debased form used by the soldiers of the
>   Dark Tower, of whom Grishnákh was the captain. *Uglúk to the
>   cesspool, sha! the dungfilth; the great Saruman-fool, skai!*

7   Where F 2 in the discussion of *Baggins* (p. 48) had Westron *labin*
     'bag', and *Labin-nec* 'Bag End', the text A has *laban, Laban-nec*.
     For the origin of 'hobbit' my father retained the form *cubuc* and
     Théoden's archaic *cûgbagu* (p. 49), noting that it meant ' "hole-
     dweller" (or "hole-builder")': see p. 69. He also gave here for
     the first time the Westron name for 'hobbits', *nathramin*, though
     later in the text the form *banathin* appears; and he provided the
     true name of Hamfast Gamgee:

>   The Gaffer's name on the other hand was *Ranadab*, meaning
>   'settled, living in a fixed abode or group of hobbit-holes',
>   and hence often 'stay-at-home', the opposite of 'wanderer'.
>   Since this closely corresponds with ancient English *hamfæst*,
>   I have translated it as *Hamfast*. The shortenings [*Sam* and
>   *Ham*] at any rate rhyme, as did *Ban* and *Ran* in the Shire.
>   Moreover neither *Banzîra* nor *Ranadab* were any longer
>   current in the Shire as ordinary words and survived only as
>   names, originally given no doubt as (not entirely complimen-
>   tary) nicknames, but used traditionally in certain families with-
>   out much more recognition than is the case today with, say,
>   Roy or Francis.

8   For *Laban-nec* 'Bag End' in A the second text B has *Laban-neg*.
     The 'hobbit' word became *kubug*, and the Rohan form *kûgbagul*,
     changed on the typescript to *cuduc* and *kûddûka*. The true
     name of Gorhendad Oldbuck became *Ogmandab*, and that of
     Meriadoc *Kalimanac*, altered to *Kalimanoc* (*Kalimac* in RK); that
     of Hamfast Gamgee became *Ranagad* (*Ranugad* in RK), and of
     Sam *Banzîra*. The Westron word for 'hobbit' became *banakil*, as
     in RK; but *Branduhîm* 'foaming beer' as the Hobbits' perversion
     of *Baranduin* remained (see note 10), as did *Carbandur* for
     Imladris (with *Karningul*, as in RK, pencilled against it).

9 It is clear that there was no intermediate text.
10 The introduction of the Hobbits' original name for the river, *Branda-nîn* 'border-water' or 'Marchbourn', transformed into *Bralda-hîm* 'heady ale', was only made in this last typescript.

III

THE FAMILY TREES

This chapter is an account of the evolution of the genealogical tables given in Appendix C to *The Lord of the Rings*; and since such a development can obviously be followed far more easily and rapidly by successive stages of the tables themselves than by any account in words, I present it here largely by redrawings of the original family trees. My father followed his usual course of emending each one (most of them being carefully, even beautifully, made) more or less roughly in preparation for its successor; I have therefore in my redrawings excluded subsequent alterations, when the distinction can be clearly made.

Baggins of Hobbiton

The first four genealogical tables of the Baggins family, to which I give the references **BA 1** to **BA 4**, are found on pp. 89–92.

BA 1 (p. 89)

This is the earliest tree of the family of Baggins of Hobbiton (by which I mean the earliest fully formed and carefully presented table, excluding such hasty genealogies as that referred to in VI.222). It was very carefully made, but was much used and corrected later, and is now a very battered document. The number of members of the Baggins family shown is still far fewer than in the published table; and the presence of *Folco Took* (with *Faramond* pencilled beside it) suggests that it belongs to the period that I have called 'the Third Phase' in the writing of the earlier chapters of *The Fellowship of the Ring*, before the emergence of Peregrin Took (see VII.31–2). It may be related therefore to the original text of the *Prologue* (see p. 3 and note 1), and to the original tree of the Took family given in VI.317. As in that table, the ages of those present at the Farewell Party are given, but not extended as a system of relative dating for all members of the family including those long dead; and dates are also given according to the Shire Reckoning (which appeared quite early, in the autumn of 1939, see VII.9).

It will be seen that virtually all the dates in BA 1 differ from those for the corresponding persons in the published form, though seldom by much.

A good deal of this genealogy was present already in the first stages of the writing of *The Lord of the Rings*, but I will not return here to the early history of the Baggins family tree, since it has been fully recounted in *The Return of the Shadow* and all the names indexed. It may be noted, however, that the maiden name of Miranda Burrows, who was described (VI.283) as the 'overshadowed wife' of Cosimo Sackville-Baggins, was never given in the narrative texts before she disappeared (VI.324); and that Flambard Took, son of the Old Took, and his wife Rosa Baggins had appeared in the original Took family tree given in VI.317.

BA 2 (p. 90)

This table was a rough working version, taking up changes marked on BA 1, and with further alterations and additions entering in the course of its making. It was immediately followed by an even hastier version without dates, hardly differing from BA 2, but introducing one or two further changes that appear in BA 3 (and changing Miranda Burrows to Miranda Noakes and then to Miranda Sandyman). I have given no number to this text, regarding it simply as an extension of BA 2.

As my father first made this table Bingo Baggins was moved down to become the youngest of the three sons of Mungo, but remained the husband of Maxima Proudfoot. While it was in progress, however, a daughter Linda Baggins was introduced above him, and she took over the Proudfoot connection, becoming the wife of Marco Proudfoot and the mother of Odo Proudfoot; while Bingo, now the youngest of a family of five, as he remained, became the husband of Fatima Chubb.

Olo Proudfoot was first named Rollo; and Rosa Baggins' husband Flambard Took becomes Hildigrim Took (the final name: see the Took genealogy T 3 on p. 110). The names Ponto, Largo, Longo, Fosco, Dora, replacing Longo, Tango, Largo, Togo, Semolina respectively, remained into the final form of the genealogy. It may also be noted that Drogo's birth-date was changed to make him a year younger than his sister Dora, though his place in the tree was not altered; it will be seen that in BA 3 he is again made older than her by a year.

BA 3 (p. 91)

The third Baggins family tree is one of a series of carefully made tables, and being the first carries an explanatory head-note, as follows:

> The dates in these Trees are given according to the 'Shire-reckoning', in the traditional Hobbit manner, calculated from the crossing of the Baranduin (Brandywine River), Year 1, by the brothers Marco and Cavallo. The persons mentioned in these tables are only a selection from many names. All are either concerned with the events recounted in the memoirs of Bilbo and Frodo; or are mentioned in them; or are persons present at the Farewell Party, or the direct ancestors of the guests on that occasion. The names of these guests (such of the 144 as room has been found for) are marked *.

Bilbo Baggins, born 1290, went on his famous journey 1341–2. At the age of 111 he gave his Farewell Party in 1401. Frodo Baggins sold Bag End in 1418 and returned at the end of 1419. He left the Shire in 1421. Meriadoc Brandybuck succeeded to Brandy Hall and the headship of the family in 1432. Peregrin became The Took (and Seventeenth Shirking) in 1434. The memoirs (and additions by Samwise Gamgee) close in 1436.

The mention here of Peregrin becoming the seventeenth Shirking relates this table at once to the texts of the *Prologue* (see pp. 5–7, 11) composed after the narrative of *The Lord of the Rings* had been completed, and suggests that the family trees followed something of the same succession as is found in the Prologue texts. – I have not included in my redrawing the stars indicating presence at the Farewell Party, for my father only put them in later and incompletely.

On the family name Gaukroger (subsequently lost), appearing in Togo Baggins' wife Selina Gaukroger, see VI.236 and note 10; and on Belisarius Bolger see note 3.

BA 4 (p. 92)

The fourth tree is the first text of another set of genealogies, and seems to belong to much the same time as BA 3. This also is finely written, with an introductory note that is virtually the same as that in the published form (RK p. 379), apart from the preservation of the names Marco and Cavallo, but then continues with the second paragraph (giving dates) of that to BA 3, and includes the reference to Peregrin's becoming the 'Seventeenth Shirking'.

This version retains the dates of BA 3 (not repeated in the redrawing), and differs from it chiefly in the addition of descendants from Bingo and Ponto Baggins; also by the loss of Togo Baggins and his wife Selina Gaukroger and their replacement by a second daughter of Inigo and Belinda, Laura, and her husband Togo Gaukroger.

The new names Polo, Porro are referred to in both texts of the original version of the Appendix on Languages (see p. 46, §43), showing that that work followed or accompanied this stage in the development of the family trees.

The starred names, indicating presence at the Farewell Party, are as in the published table, with the omission of Cosimo Sackville-Baggins and Dora Baggins: this was perhaps inadvertent, but neither name is starred in BA 3.

Sweeping changes to the existing names were entered subsequently on BA 4. In the introductory note Marco and Cavallo were changed to Marcho and Blanco (see pp. 6, 17), and 'Seventeenth Shirking' to 'Twentieth Thane' (see under BA 3). In the family tree the following changes were made, listed by generations:

Inigo Baggins > Balbo Baggins

Belinda Boffin > Berylla Boffin

Regina Grubb > Laura Grubb
Ansegar Bolger > Fastolph Bolger
Maxima Bunce > Mimosa Bunce
Cornelia Hornblower > Tanta Hornblower
Laura Baggins > Lily Baggins
Togo Gaukroger > Togo Goodbody

Bertha Baggins > Belba Baggins
Rudigor Bolger > Rudigar Bolger
Magnus Proudfoot > Bodo Proudfoot
Fatima Chubb > Chica Chubb
Robinia Bolger > Ruby Bolger

Conrad Bolger > Wilibald Bolger

Cosimo Sackville-Baggins > Lotho Sackville-Baggins
Gerda Chubb-Baggins > Poppy Chubb-Baggins
Arnor Bolger > Filibert Bolger
Porro Baggins > Porto Baggins
Crassus Burrows > Milo Burrows
Duenna Baggins > Daisy Baggins
Guido Boffin > Griffo Boffin

Flavus, Crispus, Rhoda, Fulvus Burrows > Mosco, Moro, Myrtle,
    Minto Burrows

In addition, the wife of Posco Baggins was introduced, named (as
in the final form) Gilly Brownlock; and Ponto Baggins' daughter
Angelica appeared.

On the removal of the Latin names of Peony Baggins' husband and
their offspring see p. 47, §45, and commentary (p. 69).

The nomenclature and structure of the Baggins genealogy as published was now present, except in this respect. In the final form Frodo's
aunt Dora again becomes older than her brother Drogo (see under
BA 2 above), and her husband Wilibald Bolger (see the list just given)
is removed; while Posco Baggins has a sister Prisca, born in 1306, and
she gains Wilibald as her husband.

In subsequent manuscripts (of which there were five, making nine
all told, not including incomplete drafts) these changes entered, and in
one of them the word 'spinster' was written against Dora Baggins.

Bolger of Budgeford

It is a curious fact that the genealogical tables of the families of Bolger
of Budgeford and Boffin of the Yale were already in print when they
were rejected from Appendix C, but I have not been able to find any
evidence bearing on the reason for their rejection. In a letter from the
publishers of 20 May 1955 my father was told: 'We have dropped
Bolger and Boffin from Appendix C', and on 24 May Rayner Unwin

89

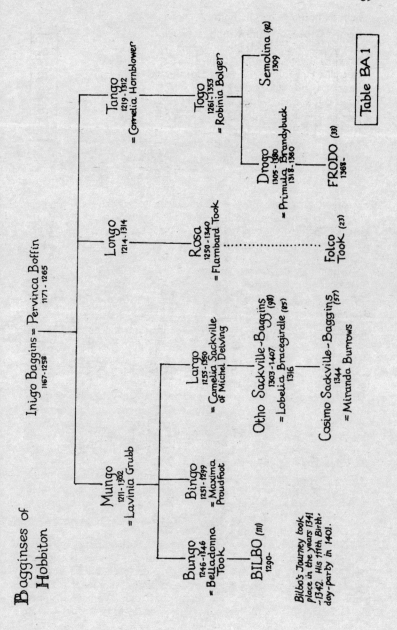

Bagginses of Hobbiton

Inigo Baggins = Pervinca Boffin
1167-1258   1171-1265

Mungo
1211-1302
= Lavinia Grubb

Longo
1214-1314

Tango
1219-1312
= Camelia Hornblower

Bungo
1246-1346
= Belladonna
Took

Bingo
1251-1299
= Maxima
Proudfoot

Largo
1255-1350
= Camelia Sackville
of Michel Delving

Rosa
1250-1340
= Flambard Took

Togo
1261-1353
= Robinia Bolger

BILBO (111)
1290-

Otho Sackville-Baggins (98)
1303-1407
= Lobelia Bracegirdle (95)
1316

**Folco
Took** (23)

Drogo
1305-1380
= Primula Brandybuck
1318-1380

Semolina (92)
1309

Casimo Sackville-Baggins (57)
1344
= Miranda Burrows

FRODO (33)
1368-

*Bilbo's Journey took
place in the years 1341
–1342. His 111th Birth-
day-party in 1401.*

Table BA 1

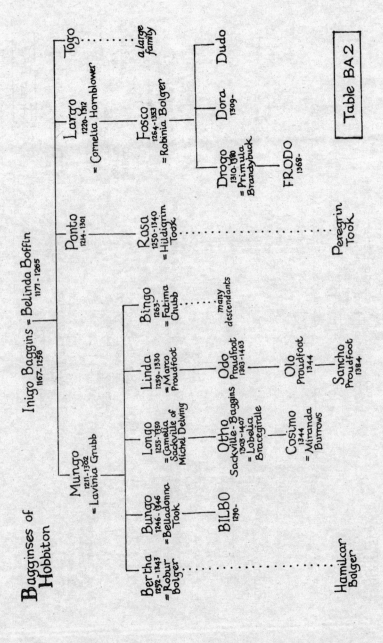

Bagginses of Hobbiton

Inigo Baggins = Belinda Boffin
1167-1256   1171-1265

Mungo 1211-1302 = Lavinia Grubb

- **Bertha** 1252-1343 = Robur Bolger .... **Hamilcar Bolger**
- **Bungo** 1246-1346 = Belladonna Took
  - **BILBO** 1290-
- **Longo** 1255-1350 = Camelia Sackville of Michel Delving
  - **Otho** Sackville-Baggins 1303-1407 = Lobelia Bracegirdle
    - **Cosimo** 1344 = Miranda Burrows
- **Linda** 1259-1330 = Marco Proudfoot
  - **Odo** Proudfoot 1303-1403
    - **Olo** Proudfoot 1344
      - **Sancho** Proudfoot 1384
- **Bingo** 1263- = Fatima Chubb .... many descendants

Ponto 1214-1301

- **Rosa** 1250-1340 = Hildigrim Took .... **Peregrin Took**

Largo 1220-1312 = Cornelia Hornblower

- **Fosco** 1264-1353 = Robinia Bolger
  - **Drogo** 1310-1380 = Primula Brandybuck
    - **FRODO** 1368-
  - **Dora** 1309-
  - **Dudo**

Togo .... a large family

Table BA2

91

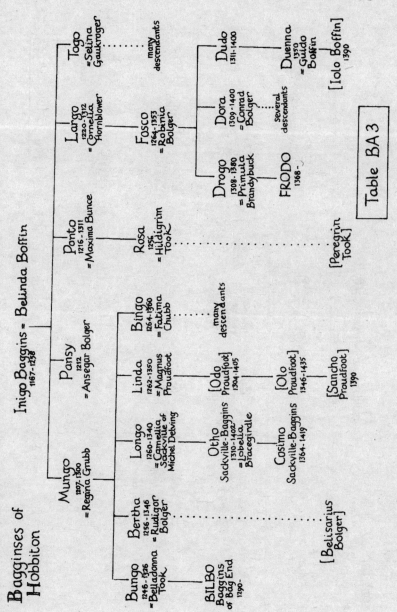

Table BA 3

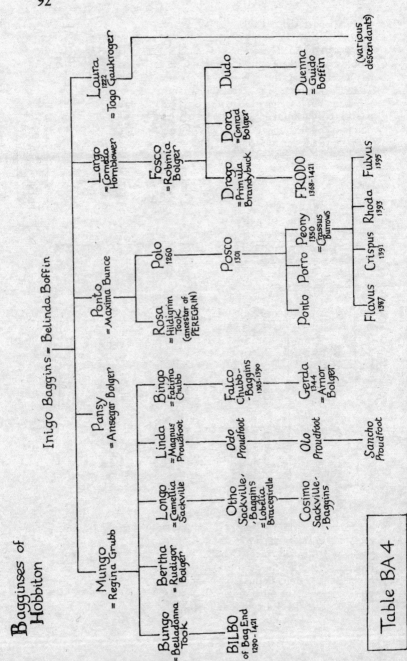

Bagginses of Hobbiton

Inigo Baggins = Belinda Boffin

Mungo = Regina Grubb

Pansy = Ansegar Bolger

Ponto = Maxima Bunce

Largo = Cornelia Hornblower

Laura 1222 = Togo Gawkroger

Bungo = Belladonna Took

BILBO of Bag End 1290-1421

Bertha = Rudigor Bolger

Longo = Camellia Sackville

Linda = Magnus Proudfoot

Bingo = Fatima Chubb

Rosa = Hildigrim Took (ancestor of PEREGRIN)

Polo 1260

Fosco = Robinia Bolger

Dudo

Otho Sackville-Baggins = Lobelia Bracegirdle

Odo Proudfoot

Falco Chubb-Baggins 1303-1390

Posco 1301

Drogo = Primula Brandybuck

Dora = Conrad Bolger?

Duenna = Guido Boffin

Cosimo Sackville-Baggins

Olo Proudfoot

Gerda 1344 = Amor Bolger

Ponto   Porro   Peony 1350 = Crassus Burrows

FRODO 1368-1421

(various descendants)

Sancho Proudfoot

Flavus 1387   Crispus 1391   Rhoda 1393   Fulvus 1395

Table BA 4

wrote: 'I have deleted the two family trees and the redundant note that introduced them' (no copy of either tree has any note specifically relating to them). These remarks might suggest that it was my father who proposed their omission, though no trace can now be found of any such request; but it is hard to see why he should have done so. That he was pressed for space, and greatly oppressed by that necessity, is certain, but it seems strange (if this is the explanation) that he should have been so limited as to abandon these genealogies in order to obtain a couple of pages elsewhere in the Appendices.

I refer to the versions of the Bolger genealogy by the letters **BG**, and the three that I have redrawn, BG 1, BG 2, and BG 4, will be found on pp. 95–7.

BG 1 (p. 95)

This earliest form of the Bolger family tree is entitled *Bolgers of Woodhall*. On my father's original map of the Shire, reproduced as frontispiece to *The Return of the Shadow*, the Bolger territory is marked as lying north of the Woody End and south of the East Road (i.e. west of the Brandywine Bridge).

The very brief table is found, together with genealogies of the Tooks and Brandybucks, on the page that carries the original Baggins family tree BA 1, and was very plainly made at the same time, at an early stage in the writing of *The Lord of the Rings* (see pp. 85, 89); but these early Bolgers, Scudamor, Cedivar, Savanna, Sagramor, are not found in those texts. Robinia Bolger in the fourth generation appears also in BA 1 as the wife of Togo Baggins; but her brother Robur is seen to have existed independently before he was introduced into the Baggins family in BA 2 (p. 90) as the husband of Bertha Baggins, Bilbo's aunt, who first emerged in that version. Rollo Bolger is that friend of Bilbo's to whom he bequeathed his feather-bed (VI.247). Olo and Odo appear in the Took genealogy given in VI.317; for my attempt to expound briefly the history of 'Odo Bolger' see VII.31–2.

BG 2 (p. 96)

The second version of the Bolger genealogy[1] is one of the group of which the Baggins table BA 3 (p. 91) is the first, carrying the explanatory head-note. The title is now changed to *Bolgers of Budgeford*. In the chapter *A Conspiracy Unmasked* (FR p. 118) Fredegar's family is said to come 'from Budgeford in Bridgefields' (the only occurrence of these names in the narrative of *The Lord of the Rings*).[2]

Apart from Odovacar, Rudigor (later Rudigar), and Fredegar (applied to a different person), none of the actual names of members of the Bolger family in this genealogy appear in the family-trees in RK, but some recur in other tables made at the same time: thus in the Baggins table BA 3 are found Ansegar (husband of Pansy Baggins),

Robinia (wife of Fosco Baggins), Conrad (husband of Dora Baggins), and Belisarius (replacing Hamilcar).[3]

Two of the names subsequently rejected are mentioned in the text F 2 of the Appendix on Languages: Celador Bolger (p. 61, note 42), and Bildad Bolger. Bildad is mentioned in F 2 (p. 51, §50) in the context of my father's not using scriptural names to 'translate' Hobbit names: it was 'a genuine Hobbit name', he explained, that bore a merely accidental resemblance to the Biblical Bildad (one of the friends of Job).

The name *Miranda* (Gaukroger) reappears after the disappearance of Miranda Burrows, wife of Cosimo Sackville-Baggins (p. 86). Robur Bolger (see under BG 1) has been replaced, as in BA 3, by Rudigor, but Robur remains as the name of Rudigor's younger brother.

BG 3

This table corresponds to BA 4 of the Baggins clan, but it repeats BG 2 exactly except in the addition of Robur's descendants, and in the change of the name *Gundobad* to *Gundahad*. I have not redrawn it, therefore, but give here the added element:

Robur = Amelia Hornblower
|
Omar = Alma Boffin
|
Arnor = Gerda Chubb-Baggins

Arnor and his wife Gerda Chubb-Baggins appear in BA 4. – The birthdates of these Bolgers are the same as those of their replacements in BG 4: Robur (Rudibert) 1260, Omar (Adalbert) 1301, Arnor (Filibert) 1342.

BG 4 (p. 97)

On the Baggins table BA 4 my father made many changes to the existing names, and in so doing brought the Baggins genealogy close to its final form. On the accompanying Bolger table BG 3 he did the same, but even more extensively, so that of the existing names none were left save Gundahad, Rudigar (altered from Rudigor), Odovacar (see VII.20), and Fredegar (who becomes the former Fredegar's grandson), and the Bolger clan have uniformly 'translated' names of Germanic origin. At the same time three children of Wilibald Bolger (formerly Conrad) were added; and the Hobbit family names Diggle and Lightfoot (not found in *The Lord of the Rings*) appear.[4]

Of those who do not appear in the published genealogies the following are marked as guests at the Farewell Party: Wilimar, Heribald, and Nora, and also their mother Prisca Baggins (see p. 88), who is not so marked in the Baggins tree. She was 95; but Frodo's still more ancient aunt Dora was present at the age of ninety-nine.

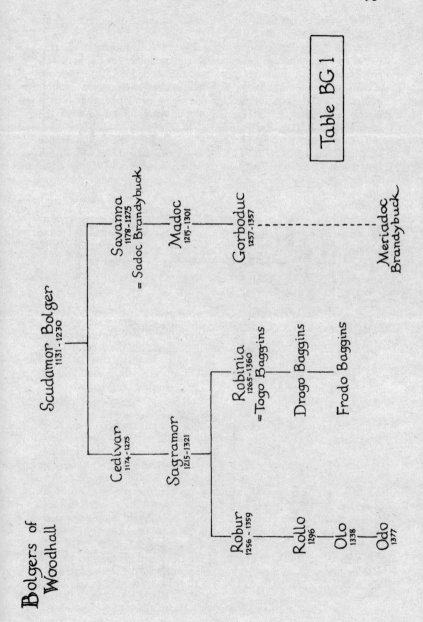

Bolgers of Woodhall

Scudamor Bolger
1131 - 1230

Cedivar
1174 - 1275

Savanna
1178 - 1275
= Sadoc Brandybuck

Sagramor
1215 - 1321

Madoc
1215 - 1301

Robur
1256 - 1359

Robinia
1265 - 1360
= Togo Baggins

Gorboduc
1257 - 1357

Rollo
1296

Drogo Baggins

Olo
1338

Frodo Baggins

Odo
1377

Meriadoc Brandybuck

Table BG 1

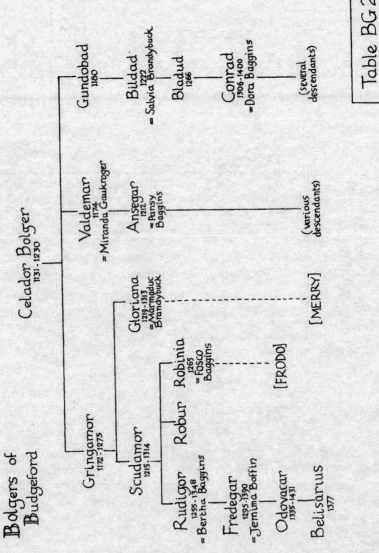

Bolgers of Budgeford

Celador Bolger
1131-1230

Gringamor
1172-1275

Gundobad
1180

Valdemar
1174
= Miranda Gaukroger

Ansegar
1212
= Pansy Baggins

(various descendants)

Bildad
1222
= Salvia Brandybuck

Bladud
1266

Conrad
1306-1400
= Dora Baggins

(several descendants)

Scudamor
1215-1314

Gloriana
1219-1313
= Marmaduc Brandybuck

- - - [MERRY]

Rudigor
1255-1348
= Bertha Baggins

Robur

Robinia
1265
= Fosco Baggins

- - - [FRODO]

Fredegar
1295-1390
= Jemima Boffin

Odovacar
1335-1431

Belisarius
1377

Table BG2

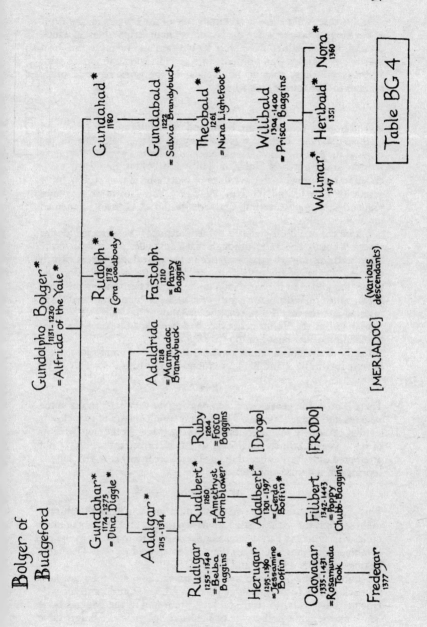

97

Bolger of Budgeford

Gundolpho Bolger* 1131-1230 = Alfrida of the Yale*

Gundahar* 1174-1275 = Dina Diggle*

Adalgar* 1215-1314

Rudigar 1255-1348 = Belba Baggins

Herugar* 1295-1390 = Jessamine Boffin*

Odovacar 1335-1431 = Rosamunda Took

Fredegar 1377

Rudibert* 1260 = Amethyst Hornblower*

Adalbert* 1301-1397 = Gerda Boffin*

Filibert 1342-1443 = Poppy Chubb-Baggins

Ruby 1264 = Fosco Baggins

[Drogo]

[FRODO]

Adaldrida 1218 = Marmadoc Brandybuck

[MERIADOC]

Rudolph* 1178 = Cora Goodbody*

Fastolph 1210 = Pansy Baggins

(various descendants)

Gundahad* 1180

Gundabald 1222 = Salvia Brandybuck

Theobald* 1261 = Nina Lightfoot*

Wilibald 1304-1400 = Prisca Baggins

Wilimar* 1347

Heribald* 1351

Nora* 1360

Table BG 4

In this case, since there is no family tree of the Bolgers in *The Lord of the Rings*, I have redrawn the last of the manuscript tables, in which the alterations made to BG 3 were set out fair; and it was in this form that the genealogy was printed.[5] In this redrawing the names with asterisks are those that do not appear in the genealogies of other families in *The Lord of the Rings*.

Boffin of the Yale

In *The Lord of the Rings* no 'homeland' of the Boffins is named, and in the First Edition there was no mention of the Yale; but on the original map of the Shire (frontispiece to Vol.VI) the name *Boffins* is written to the north of Hobbiton Hill,[6] and Boffins are clearly associated in early texts with the village of Northope in that region, 'only a mile or two behind the Hill' (VI.319, 385). Northope was subsequently renamed Overhill, and 'Mr. Boffin at Overhill' remained into FR (p. 53).

But on the first Shire-map the name Northope was corrected, not to Overhill but to The Yale, although that name does not appear in the texts; and this must be the reference in the genealogical trees, which retained 'Boffin of the Yale' into the printed form. Much later the name was added to the Shire map in the Second Edition in a different place, south of Whitfurrows and west of Stock, and a reference was inserted into the text (FR p. 86), 'the lowlands of the Yale' (see VI.387, note 10); but the Boffin genealogy had been abandoned before the publication of the First Edition (p. 88).

I refer to the Boffin family trees by the letters **BF**, and those that I have redrawn, BF 2 and BF 4, are found on pp. 100–1.

BF 1

There is no Boffin genealogy accompanying the very early tables of the Baggins and Bolger families. The earliest form consists of two closely similar, extremely rough drafts on the same pages as the two versions of BA 2 (see p. 86): so rough and so much corrected that I have not attempted to redraw either of them. They were in any case very largely repeated in the following version.

BF 2 (p. 100)

This genealogy is extant in two forms, differing only in that the first of them sets out the earliest generations separately, and begins the main table with Otto the Fat, whereas in the second form the elements are combined: for these purposes they can be treated as one. This table belongs with BA 3 (p. 91) and BG 2 (p. 96).

Hugo Boffin, whose wife was Donnamira Took, and their son Jago go back to the Took genealogy given in VI.317; Guido and his wife Duenna Baggins, with their son Iolo, are found in the Baggins table BA 3; and Jemima Boffin wife of Fredegar Bolger in the Bolger table

BG 2. Hugo Bracegirdle, who does not appear in the published genealogies, is named in FR (p. 46) as the recipient of a book-case belonging to Bilbo.

Lobelia Sackville-Baggins' dates make her 92 at her death: at the beginning of the chapter *The Grey Havens* (RK p. 301) the text had 'she was after all quite ninety years old', changed on the late type-scripts to 'more than a hundred'; and on the following version of the Boffin genealogy her dates were altered to 1318–1420.

The subsequent development of the Boffin genealogy exactly parallels that of the Bolgers, and I treat them in the same way.

BF 3

This is written on the same page as BG 3, and as in that table the previous version was followed exactly, but with the corresponding addition (see p. 94) introducing Alma Boffin, the wife of Omar Bolger. This table is not redrawn. As in the case of BG 3 (and also of the accompanying Baggins table BA 4) a great many of the names were changed on the manuscript of BF 3, and new Boffins were introduced in the second generation.

BF 4 (p. 101)

As with the Bolger genealogy, I give here the final manuscript of the Boffin table (written on the same page as BG 4), the form from which it was printed, in which the changed names and additions made on BF 3 appear in a fair copy; and here also the starred names indicate those that are not found in the genealogies of other families in *The Lord of the Rings*. Folco Boffin, who is not present in any of these, was a friend of Frodo's (FR pp. 51, 76–7, and see VII.30–2); for Hugo Bracegirdle see under BF 2 above.

Of those who do not appear in the published genealogies the following are marked as being present at the Farewell Party: Vigo, Folco, Tosto, Bruno Bracegirdle, Hugo Bracegirdle, and the 'various descendants' of Rollo Boffin and Druda Burrows.

Brandybuck of Buckland

The Brandybuck genealogies are referred to by the letters BR; for the redrawn versions BR 1 and BR 4 see pp. 104–5.

BR 1 (p. 104)

This earliest version of the Brandybuck family tree is written below the earliest of the Baggins clan (BA 1), with those of the Bolgers (BG 1) and the Tooks (not the earliest) on the reverse.

Many of the names found here are found also in the Took genealogy given in VI.317: Gorboduc Brandybuck and his wife Mirabella Took, and their six children (see VI.318) Roderic, Alaric, Bellissima, Theodoric, Athanaric, and Primula; also Caradoc, Merry's father, and

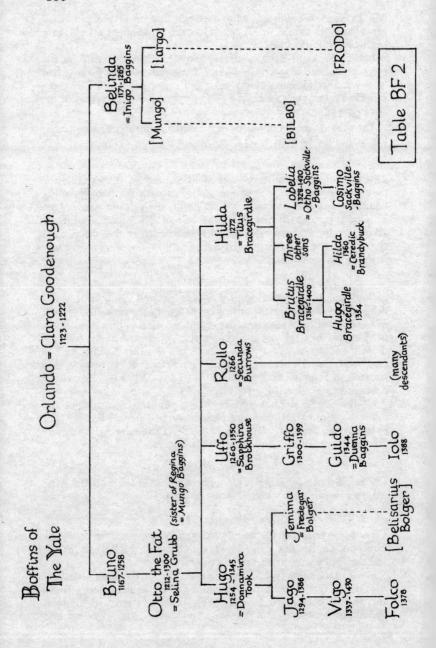

Boffins of
The Yale

Orlando = Clara Goodenough
1123 - 1222

Bruno
1167-1258

Otto the Fat
1212-1300
= Selina Grubb

(sister of Regina
= Mungo Baggins)

Belinda
1171-1265
= Inigo Baggins

[Mungo]   [Largo]

[BILBO]   [FRODO]

Hilda
1272
= Titus Bracegirdle

Brutus
Bracegirdle
1316-1400

Three
other
sons

Lobelia
1328-1420
= Otho Sackville-
- Baggins

Hugo
Bracegirdle
1354

Hilda
1360
= Ceredic Brandybuck

Cosimo
Sackville-
- Baggins

Rollo
1266
= Secunda Burrows

(many
descendants)

Uffo
1260-1350
= Sapphira Brockhouse

Griffo
1300-1399

Guido
1344
= Duenna Baggins

Iolo
1388

Hugo
1254 - 1345
= Donnamira Took

Jago
1294-1386

Jemima
= Fredegar
Bolger

Vigo
1337-1430

[Belisarius Bolger]

Folco
1378

Table BF 2

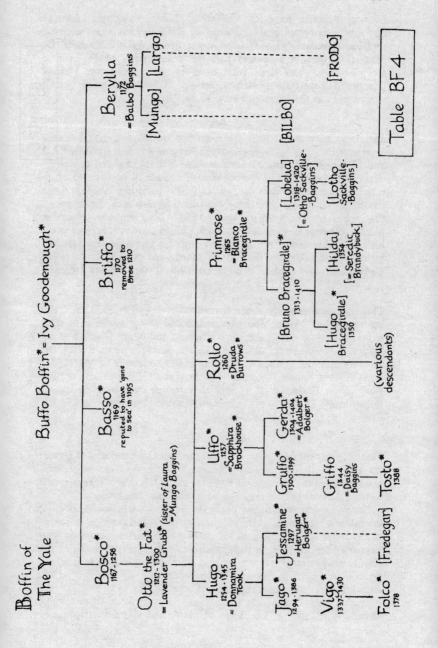

Table BF 4

his wife Yolanda Took (cf. VI.100, 251). Merry's cousin Lamorac appears in early texts of *The Lord of the Rings*,[7] where the name replaced Bercilak (VI.273) who in the genealogy is his father. Of Madoc (Gorboduc's father) and the descendants of his second son Habaccuc there is no trace in those texts, except for Melissa (afterwards replaced by Melilot, see pp. 105–6, who made herself conspicuous at the Farewell Party, VI.38, 101).

BR 2

This is an extremely rough table, written in ink over pencil on the reverse of the page carrying the rough Baggins and Bolger tables BA 2 and BF 1: here my father is seen devising a much changed genealogy of the Brandybucks. I have not redrawn it, since its names and structure largely survived into the fair copy BR 4, and it needs only to be recorded that it was here that Gorhendad Brandybuck the 'founder' first appeared, but with the dates 1134–1236, and not yet as the remote ancestor Gorhendad Oldbuck of four centuries before; while his son is Marmaduc, not as subsequently his grandson, and Madoc, Sadoc, and Marroc are the sons of Marmaduc. 'Old Rory' is called Cadwalader; and all the Latin titles (see BR 4) were already present.

BR 3

This was another rough draft, scarcely differing from BR 2 except in the reversal of Madoc and Marmaduc and in the addition of their wives: Madoc's wife is Savanna Hogpen, and Marmaduc's Sultana Bolger. In the original Bolger table (BG 1, p. 95) Savanna Bolger was the wife of Sadoc Brandybuck, while in BG 2 the wife of Marmaduc was Gloriana Bolger. Corrections to the text altered the name of 'Old Rory' from Cadwalader to Sagramor (taken over from Sagramor Bolger in BG 1), and of his wife from Matilda Drinkwater to Matilda Goold.

BR 4 (p. 105)

This carefully made version is one of the series that includes (Baggins) BA 3 (p. 91), (Bolger) BG 2 (p. 96), and (Boffin) BF 2 (p. 100). Additions were made subsequently to BR 4, but in this case it is convenient to treat them as part of the table as first written (see below).

In this new version of the Brandybuck tree, comprised in BR 2–4, my father's enjoyment of the incongruity of Hobbit customs of name-giving culminated in such marriages as that of Madoc Superbus with Savanna Hogpen, and in the grandiose epithets of the heads of the clan, with Meriadoc taking his title Porphyrogenitus from imperial Byzantium, 'born in the purple (chamber)'. In the text F 2 of the Appendix on Languages my father wrote (p. 47, §45): ' "Classical" names ... represent usually names derived by Hobbits from tales of ancient times and far kingdoms of Men', and added in a footnote:

'Thus the perhaps to us rather ridiculous subnames or titles of the Brandybucks adopted by the heads of the family, *Astyanax*, *Aureus*, *Magnificus*, were originally half-jesting and were in fact drawn from traditions about the Kings at Norbury.' Afterwards he struck out this note and rejected classical names (see p. 69, §45).

The following additions, included in the redrawing, were made to the table after it had been completed. Sadoc Brandybuck, at first said to have had 'many descendants', is given 'Two sons' and a daughter Salvia, the wife of Bildad Bolger (see BG 2, p. 96); Basilissa Brandybuck becomes the wife of Fulvus Burrows; their son Crassus Burrows is added, who on account of his marriage to Peony Baggins has appeared in BA 4 (p. 92), together with their four children; and Hilda Bracegirdle enters as the wife of Ceredic Brandybuck, with their three children. As the table was made Marmaduc's wife was still Sultana Bolger, but she was changed to Gloriana as in BG 2.

BR 5

Following the general pattern, BR 5 was recopied from BR 4 almost as it stood: the only change made was that Gorhendad was now actually named Gorhendad Oldbuck, retaining the note 'Built Brandy Hall and changed the family name to Brandybuck' (retaining also the dates 1134–1236); and then subsequently a great many of the names were altered on the manuscript.

Gorhendad Oldbuck was replaced by Gormadoc 'Deepdelver', and his wife Malva Headstrong was introduced. 'Gorhendad Oldbuck of the Marish', however, is Gormadoc's father, and his dates are 1090–1191. At this time all the Latin or Greek titles of the heads of the Brandybuck clan were replaced by English names, as in the final genealogy. Other changes were (following the generations):

Savanna Hogpen > Hanna Goldworthy

Marmaduc > Marmadoc
Gloriana Bolger > Adaldrida Bolger (see BG 4)
Bildad Bolger > Gundabald Bolger (see BG 4)

Gorboduc > Gormanac > Gorbadoc
Orgulus > Orgulas

Sagramor > Rorimac
Matilda Goold > Menegilda Goold
Bellissima > Amaranth
Carados > Saradas
Basilissa > Asphodel
Fulvus Burrows > Rufus Burrows
Priamus > Dinodas
Columbus > Gorgulas > Gorbulas

Caradoc > Saradoc

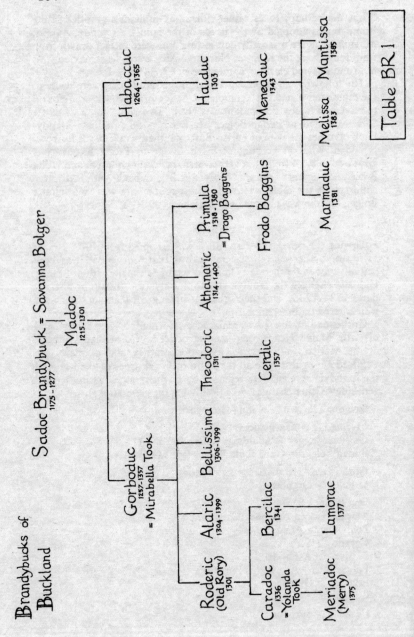

Brandybucks of
Buckland

Sadoc Brandybuck = Savanna Bolger
1175 - 1277

Madoc
1215-1301

Habaccuc
1264 - 1365

Gorboduc
1257 - 1357
= Mirabella Took

Haiduc
1303

Meneaduc
1343

Marmaduc
1381

Melissa
1383

Mantissa
1385

Roderic
(Old Rory)
1301

Alaric
1304 - 1399

Bellissima
1306 - 1399

Theodoric
1311

Athanaric
1314 - 1400

Primula
1310 - 1380
= Drogo Baggins

Bercilac
1341

Cerdic
1357

Frodo Baggins

Caradoc
1336
= Yolanda
Took

Lamorac
1377

Meriadoc
(Merry)
1375

Table BR1

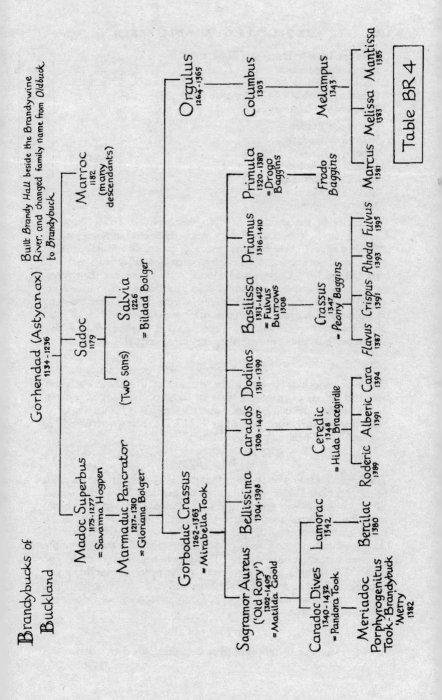

Brandybucks of Buckland

Gorhendad (Astyanax) 1134–1236   Built *Brandy Hall* beside the Brandywine River, and changed family name from *Oldbuck* to *Brandybuck*

Madoc Superbus 1175–1277 = Savanna Hogpen

Sadoc 1179

Marroc 1182 (many descendants)

Marmaduc Pancrator 1217–1310 = Gloriana Bolger

(Two sons)

Salvia 1226 = Bildad Bolger

Orgulus 1264–1565

Columbus 1303

Gorboduc Crassus 1262–1363 = Mirabella Took

Bellissima 1304–1398

Carados 1308–1407

Dodinas 1311–1399

Basilissa 1313–1412 = Fulvus Burrows 1308

Priamus 1316–1410

Primula 1320–1380 = Drogo Baggins

Melampus 1343

Sagramor Aureus ('Old Rory') 1302–1405 = Matilda Goold

Ceredic 1348 = Hilda Bracegirdle

Crassus 1347 = Peony Baggins

Frodo Baggins

Marcus 1381   Melissa 1383   Mantissa 1385

Caradoc Dives 1340–1432 = Pandora Took

Lamorac 1342

Roderic 1389   Alberic 1391   Cara 1394

Flavus 1387   Crispus 1391   Rhoda 1393   Fulvus 1395

Bercilac 1380

Meriadoc Porphyrogenitus Took-Brandybuck 'Merry' 1382

Table BR 4

Pandora Took > Esmeralda Took
Lamorac > Merimac
Ceredic > Seredic
Crassus Burrows > Milo Burrows (see p. 88)
Melampus > Marmadas

Bercilac > Berilac
Roderic > Doderic
Alberic > Ilberic
Cara > Celandine
Marcus > Merimas
Melissa > Mentha
Mantissa > Melilot

The names of the children of Milo Burrows and Peony Baggins, Flavus, Crispus, Rhoda, and Fulvus, were struck out but not replaced, since they appear in the Baggins genealogy (see p. 88 and RK p. 380).

Only in these respects does BR 5 as corrected differ from the final form (RK p. 382): Gorhendad Oldbuck is the father, not the remote ancestor of Gormadoc Brandybuck; and Merry is still named Meriadoc Took-Brandybuck. Subsequently my father altered the note on Gorhendad to begin 'c.740 began the building of *Brandy Hall*', but left in his dates as 1090–1191, which survived into the proof, as did Meriadoc Took-Brandybuck, when they were deleted.

Took of Great Smials

The final genealogy of the Tooks was achieved without the great upheaval of names that took place in those of the Baggins, Bolger, Boffin and Brandybuck families. I give the letter T to the versions, T 1 being the very early form printed in VI.317; the redrawn versions T 2, T 3, and T 4 appear on pp. 109–11.

T 2 (p. 109)

This version is found on the page that carries also the first genealogies of the Baggins, Bolger, and Brandybuck families, BA 1, BG 1, and BR 1. It is very closely related to T 1, and indeed differs from it chiefly in giving the dates according to the years of the Shire Reckoning, rather than the ages of the persons relative to the Farewell Party. If the age of each person given in T 1 is subtracted from the year of the Farewell Party, the birth-dates in T 2 agree in nearly every case.[8] The only other changes are the reversal of the order of Isambard and Flambard, sons of the Old Took;[9] the addition of Vigo's son Uffo, and of Uffo's son Prospero (see VI.38); and the change of Odo Took-Bolger to Odo Bolger.

T 3 (p. 110)

The development of this version is best understood by comparison with T 2; but it may be noted that Isembard (for earlier Isambard) has been restored to the second place among the sons of the Old Took, while Flambard, husband of Rosa Baggins, is renamed Hildigrim (a change seen also in the Baggins tables BA 1 and 2). Fosco becomes Sigismond, and rather oddly both Hildigrim and Sigismond have a son named Hildibrand (formerly Faramond and Vigo): the Hildibrand son of Hildigrim was replaced subsequently on the manuscript by Adalgrim, as he remained. Among the many changes in the third and fourth generations from the Old Took may be noted the arrival of Peregrin son of Paladin (see VII.35), while Odo Bolger becomes Hamilcar; the replacement of Merry's mother Yolanda by Pandora (cf. the Brandybuck tables BR 1 and 4); and the appearance of Odovacar Bolger (cf. BG 2).[10]

T 4 (p. 111)

At this stage (corresponding to BA 3, BG 2, BF 2, and BR 4) my father made a series of four tables all closely similar – differing scarcely at all, in fact, except in the names of the children of the Old Took, who were increased in number without thereby altering the subsequent generations as they now existed. I have redrawn the fourth of these, calling it T 4, but note below the differences in the three preceding versions.

In all four copies the first ancestor recorded in the tree is now Isengrim II, with the title 'Seventh Shirking' (in the first copy 'Shireking or Shirking'), on which see p. 87. Isengrim eldest son of the Old Took, now Isengrim III, retained through three copies the dates given to him in T 3, 1232–1282, remarkably short-lived among all the centenarians, with the note added 'no children'. In all the copies the holders of the title Shirking are underlined, as the Thains are starred in the final form (RK p. 381).

A daughter named Gloriana, following Isengrim III, was introduced in the first copy, but was changed at once to Hildigunda (see below), either because Gloriana Bolger (BG 2, BR 4) already existed or because the name Gloriana was at once transferred to her. Hildigunda had a brief life, her dates on the first copy being 1235–1255; on subsequent copies no dates were given, but she is said to have 'died young'. On the third copy her name was changed to Hildigard, as it remained.

Between Hildigunda / Hildigard and Hildigrim, a son of the Old Took named Isumbras IV (the remote ancestor being now Isumbras III) was introduced, himself the father and grandfather of subsequent Shirkings. Since Isengrim III had no descendants, on the death of the unmarried Ferumbras III the headship of the family passed to the descendants of the third son of the Old Took, Hildigrim, and thus Pippin's father Paladin became the Shirking. It seems probable that the alterations to this part of the genealogy were made in order to achieve this.[11]

After Hildigrim there enters Isembold, with no descendants indicated; and after Isembold there was in the first copy Hildigunda, changed to Hildifuns when Hildigunda replaced Gloriana (see above). On the third copy Hildifuns became Hildifons: he lived to the ripe age of 102 (see below), again with no descendants shown.

Isembard was moved down to become the seventh child of the Old Took; while Sigismond (the fourth child in T 3) changes place with his son Hildibrand. Finally, a twelfth child entered on the third copy: Isengar, about whom nothing is said.

Pippin's son Faramir I and his wife Goldilocks, daughter of Samwise, entered on the fourth copy (T 4).

The version T 4 received a number of changes of name, though far fewer than in the preceding families, and some added notes; the title was changed to 'Tooks of Great Smials'.

Isengrim II (seventh Shirking) > Isengrim II (tenth Thain of the Took line)

Bandobras: (many descendants) > (many descendants, including the Northtooks of Long Cleeve)

Isembold: [added:] (many descendants)

Hildifons 1244–1346 > Hildifons 1244– (went off and never returned)

Gorboduc Brandybuck > Gormanac Brandybuck (see below)

Isengar: [added:] said to have 'gone to sea' in his youth

Paladin II > Pharamond II (see below)

Pandora > Esmeralda (see p. 101)

Caradoc Brandybuck > Saradoc Brandybuck (see p. 103)

Diamanda > Rosamunda (see BG 4)

Prima > Pearl

Pamphila > Pimpernel

Belisarius Bolger > Fredegar Bolger

Faramond > Ferdibrand

In addition, Pippin's mother Eglantine Banks was introduced, and his wife Diamond of Long Cleeve; and 'several [> three] daughters' were given to Adelard Took.

In subsequent manuscript versions the points in which the genealogy still differed from the final form were corrected: thus Pippin's father reverted from Pharamond II to Paladin II; Gormanac Brandybuck became Gorbadoc, as also in the Brandybuck genealogy (p. 103); and Folco Boffin was omitted, perhaps because of the difficulty of fitting him in (he appeared in any case in the Boffin genealogy).

The Longfather-tree of Master Samwise

There is no very early genealogy of the Gamgees and Cottons, and the first version to appear belongs with the group beginning with the Baggins table BA 3: it is indeed written on the same page as BG 2 of

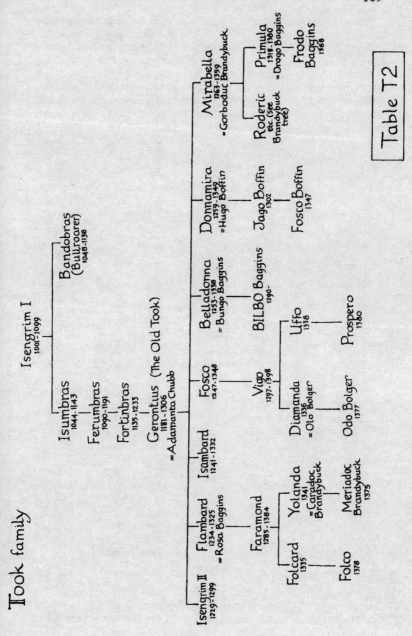

Took family

Isengrim I
1001-1099

Bandobras (Bullroarer)
1048-1138

Isumbras
1044-1143

Ferumbras
1090-1191

Fortinbras
1135-1233

Gerontius (The Old Took)
1181-1306
= Adamanta Chubb

Isengrim II
1229-1299

Flambard
1234-1325
= Rosa Baggins

Isambard
1241-1332

Fosca
1247-1348

Belladonna
1253-1356
= Bungo Baggins

Donnamira
1259-1342
= Hugo Boffin

Mirabella
1263-1359
= Gorbaduc Brandybuck

Faramond
1285-1384

Vigo
1297-1398

BILBO Baggins
1290-

Jago Boffin
1302

Roderic
etc. (see
Brandybuck
tree)

Primula
1318-1380
= Drogo Baggins

Folcard
1355

Yolanda
1341
= Caradoc Brandybuck

Diamanda
1336
= Olo Bolger

Uffo
1318

Fosco Boffin
1347

Frodo Baggins
1368

Folco
1378

Meriadoc
Brandybuck
1375

Odo Bolger
1377

Prospero
1360

Table T2

110

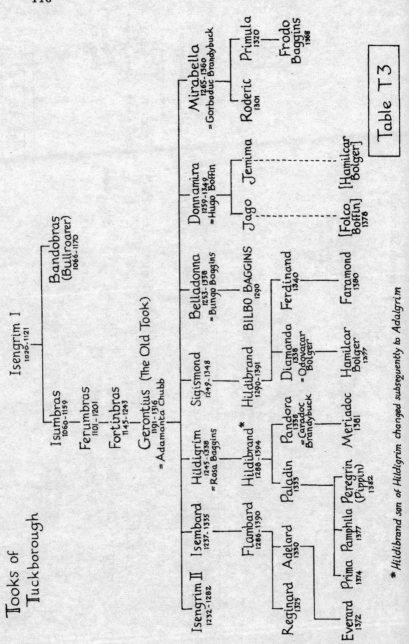

Tooks of Tuckborough

Isengrim I
1020-1121

Bandobras
(Bullroarer)
1066-1170

Isumbras
1060-1159

Ferumbras
1101-1201

Fortinbras
1145-1243

Gerontius (The Old Took)
1191-1316
= Adamanta Chubb

Isengrim II
1232-1282

Isembard
1237-1335

Hildigrim
1245-1338
= Rosa Baggins

Sigismond
1249-1348

Belladonna
1253-1338
= Bungo Baggins

BILBO BAGGINS
1290

Donnamira
1259-1349
= Hugo Boffin

Mirabella
1265-1360
= Gorbaduc Brandybuck

Flambard
1285-1390

Hildibrand*
1288-1594

Hildibrand
1290-1391

Jago   Jemima

[Folco Boffin]
1378

[Hamilcar Bolger]

Roderic
1301

Primula
1320

Frodo Baggins
1368

Adelard
1350

Paladin
1355

Pandora
1358
= Caradoc Brandybuck

Diamanda
1358
= Odovacar Bolger

Ferdinand
1340

Reginard
1325

Everard
1372

Prima
1574

Pamphila
1577

Peregrin
(Pippin)
1382

Meriadoc
1381

Hamilcar
Bolger
1577

Faramond
1380

Table T3

*Hildibrand son of Hildigrim changed subsequently to Adalgrim

Tooks of the Smials
of Tuckborough

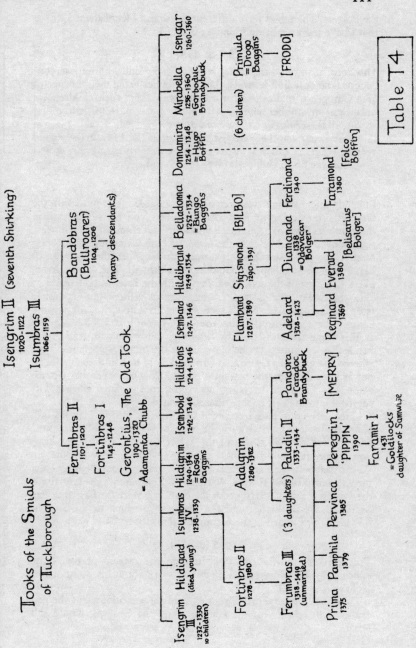

Table T4

the Bolgers. The tables have different titles, and I letter them S, those that I have redrawn being found on pp. 114–16.

S 1 (p. 114)

This consists of two brief tables set out side by side without interconnection: the only link between the two families being the marriage of Sam Gamgee with Rose Cotton. It is notable that their children are only eight in number, ending with Daisy born in 1436. In the first version of the *Epilogue* to *The Lord of the Rings*, which takes place in that year, Daisy was the youngest, in her cradle (IX.114). In the second version (IX.122) this was repeated, but corrected to say that it was Primrose, the ninth child, who was in the cradle.

S 2 (p. 115)

I include under this reference two closely related tables both with the same title (the first form, not redrawn, differs from the second only in these points: Wiseman Gamwich is absent, and Hamfast of Gamwich, who 'moved to Tighfield', is the father of Hob Gammidge the Roper; Ham Gamgee's sister May is absent; and neither the husband of Elanor nor the husband of Goldilocks is shown). The second form, like S 1, is part of the series beginning with the Baggins table BA 3.

In these texts the Cotton family is again written out separately from the Gamgees, but Sam's sister Marigold is now the wife of Rose Cotton's brother Tom ('Young Tom', RK p. 286). It will be seen that at this stage the third family, beginning with Holman 'the greenhanded' of Hobbiton (as he is named in the final form), had not yet entered the genealogy; and that Sam and Rose had fourteen children, not as later thirteen, the youngest being Lily (born when her parents were very advanced in years, according to the dates given!). Lily survived into the first proof, when she was deleted.

Later correction to S 2 replaced Goodwill Whitfoot (Elanor's husband) by Fastred Fairbairn (in the final form Fastred of Greenholm), and rejected the Whitfoots of the White Downs, adding this hasty note: 'They removed to a new country beyond the Far Downs, the Westmarch between Far Downs and Tower Hills. From them are come the Fairbairns of the Towers, Wardens of Westmarch.' The sentence in the *Prologue* (FR p. 18) 'Outside the Farthings were the East and West Marches: the Buckland; and the Westmarch added to the Shire in S.R.1462' was added in the Second Edition (see p. 17).

S 3 (p. 116)

This version, untitled, was written on the reverse of the 'Note' concerning the two versions of Bilbo's story about his meeting with Gollum (see p. 12).

Here the 'greenhanded' strain entered the genealogy, but the generations, in relation to the Gamgees and the Cottons, would subsequently be displaced 'upwards': see under S 4. This version has no note on the Fairbairns.

S 4

In this finely made tree, entitled 'Genealogy of Master Samwise, showing the rise of the family of Gardner of the Hill', the final form was reached in all but a few points. The moving up of the 'Greenhands' by a generation now entered: Hending 'greenhand' of Hobbiton remained, but was now born in 1210; his children likewise have birthdates earlier by some forty years; and Hending's daughters Rowan and Rose now marry, not Hobson Gamgee and Wilcome Cotton, but their fathers, Hob Gammidge and Cotman.

At first sight my father's alteration of names in the family trees, as here, with its baffling movement of Holmans and Halfreds, may seem incomprehensibly finicky, but in some cases the reasons can be clearly seen, and this is in fact a good example. In S 3 Ham Gamgee is said to have 'taken up as a gardener with his uncle Holman': this is Holman Greenhand the gardener, brother of his mother Rowan – and he is 'old Holman' who looked after the garden at Bag End before Ham Gamgee took on the job (FR p. 30). But with the displacement of the 'Greenhand' generations that entered in S 4 Holman Greenhand would become Ham Gamgee's great-uncle (brother of his grandmother Rowan), and so too old. It was for this reason that my father changed Holman Greenhand of S 3, born in 1292, to Halfred Greenhand (born in 1251), and gave him a son named Holman, born in 1292, described in the final genealogy as Ham Gamgee's 'Cousin Holman': he was Ham Gamgee's first cousin once removed.

In S 4 Hending's third son (Grossman in S 3) is Holman: the names of father and son were subsequently reversed. Ham Gamgee's brother Holman of Overhill remained (later Halfred of Overhill); and Wilcome Cotton becomes Holman Cotton, as in the final form, but his nickname is 'Long Holm', not 'Long Hom'. This name *Holman* is to be taken, I think, in the sense 'hole-dweller'.

Elanor's husband remains in S 4 Fastred Fairbairn, and Frodo's son, Samwise Gardner in S 3, reverts to Samlad Gardner as in S 2: this was corrected to the final name, Holfast. The dates of birth of the children of Sam Gamgee and Rose Cotton remain as they were in S 3; thus Primrose, the ninth child, was born in 1439 (see under S 1 above).

In all other respects S 4 was as the final genealogy, including the note on the Fairbairns; and it was on this manuscript that the last corrections were made (the birth-date of Sam and Rose's last child, Lily, becoming 1444).

S 4 was followed by a beautifully drawn tree, from which the genealogy in *The Lord of the Rings* was printed, and here the final title entered. As already noticed, it was on the first proof that Lily was removed.

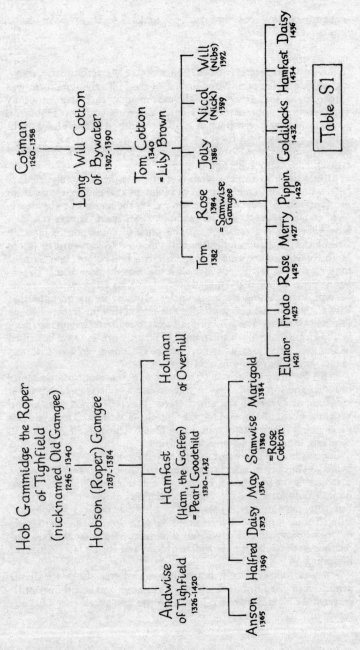

Table S1

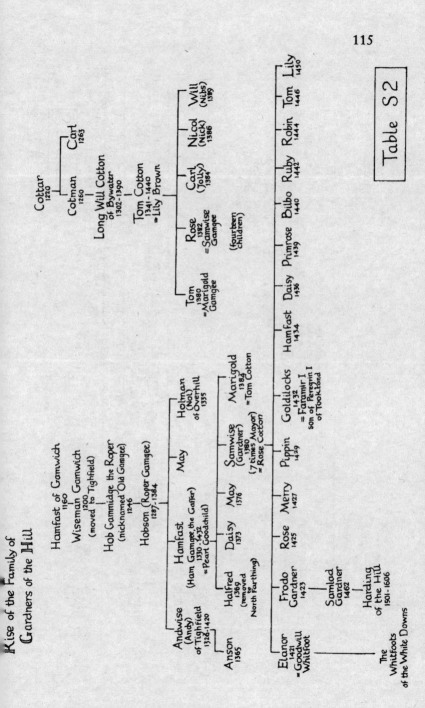

Rise of the Family of
Gardners of the Hill

115

Table S2

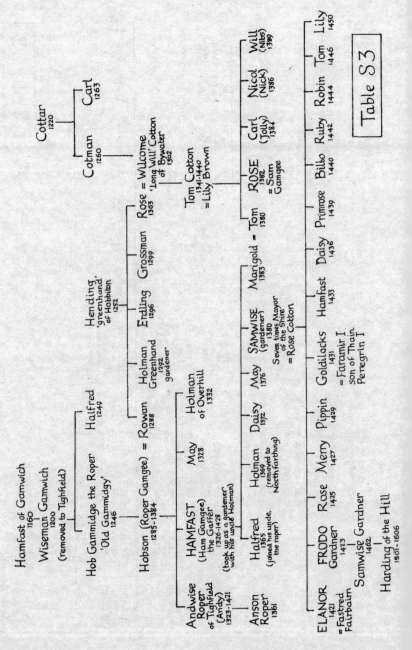

Table S3

NOTES

1 This manuscript of the Bolger family was the latest that remained in my father's possession, and he had of course no copies of the texts that went to Marquette. Years later he wrote on BG 2: 'Doesn't fit genealogies published. Fredegar should be born about 1385–8. Put in Estella 1387'. On one of his copies of the First Edition he added to the genealogy of the Tooks (Fredegar's mother being Rosamunda Took) 'Estella' as the sister of Fredegar and her birth-date 1385; and to the Brandybuck genealogy he added to Meriadoc '= Estella Bolger 1385', noting beside this that he had told a correspondent in 1965 that 'I believe he married a sister of Fredegar Bolger of the Bolgers of Budgeford'. These corrections, for a reason unknown to me, were not incorporated in the Allen and Unwin Second Edition, but they did occur in a later impression of the Ballantine edition of 1966, and hence Estella Bolger and her marriage to Merry Brandybuck are entered in *The Complete Guide to Middle-earth* by Robert Foster.

These additions to the family trees were made at the instance of Douglas A. Anderson in the Houghton Mifflin edition of 1987, to which he contributed a note on the history of the text. Estella Bolger and her marriage to Meriadoc have finally entered the British 'tradition' in the re-set edition published by HarperCollins in 1994 (see Douglas Anderson's 'Note on the Text' in this edition, p. xii).

2 My statement in VII.39, note 19, that Bridgefields does not appear on the original map of the Shire is erroneous: it is pencilled on that map (and can be seen in the reproduction, frontispiece to Vol.VI) beside the name Bolger, a region just south-west of the Brandywine Bridge. As noted in VII.39, on my large map of the Shire made in 1943 my father pencilled in the name Budgeford, this being the crossing of the Water by the road (entered on the map at the same time) from Whitfurrows on the East Road to Scary. At the same time he wrote in Bridgefields in a new position, north-west of the Brandywine Bridge and north of the East Road, as it appears on the published map of the Shire.

3 In late typescripts of the chapters in which Fredegar Bolger appears in *The Lord of the Rings* the name *Belisarius* (with the nickname *Belly*, which no doubt accounts for the choice) replaced the earlier *Hamilcar*, and was then itself replaced by *Fredegar*.

4 Jemima Boffin of BG 2 was first renamed *Jasmine*, which was replaced by the form *Jessamine*; and so also in the Boffin genealogy.

5 On one of the proofs my father corrected Fredegar's birth-date from 1377 to 1380, but the genealogy was omitted from the book

before this was introduced; in the Took table, however, the date was changed. See note 1.

6　This was in fact an alteration (VI.298 and note 1): originally my father marked the Boffins north-west of the Woody End, and the Bolgers north of Hobbiton, subsequently changing them about; cf. VI.298, 'as far west as Woodhall (which was reckoned to be in the Boffin-country)'.

7　In VI.273, 275 I printed the name as *Lanorac*, which was a misreading of the difficult manuscript.

8　In VI.316 I noted that some of the figures in T 1 were changed on the manuscript, and gave a list of them; but I said that these were 'the earlier ones', whereas they are in fact the corrected figures. See note 9.

9　In T 1 the birth-dates of Isambard and Flambard were 170 and 165 years before the Farewell Party, but these were changed (see note 8) to 160 and 167 (in T 2 1241 and 1234); hence the reversal of the positions of the brothers in T 2.

10　On T 2 Uffo Took and his son Prospero were corrected to Adelard and Everard (see VI.247, 315), Uffo becoming a Boffin name (see BF 2). It will thus be seen that they have been removed from the descent of the fourth son (Fosco > Sigismond) and given to that of the second son Isembard (formerly without any descendants named), whose son Flambard takes over the former name of Hildigrim.

11　Farmer Cotton's reference to Pippin's father as the Thain ('You see, your dad, Mr. Peregrin, he's never had no truck with this Lotho, not from the beginning: said that if anyone was going to play the chief at this time of day, it would be the right Thain of the Shire and no upstart ...') was a late addition to the text of the chapter *The Scouring of the Shire* (RK p. 289); for the original form of the passage see IX.99.

IV

THE CALENDARS

The earliest text of what became Appendix D to *The Lord of the Rings* is a brief, rough manuscript without title, which I will call **D 1**. In style and appearance it suggests association with the first of the two closely related manuscripts of the Appendix on Languages, F 1 (see p. 28), and that this is the case is shown by a reference in the text to 'the note on Languages p. 11'. This in fact refers to the second version, F 2, which was thus already in existence (see p. 136, note 2). D 1 was followed, clearly at no long interval, by a fair copy, **D 2**, exactly parallel to the manuscripts F 1 and F 2 of the Appendix on Languages; and thus the order of composition was F 1, F 2; D 1, D 2. I have no doubt at all that all four texts belong to the same time, which was certainly before the summer of 1950 (see p. 28 and note 1), and probably earlier: in fact, an envelope associated with D 1 is postmarked August 1949.

In this case, since the texts are far briefer than F 1 and F 2, and since the second manuscript D 2 was substantially altered from its predecessor, I give them both. These earliest versions of the Appendix on Calendars show, as do those of the Appendix on Languages, how far the conception still was, when *The Lord of the Rings* had been completed, from the published form. There follows here the text of the manuscript D 1.

In the Shire the Calendar was not arranged as ours is; though the year seems to have been of the same length, for long ago as those times are now, reckoned in years and men's lives, they were not (I suppose) far back in the age of Middle-earth. According to the Hobbits themselves they had no 'week' when they were a wandering people, and though they had months, reckoned by the moon, their keeping of dates and time was not particularly accurate. In Eriador (or the West-lands) when they settled down they adopted the reckoning of the Dúnedain, which was of Elvish origin. But the Hobbits of the Shire after a while altered things to suit their own convenience better. 'Shire-reckoning' was eventually adopted also in Bree.

It is difficult to discover from old records precise details about those things which everybody knows and takes for granted, nor am I skilled in such abstruse matters. But in that part of Middle-earth at that time it seems that the Eldar (who had, as Sam said, more time at their disposal) reckoned in centuries. Now they had observed – I do not know how, but the Eldar have many powers, and had observed many centuries – that a century contains, as near as no matter for practical purposes, 36524 days. They therefore divided it into 100 years (or sun-rounds) of 366 days, and dealt with the inaccuracy, not as we do by inserting at intervals an additional day to make up for the deficit, but by ejecting a few days at stated times to reduce the surplus. Every *four* years they would have used *three* days too many, if they had done nothing to correct it.

Normally they divided their year of 366 days into twelve months, six of 31 and six of 30 days. They alternated from January to June 31, 30; from July to December 30, 31. It will be observed that their months thus had the same lengths as ours, except for February, 30, and July, 30. Every *eighth* year they got rid of their excess of 6 days by reducing all months to 30 days; and these years were called ['Equal-month Years' or 'Thirty-day Years' >] 'Sixty-week Years' or 'Short Years'.

The Elvish week had only *six* days; so normal years had 61 weeks, and every eighth year had 60 weeks. The first day of the year always began on the first day of the week. In the Short (eighth) Years every month began on the first day of the week. In the normal years they progressed thus: 1, 2, 2, 3, 3, 4, 4, 4, 5, 5, 6, 6.[1]

The Eldar still at the end of a century would have had 36525 days, not 35624; so once a century they left out the last day of the last month (reducing December to 30 days). The week-day went with it: there was no sixth day of the week in the last week of the century.

The Dúnedain altered these arrangements. They favoured the number 7, and also found a seven-day week more convenient. They also preferred a system by which all the months had the same lengths and did not vary at intervals. [*Struck out later:* They had 12 months (not 13) so that the year could be divided into two exact halves.]

In Gondor, therefore, and in most regions where the Common Speech was used, the year had 365 days; there were 12 months of 30 days each; and 52 weeks of 7 days each. But the method of dealing with the extra 5 days differed in different countries.

In Gondor, between June 30 and July 1 they placed a kind of short month of 5 days, which were called *The Summer Days*, and were a time of holiday. The middle day of the Summer Days (the third) was called Midyear's Day and was a festival. Every fourth year there were 6 Summer Days, and the Midyear festival was two days long (celebrated on the third and fourth days). In the last or hundredth year of a century the additional Summer Day was omitted, bringing the total to 36524.

In the Shire (and eventually in Bree where Shire-reckoning was finally adopted) there were 3 Summer Days, called in the Shire *The Lithe* or *The Lithedays*; and 2 *Yule Days*, the last of the Old Year and the first of the New.* Every fourth year there were 4 Lithedays [*added:* except in the last year of a century]. The Lithedays and the Yuledays were the chief holidays and times of feasting. The additional Litheday, called *Overlithe*, was a day of special feasting and merrymaking. *Yule* was in full the last week of the old year and the first of the new, or in Shire-reckoning (since December had only 30 days) December 24 to January 7 inclusive; but the two middle days of the period, *Old Year's Day* or *Yearsend* (December 30) and *New Year's Day* or *Yearsday* (January 1), were the great Yuledays, or Yule proper.

The Hobbits introduced one notable innovation (the Shire-reform). They found the shifting of the weekday name in relation to dates from year to year untidy and inconvenient. So in the time of Isengrim II they arranged that the odd day, which put the succession out, should have no weekday name. So Midyear's Day (the second and middle day of the Lithe) had no weekday name, and neither had Overlithe (which followed it in every fourth year). After this reform the year always began on the first day of the week and ended on the last day of the week; and the same date in one year always had the same weekday name in all other years. In consequence of which Hobbits never troubled to put weekdays on their letters. They found this very

---

* The reckoning of the year's beginning had varied much in various times and places. The beginning after Yule (originally intended to be at the Winter Solstice) was used in the North Kingdom and eventually adopted by Hobbits. The wild Hobbits were said to have begun their year with the New Moon nearest to the beginning of Spring. The settled Hobbits for a time began their year after Harvest, roughly October 1st. This habit long endured in Bree. In Gondor after the downfall of Baraddur a new era was begun with that day reckoned as the first day of its first year.

convenient in the Shire, but of course, if they travelled further than Bree, where the reform was adopted, they found it rather confusing.

It will be observed if one glances at a Hobbit (perpetual) Calendar that the only day on which no month began was a -Friday. It was thus a jesting idiom in the Shire to speak of 'on Friday the first' when referring to a day that did not exist, or to a day on which impossible events like the flying of pigs or (in the Shire) the walking of trees might be expected to occur. In full the expression was 'Friday the first of Summerfilth', for there was no such month.

In the above notes I have used our modern month and week-day names, though of course neither the Eldar nor the Dúnedain nor the Hobbits actually did so. But dates are both important and easily confused, so that I thought a translation into our familiar names essential. These may very properly be allowed to represent the usual names in Gondor and in the Common Speech. But in fact, the Hobbits of the Shire and of Bree adhered to old-fashioned month-names, which they seem to have picked up in antiquity from the Men of the Anduin-vale; at any rate very similar names were found in Dale and in Rohan (see the note on Languages p. 11).[2] The original meanings of these had been as a rule long forgotten and they had become in consequence worn down in form, -*math* for instance at the end of four of them is a reduction of *month*. There was some varia-tion in the names. Several of the Bree-names differed from those of the Shire, and in one or two cases the East-farthingers agreed with Bree.

	Shire	Bree
January	Afteryule	Frery (also East Farthing)
February	Solmath[a]	Solmath[a]
March	Rethe[3]	Rethe
April	Astron	Chithing (also East Farthing)
May	Thrimilch[b]	Thrimidge
June	Forelithe	Lithe
	The Lithe or Lithedays	The Summer Days
July	Afterlithe	Mede
August	Wedmath	Wedmath
September	Halimath	Harvest(math) (also East Farthing)
October	Winterfilth	[Wintermath >] Wintring

| November | Blotmath[c] | Blooting |
| December | Foreyule | Yulemath |

(a) Pronounced *So'math*. (b) Pronounced *Thrimidge* and also written *Thrimich*, *Thrimidge*, the latter being already most usual in Bilbo's time. (c) Often pronounced *Blommath*. There were often jests in Bree about 'Winterfilth in the Shire', after the Breefolk had altered their name to *Wintring*; but the name had probably meant 'filling, completion' and may have derived from the time when the year ended and began in October after Harvest. Winter was indeed (as still with us) often used for 'year' in reckoning age.[4]

The Hobbit week was taken from the Dúnedain and the names were translations of the names given by the Dúnedain following the Eldar. The six-day week of the Eldar had days dedicated to the Stars, Sun, Moon, the Two Trees of Valinor, the Sky, and the Valar or Rulers, in that order, the last day being the chief or high day.

The Dúnedain kept the dedications and order, but altered the fourth day to Tree-day with reference to the Eldest Tree of which a descendant grew in Númenor, and desiring a seven day week and being great mariners they inserted a Sea-day after the Sky-day.

The Hobbits took over this arrangement, but the meanings of the days were soon forgotten and the names reduced in form. The 'translation' was made more than a thousand years before Bilbo's time. In the oldest known records of the Shire, in the earlier parts of the Great Writ of Tuckborough,[5] the names appeared in the following archaic forms.

1.	*Sterrendei*	that is	Stars' day
2.	*Sunnendei*		Sun's day
3.	*Monendei*		Moon's day
4.	*Treowesdei*		Tree's day
5.	*Heovenesdei*		Heaven's (Sky's) day
6.	*Meresdei*		Sea's day
7.	*Hihdei*		High day

But in the language of the date of the Red Book these names had become written: *Sterday* (or *Stirday*), *Sunday*, *Munday*, *Trewsday*, *Hevensday*, *Mersday*, *Hiday*; and *Hevensday* was universally pronounced *Hensdy* and often written *He'nsday*. The spelling *Stirday* (usual in the Red Book) was due to the fact that, the old meaning being forgotten, *Stirday*, which began the week again, after the holiday of *Hiday*, was popularly supposed to be connected with *Stirring*.

Since the Hobbit-names are accidentally somewhat like our own, and two are identical (in spoken form)[6] I thought it would be inconvenient to translate them according to their *order*. I have therefore translated them according to their *sound*. But it must be remembered that the associations in the Shire were different. Translated the week runs: Saturday, Sunday, Monday, Tuesday, Wednesday, Thursday, Friday. But Saturday was the first day of the week, and Friday the last. In associations Saturday was more like our Monday and Friday like our Sunday.

The month names I have, as explained above, translated. But for fear of getting into confusion I have left Bilbo's and Frodo's *dates* unchanged: that is, I have kept the Hobbit lengths of month. This only closely concerns this book at the turn of the years 1418–19. It must then be remembered by those who wish to follow the various movements of the characters that while December 1418 and January 1419 have (because of the addition of a Yule-day to each) the same length as ours, February has 30, so that e.g. March 25 would be March 27 in our reckoning.

The Leapday or Overlithe does not concern the Red Book, as it did not occur in any of the important years for the story of the Ring. It occurred in the year before Bilbo went to the Lonely Mountain, 1340; it had been missed in 1400 being the end of a century (just before Bilbo's Farewell Party in 1401), and so had not occurred from 1396 until 1404. The only years dealt with in the Red Book in which it occurred were 1420, the famous Harvest, and 1436. But though no doubt the feasting at Overlithe in 1420 was tremendous it is not mentioned specially.[7] The Book ends before the Lithe of 1436.

It will be seen that the account of the Eldarin calendar in Middle-earth given in D1 bears no relation to that in the published text. Moreover, while the Shire Calendar as described in D 1 was preserved without change, it is much more closely based on the Númenórean system than in Appendix D. In D 1 both calendars had a year of 12 months of 30 days each, and the only difference in that of the Shire was the distribution of the five Summer Days of Gondor into two Yuledays and three Summer Days or Lithedays (the leap-year day of Overlithe or fourth Litheday corresponding to the sixth Summer Day in Gondor). In Appendix D, on the other hand, the Númenórean calendar had ten months of 30 days and two of 31 (making 362), with the three 'extra days' being *yestarë* (the beginning of the year), *löendë* (the mid-day), and *mettarë* (the ending of the year).

In writing of the names of the months and days of the week my father used the word 'translation'. He was referring, of course, to the substitution of e.g. *Thursday* for *Mersday* or *March* for *Rethe*. But it is to be remembered that *Mersday*, *Rethe*, etc. were themselves feigned to be 'translations' of the true Hobbit names. We do not know what the 'real' translation of the Númenórean name *Oraearon* (RK p. 388) was; the theory is that my father devised a translation of the Hobbit name, which he knew, in archaic English form, *Meresdei* later *Mersday*, and then substituted *Thursday* in the narrative. The rhyming of 'Trewsday, Hensday, Mersday, Hiday' with our 'Tuesday, Wednesday (Wensday), Thursday, Friday' he naturally called an accidental likeness; but it was an astonishing coincidence! I am much inclined to think that the Hobbit calendar was the original conception, and that the names of the days were in fact devised precisely in order to provide this 'accidental likeness'. If this is so, then of course the earlier history of the names of the week (going back to the six-day week of the Eldar) was a further evolution in this extraordinarily ingenious and attractive conception. It is notable, I think, that the Elvish names do not appear until the text D 2 (where the Sindarin names are called, as is to be expected, Noldorin).

This second text now follows (with certain omissions, which are noted). It is a very carefully written manuscript, bearing the title *The Calendar*. I believe it to have been written soon after D 1.

The Calendar

The Calendar in the Shire differed in several features from ours. The year seems to have been of the same length, for long ago as those times are now, reckoned in years and lives of men, they were not, I suppose, very remote according to the memory of the Earth. It is recorded by the Hobbits that they had no 'week' when they were still a wandering people, and though they had 'months', governed more or less by the Moon, their keeping of dates and calculations of time were vague and inaccurate. In the west-lands of Eriador, when they had begun to settle down, they adopted the reckoning of the Dúnedain of the North-kingdom, which was ultimately of Elvish origin; but the Hobbits of the Shire introduced several minor alterations. This calendar, or 'Shire-reckoning' as it was called, was eventually adopted also in Bree, except for the Shire-usage of counting as Year 1 the year of the foundation or colonization of the Shire.

It is often difficult to discover from old tales and traditions

precise information about those things which people knew well
and took for granted in their own day, like the names of letters,
or of the days of the week, or the names and lengths of months.
I have done as well as I could, and have looked into some of the
surviving works on chronology. Owing to their general interest
in genealogy, and to the [added: later] interest of the learned
among them in ancient history, the Shire-hobbits seem to have
concerned themselves a good deal with dates; and they even
drew up complicated tables showing the relations of their own
system with others. I am not learned or skilled in these abstruse
matters, and may have made many mistakes; but at any rate the
chronology of the crucial years (Shire-reckoning 1418, 1419) is
so carefully set out in the Red Book that there cannot be much
doubt about days and times at this point.

It seems clear that the Eldar, who had, as Samwise remarks,
more time at their disposal, reckoned in centuries, and the
Quenya word *yén*, often translated 'year', really means a hundred of our years, sometimes called *quantiën* or 'full year'. Now
they observed – I do not know how or when: but the Eldar have
many powers, and they had observed many centuries – that the
century or *quantiën* contained, exactly or exactly enough for
practical purposes, 36524 days. They therefore divided it into
100 *coranári** (sun-rounds or years) of 366 days. This would
have given them 36600 days, or 76 too many; and they dealt
with the inaccuracy, not as we do by inserting at intervals an
additional day to make up for a deficit, but by ejecting a few
days at stated times to reduce the surplus. Every *four* years they
would have had (very nearly) *three* days too many, if they had
done nothing to correct this. Their method of correction may
seem complicated to us, but they favoured the numbers six and
twelve, and they were chiefly concerned to make things work
out properly at the end of their 'full year' or century.

Normally they divided their *coranar* of 366 days into twelve
months, six of 31 days and six of 30 days. The lengths alternated from January† to June 31, 30; and from July to December 30, 31. It will be observed that their months thus had the
same lengths as ours, except for February, 30 (usual in all the
calendars of this period), and July, 30. Every *eighth* year they

* Also called in less astronomical contexts *loa* 'time of growth', sc.
of plants, etc.

† The month-names are here translated to avoid confusion.

got rid of the excess of 6 days by reducing all the months to 30 days and thus having a year (or *coranar*) of only 360 days. These years they called 'Short Years' or 'Sixty-week Years'.

The Eldarin week had only *six* days, so normal years had 61 weeks, and every eighth year had 60 weeks. The first day of the *coranar* always began on the first day of the week. In the Short Years every month also began with the first day.

These eight-year cycles ran on regularly until the end of the 96th year of the *quantiën* or century. There then remained four more years to deal with, and 1460 days were required to complete the full tale of 36524. Four years of 365 days would have done this, but that would not have fitted the Elves' six-day week. Their actual arrangement, rounding off the *quantiën* neatly, was this: at the end of the century they had a half-cycle of *three* long years of 366 days (total 1098), and *one* short year (the last of the century) of 360: making 1458 and exactly completing the weeks. The two more days still required[8] were added at the end and the beginning of the *quantiën*; they had no weekday name nor month, but only their names: *Quantarië* Day of Completion, Oldyear's Day, and *Vinyarië* Newyear's Day; they were times of festival. Thus the year 1 of the Eldarin century had 367 days; Years 8, 16, 24, 32, 40, 48, 56, 64, 72, 80, 88, 96 had 360 days; Year 100 had 361; and the remainder had 366. It is thus impossible to translate an Eldarin date into our terms without a possible error of some days, unless one knows at what point in an Eldarin century a given year stands, and whether that century did in fact begin on what we should call January 1.*

* I believe that the Elves observe the Sun and stars closely, and make occasional corrections. Their *quantiéni* are arranged, I am told, to begin as nearly as possible with the first sunset after the Winter Solstice. The Eldarin 'day' or *arë* was reckoned not from midnight, but from the moment of the disappearance of the sun below the horizon as observed from the shores of the sea. Among other peoples the reckoning of the year's beginning had varied much at different times, though it was usually at mid-winter, or at a date taken as the beginning of Spring, and occasionally after Harvest. The beginning after Yule (taken as at or near the Winter Solstice) was used by the Dúnedain in the North-kingdom, and eventually was adopted by the Hobbits. The Wild Hobbits were said to have begun their year with the New Moon nearest the beginning of Spring. The settled Hobbits for some time began their year after Harvest, or after the introduction of regular fixed months on October the first. A trace of this was left in the keeping of October 1 as a minor festival in the Shire and Bree.

The Dúnedain altered these arrangements. Being mortal if long-lived the actual 'sunround' or year was their natural unit. They required therefore a system in which months had the same length from year to year. Also they much favoured the number seven. The following was the system used in Númenor, and after the Downfall in the North-kingdom, and also in Gondor until the end of the line of Kings: it is called, therefore, King's Reckoning.

The year had 365 days; there were 12 months, normally of 30 days each; but the months on either side of the mid-year and the year's-end had 31 (in our terms January, June, July, December). The 183rd day or Midyear Day belonged to no month. Every *fourth* year, except in the last year of a century, there were two Midyear Days. From this system the Shire-reckoning, described below, was derived.

But in Gondor later, in the time of the Stewards, the length of the months was equalized. Each month had 30 days, but between June 30 and July 1 were inserted 5 days, called the Summer Days. These were usually a time of holiday. The middle or third of these days, the 183rd of the year, was called Midyear Day and was a festival. As before, it was doubled in every *fourth* year (except the hundredth year of a century). This was called the Steward's Reckoning, and was usual in nearly all countries where the Common Speech was used (except among Elves, who used it only in their dealings with Men).

The Hobbits, however, remained conservative, and continued to use a form of King's Reckoning adapted to fit their own customs. Their months were all equal and had 30 days, but they had *three* Summer Days, called in the Shire the Lithe or the Lithedays between June and July; and *two* Yuledays, the last of the old year and the first of the new year. So that in effect January, June, July, December still had 31 days, but the Lithedays and Yuledays were not counted in the month (January 1st was the second and not the first day of the year). Every *fourth* year, except in the last year of the century,* there were *four* Lithedays. The Lithedays and the Yuledays were the chief holi-

* Earlier it had been the *first year* of the century, for it so happened that Hobbits adopted King's Reckoning in the last year of a Dúnedain century, probably Third Age 1300, which became the first year of their reckoning. But as Shire Reckoning 1 was found to correspond to King's Reckoning 1601 things were later adjusted to fit in with King's Reckoning.

days and times of feasting. The additional Litheday added after Midyear Day (and so the 184th day of the longer years) was called Overlithe and was a day of special merrymaking. In full 'Yuletide' was fourteen days long, the last week of the old and the first of the new year (from December 25 to January 6 inclusive), but the two middle days of the period, *Yearsend* or Oldyear's Day, and *Yearsday* or Newyear's Day were the great Yuledays.

The Hobbits introduced one small but notable innovation, the 'Shire-reform'. ...

The text continues without significant change from that of D 1 (p. 121), with the same page-reference to the text F 2 of the Appendix on Languages (see note 2), and without the Quenya names of the months which are given in Appendix D (RK p. 388). In the list of Hobbit month-names *Yulemath* (as well as *Harvest(math)*) is now included as being current in the East Farthing as well as in Bree, and the Shire-name of May becomes *Thrimidge*, as in Bree, with the note 'formerly written *Thrimich* and archaically *Thrimilch*'. The explanation of the name *Winterfilth* is altered, 'the name had probably originally meant the *filling* or *completion* of winter, or rather of the year leading up to the entry of winter', the precise meaning of which is obscure to me (see note 4).

Following the list of month-names and the notes on them the text D 2 continues:

I have not ventured to use these actual unfamiliar names in the course of the narrative; but it must be understood that the reference is always to the Shire Calendar, even where 'Shire-reckoning' is not specified, as it sometimes is. Thus the points essential to the turn of the years S.R.1418, 1419 are that October 1418 has only 30 days; while January 1st is the second day of 1419, and February 1419 has 30 days. In consequence Bilbo's birthday September 22nd being the 99th and not the 100th day from the year-end corresponds to our September 23rd; February 1st corresponds to our February 1st, but 29, 30 to our March 1, 2; and the date of the downfall of Baraddur and Sauron, S.R. March 25, corresponds to our March 27th.

The Hobbit week was taken from the Dúnedain, and the names were translations of the names given to the week-days in the old North-kingdom, those in turn deriving from the Eldar. These names were at that time almost universal among users of the Common Speech, though there were some local variations. The six-day week of the Eldar had days dedicated to, or named after, the Stars, the Sun, the Moon, the Two Trees,* the Heavens, and the Valar or Powers, in this order, the last day being the chief or high day of the week. Their Quenya names were: *Elenya, Anarya, Isilya, Aldarya, Menelya, Valarya* (or *Tárinar*). The Noldorin names were [*Argiliath >*] *Argilion, Aranor, Arithil,* [*Argelaid >*] *Argaladath, Arvenel (-fenel, -mhenel), Arvelain* (or *Ardórin*).[9]

The Dúnedain kept the dedications and order, but altered the fourth day to *Argalad* 'Tree-day' with reference to the Elder Tree only, of which the White Tree that grew in the King's Court in Númenor was a descendant. Also, desiring a seventh day, and being the greatest of mariners, they inserted a 'sea-day' *Aroeren* (Quenya *Earenya*) after the Heavens' day.

The Hobbits took over this arrangement ...

The text then follows that of D 1 (p. 123) almost exactly in the account of the names of the days of the week in the Hobbit calendar, but the Red Book spellings of *Sterrendei* and *Hihdei* are given as *Starday* and *Hiday (or Highday)*. *Starday* was then changed to *Sterday*, with the note: 'The spelling *Stirday*, sometimes found in the Red Book, was due to the forgetting of the meaning of the name. *Sterday*, which began the week, was popularly supposed to be connected with "stirring" after the holiday of *Highday*.'

D 2 then concludes thus:

I have translated these names also into our familiar names, and in deciding which name to equate with which modern name I have observed not the Hobbit order (beginning with *Sterday*), but the meanings. Thus since *Sunday* and *Munday* are practically identical with our *Sunday* and *Monday* and have the same 'dedications' in the same order, I have equated these and taken the rest in the same order as they stand in the Shire list: thus Hobbit 1, 2, 3, 4, 5, 6, 7 have been translated by our 7, 1, 2, 3, 4, 5, 6. It must be remembered, however, that the associations of the weekday names will thus be different: Saturday, for instance, will correspond closely in Hobbit-custom with our Monday, while Friday will correspond as closely as anything in the Shire did with Sunday.

The Overlithe or Leapday does not concern the Red Book since it did not occur in any of the important years in the story

---

* The Two Trees of Valinor, Silpion of silver (the Elder), and Laurelin of gold (the Younger), which gave light to the Blessed Realm.

of the Great Ring. It occurred in the year before Bilbo went to the Lonely Mountain, namely in 1340; it had been missed out in 1400,* the year before his Farewell Party (1401), and so had not occurred from 1396 to 1404. The only years dealt with in the Red Book in which it occurred were 1420, the famous Harvest, and 1436. No doubt the merrymaking of Overlithe in 1420 was as marvellous as everything else in that marvellous year, but it is not mentioned specially by Master Samwise. He had many other things to think about, and his brief account of them has not been enlarged upon. The book ends before the Lithe of 1436.

On the assumption, which I feel sure is correct, that D 2 belongs to very much the same time as D 1, my father quickly became dissatisfied with his first account of the antecedents of the Hobbit calendar (which itself remained virtually unchanged throughout). In the Eldarin calendar he now introduced the words *yén* and *quantiën*, both meaning a hundred of our years (*coranári* 'sun-rounds'), but retained the essential structure described in D 1 of 366 days to the year, divided into six months alternating between 30 and 31 days, with a reduction of all months to 30 days in every eighth year, these being called 'Short Years'. On the other hand, he altered the Eldarin treatment of the last four years of the century: whereas in D 1 (p. 120) a day was simply rejected at the very end of the century, in D 2 two were added, one at the beginning and one at the end of the century (see note 8).

The Númenórean calendar was more radically changed. In D 1 there were 12 months of 30 days each in a year of 365 days, with a period of 5 days (standing outside the months) called 'the Summer Days' between June 30 and July 1, the third of these being called 'Midyear's Day'. Every fourth year was a leap-year with six 'Summer Days' including two 'Midyear's Days'. From this calendar that of the Hobbits was derived, with the 5 'extra' days dispersed into 3 'Summer Days' ('Lithedays') and 2 'Yuledays', the leap-year day being 'Overlithe'.

In D 2, on the other hand, the Númenórean calendar had 8 months of 30 days and 4 months of 31 (January, June, July, December), requiring only one 'extra' day, Midyear Day, standing outside the months, this (as in D 1) being doubled every fourth year. This was called 'King's

---

* The determination of the centuries was ultimately taken from the reckoning of the Dúnedain. For though 'Shire-reckoning' only began with the settlement of the Shire, it was found that this had occurred in year 1601 of the Third Age according to King's Reckoning. To convert S.R. years into T.A. years one therefore adds 1600. Bree-years began 300 years earlier than Shire-years.

Reckoning'. Despite this alteration of the Númenórean calendar the Hobbit calendar (unchanged from D 1) is still, rather curiously, derived from it: for my father explained (p. 128) that they did 'in effect' retain the four 31-day months in the two Yuledays (January, December) and two Lithedays (June, July, on either side of Midyear's Day), although these in the Hobbit calendar were not counted in the months.

A further innovation in D 2 is the later revision of the calendar in Gondor, 'in the time of the Stewards', when the months were all reduced to 30 days, with 5 inserted 'Summer Days'. This was called 'Steward's Reckoning', and was widely adopted – but not by the Hobbits. 'Steward's Reckoning' is of course a reversion to the original Númenórean calendar in D 1 – which was the source of that of the Hobbits.

In Appendix D the conservative nature of the Hobbit calendar was retained, being a form of the King's Reckoning rather than of the reformed Steward's Reckoning, but these were again altered. The precise relations can best be understood from the actual texts, but the following is an attempt to summarise the essential differences.

D 1   *Númenórean*: all months of 30 days, 5 'Summer Days' outside the months. Hobbit calendar derived from this, with 2 Yule-days and 3 Lithedays outside the months.

D 2   *Númenórean 'King's Reckoning'*: 4 months of 31 days, Midyear Day outside the months. Hobbit calendar derived from this.

    Númenórean 'Steward's Reckoning': all months of 30 days, 5 'Summer Days' outside the months. Not adopted by Hobbits.

Appendix D   *Númenórean 'Kings' Reckoning'*: 2 months of 31 days, with 3 days outside the months (*yestarë, loëndë, mettarë* at the beginning, middle, and end of the year). Hobbit calendar (still as in D 1, D 2) derived from this.

    Númenórean 'Stewards' Reckoning': introduced by Mardil: all months of 30 days, with 2 further days outside the months (*tuilérë, yáviérë*, at end of March and September) added. Not adopted by Hobbits.

In D 2 there is no reference to the introduction of a new calendar in Third Age 3019 (S.R.1419), the year of the fall of Barad-dûr and the coronation of King Elessar, beginning on March 25 (RK p. 390); but in D 1 there is such a reference (p. 121, footnote) to a new reckoning, the year beginning, however, in the autumn: 'The settled Hobbits for a time began their year after Harvest, roughly October 1st. ... In Gondor after the downfall of Baraddur a new era was begun with that day reckoned as the first day of its first year.'

My father wrote two statements at this time on the subject of the new reckoning, differently arranged but virtually identical in content: I give the second version, which is somewhat clearer.

New Era

Gondor Calendar of the Fourth Age. After the downfall of Sauron and the return of the King, a new calendar was devised in Gondor and adopted throughout the realm and in all the westlands. This was calculated to begin on the day of the fall of Barad-dûr. That took place in Third Age 3019 (Shire-reckoning 1419), on March 25th according to Shire-reckoning, King's reckoning, and the Elvish calendars (March 27th in our calendar, and March 26th in Steward's reckoning).[10]

In honour of the Halflings (Hobbits) their week-day Sunday (for 25 March) was taken for the first week-day of the first year of the New Era, and so became also the first day of every week. Also the 'Shire-reform' was adopted, by which Midyear's Day had no weekday name, so that weekday names remained fixed in relation to dates, and each year began on a Sunday *(Anarya)* and ended on a Saturday *(Elenya)*.

The calendar of months and seasons was also entirely reformed. The year now began with *Spring* (25 March old style). It was divided into *five* seasons: two long (three months), and three short (two months): *Spring* (April, May); *Summer* (June, July, August); *Autumn* or *Harvest* (September, October); *Winter* (November, December, January); *Stirring* (February, March).*

Each month was 30 days long. There were thus 5 days (or in Leap-years 6) outside the months. These were: 2 'Spring-days' before April 1st, which began the new year, and were festivals.† 'Midyear's Day' fell between September and October and became now a harvest festival. In Leap-years this Day was doubled. The year ended with 2 'Stirring-days' after March 30: these days were days of preparation for the New Year and of commemoration of the dead and fallen.

Dates were usually given in official documents by the Seasons, but the old month-names (Common-speech, Noldorin or Quenya) remained in private and popular use, though their

---

* When the year was divided into two halves, Winter was held to run from October to Year's end, and Summer from Year's beginning to the end of September.

† The first Spring-Day and the first day of the Year was especially the commemoration of the fall of Sauron, since it corresponded to 25 March in earlier reckoning.

New Era

					Shire Reckoning	Steward's Reckoning
						March
Entarë Year's beginning: Tuilëar Springdays	1		1		25	26
	2		2		26	27
Víressë First Spring (April)	1	Tuilë Spring	3	Lairë or Úriën : Summer	27	28
						April
Lótessë Second Spring (May)	1		33		27	28
						May
	30		62		26	27
Nárië First Summer (June)	1		1		27	28
						June
Cermië Second Summer (July)	1	Lairë Summer	31		27	28
						July
Úrimë Third Summer (August)	1		61		24	23
						Aug.
	30		90		23	22
Yavannië First Autumn (Sept.)	1		1		24	23
						Sept.
Arendiën Midyear's Day	1	Quellë Autumn	31		24	23
Narquelië Second Autumn (Oct.)	1		32		25	24
						Oct.
	30		61		24	23
Hísimë First Winter (November)	1		1		25	24
						Nov.
Ringarë Second Winter (December)	1	Hrívë Winter	31	Hrívë or Fíriën : Winter	25	24
						Dec
Narvinyë Third Winter (January)	1		61		25	24
						Jan.
	30		90		22	23
Nendessë First Stirring (Feb.)	1		1		23	24
						Feb.
Súlimë Second Stirring (March)	1	Coirë Stirring	31		23	24
						March
	30		60		22	23
Coirëar Stirringdays	1		61		23	24
Mettarë Year's-end	2		62		24	25

Every fourth year save the last in the
Quantiën or Century there were two Arendiéni.

incidence was somewhat altered: they began and ended earlier in the year than in older calendars.

On the reverse of the page carrying the first of these accounts of the calendar of the New Era is a table made at the same time; this was struck out and replaced by another, identical in all essentials, and this latter I have redrawn (p. 134). In this table the first column of figures refers to actual dates (with the five days standing outside the months numbered 1 and 1, 2); thus the five figures given for *Tuilë* (Spring), 1, 2, 1, 1, 30, refer respectively to the two *Tuilëar* (Springdays), 1 (*Entarë*) and 2; the first day of *Víressë* (April 1); the first day of *Lótessë* (May 1); and the last day of *Lótessë* (May 30). The second column of figures is the *cumulative* total of days in each season corresponding to those in the first column: thus 1 *Lótessë* is the 33rd day of the year (2 *Tuilëar*, *Víressë* 30 days, *Lótessë* 1, = 33).

In Appendix D this elegantly balanced structure had been abandoned and replaced by a different system, somewhat obscurely recounted. But it seems extremely probable that it was here, in this original account of the calendar of the New Era, that the Quenya names of the months first entered. It will be seen that the names given in Appendix D are all present except that of February, *Nénimë*, which is here *Nendessë*; while the opening day of the year is *Entarë* (on the first form of the table written *Entalë* and then changed) for later *Yestarë*, and Midyear's Day is *Arendiën* for later *Loëndë*. The changed names were written onto the table later, probably much later.

On the back of the second table, and clearly intended to be continuous with it, is the following.

Alternative names.[11]
Autumn: *Endien* (Midyear).

April: *Ertuilë*	October: *Lasselanta (Nóquellë)*
May: *Nótuilë*	November: *Errívë*
June: *Ellairë*	December: *Norrívë*
July: *Nólairë*	January: *Meterrívë*
August: *Metelairë*	February: *Ercoirë*
September: *Erquellë*	March: *Nócoirë*

The Noldorin month names and seasons corresponding were:
Spring: *Ethuil*: April *Gwirith*. May *Lothron*.
Summer: *Loer*: June *Nórui*. July *Cerfeth*. August *Úrui*
Autumn: *Firith*: September *Ifonneth*. October *Narbeleth*.
Winter: *Rhîw*: November *Hithui*. December *Girithron*.
    January *Nerwinien*.
Stirring: *Echuir*: February *Nenneth*. March *Gwaeron*.
Occasional variants: Autumn: [*Dant, Dantilais* >] *Dannas,*

Lasbelin. June: *Ebloer*. July: *Cadloer*. December: *Ephriw*. January: *Cathriw*.

The old *Year beginning* corresponded to N[ew] E[ra] January 8, the 68th day of Winter, and 281st day of the year.

The old *Midyear* corresponded to N.E. July 6, the 36th day of Summer, and 98th day of the year.

The old *Year's-end* corresponded to N.E. January 7, the 67th day of Winter, and 280th day of the year.

The Shire *Lithedays* = N.E. July 5, 6, 7

The old Gondor *Summerdays* = N.E. July 4–8 inclusive.

Here the Noldorin (Sindarin) names first appear, and are the same as those given in Appendix D, with two exceptions: *Nerwinien* for *Narwain* (January) and *Nenneth* for *Nínui* (February). *Narwain* and *Nínui* were written in much later, together with the following changes: *Metelairë*, *Meterrívë* > *Mettelairë*, *Metterrívë*; *Cerfeth* > *Cerveth*; *Ifonneth* > *Ivanneth*; *Loer* > *Laer*, *Ebloer* > *Eblaer*, *Cadloer* > *Cadlaer*.

Together with many other tables of comparative reckoning, some beautifully made, this effectively completes all the calendar material that I can certainly identify as belonging to this primary phase of my father's work on the subject. It is remarkable that (amid abundant but very rough and difficult notes) there is no further text until the typescript (itself rough and a good deal emended) from which the text of Appendix D was printed.[12] It seems very unlikely that any intervening text should have been lost, and I am inclined to think that my father was still developing and refining his theory of the Calendars when the need to submit his text to the publishers became imperative and urgent. Of the final form I believe that what I said of Appendix F, that 'had circumstances been otherwise the form of that appendix would have been markedly different' (p. 82), can be repeated of Appendix D with greater force.[13]

NOTES

1 I have added the final 6, absent in the manuscript.

2 As noted on p. 119 this is a reference to the manuscript F 2 of the Appendix on Languages, pp. 38–9, §§23–4. The sentence at the end of §24, 'But most remarkable of all are the Hobbit monthnames, concerning which see the note on Calendar and Dates', was an addition, but one made with care near to the time of writing of F 2 – no doubt when my father reached this point in D 1.

3 *Rethe* was not the original name. On the back of this page of the manuscript is a comparative table, struck through, of Hobbit

dates and modern dates by month and day; and the third month is here *Luyde*, not *Rethe*. *Luyde* occurs also in one of the *Prologue* texts (see p. 9), but I have not found it anywhere else; nor have I found any other names preceding those in the list given here, which survived without change.

4 *Winterfylleth* was the Old English name of October. Its meaning was discussed by Bede (died 735), who explained the name by reference to the ancient English division of the year into two parts of six months each, Summer and Winter: *Winterfylleth* was so called because it was the first month of Winter, but *fylleth*, Bede supposed, referred to the full moon of October, marking the beginning of that period of the year. My father's interpretation of the name in D 1, 'the filling (completion) of the year', 'winter' being used in the sense 'year', is at variance both with Bede and apparently with that in the published text (RK p. 388, footnote), 'the filling or completion of the year *before Winter*'. In either case it must be supposed that the 'true' words underlying translated 'filth' and 'Winterfilth' could make the same pun!

On the former beginning of the Hobbit year after Harvest see p. 121, footnote.

5 The Great Writ of Tuckborough (later the Yearbook of Tuckborough) is mentioned also in the Appendix on Languages, p. 40, §27.

6 The words '(in spoken form)' refer to the spelling *Munday*. In the published text the sentence reads: 'In the language of the time of the War of the Ring these had become *Sterday, Sunday, Monday* ...', instead of 'had become written', thus avoiding the question of *Munday, Monday*: the latter being a mere peculiarity of English spelling, as in many other words with the vowel of *but*, as *monk, son*, etc. *Sunday* was once often spelt *Sonday*. – So also *Hiday* of D 1 is given the modern spelling *Highday* in the published text. But in the list of archaic (Old English) forms it should not be *Highdei* but *Hihdei*, as in D 1.

7 Contrast Appendix D (RK p. 384): 'the merrymaking in that year [1420] is said to have been the greatest in memory or record.'

8 The different computation in D 1 (p. 120), whereby the Eldarin calendar would have 36525 days in a century (leading to the removal of the last day of a century) was reached thus: the last four years of a century were computed as half of an eight-year cycle, that is 2922 (seven long years and one short year) divided by two, 1461. Added to the total (35064) of the days in 96 years this made 36525. In D 2 the last four years are not half of an eight-year cycle but three full years and one short year, that is 35064 + 1458 in a century, total 36522 (leading to the addition of the two extra days outside the structure of weeks and months, *Quantárië* and *Vinyárië*).

9   I have found no further list of the Elvish names of the days of the
week, nor any mention of individual names, before the third (and
final) text, from which Appendix D was printed (see p. 136).
There, the Quenya names of the fourth and sixth days, *Aldarya*
and *Valarya*, were still in that form (but *Tárion* had replaced
Tárinar); my father emended them very clearly, on both copies of
the typescript, to *Aldauya* and *Valanya*. On the proof of the first
of these was printed *Aldanya*, and he emended this to *Aldúya*, as
it appears in Appendix D.
    On the use of 'Noldorin' for 'Sindarin' see the Appendix on
Languages, especially p. 36, §18, and commentary, pp. 65–6.
These month-names next reappear in the final typescript, already
changed to *Orgilion, Oranor, Orithil, Orgaladhad, Ormenel,
Orebelain* (or *Rodyn*); and similarly with the name of the
'Sea-day' added by the Númenóreans, changed from *Aroeren* to
Oraearon.
10   In the Eldarin calendar (p. 126), in the long (normal) years,
January had 31 days and February 30; thus March 25th was the
86th day of the year. In the Gondorian King's Reckoning (p. 131)
the same was true. In the Shire Reckoning Yuleday preceded
January 1, but both January and February had 30 days, so that
March 25 was again the 86th day of the year.
    In the Gondorian Steward's Reckoning (p. 132), on the other
hand, the count is simply 30 days in January and 30 days in
February, so that March 25 is the 85th day of the year; while in
our calendar 31 + 28 + 25 makes March 25 the 84th day.
11   Some of these alternative names are included in the first form of
the table, with the difference that *Errívë* and *Norívë* (so spelt) are
alternatives respectively for *Ringarë* (December) and *Narvinyë*
(January).
12   It is a curious point that this typescript begins with the *printed*
'Shire Calendar for use in all years' exactly as it appears in
Appendix D (RK p. 384): my father's typescript begins below it
('Every year began on the first day of the week ...'), and the same
is true of the carbon copy. Presumably this calendar was printed
first and separately and copies were sent to my father, who used
them in this way.
    The manuscript calendar from which this was printed is
extant, and it is interesting to see that on the left-hand side there
is a column headed 'Weekday' with the names of the days of the
week set out against each of the three transverse groups of
months, thus for example in the second month *Solmath*:

Stirday	–	5	12	19	26
Sunday	–	6	13	20	27
Munday	–	7	14	21	28
Trewsday	1	8	15	22	29

and so on. This column of the days of the week would have made the calendar easier to understand; but on the manuscript it is struck through, by whom is not clear. I can see no reason for this but that of space on the page, which one would think could have been quite easily accommodated. – This manuscript table undoubtedly goes back to the original phase of my father's work on the calendars, described in this chapter.

13   Among various alterations made by my father on the proof, it may be noted that the text of Appendix D as first printed ended thus: 'Some said that it was old Sam Gardner's birthday, some that it was the day on which the Golden Tree first flowered in 1420, and some that it was the Elves' New Year. The last was (more or less) true, so all may have been.'

V

THE HISTORY OF THE AKALLABÊTH

The development of Appendix B, *The Tale of Years*, was naturally associated with and dependent on that of Appendix A, which as published bears the title *Annals of the Kings and Rulers*. But more unexpectedly, the Tale of Years of the Second Age was closely associated with the evolution of the history of Númenor and of the *Akallabêth*. In the presentation of the early forms of these Appendices I have found after trial and error that the best course is to divide the Tale of Years into two parts, the Second and the Third Ages, and to treat them separately; and also, to introduce at this point an account of the *Akallabêth*, followed by the Tale of Years of the Second Age in Chapter VI.

In the *History of Middle-earth* I have given no indication of how this work, a primary narrative of the Second Age, developed to the form given in the published *Silmarillion*, or when it first came into being. The early history of the legend, closely related to the abandoned story *The Lost Road*, was studied in Volume V, where the two original narratives of *The Fall of Númenor*, which I called FN I and FN II, were printed (V.13 ff.). In *Sauron Defeated* (IX.331 ff.) I gave a third version, FN III, which I have ascribed to a fairly early stage in the writing of *The Lord of the Rings*. The massive development of the legend in the work called *The Drowning of Anadûnê*, closely associated with *The Notion Club Papers* and the emergence of the Adûnaic language, was studied in *Sauron Defeated*, where I ascribed it to the first half of 1946 (IX.147, 389–90): this dating was subsequently confirmed by the observation of John Rateliff that W. H. Lewis recorded in his diary that my father read the work to the Inklings in August 1946 (Foreword to *Morgoth's Ring*, X.x).

In my commentary on *The Drowning of Anadûnê* I indicated and discussed at many points its relationship to the *Akallabêth*, but for the text of the latter I made use only of the final form, as printed in *The Silmarillion*, pp. 259 ff. Since the writing of the *Akallabêth* evidently post-dated the writing of *The Lord of the Rings* I postponed discussion of its history, but I found no room for it in the very long books *Morgoth's Ring* and *The War of the Jewels*.

I did, however, in *Sauron Defeated* make an extraordinary misstatement on the subject of the *Akallabêth*, which must be repaired.

When discussing (IX.406) my father's late note on *The Drowning of Anadûnê*, in which he referred it to 'Mannish tradition', I said:

> The handwriting and the use of a ball-point pen suggest a relatively late date, and were there no other evidence I would guess it to be some time in the 1960s. But it is certain that what appears to have been the final phase of my father's work on Númenor (*A Description of Númenor, Aldarion and Erendis*) dates from the mid-1960s (*Unfinished Tales* pp. 7–8);[1] and it may be that the *Akallabêth* derives from that period also.

This last remark is patent nonsense. The great extension of the line of the Númenórean kings, which entered in the course of the development of the *Akallabêth*, was present in Appendix A (and a mere glance through the texts of the work is sufficient to show, simply from their appearance, that they could not conceivably date from so late a time). How I came to write this I do not know, nor how it escaped all subsequent checking and revision. I perhaps meant to say that my father's note on *The Drowning of Anadûnê* may have derived from the same period as *Aldarion and Erendis*.

When I wrote *Sauron Defeated* I was nonetheless not at all clear about the time of the original writing of the *Akallabêth*, and I assumed without sufficient study of the texts that it was later than it proves to be.

The textual history is relatively brief and simple in itself. The earliest text, which I will call A, is a clear manuscript of 23 pages; a good deal of this text is extant also in pages that were rejected and written out again, but virtually nothing of any significance entered in the rewriting, and the two layers of this manuscript need not be given different letters.

My father then corrected A, fairly extensively in the earlier part, very little in the story of the Downfall, and made a second text, a typescript, which I will call B. He followed the corrected manuscript with an uncharacteristic fidelity, introducing only a very few changes as he typed. It cannot be demonstrated, but I think it virtually certain, that the series A, A corrected, B, belong to the same time; and there is usually no need to distinguish the stages of this 'first phase', which can be conveniently referred to as AB.

After some considerable interval, as I judge, he returned to the typescript B and emended it. This left the greater part of the text untouched, but introduced a vast extension into Númenórean history: primarily by the insertion of a long rider in manuscript, but also by transpositions of text, alteration of names, and the rewriting of certain passages.

The third and final text (C) was an amanuensis typescript (in top copy and carbon) taken from B when all alterations had been made to it. It seems to me very probable that this was made at the same time

(?1958) as the typescripts of the *Annals of Aman*, the *Grey Annals*, and the text LQ 2 of the *Quenta Silmarillion* (see X.300, XI.4). To this typescript my father made only a very few and as it were casual corrections.

The alterations (including the long inserted rider) made to B constitute a 'second phase'; and this is the final form of the *Akallabêth* (apart from the few corrections to C just mentioned). There are thus only two original texts, the manuscript A and the typescript B, but the corrections and extensions made to B represent a significantly different 'layer' in the history of the work. To make this plain I will call the typescript B *as subsequently altered* B 2.

While the development of the *Akallabêth* is of much interest in particular features, a very great deal of the text never underwent any significant change; and as I noted in IX.376, something like three-fifths of the precise wording of the second text of *The Drowning of Anadûnê* (which was printed in full in that book) survived in the *Akallabêth*. Moreover the final form of the *Akallabêth*, if with some editorial alteration, is available in *The Silmarillion*. In order to avoid an enormous amount of simple repetition, therefore, I use the *Silmarillion* text, which I will refer to as SA ('Silmarillion-Akallabêth'), as the basis from which to work back, so to speak, rather than working forward from A. To do this I have numbered the paragraphs in SA throughout, and refer to them by these numbers, together with the opening words to aid in their identification.

The *Silmarillion* text was of course that of B 2 (with the corrections made in C), but as I have said a number of editorial changes were made, for various reasons, but mostly in the quest (somewhat excessively pursued, as I now think) for coherence and consistency with other writings. Unless these changes were trivial they are noticed in the account that follows.

I do not here go into the relations of the *Akallabêth* to its sources (*The Drowning of Anadûnê*, and to a more minor degree the third version of *The Fall of Númenor*, FN III), since these are fully available in *Sauron Defeated*, where also the most crucial developments were extensively discussed.

The original title in the manuscript A was *The Fall of Númenor*, which was corrected to *The Downfall of Númenor* and so remained: none of the texts bears the title *Akallabêth*, but my father referred to the work by that name (cf. p. 255).

§§1–2   The original opening of A was almost a simple copy of the opening of FN III (IX.331–2): 'In the Great Battle when Fionwë son of Manwë overthrew Morgoth', etc.; but this was at once rejected, though appearing in revised form in SA §3, and a new opening substituted, which constitutes, with some editorial changes, that in SA (§§1–2). The authentic text begins: 'Of Men, Ælfwine, it is said

THE HISTORY OF THE AKALLABÊTH

by the Eldar that they came into the world in the time of the Shadow of Morgoth ...', and in SA I removed the address to Ælfwine.[2] The *Akallabêth* was conceived as a tale told by Pengoloð the Wise (as it must be supposed, though he is not named) in Tol Eressëa to Ælfwine of England, as becomes again very explicit (in the original) at the end; and no change was made in this respect in the 'second phase' B 2, nor on the final amanuensis typescript C.[3]

In §1 I also altered the sentence 'and the Noldor named them the Edain' to 'The Edain these were named in the Sindarin tongue'; on this change see under §9 below.

In §2, Eärendil's ship was named *Vingilot* in AB, but this was changed to the otherwise unrecorded *Eälótë* in B 2; in SA I reverted to *Vingilot*. The name *Rothinzil* is derived from *The Drowning of Anadûnê*.[4]

§3 *In the Great Battle* ...   The opening of this paragraph in AB read:

> In the Great Battle when at last Fionwë son of Manwë overthrew Morgoth and Thangorodrim was broken, the Edain fought for the Valar, whereas other kindreds of Men fought for Morgoth.

This was changed in B 2 to read:

> In the Great Battle when at last Eönwë herald of Manwë overthrew Morgoth and Thangorodrim was broken, the Edain alone of the kindreds of Men fought for the Valar, whereas many others fought for Morgoth.

In SA the reference to Eönwë was removed; and similarly later in the paragraph 'refusing alike the summons of [Fionwë >] Eönwë and of Morgoth' was changed to 'refusing alike the summons of the Valar and of Morgoth'. The reason for this lay in the treatment of the last chapter of the *Quenta Silmarillion* in the published work. The only narrative of the Great Battle at the end of the First Age (V.326 ff.) derived from the time when the Children of the Valar were an important conception, and Fionwë son of Manwë was the leader and commanding authority in the final war against Morgoth and his overthrow; but the abandonment of that conception, and the change in the 'status' of Fionwë / Eönwë to that of Manwë's herald led to doubt whether my father, had he ever returned to a real retelling of the story of the end of the Elder Days (see XI.245–7), would have retained Eönwë in so mighty and elemental a rôle. His part was in consequence somewhat diminished by omissions and ambiguous wording (as may be seen by comparing the text in Vol.V with that of the published *Silmarillion*; cf. also the editorial addition made to the *Valaquenta*, X.203). There is however no evidence for this supposition, and I now believe it to have been a mistaken treatment of the original text, and so also here in the *Akallabêth*.[5]

§4   *But Manwë put forth Morgoth* ...   In this paragraph my father
was still closely following FN III (IX.332), but at the end, after
'Andor, the Land of Gift' he turned to *The Drowning of Anadûnê*,
which was thereafter the primary source, though with some inter-
weaving of passages from FN III. In FN III the passage concerning
Morgoth, originally written in the present tense, was corrected to
the past tense, and this was followed in A; but it is curious that in
B my father reverted in one of the phrases to the present: 'and he
cannot himself return again into the World, present and visible,
while the Lords of the West *are* still enthroned.' This was retained
in SA.

After the words 'life more enduring than any others of mortal
race have possessed' I omitted in SA the following sentence in the
original: 'Thrice that of Men of Middle-earth was the span of their
years, and to the descendants of [Húrin the Steadfast >] Hador the
Fair even longer years were granted, as later is told.' This omission,
scarcely necessary, was made on account of divergent statements on
the subject (see *Unfinished Tales* p. 224, note 1). The erroneous
reference to Húrin, surviving from FN III (see IX.332 and note 1),
was only corrected in B 2.

In the original manuscript A the words of FN III concerning
Eressëa were retained: 'and that land was named anew Avallon; for
it is hard by Valinor and within sight of the shores of the Blessed
Realm.' This was corrected to the text that appears in SA ('and there
is in that land a haven that is named Avallónë ...'). On this see
further under §12 below.

§5   *Then the Edain set sail* ...   The original opening of this paragraph, not subsequently changed, was:

> Then the Edain gathered all the ships, great and small, that they
> had built with the help of the Elves, and those that were willing
> to depart took their wives and their children and all such wealth
> as they possessed, and they set sail upon the deep waters, follow-
> ing the Star.

I cannot now say with certainty why this passage (derived from *The
Drowning of Anadûnê*, IX.360, §12) was omitted from SA: possibly
on account of a passage in the 'Description of Númenor', not
included in the extracts given in *Unfinished Tales*, in which the ships
of the migration are described as Elvish:

> The legends of the foundation of Númenor often speak as if all
> the Edain that accepted the Gift set sail at one time and in one
> fleet. But this is only due to the brevity of the narrative. In more
> detailed histories it is related (as might be deduced from the
> events and the numbers concerned) that after the first expedition,
> led by Elros, many other ships, alone or in small fleets, came west
> bearing others of the Edain, either those who were at first reluc-

tant to dare the Great Sea but could not endure to be parted from those who had gone, or some who were far scattered and could not be assembled to go with the first sailing.

Since the boats that were used were of Elvish model, fleet but small, and each steered by one of the Eldar deputed by Círdan, it would have taken a great navy to transport all the people and goods that were eventually brought from Middle-earth to Númenor. The legends make no guess at the numbers, and the histories say little. The fleet of Elros is said to have contained many ships (according to some a hundred and fifty vessels, to others two or three hundred) and to have brought 'thousands' of the men, women, and children of the Edain: probably between five thousand or at the most ten thousand. But the whole process of migration appears in fact to have occupied at least fifty years, possibly longer, and finally ended only when Círdan (no doubt instructed by the Valar) would provide no more ships or guides.

In this paragraph is the first appearance of the name *Elenna* ('Starwards') of Númenor.

§6 *This was the beginning of that people* ... In the first sentence the words 'that people that in the Grey-elven speech are called the Dúnedain' were an editorial alteration from 'that people that the Noldor call the Dúnedain'.[6] Cf. the similar change made in §1, and see under §9.

§7 *Of old the chief city and haven* ... Following the words 'it was called Andúnië because it faced the sunset' A had originally the following passage:

But the high place of the King was at Númenos in the heart of the land, and there was the tower and citadel that was built by Elros son of Eärendil, whom the Valar appointed to be the first king of the Dúnedain.

Númenos survived from FN III (IX.333) and earlier (see V.25, §2). This was replaced in B by the passage in SA: 'But in the midst of the land was a mountain tall and steep, and it was named the Meneltarma,' etc. The name of the city was given here, however, as *Arminalêth* (the name in *The Drowning of Anadûnê*), with a note: 'This is the Númenórean name, for by that name it was chiefly known, *Tar Kalimos* in the Eldarin tongue.' In B 2 the name was changed here (and at the subsequent occurrences) from *Arminalêth* to *Armenelos*, and the note changed to read: '*Arminalêth* was the form of the name in the Númenórean tongue; but it was called by its Eldarin name *Armenelos* until the coming of the Shadow.' Thus the statement in Index II to *Sauron Defeated* (IX.460) that *Arminalêth* was 'replaced by *Armenelos*' is incorrect: *Armenelos* was a *substitution* in the *Akallabêth* because my father was now asserting that this was the name by which the city was known through long ages, but its Adûnaic form remained *Arminalêth*. It was *Tar Kalimos* that was replaced by *Armenelos*. – This note was omitted in SA.

§8 *Now Elros and Elrond his brother* ... The words in SA 'were descended from the Three Houses of the Edain' were an editorial change from 'were descended from the lines of both Hador and Bëor'. – Near the end of the paragraph, the span of years granted to Elros was said (in all texts) to have been 'seven times that of the Men of Middle-earth', but on one copy of C my father changed 'seven' to 'three' and placed an X against the statement that Elros lived for five hundred years. The reading 'many times' in SA was an editorial substitution.

§9 *Thus the years passed* ... In the sentence 'For though this people used still their own speech, their kings and lords knew and spoke also the Elven tongue, which they had learned in the days of their alliance' AB had 'the Noldorin tongue'. Similarly in §§1, 6 it was said that *Edain, Dúnedain* were Noldorin names, but only in the present case did my father change (in B 2) 'Noldorin' to 'Elven'. Thus the old conception that the Noldor in Beleriand retained their own tongue was still present, as it was also in the original forms of the Appendices on Languages and Calendars (see p. 138, note 9). This at once shows a relatively early date for the *Akallabêth*; and as noted earlier the adoption of Sindarin by the Exiled Noldor had already emerged in the *Grey Annals* (p. 62, §5).

The continuation of the same sentence originally read 'and they remained in great friendship with the Eldar, whether of Avallon or of the westlands of Middle-earth', but this was changed to the text in SA, 'and thus they held converse still with the Eldar, whether of Eressëa', etc. The same removal of the word 'friendship' of the relations between the Eldar and the Númenóreans is found also in §§12, 29.

§§10, 11 *For the Dúnedain became mighty* ..., *But the Lords of Valinor* ... There were no editorial alterations made to these paragraphs, which go back with no change of any significance to the earliest text.

§12 *For in those days Valinor still remained* ... In A the name of the Mountain of Númenor was *Menelmindon*; in FN III it was *Menelmin* (IX.335), and *Menelmindo, Menelminda* occur in *The Notion Club Papers*. But *Meneltarma* is found already in A at a later point in the narrative.

In A as originally written the name *Avallon* was still the new name of the isle of Eressëa, but in the rewriting of that passage (see under §4) it was corrected to *Avallónë*, now the name of the haven of the Eldar in Eressëa. In the present paragraph A had: 'But the wise among them knew that this distant land was not indeed Valinor, the Blessed Realm, but was Avallónë, the Isle of the Eldar, easternmost of the Undying Lands'; *Avallónë* was here the form first written, and thus my father moved from *Avallon* to *Avallónë* while writing the manuscript, without however changing the significance of the name (but see under §75). The text was then altered, to embody the new conception, but only by changing 'Isle' to 'Haven', to which in SA I added 'upon Eressëa' to make the meaning clear. (Much of the present passage derives fairly closely from *The Drowning of Anadûnê*, IX.361, §16: on the extremely difficult question of the meaning of *Avallôni* in that work see IX.379-80, 385-6.)

In the passage describing the coming of the Eldar to Númenor AB had:

> And thence at times the Firstborn still would come to Númenor in oarless boats, or as birds flying, for the friendship that was between the peoples.

The text of SA here is that of B 2, and here again (see §9 above) the 'friendship' of the Eldar and the Númenóreans was removed.

The conclusion of the paragraph provides further clear evidence of the early date of the *Akallabêth*. This passage began as an addition to A (following the words 'for the friendship that was between the peoples' cited above) as follows, with the changes made to it shown:

> And they brought to Númenor many gifts: birds of song, and flowers of sweet fragrance and herbs of great virtue. And a seedling they brought of the White Tree [Nimloth the Fair >] Galathilion that grew in the [courts of Avallónë >] midst of Eressëa, and was in his turn a seedling of the Eldest Tree, [Galathilion the light of Valinor >] Telperion of many names, the light of Valinor. And the tree grew and blossomed in the courts of the King in [Númenos >] Ar-minalêth; Nimloth the fair it was named, and the night-shadows departed when Nimloth was in flower.

The history of the names of the White Trees is complex, for several reasons: the names were applied to the Two Trees of Valinor and re-used as names for the later trees; the later trees (of Tirion (Túna), Eressëa, Númenor) entered at different times; and there was shifting in their applications. It is simplest to consider first the statements deriving from the major period of work on the Elder Days between the completion and the publication of *The Lord of the Rings*.

In the *Annals of Aman* (X.85, §69) Yavanna gave to the Noldor of Túna (Tirion) 'Galathilion, image of the Tree Telperion'. In the revision of the *Quenta Silmarillion* from the same period (X.176, §39) it is said of this tree that 'Yavanna made for them a tree in all things like a lesser image of Telperion, save that it did not give light of its own being'; its name is not given. It is also said in the same version of the *Quenta Silmarillion* (X.155) that *Galathilion*, a name of Telperion, was given also to the White Tree of Túna, which was known as 'Galathilion the Less'; and that 'his seedling was named *Celeborn* in Eressëa, and *Nimloth* in Númenor, the gift of the Eldar.'

As my father first wrote this addition to A he named the Tree of Eressëa *Nimloth*, saying that it was 'a seedling of the Eldest Tree, Galathilion the light of Valinor'; he thus omitted the Tree of Túna (Galathilion the Less). He immediately changed the name of the Tree of Eressëa to *Galathilion*, a seedling of Telperion, and gave the name *Nimloth* to the Tree of Númenor. (This shows incidentally that the addition preceded the writing of the account of the fate of the Tree of Númenor later in A, for there the name was *Nimloth* from the first.)

The passage as emended reappears without any further change in the second text, the typescript B. But on this text my father struck it out and rewrote it thus (B 2):

And a seedling they brought of the White Tree that grew in the midst of Eressëa, and was in its turn a seedling of the Tree of Túna, Galathilion, that Yavanna gave to the Eldar in the Land of the Gods to be a memorial of Telperion, Light of Valinor. And the tree grew and blossomed in the courts of the King in Ar-Minalêth [> Ar-Menelos]; Nimloth the Fair it was named, and flowered in the evening and the shadows of night it filled with its fragrance.

Here, in this 'second phase' of the *Akallabêth*, with the introduction of the Tree of Túna (Galathilion), the gift of Yavanna, the same succession is found as in the *Annals of Aman* and the contemporary revision of the *Quenta Silmarillion*: Telperion of Valinor; Galathilion of Túna; [Celeborn] of Eressëa; Nimloth of Númenor. The conclusion is thus inescapable that the first phase (AB) of the *Alkallabêth* was earlier than those works (the *Annals of Aman*, etc.) that can be dated with sufficient accuracy to 1951.

In SA the passage was slightly rewritten, introducing the name *Celeborn* of the Tree of Eressëa (X.155) and (unnecessarily) the word 'image' of the Tree of Túna from the *Annals of Aman* (X.85).

In this connection it is interesting to compare the passage in *The Return of the King* (p. 250, at the end of the chapter *The Steward and the King*) where the finding of the sapling tree on Mount Mindolluin is recounted. Gandalf's words are:

Verily this is a sapling of the line of Nimloth the fair; and that was a seedling of Galathilion, and that a fruit of Telperion of many names, Eldest of Trees.

It will be seen that this agrees with the emended form of the passage in the first phase (AB) of the *Akallabêth*: for Galathilion (as the parent of Nimloth) is here the Tree of Eressëa, there is no mention of the Tree of Túna, and Galathilion is a 'fruit' of Telperion (not an 'image', or a 'memorial'). The conclusion must be that this passage was not revised when the Tree of Túna entered the history.[7]

§13 *Thus it was that because of the Ban of the Valar* ... The development of the opening passage concerning the great voyage is curious. In *The Drowning of Anadûnê* (IX.362, §17) it was said that the mariners of Númenor sailed 'from the darkness of the North to the heats of the South, and beyond the South to the Nether Darkness. And the Eruhîn [Númenóreans] came often to the shores of the Great Lands, and they took pity on the forsaken world of Middle-earth.' In the *Akallabêth*, after the words 'to the Nether Darkness', my father introduced a passage from FN III (IX.334):

> They ranged from Eressëa in the West to the shores of Middle-earth, and came even into the inner seas; and they sailed about the North and the South and glimpsed from their high prows the Gates of Morning in the East.

This goes back to the earliest texts of *The Fall of Númenor* (V.14, 20, 25). But when incorporating it into the *Akallabêth* he changed this to 'and they came even into the inner seas, and sailed about Middle-earth and glimpsed from their high prows the Gates of Morning in the East' – returning to *The Drowning of Anadûnê* with 'And the Dúnedain came often to the shores of the Great Lands' (with 'often' > 'at times' in B 2).

This is the text in SA. It seems altogether impossible to say what geographical conception of the East of the World lies behind this passage.

In SA, after the words 'the Númenóreans taught them many things', the following passage (likewise derived from *The Drowning of Anadûnê*, *ibid.*) was omitted:

> Language they taught them, for the tongues of the Men of Middle-earth, save in the old lands of the Edain, were fallen into brutishness, and they cried like harsh birds, or snarled like savage beasts.

§14 *Then the Men of Middle-earth were comforted* ... to §17 *And some there were who said* ... (SA pp. 263–4). No changes entered the text in B 2, but two editorial changes were made in §17: for 'the bliss of the Great' and 'the people of Earth' I substituted 'the bliss of the Powers' and 'the people of Arda'.

§18 *The Eldar reported these words* ... A has: 'and he sent messengers to the Dúnedain, who spoke earnestly to the King, Tar-Atanamir'. My father was closely following *The Drowning of Anadûnê* in this paragraph (IX.364, §23), but in that work the king was Ar-Pharazôn: Tar Atanamir here first appears.[8] See further under §§24–5.

§19 *'The Doom of the World,' they said* ... to §23 *Then the Messengers said* ... Scarcely any changes, and none that need be

recorded, entered the text in B 2 in this part of the *Akallabêth*; there
were however some minor editorial alterations made in SA. In §21
there is in the original a complex interchange between 'thou' and
'you' in the reply of the Messengers, according as they are addressing the King or referring to the people as a whole, for example:
'thou and thy people are not of the Firstborn, but are mortal Men
as Ilúvatar made you', or 'And you, thou sayest, are punished for
the rebellion of Men'. In SA 'you' was employed throughout. In §23
'within the girdle of the Earth' was changed to 'within the Circles of
the World', and 'The love of this Earth' to 'The love of Arda'.

§§24, 25 *These things took place ..., Then Tar-Ancalimon ...*
These two paragraphs have to be considered together. AB §24
opened:

> These things took place in the days of Tar-Atanamir, and he was
> the seventh of those kings that succeeded Elros upon the throne
> of Númenor; and that realm had then endured for more than two
> thousand years ...

And AB §25 opened:

> Then [Kiryatan > Ar-Kiryatan >] Tar-Kiryatan the Shipbuilder,
> son of Atanamir, became King, and he was of like mind ...

It would be clear in any case from these new names that a development had taken place, or was taking place, in the history of the royal
house of Númenor from that in *The Drowning of Anadûnê*; but in
fact there is an extremely interesting isolated page in which my
father set forth the new conception, and it is most convenient to give
this page here.

Second Age

Elros	died	S.A.	460	
King 1	,,	c.	682	
2	,,	c.	903	
3	,,	c.	1125	
4	,,	c.	1347	
5	,,	c.	1568	
6	,,	c.	1790	[added:] In his day the Númenóreans aided Gil-glad in the defeat of Sauron
7	,,	c.	2061	

In his time the Shadow first fell on Númenor. His name was
Tar-Atanamir. To him came messages from the Valar, which
he rejected. [*Added:*] He clung to life for an extra 50 years.

8   died   S.A. c. 2233

In his time first began the division of the folk between the

King's folk and the *Nimruzîrim*[9] *(Elendilli)* or Elf-friends. The King's folk and Royal House cease to learn or use Elvish speech and are more usually known by their Númenórean names. This king was *Tar-Kiryatan* (Shipwright) or in Númenórean *Ar-Balkumagän*. Settlements of *dominion* in Middle-earth begin.

    9   died   S.A. c. 2454

Estrangement of Elf-friends and King's Men deepens. The King makes the Elf-friends dwell in East, and their chief place becomes Rómenna. Many depart to settle on shores of N.W. of Middle-earth. The King's folk as a rule go further south.

    10   died   S.A. c. 2676
    11   ,,   c. 2897
    12   ,,   c. 3118

Power but not bliss of Númenor reaches zenith.

    13 and last *Tarkalion* or *Arpharazôn*. Challenges Sauron and lands at Umbar 3125

        Downfall of Númenor   3319

General aspects of this text are discussed later (pp.171–2 and note 4). There can be no doubt that it is a scheme that my father had beside him when writing the original manuscript A of the *Akallabêth*. For the moment, it can be observed that, as in A, Atanamir (to whom the Messengers came) was the father of Kiryatan; and that when my father wrote in A that Atanamir 'was the seventh of those kings that succeeded Elros' he meant this precisely: for in the 'Scheme' (as I will refer to it) he is numbered 7, and Kiryatan is numbered 8, while Elros has no number.

In B 2 the openings of these two paragraphs, §§24–5, were changed to the text given in SA: 'These things took place in the days of Tar-Kiryatan the Shipbuilder, and of Tar-Atanamir his son ...', and 'Then Tar-Ankalimon, son of Atanamir, became King ...' In this 'second phase' not only was the order of Atanamir and Kiryatan reversed, but (although it was still to him that the Messengers came) Atanamir becomes the thirteenth king (the original words in A, 'of those kings *that succeeded Elros*' being now removed: in *The Line of Elros* in *Unfinished Tales* (p. 221) Kiryatan was the twelfth and Atanamir the thirteenth, with Elros counted as the first). The second phase (B 2) of the *Akallabêth* thus represents, or rather rests on, a further large development of the Númenórean history from that seen in the first phase, or AB.

At the end of §25 there is a paragraph in AB which was omitted in its entirety in B 2 (i.e. it was struck out on the B typescript):

The Elendili dwelt mostly near the west coasts of the land; but as the shadow deepened in men's hearts, the estrangement between the two parties grew greater, and the king commanded them to remove and dwell in the east of the island, far from the haven of Andúnië, to which the Eldar had been wont to come; and thereafter the Eldar visited them only seldom and in secret. The chief dwelling of the Elf-friends in the later days was thus about the harbour of Rómenna; and thence many set sail and returned to Middle-earth, where they might speak with the Elves in the Kingdom of Gil-galad. For they still taught to their children the Eldarin tongues, whereas among the King's Men these tongues fell into disuse, and even the heirs of Eärendil became known to their people by names in the Númenórean tongue. And the kings desired to put an end to all friendship between their people and the Eldar (whom they called now the Spies of the Valar), hoping to keep their deeds and their counsels hidden from the Lords of the West. But all was known to Manwë that they did, and the Valar were wroth with the Kings of Númenor and gave them counsel no more.

For the explanation of this omission see p. 155. B 2 now continues with SA §26.

§26   *Thus the bliss of Westernesse became diminished* ...   At the end of this paragraph AB has 'after the days of [Ar-Kiryatan >] Tar-Kiryatan' (Kiryatan being then the son of Atanamir); in B 2 this became 'after the days of Tar-Ankalimon' (who has already appeared in §25 as the son of Atanamir).

There is extant some original drafting for the passage concerning the mounting obsession with death among the Númenóreans, including the following passage that was not taken up in A:

And some taught that there was a land of shades filled with the wraiths of the things that they had known and loved upon the mortal earth, and that in shadow the dead should come there bearing with them the shadows of their possessions.

§27   *Thus it came to pass* ...   This paragraph in SA goes back without change to the earliest text.

§28   *In all this the Elf-friends had small part* ...   The end of this paragraph, from 'lending them aid against Sauron', was altered in SA; the authentic text reads:

But the King's Men sailed far away to the south, and though the kingdoms and strongholds they made have left many rumours in the legends of Men, the Eldar know naught of them. Only Pelargir they remember, for there was the haven of the Elf-friends above the mouths of Anduin the Great.

Pengoloð implied, no doubt, that after the great division arose among the Númenóreans the Elves of Eressëa were cut off from any

knowledge of the imperial enterprises of the King's Men in the
further south of Middle-earth. But with the removal of Pengoloð
and Ælfwine from the published text, the *Akallabêth* lost its
anchorage in expressly Eldarin lore; and this led me (with as I now
think an excess of vigilance) to alter the end of the paragraph. – This
was the first appearance of Pelargir in the narratives of Númenor.

§29   *In this Age, as is elsewhere told ...*   In AB the second sentence
of this paragraph ran: 'It was indeed in the days of Atanamir in
Númenor that in Mordor the Tower of Barad-dûr was full-wrought,
and thereafter Sauron began to strive for the dominion of Middle-
earth ...' In B 2 this was altered to the text of SA, 'Already in the
days of Tar-Minastir, the eleventh King of Númenor, he had fortified
the land of Mordor and had built there the Tower of Barad-dûr ...'
The appearance here of Tar-Minastir the eleventh king is of course
a further element in the enlarged history already encountered in
§§24–6. So also in this paragraph the text of AB 'nor did he
forget the aid that they [the Númenóreans] had rendered to Gil-
galad of old' was changed in B 2 to 'the aid that Tar-Minastir had
rendered ...'

In the sentence 'And Sauron hated the Númenóreans, because of
the deeds of their fathers and their ancient alliance with the Elves'
the word 'alliance' was an early change from the original word
'friendship'; see under §9 above.

The words in SA 'in that time when the One Ring was forged and
there was war between Sauron and the Elves in Eriador' were an
editorial addition.

§30   *Yet Sauron was ever guileful ...*   This paragraph goes back to
A unaltered, except for the early change of 'great lords of Númenor'
to 'great lords of Númenórean race'. – The name *Úlairi* of the Ringwraiths seems to mark a period in my father's work: it is found also
in a text of the Tale of Years (p. 175); in *The Heirs of Elendil*
(Chapter VII); and in *Of the Rings of Power and the Third Age*
(published in *The Silmarillion*).

At the end of the paragraph my father wrote on the typescript C,
to follow 'he began to assail the strong places of the Númenóreans
upon the shores of the sea': 'but Umbar he could not yet take'. See
§41 below.

After SA §30 there is a second passage in AB (see p. 151) that was
excluded in B 2:

In those days there arose and took the throne of the Sea-kings the
great Tar-Calion, whom men called Ar-Pharazôn the Golden, the
mightiest and the proudest of all his line. And twelve kings
had ruled the Númenóreans between Elros and Ar-Pharazôn,
and slept now in their deep tombs under the mount of the
Meneltarma, lying upon beds of gold. Great and glorious was
Ar-Pharazôn, sitting upon his carven throne in the city of

Ar-minalêth in the noon-tide of his realm; and to him came the masters of ships and men returning out of the East, and they spoke of Sauron, how he named himself the Great, and purposed to become master of all Middle-earth, and to destroy even Númenor, if that might be.

Then great was the anger of Ar-Pharazôn hearing these tidings, and he sat long in thought, and his mood darkened. And he determined without the counsel of the Valar, or the aid of any wisdom but his own, that he would demand the allegiance and homage of this lord; for in his pride he deemed that no king should ever arise so mighty as to vie with the Heir of Eärendil.

Ar-Pharazôn is here named the fourteenth king, since 'twelve kings had ruled the Númenóreans *between* Elros and Ar-Pharazôn'; and this agrees with *The Drowning of Anadûnê*[10] and also with the Scheme on p. 151, where Ar-Pharazôn is numbered 13 and Elros is not counted.

At this point (i.e. following the conclusion of SA §30) there is a direction on the typescript B to take in a rider, this being a finely-written manuscript of four sides.

§31   *In those days the Shadow grew deeper* ... to §40 *Great was the anger* ...   This passage in SA (pp. 267–70) follows almost exactly the text of the rider just referred to. Here there entered the narrative of Númenor the story of the reigns of Ar-Adûnakhôr and Ar-Gimilzôr; of the Lords of Andúnië, who were of the Line of Elros; of the sons of Ar-Gimilzôr, Inziladûn and Gimilkhâd, and their conflict; of the unhappy reign of Inziladûn (Tar-Palantir); and of the forced marriage of his daughter Míriel (Ar-Zimraphel), the rightful Queen, to Pharazôn son of Gimilkhâd, who seized the sceptre for himself.

The few significant points in which the text of the rider was changed in SA are as follows.

In §31 I altered 'the twentieth king' (Ar-Adûnakhôr) and 'the twenty-third king' (Ar-Gimilzôr) to 'nineteenth' and 'twenty-second', and in §38 I altered 'four and twenty Kings and Queens had ruled the Númenóreans' before Ar-Pharazôn to 'three and twenty'. My reason for making these (incorrect) changes (an omission in the list of the rulers of Númenor given in Appendix A (I, i)) has been fully explained in *Unfinished Tales* p. 226, note 11.

In §33 I omitted two notes (belonging to the same time as the manuscript and forming part of it) concerning the Lords of Andúnië. The first of these refers to the words 'for they were of the line of Elros' and reads: 'And they took names in Quenya, as did no other house save the kings'; the second refers to the following words, 'being descended from Silmarien, daughter of Tar-Elendil the fourth king':

And in their line the sceptre would indeed have descended had the

law been in his day as it was later made. For when Tar-Ankalimë
became the first ruling Queen, being the only child of Tar-
Aldarion the Sixth King, the law was made that the oldest child
of the King whether man or woman should receive the sceptre
and the kingly authority; but Silmarien was older than her
brother Meneldur who succeeded Tar-Elendil.

On this see *Unfinished Tales* p. 208, where the different formulations of the new law brought in by Tar-Aldarion are discussed.
The law is stated here in the same words as in Appendix A (I, i), i.e.
simple primogeniture irrespective of sex (rather than inheritance of
the throne by a daughter only if the Ruler had no son).[11]

In §37 the Adûnaic name of Tar-Míriel is not *Ar-Zimraphel* in the
long rider, but *Ar-Zimrahil*, and this is the form in all the sources:
in *The Drowning of Anadûnê* (IX.373, §48), in *Akallabêth* AB (see
§78 below), in *The Line of Elros* (*Unfinished Tales* p. 224), and in
Aldarion and Erendis (*ibid.* p. 190). *Ar-Zimraphel* actually occurs
in one place only, a change made by my father in the present paragraph on the amanuensis typescript C. This I adopted in SA, and the
change to *Ar-Zimraphel* was also made silently to the passages in
The Line of Elros and *Aldarion and Erendis*.

Under §§24–5 and 30 above I have given two passages in AB that
were struck out when the long rider was introduced. The first of
these, following SA §25 and beginning 'The Elendili dwelt mostly
near the west coasts ...' (p. 151) was largely re-used in the rider (SA
§32, *Now the Elendili dwelt mostly in the western regions* ...), but
the forced removal of the Elf-friends to the east of Númenor was
now carried out by Ar-Gimilzôr, whereas in AB the king who commanded it is not named. The second omitted passage, following SA
§30 and beginning 'In those days there arose and took the throne of
the Sea-kings the great Tar-Calion' (p. 153), was postponed to the
end of the rider, where it reappears in revised form (SA §§38–40,
p. 270). At the words in §40 'so mighty as to vie with the Heir of
Eärendil' the rider ends, and the AB or 'first phase' text takes up
again with 'Therefore he began in that time to smithy great hoard
of weapons ...'.[12]

Several pages were placed with the rider, written on the same
paper, in which my father is seen devising a different story of the
marriage of Pharazôn and Míriel. For this see pp. 159 ff.

§41 *And men saw his sails coming up out of the sunset* ... In the
first sentence the words 'gleaming with red and gold' (of the sails of
the ships of Ar-Pharazôn) should read 'gleaming with red gold' (a
phrase that goes back to *The Drowning of Anadûnê*, IX.389, §28).

In the second sentence I altered the original text 'Umbar, where
there was a mighty haven that no hand had wrought' to 'Umbar,
where was the mighty haven of the Númenóreans that no hand had
wrought', in view of Appendix B, Second Age 2280: 'Umbar is made

into a great fortress of Númenór' (nearly a thousand years before the coming of Ar-Pharazôn). For the same reason I changed the original text in the following sentence, from 'Empty and silent under the sickle moon was the land when the King of the Sea set foot upon the shore' to 'Empty and silent were all the lands about when the King of the Sea marched upon Middle-earth'. (It is probable that when my father wrote this he did not yet suppose that Umbar was a Númenórean fortress and harbour at the time of Ar-Pharazôn's landing.)

§§42 ff.   In the remainder of the *Akallabêth* the text of the original manuscript A underwent very little change indeed at any subsequent stage; there is thus no further need to comment on the text paragraph by paragraph. Only occasional editorial alteration was made in SA, and in the rest of this account it can be understood that except as stated the published work follows the original exactly, or at most with very slight modification not worth recording.[13]

§44   *Yet such was the cunning of his mind ...*   (p. 271). The text of AB reads 'all the councillors, save Valandil only, began to fawn upon him'. In B 2 my father changed *Valandil* to *Amandil* here and at all subsequent occurrences. Since Amandil had not been mentioned in the text previously I added the words 'lord of Andúnië' in SA. – It is curious that the naming of Elendil's father *Valandil* was a reversion to *The Lost Road* (V.60, 69). In the course of the writing of *The Lord of the Rings* the name was variously and fleetingly applied to a brother of Elendil, to a son of Elendil, and to Elendil himself (VI.169, 175; VII.121, 123–4).

§53   *Nonetheless for long it seemed to the Númenóreans ...*   (p. 274). In the last sentence 'the kindly kings of the ancient days' is an editorial change from 'the kindly kings of the Elder Days'.

§57   *'The days are dark, and there is no hope for Men ...*   (p. 275). The text has 'there is no hope in Men', and the reading in SA appears to be a mere error, since there is no reason for the change. In the speeches of Amandil and Elendil that follow my father evidently intended a distinction between 'thou' from father to son and 'you' from son to father, but his usage was not consistent. In SA I substituted 'you' throughout.

§73   *Then Ar-Pharazôn hardened his heart ...*   (p. 278). The name of the great ship of Ar-Pharazôn is *Aglarrâma* in AB (as in *The Drowning of Anadûnê*, IX.372, §44), changed in B 2 to *Alkarondas*.

§75   *But the fleets of Ar-Pharazôn ...*   (p. 278). In the original text (at all stages) this paragraph begins:

But who among Men, Ælfwine, can tell the tale of their fate? For neither ship nor man of all that host returned ever to the lands of the living; and the world was changed in that time, and in Middle-earth the memory of all that went before is dim and unsure. But among the Eldar word has been preserved of the deeds and things that were; and the wisest in lore among them tell this tale, Ælfwine, that I tell now to thee. And they say that the fleets of Ar-Pharazôn came up out of the deeps of the Sea and encompassed Avallónë and all the Isle of Eressëa ...

Since this last phrase is found already in A it is clear that the changed meaning of *Avallónë* (signifying the eastern haven in Eressëa, not the Isle itself) had entered during the writing of A (see under §12 above).

In SA 'Taniquetil' is an editorial change from 'the Mountain of Aman', and 'the light of Ilúvatar' from 'the light of God'.

§76 *Then Manwë upon the Mountain ...* In the first sentence 'their government of Arda' was a change in SA from 'their government of the Earth'.

§77 *But the land of Aman ...* Two changes were made here in SA. The original text has 'were taken away and removed from the circles of the world beyond the reach of Men for ever', and 'there is not now within the circles of the world any place abiding ...'.

§78 *In an hour unlooked for by Men ...* AB has 'Ar-Zimrahil', changed in B 2 to 'Tar-Míriel'; see note 12.

§80 *Nine ships there were ...* All the texts have 'Twelve ships there were: six for Elendil, and for Isildur four, and for Anárion two', but on the amanuensis typescript C my father changed the numbers to 'nine: four, three, two', noting in the margin: 'Nine, unless the rhyme in LR is altered to *Four times three*.' The reference is to the song that Gandalf sang as he rode on Shadowfax with Pippin across Rohan on their way to Minas Tirith (*The Two Towers* p. 202):

> Tall ships and tall kings
> Three times three,
> What brought they from the foundered land
> Over the flowing sea?

§81 *Elendil and his sons ...* The opening of this paragraph was altered in SA to remove a reference to Ælfwine: 'And here ends the tale, Ælfwine, to speak of Elendil and his sons, who later founded kingdoms in Middle-earth ...'.

§83 *But these things come not into the tale ...* B had 'the Drowning of Anadûnê', corrected to 'the Drowning of Númenor' (a reversion to the reading of A). At the end of the paragraph AB had 'spoke of Akallabêth that was whelmed in the waves, the Downfallen, Atalantë in the Eldarin tongue', with *Akallabêth* changed to *Mar-nu-Falmar* in B 2. The removal of *Akallabêth* (restored in SA) belongs with the general replacement of Adûnaic by Elvish names: see under §78 above, and note 12. – On one of the copies of the typescript C my father wrote this note on the name *Atalantë*:

The Adûnaic or Númenórean name of the same meaning was *Akallabêth*, √KALAB. By a curious coincidence (not consciously prepared) before this tale was written a base √TALAT 'collapse, fall in ruin' had already been invented, and from that base *atalantë* 'it has fallen down' was a correct formation according to grammatical rules devised before Númenor had been thought of. The resemblance to *Atlantis* is thus by chance (as we say).

Against this note is written '71', which must mean '1971' (see XI.187, 191). With this statement on the subject cf. Lowdham's remarks in *The Notion Club Papers*, IX.249; my father's letter of July 1964 cited in V.8 (footnote); and the *Etymologies*, V.390, stem TALÁT.

§§84–6   The concluding section of the *Akallabêth*, beginning in SA *Among the Exiles many believed …*' (pp. 281–2), was headed in A *Epilogue*; this was omitted in B. There is a full discussion of this section in relation to *The Drowning of Anadûnê* in IX.391–6.

§84   *Among the Exiles many believed …*   The original text, not changed from A, reads:

> But if thou wouldst know, Ælfwine, ere thou goest, why it is that men of the seed of Eärendil, or any such as thou to whom some part, however small, of their blood is descended, should still venture upon the Sea, seeking for that which cannot be found, this much I will say to thee.
>
> The summit of the Meneltarma, the Pillar of Heaven, in the midst of the land, had been a hallowed place, and even in the days of Sauron none had defiled it. Therefore among the Exiles many believed that it was not drowned for ever, but rose again above the waves, a lonely island lost in the great waters, unless haply a mariner should come upon it. And some there were that after sought for it, because it was said among lore-masters that the far-sighted men of old could see from the Meneltarma a glimmer of the Deathless Land.

§86   *Thus in after days …*   The sentence 'until it came to Tol Eressëa, the Lonely Isle' was a change in SA from the original 'until it came to Eressëa where are the Eldar immortal'. Immediately following, 'where the Valar still dwell and watch the unfolding of the story of the world' was an early change from the reading of A, 'where the Valar still dwell but watch only and meddle no longer in the world abandoned to Men'.

In the last sentence 'and so had come to the lamplit quays of Avallónë' was an editorial change from 'and so had come to Avallónë and to Eressëa' ('to Eressëa and to Avallónë' A). For the 'lamplit quays of Avallónë' see V.334.

After the conclusion of the *Akallabêth* in SA the following lines were omitted:

And whether all these tales be feigned, or whether some at least be true, and by them the Valar still keep alight among Men a memory beyond the darkness of Middle-earth, thou knowest now, Ælfwine, in thyself. Yet haply none shall believe thee.

Note on the marriage of Míriel and Pharazôn

My father did much work on this story, but it is not easy to see how it is to be related to the paragraph (SA §37, *And it came to pass that Tar-Palantir grew weary ...*) in the long rider inserted into the typescript B, which is exactly repeated in SA except for the change of *Ar-Zimrahil* to *Ar-Zimraphel* (p. 155). It will in any case be clearer if the genealogy is set out (cf. *The Line of Elros* in *Unfinished Tales*, p. 223).

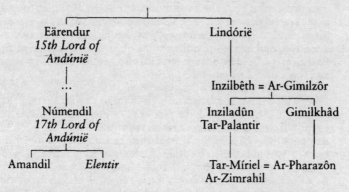

The significance of Amandil's brother Elentir will be seen in the texts given here: so far as I am aware he appears nowhere else. These texts were written on the same paper as the long rider and were inserted with it into the typescript B.

(a)

This is a very rough manuscript written in such haste that it has proved extraordinarily difficult to decipher. The text that follows is uncertain in many points, but these do not affect the narrative and I have largely dispensed with brackets and queries; it does not convey at all the appearance of the original.

He [Ar-Pharazôn] was a man of great beauty and strength/stature after the image of the first kings, and indeed in his youth was not unlike the Edain of old in mind also, though he had strength of will rather than of wisdom as after appeared, when he was corrupted by the counsels of his father and the acclaim of the people. In his earlier days he had a close friendship with Amandil who was afterwards Lord of Andunië,[14] and he had loved the people of the House of

Valandil with whom he had kinship (through Inzilbêth his father's mother). With them he was often a guest, and there came Zimrahil his cousin, daughter of Inziladûn who was later King Tar-Palantir. Elentir the brother of Amandil loved her, but when first she saw Pharazôn her eyes and her heart were turned to him, for his beauty, and for his wealth also.

But he went away[15] and she remained unwed. And now it came to pass that her father Tar-Palantir grew weary of grief and died, and as he had no son the sceptre came to her, in the name of Tar-Míriel, by right and the laws of the Númenóreans. But Pharazôn [?arose] and came to her, and she was glad, and forsook the allegiance of her father for the time, being enamoured of Pharazôn. And in this they broke the laws of Númenor that forbade marriage even in the royal house between those more nearly akin than cousins in the second degree. But they were too powerful for any to gainsay them. And when they were wedded she yielded the sceptre to Pharazôn, and he sat upon the throne of Elros in the name of Ar-Pharazôn the Golden, but she retained also her title as hers by right, and was called Ar-Zimrahil.[16]

The Elendili alone were not subservient to him, or dared to speak against his wishes, and it became well-known to all in that time that Amandil the Lord of Andúnië was head of their party though not openly declared. Therefore Ar-Pharazôn persecuted the Faithful, stripping them of any wealth that they had, and he deprived the heirs of Valandil of their lordship. Andúnië he took then and made it a chief haven for the king's ship-building, and Amandil who was now the Lord he commanded to move and dwell also in Rómenna. Yet he did not otherwise molest him [?at this time], nor dismiss him from the Council of the Sceptre, because he remembered still in his heart their friendship of old; and Amandil was well beloved also by many who were not of the Elendili.

And now when he deemed himself [?firm] upon the throne and beyond all gainsaying he sat in A[rmenelos] in the glory of his power, and he found it too little to appease his [?lust], and amid all his splendour he brooded darkly upon war.

There are a number of phrases in this text that are identical or almost so to those found in the long rider ('Tar-Palantir grew weary of grief and died', 'by right and the laws of the Númenóreans', 'those more nearly akin than cousins in the second degree', 'he brooded darkly upon war', SA §§37, 39). It would be natural to suppose that these phrases made their first appearance in this text, which was dashed down on the page, and that they were repeated in the rider, which was a manuscript written with great care; and in that case it would have to be concluded that my father discarded this story of the love of Amandil's brother Elentir for Zimrahil, and of her turning away from

him and from the Elf-friends and glad acceptance of Pharazôn, before
writing the final version. But I doubt that this was the case.

(b)

A second page is in handwriting even more obscure, and I have not
been able to make out the whole of it after repeated attempts.

> In his boyhood he had a close friendship with Amandil son of
> Númendil Lord of Andúnië, who being one of the chief councillors
> of the Sceptre dwelt often in Armenelos.

Cut out friendship. Ar-Pharazôn's policy to Amandil was due to
his wife?

> Now Zimrahil, whom her father called Míriel, only daughter of
> Tar-Palantir, was a woman of great beauty, smaller [?in ... stature]
> than were most women of that land, with bright eyes, and she had
> great skill in ... She was older than Ar-Pharazôn by one year,[17] but
> seemed younger, and his eyes and heart were turned to her; but the
> laws of Númenor lay between, beside the displeasure of her father
> whom Gimilkhâd opposed in all ways that he could. For in
> Númenor cousins in the first degree did not marry even in the royal
> house. And moreover Zimrahil was betrothed to Elentir Amandil's
> [?older] brother and heir of Númendil.[18]

From a distance,[19] for Gimilkhâd and his son were not welcome
in the house of the king.

In the remainder of the text there are a number of whole sentences,
clearly essential to the briefly sketched narrative, in which I can
decipher virtually nothing.

> Now it came into his heart that he would .... Pharazôn was not
> disposed to admit hindrance to his desires, and he asked leave there-
> fore of Amandil to be a guest in his house, learning ..... Zimrahil
> was at the time in Andúnië. Gimilkhâd was little pleased with this,
> for the Lords of Andúnië were his chief opponents. But Pharazôn
> [?laughed] saying he would do as he would, and ....

> And Amandil and Pharazôn rode in Andúnië and Elentir and
> Zimrahil saw them afar as they [?stood] ..... for Elentir loved his
> brother. But when Zimrahil saw Pharazôn in the splendour of his
> young manhood come riding [?in] .... Suddenly Zimrahil's heart
> turned towards him. And when Pharazôn was greeted upon the
> steps of the house their eyes met .... and were abashed.

I take this to be a further movement in the story struggling to emerge,
in which my father was considering a different treatment of
Pharazôn's intrusion into the relationship of Míriel and Elentir (who
are now said to be betrothed); but the sketch is so rapid, and so much
is indecipherable, that the actual course of the story is obscure.

(c)

A brief, clearly written text is the third of these papers associated with the rider inserted into the text of the *Akallabêth*.

> For Pharazôn son of Gimilkhâd had become even more restless and eager for wealth and power than his father. He was a man of great beauty and stature, in the likeness of the first kings of men; and indeed in his youth he was not unlike the Edain of old in mind also, though he had courage and strength of will rather than of wisdom, as after appeared, when he was corrupted by the counsels of his father, and the acclaim of the people. In his earlier days he had a close friendship with Amandil son of Númendil, Lord of Andúnië, and he loved the people of that House, with whom he himself had kinship (through Inzilbêth his father's mother). With them he was often a guest, and there also his cousin, daughter of Inziladûn, was often to be found. For Elentir Amandil's brother loved her, and she had turned her heart to him, and it was known that soon they would be betrothed.

In this my father was closely following the opening of text *(a)*, but the last sentence of the text, before it was abandoned, turns away, with the mention of the approaching betrothal of Elentir and Zimrahil, and was perhaps about to take a different course.

(d)

Finally, my father wrote the following passage in the margin of the inserted rider against §37, though without indication of its placing: most probably at the end of the paragraph ('... and the name of his queen he changed to Ar-Zimrahil').

> And he persecuted the Faithful, and deprived the Lords of Andúnië of their lordship, since they had aided Tar-Palantir and supported his daughter. Andúnië he took then and made it the chief harbour of the king's ships, and Amandil the Lord he commanded to dwell in Rómenna. Yet he did not otherwise molest him, nor dismiss him yet from his Council. For in the days of his youth (ere his father corrupted him) Amandil had been his dear friend.

This is very closely related to the end of text *(a)*, p. 160, 'Therefore Ar-Pharazôn persecuted the Faithful ...'; on the other hand, it seems clear from the words 'and supported his daughter' that the story of Zimrahil's love for Pharazôn is not present.

It is not perfectly clear to me how the textual puzzle presented by these writings is to be resolved, but I am inclined to think that, contrary to appearance, the texts *(a)*, *(b)*, and *(c)* in fact followed the writing of the long rider to the *Akallabêth*, and that they represent the emergence of a doubt in my father's mind whether the marriage of Pharazôn and Zimrahil was indeed 'against her will', and the sketching of a new story on the subject. The close agreement of phrases in *(a)* with those in the rider (see pp. 160–1) must then be interpreted as simple repetition of what was already present there, rather than as drafting for it. Finally, on this view, he abandoned the new story, and returned to that already present in §37. Amandil's brother Elentir was lost, at any rate in the recorded tradition.

It may be noted that the youthful friendship of Pharazôn and Amandil is referred to in SA §47 (*Then Ar-Pharazôn the King turned back* ..., p. 272), and this indeed goes back to the original manuscript of the *Akallabêth*: 'In the days of their youth together Valandil [> Amandil] had been dear to Ar-Pharazôn, and though he was of the Elf-friends he remained in his council until the coming of Sauron.'

NOTES

1 I think now that such slight evidence as there is points rather to about 1960 as the date of these works.

2 In §1 I altered the original 'yet they came at last to the lands that look upon the Sea. These are indeed that folk *of whom thou hast heard* that came into Beleriand in the days of the war of the Noldor and Morgoth' in order to remove the italicised words (the alteration of the last sentence to 'entered Beleriand in the days of the War of the Jewels' was a very late change, one of the very few that my father made to the typescript C). In §2, similarly, I changed 'and *thou hast heard* how at the last' to 'and in the *Lay of Eärendil* it is told how at the last'.

3 *The Line of Elros* ends with the words (*Unfinished Tales* p. 224): 'Of the deeds of Ar-Pharazôn, of his glory and his folly, more is told in the tale of the Downfall of Númenor, *which Elendil wrote*, and which was preserved in Gondor.'

4 In A my father added a footnote here, omitted in B: '*Rothinzil* is a name in the Númenórean tongue, and it has the same meaning as *Vingilot*, which is Foamflower.'

5 It is true that in the opening sentence of the Tale of Years my father substituted in the final typescript 'The *First Age* ended with the Great Battle, in which the Host of Valinor broke Thangoro-drim and overthrew Morgoth', replacing a reference to 'Fionwë and the sons of the Valar' of preceding versions (see pp. 172–3); but he may not have removed the name Fionwë (Eönwë) for the same reason as I did in the *Akallabêth*.

6 The manuscript A had 'called', which became 'call' in B.

7 Cf. Elrond's words in *The Council of Elrond* (FR p. 257): 'There in the courts of the King [in Minas Anor] grew a white tree, from the seed of that tree which Isildur brought over the deep waters, and the seed of that tree before came from Eressëa, and before

that out of the Uttermost West in the Day before days when the
world was young.'

8 'Tar-Atanamir' was struck out in A and does not appear in B, but
this seems to have been due only to my father's wish to postpone
the naming of the king to §24.

9 *Nimruzîrim*: *Nimruzîr* is the name of Elendil in *The Drowning of
Anadûnê*.

10 In *The Drowning of Anadûnê* (IX.363, §20) 'seven kings had
ruled ... between Indilzar [Elros] and Ar-Pharazôn', but 'seven'
was changed to 'twelve' (IX.381).

11 Other footnotes (on the inscription of the Quenya name *Herunú-
men* of Ar-Adûnakhor in the Scroll of Kings, §31, and on the
explanation of the name Tar-Palantir, §35, with which cf. *The
Line of Elros* in *Unfinished Tales* p. 223) were incorporated into
the body of the text in SA. At the end of §35 I extended the words
of the original text 'the ancient tower of King Minastir upon
Oromet' to '... upon the hill of Oromet nigh to Andúnië', this
being taken from *The Line of Elros*, p. 220; and in §37 after
'Míriel' I added the words 'in the Elven-tongue'.

12 Before the second of these passages was struck out (and so before
the insertion of the rider) my father went through it and all the
remainder of the typescript B and replaced *Ar-Pharazôn* by
Tar-Kalion (in the rejected passage, p. 153, he cut out the words
'whom men called Ar-Pharazôn', thus leaving 'Tar-Calion the
Golden'). His intention, presumably, was to use Elvish names
exclusively; nonetheless, in the inserted rider he named the king
Ar-Pharazôn. The typist of C therefore moved from one name
to the other; and seeing this my father began on C to change
Tar-Kalion back to *Ar-Pharazôn*, but soon wearied of it. In SA I
adopted *Ar-Pharazôn*.

13 Throughout this concluding part of the *Akallabêth* I substituted
the name Ar-Pharazôn for Tar-Kalion, as explained in note 12.
Arminalêth was changed to *Armenelos* on B, and this was taken
up in SA.

14 The following is written in the margin here: '3rd in line from
Eärendur and 18th from Valandil the First Lord of Andúnië'.

15 Above 'he went away' is written '[?Pharazôn] went to the wars';
cf. SA §36 (*Now Gimilkhâd died* ...): 'He [Pharazôn] had fared
often abroad, as a leader in the wars that the Númenóreans made
then in the coastlands of Middle-earth'.

16 At this point in the manuscript stands the following: 'And his
love therefore of the Lords of Andúnië turned to hate, since they
alone were powerful or wise enough to restrain him and give
counsel against his desires.' A second version following this was
struck out, and no doubt my father intended the rejection of the
first also.

17 In *The Line of Elros* Ar-Pharazôn was born in 3118, and Tar-Míriel in 3117 (*Unfinished Tales* p. 224).

18 The word I have given as 'older' is scarcely interpretable at all as it stands, but 'older' or 'elder' seems inevitable, since Elentir is called the heir of Númendil, Lord of Andúnië, apparently displacing Amandil.

19 'From a distance' presumably refers back to the words 'his eyes and heart were turned to her'.

VI

THE TALE OF YEARS OF
THE SECOND AGE

The chronology of the Second Age can be traced back to its origin in two small half-sheets of paper. That these are not only the first written record of such a chronology, but represent the actual moment of its establishment, seems certain from the obviously experimental nature of the calculations. I will refer to the various texts of the Tale of Years by the letter T, and call the first of these pages, given below, T(a) to indicate its primary nature. The rejected figures, being overwritten, are in some cases hard to make out, but I believe this to be a substantially correct representation of the text as it was first written; following it, I give the subsequent changes.

Time Scheme

'Ages' last *about* 3000 years.
The 'Black Years' or the age between the Great Battle and defeat of Morgoth, and the Fall of Númenor and the overthrow of Sauron lasted about 3500.
Thus:
Great Battle

Judgement of Fionwë and establishment of Númenor	10
Reign of Elros	410
11 other kings averaging 240 each	2640
Last 13th king	220
	3280

Elendil (very long-lived) was [*many rejected figures*] 200 years old at Fall of Númenor, and Isildur 100. The new realms lasted 100 years before Sauron opened war. 100
The gathering of Alliance 3 years, the Siege 7 10

          3390

The Third Age was 'drawing to its end' in Frodo's time. So that *Loss of Ring* was about 3000 years ago. For 500 years Sauron remained quiet and then began slowly to grow in Mirkwood – that stirred events and wakened the Ring to come back.
So Smeagol and Deagol's finding occurred about 600 years after

Isildur's death. Gollum therefore had the Ring near[ly] 2400 years.

Average life of a Númenórean   210 years (3×70)
Average life of royal house   350 years (5×70)
A King of Númenor usually acceded when about 100–120 and ruled about 250 years.

These dates seem to have been changed in this order. First, the duration of the new realms before Sauron assailed them was changed from 100 to 110 years, giving a total of 3400 (and at the beginning of the text the figure of 'about 3500' for the length of the Black Years, i.e. the Second Age, was changed to 'about 3400', and not subsequently altered). Then the establishment of Númenor was changed from 10 to 50, giving the date 3320 for the Fall of Númenor, and a total of 3440 years in the Second Age.

Sauron's 'remaining quiet' (in the Third Age) was changed from 500 to 1000 years, the finding of the Ring in the Anduin from 600 to 1100 years after Isildur's death, and Gollum's possession of it from 2400 to 1900 years.

A pencilled note, very probably of the same time, on this page reads: 'In character Aragorn was a hardened man of say 45. He was actually 90, and would live at least another 50 (probably 70) years. Aragorn was a Númenórean of pure blood but the span had dwindled to double life.'

The second of these two primary pages, unquestionably written at the same time as the first (as is shown by the paper used), is headed 'The Second Age and the Black Years', and gives dates from 'B.Y.' 0 (the end of the Great Battle) to the loss of the One Ring and the end of the Second Age, the date of which (3440 in T(a)) now becomes 3441, which was never changed. This page, being the earliest version of an actual 'Tale of Years', I will call T 1. In its earlier part T 1 was so much corrected and reworked as my father proceeded that it is scarcely possible to analyse the successive stages of its endlessly changed chronology; but in a subsequent text he followed the final form of T 1 so closely that it can be given in its place. The chief point to notice in it is the entry 'Foundation of Tarkilion', which was changed (probably at once) to 'Foundation of Artheden (Dunhirion) and Gondor'. The name *Dunhirion* is also found, but not so far as I know elsewhere, in a late text of the chapter *The Council of Elrond*, where it was corrected to *Annúminas*; while *Tarkilion* is found in the original manuscript of *Of the Rings of Power and the Third Age*, likewise corrected to *Annúminas*, and likewise apparently not found elsewhere. *Artheden* is clearly the first appearance of Arthedain, though not with its later significance.

The page T 1 (in its final form) was followed so closely by the next text that it seems probable that no long interval had elapsed. This is a clearly written manuscript on two sides of a single sheet; I will refer to it as T 2. A few changes were made to it in red ink, but they were made after the subsequent version had been written (since the same changes were made to that, also in red ink), and I do not notice them here.

Of the Tale of Years
in the latter ages

The 'First Age'[1] ended with the Great Battle and the departure of the Elves and Fathers of Men, and the foundation of Númenor.

The 'Second Age' ended with the overthrow of Sauron, and the Loss of the One Ring.

The 'Third Age' is drawing to its end in the tales of the Shire and of the Hobbits.

Each 'Age' last[ed] somewhat more or less than 3000 years; so that the Loss of the Ring was about 3000 years before Frodo's time. Deagol finds it about 1100 years after Isildur's death. 'Gollum' therefore had the Ring for about 1900 years.

The Second Age or the Black Years
reckoned from the overthrow of Morgoth

End of the Great Battle.

10   Foundation of the Havens, and the kingdom of Lindon.

50   Foundation of Númenor.

460   Death of Elros, Ëarendel's son, first king of Númenor.

500   Reawakening[2] of Sauron in Middle-earth.

700   First ships of the Númenóreans return to Middle-earth. Others come at times, but seldom, and they do not stay.

750   Foundation of Imladrist[3] (Rivendell) and Eregion (Hollin).

900–   Sauron begins in secret to build the fortress of Barad-dûr in Mordor, and makes the forges of Orodruin.

1200–1500   The Rings of Power are made in Eregion.

1550   War of the Elves and Sauron. The 'Days of Flight' begin, or the Black Years properly so called.

1600   Gil-galad defends Lindon; and Imladris is besieged but holds out. Eregion is laid waste.

1700   The great voyages of the Númenóreans begin. They come in many ships to Lindon, and they aid Gil-galad and Elrond.

1900   Barad-dûr is completed.

2000–3000 Sauron's dominion slowly extends over all Middle-earth, but it is withheld from the North-West, and all along the West-shores, even far southwards, the Númenóreans have fortresses and outposts.

3118 Tar-kalion the young king, the thirteenth of his line, ascends the throne of Númenor. He resolves to challenge Sauron the Great, and begins an armament (3120).

3125 Tar-kalion sets sail to Middle-earth. Sauron is obliged to yield and is taken to Númenor.

3319 Downfall of Númenor. Elendil, Anárion and Isildur fly to Middle-earth. Foundation of Arthedain (with the city Annúminas) in the North; and of Gondor (with the city Osgiliath) in the South.

3320 Sauron returns to Mordor.

3430–3 Sauron at last being ready makes war in Gondor. The Last Alliance is formed.

3433 [> 3434] Battle of Dagorlad. Siege of Barad-dûr begun.

3441 Sauron overthrown. Ring taken and lost. End of the Second Age.

The following are the only differences in the chronology of T 2 from its forerunner. In T 1 Sauron's departure to Númenor is given a separate entry under the year 3128; and (while T 1 already has the final date 3319 for the Downfall, where T(a) had 3320) the flight of Elendil and his sons is placed, most strangely, a year later, in 3320.

It will be seen that the dates of events in the Second Age are for the most part at variance with those in Appendix B, in many cases very widely so (thus Imladris was founded at the same time as Eregion, in 750, but in Appendix B not until 1697, in the War of the Elves and Sauron, when Eregion was laid waste). The most extreme of these differences refers in fact to the Third Age, in the headnote to the text, where the statement in T(a) that Déagol found the Ring in about Third Age 1100 and therefore Gollum possessed it for some 1900 years (p. 167) is repeated: in Appendix B Déagol finds the Ring in T.A.2463, by which reckoning Gollum had it for 478 years, until Bilbo found it in 2941.

There are a number of points of agreement between T 2 (under which I include here the closely similar T 1) and the 'Scheme' of the Númenórean kings accompanying the original manuscript A of the *Akallabêth*, given on pp. 150–1. In both, the death of Elros is placed in the year 460 (not as later in 442); in T 2 the coming of the Númenóreans to the aid of Gil-galad in Lindon is dated 1700, while in the 'Scheme' this is said to have occurred in the days of the unnamed sixth king (after Elros), who died in 1790; in T 2 the accession of Tar-kalion is placed in 3118, and in the 'Scheme' his father, the unnamed

twelfth king (after Elros) died in that year; and in both the date of Tar-
kalion's landing in Middle-earth is 3125. A further point of agreement
between both, and also with the manuscript A of the *Akallabêth*, concerns the completion of Barad-dûr: in T 2 this is dated 1900; in
Akallabêth A (see p. 153, §29) it is said to have occurred in the days
of Atanamir; and in the 'Scheme' Atanamir is said to have died in
2061, his father having died in 1790.

Two other points in this earliest version (or strictly versions) of the
Tale of Years of the Second Age remain to be mentioned. The loss of
the One Ring is expressly placed in the last year of the Second Age,
3441; whereas in Appendix B the headnote states that that Age 'ended
with the first overthrow of Sauron ... and the *taking* of the One Ring'
(cf. also the last words of section I (i) of Appendix A, RK p. 318),
while the planting of the White Tree in Minas Anor, the handing over
of the South Kingdom to Meneldil, and the death of Isildur are placed
in the year 2 of the Third Age. Secondly, in the entry for 3319 Anárion
is placed before Isildur, and it will be seen shortly that this does indeed
mean that Anárion was the elder of Elendil's sons (cf. the text FN III
in IX.335: 'his sons Anárion and Isildur'). In *Akallabêth* A and subsequently Isildur had four ships and Anárion two (p. 157, §80), from
which it seems clear that the reversal of this had already taken place.
On the other hand, in an early version of the chapter *The Council of
Elrond* Isildur was expressly stated to be the elder (VII.126).

Found with T 2 and to all appearance belonging to the same time
is another page in which my father restated in the same or closely
similar terms a part of his notes on Númenor and the aftermath of the
Downfall in T(a), pp. 166–7. This page I will call T(b). Corrections to
it were made at the same time as those to T 2, and are not noticed here.

Average life of a Númenórean before the fall was about 210
years (3 × 70). Average life of the royal house of the line of
Ëarendel was about 350 years (5 × 70). A king of Númenor
usually came to the throne when about 120 years old and
reigned 200 years or more.

50	Númenor founded
410	years Elros reigned
2640	11 other kings (averaging 240 each)
220	Last king (Tarkalion)
3320	

Elendil was very long-lived (being of Ëarendel's line). He was
about 200 years old at the time of the Fall of Númenor and
Anárion 110, Isildur 100. The new realms of Arnor and Gondor lasted about 110 years before Sauron made his first attacks
on them. The gathering of the Last Alliance, the march, battle

and siege, lasted about 11 years. (121)
3320 + 121, 3441.

The remainder of this page and its verso are taken up with the earliest version of the Tale of Years of the Third Age, obviously written continuously from T(b) just given; for this see p. 225.

These initial computations of the chronology of the Second Age are remarkable in themselves and perplexing in the detail of their interrelations.

The text T(a), self-evidently the starting-point, made 3320 the date of the Downfall. After a lapse of 110 years Sauron opened war on the new kingdoms (3430), and a further ten passed before his overthrow in 3440, the last year of the Second Age.

In T 1, written at the same time as, but after, T(a), the Downfall is placed in 3319 (no reason for the change being evident), but the flight of Elendil and his sons is incomprehensibly placed in the following year, 3320 (p. 169). Again after 110 years Sauron attacked Gondor (3430), but now *eleven* years passed before his overthrow in 3441.

In T 2, which is little more than a fair copy of T 1, the founding of the kingdoms in Middle-earth is placed in the year of the Downfall, which is now 111 years before Sauron's attack in 3430; as in T 1, eleven years passed before the overthrow of Sauron in 3441.

Finally, the extremely puzzling text T(b) goes back to T(a) in placing the Downfall in 3320, and 110 years passed before the war began in 3430; but the total of 3441 is reached as in T 1 and T 2 by the lapse of eleven years before the overthrow. T(b) is apparently a companion page to T 2, and must be later than the other texts, since the Northern Kingdom is here called Arnor, not Arthedain, and this change only entered after a further text of the Tale of Years had been written.

If we now turn to the *Akallabêth* 'Scheme' (pp. 150–1) it will be seen that the date 3319 of the Downfall is reached by an entirely different route. In the 'Scheme' the intervals between the death-dates of the kings are in every case either 221 or 222 years, except for those between the unnamed sixth king and Atanamir, the seventh, which was 50 years longer (271 years), and between Atanamir and his son Kiryatan which was 50 years shorter (172 years). If all these intervals are added together they reach a total of 2658 years; and if to this is added the year of the death of Elros (460) and the length of the reign of Tar-kalion (201 years) we reach 3319, the date of the Downfall.[4] In the 'Scheme' Tar-kalion is numbered '13', but he is expressly the thirteenth king *excluding* Elros, as he is also in *Akallabêth* A and *The Drowning of Anadûnê* as revised (see p. 154 and note 10), so that there were fourteen kings of Númenor in all.

In the texts T(a) and T(b), on the other hand, 'eleven other kings' ruled between Elros and Tar-kalion, making thirteen in all; and the average length of their reigns being here 240 years, the total is 2640.

When to this is added 460 and Tar-kalion's reign of 220 years the total is 3320.

A final element is the fact that in T 1, the companion page to T(a), Tar-kalion ascended the throne in 3118 and reigned for 201 years, just as in the 'Scheme'.

Every explanation of this extraordinary textual puzzle seems to founder. It is not in itself perhaps a matter of great significance, though one certainly gets the impression that there is more to the date 3319 (and possibly also to 3441) than the evidence reveals. It is clear, at any rate, that all these texts, the original manuscript of the *Akallabêth* and its associated 'Scheme', the computations in the texts T(a) and T(b), and the initial version of the Tale of Years, arose at the same time, before the narrative of *The Lord of the Rings* was in final form; while the evidence suggests that it was these computations of the Númenórean kings, formulaic as they were, that provided the chronological 'vehicle' of the Second Age, established at that time. It can be seen from the text T 1 that the Númenórean history provided the fixed element, while the dating of events in Middle-earth before the Downfall were at first of an extreme fluidity (the making of the Rings of Power, for instance, was moved from 1000–1200 to 1200–1500, and the War of the Elves and Sauron from 1200 to 1550).

The third text of the Tale of Years, which I will call T 3, is (so far as the Second Age is concerned) little more than a copy of T 2, with a number of entries somewhat expanded, and one sole additional entry: '3440 Anárion is slain'; no dates were altered. Anárion and Isildur still appear in that order, and the North Kingdom is still named Arthedain, though both were subsequently corrected. The statement in the opening passage of T 2 concerning the length of the Ages and the finding of the Ring by Déagol was omitted, and in its place the following was introduced:

The *Fourth Age* ushered in the Dominion of Men and the decline of all the other 'speaking-folk' of the Westlands.

Following the usual pattern, a number of additions, some of them substantial, were made to the manuscript T 3, but virtually all of them were taken up into the following version, the greatly expanded T 4, whose entries for the Second Age are given here. This is a good clear manuscript with few subsequent alterations in this part of the text; those which were made before the following text was taken from it are noticed if significant.

The Tale of Years
in the
Latter Ages

The *First Age* was the longest. It ended with the Great Battle in which Fionwë and the sons of the Valar broke Thangorodrim and overthrew Morgoth.[5] Then most of the exiled Elves returned into the West and dwelt in Eressëa that was afterwards named Avallon, being within sight of Valinor.[6] The Atani or Edain, Fathers of Men, sailed also over Sea and founded the realm of Númenor or Westernesse, on a great isle, westmost of all mortal lands.

The *Second Age* ended with the first overthrow of Sauron and the loss of the One Ring.

The *Third Age* came to its end in the War of the Ring, and the destruction of the Dark Tower of Sauron, who was finally defeated.

The *Fourth Age* ushered in the Dominion of Men and the decline of all other 'speaking folk' of the Westlands.

[*Added:* The first three ages are now by some called *The Elder Days*, but of old and ere the Third Age was ended that name was given only to the First Age and the world before the casting forth of Morgoth.][7]

The Second Age

These were the *Dark Years* of Middle-earth, but the high tide of Númenor. Of events in Middle-earth scant record is preserved even among the Elves, and their dates here given are only approximate.

10   Foundation of the Grey Havens, and the Kingdom of Lindon. This was ruled by Gil-galad son of Felagund,[8] chief of all the Noldor who did not yet depart to Avallon.

50   Foundation of Númenor. [*Added:* About the same time the works of Moria were begun by Durin the Dwarf and his folk from the ruins of the ancient dwarf-cities in the Blue Mountains. *This was struck out and replaced by:* About this time many dwarves fleeing from the ruins of the dwarf-cities in the Blue Mountains came to Moria, and its power and the splendour of its works were greatly increased.][9]

460   Death of Elros Eärendil's son, first King of Númenor.

500   Sauron, servant of Morgoth, begins to stir again in Middle-earth.

700   First ships of the Númenóreans return to Middle-earth. At first they came only seldom, and the Númenóreans did not stay long in any place.

750   Foundation of Imladris (or Rivendell) and of Eregion
      (or Hollin) as dwellings of the Noldor or High Elves.
      Remnants of the Telerian Elves (of Doriath in ancient
      Beleriand) establish realms in the woodlands far east-
      ward, but most of these peoples are Avari or East-elves.
      The chief of these were Thranduil who ruled in the
      north of Greenwood the Great beyond Anduin, but
      Lórien was fairer and had the greater power; for Cele-
      born had to wife the Lady Galadriel of the Noldor, sister
      of Gil-galad [> sister of Felagund Gil-galad's sire].[10]

900   Sauron in secret begins the building of the fortress,
      Barad-dûr, in Mordor, and makes there the forges of
      Orodruin, the Mountain of Fire. But he professes great
      friendship with the Eldar, and especially with those of
      Eregion, who were great in smith-craft.

1200–1500   The Rings of Power are forged in Eregion; but the
      Ruling Ring is forged by Sauron in Orodruin.

1550 War of the Elves and Sauron begins. The 'Days of Flight'
      begin, or the 'Dark Years' properly so called, being
      the time of the dominion of Sauron. Eregion is laid
      waste. The Naugrim (or Dwarves) close the gates of
      Moria. Many of the remaining Noldor depart west over
      Sea.

1700 The great voyages of the Númenóreans begin. Gil-galad
      defends Lindon and the Grey Havens. Imladris is
      besieged but holds out under the command of Elrond
      Eärendil's son. The Númenóreans come with many
      ships to Lindon and they aid Gil-galad and Elrond.
      Sauron retreats from Eriador (west of the Misty Moun-
      tains).

1900 Barad-dûr is completed with the power of the Ruling
      Ring.

c.2000   The Shadow falls on Númenor. The Númenóreans
      begin to murmur against the Valar, who will not permit
      them to sail west from their land; and they become
      jealous of the immortality of the Eldar. [Added:
      (c.2250).] A division appears among the Númenóreans
      between the Elf-friends, the smaller party, and the King's
      Folk. The latter become slowly estranged from the Valar
      and the Eldar, and abandon the use of the Elven tongues;
      the kings take names of Númenórean form. The Elf-
      friends, dwelling most in the east of Númenor,[11] remain

loyal to the kings except in the matter of rebellion against the decrees of the Valar.

2000–3000 The Númenóreans now make permanent dwellings on the shores of Middle-earth, seeking wealth and dominion; they build many havens and fortresses. The Elf-friends go chiefly to the North-west, but their strongest place is at Pelargir above the Mouths of Anduin. The King's Folk establish lordships in Umbar[12] and Harad and in many other places on the coasts of the Great Lands.

During the same time Sauron extends his dominion slowly over the great part of Middle-earth; but his power reaches out eastward, since he is withheld from the coasts by the Númenóreans. He nurses his hatred for them, but cannot yet challenge them openly. Towards the end of this time the *Úlairi*, the Ringwraiths, servants of Sauron and slaves of the Nine Rings first appear.

3118 Tar-kalion, calling himself Ar-Pharazôn the Golden, thirteenth king of the line of Eärendil, ascends the throne of Númenor. He resolves to challenge Sauron the Great, and builds an armament.

3125 Ar-Pharazôn sets sail for Middle-earth. The might and splendour of the Númenóreans fills the servants of Sauron with fear. Ar-Pharazôn lands at Umbar, and in pursuance of his own secret design Sauron humbles himself and submits. Sauron is taken as a hostage to Númenor.

3140–3310 Sauron slowly gains the confidence of Ar-Pharazôn, until he dominates his counsels. He urges Ar-Pharazôn to make war on the Lords of the West to gain everlasting life.

Most of the Númenóreans fall under the sway of Sauron, and they persecute the Elf-friends; and they become tyrants over men in Middle-earth.

3310 Ar-Pharazôn feeling the approach of death at last takes the counsel of Sauron and prepares a vast fleet for an assault upon Avallon and Valinor. Valandil [> Amandil][13] the faithful breaks the ban of the Valar and sails west, hoping to repeat the embassy of Eärendil, and obtain the help of the Lords of the West. He is never heard of again. His son Elendil, as his father had bidden, makes ready ships on the east coast of Númenor, preparing for flight with all the faithful that he can gather.

3319   The great fleet of Ar-Pharazôn sets sail into the West and encompassing Avallon assails the shores of Valinor. Númenor is destroyed, and swallowed up by the sea. The world is broken and Valinor separated from the lands of the living.

Elendil and his sons Isildur and Anárion escape and fly east with nine great ships[14] to Middle-earth. They bring with them the Seven Stones or *Palantíri*, gifts of the Eldar of Avallon, and Isildur brings also a seedling of the White Tree of Avallon.

3320   Foundation of the realm of Arnor in the north of the Westlands, with the city Annúminas; and of Gondor about the waters of Anduin in the south, with the city Osgiliath. The Stones are divided: Elendil retains three in the North-kingdom, at Annúminas, and on Amon Súl, and in the tower of Emyn Beraid (the Tower Hills).[15] His sons take four, and set them at Minas Ithil, at Minas Anor, at Osgiliath, and at Orthanc.

In the same year Sauron returns to Middle-earth, and being at first filled with fear by the power and wrath of the Lords of the West he hides himself in Mordor and is quiet.

3430–3 [> 3429–30]   Sauron, being at last ready again, makes war upon Gondor. Orodruin bursts into smoke and flame, and Men of Gondor seeing the sign re-name it Amon Amarth, Mount Doom.[16] Sauron comes forth and assails Minas Ithil, and destroys the White Tree that Isildur planted there. Isildur takes a seedling of the Tree and escapes by ship down Anduin with his wife and sons. He sails to Elendil in the North. The Last Alliance is formed between Gil-galad Elven-king and Elendil and his sons. They march east to Imladris summoning all folk to their aid.

3434   The Host of the Alliance crosses the Misty Mountains and marches south. They encounter the host of Sauron upon Dagorlad north of the gates of Mordor, and they are victorious. Sauron takes refuge in Barad-dûr.

3434–   Siege of Barad-dûr begins and lasts seven years.

3440   Anárion is slain in Gorgoroth.

3441   Sauron comes forth, and wrestles with Elendil and Gil-galad. They overthrow him but are themselves slain.

The One Ring is taken from the hand of Sauron by Isildur as the weregild of his father, and he will not permit it to be destroyed. He plants the seedling of the White Tree in Minas Anor in memory of his brother Anárion, but he will not himself [*added:* long] dwell there. He delivers the South-kingdom to Meneldil son of Anárion and marches north up the vale of Anduin, purposing to take up the realm of Elendil. He is slain by Orcs near the Gladden fields and the Ring is lost in the River.[17] The Ringwraiths fall into darkness and silence. The Second Age ends.[18]

In this fourth text of the Tale of Years the pattern of dating seen in T 1, T 2, with its great differences from the final form in Appendix B, is preserved. Thus Rivendell was still founded far earlier, in 750; Barad-dûr was begun in 900 and its building still took a thousand years; the making of the Rings of Power in Eregion, and the War of the Elves and Sauron, are dated as they were, extending over far greater periods of time. The work was becoming a condensed history rather than a list of dates; but scarcely any new dates were introduced.

In new material in the entry for c.2000 the sentence 'The Shadow falls on Númenor' is clearly related to the *Akallabêth* 'Scheme' (p. 150), where it is noted of the reign of Tar-Atanamir (c.1790–c.2061) that 'In his time the Shadow first fell on Númenor'. The fullness of the entries concerning the reign of Ar-Pharazôn reinforces the view that my father made these early versions of the Tale of Years when he was writing the *Akallabêth*, as do a number of particular features, such as the sentence concerning the Great Battle in the headnote to T 4 (see note 5) and the occurrence of the name *Úlairi* of the Ringwraiths in the entry for 2000–3000 (see p. 153, §30). The fact that *Avallon* was still the name of Eressëa (and not that of the haven) shows beyond doubt that the *Akallabêth* was still at the stage of the earliest manuscript (see note 6).

I think it extremely probable that this text T 4 (of which the part pertaining to the Third Age is very much longer) belongs in time with the texts F 2 and D 2 of the Appendices on Languages and on Calendars, and with the third text of *The Heirs of Elendil*, given in the next chapter. But external evidence of date seems to be entirely lacking.

From T 4 an amanuensis typescript T 5 was made, carefully following the original. At some stage my father subjected one of the copies to very heavy correction, but his chief (though not the only) purpose in doing so seems to have been to abbreviate it by the omission of phrases. By this time the 'second phase' of the *Akallabêth* (see p. 154, §31) had entered, and the last years of Númenor were altered on the typescript (cf. p. 175):

3118   Birth of Ar-Pharazôn.
3255   Ar-Pharazôn the Golden, twenty-fifth king of the line of Elros, seizes the sceptre of Númenor. He resolves to challenge Sauron the Great, and builds an armament.
3261   Ar-Pharazôn sets sail for Middle-earth. The might of the Númenóreans fills the servants of Sauron with fear. Ar-Pharazôn lands at Umbar, and Sauron humbles himself and submits. Sauron is taken as a hostage to Númenor.
3262–3310   Sauron slowly gains the confidence of Ar-Pharazôn ...

The opening dates of the Second Age were also changed: Year 1, Foundation of the Grey Havens; 32 Foundation of Númenor; 442 Death of Elros; 600 First ships of the Númenóreans return to Middle-earth. Other changes were the replacement of *Úlairi* by *Nazgûl* in the entry for 2000–3000 (changed to 2200–3000), and the removal of *Avallon* at all occurrences, either by altering it to *Eressëa* or by the omission of any name.

The evident reason for the revision of the typescript (in respect of the abbreviation of the text) is discussed later (see p. 246). The next stage in the development was an attempt to reduce the Tale of Years much more drastically. This is represented by a confused collection of typescript pages (from which a good deal of the Third Age is missing) made very evidently under stress: the deadline for the publication of *The Return of the King* was fast approaching, and the situation was indeed afflicting. Not only must the record of events be further pruned and curtailed, but fundamental features of the chronology of the Second Age were not yet established; and this work must be done against time.

I give in illustration a portion of the first version of the Second Age chronology comprised in this material. My father was typing very rapidly, faster than he could manage, and there are very many errors, which I have of course corrected; I have also introduced divisions to indicate successive shifts in the dating, though there is no suggestion of these in the typescript, where the rejected passages are not even struck through. Thus the text that follows has a very much more ordered appearance than does the original.

900   Sauron secretly begins the building of Barad-dûr. He makes the forges of the Mountain of Fire.
1200   Sauron seeks the friendship of the Elves, especially those of Eregion, who are great in smith-craft.
1200–1500   The Rings of Power are forged in Eregion; but the Ruling Ring is forged by Sauron in Mordor.
1550   The war of Sauron and the Elves begins. The 'Dark Years' follow, the time of the dominion of Sauron. Many of the remaining Eldar depart west over Sea. The great voyages of the Númenóreans begin.

1600   Eregion is laid waste. The gates of Moria are shut. The forces
        of Sauron overrun Eriador. Imladris is besieged, but holds out
        under the command of Elrond Eärendil's son, sent from
        Lindon. The forces of Sauron overrun Eriador. Gil-galad
        defends Lindon and the Grey Havens.

1603   A Númenórean navy comes to the Grey Havens. The
        Númenóreans aid Gil-galad, and Sauron's forces are driven
        out of Eriador and Sauron retreats from Eriador. The West-
        lands have peace for some while.

        From the time of the defeat in Eriador Sauron does not
        molest the Westlands for many years, but plots in secret. He
        slowly extends his dominion eastward, since he is withheld
        from the coasts by the Númenóreans. He nurses his hatred for
        them, but cannot yet challenge them openly.

1700   Barad-dûr is completed with the power of the Ruling Ring.

1200   Sauron seeks the friendship of the Elves (in hope to subject
        them). He is still fair to look on, and the Elves become en-
        amoured of the knowledge he can impart.

1300   The Elves begin the forging of the Rings of Power. It is said that
        this took many long years. S[auron] secretly makes the forges
        [sic]

1500   The Three Great Rings are made by Celebrimbor of the Silver
        Grasp (celebrin 'silver', paur 'the fist or closed hand'). The
        Ruling Ring is made secretly by Sauron in Mordor.

1000   Sauron begins the building of Barad-dûr in Mordor.

1200   Sauron courts the friendship of the Elves, hoping to get them,
        the chief obstacle to his dominion, into his power. Gil-galad
        refuses to treat with him. But Sauron is still fair to look on and
        the Elves of Eregion are won over by their desire of skill and
        knowledge.

1500   The Elves of Eregion under the guidance of Sauron begin the
        forging of the Rings of Power. This takes many long years.
        Sauron secretly forges the One Ring in Orodruin.

1690   The Three Rings are completed. Celebrimbor becomes aware
        of the designs of Sauron. Barad-dûr is completed with the
        power of [sic]

1695   The War of the Elves and Sauron begins. Many of the remain-
        ing Eldar depart west over Sea.

1696   Elrond Eärendil's son is sent to Eregion by Gil-galad.

1697   Eregion is laid waste. The gates of Moria are shut. Elrond
        retreats with the remnant of the Eldar to Imladris.

1600   The great voyages of the Númenóreans begin. The ships are
        welcomed by Gil-galad and Círdan.

1699   Imladris is besieged but holds out under the command of
        Elrond. Sauron overruns Eriador. Gil-galad defends Lindon

and the Grey Havens.
1700   A great navy of the Númenóreans comes to the Grey Havens.

Here this text seems to have been abandoned and replaced by another and more coherent version, with entries further reduced and dates following the latest formulations in the text just given. These dates from 1500 to 1700 were then corrected on the typescript, being reduced (advanced) by a hundred years, and so moving them away from those in Appendix B, as seen in the following table (in which I give only brief indications of the actual entries).

		Appendix B
1500 [> 1400]	(Forging of the Three Rings begun)	c.1500
1600 [> 1500]	(Forging of the One Ring)	c.1600
1690 [> 1590]	(Three Rings completed)	c.1590
1690 [> 1590]	(Barad-dûr completed)	c.1600
1695 [> 1595]	(War of Elves and Sauron begins)	1693
1697 [> 1597]	(Eregion laid waste)	1697
1699 [> 1599]	(Sauron overruns Eriador)	1699
1700 [> 1600]	(Coming of Númenórean navy)	1700

At this stage Imladris was still founded in the year 750. The correction of all the entries from 1500 to 1700 was subsequently abandoned; the dates before correction were now those of the final chronology or very close to them, with the exception of the completion of Barad-dûr and the completion of the Three Rings. In this text, by either dating, the Three Rings were not achieved for a further ninety years after the forging of the One Ring, whereas in the final chronology (by adopting in this one case the revised date, 1590) the One Ring was made ten years after the Three.

This second text then continues:

1869   Tar-Ciryatan, twelfth king of Númenor, receives the sceptre. The first shadow falls on Númenor. The Kings become greedy of wealth and power.

2060–2251   Reign of Tar-Atanamir the Great, thirteenth King of Númenor.[19] The shadow deepens. The King's ships exact heavy tribute from Men on the coasts of Middle-earth. The Númenóreans become jealous of the immortality of the Eldar; and the King speaks openly against [the] command of the Valar that they should not sail west from their land.

2250–3000   During this time the power and splendour of the Númenóreans continues to increase; and they build many fortresses on the west shores of Middle-earth. Sauron extends his power eastward, being withheld from the coasts, and nurses his hatred of Númenor. But the Númenóreans become divided against

Here the entry breaks off, and is immediately followed by a long account (more than 2000 words) of the Númenóreans, of their origin, their division, the coming of Sauron, and the Downfall.

I believe that this strange development can be explained in this way. At that time, as things stood, The Lord of the Rings would be published without any account, however brief, of the story of Númenor. In the manuscript T 4 my father had written (pp. 174–6) what I have called 'a condensed history rather than a list of dates'; for it is to be remembered that in the narrative of The Lord of the Rings, despite all the many mentions of the names Númenor and Westernesse, he had told nothing of its history, and of the Downfall no more than Faramir's words in Minas Tirith, when he told Éowyn that he was thinking 'of the land of Westernesse that foundered, and of the great dark wave climbing over the green lands and above the hills'. He must now attempt to contract even what he had written in T 4, and as a comparison of the last entries in the present text just given with those in T 4 (pp. 174–5) shows, he was not succeeding. The reduction into a mere chronological scheme of a large history that could not be understood by a recital of events was a task profoundly uncongenial to him. He despaired of it, and broke off in mid-sentence.

It may well have been at that point, having typed the words 'But the Númenóreans become divided against', that he decided that The Lord of the Rings must contain some account of the story of Westernesse, separate from the Tale of Years, and set it down there and then, beginning with the words 'As a reward for their sufferings in the cause against Morgoth, the Valar, the Guardians of the World, granted to the Edain a land to dwell in, removed from the dangers of Middle-earth.' Removed from the Tale of Years, it found a place in Appendix A, Annals of the Kings and Rulers, RK pp. 315–18.[20]

There are in fact two typescripts of this text, both composed ab initio on the typewriter; the second of these my father described in a pencilled note as a 'variant' of the first, and it was this that he used, with many minor alterations of wording and some omissions, in Appendix A. Neither version has the list of the Kings and Queens of Númenor (RK p. 315), and both have a more detailed account of the rebellion against Tar-Palantir and the marriage of Míriel his daughter to Pharazôn (said in both texts to have been 'by force'), which was omitted in Appendix A. Both versions, also, have an account of Sauron's policy in his attack on the coastal fortresses and harbours of the Númenóreans which was likewise omitted, and is not found in the Akallabêth. I cite here two passages from the first version of the text.

Proudest of all the Kings was Ar-Pharazôn the Golden, and no less than the kingship of all the world was his desire. But still he retained enough wisdom to fear the Lords of the West, and turned therefore his thoughts to Middle-earth. Now Sauron knowing of the dissension in Númenor thought how he might use it to achieve his revenge. He began therefore to assail the havens and forts of the Númenóreans, and invaded the coastlands under their dominion. As he foresaw this aroused the great wrath of the King, who resolved to challenge Sauron the Great for the lordship of Middle-earth. For five years Ar-Pharazôn prepared, and at last he himself set sail with a great navy and armament, the greatest that had yet appeared in the world.

If Sauron had thought thus to decoy the King to Middle-earth and there destroy him, his hope deceived him. And Ar-Pharazôn landed at Umbar, and so great was the splendour and might of the Númenóreans at the noon of their glory that at the rumour of them alone all men flocked to their summons and did obeisance; and Sauron's own servants fled away. The land of Mordor he had indeed fortified and made so strong that he need fear no assault upon it; but he was in doubt now, and even the Barad-dûr seemed no longer secure.

Sauron therefore changed his design, and had recourse to guile. He humbled himself, and came himself on foot before Ar-Pharazôn, and did him homage and craved pardon for his offences. And Ar-Pharazôn spared his life; but took from him all his titles, and made him prisoner, and carried him at length back to Númenor to be hostage for the submission and faith of all who had before owed him allegiance.

'This is a hard doom,' said Sauron, 'but great kings must have their will', and he submitted as one under compulsion, concealing his delight; for things had fallen out according to his design.

Now Sauron had great wisdom and knowledge, and could find words of seeming reason for the persuasion of all but the most wary; and he could still assume a fair countenance when he wished. He was brought as a prisoner to Númenor in 3261, but he had not been there five years before he had the King's ear and was deep in his counsel.

'Great kings must have their will': this was the burden of all his advice; and whatever the King desired he said was his right, and devised plans whereby he might gain it.

Then darkness came upon the minds of the Númenóreans, and they held the Guardians in hatred, and openly denied the One who is above all; and they turned to the worship of the Dark, and of Morgoth the Lord of the Darkness. They made a great temple in the land and there did evil; for they tormented the remnant of the faithful, and there slew them or burned them. And the like they did in Middle-earth, and filled the west coasts with tales of dread, so that men cried 'Has then Sauron become King of Númenor?'

So great was his power over the hearts of the most of that people that maybe had he wished he could have taken the sceptre; but all that he wished was to bring Númenor to ruin. Therefore he said to the King: 'One thing only now you lack to make you the greatest King in the world, the undying life that is withheld from you in fear and jealousy by the lying Powers in the West. But great kings take what is their right.' And Ar-Pharazôn pondered these words, but for long fear held him back.

But at last even Ar-Pharazôn the Golden, King of kings, having lived one hundred and ninety-two years,[21] felt the waning of his life and feared the approach of death and the going out into the darkness that he had worshipped. Therefore he began to prepare a vast armament for the assault upon Valinor, that should surpass the one with which he had come to Umbar even as a great galleon of Númenor surpassed a fisherman's boat.

There follows a brief account of the expulsion of those of doubtful loyalty from the western coasts of Númenor, the voyage of Amandil into the West,[22] the sailing of the Great Armament, and the cataclysm of the Downfall. At the end of this, following the words 'But Elendil and his sons escaped with nine ships, and were borne on the wings of a great storm and cast up on the shores of Middle-earth', is a notable statement of the destruction caused by the drowning of Númenor:

These were much changed in the tumult of the winds and seas that followed the Downfall; for in some places the sea rode in upon the land, and in others it piled up new coasts. Thus while Lindon suffered great loss, the Bay of Belfalas was much filled at the east and south, so that Pelargir which had been only a few miles from the sea was left far inland, and Anduin carved a new path by many mouths to the Bay. But the Isle of Tolfalas was almost destroyed, and was left at last like a barren and lonely mountain in the water not far from the issue of the River.

No such statement is found elsewhere.[23] In the *Akallabêth* (*The Silmarillion* p. 280), in a passage taken virtually without change from *The Drowning of Anadûnê* (IX.374, §52), there is no reference to any named region or river.[24]

There is no further text of the Tale of Years extant before the typescript from which Appendix B was printed. Of this it may be noted that in the preamble to the entries for the Second Age the reference to *mithril* reads:

> This they did because they learned that *mithril* had been discovered in Moria. It had been believed before that this could only be got in the Ered Luin; but no more could now be found there in the old dwarf-mines.

My father struck out the second sentence on the proof.

NOTES

1   Against this opening statement concerning the Three Ages my father later scribbled 'These Ages are called the Elder Days'. On this see p. 173 and note 7.

2   T 1 has the more natural 'Arising of Sauron'.

3   *Imladrist* was corrected at once to *Imladris*. In T 1 the form is *Imladris*, as also in T 2 in the entry for 1600, so that this was a mere casual reversion to the earlier form.

4   It is plain that in the 'Scheme' the death-date of one king indicates also the accession of the next, and thus the interval between two death-dates is the length of the reign of the king: for example, the fourth king died in 1347, and the fifth in 1568, and thus the fifth king reigned for 221 years.

It certainly seems most natural to suppose that the 'Scheme' was precisely that, and that the representation of the reigns as all of the same length (differing only by one year) was a mere formula of convenience for working out the chronology as a whole. But Atanamir reigned for 50 years longer than any other, and his son for 50 years less; and this obviously relates to the passage in the *Akallabêth* (SA §24, going back to the original manuscript):

> And Atanamir lived to a great age, clinging to his life beyond the end of all joy; and he was the first of the Númenóreans to do this, refusing to depart until he was witless and unmanned, and denying to his son the kingship at the height of his days.

The much greater age of Atanamir must imply that all the other kings died by act of their own will long before the end of their physical span, and thus allowed their sons a period of rule equivalent to their own. It would be mistaken to press this early and experimental text too closely on the matter, but it certainly suggests a difference from the developed conception in *The Line of Elros*, where it is said (*Unfinished Tales* p. 218) that it was the custom 'until the days of Tar-Atanamir that the King should yield the sceptre to his successor before he died'; there were thus a number of years (recorded in the entries of *The Line of Elros*) between the king's surrender of the sceptre and his death.

5   With this sentence cf. the original version of the *Akallabêth*, p. 143, §3.

6   It is notable that here and subsequently *Avallon* is still the name of the whole Isle of Eressëa, as it was in the original manuscript A of the *Akallabêth*, although the later form *Avallónë* and the later meaning (the Haven) entered before that manuscript was completed (see p. 146, §12).

7   Cf. the preamble to the Tale of Years in Appendix B: 'In the Fourth Age the earlier ages were often called the *Elder Days*; but that name was properly given only to the days before the casting out of Morgoth.' In the *Akallabêth* 'the Elder Days' was apparently used of the earlier part of the Second Age (p. 156, §53).

8   For other references to the abandoned idea that Gil-galad was the son of Felagund see XI.242–3, and pp. 349–50.

9   It looks as if the added passage concerning the Dwarves was rejected and replaced immediately. It is strange that my father should have written first that Durin founded Moria at the beginning of the Second Age, with 'his folk' coming from the ruins of Nogrod and Belegost.

10 With this entry compare the headnote to the Second Age in Appendix B. – The words 'the Lady Galadriel of the Noldor, sister of Gil-galad' were not, as might be thought, a slip, but record a stage in her entry into the legends of the First Age. In one of the earliest texts of the work *Of the Rings of Power and the Third Age* my father wrote of Galadriel: 'A Queen she was and lady of the woodland elves, yet she was herself of the Noldor and had come from Beleriand in the days of the Exile.' To this he added subsequently: 'For it is said by some that she was a hand-maid of Melian the Immortal in the realm of Doriath'; but striking this out at once he substituted: 'For it is said by some that she was a daughter of Felagund the Fair and escaped from Nargothrond in the day of its destruction.' In the following text this was changed to read: 'And some have said that she was the daughter of Felagund the Fair and fled from Nargothrond before its fall, and passed over the Mountains into Eriador ere the coming of Fionwë'; this in turn was altered to: 'For she was the daughter of Felagund the Fair and the elder sister of Gil-galad, though seldom had they met, for ere Nargothrond was made or Felagund was driven from Dorthonion, she passed east over the mountains and forsook Beleriand, and first of all the Noldor came to the inner lands; and too late she heard the summons of Fionwë.' – In the *Annals of Aman* and the *Grey Annals* she had become, as she remained, the sister of Felagund.

11 In the *Akallabêth* the Elendili dwelt mostly in the west of Númenor, and were forced to remove into the east (p. 152); but

the statement here that they dwelt mainly in the east may be due simply to compression.

12 This is the first reference to the establishment of a Númenórean settlement at Umbar before the landing of Ar-Pharazôn (see p. 156, §41).

13 On the name *Valandil* for *Amandil* (as in the first version of the *Akallabêth*) see p. 156, §44.

14 It is curious that all the texts of the *Akallabêth* have twelve ships, and only on the late amanuensis typescript did my father change the number to nine (see p. 157, §80); whereas in the present text T 4, certainly no later than the earliest text of the *Akallabêth*, the number is nine as first written.

15 The statement in this entry concerning the division of the *palantíri* appeared first in additions to the preceding text T 3; and there they are called *Gwahaedir*, while the Tower Hills are called *Emyn Gwahaedir*, replaced by *Emyn Hen Dúnadan*, and then again by *Emyn Beraid*. This last name does not appear in the actual narrative of *The Lord of the Rings*.

16 This was probably the first appearance of *Amon Amarth*, which only occurs in Appendix A (I, i, at end, RK p. 317).

17 All the material in these last entries first appears as rough and complex marginal additions to the manuscript T 3, but at this point there is an addition in T 3 which my father did not take up, perhaps because he missed it:

> The shards of the Sword of Elendil are brought to Valandil Isildur's heir at Imladris. He becomes king of the North Kingdom of Arnor, and dwells at Fornost.

The name Valandil of Isildur's heir thus does not appear in T 4; but the entry for 3310 was not added to T 3, and thus Valandil as the name of Elendil's father does not appear in that text.

18 On the ending of the Second Age with the death of Isildur and the loss of the One Ring in the Anduin see p. 170.

19 In Appendix B the entry for S.A.2251 begins 'Tar-Atanamir takes the sceptre. Rebellion and division of the Númenóreans begins.' In *Unfinished Tales* (p. 226, note 10) I discussed this, concluding that the entry was certainly an error, although at that time I was apparently unaware of the present text, or at any rate did not consult it; I suggested that the correct reading should be: '2251 Death of Tar-Atanamir. Tar-Ancalimon takes the sceptre. Rebellion and division of the Númenóreans begins.' No further text is extant before the final typescript from which Appendix B was printed, and it cannot be said how the error arose, moving from '2060–2251 Reign of Tar-Atanamir' to '2251 Tar-Atanamir takes the sceptre'.

20 I have found nothing in the correspondence of that time touching

on Appendix A, and I cannot answer the question how it was possible, if the Tale of Years had to be so contracted for reasons of space, to include a further long section in that Appendix at that stage.

21 'having lived one hundred and ninety-two years': from 3118 to 3310. In the text T 4 3118 was the year of his accession, corrected in the later revision of the typescript T 5 (p. 178) to the year of his birth.

22 The date of Amandil's voyage is given in this text, 3316; it was added also in the revision of the typescript T 5, entry 3310.

23 This appears to be the sole reference in any text to Tolfalas, apart from a mention of its capture by Men of the South in an outline made in the course of the writing of *The Two Towers* (VII.435). The isle and its name appeared already on the First Map of Middle-earth (VII.298, 308), but on all maps its extent appears much greater than in the description of it here.

24 On the extremely difficult question of the relation between the destruction caused in Middle-earth in the Great Battle at the end of the First Age, and that caused by the Drowning of Númenor, see V.22–3, 32–3, 153–4.

VII

THE HEIRS OF ELENDIL

While the development of the Appendices as a whole, and the *Prologue*, was to some degree an interconnected work, the Tale of Years was of its nature (since chronology became a paramount concern of my father's) closely interwoven with the evolution of the history of Númenor and the Númenórean kingdoms in Middle-earth, as has been seen already in the relation of the Tale of Years of the Second Age to the development of the *Akallabêth*. For the history and chronology of the Realms in Exile the primary document is a substantial work entitled *The Heirs of Elendil*.

The textual history of this is not easy to fathom. It is divided into two parts, the Northern Line (the Kings and the Chieftains) and the Southern Line (the Kings and the Stewards). The oldest manuscript, which I will call A, is headed *The Heirs of Elendil   The Southern Line of Gondor*; it is clearly if rapidly written for the most part, but in the concluding section recounting the names and dates of the Stewards of Gondor becomes very rough and is obviously in the first stage of composition.

The second manuscript, B, has both the Northern and the Southern Lines, in that order; but though my father fastened the two sections together, they are distinct in appearance. I believe that the second part began as a fair copy of A, but quickly developed and expanded into a much fuller (and increasingly rough) text. To this he added the Northern Line. This section in B seems to be in the first stage of composition (a rejected page shows the names of the later kings and chieftains in the process of emergence) – and there is no trace of any earlier work on the Northern Line, a companion text to A. On the other hand there are clear indications that the Northern Line and its history did already exist when A was set down.

Heavily emended, the composite text B paved the way for a fine manuscript, C; this in turn was much emended in the Northern Line, less so in the remainder, and an amanuensis typescript D was made (much later) from the corrected text (see p. 190).

There is as usual no hint or trace of external dating for any of this work on *The Heirs of Elendil*, and the most that can be done is to try to relate it to other texts. The relative date of B is shown by the fact that the North Kingdom was still called *Arthedain* and that Anárion was still the elder son of Elendil, for this was also the case in the third text of the Tale of Years, T 3 (p. 172). The name of the tenth king of the Northern Line is in B *Eärendil*, which is found in the early texts F 1, F 2 of the Appendix on Languages as that of the tenth king (p. 32, footnote to §9). In the fourth text T 4 of the Tale of Years the name of the realm is *Arnor*, Isildur is the elder son, and King Eärendur enters.

There can be no doubt therefore that all the fundamental structure and chronology of the Realms in Exile reached written form in the first phase of the work on what would become the Appendices (cf. p. 177). That the final text C, and many at least of the corrections and additions made to it, belongs to the same time is equally clear. One might suppose this to be the case on general grounds: from the care and calm that are evident in the fine manuscript as it was originally made, in contrast to the latter ragged and chaotic work on the Appendices, and from the fact that corrections to the preceding text B were made (according to my father's constant practice) in preparation for this further version. But the occurrence on the first page of C of the names *Valandil* of Elendil's father and of *Avallon* for *Eressëa* (the latter remaining uncorrected) shows that it belongs to the time when the original text of the *Akallabêth* still stood and T 4 of the Tale of Years had not yet been revised, for both of these have *Valandil* (pp. 156, 175) and *Avallon* (p. 173 and note 6). To this may be added the use of 'Noldorin' for 'Sindarin'.

Work on *The Heirs of Elendil* gave rise to alterations in the text of *The Lord of the Rings*. A good example of this is found in the passage of the chapter *A Knife in the Dark* (FR p. 197) where Strider speaks of the history of Weathertop. As this passage stood at the end of work on the chapter (scarcely differing from the original text, VI.169) he said:

> There is no barrow on Weathertop, nor on any of these hills. The Men of the West did not live here. I do not know who made this path, nor how long ago, but it was made to provide a road that could be defended, from the north to the foot of Weathertop; some say that Gil-galad and Elendil made a fort and a strong place here in the ancient days, when they marched into the East.

This was altered and expanded, in a late typescript, to the passage in FR, where Strider's account of the great tower of Amon Sûl that was burned and broken derives from the addition made to the entry for Arveleg I (eighteenth king of the Northern Line) in *Heirs of Elendil* B, reappearing in the final text C (see pp. 194, 209). But the addition made to C in the entry for Argeleb I, seventeenth king, 'Argeleb fortifies the Weather Hills', belongs with the alteration of Strider's words about the path, which now became:

> The Men of the West did not live here; though in their latter days they defended the hills for a while against the evil that came out of Angmar. This path was made to serve the forts along the walls.

The date of the making of the typescript D, however, is very much later. It is a good text, in top copy and carbon, made by an experienced typist, which fact alone would strongly suggest that it comes from the time after the publication of *The Lord of the Rings*; but in addition it was made on the same machine as that used for the *Annals of Aman*, the *Grey Annals*, the text LQ 2 of the *Quenta Silmarillion*, and the *Akallabêth*, about 1958 (see pp. 141–2). It is remarkable (seeing that all the essential material of C had been taken up into Appendix A, if presented there in a totally different form) that my father should have selected this text as one of those to be copied 'as a necessary preliminary to "remoulding" [of *The Silmarillion*]', as he said in his letter to Rayner Unwin of December 1957 (X.141). He did indeed make use of it later still, writing on the folded newspaper that contains the texts of *The Heirs of Elendil* 'Partly revised August 1965' – i.e. in preparation for the Second Edition of *The Lord of the Rings* published in 1966: from this time comes a long insertion in typescript greatly expanding the account of the events leading to the Kin-strife in Gondor, which in somewhat contracted form was introduced into Appendix A in the Second Edition (see further p. 259).

It has been difficult to find a satisfactory way of presenting this complex material, especially in view of the lack of correspondence in the texts of the Northern and Southern Lines (B–C; A–B–C). As with the two texts F 1 and F 2 of the Appendix on Languages, it has seemed best to give first the full text of C, with the corrections and expansions noted as such (though without any attempt to distinguish the relative times of their making), and to indicate significant differences in B in the Commentary following the text. In addition, I give an account of the brief manuscript A of the Southern Line at the beginning of the Commentary on that part of the work (p. 211).

As I have already mentioned, there is no writing extant before the manuscript A. It will be seen, however, that the names of the southern kings and their dates were already very largely fixed in A as first written down, and that (although the historical notes are very scanty and brief by comparison with the final form) such matters as the Kin-strife and the claim of Arvedui (last king in the North) to the southern crown were fully if not very substantially present; it may be supposed therefore that initial notes and lists have not survived (see also p. 216, under *Ondohir*). It is generally impossible to say how much of the matter that entered at each successive stage had newly arisen, and how much was present but at first, when the scope of the work was not yet fully realised, held in abeyance. But there is reason to think (see p. 213) that a firm if undeveloped structure of the history of the Realms in Exile had arisen a good while before the first texts of *The Heirs of Elendil* were composed. There are cases in text B where the actual working out of the history can be clearly seen, but always within that structure.

The Heirs of Elendil

Summary of the Annals in the 'Book of the Kings' and the 'Roll of Stewards of Gondor'. The dates are corrected to the reckoning of the Ages according to the Eldar, as also used in Arnor. In Gondor the dates were reckoned from the foundation of Osgiliath, Second Age 3320. Twenty-one years thus have to be added to the year-numbers here given to find the dates of the first Gondor era.

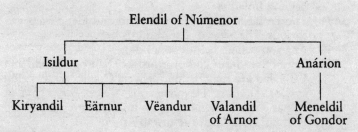

Elendil of Númenor

Isildur — Anárion

Kiryandil   Eärnur   Vëandur   Valandil of Arnor   Meneldil of Gondor

Year
Second Age

3119   Elendil born in Númenor. His father was Valandil [> Amandil] chief of the party of the Elf-friends.

3209   Isildur, elder son of Elendil, born in Númenor.

3219   Anárion, second son of Elendil, born in Númenor.

3299   Kiryandil, son of Isildur, born in Númenor.

3318   Meneldil, son of Anárion, born. He was the last man to be born in Númenor.

3319   Downfall of Númenor.

3320   Establishment of the Númenórean 'realms in exile' in the west of Middle-earth: Arnor in the north of the westlands (with chief city at Annúminas) by Elendil; Gondor in the south (with chief city at Osgiliath) by his sons. Isildur planted a seedling of the White Tree of Avallon, gift of the Eldar, in Minas Ithil. The *Palantíri*, or Seven Stones of Sight, were divided, and set up in towers: three in Arnor, at Annúminas, and at Amon Sûl, and upon the Emyn Beraid looking towards the Sea; four in the realm of Gondor, at Osgiliath, at Minas Ithil, at Minas Anor, and at Orthanc in Angrenost (Isengard).

3339   Eärnur, second son of Isildur, born in Gondor.

3379   Vëandur, third son of Isildur, born in Minas Ithil.

3429   Sauron attacks Gondor from the neighbouring land of Mordor. He destroys Minas Ithil and burns the White

Tree. Isildur escapes by ship down Anduin, and sails
north from Anduin's Mouths to Elendil in Arnor, with
his wife and sons; he bears with him a seedling of the
White Tree, grown from its first fruit in Middle-earth.
Anárion holds out in Osgiliath.

3430 The last Alliance is begun. Elendil and Isildur obtain the
help of Gil-galad and Elrond and gather great forces.
They march east to Imladris. Valandil son of Isildur
born in Imladris.

3434 The Battle of Dagorlad. Gil-galad and Elendil are victorious. The Siege of Barad-dûr is begun.

3440 Anárion is slain before Barad-dûr.

3441 Fall of Barad-dûr and overthrow of Sauron. Elendil and
Gil-galad are slain. Isildur delivers Gondor to Meneldil
son of Anárion. He plants the White Tree again in
Minas Anor in memory of his brother, and marches up
Anduin, intending to return to Arnor.

Isildur and his three elder sons are slain by Orcs in the
Gladden Fields. His fourth son Valandil succeeds to
Arnor, but being a child remains for a time with Elrond
at Imladris.

The Second Age ends and the Third Age begins

Here follows the roll of the Kings of the Northern Line, and
after the ending of the kings the names of the chieftains of the
Dúnedain of the North who maintained throughout this Age
the line of Valandil son of Isildur unbroken.

In the tenth year of the Third Age Valandil being come to
manhood took up the kingship of Arnor and dwelt at Annúminas by Lake Nenuial.

The Heirs of Elendil
The Northern Line of Arnor: the Isildurioni

#	Name	born	lived	
1	Elendil	born S.A.3119	lived 322 years	†slain 3441 or T.A.1
2	Isildur	3209	232	†slain 3441 or T.A.1
3	Valandil	3430	260	died T.A.249
4	Eldakar	T.A. 87	252	339
5	Arantar	185	250	435
6	Tarkil	280	235	515
7	Tarondor	372	230	602

8	Valandur	462	190	†slain	652
9	Elendur	552	225	died	777
10	Eärendur	640	221		861

After Eärendur the Northern Kingdom of Arnor was broken up. The sons of the king established smaller independent kingdoms. The direct line of the eldest son ruled the realm of Arthedain in the north-west; their city was Fornost. Annúminas became deserted owing to the dwindling of the people. The chief of the lesser realms were [Cardolan east of the Baranduin; and Rhudaur north of the Bruinen. Arthedain still claimed the overlordship, but this was disputed. >] Cardolan south of the Great Road and east of the Baranduin; and Rhudaur north of the Great Road between the Weather Hills and the Bruinen. There was often strife between the kingdoms; the chief matter of debate was the possession of the Weather Hills and the land westward thence towards Bree. For both Rhudaur and Cardolan desired to control Amon Sûl (which stood upon their borders), because of the Tower built there by Elendil, in which was kept the chief *palantír* of the North. / From this time on the official names of the kings were no longer given, after the manner of Númenor, in High-elven or 'Quenya' form; but the kings of Arthedain used Elvish names of Noldorin form and still maintained their friendship with the Eldar of Lindon and Imladris.

11	Amlaith of Fornost	born 726	lived 220 years	died 946
12	Beleg	811	218	1029
13	Mallor	895	215	1110

In his time an evil shadow fell upon Greenwood the Great, and it became known as Mirkwood. The Sorcerer of Dol Guldur (later known to be Sauron returned) begins to work evil. The Periannath cross the Mountains and come into Arnor.

14	Celepharn	born 979	lived 212 years	died 1191
15	Celebrindol [> Celebrindor]	1062	210	1272
16	Malvegil	1144	205	1349

In the days of Malvegil Orcs again became a menace, and invaded the lands of Arnor. The Úlairi or Ringwraiths began to stir again. The chief of the Úlairi comes north and establishes himself as a king of evil men in Angmar in the far north regions. The Witch-king makes war on the realms of the Dúnedain, which are disunited. The lesser realms resist the claim of the King at Fornost to be overlord of all the former lands of Arnor. In token of this claim all the kings of Arthedain, and the chieftains after them, take names with the prefix *aran*, *ar(a)* signifying 'high king'. [*Added:* The purpose of the Witch-king is to destroy

Arnor, for there is more hope of success in the North (where the realm is disunited) than in the South while Gondor remains strong. At this time no descendants of Isildur remain in Rhudaur or Cardolan; therefore the kings of Arthedain again claim over-lordship in all Arnor. The claim is rejected by Rhudaur, in which power has been seized by men in secret league with Angmar.]
[*Struck out:* The kings of Arthedain also claim to be guardians of the *palantír* of Amon Sûl, though this is outside their territory, standing on the borders of Cardolan and Rhudaur between whom also it is a matter of bitter dispute.]

17   Argeleb I   born 1226   lived 130 years   †slain 1356
[He was slain in battle with Cardolan in the strife of the *palantír* of Amon Sûl. >] Argeleb fortifies the Weather Hills. He was slain in battle with Rhudaur (with secret aid of Angmar); the enemy tries to seize the *palantír* of Amon Sûl.

18   Arveleg I   born 1309   lived 100 years   †slain 1409
The Witch-king of Angmar taking advantage of war among [the Númenóreans or Dúnedain >] the Dúnedain comes down out of the North. He overruns Cardolan and Rhudaur. [Cardolan is ravaged and destroyed and becomes desolate. The Tower of Amon Sûl is razed and the *palantír* is broken. Evil spirits come and take up their abode in the mounds of the hills of Cardolan. In Rhudaur an evil folk, workers of sorcery, subjects of Angmar, slay the remnants of the Dúnedain and build dark forts in the hills. But the Dúnedain of Fornost, in spite of the death of their king, hold out, and repel the forces of Angmar with the help of Cirdan of Lindon. >] Cardolan is ravaged; the Tower of Amon Sûl is razed and the *palantír* is removed to Fornost. In Rhudaur an evil folk ... [*as above*] build dark forts in the hills, while the remaining Dúnedain of Cardolan hold out in the Barrow Downs and the Forest; the Dúnedain of Arthedain repel the forces of Angmar from Fornost with the help of Cirdan of Lindon.

19   Araphor   born 1391   lived 198 years   died 1589
20   Argeleb II   1473   197   1670
In his day the people of the old lands of Arnor become further diminished by the coming of the plague out of the south and east, which also devastated Gondor. [The plague does not pass beyond the Baranduin. >] The plague lessens in deadliness as it goes north; but Cardolan becomes desolate. Evil spirits come out of Angmar and take up their abode in the mounds of Tyrn Goerthaid. / It was Argeleb II who granted the land west of the Baranduin to the Periannath; they crossed the river and entered the land in 1601.

21   Arvegil   born 1553   lived 190 years   died 1743
22   Arveleg II   1633   180   1813

23 Araval 1711 180 1891

With the help of Lindon and Imladris he won a victory over Angmar in 1851, and sought to reoccupy Cardolan, but the evil wights terrify all who seek to dwell near.

24 Araphant born 1789 lived 175 years died 1964

Angmar recovers and makes war on the Dúnedain. Araphant seeks to renew ancient alliance and kinship with Gondor. In 1940 his heir Arvedui wedded Fíriel daughter of King Ondohir [> Ondonir] of Gondor. But Gondor is engaged in the long Wars of the Wainriders, and sends little help. Ondohir [> Ondonir] and his sons fell in battle in 1944, and Arvedui claimed the crown of Gondor, on behalf of Fíriel and himself as representing 'the elder line of Isildur', since no close male claimant to the throne in Gondor could at first be found. The claim was rejected by Gondor, but Arvedui and his descendants continued to consider themselves as the true heirs of Anárion as well as of Isildur.

25 Arvedui

born 1864 lived 110 years †drowned 1974 [> 1975]

He was the last king at Fornost. In [added: the winter of] 1974 the Witch-king destroyed Fornost, laid Arthedain waste, and scattered the remnants of the Dúnedain. Arvedui escaped from Fornost and fled north, taking the *palantíri* of Annúminas and Emyn Beraid. He attempted to go by ship from Forochel to Gondor but was wrecked and the Stones were lost. The sons of Arvedui took refuge with Cirdan of Lune. The following year Elrond and Cirdan, with some belated help from Gondor, sent by sea, defeated the forces of Angmar. The Witch-king was overthrown by Elrond, and his realm brought to an end. The northern lands though desolate were now made somewhat more wholesome again. But it was found later that the Witch-king had fled away secretly southwards, and had entered Minas Ithil (now called Minas Morgul) and become Lord of the Ringwraiths.

The remnants of the Dúnedain of the North become rangers and errants, living largely in hiding, but waging ceaseless war on all evil things that still are abroad in the land. The sons of their chieftains are usually fostered in Imladris by Elrond, to whose keeping are given the chief remaining heirlooms of their house, especially the shards of Elendil's sword, Narsil.

End of the North Kingdom

Here follows the roll of the Chieftains of the Dúnedain
of Eriador, heirs of Isildur
Little is preserved of the tale of their wanderings and deeds,
until the end of the Third Age.

The Chieftains of the Dúnedain

26 (and 24th heir of Isildur)

	1	Aranarth	born 1938	lived 168 years	died 2106		
27	2	Arahail	2012	165	2177		
28	3	Aranuir	2084	163	2247		
29	4	Aravir	2156	163	2319		
30	5	Aragorn I	2227	100	†slain 2327		

Aragorn was slain by wolves which infested eastern Eriador.

31	6	Araglas	born 2296	lived 159 years	died 2455		
32	7	Arahad I	2365	158	2523		
33	8	Aragost	2431	157	2588		
34	9	Aravorn	2497	157	2654		
35	10	Arahad II	2563	156	2719		
36	11	Arassuil	2628	156	2784		

In his time there was much war with Orcs that infesting the Misty Mountains harried Eriador. The chief battles were in 2745–8. In 2747 the Periannath (Halflings) defeated a westerly ranging force of the invaders that came down from the north into their land west of Baranduin.

37	12	Arathorn I	born 2693	lived 155 years	died 2848		
38	13	Argonui	2757	155	2912		
39	14	Arador	2820	110	†slain 2930		

He was slain by trolls in the mountains north of Imladris.

40 15   Arathorn II   born 2873   lived 60 years   †slain 2933

He wedded Gilrain daughter of Dirhael, a descendant also, but by a younger branch, of Arathorn I. He was slain by an orc-arrow when hunting Orcs in the company of Elladan and Elrohir, the sons of Elrond. He wedded in 2929. His infant son (aged 2 at his father's death) was fostered and brought up at Imladris.

41 16   Aragorn II   born 2931   lived 190 years   died 3121
or the Fourth Age 100

Aragorn became King of Arnor and Gondor in the name of *Elessar*. He played a great part in the War of the Ring in which at last Sauron and the power of Mordor was destroyed. He wedded Arwen Undómiel daughter of Elrond and restored the majesty and blood of the Númenóreans. The Third Age ended with the departure of Elrond in 3022 [> 3021]; and the descendants of Elessar through Arwen became also heirs of the elf-realms of the westlands.

The Heirs of Elendil
The Southern Line of Gondor: the Anárioni

1	Elendil			
	born S.A.3119	lived 322 years	†slain 3441 = T.A.1	
2	Anárion 3219	221	†slain 3440	
3	Meneldil 3318	280	died T.A.158	
	[added: 4th child]			
4	Kemendur 3399	279		238
5	Eärendil T.A. 48	276		324
6	Anardil 136	275		411
7	Ostohir [> Ostonir]			
	222	270		492

He rebuilt and enlarged Minas Anor, where afterwards the kings dwelt always in summer rather than at Osgiliath.

8 Rómendakil I   born 310   lived [231] years †slain 541
His original name was *Tarostar*. In his father's time wild men out of the East first assailed Gondor. Tarostar defeated them and drove them out, and took the name *Rómendakil*, East-slayer. He was, however, later slain in battle with fresh hordes of Easterlings.

9 Turambar   born 397   lived 270 years   died 667
He avenged his father, and conquered much territory eastwards.

10 Atanatar I   born 480   lived 268 years   died 748
11 Siriondil   570   260   830
12 Falastur   654   259   913
He was first called *Tarannon*. He took the name *Falastur*, on coming to the throne, to commemorate his victories that had extended the sway of Gondor far along the shore-lands on either side of the Mouths of Anduin. He was the first childless king. He was succeeded by the son of his brother Tarkiryan.

13 Eärnil I   born 736   lived 200 years
                                          †drowned 936
He began the building of a great navy, and repaired the ancient havens of Pelargir [added: and seized and fortified Umbar, 933]. He was lost with many ships and men in a great storm off Umbar.

14 Kiryandil   born 820   lived 195 years   †slain 1015
He continued to increase the fleets of Gondor; but he fell in a battle with the Men of Harad [who contested the designs of Gondor to occupy Umbar and there make a great fort and haven. >] They contested the designs of Gondor to occupy the coast-lands beyond R. Harnen; they therefore tried to take Umbar, where Gondor maintained a great fort and haven.

15 Hyarmendakil I
                   born 899   lived 250 years   died 1149

At first called *Kiryahir*, he avenged his father, defeated the kings
of Harad, and made them acknowledge the overlordship of
Gondor, 1050. Gondor occupied all the land south of the
Mouths of Anduin up to [Umbar and the borders of Near
Harad; >] the River (Poros >) Harnen and the borders of Near
Harad; and also all the coast-lands as far as Umbar. / Umbar
became a great fortress and haven of fleets. After his victory
Kiryahir took the name of Hyarmendakil 'South-slayer'. He
reigned 134 years, the longest of all save Tarondor (twenty-
seventh king).

16   Atanatar II   born 977   lived 249 years   died 1226
Surnamed *Alkarin*, the Glorious. In his time, owing to the vigour
of the 'Ship-kings', the line from Falastur onwards, Gondor
reached the height of its power. This extended in direct rule as
far north as Celebrant and the south-eaves of Mirkwood, east to
the Sea of [Rúnaer >] Rhúnaer, and south to Umbar, and westward to the River Gwathlo or Greyflood. In addition many other
regions were tributary: the Men of Anduin Vale as far as its
sources, and the folk of Harad in the South. But Atanatar in fact
did nothing to increase this power, and lived mostly in splendour
and ease. The waning of Gondor began before he died, and the
watch on the borders was neglected.

17   Narmakil I   born 1049   lived 245 years   died 1294
The second childless king. He was succeeded by his younger
brother.

18   Kalmakil   born 1058   lived 246 years   died 1304
19   Rómendakil II   1126   240   1366
20   Valakar   1194   238   1432
In his time there broke out the disastrous civil war called the
Kin-strife. After the death of Atanatar the Glorious the Northmen of Mirkwood and the Upper Anduin, who had increased
much in the peace brought by the power of Gondor, became
powerful. Though these people were ultimately related in speech
and blood to the Atani (and so to the Númenóreans), and were
usually friendly, they now became restless. Rómendakil was
forced to withdraw his northern border east of Anduin to the
Emyn Muil. He there built the Gates of Argonath with images of
Isildur and Anárion beyond which no stranger was allowed to
come south without leave. But Rómendakil being at this time
much troubled by assaults of Easterlings sought to attach the
Northmen more closely to his allegiance. He took many into his
service and gave them high rank. His son Valakar dwelt long
among them in the house of [*added:* Vidugavia] the King of
Rhovannion. Rómendakil permitted him to wed the king's
daughter. The marriage of the heir to a woman of an alien people

and without any Númenórean blood had never occurred before, and caused great displeasure. Before Valakar died there was already open rebellion in the southern fiefs. Various claimants to the crown appeared, descendants of Atanatar II. The most favoured especially by the fleet, and ship-folk of the southern shores, was the Captain of the Ships, Kastamir [great-grandson >] grandson of Kalmakil's second son Kalimehtar.

21(a) Eldakar   born 1255   deposed 1437

When Valakar died his son, who had the alien name of *Vinitharya*, took the name *Eldakar*, and succeeded. At first he held Osgiliath, and Minas Anor, but he was driven out and deposed by Kastamir, and fled to the north. In this war Osgiliath suffered much damage, and the tower of the *palantir* was destroyed and the *palantir* lost.

22 Kastamir born 1259 seized throne 1437   †slain 1447

After ten years Eldakar defeated Kastamir with the help of his mother's kin. Kastamir was slain [*added:* by Eldakar in battle in Lebennin, at Ethraid Erui], but his sons and many of his kin and party fled to Umbar, and long held it as an independent realm at war with Gondor.

21(b) Eldakar

  regained the kingdom 1447   lived 235 years   died 1490

After Eldakar's return the blood of the kingly house and kindred became more mixed, for many Northmen settled in Gondor, and became great in the land, and high officers in its armies. But the friendship with the Northmen, which continued as part of the policy of the kings, proved of great service in later wars.

23 Aldamir   born 1330 lived 210 years †slain 1540

He was the second son and third child of Eldakar. His elder brother Ornendil was slain in the wars of the Kin-strife (1446). Aldamir fell in battle with the rebelling kings of Harad allied with the rebels of Umbar.

24 Vinyarion   born 1391 lived 230 years   died 1621

He later (1551) took the name *Hyarmendakil II*, after a great victory over Harad in vengeance for his father.

25 Minardil   born 1454 lived 180 years †slain 1634

The rebels of Umbar had never ceased to make war on Gondor since the death of Kastamir, attacking its ships and raiding its coast at every opportunity. They had however become much mixed in blood through admission of Men of Harad, and only their chieftains, descendants of Kastamir, were of Númenórean race. Learning through spies that Minardil was at Pelargir, suspecting no peril since the crushing of Harad and Umbar by his father, Angomaitë and Sangahyanda, leaders of the Corsairs of Umbar, great-grandsons of Kastamir, made a raid up Anduin, slew the king, ravaged Pelargir and the coasts, and escaped with great booty.

26   Telemnar   born 1516   lived 120 years   died 1636
Telemnar immediately began to fit out a fleet for the reduction of Umbar. But a deadly plague or sickness, coming with dark winds out of the East, fell on the land. Great numbers of the folk of Gondor, especially those that dwelt in Osgiliath, and other cities and towns, took sick and died. The White Tree of Minas Anor withered and died. Telemnar and all his children perished. The crown was taken by his nephew.

27   Tarondor   born 1577   lived 221 years   died 1798
He was the eldest son of Minastan, second son of Minardil. He removed the king's house permanently to Minas Anor, and there replanted a seedling of the White Tree in the citadel. During the plague in Osgiliath those folk that survived fled from the city to the western dales or into the woods of Ithilien, and few were willing to return. Osgiliath became largely deserted and partly ruinous. Tarondor had the longest reign of all the Kings of Gondor (162 years), but was unable to do more than attempt to re-establish life and order within his borders. Owing to the fewness of his people the watch on Mordor was neglected and the fortresses guarding the passes became emptied.

28   Telumehtar   born 1632   lived 218 years   died 1850
He took the title *Umbardakil* after the storming and destruction of the haven and stronghold of the Corsairs of Umbar (1810). But this was later reoccupied and rebuilt in the troublous times that later befell Gondor.

29   Narmakil II   born 1684   lived 172 years   †slain 1856
In his time it is said that the Úlairi or Ringwraiths re-entered Mordor, owing to the ceasing of the vigilance, and there they secretly prepared in the darkness for the return of their Dark Lord. Men out of the East appeared of a new sort, stronger, better armed, journeying in huge wains, and fighting in chariots. Stirred up maybe by Sauron they made a great assault on Gondor, and continued to be a great peril for very many years. Narmakil was slain in battle with their host beyond Anduin, north-east of the Morannon.

30   Kalimehtar   born 1736   lived 200 years   died 1936
He continued the War of the Wainriders, and in 1899 won a great victory over them on Dagorlad, which checked their attacks for some time. He built the White Tower in Minas Anor to house the *palantír*.

31   Ondohir
        [> Ondonir]   born 1787   lived 157 years   †slain 1944

War continued with the Wainriders. In 1940 Ondohir [> Ondonir] gave the hand of his daughter Fíriel (born 1896), his third child, to Arvedui heir of Araphant, King of the North-kingdom; but he was unable to send any help to the north against the evil realm of Angmar, because of his own peril. In 1944 Ondohir [> Ondonir] and both his sons Faramir and Artamir fell in battle against an alliance of the Wainriders and the Haradrim. The king and his sons fell in battle in the north and the enemy poured into Ithilien. But in the meantime Eärnil Captain of the southern army won a victory in South Ithilien, destroyed the army of Harad, and hastening north succoured the retreating remnants of the northern army, and drove the Wain-riders off. In the great rout that followed most of the enemy were driven into the Dead Marshes.

On the death of Ondohir [> Ondonir] and his sons Arvedui of the North claimed the crown of Gondor as the 'direct descendant of Elendil', and as husband of Fíriel. The claim was rejected by Gondor. At length Eärnil the victorious Captain received the crown (in 1945), since he was of the royal house.

32   Eärnil II   born 1883   lived 160 years   died 2043
He was son of Siriondil, son of Kalimmakil, son of Narmakil II. In his time the North-kingdom came to an end with the over-throw and death of Arvedui, claimant to both crowns. He sent [some help north by sea >] his son Eärnur north with a fleet, and so aided in the destruction of the realm of Angmar. But, though not revealed until later, the Witch-king fled south and joined the other Ringwraiths in Mordor, becoming their Lord. When they were ready the Úlairi suddenly issued from Mordor over the pass of Kirith Ungol. They took Minas Ithil, and were never again expelled from it during that Age. It became a place of great fear, and was renamed Minas Morgul. Few people were willing any longer to dwell in Ithilien, but this was still held and garrisoned by Gondor. At this time probably the *palantír* of Minas Ithil was captured and so came to the hands of Sauron.

33   and last of the Third Age
Eärnur   born 1928   lived 122 years   †slain 2050
He renamed Minas Anor Minas Tirith, as the city on guard against the evil of Minas Morgul. On the death of his father the Lord of the Ringwraiths challenged Eärnur to single combat to make good his claim to the throne. Mardil the Steward restrained him.

The challenge was repeated with taunts in 2050, seven years later, and against the counsel of Mardil Eärnur accepted. He rode with a small escort of knights to Minas Morgul, but neither he nor his company were ever heard of again. It was thought that the faithless enemy had merely decoyed him to the gates and then trapped him and either slain him or kept him in torment as a prisoner.

Since his death was not certain Mardil the Good Steward ruled Gondor in his name for many years. In any case no male descendants of the royal line, among those whose blood was little mixed, could be found.

For a long time before Mardil's day the Stewardship had usually been held by a member of his family (the *Hurinionath*, descended from Húrin, Steward to King Minardil). It now became hereditary like a kingship; but each new Steward took office with the formula: 'to hold rule and rod in the King's name and until the King's return'. Though this soon became a mere formality and the Stewards exercised all the power of kings, it was believed by many in Gondor that a king would return, and the Stewards never sat on the ancient throne nor used the royal standard and emblems. The banner of the Stewards was plain white. The royal standard was sable with a silver tree in blossom beneath seven stars.

34   Elessar   born 2931   lived 190 years   died 3121
                                             or the Fourth Age 100

After a lapse of 969 years Aragorn, son of Arathorn, 16th chieftain of the Dúnedain of the North, and 41st heir of Elendil in the direct line through Isildur, being also in the direct line a descendant of Fíriel daughter of Ondohir [> Ondonir] of Gondor, claimed the crown of Gondor and of Arnor, after the defeat of Sauron, the destruction of Mordor, and the dissolution of the Ringwraiths. He was crowned in the name of *Elessar* at Minas Tirith in 3019. A new era and calendar was then begun, beginning with 25 March (old reckoning) as the first day. He restored Gondor and repeopled it, but retained Minas Tirith as the chief city. He wedded Arwen Undómiel, daughter of Elrond, brother of Elros first King of Númenor, and so restored the majesty and high lineage of the royal house, but their life-span was not restored and continued to wane until it became as that of other men.

The Third Age ended according to the reckoning of the Eldar in 3021 and the same year Elrond departed. In 3022 the Fourth Age started and the Elder Days and their Twilight were over.

The son of Elessar and Arwen was Eldarion, first king of the Fourth Age, whose realm was great and long-enduring, but this roll does not contain the names of the Fourth Age.

Here follows the roll of the Stewards of Gondor
that ruled the realm and city between the going of Eärnur

and the coming of Elessar
The Ruling Stewards of Gondor

The names of these rulers are here added; for though the *Hurinionath* were not in the direct line of descent from Elendil, they were ultimately of royal origin, and had in any case kept their blood more pure than most other families in the later ages.

They were descended, father to son, from Húrin, Steward to King Minardil, who had laboured greatly for the ordering of the realm in the disastrous days of the plague, when King Telemnar died within two years of the slaying of King Minardil by the Corsairs. From that time on the kings usually chose their steward from this family, though a son did not necessarily succeed a father. But in fact it had descended from father to son since Pelendur, Steward to King Ondohir, and after the ending of the kings it became hereditary, though if a Steward left no son, the office might pass in the female line, that is to his sister-son, or to his father's sister-son.

The choice was made according to their worth among the near kin by the Council of Gondor. But the Council had no power of choice if there was a son living.

The Stewards belonged to a family of the ancient Elf-friends who used (beside the Common Speech) the Noldorin tongue after the fashion of Gondor.* Their official names (after Mardil) were in that tongue and drawn mostly from the ancient legends of the Noldor and their dealings with the Edain.

All the time of the Stewards was one of slow dwindling and waning both of the power and numbers of the Men of Gondor, and of the lore and skill of Númenor among them. Also the life-span of those even of the purer blood steadily decreased. They were never free from war or the threat of war with the evil that dwelt in Minas Morgul and watched them. They counted it glory and success to hold that threat at bay. Osgiliath became a ruin, a city of shadows, often taken and re-taken in petty battles. For a while, during the 300 years peace, after the

---

* Since this had long ceased to be a 'cradle-tongue' in Gondor, but was learned in early youth (by those claiming Númenórean descent) from loremasters, and used by them as a mark of rank, it had changed very little since the Downfall; and though the Men of Gondor altered a little some of the sounds, they could still understand the Eldar and be understood by them. In the later days, however, they saw them seldom.

formation of the White Council, Ithilien was reoccupied and a hardy folk dwelt there, tending its fair woods and fields, but after the days of Denethor I (2435–77) most of them fled west again. But it is true that but for Minas Tirith the power of Mordor would much sooner have grown great and would have spread over Anduin into the westlands. After the days of Eärnur the White Tree waned and seldom flowered. It slowly aged and withered and bore no fruit, so far as men knew.

Pelendur   born 1879   lived 119 years   died 1998

He was steward to King Ondohir and advised the rejection of the claim of Arvedui, and supported the claim of Eärnil who became king in 1945. He remained steward under Eärnil, and was succeeded by his son.

Vorondil   born 1919   lived 110 years   died 2029

He was succeeded by his son. [*Added:* Vorondil was a great hunter and he made a great horn out of the horn of the wild oxen of Araw, which then still roamed near the Sea of Rhûn.]

1   Mardil Voronwë ('steadfast')

born 1960   lived 120 years   died 2080

He became steward to King Eärnil in his later days, and then to King Eärnur. After the disappearance of Eärnur he ruled the realm for thirty years from 2050, and is reckoned the first of the line of *Ruling Stewards* of Gondor.

		born	lived	died
2	Eradan	born 1999	lived 117 years	died 2116
3	Herion	2037	111	2148
4	Belegorn	2074	130	2204
5	Húrin I	2124	120	2244
6	Túrin I	2165	113	2278

He was the third child of Húrin. He was wedded twice and had several children (a thing already rare and remarkable among the nobles of Gondor); but only the last, a child born in his old age, was a son.

7   Hador   born 2245   lived 150 years   died 2395

The last recorded Man of Gondor to reach such an age. After this time the life-span of those of Númenórean blood waned more rapidly.

8	Barahir	born 2290	lived 122 years	died 2412
9	Dior	2328	107	2435

He was childless and was succeeded by the son of his sister Rían.

10   Denethor I   born 2375   lived 102 years   died 2477

Great troubles arose in his day. The Morgul-lords having bred in secret a fell race of black Orcs in Mordor assail Ithilien and overrun it. They capture Osgiliath and destroy its renowned bridge.

Boromir son of Denethor in 2475 defeated the host of Morgul and recovered Ithilien for a while.

11   Boromir
  born 2410   lived [89 >] 79 years   died [2499 >] 2489
He was third child of Denethor. His life was shortened by the poisoned wounds he received in the Morgul-war.

12   Cirion   born 2449   lived 118 years   died 2567
In his time there came a great assault from the North-east. Wild men out of the East crossed Anduin north of the Emyn Muil and joining with Orcs out of the Misty Mountains overran the realm (now sparsely populated) north of the White Mountains, pouring into the wold and plain of Calenardon. Eorl the Young out of Éothéod brings great help of horsemen and the great victory of the Field of Celebrant (2510) is won. Eorl's people settle in Calenardon, which is after called Rohan, a free folk but in perpetual alliance with the Stewards of Gondor. (According to some Eorl was a descendant of the Northmen that were allied with the royal house in the days of Eldakar.) [Added: Eorl was slain in battle in the 'Wold of Rohan' (as it was later called), 2545.]

13   Hallas   born 2480   lived 125 years   died 2605
14   Húrin II   2515   113   2628
15   Belecthor I   2545   110   2655
16   Orodreth   2576   109   2685
17   Ecthelion I   2600   98   2698
He repaired and rebuilt the White Tower in Minas Tirith, which was afterwards often called Ecthelion's Tower. He had no children and was followed by Egalmoth, grandson of Morwen sister of Orodreth.

18   Egalmoth   born 2626   lived 117 years   died 2743
In this time there was renewed war with the Orcs.

19   Beren   born 2655   lived 108 years   died 2763
In his time [there was a renewed attack on Gondor by the pirates of Umbar. >] there was a great attack on Gondor (2758) by three fleets of the pirates of Umbar. All the coasts were invaded. / Gondor received no help from Rohan, and could send no help thither. Rohan was invaded from the North-east, and also from the West (by rebelling Dunlendings). The Long Winter 2758–9. Rohan lies for five months under snow. [Added: Saruman comes to Orthanc.]

20   Beregond   born 2700   lived 111 years   died 2811
In his time the War of the Dwarves and Orcs in the Misty Mountains occurred [(2766–9) >] (2793–9). Many Orcs flying south are slain and they are prevented from establishing themselves in the White Mountains.

21   Belecthor II   born 2752   lived 120 years   died 2872

Only child, late-born, of Beregond. The last of his line to pass the age of 100 years. At his death the White Tree finally dies in the citadel, but is left standing 'until the King come'. No seedling can be found.

22   Thorondir   born 2782   lived 100 years   died 2882

23   Túrin II   2815   99   2914

In his time [folk finally fled >] many more folk removed west over Anduin from Ithilien, which became wild and infested by Mordor-orcs. But Gondor makes and keeps up secret strongholds there, especially in North Ithilien. The ancient refuge of Henneth Annûn is rebuilt and hidden. The isle of Cair Andros in Anduin is fortified. The Men of Harad are stirred up by the servants of Sauron to attack Gondor. In 2885 Túrin fought a battle with the Haradrim in South Ithilien and defeated them with aid from Rohan; but the sons of King Folcwine of Rohan, Folcred and Fastred, fell in this battle. Túrin paid Folcwine a rich weregild of gold.

24   Turgon   born 2855   lived 98 years   died 2953

In the last year of his rule Sauron declared himself again, and reentered Mordor, long prepared for him. Barad-dûr rose again. Mount Doom long dormant bursts into smoke and flame. [*Added*: Saruman takes possession of Orthanc, and fortifies it.]

25   Ecthelion II   born 2886   lived 98 years   died 2984

He is visited by Mithrandir (Gandalf) to whom he is friendly. Aragorn of the North serves as a soldier in his forces. He strengthens Pelargir again, and refortifies Cair Andros.

26   Denethor II

               born 2930   lived 89 years   †slew himself 3019

He was first son and third child of Ecthelion and more learned in lore than any Steward for many generations. He was very tall and in appearance looked like an ancient Númenórean. He wedded late (for his time) in 2976 Finduilas daughter of Prince Adrahil of Dol Amroth, a noble house of southern Gondor of Númenórean blood, reputed also to have Elven-blood from ancient days: the Elven-folk of Amroth of Lórien dwelt in the region of Dol Amroth before they sailed over sea. His elder son Boromir (2978) was slain by orcs near Rauros in 3019. His younger son Faramir (2983) became the last Ruling Steward. His wife Finduilas died untimely in 2987.

In his time the peril of Gondor steadily grew, and he awaited always the great assault of Sauron that he knew was preparing. It is said that he dared to use the *palantir* of the White Tower, which none since the kings had looked in, and so saw much of the mind of Sauron (who had the Stone of Ithil), but was aged prematurely by this combat, and fell into despair.

The attack began in the summer of 3018. The Ringwraiths issued once more from Minas Morgul in visible form. The sons of Denethor resisted them but were defeated by the Black Captain, and retreated over Anduin; but they still held West Osgiliath.

Boromir departed to Imladris soon after on a mission to seek the counsel of Elrond. He was slain as he returned. Minas Tirith was besieged in March 3019, and Denethor burned himself on a pyre in the Tomb of the Stewards.

27 Faramir   born 2983   lived 120 years   died 3103
                                                   = Fourth Age 82

He succeeded by right on the death of his father, but in the same year surrendered rod and rule to the King Elessar, and so was the last Ruling Steward. He retained the title of Steward, and became Prince of the restored land of Ithilien, dwelling in the Hills of Emyn Arnen beside Anduin. He wedded in 3020 Éowyn sister of King Éomer of Rohan.

So ends the tale of
the Ruling
Stewards of Gondor

The manuscript C of *The Heirs of Elendil* ends here, but clipped to it is a genealogy of the line of Dol Amroth: for this see p. 220.

Commentary

As I have explained (p. 188), the manuscript B is for the Northern Line the earliest text, and the commentary to this part is largely a record of significant differences from the text printed (C). Corrections to B are not as a rule noticed if they merely bring it to the form in C (in substance: usually not in the precise expression), nor are additions to B as first written necessarily noticed as such.

References to the historical accounts following the names and dates of the kings and rulers are made simply by the name, with the page-reference to the C text. A notable feature of *The Heirs of Elendil* is the record of the birthdates of the rulers, which were excluded from Appendix A; other dates are in all cases the same as those in Appendix A unless the contrary is noted.

The preamble concerning dates in C (p. 191) is absent from B, which begins with the genealogy. This differs from that in C in showing Anárion as the elder son of Elendil, and in naming 'Valandil of Arthedain': thus B belongs with the early texts of the Tale of Years, as already noted (pp. 188–9).

Only Isildur's youngest son, Valandil, is named in *The Lord of the Rings*. In the very late work *The Disaster of the Gladden Fields* the three elder are named Elendur, Aratan, and Ciryon (*Unfinished Tales* p. 271 and note 11); on one of the copies of the typescript D (p. 190) my father pencilled a note remarking on this, and saying that the names found in 'Gladdenfields' were to be accepted.

In the chronological outline that follows in B as in C, the birth-date of Anárion is 3209 and of Isildur 3219; Meneldil was born in 3299, and it was Kiryandil son of Isildur who was the last man to be born in Númenor (3318). Arthedain appears for Arnor in 3320; the birth-dates of Eärnur and Vëandur are 3349 and 3389; and Valandil was born in Annúminas, not Imladris.

In both texts Isildur died in 3441 (which in the list of the Northern kings that follows is made equivalent to Third Age 1), the same year as the overthrow of Sauron (see pp. 170, 177).

Following the words 'The Second Age ends and the Third Begins' B continues at once with the naming of the kings of the Northern Line (without the name *Isildurioni*). The list of these kings up to the disintegration of the North Kingdom was the same in B as in C with the sole difference (apart from the different date of Isildur's birth, 3219) that the tenth king Eärendur is named Eärendil in B: on this see p. 189.

Valandil (p. 192)   In B there was a note here: 'Removed to Fornost and Annúminas was deserted'; this was struck out, and 'Annúminas became deserted' added to the note following King Eärendil.

Eärendur (p. 193)   The note in B begins 'After Eärendil the Northern Kingdom of Arthedain disintegrated', and the north-western kingdom ruled by Amlaith is referred to by the name of the city of its kings: 'Fornost still claimed the overlordship, but this was disputed.' The other realms are thus described in B: 'Cardolan (where later were Bree and the Barrowdowns) and Rhudaur north of the R. Bruinen (where later were the Trollshaws).'

Mallor (p. 193)   In B the corresponding note follows Beleg the twelfth king: 'In his reign Sauron took shape again in Mirkwood and evil things began again to multiply.'

Celebrindor (p. 193)   The name of the fifteenth king in B as first written was *Celem...gil*, perhaps *Celemenegil*; this was struck out and replaced by *Celebrindol*, as in C before correction to *Celebrindor*.

Malvegil (p. 193)   The note in B is, as generally, briefer but has all the essentials of that in C; here it is said that 'Fornost is at war with the lesser kingdoms, the chief dispute being about the *palantir* of Amon Sûl'. The conclusion of the note in C, concerning this, was rejected when the disputed claim to Amon Sûl was introduced much earlier, at the disintegration of Arnor after the death of Eärendur. – On the name *Úlairi* see p. 153.

The kings from Argeleb I to Arvedui (pp. 194–5)   An earlier form of the page in B that begins with the last sentence of the note following

Malvegil, the taking of the prefix *aran*, *ar(a)* by the kings at Fornost, is extant, and here the names of these kings are seen evolving. The original names were as follows (it is curious that despite the words at the head of the page the first three kings do not have the prefix *Ar*):

17 Celebrindol (> Argeleb I)
18 Beleg II   (> Arveleg I)
19 Malvegil II (> Araphor)
20 Arveleg   (> Argeleb II)
21 Arvegil
22 Argeleb   (> Arveleg II)
23 Arvallen (> Araval)
24 Araphant
25 Arvedui

But the dates of these kings underwent no change. The original name of the seventeenth king, Celebrindol, was given to the fifteenth, originally Celemenegil (?), as noted above.

Argeleb I (p. 194) On the rejected page of B the note following this king states only: 'slain in battle 1356. Angmar is repulsed but turns upon the lesser kingdoms.' The replacement page has: 'Slain in battle with subkingdoms of Cardolan and Rhudaur'. Neither text refers to the *palantir* of Amon Sûl. On the mention in the altered text in C of Argeleb's fortifying of the Weather Hills see p. 189.

Arveleg I (p. 194) The rejected page of B has no note here; in the replacement page it reads:

Angmar taking advantage of war among the Númenóreans comes down and overruns Cardolan and Rhudaur. These realms become subject to the Sorcerer-king and full of evil things, especially Cardolan. But Fornost in spite of death of King Arveleg holds out with aid from Lindon and Imladrist.

An addition concerning the *palantir* of Amon Sûl was made to this:

The tower of the *palantir* on Amon Sûl is destroyed, but no one knows what became of the Stone. Maybe it was taken by the Witch-king.

This addition was probably made in revision of the original statement in C that the *palantir* was broken.

Argeleb II (p. 194) In B there was no note here and so no mention of the plague, but the following was added in: 'He gave "the Shire" to the Hobbits.' This is stated in an addition to an early text of the *Prologue* (p. 9): 'In the Year 1 ... the brothers Marco and Cavallo, having obtained formal permission from the king Argeleb II in the waning city of Fornost, crossed the wide brown river Baranduin.'

Araval (p. 195) The statement in B reads: 'With help of Lindon and Imladrist Araval wins great victory over Angmar, and drives the evil wights north. He reoccupies Cardolan.' In the rejected page of B this victory is ascribed to the next king, Araphant, who 'drives back the

Sorcerer-king and in 1900 destroys Cardolan.' There is no reference to the victory of Araval in the history of the North Kingdom in Appendix A.

Araphant (p. 195)   More briefly, B has here:

Angmar recovers, and makes war again. Araphant seeks alliance with Gondor and weds his son Arvedui to daughter of King Ondohir of Gondor; so that his descendants come also from the southern line of Anárion. But Gondor is waning and fallen on evil days, and sends little help.

The original note to Araphant has been given under Araval, but an addition to this mentions the marriage of Araphant's son Arvedui to Ondohir's daughter, and here she is named: *Ilmarë* (see further pp. 215–16, *Ondohir*). The change of *Ondohir* to *Ondonir* in C was made also at all occurrences of the name in the Southern Line, and also that of the seventh king of Gondor, *Ostohir*, was altered to *Ostonir*. These changed names appear in the late typescript D, where my father let them stand; but *Ostohir*, *Ondohir* reappear in Appendix A. In the Second Edition he changed them to *Ostoher*, *Ondoher* (and also the original name of Hyarmendacil I, *Ciryahir* (*Kiryahir*), which was altered to *Ciryaher*). In an isolated note on these changes he said that *Ondohir* was a hybrid name: in pure Quenya it should be *Ondoher* (Q. *heru*, *hēr-* 'lord'), and *-hir* seems to be due to the influence of Sindarin *hīr* 'lord', and also that of other names ending in *-ir*, especially *-mir*, *-vir*.

Arvedui (p. 195)   The statement in B here lacks very little that is told in C, although as my father first wrote it there was no mention of Arvedui's fate: his death is given as 'slain 1974'. In a subsequent addition the same is said of his flight by ship and drowning as in C, and the loss of the *palantíri* in the shipwreck is mentioned, but they are not identified: they are called simply 'the two that remain'. In this text that of Amon Sûl was lost when the tower was destroyed ('Maybe it was taken by the Witch-king', p. 209, *Arveleg I*). So also in C the *palantíri* taken by Arvedui are those of Annúminas and Emyn Beraid, for in that text the Stone of Amon Sûl was said to have been broken (p. 194, *Arveleg I*). C was emended to say that it was saved and removed to Fornost (*ibid.*): this was the final version of the history, with the Stones lost in the sea becoming those of Annúminas and Amon Sûl, while that of Emyn Beraid, which had a special character, remained in the North (see RK p. 322, footnote, and *Unfinished Tales* p. 413, note 16). But the C text was not emended in the present passage.

Of the tale told in Appendix A of Arvedui's sojourn among the Lossoth, the Snowmen of Forochel, there is here no trace.

The Chieftains of the Dúnedain (p. 195)   The rejected page of B carries the names of the Chieftains, and some of these as first written were corrected on the manuscript, thus:

27 Araha[n]til (sixth letter illegible) > Arahail
28 Aranuil > Aranuir
31 Arallas > Araglas
33 Arandost > Aragost
35 Arangar > Arahad II
36 Arasuil > Arassuil
39 Arv[or]eg (fifth and sixth letters uncertain) > Arador

The dates were also different from the final chronology, save for those of Aranarth and Aragorn II, in both versions of B; they were corrected on the replacement page of B to those of C. The original dates were:

Arahail	2011–2176	Aravorn	2490–2647
Aranuir	2083–2246	Arahad II	2555–2711
Aravir	2154–2316	Arassuil	2619–2775
Aragorn I	2224–2324	Arathorn I	2683–2838
Araglas	2292–2451	Argonui	2746–2901
Arahad I	2359–2517	Arador	2808–2912
Aragost	2425–2583	Arathorn II	2870–2933

These changes of date were carefully made, in several cases in more than one stage; in the result the length of the lives of the Chieftains remained the same, except in the cases of Aravir, Aragost, Arador, and Arathorn II.

Aragorn I (p. 196)   In the rejected page of B he was 'lost in wilderness while hunting'; in the replacement page he was 'lost in the wilderness; probably slain by orcs [> wolves].'

Arassuil (p. 196)   The victory of the Hobbits in 2747 was the Battle of Greenfields.

Arador (p. 196)   Arador's death is referred to at the beginning of the tale of Aragorn and Arwen in Appendix A, as also is that of Arathorn II (RK pp. 337–8).

Aragorn II (p. 196)   B has here: 'Became King Elessar of Gondor and Arthedain, aided in the overthrow of Sauron with which Third Age ended in 3019. He wedded Arwen Undómiel, daughter of Elrond. His descendants became thus heirs of the Númenórean realms, and of Lúthien and the Elf-kingdoms of the West.' The statement in C that 'The Third Age ended with the departure of Elrond in 3022' was presumably a mere slip, since the date of Aragorn's death is given immediately above as 3121 = Fourth Age 100, which assumes the beginning of that Age in 3022. Later in C, when Aragorn appears at the end of the roll of the kings of the Southern Line (p. 202), the departure of Elrond is given as 3021, the Fourth Age is said to have begun in 3022, and 3121 is again equated with Fourth Age 100.

The Southern Line of Gondor

The earliest extant list of the rulers of Gondor is the manuscript A briefly described on p. 188. This has precisely the same form as the two later texts of *The Heirs of Elendil*, with the dates of birth and death (and the manner of death) of each king, and the length of his life. There is only one difference of name in A, that of the fourteenth king (p. 197), who was first called *Kiryahir* but subsequently renamed *Kiryandil* (at the same time *Kiryahir* entered as the original name of Hyamendakil I). There are only two differences in the succession, the first being in that following the sixteenth king Atanatar II (p. 198), which in A as first written went:

16   Atanatar II   977–1226
17   Alkarin   1049–1294
18   Narmakil I

It was evidently at this point that my father stopped, moved 'Alkarin' to stand beside Atanatar II with the words 'also named', and changed Narmakil I from 18 to 17, entering as his dates those previously given to 'Alkarin'. The next king, Kalmakil, was then entered as 18. I have no doubt whatever that this was a mere slip, *Alkarin* being an honorific name; and this is significant, for it shows that my father was copying from an existing text, or existing notes. There is no trace now of anything of the sort, and it must be concluded that the written origin of the history of the rulers of Gondor is lost.

The other difference in the succession occurs after the thirtieth king Kalimehtar (p. 200), where A has:

31   Ostohir II   1787–1985, lived 198 years
32   Ondohir   1837–1944 (slain), lived 107 years

Eärnil II and Eärnur the last king are numbered 33 and 34. The death of Ostohir II is thus placed 41 years *after* that of his successor Ondohir. How this peculiar anomaly arose can only be surmised: the likeliest explanation is that there were variant and contradictory conceptions in the text that my father was using, and that he failed to observe it. It was not corrected in A, and indeed the same succession survived into B, with Eärnur numbered the thirty-fourth king. When he did observe it he resolved it by simply striking out Ostohir II and giving his birth-date of 1787 to Ondohir, so that he lived for 157 and not 107 years.

A also differed from the final chronology in the dates of the kings from Anárion to Anardil (see p. 197), which were:

Anárion   S.A.3209–3440
Meneldil   S.A.3299–T.A.139
Kemendur   S.A.3389–T.A.228
Eärendil   T.A.40–316
Anardil   T.A.132–407

The dates of these five kings remained in B as they were in A, but were then corrected to those found in C; after correction the life-span of each king remained the same as before, with the exception of Anárion, since he became the younger son of Elendil while the date of his death was fixed. All other dates in A were retained into the final chronology.

The notes in A were brief and scanty until Valakar the twentieth king (and those to Rómendakil I and Hyarmendakil I were subsequent additions):

7   Ostohir I   Rebuilt and enlarged Minas Anor.

8   Rómendakil I   At this time Easterlings assailed kingdom.

13   Eärnil I   Began rebuilding the neglected navy. Lost at sea in a storm.

15   Hyarmendakil I   Defeated Harad and made them subject.

16   Atanatar II   In his day Gondor reached its widest extent owing to the vigour of the 'line of Eärnil'. But he loved life of ease and began to neglect the guards in the East. Waning of Gondor began.

There are also some notes on the nature of the succession: Falastur had no son, and his successor Eärnil I was the son of Falastur's brother Tarkiryan; Narmakil I had no children, and his successor Kalmakil was his brother.

It seems plain that a firm structure at least in outline had already arisen: that my father had in his mind a clear picture of the chronology, the major events, the triumphs and vicissitudes of the history of Gondor, whether or not it was committed to writing now lost.

From Valakar the notes in the A text as written become more frequent and some of them much fuller, a pattern still reflected in the entries in the greatly expanded C text. Some of these entries are given in the commentary on the Southern Line in C that now follows.

Ostohir (p. 197)   In all three texts Ostohir is the first of that name, but the figure I was struck out in C: see p. 212. On the change of the name to *Ostonir* see p. 210, *Araphant*.

Rómendakil I (p. 197)   In Appendix A *Rómendakil* is translated 'East-victor', but in texts B and C 'East-slayer'; so also in the case of *Hyarmendakil*, translated 'South-slayer' in B and C.

Falastur (p. 197)   This king's former name *Tarannon* first appears in C, though the reason for *Falastur* is recorded in B.

Kiryandil (p. 197)   B has only 'Continued to increase fleets, but fell in a sea-battle against the Kings of Harad'. The alterations to C under Eärnil I and Kiryandil bring the history to its form in Appendix A, where it was Eärnil who captured Umbar.

Valakar (p. 198)   As the first extant account of the Kin-strife in Gondor I give here the entry in A, where the whole history of the civil war is placed in the note following Valakar:

In 1432 broke out the Kin-strife. Valakar had wedded as wife a daughter of the King of Rhovannion, not of Dúnedain blood. The succession of his son Eldakar was contested by other descendants of Kalmakil and Rómendakil II. In the end Eldakar was driven into exile and Kastamir, great-grandson of Kalmakil's second son

Kalimehtar, became king. But Eldakar drove him out again, and after that time the blood of the kingly house became more mixed, for Eldakar had the assistance of the Northmen of the Upper Anduin his mother's kin, and they were favoured by the kingly house afterwards, and many of them served in the armies of Gondor and became great in the land.

Thus nothing was told of the political and military circumstances that led to the marriage of Valakar to the daughter of the (as yet unnamed) King of Rhovannion. In B something is said of this:

Since the days of Atanatar II the Northmen of Mirkwood and upper Anduin had been increasing greatly in numbers and power, and in Rómendakil's time hardly acknowledged the overlordship of Gondor. Rómendakil having enough to do with Easterlings sought to attach the Northmen more closely to their allegiance, and arranged that his son Valakar should wed the daughter of the King of Róvannion (Wilderland).

B then follows A in placing the whole history of the Kin-strife in the note following Valakar, and makes only the additional statements that such a marriage was unheard of, and that Valakar's son bore before his accession the alien name *Vinthanarya*. In both texts it is said that Kastamir was slain by Eldakar in 1447, but there is no mention in either of the flight to Umbar by his defeated adherents and the arising there of an independent pirate realm (see below under *Minardil*).

Aldamir (p. 199)   In A it is said that 'his elder son Ornendil was slain with him in battle with rebels of Harad'; B is the same as C, making Ornendil the brother of Aldamir who had been slain in the Kin-strife, but without the reference to 'the rebels of Umbar' (see under *Minardil*).

Vinyarion (p. 199)   The victory of Vinyarion in Harad in vengeance for his father, mentioned in almost the same words in all three texts, is not referred to in the account in Appendix A, and thus the reason for his taking the name Hyarmendakil II is not given; but the event is recorded in the Tale of Years, Third Age 1551.

Minardil (p. 199)   In A the story of the founding of the hostile lordship of the Corsairs of Umbar by the followers of Kastamir does not appear and had probably not yet arisen: this is suggested by the fact that in B it first enters long after the event in the note on Minardil:

The sons of Kastamir and others of his kin, having fled from Gondor in 1447, set up a small kingdom in Umbar, and there made a fortified haven. They never ceased to make war upon Gondor, attacking its ships and coasts when they had opportunity. But they married women of the Harad and had in three generations lost most of their Númenórean blood; but they did not forget their feud with the house of Eldakar.

The entry in B then continues with the account (much fuller than that in Appendix A) of the slaying of Minardil at Pelargir, which was repeated almost exactly in C.

The names *Angomaitë* and *Sangahyanda* were changed to *Angamaitë* and *Sangahyando* in the Second Edition.

Telemnar, Tarondor, Telumehtar (p. 200) In B the text of these entries closely approached those in C; but most of the entry concerning Tarondor, including the account of the desertion of Osgiliath and the removal of the king's house to Minas Anor, was a later addition.

Narmakil II (p. 200) The note in A read: 'Battle with the Ringwraiths who seized Mordor. Osgiliath ceases to be the chief seat of the kings'. In B this was somewhat developed:

> At this time the Úlairi (or Ringwraiths) who had seized Mordor long before began to assail Ithilien. Narmakil was slain by the Sorcererking. Osgiliath ceased to be the seat of the kings.

This was roughly rewritten to read:

> In his time it is said that the Úlairi (or Ringwraiths) arose again and re-entered Mordor secretly. There they prepared in the darkness for the return of their Dark Lord. Men out of the East, a fierce people riding in great wains, came against Gondor, doubtless stirred up by Sauron and Úlairi. Narmakil slain in battle.

This was the first appearance of the Wainriders.

Kalimehtar (p. 200) The note in A recorded only that Kalimehtar 'built the White Tower of Minas Anor and removed his court thither'. B repeated this, and continued: 'Minas Anor becomes called Minas Tirith, since Minas Ithil is lost and becomes a stronghold of the Úlairi, and is called Minas Morgul.' This was struck out immediately, and the fall of Minas Ithil postponed to the time of King Ondohir; subsequently the entry was replaced by the following:

> Built the White Tower of Minas Anor. Continued war against the Wainriders, and defeated them before the Morannon.

The building of the White Tower by Kalimehtar is not referred to in Appendix A, but is recorded in the Tale of Years, Third Age 1900. – For Ostohir II who followed Kalimehtar in A and (before correction) in B see p. 212.

Ondohir (pp. 200–1) A has here a more substantial entry, though very largely concerned with the claim of Arvedui:

> His sons Faramir and Artamir were both slain in the war with Mordor. Minas Ithil fell and became Minas Morgul. In 1940 his daughter (third child), born 1896, wedded Arvedui (son of Araphant) last king of the North. Arvedui in 1944 claimed the Southern crown, but this was refused. There was a time without a king and the steward Pelendur governed. The claim of Arvedui lapsed with his death in battle in 1974, but though too weak ever to press their claim the descendants of Arvedui and Fíriel daughter of Ondohir, chieftains of the Dúnedain of the North, continued to

claim the Southern crown; though in fact it passed after an interregnum to Eärnil II, a descendant (great-grandson) of Narmakil II's
second son Kalimmakil.

The omission in the note of the death of Ondohir was a mere oversight
in rapid writing: he is marked as 'slain' in 1944. Ondohir's daughter
is here named *Fíriel*, as in B and C; the name *Ilmarë* in the rejected
page of B in the section on the Northern Line (p. 210, *Araphant*) can
then only be explained as a passing change of name. The fact that the
Northern kings Araphant and Arvedui are named in A (and the date
of Arvedui's death given) shows that work on the history of the Northern Line existed before the writing of B, the earliest extant text for that
part (see p. 188).

In B the entry for Ondohir, as first written, began thus:

War continued with the Úlairi. Minas Ithil fell and became a stronghold of the enemy, and was renamed Minas Morgul. Minas Anor
became Minas Tirith.

This followed the original entry in B under Narmakil II, in which the
assault of the Úlairi on Ithilien was recorded (before the entry into the
history of the Wainriders). The fall of Minas Ithil and the renaming
of the two cities was now moved on from its placing in the reign of
Kalimehtar (and thus returns to the text of A, given above).

The opening of B was subsequently struck out, apart from the first
sentence, which was corrected to 'War continued with the Wainriders',
as in C. The rest of the original entry in B records the fall of Ondohir
and his sons 'in battle in Ithilien' (which as written referred to battle
with the Ringwraiths, but which was subsequently extended to read 'in
battle in Ithilien against an alliance of the Wainriders and the Harad
that assailed eastern Gondor from north and south'), and then recounts
the claim of Arvedui, closely following A. The statements in A that
'there was a time without a king' when the Steward Pelendur governed,
and that the crown passed to Eärnil after an 'interregnum', were
retained but then struck out (see below under *Eärnil II*). There is thus
no mention in B of the great victory of Eärnil in South Ithilien followed
by his rout of the Wainriders, which led to his accession as king.

On the correction of *Ondohir* to *Ondonir* see p. 210, *Araphant*.

Eärnil II (p. 201) In A it is said only that he was 'son of Kiryandil
son of Siriondil son of Kalimmakil son of Narmakil II', and that he
came to the throne in 1960 (thus after an interregnum of sixteen
years). This was repeated without change in B, and allowed to stand,
although my father had rejected the references to an interregnum,
when Pelendur governed, in the entry for Ondohir. Kiryandil was later
removed, and Siriondil became the father of Eärnil. In all three texts
Kalimmakil was the son of Narmakil II, but in Appendix A (RK
p. 330) the son of Arciryas the brother of Narmakil.

Nothing further is said of Eärnil in B as originally written, but in an
addition the flight of the Sorcerer-king out of the North is recorded

(though without any mention of the great fleet from Gondor under Eärnil's son Eärnur which in large part brought about the destruction of Angmar), and the fall of Minas Ithil moves to its final place in the history:

> In his time the Sorcerer-king of Angmar, chief of the Úlairi, fled from the North and came to Mordor, and built up a new power. Under his leadership the Úlairi took Minas Ithil, and made it their city and stronghold, from which they were never expelled. S. Ithilien abandoned by Gondor, but a garrison holds the bridges of Osgiliath. Minas Ithil becomes called Minas Morgul, and Minas Anor is renamed Minas Tirith.

In C, as in Appendix A (RK p. 332), the renaming of Minas Anor took place in the time of Eärnur. – A further, later addition in B notes: 'The Nazgûl seize the Ithil-stone'.

Eärnur (p. 201)   This final note in A reads:

> The last king. He went to war with Minas Ithil and Mordor and never returned; nor was his body ever recovered. Some said he was carried off alive by the evil king. He left no children. No male descendants of clear title (or nearly pure blood) of Elendil could be discovered. Mardil the Steward, grandson of Pelendur, governed nominally 'until the King's return', and this became an habitual formula. There had been a tendency (but no rule) for the Stewardship to be hereditary or at least chosen from one family. It now became hereditary like a kingship.

Here the A text of the Southern Line ends. In B this note was repeated without change of substance, but continues after the words 'hereditary like a kingship':

> But the Stewards no longer took official names of Quenya form, and their names were all of Noldorin origin, that tongue still being used by the noble houses of Gondor.
>
> After the time of Eärnur the White Tree never [> seldom] again bore fruit, and ever its blossom grew less as it slowly died [> aged].

It is clear that the story of the challenge to Eärnur by the Lord of the Ringwraiths had not emerged. Later, the opening of the passage in B was rejected and the following substituted:

> He accepted the challenge [*added:* to fight for the *palantir* of Ithil?] of the Lord of the Úlairi and rode over the bridge of Osgiliath [> to the gates of Morgul] to meet him in single combat, but was betrayed and taken, and was never again seen by men.

The two challenges to Eärnur, and the restraint on the king exercised by Mardil the Steward, did not appear until the text C.

Elessar (p. 202)   The text in B is very close to its form in C, but lacks the reference to the continued waning of the life-span of the royal house. After the words 'and so restored the majesty and high blood of the royal house' B concludes:

Here ends the Red Book. But it was foretold that Eldarion the son of Elessar should rule a great realm, and it should endure for a hundred generations of men; and from him should come the kings of many realms in after days.

I have said (p. 190) that 'it is generally impossible to say how much of the matter that entered at each successive stage had newly arisen, and how much was present but at first ... held in abeyance.' Nonetheless, from this (inevitably complex) account of the development of the history of the kings of Gondor recorded in increasing detail through the texts, new elements can be seen emerging and becoming established, as the founding of the corsair-kingdom of Umbar, the invasions of the Wainriders, or the sending of the fleet from Gondor to assail Angmar.

The Stewards of Gondor

The earliest text recording the names and dates of the Stewards of Gondor is constituted by two pages attached to the manuscript A of the Southern Line. These pages were obviously written on continuously from the preceding section, but the text becomes very rapid and rough in its latter part and ends in a scrawl of confused dates.

For the C-text of the Stewards see pp. 202 ff. The B-text is headed: 'Appendix. The Stewards of Gondor', with a brief preamble:

These may be added, for though not in the direct line, the *Hurinionath*, the family to which Pelendur and Mardil belonged, were of Númenórean blood hardly less pure than that of the kings, and undoubtedly had some share in the actual blood of Elendil and Anárion.

To this was added later:

During all the days of the Stewards there was unceasing war between Minas Morgul and Minas Anor. Osgiliath was often taken and retaken. In North Ithilien a hardy folk still dwelt as borderers and defenders, but slowly they dwindled and departed west over the River.

The notes in B as originally written were few, and those mostly concerned (as in A) with individual Stewards as their lives and life-spans affected the nature of the succession. References to other events were in nearly all cases subsequent additions.

Pelendur   B has here, almost exactly following A: 'Became Steward 1940; ruled the realm during the interregnum 1944–1960, when he surrendered authority to Eärnil II.' On this see *Eärnil II*, p. 216. That Pelendur did become briefly the ruler of Gondor is not stated in C (as it is in Appendix A, RK p. 319), but that there was an interregnum for a year is implied by the revised dating (Ondohir slain in 1944, Eärnil's accession in 1945).

Vorondil   There is no note on Vorondil in A and B. With the addition in C cf. the chapter *Minas Tirith*, RK p. 27, where it is not said (though no doubt implied) that Vorondil was the actual maker of the horn last borne by Boromir: 'since Vorondil father of Mardil hunted the wild kine of Araw in the far fields of Rhûn' (on this passage see VIII.281 and note 14).

Mardil Voronwë A has a note here, which was not repeated in B, 'After his time the names are usually Noldorin not Quenya. Few are left who know Quenya.' Cf. Appendix A (RK p. 319): 'His successors ceased to use High-elven names.'

Belegorn In A the name of the fourth Ruling Steward was *Bardhan*, later changed to *Belgorn*; *Belegorn* in B.

Túrin I The same note is present in all three texts.

Hador In A the name of the seventh Ruling Steward was *Cirion*, and *Hador* that of the twelfth; this was retained in B, but the names were later reversed. A has simply 'lived to great age 150'; B is as C, but the note ends 'the life-span of the nobles is waning steadily.'

Dior In A and B the same is said as in C, but Dior's sister (*Rían* in C) is not named.

Denethor I The note in A reads: 'Great troubles arose. Enemy destroyed Osgiliath. Boromir son (third child) of the Steward defeats them, and for a time recovers Ithilien.' B repeated this, but the text was altered to read: 'Enemy overran all Ithilien and destroyed the bridges of Osgiliath.'

Boromir A has: 'Death hastened by wounds got in the war'; B: 'His life was shortened by wounds received from the poisoned weapons of Morgul.'

Cirion In neither A nor B was there a note following Cirion (first written *Hador*), but the following was added in B: 'War with Orcs and Easterlings. Battle of Celebrant' (with the date 2510 put in subsequently), and also:

> Sauron stirs up mischief, and there is a great attack on Gondor. Orcs pour out of the Mountains and of Mirkwood and join with Easterlings. Hador [> Cirion] gets help from the North. Eorl the Young wins the victory of the Field of Celebrant and is given Calenardon or Rohan.

Since the mentions of the Field of Celebrant in the narrative of *The Lord of the Rings* were all late additions (see e.g. IX.72, note 16) it may be that the story was evolving at the time of the writing of *The Heirs of Elendil*.

Ecthelion I A's note here makes Egalmoth, successor of the childless Ecthelion, the grandson of Morwen sister of Belecthor I. This introduces a generation too many, and was obviously due to the mention of Egalmoth under his predecessor Ecthelion – a testimony to the rapidity with which my father sketched out the dates and relations of the later Stewards in this earliest text. In B Morwen becomes the sister of Orodreth, Ecthelion's father.

Egalmoth   In B a note was added (repeated in C): 'Orc-wars break out'. This is referred to in the Tale of Years in Appendix B: '2740 Orcs renew their invasions of Eriador.' A later pencilled note in B says 'Dwarf and Orc war in Misty Mountains' (see under *Beregond* below).

Beren   There was no note in B, but these were added: 'Long winter 2758', and 'In his reign there is an attack on Gondor by [Pirates >] Corsairs of Umbar [2758 >] 2757'.

Beregond   In A and B his name was *Baragond*, with the note that he was the third child of Beren. A pencilled note in B repeats the notice of the War of the Dwarves and the Orcs from the entry under Egalmoth, with the date '2766–'.

The Stewards from Belecthor II to Ecthelion II   By this point A has become no more than a working-out of dates; and the brief notes in B can be collected together. That to Belecthor II is the same as in C but without mention of the death of the White Tree; that to Túrin II is 'Bilbo was born in the Shire during his rule'; and that to Turgon is 'Aragorn born in Eriador during his rule'. Very rough and hasty additions were made later in preparation for the much fuller notes in C.

The statement in C under Ecthelion II that 'Aragorn of the North serves as a soldier in his forces' is the first mention of Aragorn's years of service in disguise in Rohan and Gondor.

Denethor II   B has only a statement of dates and relationships, including that of Denethor's marriage to Finduilas daughter of Adrahil of Dol Amroth: this is seen in A (where the father of Finduilas is named *Agrahil*) at the moment of its emergence.

Faramir   The note in B is the same in substance as that in C, but adds that as the Prince of Ithilien he 'dwelt in a fair new house in the Hills of Emyn Arnen, whose gardens devised by the Elf Legolas were renowned.'

The Line of Dol Amroth

Arising from the reference to Denethor's marriage to Finduilas, at the foot of the last page of the B manuscript my father began working out the genealogy of the descendants of Adrahil of Dol Amroth; and a carefully made table beginning with Angelimir the twentieth prince was attached by my father to the manuscript C of *The Heirs of Elendil*. This I have redrawn on p. 221 (the Princes are marked with crosses as in the original). Beneath the table is a note on the origins of the house of Dol Amroth, telling that Galador the first lord was the son of Imrazôr the Númenórean, who dwelt in Belfalas, and Mith-

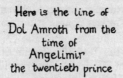

Here is the line of
Dol Amroth from the
time of
Angelimir
the twentieth prince

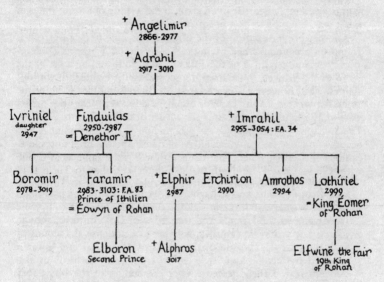

⁺Angelimir
2866-2977

⁺Adrahil
2917-3010

Ivriniel
daughter
2947

Finduilas
2950-2987
=Denethor II

⁺Imrahil
2955-3054 : F.A. 34

Boromir
2978-3019

Faramir
2983-3103: F.A. 83
Prince of Ithilien
=Éowyn of Rohan

⁺Elphir
2987

Erchirion
2990

Amrothos
2994

Lothíriel
2999
=King Éomer
of Rohan

Elboron
Second Prince

⁺Alphros
3017

Elfwine the Fair
19th King
of Rohan

In the tradition of his house *Angelimir* was the twentieth in unbroken descent from *Galador* first Lord of Dol Amroth (c. T.A. 2004-2129). According to the same traditions *Galador* was the son of *Imrazôr* the Númenórean who dwelt in *Belfalas*, and the Elven-lady *Mithrellas*. She was one of the companions of *Nimrodel*, among many of the Elves of *Lórien* that fled to the coast about T.A. 1980, when evil arose in *Moria*; and *Nimrodel* and her maidens strayed in the wooded hills, and were lost But in this tale it is said that *Imrazôr* harboured *Mithrellas*, and took her to wife But when she had borne him a son, *Galador*, and a daughter, *Gilmith*, she slipped away by night, and he saw her no more. But though *Mithrellas* was of the lesser silvan race (and not of the High Elves or the Grey) it was ever held that the house and kin of the Lords of Dol Amroth were noble by blood, as they were fair in face and mind.

rellas one of the companions of Nimrodel. This note is printed in *Unfinished Tales*, p. 248, with the unaccountable error of *Angelimar* for *Angelimir* (an editorial mistake, since it occurs twice in the text and again in the index).

The page obviously belongs with the writing of C to which it is attached, since on the reverse are the first entries for the Southern Line in exactly the same form as they appear in the text, but abandoned, as it appears, simply because of an error in the writing out of the dates in what was designed to be a fine manuscript.

Another briefer account of the origin of the Line of Dol Amroth is found on a page attached by my father to the (as I believe, contemporary) manuscript T 4 of the Tale of Years, followed by a list of the dates of the Princes, those from the second to the eighteenth without names. This, however, is much later; for there is another form of the same list written on the back of a college document from the earlier part of 1954, and this is plainly the earlier of the two (see p. 223).

The House of Dol Amroth

Amroth brother of Celeborn flies from northern Lórien when the Balrog drives out the Dwarves about 1980 T.A.

Mithrellas, one of the companions of Nimrodel, is lost in the woods of Belfalas, and is harboured by Imrazôr the Númenórean [*added in margin*: Imrazôr 1950–2076], who takes her to wife (according to the legends and traditions of Dol Amroth); though after a few years she vanishes, whether to wander in the woods or seek the havens. The son of the union of Mithrellas and Imrazôr received the elven-name of Galador; from him the lords of Dol Amroth traced their descent. After the ending of the kings they became virtually independent princes, ruling over Belfalas, but they were at all times loyal to the Steward as representing the ancient crown.

1	Galador	2004–2129	(125)	
2	...	2060–2203	(143)	
3	...	2120–2254	(134)	
4	...	2172–2299	(127)	
5	...	2225–2348	(123)	
6	...	2274–2400	(126)	
7	...	2324–2458	(134)	
8	...	2373–2498	(125)	
9	...	2418–2540	(122)	
10	...	2463–2582	(119)	
11	...	2505–2623	(118)	
12	...	2546–2660	(114)	
13	...	2588–2701	(113)	
14	...	2627–2733	(106)	
15	...	2671–†2746	(75)	slain by Corsairs of Umbar

16	...	2709–†2799	([90]) slain in battle
17	...	2746–2859	(113)
18	...	2785–2899	(114)
19	Aglahad	2827–2932	(105)
20	Angelimir	2866–2977	(111)
21	Adrahil	2917–3010	(93)
22	Imrahil	2955–3054	(99)
23	Elphir	2987–(3087 =) F.A.57	(100)
24	Alphros	3017–(3115 =) F.A.95	(98)

In contrast to this carefully written page, the other form of this list (that written on the back of the document of 1954) has a scrawled note at its head, the same as that in the text just given but extending only to the words 'harboured by Imrazôr the Númenórean, who weds her'; and the dates are written in pencil, with some corrections. Imrazôr is numbered 1, so that Angelimir is the twenty-first prince; but this was corrected. The life-span of the sixteenth prince was given as 91 years instead of 90, and my father followed this in the second text; and where the second text has 'slain in battle' the first has 'Battle with Orcs'.

The statement here that Amroth was the brother of Celeborn appears to be unique (for other accounts of him see *The History of Galadriel and Celeborn* in *Unfinished Tales*: but all the material concerning Amroth collected there comes from after, much of it long after, the publication of *The Lord of the Rings*). On both forms of the present text the words were struck out, and on the second my father pencilled 'was a Sinda from Beleriand'. With the time of Amroth's flight from Lórien cf. the entry for 1981 in Appendix B: 'The Dwarves flee from Moria. Many of the Silvan Elves of Lórien flee south. Amroth and Nimrodel are lost'; also *Unfinished Tales* pp. 240, 245.

No events are recorded elsewhere in the years 2746 and 2799 that cast light on the deaths in battle of the fifteenth and sixteenth Princes of Dol Amroth.

The dates of the deaths of Prince Imrahil and of Faramir Prince of Ithilien in the genealogy redrawn on p. 221 (3054 = Fourth Age 34, and 3103 = F.A.83) place the beginning of the Fourth Age in 3021; similarly in the list of the princes given above the dates of the deaths of Elphir and Alphros, 3087 and 3115, and equated with F.A.67 and 95. In text C of *The Heirs of Elendil* the Fourth Age began in 3022, and in text B the Third Age ended in 3019 (see pp. 196, 211).

The Princes Aglahad, Angelimir, Elphir, and Alphros are only recorded in these texts, as also are other members of the line of Dol Amroth in the genealogical table, Ivriniel, Erchirion, and Amrothos. Faramir's son Elboron likewise only appears in this genealogy. In him an old name reappears: Elboron and Elbereth were the original names of the young sons of Dior Thingol's Heir who were murdered by the followers of Maidros (IV.307, V.142). Later the sons of Elrond were named Elboron and Elbereth, before they became Elladan and Elrohir (VIII.297, 301, 370).

The further development of Appendix A is postponed to Chapter IX.

VIII

THE TALE OF YEARS OF
THE THIRD AGE

The earliest text of the Tale of Years of the Third Age is a brief manuscript apparently closely associated with the very early form of that of
the Second Age which I have called T 2 (see pp. 168–70); and although
they are separate texts and not continuous it is convenient to refer to
this likewise as T 2.

Though subsequently covered with somewhat haphazard accretions, for the most part obviously associated with work on the
chronology of the Realms in Exile, it is possible to extricate with fair
certainty the text of T 2 as originally set down, and I give it in this
form here.

Of the History of the Third Age
little is known

0   If we reckon from the death of Isildur.

Years of Third Age

1000–   Sauron wakes again, and enters Mirkwood. Establishes a stronghold at Dol Dûgul[1] and slowly grows.

c.1100   Deagol finds the One Ring and is slain by Smeagol.[2]
Smeagol becomes Gollum.

c.1105   Gollum enters eaves of Misty Mountains.

c.1300   The people of Smeagol grow and begin to multiply.
They cross the Misty Mountains and journey westward. They become Hobbits.[3] Orcs begin to reappear.

c.1500   Hobbits settle at Bree.

c.1600   (S.R.1)[4] Marco and Cavallo cross the Baranduin
(Brandywine) and are given 'the Shire' to live in by the
king at Northworthy[5] (Fornost). 'Shire-reckoning'
begins.

c.1900   Last 'king at Northworthy'. The Dúnedain or Rangers
(last of the Númenóreans in the North) wander in the
wild; but the heirs of the kings live at Imladris (Rivendell) with Elrond.

c.2000   The line of the Kings of Gondor becomes extinct with
death of Eärnur.[6] The Line of the Stewards begins with
Mardil the Good Steward.

c.2500   Elrond who had never before been wed, wedded Cele-
          brían daughter of Galadriel of Lórien.[7] His children
          were Elrohir and Elladan and a daughter Finduilas[8]
          in whom the likeness of Lúthien reappeared. These
          children are of men's stature but Elven-blood.[9]
c.2600   Celebrían is slain by Orcs on the road over the Moun-
          tains to visit Galadriel.
c.2620   Isengrim Took the First establishes the Took family in
          the Shire.
c.2890   Bilbo born.
  2910   Aragorn son of Arathorn heir of Isildur born.
  2940   Bilbo goes on his adventures.
  2950   Sauron re-enters Mordor.
  3001   Bilbo's Farewell Party.
  3018   Frodo sets out.

Whatever may have been the reasons for the selection of these particular events, it is striking that there are no entries referring to the
history of Arnor and Gondor except those to the last king in the North
and to the last king in the South (Eärnur), with the beginning of the
line of Stewards; and the dates of these entries show that this text
preceded the earliest extant forms of *The Heirs of Elendil*.

The next version was the manuscript T 3 (see p. 172), which in the
part of it treating the Second Age, as I have said, was 'little more than
a copy of T 2, with a number of entries expanded'. This is not at all
the case, however, with the Third Age. It was here that my father introduced a comprehensive and coherent chronology of the Age, and set
his course, in this work that he called 'the Tale of Years', in a direction
remarkably unlike its ultimate appearance in Appendix B to *The Lord
of the Rings*. That it was closely associated with *The Heirs of Elendil*
is very plain. The manuscript was covered with alterations, expansions and additions, and became a working draft for the major
text T 4 which I have no doubt soon followed it.

As will be seen subsequently, T 4 was and remained for a long time
the form of the Tale of Years that my father thought appropriate, and
was indeed proposed to the publishers in 1954. I shall here pass over
the text T 3, though with some reference to it in the notes at the end
of the chapter, and give that of T 4 in its entirety.

This is a very clear manuscript with a notable lack of hesitation or
second thoughts. That it was intended to be a final and publishable
text is shown also by the fact that, when my father came to the conclusion that the establishment of the White Council was placed four
hundred years too early, he rejected two pages and wrote two new
ones in such a way that they fitted precisely into the original text. I give
it here as it was written, say in the years 1949–50 (as I believe), but

with the text of the substituted pages, since it seems probable that they were written before the manuscript was completed, or at any rate soon after. It was a good deal altered later, chiefly with respect to certain matters: the migrations of the Stoors; the machinations of Saruman; and the movements of Gollum. I have not included any revisions in the text, but give an account of them at the end of the chapter (p. 250).

The opening statement concerning the Four Ages, and the entries for the Second Age, have been given on pp. 172–7.

The Third Age

These were the Fading Years. Of this Age in its beginnings little is now known, save for the traditions of the realm of Gondor. For a thousand years and more the Eldar in Middle-earth, protected by the Three Rings, were content and at peace, while Sauron slept; but they attempted no great deeds, and made no new things of wonder, living mostly in memory of the past. In all this time the things of old were slowly fading, and new things were stirring, though few observed the signs.

The Dwarves became ever more secretive, and hid themselves in deep places, guarding their hoards from their chief enemies, the dragons and the Orcs. One by one their ancient treasuries were plundered, and they became a wandering and dwindling people. In Moria the Dwarves of the race of Durin long held out, but this people once numerous steadily waned, until their vast mansions became dark and empty.

The might and lore and the life-span of the Númenóreans (or Dúnedain as they were called by the Elves) also waned as the years passed and their blood became mingled with that of lesser Men.[10] More swift was the waning in the North-kingdom, for the lands of Eriador, as that region was now called, became colder and less friendly to Men in that time. There the Dúnedain became ever less. After the days of Eärendur[11] of Arnor the North-kingdom became divided into petty realms, and the Heirs of Isildur of the direct line ruled only over Arthedain in the far North-west. In Gondor the power of the kings of Anárion's line endured longer, and their sway extended over many lands of Men; but there was little coming and going between the realms except in times of need.

1 Ohtar Isildur's esquire escapes with two other men only from the slaughter of the Gladden Fields.[12] He brings the shards of Elendil's sword, Narsil, which Isildur had saved, and delivers it to Valandil Isildur's son

in Imladris. Valandil was a child, fourth son of Isildur. His brothers perished with their father.

10   Valandil Isildur's son becomes King of Arnor and dwells at Annúminas.

420–30   Ostohir King of Gondor rebuilds and enlarges Minas Anor.

490   First invasion of Gondor by Easterlings.

500   Tarostar defeats the Easterlings and takes the name of Rómendakil, East-slayer.

541   Rómendakil slain in battle with a second invasion of Easterlings, who are driven out by his son Turambar.

861   Death of Eärendur last and tenth king of Arnor. The North-kingdom becomes divided among Eärendur's sons. The direct line of the eldest son, Amlaith of Fornost, rules the realm of Arthedain. Annúminas is deserted. The other realms were Cardolan (where later was Bree and the Barrowdowns) and Rhudaur, north of the River Baranduin. From this time the official names of the kings at Fornost were no longer given in High-elven form, but in Noldorin. Amlaith and his descendants maintained friendship with the Eldar, especially with Cirdan at the Havens.[13]

c.1000   About this time the *Istari*, that is the Wise Men or wizards, appeared in the westlands of Middle-earth. It was not known whence they came (unless to Cirdan and Elrond). But afterwards, when it was revealed that the shadow of Sauron had first begun to take new shape at this same time, it was said by many that they came out of the Far West, and were messengers sent to contest the power of Sauron, if he should arise again, and to move all good folk and kindly creatures to resist him.

The Wizards appeared nonetheless in the likeness of Men, and resembled Men in most things, save that they were never young and aged but slowly, and had many powers of mind and hand. For long they journeyed far and wide among Elves and Men and all speaking-folk, and held converse also with beasts and birds. They did not reveal their true names, but used those that the peoples of Middle-earth gave to them, and they were many. The chief of this order were the two whom the Eldar called Mithrandir and Curunír, but Men in the North named Gandalf and Saruman. Of them Mithrandir was closest in counsel with the Eldar and with Elrond; he wandered far in the North and West and never made for himself any lasting abode. But Curunír journeyed often far into the East, and when he returned he dwelt at Orthanc in the Ring of Isengard.[14]

About this time also the *Periannath*, of whom there are no earlier accounts among Elves or Men, are first mentioned in ancient tales. These were a strange small people, called by Men[15] Halflings, but by themselves (later in the west of Eriador) Hobbits. They are thought to have long dwelt in Greenwood the Great or near its western eaves, and in the vale of the upper Anduin. But at this time they began to move westward over the Misty Mountains into Eriador. It is said that they moved from their earlier dwellings because Men increased much at that time; and because a shadow fell on Greenwood, and it became darkened, and was called Mirkwood, for an evil spirit stirred there.[16] The Harfoots were the first clan of Hobbits to enter Eriador.[17]

c.1100 It becomes known to the Wise (being the chieftains of the Eldar and the Istari) that an evil power had arisen in Mirkwood and had established a stronghold on the hill of Dol Guldur in the southern forest. But it was still some time before they knew for certain that this was the shadow of Sauron himself and that he was awake again.

c.1150 The Fallohides, a clan of the Periannath, crossed into Eriador and came down from the North along the River Hoarwell. About the same time the Stoors, another clan, came over the Redhorn Pass and moved south towards Dunland.[18]

c.1200 Under Atanatar the Glorious Gondor reaches the height of its power, and its sway extends from the Greyflood in the West to the Sea of Rhúnaer in the East, and from the south-eaves of Mirkwood in the North to the land of the Haradrim in the South. The Haradrim acknowledge the overlordship of Gondor for many years.

c.1300 The western Periannath, now for the most part mingled together, move westward from the region of Amon Sûl (Weathertop), and begin to make small settlements among the remnants of the peoples of the old North-kingdom. Their chief settlement was on and about the Hill of Bree.

c.1350   Evil things begin to multiply again. Orcs increase rapidly and delve in the Misty Mountains, and attack the Dwarves. The Ringwraiths stir once more. The chief of these, the wielders of the Nine Rings, becomes the Witch-king of the realm of Angmar in the North beyond Arnor, and makes war on the remnants of the Dúnedain.

1356   Argeleb king at Fornost is slain in battle with the realms of Cardolan and Rhudaur, which resist his claim to overlordship.

c.1400   About this time, owing to dissensions and to the unfriendliness of the lands and clime of eastern Eriador, some of the Stoors return to Wilderland and dwell beside the R. Gladden that flows into Anduin. They become a riverside people, fishers and users of small boats. Others of the Stoors move north and west and join with the Harfoots and Fallohides.

1409   The Witch-king of Angmar taking advantage of the civil war among the Dúnedain comes out of the North and overwhelms the petty realms of Cardolan and Rhudaur and destroys the remnants of the Númenóreans that dwelt there. Cardolan is forsaken. The deserted mounds of Cardolan become filled with deadly spirits; but in Rhudaur for long there dwelt an evil people out of the North, much given to sorcery. The Men of Bree and the Periannath of the same region maintain their independence.

In this year 1409 King Arveleg I of Fornost was slain in battle by the Witch-king, but the Heirs of Isildur still hold out at Fornost with aid from Lindon. Arveleg is succeeded by Araphor.

In this war the Palantír of Amon Sûl was destroyed. Help did not come from the South-kingdom for their peace also was troubled by dissensions. King Valakar took to wife the daughter of an alien king of the Northmen of Anduin, with whom Gondor had sought alliance and aid in their war with the Easterlings. No king or heir to the throne of Gondor had before done such a thing.

1432   War of the Kin-strife breaks out in Gondor. Valakar dies and the succession of his son, half of alien blood, is contested by other descendants of Atanatar the Glorious. The war lasts till 1447. Kastamir who had driven out Valakar's son Eldakar was ejected by Eldakar and slain. The sons of Kastamir flee from Gondor and set up a pirate fortress at Umbar, and remain at war with the king.

1601 (S.R.1)[19]   A host of Periannath migrates from Bree westward, and crosses the R. Baranduin (Brandywine). The land beyond, between the Baranduin and Emyn Beraid, had been a demesne of the Kings of Arnor, where they had both chases and rich farms; but they were now untended and falling into wilderness. The king Argeleb II therefore allowed the Periannath to settle there, for they were good husbandmen.[20] They became his subjects in name but were virtually independent and ruled by their own chieftains. Their numbers were swelled by Stoors that came up from southern Eriador and entered the land from the south and dwelt mostly near to the Baranduin. This land the Periannath or Halflings called 'The Shire'. Shire-reckoning begins with the crossing of the Baranduin in this year.

1634   The Corsairs of Umbar slew King Minardil and ravaged Pelargir. They were led by Angomaitë and Sangahyanda grandsons of Kastamir.[21]

1636   A great plague comes out of the East, and devastates Gondor. King Telemnar and all his children died. The White Tree of Isildur in Minas Anor withered and died. The power of Gondor dwindles.

1640   King Tarondor removed the king's house to Minas Anor. He planted there again a seedling of the White Tree. Osgiliath becomes deserted owing to the fewness of the people, and begins to fall into ruin. The watch on Mordor is relaxed, and the fortresses at the passes become empty.

    The plague spreads north and west, and wide regions of Eriador become desolate. But the virulence of the plague decreases as it passes west and the Periannath in the Shire suffer little loss.[22]

c.1700   Mordor being now left unguarded evil things enter in again and take up their abode there secretly. Communication between the North and South kingdoms ceases for a long while.

1850   Assault of the Wainriders out of the East upon Gondor. War lasts for many years.

1900   Kalimehtar of Gondor builds the White Tower in Minas Anor.

1940   Messengers pass between the two kingdoms, since both are in peril: the South from the Wainriders of the East, and the North from renewed attacks of Angmar. Arvedui heir of Araphant of Arthedain weds Fíriel, the daughter of King Ondohir of Gondor.

1944   Ondohir with both his sons, Faramir and Artamir, slain in battle against a great alliance of the Wainriders and the Men of Harad. Arvedui of the North claims the southern crown, both on his wife's behalf and on his own as representing 'the elder line of Isildur'. The claim is refused by Gondor and lapses with the death of Arvedui; but all his descendants, though too weak to press their claim, continue to maintain that they are also by rights kings of Gondor, being descended both from Isildur and Anárion (through Fíriel).

1960   Pelendur the king's steward for a time ruled Gondor, but after a while Eärnil, descendant of a previous king, receives the crown.[23]

1974   End of the North-kingdom. The Witch-king destroys Fornost, lays the land waste, and scatters the remnants of the Dúnedain. Arvedui flies north taking the Palantíri (the two that remain). He attempts to escape by ship to Gondor from Forochel, but is lost at sea, and the Stones disappear. His sons take refuge with Cirdan.[24]

1975   Cirdan of Lune and Elrond, with belated help sent by sea from King Eärnil, defeat Angmar. The Witch-king is overthrown and his realm destroyed. He flies south and comes at last to Mordor.

1976   Aranarth son of Arvedui takes refuge with Elrond at Imladris. He abandons the title of 'king', since he now has no people, but the chieftains of the Dúnedain descended from him continue to bear names with the royal prefix Ar, Ara. The Periannath sent archers to the Battle of Fornost, but after the end of the kingdom they claim the Shire as their own. They elect a Thain to take the place of the king.[25] According to their tradition the first independent Shire-thain was one Bucca of the Marish, from whom later the Oldbuck family claimed descent. The beginning of his office dated from S.R.379.

1980–2000 The Witch-king gathers the other eight Ring-wraiths to him and they issue from Mordor, and folk flee from Ithilien in terror. The Úlairi captured Minas Ithil and made it their stronghold, from which they were not again expelled while the Third Age lasted. The Palantír of Minas Ithil is captured. Minas Ithil is re-named Minas Morgul (Tower of Sorcery), and Minas Anor is called Minas Tirith (the Tower of Guard).

About this time also other evil things were roused. A terror of the Elder Days, a Balrog of Thangorodrim, appeared in Moria. Some say that the Dwarves delving too deep in their search for *mithril* or true-silver disturbed this evil creature from its sleep far under the world. The remnants of Durin's folk are slain by the Balrog or driven out of Moria. Many of them wandered into the far North, as far as the Grey Mountains or the Iron Hills.

c.2000 Curunír (Saruman), returning out of the East, takes up his abode in the Tower of Orthanc in the Ring of Isengard.[26] This had been an ancient stronghold of Gondor, guarding their north-west frontier, but the northern parts of the realm were now largely empty and King Eärnil was glad to have the aid of Curunír against the Ringwraiths, and gave Isengard to him for his own.

About this time it is thought that Déagol the Stoor found the Ring in Anduin near the Gladden Fields where Isildur was slain as he swam. Déagol was murdered by his friend Sméagol, who took the Ring.

c.2010? Sméagol, now called Gollum, is cast out by his own people, and hides in the Misty Mountains. He vanishes out of all knowledge taking the Ring with him.[27]

2043 Death of King Eärnil. His son Eärnur (the Last King of Gondor in that Age) comes to the throne. The Lord of the Ringwraiths challenged him to battle.

2050 Against the counsel of Mardil his Steward King Eärnur accepts the renewed challenge of the Lord of Morgul to single combat. He rides to the gates of Minas Morgul, but he was betrayed and taken and never again seen by mortal men. Eärnur left no children. No male descendants (of clear title or nearly pure blood) of Anárion could be discovered. Mardil the good Steward governed the realm, nominally 'until the King's return'. For a long time previously the stewardship had usually been held by a member of the same family (one of nearly pure Númenórean descent). It now became hereditary in that family like a kingship. But each Steward took office with the formula 'to hold the rule and rod until the King's return'; and they did not take official names of Quenya or High-elven form. Their names were mostly of Noldorin kind, that tongue being still used by those descended from the Elf-friends of Númenor.

After the disappearance of Eärnur and the ending of the kings the White Tree seldom again bore fruit, and each year its blossom grew less as it slowly aged.

2060   The fear of the Ringwraiths, or Úlairi, spreads far and wide. The Elves deem that the Power in Dol Guldur is one of these; but in the hearts of Elrond and Gandalf the fear grows that the darkness in Mirkwood should prove to be the shadow of Sauron himself awakening.[28]

2063   Gandalf goes alone to Dol Guldur in secret, to discover the truth concerning the Sorcerer. But the Sorcerer is aware of him; and being not yet grown to great power, he fears the eyes of Gandalf, and the strength of the Wise, and he deserts Dol Guldur and hides in the East again for a while.

Here begins a time that is called the Watchful Peace. For there was a long quiet, but no certainty. During that time the Ringwraiths never again appeared in visible shape beyond the walls of Minas Morgul; but the Wise were in doubt what should yet come to pass, and Gandalf made great journeys to discover the plans and devices of their enemies.

2300   Elrond, who had remained unwed through all his long years, now took to wife Celebrían, daughter of Galadriel and Celeborn of Lórien. His children were the twin brethren, Elladan and Elrohir, and Arwen Undómiel, the fairest of all the maidens of the Third Age, in whom the likeness of Lúthien her foremother returned to Middle-earth. These children were three parts of Elven-race, but the doom spoken at their birth was that they should live even as the Elves so long as their father remained in Middle-earth; but if he departed they should have then the choice either to pass over the

Sea with him, or to become mortal, if they remained behind.

2340   Isumbras I, head of the Took family in the Shire, becomes thirteenth Thain, the first of the Took line.[29] After his day the office became hereditary in the family of the Tooks of the Great Smials. About this time the Oldbucks occupied the Buckland, east of the River Brandywine and on the edge of the Old Forest.

2349   Birth of Elladan and Elrohir, sons of Elrond, in Imladris.[30]

2349   Birth of Arwen Undómiel.

2460   After a space of nearly four hundred years the Watchful Peace ends, and the powers of evil move again. The Sorcerer returns to Dol Guldur with increased strength, and gathers all evil things under his rule.

2463   The White Council is formed to unite and direct the forces of the West, in resistance to the shadow. Curunír (or Saruman the White) is chosen to be the head of the Council, since he has studied all the arts and ways of Sauron and his servants most deeply. Galadriel of Lórien wishes Gandalf to be made chief, but he refuses. Saruman begins his study of the Rings of Power and their uses and history.

2475   The attack upon Gondor is begun again with new vigour, in the days of Denethor I, son of Dior,[31] the tenth Steward. His son Boromir defeats the enemy before East Osgiliath, but Osgiliath is finally ruined in this war, and the ancient and marvellous stone-bridge is broken. The Men of Gondor still maintain their hold upon Ithilien, but little by little its people desert it and pass west over Anduin to the valleys of the White Mountains.

2480 onwards   Orcs again multiply in secret and occupy many deep places (especially those anciently made by the Dwarves) in the Misty Mountains. They do this so stealthily that none are aware of it, until they have great forces hidden and are ready to bar all the passes from Eriador into Anduin's vales, according to the plan of their master in Dol Guldur. Orcs and Trolls occupy parts of the now empty Mines of Moria.

2509   Celebrían, wife of Elrond, journeys to Lórien to visit Galadriel, her mother; but she is taken by Orcs in the passes of the mountains. She is rescued by Elrond and his sons, but after fear and torment she is no longer willing to remain in Middle-earth, and she departs to the Grey Havens and sails over Sea.[32]

2510   A great host of Orcs, with Easterlings as allies, assail the northern borders of Gondor, and occupy a great part of Calenardon. Gondor sends for help. Eorl the Young leads his people, the Éothéod or Rohirrim, out of the North from the sources of Anduin, and rides to the help of Cirion, Steward of Gondor. With his aid the great victory of the Field of Celebrant is won. Elladan and Elrohir rode also in that battle. From that time forth the brethren never cease from war with the Orcs because of Celebrían. Eorl and his people are given the plains of Calenardon to dwell in, and that land is now called *Rochann* (Rohan). There the Rohirrim live as free men under their own kings, but in perpetual alliance with Minas Tirith.

2569   The Golden Hall of Meduseld is built by Brego son of Eorl.

2570   Baldor son of Brego takes a rash vow to enter the Forbidden Door in Dunharrow, and is never seen again.

2590   Thrór the Dwarf (of Dúrin's race) founds the realm of Erebor (the Lonely Mountain), and becomes 'King under the Mountain'.[33] He lives in friendship with the Men of Dale, who are nearly akin to the Rohirrim.

2620   Isengrim II, tenth Thain of the Took-line, born in the Shire.

2698   Ecthelion I, Steward of Gondor, repairs and rebuilds the White Tower of Minas Tirith, afterwards often called the Tower of Ecthelion.[34]

2740–   Wars with the Orcs break out again.

2747   Orcs passing far to the north raid down into Eriador. A large force invades the Shire. Bandobras Took, second son of Isumbras III, defeats them at the Battle of the Greenfields in the Northfarthing and slays the Orc-chief Golfimbul. This was the last battle in which Hobbits (Periannath) were engaged until the end of the Third Age.

2757   Rohan is overrun by Orcs and Easterlings. At the same time Gondor is attacked by the Corsairs of Umbar.

2758–9   The Long Winter. Helm of Rohan takes refuge from his enemies in Helm's Deep in the White Mountains.

2763   New line of kings in Rohan is begun with Fréaláf Hildeson (sister-son of Helm). The second row of King's Mounds is begun.

2765   Smaug the Dragon descends on Erebor and destroys the realm of Thrór the Dwarf, and lays waste the town and lordship of Dale. Thrór and his son Thráin escape with a few only of their people.

2766   Thrór the Dwarf, descendant of Durin, being now homeless and robbed of his treasure, ventures into Moria, but is slain by an Orc in the dark. Thráin and Thorin escape. In vengeance for Thrór and in hope of re-establishing a kingdom the scattered Dwarves of Durin's race gather together out of the North and make war on the Orcs of the Misty Mountains. The War of the Dwarves and Orcs was long and terrible and fought largely in the dark in deep places.

2769   The War of Orcs and Dwarves comes to an end in a great battle before the East-gate of Moria: the Battle of the Dimrill Dale (Nanduhirion). The Orcs were almost annihilated, and Moria is once more emptied, but the Dwarves also lost very heavily and were too few at the end to reoccupy Moria or face the hidden terror. Dáin returns to the Iron Hills; but Thráin and Thorin become wanderers.[35]

2790   Birth of Gerontius Took: later the fourteenth Thain,[36] and known as 'the Old Took' because of his great age (he lived to be 130 years old).

2850   Gandalf visits Dol Guldur again to discover the purposes of the Sorcerer. He finds there Thráin the Dwarf son of Thrór and receives from him the secret key of Erebor. Thráin had come thither seeking for one of the Seven Rings; but he dies in Dol Guldur.[37] Gandalf discovers beyond doubt that the Sorcerer is none other than Sauron himself, and that he is gathering again all the Rings of Power, and seeking to learn the fate of the One, and the dwelling of Isildur's Heirs.

2851   Gandalf urges the White Council to assail Dol Guldur, but he is overruled by Saruman. For Saruman has begun to lust for power and desires himself to discover the One Ring. He thinks that it will come to light again, seeking its Master, if Sauron is let be for a while. He does not reveal his thought to the Council, but feigns that his studies have led him to believe that the Ring has been rolled down Anduin and into the deeps of the Sea. But Saruman himself keeps a watch upon Anduin and the Gladden Fields and he fortifies Isengard.

2872 Belecthor II, twenty-first Steward of Gondor, dies.[38] The White Tree dies in the court of Minas Tirith. No seedling can be found. The dead tree is left standing in the court under the White Tower.

c.2880 Ithilien becomes desolate and untilled and the remnant of its people remove west over Anduin to Lossarnach and Lebennin. But the Men of Minas Tirith still hold Ithilien as a border country and patrol it; they keep forces in the ruins of Osgiliath and in secret places in Ithilien.[39]

2885 In the days of Túrin II, twenty-third Steward, the Haradrim attack Gondor and ravage South Ithilien. The Rohirrim send help. Folcred and Fastred sons of King Folcwine of Rohan fall in battle in the service of Gondor.

2891 Bilbo born in the Shire (his mother was a daughter of the Old Took).

2911 The Fell Winter. White Wolves invade the Shire over the frozen Brandywine River. About this time Saruman discovers that Sauron's servants are also searching the Great River near the Gladden Fields. He knows then that Sauron has learned the manner of Isildur's end (maybe from Orcs), and he is afraid. He withdraws to Isengard and fortifies it, but he says nothing to the Council.

2920 Death of Gerontius Took at age of 130.

2929 Arathorn, son of Arador chieftain of the Dúnedain, weds Gilrain daughter of Dirhoel [> Dirhael].

2930 Arador slain by Trolls.

2931 Aragorn son of Arathorn born.

2933 Arathorn II chief of the Dúnedain slain by Orcs when riding with Elladan and Elrohir. His infant son Aragorn is fostered by Elrond. Elrond keeps the heirlooms of his father, but his ancestry is kept secret, since the Wise know that Sauron is seeking for the Heir of Isildur.

2940 Thorin Oakenshield the Dwarf, son of Thráin, son of Thrór of Erebor visits Bilbo in the Shire in the company of Gandalf. Bilbo sets out for Dale with Gandalf and the

Dwarves. Bilbo meets Sméagol-Gollum and becomes possessed of the Ring; but it is not guessed what Ring this is.

Meeting of the White Council. Saruman, since he now wishes to prevent the Sorcerer from searching the River, agrees to an attack on Dol Guldur. The Sorcerer is driven out of Mirkwood. The Forest for a time becomes wholesome again. But the Sorcerer flies east, and returns in secret.

Battle of the Five Armies fought in Dale. Thranduil of Mirkwood, the Men of Esgaroth, and the Dwarves, with the help of the Eagles of the Misty Mountains, defeat a great host of Orcs. Bard of Esgaroth slays Smaug the Dragon. Thorin Oakenshield dies of wounds. Dáin of the Iron Hills re-enters Erebor and becomes 'King under the Mountain'.

2941   Bilbo returns to the Shire with a share of the treasure of Smaug, and the Ring.

2948   Théoden son of Thengel king of the Rohirrim is born in Rohan.

2953   Aragorn returns from errantry in the company of Elladan and Elrohir. Elrond reveals to him his ancestry and destiny and delivers to him the Shards of Narsil, the Sword of Elendil. Elrond foretells that in his time either the last remnant of Númenor shall pass away, or the kingdoms of Arnor and Gondor shall be united and renewed. He bids Aragorn prepare for a hard life of war and wandering.

Arwen Undómiel had now long dwelt with Galadriel in Lórien, but she desired to see her father again, and her brethren, Elladan and Elrohir, brought her to Imladris. On the day in which his ancestry was revealed to him Aragorn met her at unawares walking under the trees in Rivendell, and so began to love her. Elrond is grieved, for he foresees the choice that will lie before her; and says that at least Aragorn must wait until he has fulfilled his task. He reveals that as one of the pure blood of Númenor, born to a high purpose, Aragorn will have a long life-span. Aragorn says farewell to Rivendell and goes out into the world.

At this time Sauron, having gathered fresh power, declares himself and his true name again, and he re-enters Mordor which the Ringwraiths have prepared for him, and rebuilds Barad-dûr. This had never been wholly destroyed, and its foundations were unmoved; for they were made by the Power of the One Ring. But Mithrandir (Gandalf) journeys far and wide to counter the plans of Sauron and prepare Elves and Men for war against the Lord of Barad-dûr.

2954   Orodruin (Mount Doom), long dormant, bursts into smoke and flame again, and fear falls on Minas Tirith.

2956   Aragorn meets Gandalf, and their great friendship begins. Aragorn undertakes great journeys, even far into the East and deep into the South, exploring the purposes of Sauron and all his movements. As an unknown warrior he fights in the service of Gondor and of Rohan. Because of his high race, the noblest among mortal men, his fostering by Elrond, and his learning from Mithrandir, and his many deeds and journeys he becomes the most hardy of Men, both Elven-wise and skilled in craft and lore.

2980   Aragorn returning on a time to Rivendell from perils on the borders of Mordor passes through Lórien, and there again meets Arwen Undómiel. He is now a mighty man and she returns his love. They plight their troth on the hill of Cerin Amroth in Lórien. Théoden becomes King of Rohan.

2984   Denethor II becomes the twenty-sixth Steward of Gondor on the death of his father Ecthelion II. He married (late) Finduilas daughter of Adrahil, Prince of Dol Amroth. His elder son Boromir was born in 2978. His younger son Faramir was born in 2983. His wife Finduilas died untimely in 2987.

2989   In the spring of this year Balin the Dwarf with Óin and Ori and other folk of Erebor went south and entered Moria.

2993   Éomer Éomundsson born in Rohan. His mother was Théodwyn youngest sister of Théoden.

2996   Éowyn sister of Éomer born.

c.3000 onwards   The Shadow of Mordor creeps over the lands, and the hearts of all the folk in the Westlands are darkened. About this time it is thought that Saruman dared to use the Palantir of Orthanc, but was ensnared thus by Sauron who had possession of the Stone of

Minas Ithil (captured long before by the Úlairi). Saruman becomes a full traitor to the Council and his friends; but still schemes to acquire power for himself, and searches all the more eagerly for the One Ring. His thought turns towards Bilbo and the Shire, and he spies on that land.

3001 Bilbo gives a farewell feast and banquet in Hobbiton and vanishes from the Shire. He goes, after some journeying and a visit to Erebor, back in secret to Rivendell, and there is given a home by Elrond. Gandalf at last also suspects the nature of the Ring of Gollum, which Bilbo has handed on to his kinsman and heir, Frodo.

3002 Gandalf begins to explore the history of Bilbo's Ring, and with the aid of Aragorn searches for news of Gollum.

3004 Gandalf visits the Shire again, and continues to do so at intervals, to observe Frodo, for some years.

3009 Last visit of Gandalf to Frodo before the end. The hunt for Gollum begins. Aragorn goes to the confines of Mordor.

3016 Elrond sends for Arwen and she returns to Rivendell; for the Misty Mountains and all lands east of them are becoming full of peril and threat of war.

3018 Gandalf visits Frodo and reveals the true nature of the Ring that he possesses. Frodo decides to fly from the Shire to Rivendell, but will wait till the autumn, or until Gandalf returns. Saruman the traitor decoys Gandalf and takes him prisoner in Isengard (shortly after midsummer). The Ringwraiths appear again. At midsummer Sauron makes war on Gondor. The Witch-king appears again in person as the Black Captain of the hosts of Mordor. The sons of Denethor hold off the attack. Words in a dream bid Denethor to seek for counsel in Imladris where Isildur's Bane shall be revealed and strength greater than that of Morgul shall be found. Boromir sets out for Imladris from Minas Tirith.

Gandalf is aware of the coming of the Ringwraiths, but being imprisoned in Orthanc cannot send warning or help to Frodo.

Frodo leaves the Shire in autumn, but barely escapes the Ringwraiths that in the shape of Black Riders have come north to hunt for the Ring. Assisted by Aragorn he and his companions reach Rivendell at the end of October. At the same time Boromir arrives there, and also messengers from Erebor (Glóin and his son Gimli) and from Thranduil of Mirkwood (his son Legolas). Gandalf escapes from Isengard and reaches Rivendell.

A great council is held in the House of Elrond. It is resolved to attempt the destruction of the Ring by sending it to the fire of Orodruin in Sauron's despite. Frodo the Halfling accepts the perilous office of Ringbearer.

At the end of the year the Company of the Ring ('The Nine Walkers') leave Rivendell.

3019   The War of the Ring begins, between Sauron and his creatures, and their allies in the East and South (among all Men that hate the name of Gondor), and the peoples of the Westlands. Saruman plays a treacherous part and attacks Rohan. Théodred son of Théoden is slain in war with Saruman. Boromir son of Denethor is slain by Orcs near the Falls of Rauros. Minas Tirith is besieged by great forces led by the Black Captain, and is partly burnt. Denethor slays himself in despair. The Rohirrim by a great ride break the siege, but Théoden is slain by the Witch-king. The Battle of the Pelennor Fields followed, of which the full tale is told elsewhere. The greatest deed of that day was the deed of Éowyn Éomund's daughter. She for love of the King rode in disguise with the Rohirrim and was with him when he fell. By her hand the Black Captain, the Lord of the Ringwraiths, the Witch-king of Angmar, was destroyed.

Even so the battle would have been lost but for the coming of Aragorn. In the hour of need he sailed up Anduin from the south, in the fleet which he captured from the Corsairs of Umbar, bringing new strength; and he unfurled the banner of the kings.

After taking counsel the Host of the West marches to the Black Gate of Mordor. There it is trapped and surrounded by the forces of Sauron. But in that hour Frodo the Halfling with his faithful servant reached Mount Doom through perils beyond hope and cast the Ring into the Fire. Then Sauron was unmade and his power passed away like a cloud and the Dark Tower fell in utter ruin. This is that Frodo who was long remembered in the songs of Men as Frodo of the Nine Fingers, and renowned as one of the greatest heroes of Gondor; but though often later this was forgotten he was not a Man of Gondor but a Halfling of the Shire.

The Host of the West enters Mordor and destroys all the Orc-holds. All Men that had allied themselves with Sauron were slain or subjugated.

In the early summer Aragorn was crowned King of Gondor in Minas Tirith taking the name of Elessar (the Elfstone). He became thus King both of Arnor and Gondor, and overlord of the ancient allies of Mordor to whom he now granted mercy and peace. He found a seedling of the White Tree and planted it.

At midsummer Arwen came with Elrond and Galadriel and her brethren, and she was wedded with Aragorn Elessar, and made the choice of Lúthien.

In Gondor a new era and a new calendar was made, to begin with the day of the fall of Barad-dûr, March 25, 3019. But the Third Age is not held to have ended on that day, but with the going of the Three Rings. For after the destruction of the Ruling Ring the Three Rings of the Eldar lost their virtue. Then Elrond prepared at last to depart from Middle-earth and follow Celebrían.

3021   In the autumn of this year Elrond, Galadriel, and Mithrandir, the guardians of the Three Rings, rode westward through the Shire to the Grey Havens. With them went, it is said, the Halflings Bilbo and Frodo, the Ringbearers. Círdan had made ready a ship for them, and they set sail at evening and passed into the uttermost West. With their passing ended the Third Age, the twilight between the Elder Days and the Afterworld which then began.

Here ends the main matter of the Red Book. But more is to be learned both from notes and additions in later hands in the Red Book (less trustworthy than the earlier parts which are said to have been derived from the Halflings that were actual witnesses of the deeds); and from the Annals of the House of Elessar, of which parts of a Halfling translation (made it is said by the Tooks) are preserved.

So much may here be noted. The reign of King Aragorn was long and glorious. In his time Minas Tirith was rebuilt and made stronger and fairer than before; for the king had the

assistance of the stone-wrights of Erebor. Gimli Glóin's son of
Erebor had been his companion and had fought in all the battles
of the War of the Ring, and when peace was made he brought
part of the dwarf-folk and they dwelt in the White Mountains
and wrought great and wonderful works in Gondor. And the
Dwarves also forged anew great gates of *mithril* and steel to
replace those broken in the siege. Legolas Thranduil's son had
also been one of the king's companions and he brought Elves
out of Greenwood (to which name Mirkwood now returned)
and they dwelt in Ithilien, and it became the fairest region in all
the Westlands. But after King Elessar died Legolas followed at
last the yearning of his heart and sailed over Sea. It is said in the
Red Book that he took Gimli Glóin's son with him because of
their great friendship, such as had never else been seen between
Elf and Dwarf. But this is scarcely to be believed: that a dwarf
should be willing to leave Middle-earth for any love, or that the
Elves should admit him to Avallon if he would go, or that the
Lords of the West should permit it. In the Red Book it is said
that he went also out of desire to see again the Lady Galadriel
whose beauty he revered; and that she being mighty among the
Eldar obtained this grace for him. More cannot be said of this
strange matter.

It is said also that in 3020 Éowyn Éomund's daughter wedded
Faramir, last Steward of Gondor and first Prince of Ithilien, in
the king's house of Rohan. Éomer her brother received the kingship upon the field of battle from Théoden ere he died. In 3022
(or Fourth Age 1) he wedded Lothíriel daughter of Imrahil of
Dol Amroth, and his reign over Rohan was long and blessed,
and he was known as Éomer Éadig.

King Elessar and Queen Arwen reigned long and in great
blessedness; but at the last the weariness came upon the King,
and then, while still in vigour of mind and body, he laid himself
down after the manner of the ancient kings of Númenor, and
died, in the hundred and second year of his reign and the
hundred and ninetieth year of his life.

Then Arwen departed and dwelt alone and widowed in the
fading woods of Loth-lórien; and it came to pass for her as
Elrond foretold that she would not leave the world until she had
lost all for which she made her choice. But at last she laid herself to rest on the hill of Cerin Amroth, and there was her green
grave until the shape of the world was changed.

Of Eldarion son of Elessar it was foretold that he should rule

a great realm, and that it should endure for a hundred generations of Men after him, that is until a new age brought in again
new things; and from him should come the kings of many
realms in long days after. But if this foretelling spoke truly, none
now can say, for Gondor and Arnor are no more; and even the
chronicles of the House of Elessar and all their deeds and glory
are lost.

The account of the history of the Realms in Exile in *The Heirs of
Elendil*, where it is set out in the framework of the succession of the
kings and rulers, necessarily overlaps with that in the Tale of Years,
where it forms part of a general chronology of the Westlands. It would
therefore be interesting to know whether my father wrote the latter
before or after the final (unrevised) manuscript C of *The Heirs of
Elendil*; but the evidence on this question is strangely conflicting. On
the one hand, the entry in T 4 for the year 1960 seems to establish that
it preceded C, where the interregnum after the death of King Ondohir
was only of one year and Eärnil II came to the throne in 1945, and the
correction to the text (see note 23) was plainly made after the manuscript was completed. There are other pointers to the same conclusion;
thus the passage under 2050 concerning the Stewards was taken
straight from the B text of *The Heirs of Elendil* (see p. 217). On the
other hand, there are a number of features in T 4 that seem to show
that my father had C in front of him: as for example the statement
under 1409 that the *palantir* of Amon Sûl was destroyed, where C
(before correction) had 'the *palantir* is broken', but B (in an addition)
had 'no one knows what became of the Stone' (pp. 194, 209); or again
the two challenges made by the Lord of the Ringwraiths to Eärnur, in
2043 and 2050, which very clearly first entered *The Heirs of Elendil*
in C (pp. 201, 217). Close similarities of wording are found between
entries in T 4 and both B and C.

One might suppose that the writing of T 4 and the writing of C proceeded together; but the two manuscripts are at once very distinct in
style, and very homogeneous throughout their length. Each gives the
impression that it was written from start to finish connectedly. On the
other hand, there can be little doubt that T 3 and T 4 belong to very
much the same time as *The Heirs of Elendil*.

My father may not have precisely intended such near-repetition
between the two works as occurs, but it is possible to regard it as the
necessary consequence of his design at that time. This long Tale of
Years, ample in expression, seems to me to show that he wished,
having at long last brought the story to its end, to provide for the
reader a clear and accessible (still in the manner of the story) 'con-
spectus' of all the diverse threads and histories that came together in
the War of the Ring: of the Hobbits, the Wizards, the Dúnedain of the
North, the rulers of Gondor, the Rohirrim, the Ringwraiths, the Dark

Lord; the High-elves of Rivendell and Lindon also, the Dwarves of Erebor and Moria, and further back the lost world of Númenor. This account (a chronology, but with a narrative view and tone) was to be read at the end of the book, a Tale of Years in which the story of the Fellowship and the quest of the Ringbearer could be seen, when all was over, as the culmination of a great and many-rooted historical process – for which chronology was a prime necessity. And so also, at the end of this Tale of Years, he moved 'outside the frame' of the story, and looked further on to the later lives of Gimli and Legolas, of Faramir and Éowyn and Éomer, the reign and the deaths of Elessar and Arwen, and the realm of their son Eldarion in 'the Afterworld'.

I have mentioned when discussing the Tale of Years of the Second Age (p. 177) that an amanuensis typescript in two copies (T 5) – very intelligently and professionally done – was made from the manuscript T 4; and that one of them was emended in a most radical fashion by my father, chiefly if by no means exclusively in order to abbreviate the text by the omission of phrases that could be regarded as not strictly necessary. This cutting out of phrases ceases altogether towards the end, at the beginning of the entry for 3019.

There is no certain evidence to show when the typescript was made, but I think that it was a long while after the writing of the manuscript. The question is in any case not of much importance, for what is certain is that the typescript was sent to the publishers in 1954; in a letter of 22 October in that year Rayner Unwin said:

> The Tale of Years which I am returning herewith was interesting, but as you, I think, agree, probably too long for the appendices as it stands. I suggest that considerable reduction be made in the accounts of events already told in The Lord of the Rings, and a somewhat more staccato style be adopted (make less of a narrative of the events of the Third Age).

It was of course the typescript in its unrevised form that he had sent: the revision (in so far as it entailed abbreviation) was obviously undertaken in response to Rayner Unwin's criticism.

If my interpretation of my father's intention for the Tale of Years is at all near the truth, it may be supposed that he carried out this work of shortening with reluctance; certainly, in the result, the amount lost from the original text was not proportionately very great, the long concluding passage was not touched, and the rounded, 'narrative' manner was little diminished. But after this time there is no external evidence that I know of to indicate whether there was further discussion of the matter – whether, for instance, my father was given a more express limitation with regard to length. There is indeed nothing actually to show that the subsequent far more drastic compression was not his own idea. But there is also nothing to bridge the gap before the next text, a typescript (from which the entries before 1900 are missing, and which breaks off in the middle of that for 2941) already in full 'staccato' mode, and approaching (after a good deal of correction) closely the text in Appendix B. After this the only further extant text is the typescript from which Appendix B was printed.

NOTES

1   On the name *Dol Dûgul* for later *Dol Guldur* see VIII.122. In the manuscripts of *The Lord of the Rings* it is always spelt *Dol Dûghul* (replacing original *Dol Dûgol*).

2   On the date of Déagol's finding the One Ring see pp. 166–7.

3   'They become Hobbits': cf. the passage in *The Shadow of the Past*, later revised, cited on p. 66, §20.

4   From this point all the dates are given also in the years of the Shire Reckoning, but I do not include these in the text. Here 1600 is made S.R.1, but in all the following annals the final figure of the year corresponds in both reckonings, as '2940 (S.R.1340)', as if S.R.1 = 1601. The correction to 1601 was not made until the third text, T 4.

5   On *Northworthy* see p. 5 and note 3.

6   King Eärnur is named in the text of *The Lord of the Rings*, in the chapter *The Window on the West* (TT p. 278), where it was a late change from *Elessar* (VIII.153).

7   In Appendix B Elrond wedded Celebrían 2400 years before, in Third Age 100 (changed to 109 in the Second Edition).

8   Finduilas, earlier name of Arwen: see VIII.370, etc.

9   This was changed later to 'three parts Elven-blood'.

10   To this point the text was retained in abbreviated form in the preamble to the annals of the Third Age in Appendix B.

11   Eärendur: T 3 has here Eärendil (see p. 189).

12   In this text Isildur's death had been recorded under Second Age 3441 (p. 177).

13   In T 3 there are no entries at all before the coming of the Istari c.1000, but my father noted on that manuscript that more should be said here of Gondor and Arnor.

14   This entry concerning the Istari was preserved with some alteration in the preamble to the annals of the Third Age in Appendix B.

15   T 3 had here '(of whose kindred they were maybe a branch)', which was struck out.

16   With this passage concerning the region in which the Hobbits anciently dwelt and the reasons for their westward migration cf. the *Prologue*, FR p. 12.

17   T 3 has here: 'The families of the Harfoots, the most numerous of the Periannath (though this people were ever small in number),

crossed the Misty Mountains and came into eastern Eriador.
The Fallowhides, another and smaller clan, moved north along
the eaves of the Forest, for the shadow was deeper in its southern
parts. The Stoors tarried still beside the River.'

18   In T 3 the same is said concerning the 'Fallowhides', but the
Stoors 'came over the Redhorn Pass into the desolate land of
Hollin'.

19   On the date 1601 see note 4. Subsequent entries for some distance are given also in Shire-reckoning, but I have not included
these dates in the text printed.

20   With this passage cf. the *Prologue* text given on p. 9. The entry in
T 3 here begins: 'Owing to an increase in their numbers, which
became too great for the small Bree-land, many of the Periannath
crossed the R. Baranduin'; the text is then as in T 4, but without
the reference to the Stoors.

21   In both the B and C texts of *The Heirs of Elendil* Angomaitë and
Sangahyanda were the great-grandsons of Kastamir (so also in
Appendix A, RK p. 328).

22   T 3 ends the entry for 1640 'The Periannath were little harmed,
for they mingled little with other folk.'

23   This entry belongs to the stage in the history of Gondor when
there was an interregnum of sixteen years before Eärnil II came
to the throne, during which time Pelendur the Steward ruled the
realm (see p. 216). It was later corrected to read: '1945   Eärnil,
descendant of a previous king, receives the crown of Gondor.'

24   In T 3 it is said that Arvedui was slain by the Witch-king; this
apparently agrees with the original form of the B text of *The
Heirs of Elendil* (p. 210).

25   T 3 has here: 'but after the end of the kingdom they claim "The
Shire" as their own land, and elect a "Shire-king" from among
their own chieftains.' On the name *Shireking* or *Shirking* see
pp. 5–6, 87, 107. It seems to have been in this entry in T 3 that
Bucca of the Marish first emerged.

26   This record of Saruman's coming to Orthanc is far earlier than in
the additions made to text C of *The Heirs of Elendil*, where
(pp. 205–6) 'Saruman comes to Orthanc' during the rule of the
Steward Beren (2743–63), and in that of the Steward Turgon
(2914–53) 'Saruman takes possession of Orthanc, and fortifies
it'. In Appendix B 'Saruman takes up his abode in Isengard' in
2759.

27   These two entries concerning the finding of the Ring and
Gollum's disappearance in the Misty Mountains are nine hundred years later than in the earliest text (p. 225).

28   With the entry for 2060 the substituted pages (see pp. 226–7)
begin. The original entry for this year began:

The White Council is formed to unite and direct the resistance to the growing forces of evil, which the Wise perceive are all being governed and guided in a plan of hatred for the Eldar and the remnants of Númenor. The Council believe that Sauron has returned. Curunír, or Saruman the White, is chosen to be head of the White Council ...

The original text was then the same as that in the entry that replaced it under the year 2463.

29 The opening of this entry in T 3 seems to have been written first: 'Isumbras I, head of the rising Took family, becomes first Shire-king (Shirking) of the Took-line', then changed immediately to 'becomes seventeenth [> thirteenth] Shire-king and first of the Took-line.'

30 The dates of the births of Elladan and Elrohir, and of Arwen, are given thus as two separate entries for the same year 2349 in the replacement text, with Arwen's birth subsequently changed to 2359. In the rejected version her birth was placed in 2400. Concomitantly with the far earlier date introduced much later for the wedding of Elrond and Celebrían (see note 7), in Appendix B Elladan and Elrohir were born in 139 (changed to 130 in the Second Edition) and Arwen in 241.

31 In The Heirs of Elendil Denethor I was the son not of Dior the ninth Steward but of Dior's sister (called in the C text Rían): pp. 204, 219. – The rejected text having placed the forming of the White Council four hundred years earlier, under 2060 (note 28), at this point it moved directly from the end of the Watchful Peace and the return of Sauron to Dol Guldur in 2460 to the attack on Gondor in the days of Denethor I. The postponement of the establishment of the White Council was the primary reason for the rejection and replacement of the two pages in the original manuscript, and the entries following 2463 were copied with little change into the new text to the point where it rejoins the old, near the end of the entry for 2510.

32 As in the earliest text (p. 226), T 3 states that Celebrían was slain by the Orcs.

33 'Thrór ... founds the realm of Erebor': the history of Thrór's ancestors had not yet emerged.

34 The year 2698 was the date of the death of Ecthelion I in the texts of The Heirs of Elendil.

35 The War of the Dwarves and Orcs entered the history at this time. In very difficult scribbled notes at the end of T 3 my father asked himself: 'When were the Dwarf and Goblin wars? When did Moria become finally desolate?' He noted that since the wars were referred to by Thorin in The Hobbit they 'must have been recent', and suggested that there was 'an attempt to enter Moria in Thráin's time', perhaps 'an expedition from Erebor to Moria'. 'But the appearance of the Balrog and the desolation of Moria

must be more ancient, possibly as far back as c.1980–2000'. He then wrote:

> 'After fall of Erebor Thrór tried to visit Moria and was killed by a goblin. The dwarves assembled a force and fought Orcs on east side of Moria and did great slaughter, but could not enter Moria because of "the terror". Dáin returns to the Iron Hills, but Thorin and Thráin wander about.'

Entries were then added to the text of T 3 which were taken up into T 4. At this time the story was that Thráin and Thorin accompanied Thrór, but made their escape. – Much later the dates of the war were changed from 2766–9 to 2793–9.

36   'the fourteenth Thain': that is, of the Took line.

37   The statement here that Thráin had come to Dol Guldur seeking for one of the Seven Rings is strange, for the story that he received Thrór's ring and that it was taken from him in the dungeons of Sauron goes back to the earliest text of *The Council of Elrond* (VI.398, 403). It seems to be a lapse without more significance; see further p. 252.

38   The date of the death of the Steward Belecthor II in all three texts of *The Heirs of Elendil* is 2872. The date 2852 in the later type-scripts of the Tale of Years and in Appendix B is evidently a casual error.

39   In text C of *The Heirs of Elendil* (p. 206) the final desolation of Ithilien, where however Gondor keeps hidden strongholds, is placed in the time of the Steward Túrin II (2882–2914). In Appendix B the corresponding entry is given under 2901.

Note on changes made to the manuscript T 4 of the Tale of Years

(i) The Stoors

c.1150   The original entry was covered by a pasted slip that cannot be removed, but the underlying text as printed (p. 229) can be read with fair certainty. The replacement differs only in the statement concerning the Stoors: after coming into Eriador by the Redhorn Pass 'some then moved south towards Dunland; others dwelt for a long time in the angle between the Loudwater and the Hoarwell.'

c.1400   This entry was struck out and replaced by another under the year 1600, but the date was then changed to 1550. This was almost the same as the rejected form, but for 'some of the Stoors return to Wilderland' has 'the northern Stoors leave the Angle and return to Wilderland'.

On the evolution of the early history of the Stoors see pp. 66–7, §§22–3.

(ii) Saruman

c.2000   The far earlier coming of Saruman to Isengard (see note 26) was allowed to stand, but the reference to his becoming the head of the White Council in 2060 (note 28) was removed with the displacement of its forming to four hundred years later (2463). See p. 262, note 5.

2851   Saruman next appears in this entry, which was changed to read:

> He does not reveal his thought to the Council, but sets a watch upon Anduin and the Gladden Fields, where he himself secretly searches for the One Ring.

The words of the original text 'and he fortifies Isengard' were presumably struck out while the manuscript was in progress, since they reappear under 2911 (where they were again removed).

2911   The last sentence in the original text was altered to 'He redoubles the search for the Ring, but he says nothing to the Council.'

2940   This entry was not changed.

2953   The conclusion of this long entry, after the words 'the Power of the One Ring', was expanded thus:

> The White Council meets and debates concerning the Rings, fearing especially that Sauron may find the One. Saruman feigns that he has discovered that it passed down Anduin to the Sea. He then withdraws to Isengard and fortifies it, and consorts no more with members of the Council. But Mithrandir (Gandalf) journeys far and wide ...

The new text then returns to the original. (Saruman's pretence that he knew that the Ring had gone down Anduin to the Sea had been cut out of the entry for 2851, and the reference to his fortifying Isengard from that for 2911.)

c.3000   The last sentence of the original text was replaced thus:

> His spies bring him rumours of Sméagol-Gollum and his ring, and of Bilbo of the Shire. He is angry that Gandalf should have concealed this matter from him; and he spies upon Gandalf, and upon the Shire.

(iii) Gollum

c.2000 and c.2010   These entries concerning the finding of the Ring and Gollum's disappearance were struck out and replaced by additions under 2463 and 2470 (the dates in Appendix B). Many other additions were made concerning Gollum, but these are closely similar to those in Appendix B. There is no mention of his 'becoming acquainted with Shelob' under 2980, but an addition to the original entry for 3001 says 'About this time Gollum was captured and taken to Mordor and there held in prison.'

(iv) The return of Sauron to Mordor

In the original text of T 4 it was said in the entry for 2953 that Sauron declared himself and his true name, re-entered Mordor prepared for him by the Ringwraiths, and rebuilt Barad-dûr. In the revision, an addition was made to 2941: 'The Sorcerer returns in secret to Mordor which the Ringwraiths have prepared for him'; and at the same time the entry for 2953 was altered to read: 'At this time Sauron, having gathered fresh power, openly declares himself and his true name again, and claims Lordship over the West. He rebuilds Barad-dûr ...'

The corresponding dates in Appendix B are 2942 and 2951.

(v) The Dwarves

The statement under 2850 that Thráin went to Dol Guldur seeking one of the Seven Rings (see note 37) was replaced thus: 'Thráin was the possessor of the last of the Seven Rings of Power to survive destruction or recapture; but the ring was taken from him in Dol Guldur with torment, and he died there.' At the same time a new entry was added for the year 2840: 'Thráin the Dwarf goes wandering and is captured by the Sorcerer (about 2845?)'.

The entry for 2590 recording the founding of the realm of Erebor was changed to read: 'In the Far North dragons multiply again. Thrór ... comes south and re-establishes the realm of Erebor ...' At the same time, at the end of the entry, this addition was made: 'He was the great-great-grandson of Thráin I Náin's son' (which does not agree with the genealogical table in Appendix A, RK p. 361: see pp. 276–7).

For the correction of the entry for 1960 (the accession of Eärnil II to the throne of Gondor after a long interregnum) see note 23.

All the revisions of T 4 given above were taken up into the typescript T 5 as it was first made.

IX

THE MAKING OF APPENDIX A

(I) THE REALMS IN EXILE

As with the major manuscript T 4 of the Tale of Years given in the last chapter, I believe that years passed after the making of the manuscript C of *The Heirs of Elendil* (pp. 191 ff.) before my father took up the matter again, with a view to its radical alteration, when *The Lord of the Rings* was assured of publication. His later work on this, almost entirely in typescript, is extremely difficult to explain.

The earliest text, which I will call I, of the later period is a very rough typescript which begins thus:

The Heirs of Elendil

There is no space here to set out the lines of the kings and lords of Arnor and Gondor, even in such brief form as they appear in the Red Book. For the compiling of these annals the Hobbits must have drawn both on the books of lore in Rivendell, and on records made available to them by King Elessar, such as the 'Book of the Kings' of Gondor, and the 'House of the Stewards'; for until the days of the War of the Ring they had known little of such matters, and afterwards were chiefly interested in them in so far as they concerned Elessar, or helped in the correction of the dating of their own annals.

The line of Arnor, the Heirs of Isildur. After Elendil and Isildur there were eight high kings in Arnor, ending with Eärendur. The realm of Arnor then became divided, and the kings ceased to take names in High-elven form. But the line was maintained by Amlaith son of Eärendur, who ruled at Fornost.

After Amlaith there were thirteen kings[1] at Fornost, of whom the last was Arvedui, the twenty-fifth of the line. When he was lost at sea, the kingship came to an end in the North, and Fornost was deserted; but the line was continued by the Lords of the Dúnedain, who were fostered by Elrond.

Of these the first was Aranarth son of Arvedui, and after him there followed fifteen chieftains, ending with Aragorn II, who became king again both of Arnor and Gondor.

It was the token and the marvel of the Northern line that, though their power departed and their people dwindled to few, through all the many generations the succession was unbroken from father to son. Also, though the length of the lives of the Dúnedain grew ever less in Middle-earth, and their waning was swifter in the North, while the kings lasted in Gondor, afterwards it was otherwise; and many of the chieftains of the North lived still to twice the age of the oldest of other Men. Aragorn indeed lived to be one hundred and ninety years of age, longer than any of his line since Arvegil son of King Argeleb II; but in Aragorn the dignity of the kings of old was renewed, and he received in some measure their former gifts.

In his opening words 'There is no space here to set out the lines of the kings and lords of Arnor and Gondor' my father was surely thinking of *The Heirs of Elendil* in the elaborate form it had reached in the manuscript C. Merely to set out the names and dates of the rulers would take little enough space, yet that would serve little purpose in itself. It seems plain that he either knew or feared that he would be under severe constraint in the telling of the history of the Realms in Exile; but it seems extraordinary that he should have felt impelled to reduce the history of Arnor and the later petty realms almost to vanishing point.

After the passage given above, however, he continued with *The line of Gondor, the Heirs of Anárion*, and here he adopted another course: to give 'excerpts' from the history of Gondor. He began with a passage that remained with little change as the opening paragraph of the section *Gondor and the Heirs of Anárion* in Appendix A (I, iv); but then passed at once to 'the first great evil' that came upon Gondor, the civil war of the Kin-strife, thus omitting the first fourteen centuries of its history. This was quite briefly told, and was followed by a short account of 'the second and greatest evil', the plague that came in the reign of Telemnar; and that by 'the third evil', the invasion of the Wainriders. He had recounted the marriage of Arvedui, last king in the North, to the daughter of King Ondohir, and the great victory of Eärnil in 1944, when he abandoned the text.

One might suppose that he perceived that, in so short a space as he had determined was necessary, this would not work. The 'excerpts' could not stand in isolation without further explanation. At the end of this text he had written that the northern kingdom could send no aid to Gondor 'for Angmar renewed its attack upon Arthedain': yet neither Angmar nor Arthedain had been mentioned. What was required (one might think) was a brief précis of the whole history of the two kingdoms; but as will be seen in a moment, this was not at all what he had in mind.

It is notable that at this stage he said very little about the sources for the history; and it seems probable that his conception of them was still very undeveloped.

In a second text, II, still with the same title, he substantially expanded the opening passage:

Until the War of the Ring the people of the Shire had little knowledge of the history of the Westlands beyond the traditions of their own wanderings; but afterwards all that concerned the King Elessar became of deep interest to them, while in the Buckland the tales of Rohan were no less esteemed. Thus the Red Book from its beginning contained many annals, genealogies, and traditions of the realms of the South, drawn through Bilbo from the books of lore in Rivendell, or through Frodo and Peregrin from the King himself, and from the records of Gondor that he opened to them: such as 'The Book of the Kings and Stewards' (now lost), and the *Akallabêth*, that is 'The Downfall of Númenor'.[2] To this matter other notes and tales were added at a later date by other hands, after the passing of Elessar.

There is no space here to set out this matter, even in the brief forms in which it usually appears in the Book; but some excerpts are given that may serve to illustrate the story of the War of the Ring, or to fill up some of the gaps in the account.

My father now expressly referred to 'excerpts' from the Red Book. He retained from text I the very brief statement concerning the Northern Line; and in the section on the Southern Line he did as he had done in I, omitting all the history of Gondor before the Kin-strife. But when he came to the story of the civil war he expanded it to ten times its length in I. One may wonder what his intention now was in respect of the shape and length of this Appendix; but I doubt whether he was thinking of such questions when he wrote it. The historian of Gondor reasserted himself, and he told the story as he wished to tell it.

The remarkable thing is that this text was the immediate forerunner of the story of the Kin-strife as it was published in Appendix A (in the First Edition: in the Second Edition the events leading to it were altered and expanded, see p. 258).[3] And at the words 'Eldakar ... was king for fifty-eight years, of which ten were spent in exile' (RK p. 328) text II was abandoned in its turn.[4]

In a third text, III, my father retained the actual first page of II, carrying the opening remarks on the sources and the scanty statement on the Northern Line. For the Southern Line he entered, as before, immediately into the history of the Kin-strife, and brought the text virtually word for word to its form in Appendix A in the First Edition. Then, having recounted the plague and the invasion of the Wainriders without much enlarging what was said in text I, he wrote a very full account of the claim of Arvedui on the southern crown: and this was for most of its length word for word the text in Appendix A, beginning 'On the death of Ondohir and his sons ...' (RK p. 329), with the record of the exchanges between Arvedui and the Council of Gondor, and the appearance of Malbeth the Seer who named him Arvedui at his birth. The only difference is the absence of the reference to the Steward Pelendur, who in the Appendix A text is said to have 'played the chief part' in the rejection of the claim.

He then went on, in a passage that was again retained in Appendix A (RK pp. 330–1), to describe the message of Eärnil to Arvedui, the fleet sent into the North under Eärnur, and the destruction of Arthedain by Angmar. The story of the defeat of the Witch-king (RK pp. 331–2) had not yet been written; and with a brief reference to the overthrow of Angmar my father continued with 'It was thus in the reign of King Eärnil, as later became clear, that the Witch-king escaping from the North came to Mordor ...' With the account of the character of Eärnur (RK p. 332) text III ends.[5]

By now it can be seen how the long account of the Realms in Exile in Appendix A came into being. Strange as it seems, the evidence of the texts described above can lead only to this conclusion: that what began as an attempt (for whatever reason) to reduce the rich material of *The Heirs of Elendil* in a more than drastic fashion developed by steps into a long and finely written historical essay taking up some twenty printed pages. What considerations made this acceptable in relation to the requirements of brevity, in the absence of any evidence external to the texts themselves I am entirely unable to explain.

There are three versions of a brief text, which I will call IV for it certainly followed III, in which the opening section of Appendix A (I *The Númenórean Kings*. (i) *Númenor*), RK pp. 313 ff., is seen emerging. The opening paragraph 'Fëanor was the greatest of the Eldar in arts and lore ...', very briefly recounting the history of the Silmarils, the rebellion of Fëanor, and the war against Morgoth, was not present in the First Edition, where, as here in IV, the section opened with the words 'There were only three unions of the High Elves and Men ...'; but at this stage my father had not yet introduced the brief history of Númenor (RK pp. 315 ff., beginning 'As a reward for their sufferings in the cause against Morgoth ...'), which arose from his attempt to curtail and compress the Tale of Years of the Second Age (see pp. 180–1), and the passage concerning the Choice of Elros and Elrond, here called *i·Pheredhil*, differed from that published.

At the end of the First Age an irrevocable choice was given to the Half-elven, to which kindred they would belong. Elros chose to be of Mankind, and was granted a great life-span; and he became the first King of Númenor. His descendants were long-lived but mortal. Later when they became powerful they begrudged the choice of their forefather, desiring the immortality within the life of the world that was the fate of the Elves. In this way began their rebellion which, under the evil teaching of Sauron, brought about the Downfall of Númenor and the ruin of the ancient world.

Elrond chose to be of Elvenkind, and became a master of wisdom. To him therefore was granted the same grace as to those of the High Elves that still lingered in Middle-earth: that when weary at last of the mortal lands they could take ship from the Grey Havens and pass into the Uttermost West, notwithstanding the change of the world. But to the children of Elrond a choice was also appointed: to pass with him from the circles of the world; or if they wedded with one of Mankind, to become mortal and die in Middle-earth. For Elrond, therefore, all chances of the War of the Ring were fraught with sorrow.

Elros was the first king of Númenor, and was afterwards known by the royal name of Tar-Minyatur.

The fourth king of Númenor was Tar-Elendil. From his daughter Silmarien came the line of the Lords of Andúnië, of whom Amandil the Faithful was the last.

Elendil the Tall was the son of Amandil. He was the leader of the remnant of the Faithful who escaped from the Downfall with the Nine Ships, and established realms in exile in the North-west of Middle-earth. His sons were Isildur and Anárion.

Then follows in IV the lists of the kings, chieftains, and stewards of the Realms in Exile much as they are given in Appendix A (RK pp. 318–19). The references to Númenor in the passage just given were of course removed when the much longer account was introduced.

The Choice of the Children of Elrond as stated here differs notably from that in the final form, in the express statement that they would choose mortality if they chose to wed a mortal. In the text T 4 of the Tale of Years (p. 234, entry for the year 2300), as also in T 3, the choice is (as here in Appendix A): 'if [Elrond] departed they should have then the choice either to pass over the Sea with him, or to become mortal, if they remained behind.'[6]

After the abandoned text III, in which the account of the Northern Line was still confined to half a page, there is scarcely any rejected, preliminary material before the final typescript from which section I (iii) of Appendix A was printed, *Eriador, Arnor, and the Heirs of Isildur*. On the evidence of the extant texts this final typescript was the very one in which my father first set down the history of the North Kingdom in continuous narrative form. The story of Arvedui and the Lossoth, the Snowmen of Forochel, RK pp. 321–2, 'wrote itself' in precisely the form in which it was printed. But this is scarcely credible (see p. 279).

At the end of the story of the Lossoth, however, my father is seen in rejected pages taking a course that he decided against. At the end of the penultimate paragraph of this section (concerning the journeys of King Elessar to Annúminas and the Brandywine Bridge, RK p. 324) he continued: 'Arador was the grandfather of the king', and typed out part of a new text of the story of Aragorn and Arwen, which after some distance was abandoned. On this matter see the next section of this chapter, pp. 268 ff.

The next section of Appendix A, I (iv), *Gondor and the Heirs of Anárion*, is a fearful complex of typescript pages. Though it is possible to unravel the textual history up to a point,[7] it defies presentation, which is in any case unnecessary. The whole complex clearly belongs to one time. It was now that new elements entered the history, notably the story of the overthrow of the Witch-king of Angmar (RK pp. 331–2), and the account of the service of Aragorn under the name Thorongil with the Steward Ecthelion II (only referred to in a brief sentence in *The Heirs of Elendil*, p. 206), and of his relations with Denethor (RK pp. 335–6).

Note on the expansion of the tale of the Kin-strife in the Second Edition

In the First Edition of *The Lord of the Rings* the account of the Kin-strife (or more accurately of the events leading to it) was much briefer than that in the Second Edition, and read as follows (RK pp. 325–6 in both editions):[8]

Nonetheless it was not until the days of Rómendacil II that the first great evil came upon Gondor: the civil war of the Kin-strife, in which great loss and ruin was caused and never fully repaired.

'The Northmen increased greatly in the peace brought by the power of Gondor. The kings showed them favour, since they were the nearest in kin of lesser Men to the Dúnedain (being for the most part descendants of those peoples from whom the Edain of old had come); and they gave them wide lands beyond Anduin south of Greenwood the Great, to be a defence against men of the East. For in the past the attacks of the Easterlings had come mostly over the plain between the Inland Sea and the Ash Mountains.

'In the days of Rómendacil II their attacks began again, though at first with little force; but it was learned by the King that the Northmen did not always remain true to Gondor, and some would join forces with the Easterlings, either out of greed for spoil, or in the furtherance of feuds among their princes.

'Rómendacil therefore fortified the west shore of Anduin as far as the inflow of the Limlight, and forbade any stranger to pass down the River beyond the Emyn Muil. He it was that built the pillars of the Argonath at the entrance to Nen Hithoel. But since he needed men, and desired to strengthen the bond between Gondor and the Northmen, he took many of them into his service and gave to some high rank in his armies.

'In return he sent his son Valacar to dwell for a while with Vidugavia, who called himself the King of Rhovanion, and was indeed the most powerful of their princes, though his own realm lay between Greenwood and the River Running. There Valacar was wedded to Vidugavia's daughter, and so caused later the evil war of the Kin-strife.

'For the high men of Gondor already looked askance at the Northmen among them ...

From here the text of the Second Edition returns to that of the First, but there was a further alteration in the next paragraph, where the First Edition had: 'To the lineage of his father he added the fearless spirit of the Northmen. When the confederates led by descendants of the kings rose against him ...', inserting the sentence 'He was handsome and valiant, and showed no sign of ageing more swiftly than his father.'

As I have mentioned earlier (p. 190), in 1965, the year before the publication of the Second Edition, my father wrote a new version of this account; this he inserted into the late typescript copy D of *The Heirs of Elendil*. It is remarkable that though this new text was incorporated, in more concise form, into Appendix A, he actually wrote it as an addition to the text of *The Heirs of Elendil*, to be placed beneath the nineteenth king Rómendakil II, whose entry (see p. 198) he emended, on the typescript D, thus (the dates refer to birth, lifespan, and death):

19	Rómendakil II	1126	240	1366
	(Minalkar) (Lieutenant of the King 1240, King 1304)			

In the text of the First Edition there was no reference to the name Rómendacil as having been taken by Calmacil's son after his victory over the Easterlings in 1248, and indeed there was no mention of the victory. In the Second Edition, in the list of the Kings of Gondor (RK p. 318), the original text 'Calmacil 1304, Rómendacil II 1366, Valacar' was altered to 'Calmacil 1304, Minalcar (regent 1240–1304), crowned as Rómendacil II 1304, died 1366, Valacar'.

There is no need to give the whole of the new version, since the substance of it was largely retained in the revised text of Appendix A, but there are some portions of it that may be recorded. As originally composed, it opened:

Narmakil[9] and Kalmakil were like their father Atanatar lovers of ease; but Minalkar elder son of Kalmakil was a man of great force after the manner of his great-grandsire Hyarmendakil, whom he revered. Already at the end of Atanatar's reign his voice was listened to in the councils of the realm; and in 1240 Narmakil, wishing to be relieved of cares of state, gave him the new office and title of *Karma-kundo* 'Helm-guardian', that is in terms of Gondor Crown-lieutenant or Regent. Thereafter he was virtually king, though he acted in the names of Narmakil and Kalmakil, save in matters of war and defence over which he had complete authority. His reign is thus usually dated from 1240, though he was not crowned in the name of Rómendakil until 1304 after the death of his father. The Northmen increased greatly in the peace brought by the power of Gondor. ...

In the long version there is a footnote to the name *Vinitharya*: 'This, it is said, bore much the same meaning as *Rómendakil*.' After the birth of Vinitharya this version continues:

Rómendakil gave his consent to the marriage. He could not forbid it or refuse to recognize it without earning the enmity of Vidugavia. Indeed all the Northmen would have been angered, and those in his service would have been no longer to be trusted. He therefore waited in patience until 1260, and then he recalled Valakar, saying that it was now time that he took part in the councils of the realm and the command of its armies. Valakar returned to Gondor with his wife and children; and with them came a household of noble men and women of the North. They were welcomed, and at that time all seemed well. Nonetheless in this marriage lay the seeds of the first great evil that befell Gondor: the civil war of the Kin-strife, which brought loss and ruin upon the realm that was never fully repaired.

Valakar gave to his son the name Eldakar, for public use in Gondor; and his wife bore herself wisely and endeared herself to all those who knew her. She learned well the speech and manners of Gondor, and was willing to be called by the name Galadwen, a rendering of her Northern name into the Sindarin tongue. She was a fair and noble lady of high courage, which she imparted to her children; but though she lived to a great age, as such was reckoned among her people, she died in 1344 [*in one copy* > 1332]. Then the heart of Rómendakil grew heavy, foreboding the troubles that were to come. He had now long been crowned king, and the end of his reign and life were drawing nearer. Already men were looking forward to the accession of Valakar when Eldakar would become heir to the crown. The high men of Gondor had long looked askance at the Northmen among them, who had borne themselves more proudly since the coming of Vidumavi. Already among the Dúnedain murmurs were heard that it was a thing unheard of before that the heir to the crown, or any son of the King should wed one of lesser race, and short-lived; it was to be feared that her descendants would prove the same and fall from the majesty of the Kings of Men.

| 20 | Valakar | 1194 | 238 | crowned 1366 | 1432 |

Valakar was a vigorous king, and his son Eldakar was a man of great stature, handsome and valiant, and showed no sign of ageing more swiftly than his father. Nonetheless the disaffection steadily grew during his reign; and when he grew old there was already open rebellion in the southern provinces. There were gathered many of those who declared that they would never accept as king a man half of foreign race, born in an alien country. 'Vinitharya is his right name,' they said. 'Let him go back to the land where it belongs!'

NOTES

1 'thirteen kings' is an error for 'fourteen kings'.

2 This was almost exactly retained as the opening to Appendix A in the First Edition, as far as the reference to the *Akallabêth*, but *The Book of the Kings and Stewards* was separated into two works, which were not said to be lost. (The old opening to Appendix A was replaced in the Second Edition by an entirely new text, and the *Note on the Shire Records* was added at the end of the Prologue.) The published text then continued:

> From Gimli no doubt is derived the information concerning the Dwarves of Moria, for he remained much attached to both Peregrin and Meriadoc. But through Meriadoc alone, it seems, were derived the tales of the House of Eorl; for he went back to Rohan many times, and learned the language of the Mark, it is said. For this matter the authority of Holdwine is often cited, but that appears to have been the name which Meriadoc himself was given in Rohan. Some of the notes and tales, however, were plainly added by other hands at later dates, after the passing of King Elessar.
>
> Much of this lore appears as notes to the main narrative, in which case it has usually been included in it; but the additional material is very extensive, even though it is often set out in brief and annalistic form. Only a selection from it is here presented, again greatly reduced, but with the same object as the original compilers appear to have had: to illustrate the story of the War of the Ring and its origins and fill up some of the gaps in the main account.

The absence in the present text of the references to Gimli and Meriadoc as sources possibly suggests that my father had not yet decided to include sections on Rohan and the Dwarves in this

Appendix (although brief texts entitled *The House of Eorl* and *Of Durin's Race* were in existence).

3   This version lacked the account (RK pp. 327–8) of the great white pillar above the haven of Umbar set up in memorial of the landing of Ar-Pharazôn in the Second Age. The name of the King of Rhovanion was Vinitharya; this was corrected on the typescript to Vidugavia, and the name Vinitharya made that of Eldakar in his youth.

4   At the top of the page on which this account begins my father wrote, then or later, 'Hobbit-annal of the Kin-strife'.

5   After the words 'Many of the people that still remained in Ithilien deserted it' text III continues 'It was at this time that King Eärnil gave Isengard to Saruman.' This agrees with the statement in the text T 4 of the Tale of Years in the entry c.2000: see p. 233 and note 26, and p. 251.

6   In the two earlier versions of text IV the conclusion of the passage was extended, that of the first reading:

> Therefore to Elrond all chances of the War of the Ring would bring grief: to fly with his kin from ruin and the conquering Shadow, or to be separated from Arwen for ever. For either Aragorn would perish (and he loved him no less than his sons); or he would wed Arwen his daughter when he had regained his inheritance, according to the condition that Elrond himself had made when first their love was revealed. (See III.252, 256).

7   My father's almost exclusive use of a typewriter at this time greatly increases the difficulty of elucidating the textual history. His natural method of composition in manuscript was inhibited; and he constantly retyped portions of pages without numbering them.

8   The quotation marks indicated 'actual extracts from the longer annals and tales that are found in the Red Book'.

9   My father reverted to the use of *k* instead of *c* in this text.

(II) THE TALE OF ARAGORN AND ARWEN

Of the texts of *Aragorn and Arwen* the earliest in succession is also very plainly the first actual setting down of the tale. It was not 'a part of the tale', as it came to be called in Appendix A, and was indeed quite differently conceived. It is a rough, much corrected manuscript, which I will call 'A', and a portion of it is in typescript (not separate, but taking up from manuscript and returning to it on the same pages). Unless this peculiarity itself suggests that it belongs with the late work on the Appendices, there seems to be no clear and certain evidence of its relative date; but its peculiar subsequent history may indicate that

it had been in existence for some time when my father was working on
the narrative of the Realms in Exile described in the preceding section.

The manuscript, which bears the title *Of Aragorn and Arwen
Undómiel*, begins thus.

In the latter days of the last age [> Ere the Elder Days were
ended],[1] before the War of the Ring, there was a man named
Dirhael [> Dirhoel], and his wife was Evorwen [> Ivorwen]
daughter of Gilbarad, and they dwelt in a hidden fastness in the
wilds of Eriador; for they were of the ancient people of the
Dúnedain, that of old were kings of men, but were now fallen
on darkened days. Dirhael [> Dirhoel] and his wife were of high
lineage, being of the blood of Isildur though not of the right line
of the Heirs. They were both foresighted in many things. Their
daughter was Gilrain, a fair maid, fearless and strong as were all
the women of that kin. She was sought in marriage by Arathorn,
the son of Arador who was the Chieftain of the Dúnedain of the
North.

Arathorn was a stern man of full years; for the Heirs of Isildur, being men of long life (even to eight score years and more)
who journeyed much and went often into great perils, were not
accustomed to wed until they had laboured long in the world.
But Gilrain was younger than the age at which women of the
Dúnedain were wont at that time to take husbands; and she did
not yet desire to be a wife, and sought the counsel of her
parents. Then Dírhael said: 'Arathorn is a mighty man, and he
will be Lord of the Dúnedain sooner than men look for, yet soon
again he will be lord no longer; for I forebode that he will be
short-lived.' But Evorwen said: 'That may well be, yet if these
two wed, their child shall be great among the great in this
age of the world, and he shall bring the Dúnedain out of the
shadows.'

Therefore Gilrain consented and was wedded to Arathorn;
and it came to pass that after one year Arador was taken by
trolls and slain in the Coldfells, and Arathorn became Lord of
the Dúnedain; and again after one year his wife bore a son and
he was named Aragorn. And Aragorn being now the son of the
Heir of Isildur went with his mother and dwelt in the House of
Elrond in Imladris, for such was the custom in that day, and
Elrond had in his keeping the heirlooms of the Dúnedain, chief
of which were the shards of the sword of Elendil who came to
Middle-earth out of Númenor at its downfall. In his boyhood
Arathorn also had been fostered in that house, and he was a

friend of Elladan and Elrohir, the sons of Elrond, and often he went a-hunting with them. Now the sons of Elrond did not hunt wild beasts, but they pursued the Orcs wherever they might find them; and this they did because of Celebrían their mother, daughter of Galadriel.

On a time long ago, as she passed over the Mountains to visit her mother in the Land of Lórien, Orcs waylaid the road, and she was taken captive by them and tormented; and though she was rescued by Elrond and his sons, and brought home and tended, and her hurts of body were healed, she lay under a great cloud of fear and she loved Middle-earth no longer; so that at the last Elrond granted her prayer, and she passed to the Grey Havens and went into the West, never to return.

Thus it befell that when Aragorn was only two years of age Arathorn went riding with the sons of Elrond and fought with Orcs that had made an inroad into Eriador, and he was slain, for an orc-arrow pierced his eye; and so he proved indeed short-lived for one of his race, being no more than sixty winters when he fell.

But the child Aragorn became thus untimely Chieftain of the Dúnedain, and he was nurtured in the House of Elrond, and there he was loved by all, and Elrond was a father to him. Straight and tall he grew with grey eyes both keen and grave, and he was hardy and valiant and strong of wit, and eager to learn all lore of Elves and Men.

And when he was still but a youth, yet strong withal, he went abroad with Elladan and Elrohir and learned much of hunting and of war, and many secrets of the wild. But he knew naught of his own ancestry, for his mother did not speak to him of these things, nor any else in that House; and it was at the bidding of Elrond that these matters were kept secret. For there was at that time a Shadow in the East that crept over many lands, and filled the Wise with foreboding, since they had discovered that this was indeed the shadow of Sauron, the Dark Lord that had returned to Middle-earth again, and that he desired to find the One Ring that Isildur took, and sought to learn if any heir of Isildur yet lived upon earth; and the spies of Sauron were many.

But at length, when Aragorn was twenty years of age, it chanced that he returned to Imladris ...

I leave the original manuscript here, for this is sufficient to show the nature of its relation to the published text: the latter being marked by a general reduction, compression of what was retained and omission of allusive passages, notably the story of Celebrían.[2] But as will be seen, the reason for this was not, or was not primarily, the result of a critical view taken by my father of the telling of the tale, but of the use to which he later thought of putting it.

From this point the final version offers no contradiction to the original text, and in fact remains closer to it than in the part that I have cited,[3] until the plighting of troth by Aragorn and Arwen on the hill of Kerin Amroth (RK p. 341); soon after this, however, it diverges altogether.

And there upon that hill they looked east to the shadow and west to the twilight, and they plighted their troth and were glad. Yet many years still lay between them.[4]

For when Elrond learned the choice of his daughter he did not forbid it; but he said to Aragorn: 'Not until you are come to your full stature shall you wed with Arwen Undómiel, and she shall not be the bride of any less than a king of both Gondor and Arnor.'

But the days darkened in Middle-earth, as the power of Sauron grew, and in Mordor the Dark Tower of Barad-dûr rose ever taller and stronger. And though Aragorn and Arwen at times met briefly again their days were sundered. For the time drew on now to the War of the Ring at the end of that age of the world ...

There follows now a long passage (more than 500 words, with a part of it rejected and replaced by a new version) in which the history of the war is given in summary: telling of Mithrandir and the Halflings, the doubts of the Wise, the Ringwraiths, the Company of the Ring, and the quest of the Ringbearer; and then more expressly of Aragorn, of the Paths of the Dead, the Pelennor Fields, the battle before the Morannon, and his crowning at the gates of Minas Tirith. At the end of this the tale moves quickly to its conclusion.

And when all this was done Elrond came forth from Imladris and Galadriel from Lórien, and they brought with them Arwen Undómiel Evenstar of her people. And she made the choice of Lúthien, to become mortal and abide in Middle-earth, and she was wedded to Aragorn Arathornsson, King of Gondor and Arnor, and she was Queen and Lady of Elves and Men.

Thus ended the Third Age. Yet it is said that bitterest of all the sorrows of that age was the parting of Arwen and Elrond. For they were sundered by the Sea and by a doom beyond the end of the world. For when the Great Ring was unmade the Three Rings of the Elves failed also, and Elrond was weary of Middle-earth at last and departed seeking Celebrían, and returned never again. But Arwen became a mortal woman, and yet even so it was not her lot to die until she had lost all that she gained. For though she lived with Aragorn for five score years after and great was their glory together, yet at the last he said farewell and laid him down and died ere old age unmanned him. But she went from the city and from her children, and passed away to the land of Lothlórien, and dwelt there alone under the fading trees: for Galadriel also was gone and Lórien was withering. And then at last, it is said, she laid herself to rest upon Kerin Amroth; and there was her green grave, until all the world was changed, and all the days of her life utterly forgotten by men that came after, and elanor and nifredil bloomed no more east of the Sea.[5]

This earliest manuscript was followed by a fair copy of it in type-script ('B'), in which only a few and minor changes were introduced.[6] But the whole of the latter part of it, from the beginning of the account of the War of the Ring and its origins, was struck out, and my father clipped to the typescript new pages, in which he extended that account to nearly twice its original length. Most of this new version was then again rewritten, at even greater length, and attached as a rider to the typescript. It was now much less of a résumé than it was at first, and its purpose in the work as a whole is clearly seen. 'It was the part of Aragorn,' my father wrote, 'as Elrond foresaw, to be the chief Captain of the West, and by his wisdom yet more than his valour to redress the past and the folly of his forefather Isildur.' I cite a part of it from this final form.

Thus the War of the Ring began; and the shards of the sword of Elendil were forged anew, and Aragorn Arathorn's son arose and fulfilled his part, and his valour and wisdom were revealed to Men. Songs were made after in Gondor and Arnor concern-ing his deeds in that time which long were remembered, but are not here full-told. It was not his task to bear the burden of the Ring, but to be a leader in those battles by which the Eye of Sauron was turned far from his own land and from the secret peril which crept upon him in the dark. Indeed, it is said that Sauron believed that the Lord Aragorn, heir of Isildur, had found the Ring and had taken it to himself, even as his fore-father had done, and arose now to challenge the tyrant of Mordor and set himself in his place.

But it was not so, and in this most did Aragorn reveal his strength; for though the Ring came indeed within his grasp, he took it not, and refused to wield its evil power, but surrendered it to the judgement of Elrond and to the Bearer whom he appointed. For it was the hard counsel of Elrond that though their need might seem desperate and the time overlate, nonetheless the Ring should even now be taken in secret, if it might be, to the land of their Enemy and there cast into the fire of Mount Doom in Mordor where it was made. Aragorn guided the Ringbearer on the long and perilous journey from Imladris in the North, until he was lost in the wild hills and passed beyond the help of his friends. Then Aragorn turned to war and the defence of the City of Gondor, Minas Tirith upon Anduin, the last bulwark of the westlands against the armies of Sauron.

In all this time, while the world darkened and Aragorn was abroad in labour and danger, Arwen abode in Imladris; and there from afar she watched over him in thought, and in hope under the Shadow she wrought for him a great and royal standard, such as only one might display who claimed the lordship of the Númenóreans and the inheritance of Elendil and Isildur. And this she sent to him by the hands of his kinsfolk, the last of the Dúnedain of the North; and they came upon Aragorn on the plain of Rohan, after the battles in which Saruman the traitor was overcome and Isengard destroyed, and they delivered to Aragorn the standard of Arwen and her message; for she bade him look to the peril from the sea, and to take the Paths of the Dead. Now this was a way beneath the White Mountains of Gondor that no man dared to tread, because of the fell wraiths of the Forgotten Men that guarded it. But Aragorn dared to take that way with the Grey Company of the North, and he passed through, and so came about by the shores of the sea, unlookedfor by foe or by friend. Thus he captured the ships of the Enemy, and came up out of the deep by the waters of Anduin to the succour of Gondor in the hour of its despair; for the city of Minas Tirith was encircled by the armies of Mordor and was perishing in flame. Then was fought and won beyond hope the great battle of the Fields of Pelennor, and the Lord of the Black Riders was destroyed; but Aragorn unfurled the standard of Arwen, and in that day men first hailed Aragorn as king.

At the end of this account of Aragorn's commanding significance in the War of the Ring, the revised ending of the story in the typescript B concludes with his farewell to Arwen at his death almost exactly as it stands in Appendix A.[7] The original manuscript pages in which my father first set down this inspired passage are preserved. He wrote them so fast that without the later text scarcely a word would be interpretable.

The revised text in B ends with the words 'Here endeth the tale of the Elder Days'. My father altered this in manuscript to 'Here endeth the Tale, and with the passing of the Evenstar all is said of the Elder Days.'

Briefly to recapitulate, the typescript B as originally made had been scarcely more than a clear text of the original rough manuscript A. The latter part of it was rewritten and expanded (Aragorn's part in the War of the Ring, his dying words with Arwen) and incorporated into the typescript. My father then made a further typescript ('C'), which was a fair copy of the text as it now stood in B, much of it indeed scarcely necessary. At this stage, therefore, none of the compression and small stylistic changes that distinguish the original manuscript from the final form in Appendix A had yet entered. It still began 'Ere the Elder Days were ended', still included the story of Celebrían, and of course the major element of Aragorn's part in the War of the Ring; in relation to the final version all it lacked was Aragorn's parting from his mother Gilrain (RK p. 342).

It is hard to say how my father saw *Aragorn and Arwen* at that time, when he clearly felt that it was in finished form, or where it should stand. He took great pains with the story of Aragorn which was after-wards lost. He ended it with great finality: 'Here endeth the Tale, and with the passing of the Evenstar all is said of the Elder Days.' Can it have been his intention that it should stand as the final element of *The Lord of the Rings*?

The subsequent history is very curious. I have mentioned (p. 258) that when writing the narrative of the North Kingdom he experimented with the introduction of the story of Aragorn and Arwen. This was to follow the account of how, when King Elessar came to the North, Hobbits from the Shire would visit him in his house in Annúminas (RK p. 324); and it enters on the typescript page with extraordinary abruptness (even allowing for the device of supposed extracts from written sources to account for such transitions):

> ... and some ride away with him and dwell in his house as long as they have a mind. Master Samwise the Mayor and Thain Peregrin have been there many times.
>   Arador was the grandfather of the King. ...

It may seem that my father did not know what to do with the story, or perhaps rather, did not know what it might be possible to do with it. But it was here, strangely enough, that the abbreviation and com-pression and stylistic 'reduction' that distinguishes the final form of *Aragorn and Arwen* from the original version first entered. The text in these abandoned pages of 'The Realms in Exile' is (if not quite at all points) that of the story in Appendix A.[8] It extended only to the words 'She shall not be the bride of any Man less than the King of both Gondor and Arnor' (RK p. 342); but in manuscript notes accompanying it my father sketched out a reduction of the story of Aragorn's part in the War of the Ring to a few lines: for this element in the original story was obviously wholly incompatible with such a placing of it – which would seem in any case unsuitable and unsatisfactory. He obviously thought so too. But it is interesting to see that in the final typescript from which the story as it stands in Appendix A was printed the page on which it begins still carries at the top the words 'Master Samwise the Mayor and Thain Peregrin have been there many times', struck out and replaced by 'Here follows a part of the Tale of Aragorn and Arwen'. 'A part', presumably, because so much had gone.

A few changes were made to this last typescript of the tale, among them the substitution of *Estel* for *Amin* (see note 8) at all occurrences, and the introduction of the departure of Gilraen from Rivendell (RK p. 342) and her parting with Aragorn, with the words *Onen i-Estel Edain, ú-chebin estel anim.*

Thus the original design of the tale of Aragorn and Arwen had been lost; but the actual reason for this was the abandoned experiment of inserting it into the history of the North Kingdom. I can say no more of this strange matter.

NOTES

1 So also Aragorn declared to Arwen on his deathbed that he was 'the latest King of the Elder Days' (RK p. 343), and at the end of text B of the primary version 'with the passing of the Evenstar all is said of the Elder Days' (p. 268). See p. 173 and note 7.

2 On the other hand, while the concealment of Aragorn's ancestry from him in his youth was present in the original form of the tale, the giving to him of another name (*Estel* in the final version, see note 8) was not.

3 The distinction between 'thou' and 'you' was clearly made in the original manuscript, though sometimes blurred inadvertently, and it was retained and made precise in the text that followed it: thus Aragorn uses 'you' to Elrond, and to Arwen at their first meeting, whereas Elrond and Arwen address him with 'thou, thee'.

4 Thus their words together on Kerin Amroth, concerning the Shadow and the Twilight, were not yet present; see note 6.

5 The last sentences are put in the present tense in the published text. But when my father wrote *Aragorn and Arwen* he did not conceive it as a citation from an ancient source, and did not place it all within quotation marks.

6 To this text were added in a rider the words of Aragorn and Arwen on Kerin Amroth (see note 4); but after Arwen's words the passage

ended: 'For very great was her love for her father; but not yet did Aragorn understand the fullness of her words.'

7 There were a few differences from the final form. When Arwen spoke of 'the gift of Eru Ilúvatar' which is bitter to receive, Aragorn answered: 'Bitter in truth. But let us not be overthrown at the final test, who fought the Shadow of old. In sorrow we must go, for sorrow is appointed to us; and indeed by sorrow we do but say that that which is ended is good. But let us not go in despair.' He named himself 'the latest King of the Elder Days' (see note 1), but when he was dead 'long there he lay, an image of the splendour of the Kings of Men in glory undimmed, before the passing of the Elder Days and the change of the world': this was altered on the typescript to 'before the breaking of the world'. And at the moment of his death Arwen did not cry 'Estel, Estel!', for the name given to him in his youth had not yet arisen (see notes 2 and 8).

8 It was in this text that Aragorn's name in Rivendell entered, but here it was *Amin*, not *Estel*, though likewise translated 'Hope'. Here Aragorn's mother's name became *Gilraen* for earlier *Gilrain*, and Ivorwen's father Gilbarad disappeared.

(III) THE HOUSE OF EORL

The history of Appendix A II, *The House of Eorl*, has no perplexities. From the early period of my father's work on the Appendices there are three brief texts, which I will refer to as I, II, and III, probably written in close succession, and with the third he had evidently achieved a satisfactory formulation of all that he wished to say of the rulers of the Mark. As I judge, he then put it aside for a long time.

It seems that the names of the Kings of the Mark were first set down on paper in the course of the writing of the chapter *The Last Debate*: when Gimli in his story of the Paths of the Dead (at that time placed at this point in the narrative) spoke of the mailclad skeleton by the closed door and Aragorn's words 'Here lies Baldor son of Brego', my father interrupted the story with the list of names, to which he added dates in the Shire-reckoning (see VIII.408). I concluded that it was only the dates of Fengel, Thengel, and Théoden that belong with the writing of the manuscript; but it is a striking fact that already at that time the dates of those kings were not greatly different from those in Appendix A (RK p. 350). Particularly noteworthy is that of the birth of Théoden, S.R.1328 = 2928. In text I it remains 2928 (in both I and II the dates were all still given in Shire-reckoning, but it is more convenient to convert them); so also in II, but corrected to 2948 (the final date). In the draft manuscript T 3 of the Tale of Years it was 2928, but in T 4 (p. 239) it was 2948. This is sufficient to show that these early texts of *The House of Eorl* were contemporary with those texts of the Tale of Years.

In the first two texts my father was chiefly concerned with the elaboration of the chronology in detail, and they consist only of the names of the kings and their dates,[1] with notes added to a few of them. In I, which was written very rapidly on a small sheet, under Eorl the Field of Celebrant and the gift of Rohan are mentioned, and it is said that he began the building of Meduseld and died in battle against Easterlings in the Wold in 2545; of Brego that he drove them out in 2546, completed Meduseld, and died of grief for his son Baldor in 2570; of Aldor the Old that 'he first established Dunharrow as a refuge-fort'. In the note on Helm, however, is seen the first appearance of the tale told in Appendix A, very hastily written and still undeveloped:

> In his day there was an invasion from west of Dunlanders and of S. Gondor by pirates and by Easterlings and Orcs. In 2758 in the Long Winter they took refuge in Helm's Deep.[2] Both his sons Háma and Haeleth were killed (lost in snow). At his death there was in the kingdom an upstart king Wulf not of Eorl's line [who] with help of Dunlanders tried to seize throne. Eventually Fréalaf son of Hild his sister and nearest heir was victorious and became king. A new line of mounds was started to symbolize break in direct line.

There are no notes on the Kings of the Second Line save Fengel, of whom it is recorded that he was the youngest son of Folcwine, for his elder brothers, named here Folcwalda and Folcred, were 'killed in battle in service of Gondor against Harad'. The final note in I states that Éomer was the son of Théoden's sister Théodwyn (who does not appear in the narrative), and that 'he wedded Morwen daughter of Húrin of Gondor'. This is Húrin of the Keys, who was in command of Minas Tirith when the host of the West rode to the Black Gate (RK p. 237); I do not think that there is any other reference to the marriage of Éomer with his daughter, who was corrected on the text to Lothíriel daughter of Prince Imrahil.

The second text II was a fair copy of I, with scarcely any change in content other than in detail of dates. Where in I it was said only that Eorl was 'born in the North', in II he was 'born in Irenland in the North'. This name was struck out and replaced by *Éothéod*, and this is very probably where that name first appeared (it is found also in both texts of the original 'Appendix on Languages', p. 34, §14). It was now further said of Éomer that he 'became a great king and extended his realm west of the Gap of Rohan to the regions between Isen and Greyflood, including Dunland.'[3]

The last text (III) of this period was a finely written manuscript which begins with a brief account of the origin of the Rohirrim in the Men of Éothéod and their southward migration.

The House of Eorl

Eorl the Young was lord of the Men of Éothéod. This land lay near the sources of the Anduin, between the upper ranges of the Misty Mountains and the northernmost parts of Mirkwood. Thither the Éothéod had removed some hundreds of years before from lands further south in the vale of Anduin. They were originally close kin of the Beornings and the men of the west-eaves of the forest; but they loved best the plains and wide fields, and they delighted in horses and in all feats of horseman-ship. In the days of Garman father of Eorl they had grown to a numerous people somewhat straitened in the land of their home.

In the two thousand five hundred and tenth year of the Third Age a great peril threatened the land of Gondor in the South and wild men out of the East assailed its northern borders, allying themselves with Orcs of the mountains. The invaders overran and occupied Calenardon, the great plains in the north of the realm. The Steward of Gondor sent north for help, for there had ever been friendship between the men of Anduin's vale and the people of Gondor. Hearing of the need of Gondor from afar Eorl set out with a great host of riders; and it was chiefly by his valour and the valour of the horsemen of Éothéod that victory was obtained. In the great battle of the Field of Celebrant the Easterlings and Orcs were utterly defeated and the horsemen of Eorl pursued them over the plains of Calenardon until not one remained.

Cirion Steward of Gondor in reward gave Calenardon to Eorl and his people, and they sent north for their wives and their children and their goods, and they settled in that land. They named it anew the Mark of the Riders, and themselves they called the Eorlingas; but in Gondor the land was called Rohan, and the people the Rohirrim (that is the Horse-lords). Thus Eorl became the first King of the Mark, and he chose for his dwelling a green hill before the feet of the White Mountains that fenced in that land at the south.

This is the origin of the opening, greatly expanded, of *The House of Eorl* in Appendix A (RK pp. 344–5). In the remainder of the text, the line of the Kings of the Mark, there was very little further develop-ment: the story of Helm Hammerhand remained in substance exactly as it was, and nothing further was said of any of the kings except Thengel, Théoden, and Éomer. Of Thengel it is recorded that he married late, and had three daughters and one son, but his long sojourn in Gondor (and the character of his father Fengel that led to it) had not emerged. The death of Éomund chief Marshal of the Mark in an Orc-raid in 3002 is recorded, with the note that 'Orcs at this time began often to raid eastern Rohan and steal horses', and the fostering of his children Éomer and Éowyn in the house of Théoden. The note on Théoden that entered in III was retained almost unchanged in Appendix A.[4]

A long note was now appended to Éomer, with the same passage as is found in Appendix A (RK p. 351, footnote) concerning Éowyn, 'Lady of the Shieldarm', and the reference to Meriadoc's name Hold-wine given to him by Éomer; and the statement of the extent of his realm appearing in II (p. 271) was rewritten: 'In Éomer's time the realm was extended west beyond the Gap of Rohan as far as the Greyflood and the sea-shores between that river and the Isen, and north to the borders of Lórien, and his men and horses multiplied exceedingly.'

There is no other writing extant before the final typescript of *The House of Eorl* from which the text in Appendix A was printed, save for a single typescript page. This is the first page of the text, beginning 'Eorl was the lord of the Men of Éothéod', and my father wrote it with the old version III, given above, before him; but he expanded it almost to the form that it has in Appendix A.[5] It includes, however, the following passage (struck out on the typescript) after the words 'the Riders hunted them over the plains of Calenardhon':

> In the forefront of the charge they saw two great horsemen, clad in grey, unlike all the others, and the Orcs fled before them; but when the battle was won they could not be found, and none knew whence they came or whither they went. But in Rivendell it was recorded that these were the sons of Elrond, Elladan and Elrohir.[6]

There is also the curious point that where in Appendix A it is said that 'Cirion ... gave Calenardhon between Anduin and Isen to Eorl and his people' this text had (before correction) 'Cirion ... gave Calenardhon, and Dor Haeron between Entwash and Isen, to Eorl and his people'. I do not know of any other occurrence of this name, or of any other suggestion that the name Calenardhon applied only to the region east of the Entwash.

The father of Eorl was still named Garman, as in the old version III (p. 272), and that name appeared in the final text, where it was emended to Léod.

It is, once again, possible and indeed probable that this page survived for some reason from a complete or more complete draft, which has been lost; for if no text has been lost it would have to be concluded that my father composed *ab initio* on the typewriter the whole narrative of *The House of Eorl*, with the stories of Léod and the horse Felaróf, and of Helm Hammerhand, exactly as it stands in Appendix A.

NOTES

1   As far as Folcwine the fourteenth king the dates were already in I almost the same as those in Appendix A, though in many cases differing by a year; it was only with the last kings that there was much movement in the dates.

2   Cf. the entry in the text T 4 of the Tale of Years, entry 2758–9 (p. 236): 'Helm of Rohan takes refuge from his enemies in Helm's Deep in the White Mountains'; and also the note to the Steward Beren in *The Heirs of Elendil*, p. 205.

3   In text II Helm's son Haeleth became Haleth; and the eleventh king Léof was replaced probably at the time of writing by Brytta (on this see IX.68 and note 11). The sons of Folcwine (Folcwalda and Folcred in I) were not named in II, but my father changed Fengel to Fastred; he then added in the names of Folcwine's sons as Folcred and Fastred and changed that of the king to Felanath, before finally reverting to Fengel. In the manuscript T 4 of the Tale of Years (p. 238, year 2885) the death of Folcwine's sons 'in the service of Gondor' is recorded, and there their names are Folcred and Fastred.

4   The note on Théoden in III ends with the statement that his only child and son was Théodred 'whose mother Elfhild of Eastfold died in childbirth', and a record of Théodred's death in battle against Saruman. Théoden's name *Ednew* ('Renewed') is here given in the Old English form *Edníwe*; and Minas Tirith is called *Mundberg* (although text II has *Mundburg*: on which see VII.449, note 7, and VIII.356, note 9).

5   In the First Edition there were no notes, in the list of the Kings of the Mark, to the eleventh, twelfth, and thirteenth kings, Brytta, Walda, and Folca.

6   Cf. p. 236, annal 2510.

(IV) DURIN'S FOLK

My father's original text of what would become the section *Durin's Folk* in Appendix A is extant: a brief, clear manuscript written on scrap paper entitled *Of Durin's Line*, accompanied by a genealogy forming a part of the text. It was corrected in a few points, and one substantial passage was added; these changes were made, I think, at or soon after the writing of the manuscript. I give this text in full, with the changes shown where they are of any significance.

Durin was the name of one of the fathers of all the race of the Dwarves. In the deeps of time and the beginning of that people he came to Azanulbizar, the Dimrill Dale, and in the caves above Kibil-nâla [> Kheled-zâram],[1] the Mirrormere, in the east of the Misty Mountains, he made his dwelling, where after were the Mines of Moria renowned in song. There long he dwelt: so long that he was known far and wide as Durin the Deathless. Yet he died indeed at the last ere the Elder Days were ended, and his tomb was in Moria; but his line never failed, from father to son, and ever and anon [> thrice][2] there was born an heir to that house so like unto his Forefather that he received the name of Durin, being held indeed by the Dwarves to be the Deathless that returned. It was after the end of the First Age that the great power and wealth of Moria began, for it was enriched by many folk and much lore and craft, when the ancient cities of Nogrod and Belegost were ruined in the change of the western world and the breaking of Morgoth. And it came to pass that / at the height of the glory of Moria [> in the midst of the Third Age, while the wealth of Moria was still undiminished] Durin was the name of its king, being the second since the Forefather that had borne that title. And the Dwarves delved deep in his days, seeking ever for *mithril*, the metal beyond price that was found in those mines alone, beneath Barazinbar, the mighty Redhorn Mountain. But they roused thus from sleep a thing of terror that had lain hidden at the foundations of the world, and that was a Balrog of Morgoth. And Durin was slain by the Balrog, and after him Náin his son was slain, and the glory of Moria passed, and its people were destroyed or fled far away. For the most part they passed into the North; but Thráin Náin's son, the king by inheritance, came to Erebor, the Lonely Mountain, nigh to the eastern eaves of Mirkwood, and established his realm for a while.

But Glóin his grandson [> Thorin his son] removed and abandoned Erebor, and passed into the far North where the most of his kin now dwelt. But it came to pass that dragons arose and multiplied in the North, and made war upon the Dwarves, and plundered their works and wealth; and many of the Dwarves fled again southward and eastward. Then Thrór Dáin's son, the great-great-grandson of Thráin, returned to Erebor and became King-under-the-Mountain, and prospered exceedingly, having the friendship of all that dwelt near, whether Elves or Men or the birds and beasts of the land.

But Smaug the Golden heard rumour of his treasure and came upon him at unawares, and he descended upon the Mountain in flame, and destroyed all that region, and he entered the deep halls of the Dwarves and lay there long upon a bed of gold. / And it is elsewhere told how the Dwarves were avenged, [> From the sack and the burning Thrór escaped, and being now homeless he returned to Moria, but there was slain in the dark by an Orc. Thráin his son and Thorin his grandson gathered then the scattered folk of Durin's race and made war on the Orcs of the Misty Mountains in revenge for Thrór. They were victorious but their people were so diminished that they could not and dared not re-enter Moria. Dáin their kinsman went away to the Iron Hills, but Thráin and Thorin became wanderers. Thráin, it is said, was the possessor of the last of the Seven Rings of the Dwarf-lords of old, but he was captured by the Sorcerer and taken to Dol Guldur, and there perished in torment. Elsewhere is told of the wanderings of Thorin Oakenshield, last of the direct line of Durin,[3] in search of revenge and the restoration of his fortune; and how by the help of Gandalf the Grey he was indeed avenged at last,][4] and Smaug was slain, and after the Battle of Five Armies the kingship under the Mountain was restored. Yet Thorin Oakenshield, grandson of Thrór, was slain in that battle, and the right line was broken, and the crown passed to Dáin, a kinsman of Thorin. And the line of Dáin and the wealth and renown of the kingship endured in Erebor until the world grew old, and the days of the Dwarves were ended.

In this text and its accompanying genealogical table (which I have here redrawn) it is seen that an important advance had been made from the text T 4 of the Tale of Years, where it was told under the year 2590 that Thrór 'founded the realm of Erebor' (p. 236): as I said in a note on that entry, 'the history of Thrór's ancestors had not yet emerged'.[5] Here that history is present, but not yet precisely in the final form; for the names of 'the kings of Durin's folk' in the genealogical table here run Thorin I : Glóin : Dáin I, whereas in that in Appendix A they are Thorin I : Glóin : Óin : Náin II : Dáin I; thus in the present text Thrór is called 'the great-great-grandson of Thráin [I]'. While the history was at this stage the corrections and additions were made to T 4: see p. 252, The Dwarves.

Various names found in the later genealogy are absent here, Thrór's brother Frór and Thorin Oakenshield's brother Frerin; most notably, the brother of Dáin I is not Borin but Nár (and of his descendants only Óin and Glóin are shown). Nár was the name of the sole companion

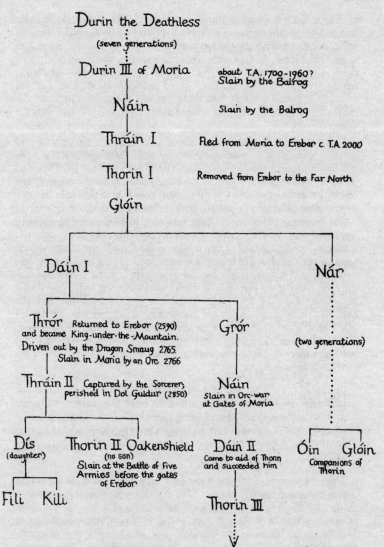

Durin the Deathless

(seven generations)

Durin III of Moria — about T.A. 1700–1960?
Slain by the Balrog

Náin — Slain by the Balrog

Thráin I — Fled from Moria to Erebor c. T.A. 2000

Thorin I — Removed from Erebor to the Far North

Glóin

Dáin I

Nár

Thrór — Returned to Erebor (2590) and became King-under-the-Mountain. Driven out by the Dragon Smaug 2765. Slain in Moria by an Orc 2766

Grór

(two generations)

Thráin II — Captured by the Sorcerer, perished in Dol Guldur (2850)

Náin — Slain in Orc-war at Gates of Moria

Dís (daughter)

Thorin II Oakenshield (no son) — Slain at the Battle of Five Armies before the gates of Erebor

Dáin II — Came to aid of Thorin and succeeded him

Óin   Glóin — Companions of Thorin

Fili   Kili

Thorin III

of Thrór on his ill-fated journey to Moria (RK pp. 354–5), who brought to Thráin the news of his father's slaying by Azog; he is called 'old', but there is no suggestion that he was Thrór's uncle. Since *Nár* is an Old Norse dwarf-name (occurring in the Völuspá), and since there is no evidence that the story of Thrór's death (apart of course from the fact of his having been killed in Moria by an Orc) had yet emerged, it seems unlikely that there was any connection between the two. – It will also be seen that while Thorin III appears, Durin the Last does not.

This text was followed by a second version, a well-written and scarcely corrected manuscript with the title *Of Durin's Race*, very similar in appearance to text III of *The House of Eorl* (p. 272) and probably contemporary with it. So closely did my father preserve the original text (as emended and expanded) that I think that it must have followed at once, or at any rate after no long interval.

The passage added to the first version was slightly filled out and improved, but the only difference worth noticing here lies in the sentences following the words 'made war on the Orcs of the Misty Mountains in revenge for Thrór', which now read: 'Long and deadly was that war, and it was fought for the most part in dark places beneath the earth; and at the last the Dwarves had the victory, and in the Battle before the Gate of Moria ten thousand Orcs were slain. But the Dwarves suffered also grievous loss and his folk were now so diminished that Thráin dared not to enter Moria, and his people were dispersed again.' The only really significant difference from the first version, however, lies in the final sentence, which became:

> And the line of Dáin prospered, and the wealth and renown of the kingship was renewed, until there arose again for the last time an heir of that House that bore the name of Durin, and he returned to Moria; and there was light again in deep places, and the ringing of hammers and the harping of harps, until the world grew old and the Dwarves failed and the days of Durin's race were ended.

Thus it was here that 'Durin the Last' emerged, and it is said of him that he returned from Erebor to Moria and re-established it (as is said in the accompanying genealogical table). To this my father never referred again; as Robert Foster noted in *The Complete Guide to Middle-earth*, 'There is no mention of a recolonization of Khazad-dûm in the Fourth Age, despite the death of the Balrog.' It is impossible to discover whether my father did in fact reject this idea, or whether it simply became 'lost' in the haste with which the Appendices were finally prepared for publication. The fact that he made no reference to 'Durin VII and Last', though he appears in the genealogy in Appendix A, is possibly a pointer to the latter supposition.

There are two copies of the genealogical table accompanying the second version, but they are essentially the same: my father made the second one simply because he had not left enough space in the first and the names on the right-hand side had to be cramped (as with the other 'finished' manuscripts of that time he clearly intended this to be in publishable form as it stood, or at any rate to be in a form from which a perfectly accurate typescript could be made). In these tables he did little more than copy the preceding version (p. 277), but there are certain differences. He retained 'seven generations' between Durin the Deathless and Durin III of Moria, but carefully erased 'seven' and replaced it by 'twelve' (later pencilling 'many'). The name Nár of the brother of Dáin I was replaced by Borin, and where the original table only marks 'two generations' between Nár and Óin and Glóin this is now filled out as in the final table, with Fundin the father of Balin and Dwalin and Gróin the father of Óin and Glóin; but a space is left blank for Borin's son Farin. The notes and dates in the original table remain the same, with no additions that need be recorded, save 'Balin returned to Moria and there perished (2994)', and the same note concerning Ori, Nori, Dori, Bifur, Bofur, and Bombur as appears in the final genealogy. Thorin III is now called 'Stonehelm', and 'Durin the Last' is shown as his son, 'who re-established the Realm of Moria'; beneath his name is a dotted arrow (as beneath Thorin III in the original table) indicating unnamed descendants.

There is no other writing on this subject from the early period of work on the Appendices. But unlike the textual situation in the case of the Northern Line of the Realms in Exile and of *The House of Eorl*, in which the final typescripts have virtually no antecedents (see pp. 257–8, 273–4), a substantial part of *Durin's Folk* is extant in a draft typescript leading directly to that sent to the printer. My father did indeed achieve in that draft a form that required little further work, but it was achieved through much rewriting as he typed.[6] This underlines, I think, the extreme improbability that those other texts came into being at once in a form that required scarcely any further change; and therefore supports the conclusion that a good deal of the late drafting in typescript has been lost.

But in this case, at any rate, the loss of the draft typescript would have done little more than distort the textual development in some details; it would have deprived this history only of the Dwarvish name *Zigilnâd* of the Silverlode (cf. *Zirak-zigil* 'Silvertine', VII.174–5, note 22) – in itself surprising, in view of *Kibil-nâla* in *The Lord of the Rings* (see note 1).

The draft typescript, however, became rough manuscript, though still closely approaching the final form (RK pp. 356–7), with the story of the great burning of the dead at the end of the Battle of Azanulbizar, and the departure of Thráin and Thorin Oakenshield to Dunland and afterwards to a new home in exile in the Blue Mountains, where they prospered, though forced to work with iron. This section ends, as in the published text, 'But, as Thrór had said, the Ring needed gold to breed gold, and of that or any other precious metal they had little or none.' My father drew a line here, as if the text were completed; but the mention of the Ring of Thráin led him to say something further about it. From this point the manuscript becomes rougher, and as it proceeded he wrote so fast that it is only barely legible and with much difficulty; and from this point also the published text soon departs from it altogether.

This Ring was the last of the Seven. It may well be that this was known to Sauron, and that the singular misfortunes of his House were due to that. For the days were passed when it would bring profit, but demanded payment rather, and its possession brought only the hate of Sauron. For the Dwarves had proved hard to tame. They were too tough, being made of a purpose to resist such onslaughts of evil will and power, and though they could be slain or broken they could not be made into shadows or slaves of any other will; and for like reason their lives were little affected, to live either longer or shorter because of the Ring.[7] The more did Sauron hate them. Nonetheless each possessor kept his ring as a secret unless he surrendered it; and though those about him doubtless guessed it, none knew for certain that Thráin had the Ring.

Partly by the very power of the Ring therefore Thráin after some years became restless and discontented. He could not put the thought of gold and gems out of his mind. Therefore at last when he could bear it no longer his heart turned again to Erebor and he resolved to return. He said little to Thorin of what was in his heart. But with Balin and Dwalin and a few others he arose and said farewell and departed (2841).

Little indeed is known of what happened to him afterwards. It would seem (from afterknowledge) that no sooner was he abroad with few companions (and certainly after he came at length back into Rhovanion) he was hunted by the emissaries of Sauron. Wolves pursued him, orcs waylaid him, evil birds shadowed his path, and the more he tried to go north the more he was driven back. One dark night, south of Gladden and the eaves of Mirkwood, he vanished out of their camp, and after long search in vain his companions gave up hope (and returned to Thorin). Only long after was it known that he had been taken alive and brought to the pits of Dol Guldur (2845). There he was tormented and the Ring taken from him; and there at last (2850) he died.[8]

So it would seem that Moria had ended and the line of Durin. After the sack of Erebor Thorin Oakenshield was but 24 (and not yet war-worthy according to Dwarf-custom); but he was 53 at Nanduhirion, and there fought in the van of the assault. But as has been told the first assault was thrown back, and Thráin and Thorin were driven for refuge in a thicket that grew in the valley not far from Kheledzâram before the great burning. There Frerin Thráin's son fell and Fundin his cousin and many others, and both Thráin and Thorin were wounded. Thorin's shield was cloven and he cast it away, and hewing with an axe a branch of an oak tree he held it in his left hand to ward off the strokes of his foes or to wield as a club. Thus he got his name, or also because in memory of this he bore ever after at his back a shield made of oak wood without colour or device, and vowed to do so until he was hailed again as king.[9]

When Thráin went away Thorin was 95, a great dwarf of proud bearing and full manhood. Maybe because rid of the Ring, Thorin long remained in Ered Luin, labouring and journeying and gathering such wealth as he could, until his people had fair houses in the hills, and were not [? ill content], though in their songs they spoke ever of the Lonely Mountain and the wealth and bliss of the Great Hall and the light of the Arkenstone. But the years lengthened, and the embers of his heart began to grow hot as Thorin brooded on the wrongs of his house and people. Remembering too that Thrór had lain upon him the vengeance due to Smaug.

But Erebor was far away and his people only few; and he had little hope that Dáin Ironfoot would help in any attempt upon the dragon. For Thorin thought ever after the manner of his kingly forefathers, counting forces and weapons and the chances of war, as his hammer fell on the red iron in his forge.

It was at this point that Mithrandir entered the story of the House of Durin. He had before troubled himself little with Dwarves. He was a friend to those of good will, and liked well the exiles of Durin's Folk that dwelt in the west. But on a time it happened that Mithrandir was passing west through Eriador (journeying to see Círdan, maybe, or to visit the Shire which he had not entered for some years) when he fell in with Thorin Oakenshield going the same way, and they spoke much together on the road, and at Bree where they rested.

In the morning Mithrandir said to Thorin: 'I have thought much in the night. Now if that seems good to you I will come home with you for a while and we will talk further in greater privacy.' From this meeting there came many events of great moment in the matter of the War of the Ring. Indeed it led to the finding of the Ring and to the involvement of the Shire-folk and the means whereby the Ring was at last destroyed. Wherefore many have supposed that all this Mithrandir purposed and foresaw. But we believe that is not so. For Frodo wrote this passage in the first copy of the Red Book, which because of its length was not included in the tale of the War: Those were glad days when after the crowning we dwelt in the fair house in Minas Tirith with Gandalf ...

I have given the text thus far in order to make clearer than I did, or indeed was able to do, in the section *The Quest of Erebor* in *Unfinished Tales* how my father originally introduced the story of Gandalf and Thorin, and the taking of Bilbo on the journey to the Lonely Mountain, into the appendix on *Durin's Folk*. At that time I was unaware of this text, and have only recently put it together from its dismembered parts, not having realised what they were. I assumed that the manuscript which I called A in *Unfinished Tales* was the original text; but the story that follows from the point where I have left it above was my father's first expression of the idea, and A was a (moderately) fair copy, much rewritten if not essentially changed.[10]

He did a great deal of work on this story before 'it had to go', as he said years later (*Unfinished Tales* p. 11). From the manuscript A he developed the typescript B (of which long extracts were given in *Unfinished Tales*), and B was clearly designed to fit into the text of *Durin's Folk* as it existed by then (see *Unfinished Tales* pp. 327–8).[11] I shall not follow here the evolution in expression and structure through the texts, but I give two notes that belong with the original manuscript, the first of which shows my father's initial thoughts on the story before he wrote it.

From 2842 onwards Thorin lives in exile, but a good many of Durin's Folk gather to him in Ered Luin. They are reduced to poverty (since mines are poor) and travel about as metalworkers. Thorin begins to think of vengeance on Smaug and recovery of his wealth, but he can only envisage this in terms of war – a gathering of all his people and an attempt to slay Smaug. But it is difficult to do. The Iron Hills are a long way away and elsewhere Durin's Folk are widely scattered.

Gandalf now takes a hand. (Since his action led ultimately to the finding of the Ring, and the successful part played by the Hobbits in its destruction, many suppose that all this was in his conscious purpose. Probably not. He himself would say he was 'directed', or that he was 'meant' to take this course, or was 'chosen'.[12] Gandalf was incarnate, in [?real] flesh, and therefore his vision was obscured: he had for the most part (at any rate before his 'death') to act as ordinary people on reason, and principles of right and wrong.) His immediate conscious purposes were probably various. Largely strategic. He knows it is Sauron in Dol Guldur.[13] Knowing the situation in Gondor he may very well have feared the reoccupation of Mordor (but not yet). At present he is concerned with Lórien and Rivendell – Sauron will certainly proceed to war. The presence of Smaug and the depression of Men in the North makes an attack that way toward Angmar and against Rivendell likely. Also he knew and approved of Durin's Folk. Also he was very fond of the Shire-folk and appreciated ..... Bilbo. He wished the Shire-folk to be 'educated'[14] before evil days came, and chose Bilbo (unattached) as an instrument.

In the second passage he was revolving questions arising from Gandalf's finding of Thráin dying in Dol Guldur.

'Your plan is grandiose and belongs to an earlier day. If you wish to regain your wealth or any part of it, you will have to go yourself – with a small band of your most faithful kinsfolk and following.' [*Struck out*: He then reveals to Thorin that] Why did he not then (or much earlier) reveal to Thorin that he had met Thráin in Dol Guldur? Two answers. He had not met him [Thorin] and did not even know where he was. From 2850 on his chief concern had been with Dol Guldur (Saruman) and the Council. He had not been west for a long time (*Hobbit* pp. 13–14. The Old Took died in 2920, so Gandalf had not in 2942 been in the Shire for 22 years and then probably only briefly).[15] He was probably unaware who the Dwarf was in Dol Guldur, since the 7th Ring would be no clue (Dwarves kept the possession of Rings very secret), and Thráin did not know his own name (*Hobbit* p. 35). It was probably only from Thorin's conversation that he guessed – and produced the evidence characteristically at a suitable chance.

In the earliest version of the story (and also in the second text A) Gandalf made no mention of his finding Thráin in Dol Guldur until the very end of the text, in response to a question from Merry about the map and the key; and my father clearly introduced it when the problem discussed in this note presented itself.

'But about that map and key,' said Merry. 'They proved useful, but you never said anything to Thorin about this beforehand. Why, you must have kept them by your own account 100 years without a word!'

'I did,' said Gandalf, 'very nearly. 91 to be exact. But I assure you I could have done little else. Thráin did not know his own name when I found him; and I certainly did not know his. By what toughness of resistance he had kept the key and map hidden in his torments I don't know. Maybe having got the Ring Sauron troubled no further, but left him to rave and die. But of course the map told me the key had something to do with Erebor. But it was far from my concerns at the time. And for long after I was concerned with other matters, with Saruman and his strange reluctance to disturb Sauron in Dol Goldur. It was not until my meeting with Thorin and conversation that I suddenly guessed who the dying Dwarf must have been. Well, well, after that I kept the things back to the last moment. They just turned the scale, and began to make Thorin accept the idea.'[16]

Among other material for *Durin's Folk* are many versions of the genealogical table, beginning with one associated with the draft typescript in which the original form (see pp. 276–8) was still retained, with only five generations between Durin VI (formerly Durin III) and Thrór. The addition of (the first) Óin and Náin II arose when my father formulated a specific pattern of aging and life-span on a page headed 'Notes on Chronology of Durin's Line', from which I cite some extracts, very slightly edited for clarity.

Dwarves of different 'breeds' vary in their longevity. Durin's race were originally long-lived (especially those named Durin), but like most other peoples they had become less so during the Third Age. Their average age (unless they met a violent death) was about 250 years, which they seldom fell far short of, but could occasionally far exceed (up to 300).[17] A Dwarf of 300 was about as rare and aged as a Man of 100.

Dwarves remained young – e.g. regarded as too tender for really hard work or for fighting – until they were 30 or nearly that (Dáin II was very young in 2799 (32) and his slaying of Azog was a great feat). After that they hardened and took on the appearance of age (by human standards) very quickly. By forty all Dwarves looked much alike in age, until they reached what they regarded as old age, about 240. They then began to age and wrinkle and go white quickly (baldness being unknown among them), unless they were going to be long-lived, in which case the process was delayed. Almost the only physical disorder they suffered from (they were singularly immune from diseases such as affected Men, and Halflings) was corpulence. If in prosperous circumstances, many grew very fat at or before 200, and could not do much (save eat) afterwards. Otherwise 'old age' lasted not much more than ten years, and from say 40 or a little before to near 240 (two hundred years) the capacity for toil (and for fighting) of most Dwarves was equally great.

This is followed by the information attributed to Gimli concerning the Dwarf-women, which was preserved in Appendix A (RK p. 360). There is no difference in substance in the present text, except for the statements that they are never forced to wed against their will (which 'would of course be impossible'), and that they have beards. This latter is said also in the 1951 revision of the *Quenta Silmarillion* (XI.205, §5).

It is then said that Dwarves marry late, seldom before they are ninety or more,[18] that they have few children (so many as four being rare), and continues:

To these they are devoted, often rather fiercely: that is, they may treat them with apparent harshness (especially in the desire to ensure that they shall grow up tough, hardy, unyielding), but they defend them with all their power, and resent injuries to them even more than to themselves. The same is true of the attitude of children to parents. For an injury to a father a Dwarf may spend a life-time in achieving revenge. Since the 'kings' or heads of lines are regarded as 'parents' of the whole group, it will be understood how it was that the whole of Durin's Race gathered and marshalled itself to avenge Thrór.

Finally, there is a note on the absence of record concerning the women of the Dwarves:

They are seldom named in genealogies. They join their husbands' families. But if a son is seen to be 110 or so years younger than his father, this usually indicates an elder daughter. Thorin's sister Dís is named simply because of the gallant death of her sons Fili and Kili in defence of Thorin II. The sentiment of affection for sister's children was strong among all peoples of the Third Age, but less so among Dwarves than Men or Elves among whom it was strongest.

The concluding passage in Appendix A, concerning Gimli and Legolas, was derived from the old text of the Tale of Years (p. 244), which had now of course been abandoned.

NOTES

1 Since *Kheled-zâram* and *Kibil-nâla* as the Dwarvish names of Mirrormere and Silverlode entered early in the history of the writing of *The Lord of the Rings* (see VII.167, 174), it seems clear that the naming of Mirrormere *Kibil-nâla* here was a slip without significance, and is unlikely to have any connection with the curious appearance of the name *Zigilnâd* for Silverlode in the draft typescript of *Durin's Folk* (p. 279).

2 'thrice': the Durin who was slain by the Balrog in Moria is named in the accompanying genealogical table 'Durin III'.

3 Thorin Oakenshield was not the 'last of the direct line of Durin'; no doubt my father meant that he was the last in the unbroken descent of the kings from father to son (cf. 'the right line was broken' a few lines below).

4 This addition was roughly written in the margins, with a number of corrections, and the passage from 'They were victorious ...' to 'Dáin their kinsman went away to the Iron Hills' is put in the present tense.

5 The extension of the line beyond Thrór appears to have had its starting-point in my father's explanation of the words on Thrór's Map in *The Hobbit* ('Here of old was Thrain King under the Mountain') as referring not to Thráin son of Thrór but to a remote ancestor also named Thráin: see VII.160.

6 My father's method of composition at this time was to continue typing, without rejecting anything, as the sentences developed. A characteristic if extreme case is seen in Dáin's words to Thráin at the end of the Battle of Azanulbizar:

> Only I have passed seen looked through the Shadow of the Gate. Beyond the Shadow it waits for you still. The world must change and some other power than ours must come,   Durin's Bane   before   Some other power must come than ours must come, before Khazad-dûm   Durin's folk walk again in

By crossing out unwanted words and putting directions on the typescript he produced the passage that stands in Appendix A (RK p. 356).

7 In a draft for this passage my father wrote at this point the following, which was not repeated: 'The Ring-wearer became rich especially in gold: that is his dealings brought him wealth according to what he traded in: if in lead, lead, if in silver, silver, if in gems, then gems more abundant and of greater size and worth.'

8   This is where the story of how Thráin came to Dol Guldur was
    first told.

9   The deaths of Frerin and Fundin, and the retreat to the wood
    where Thorin cut the oak-bough from which he got his name (RK
    p. 355 and footnote), had not been mentioned in the draft type-
    script in the account of the Battle of Azanulbizar. The story that
    Thorin carried an unpainted shield of oak wood disappeared.

10 The tone and total effect of the original version, as my father
    dashed it down, is rather different from that of the subsequent
    texts, where the expression becomes a little more reserved. To
    give a single example, when Thorin (later Glóin) sneered at 'those
    absurd little rustics down in the Shire' (cf. *Unfinished Tales*
    p. 333), Gandalf riposted: 'You don't know much about those
    folk, Thorin. If you think them all that simple because they pay
    you whatever you ask for your bits of iron and don't bargain hard
    like some Men, you're mistaken. Now I know one that I think
    is just the fellow for you. Honest, sensible, and very far from
    rash – and brave.'

11 A begins with the words 'In the morning Thorin said to
    Mithrandir ...', and continues as in the third version B (*Un-
    finished Tales* p. 328): here it was Thorin who invited Gandalf
    to his home in the Blue Mountains, whereas in the earliest text
    (p. 282) it was Gandalf who proposed it. I do not know why A
    should have begun at this point.

12 There is here a direction to 'see LR I 65/71' (read '70'), which was
    thus already in print.

13 From this was derived a passage in the earliest version of the
    story:

    'Well then, I was I suppose "chosen". But as far as I was aware,
    I had my reasons for what I did. Don't be abashed if I say that
    the chief in my mind was unconcerned with you: it was, well
    "strategic". When I met Thorin at Bree I had long known
    that Sauron was arisen again in Dol Guldur, and every day I
    expected him to declare himself.'

14 'Educated' is the word that Gandalf used in the original version
    of the passage given from the text B in *Unfinished Tales* p. 331.

    'In 2941 I already saw that the Westlands were in for another
    very bad time sooner or later. Of quite a different sort. And I
    would like the Shire-folk to survive it, if possible. But to do that
    I thought they would want something a bit more than they
    had had before. What shall I say – the clannish sort of stocky,
    sturdy family feeling was not quite enough. They were become
    a bit parochial, forgetting their own stories, forgetting their
    own beginnings, forgetting what little they had known about
    the greatness and peril of the world – or of the allies they had

in it. It was not buried deep, but it was getting buried: memory of the high and noble and beautiful. In short, they needed education! I daresay he was "chosen", and I was chosen to choose him, but I picked on Bilbo as an instrument. You can't educate a whole people at once!'

15   The reference is to Gandalf's first appearance in *The Hobbit*: 'He had not been down that way under The Hill for ages and ages, not since his friend the Old Took died, in fact, and the hobbits had almost forgotten what he looked like.' – On the date of 'The Quest of Erebor' given here, 2942, see the Note below.

16   It was not until text B of *The Quest of Erebor* that Gandalf's account of his finding Thráin in Dol Guldur was moved back in the story (see *Unfinished Tales* p. 324), though still in that version Gandalf returned to it again at the end (*ibid.* p. 336).

17   It will be found in the genealogical table that the life-span of all the 'kings of Durin's Folk' from Thráin I to Náin II varied only between 247 and 256 years, and no Dwarf in the table exceeded that, save Borin (261) and Dwalin, who lived to the vast age of 340 (the date of his death appears in all the later texts of the table, although the first to give dates seems – it is hard to make out the figures – to make him 251 years old at his death).

18   In the genealogical table all the 'kings of Durin's Folk' from Náin I to Thorin Oakenshield were born either 101 or 102 (in one case 100) years after their fathers.

Note on the date of the Quest of Erebor

Among the papers associated with the original manuscript of the story my father set down some notes headed 'Dates already fixed in *printed* narrative are these:'

Bilbo born 2891 (1291). He was visited in 2942 by Thorin II, since that autumn he was 51 (*Lord of the Rings* Chapter I): therefore Battle of Five Armies was in same year, and Thorin II died then.

Thráin must have 'gone off' (to seek Erebor) in 2842 ('a hundred years ago', *Hobbit* p. 35). (It is thus assumed that after wandering he was caught in 2845 and died in dungeons 2850.)

Dáin II is said (LR I p. 241) 'to have passed his 250th year' in 3018. He was then, say, 251, therefore he was born in 2767 [the date given in the genealogy, RK p. 361].

My father had given the date of Bilbo's birth in 2891 in the Tale of Years (p. 238), and he here referred to it as a date 'fixed in printed narrative' (*The Fellowship of the Ring* was published in July 1954, and *The Two Towers* in November). But without Volume III the date is fixed in the following way: Frodo left Bag End in September 3018 (Gandalf's letter that he finally received at Bree was dated 'Midyear's Day, Shire Year, 1418'), and he left on his fiftieth birthday (FR p. 74), which was seventeen years after Bilbo's farewell party (when Frodo was 33); the date of the party was therefore 3001. But that was Bilbo's 111th birthday; and therefore he was born in — 2890. It seems only possible to explain this as a simple miscalculation on my father's part which he never checked, – or rather never checked until now, for in another note among these papers he went through the evidence and arrived at the date 2890 for Bilbo's birth, and therefore 2941 for Thorin's visit to him at Bag End. This new date had been reached by the time that the earliest version of *The Quest of Erebor* was written.

PART TWO

LATE WRITINGS

LATE WRITINGS

It is a great convenience in this so largely dateless history that my father received from Allen and Unwin a quantity of their waste paper whose blank sides he used for much of his late writing; for this paper consisted of publication notes, and many of the pages bear dates: some from 1967, the great majority from 1968, and some from 1970. These dates provide, of course, only a *terminus a quo*: in the case, for instance, of a long essay on the names of the rivers and beacon-hills of Gondor (extensively drawn on in *Unfinished Tales*) pages dated 1967 were used, but the work can be shown on other and entirely certain grounds to have been written after June 1969. This was the period of *The Disaster of the Gladden Fields*, *Cirion and Eorl*, and *The Battles of the Fords of Isen*, which I published in *Unfinished Tales*.

It was also a time when my father was moved to write extensively, in a more generalised view, of the languages and peoples of the Third Age and their interrelations, closely interwoven with discussion of the etymology of names. Of this material I made a good deal of use in the section *The History of Galadriel and Celeborn* (and elsewhere) in *Unfinished Tales*; but I had, of course, to relate it to the structure and content of that book, and the only way to do so, in view of the extremely diffuse and digressive nature of my father's writing, was by the extraction of relevant passages. In this book I give two of the most substantial of these 'essays', from neither of which did I take much in *Unfinished Tales*.

The first of these, *Of Men and Dwarves*, arose, as my father said, 'from consideration of the Book of Mazarbul' (that is, of his representations of the burnt and damaged leaves, which were not in fact published until after his death) and the inscription on the tomb of Balin in Moria, but led far beyond its original point of departure. From this essay I have excluded the two passages that were used in *Unfinished Tales*, the account of the Drúedain, and that of the meeting of the Númenórean mariners with the Men of Eriador in the year 600 of the Second Age (see pp. 309, 314). The second, which I have called *The Shibboleth of Fëanor*, is of a very different nature, as will be seen, and from this only a passage on Galadriel was used in *Unfinished Tales*; I have included also a long excursus on the names of the descendants of Finwë, King of the Ñoldor, which was my father's final, or at any rate last, statement on many of the great names of

Elvish legend, and which I used in the published *Silmarillion*. I have also given a third text, which I have called *The Problem of Ros*; and following these are some of his last writings, probably in the last year of his life (p. 377).

A word must be said of these 'historical-philological' essays. Apart from the very last, just referred to, they were composed on a typewriter. These texts are, very clearly, entirely *ab initio*; they are not developments and refinements of earlier versions, and they were not themselves subsequently developed and refined. The ideas, the new narrative departures, historical formulations, and etymological constructions, here first appear in written form (which is not to say, of course, that they were not long in the preparing), and in that form, essentially, they remain. The texts are never obviously concluded, and often end in chaotic and illegible or unintelligible notes and jottings. Some of the writing was decidedly experimental: a notable example is the text that I have called *The Problem of Ros*, on which my father wrote 'Most of this fails', on account of a statement which had appeared in print, but which he had overlooked (see p. 371). As in that case, almost all of this work was etymological in its inspiration, which to a large extent accounts for its extremely discursive nature; for in no study does one thing lead to another more rapidly than in etymology, which also of its nature leads out of itself in the attempt to find explanations beyond the purely linguistic evolution of forms. In the essay on the river-names of Gondor that of the Gwathló led to an account of the vast destruction of the great forests of Minhiriath and Enedwaith by the Númenórean naval builders in the Second Age, and its consequences (*Unfinished Tales* pp. 261–3); from the name *Gilrain* in the same essay arose the recounting of the legend of Amroth and Nimrodel (*ibid*. pp. 240–3).

In the three texts given here will be found many things that are wholly 'new', such as the long sojourn of the People of Bëor and the People of Hador on opposite sides of the great inland Sea of Rhûn in the course of their long migration into the West, or the sombre legend of the twin sons of Fëanor. There will also be found many things that run counter to what had been said in earlier writings. I have not attempted in my notes to make an analysis of every real or apparent departure of this kind, or to adduce a mass of reference from earlier phases of the History; but I have drawn attention to the clearest and most striking of the discrepancies. At this time my father continued and intensified his practice of interposing notes into the body of the text as they arose, and they are abundant and often substantial. In the texts that follow they are numbered in the same series as the editorial notes and are collected at the end of each, the editorial notes being distinguished by placing them in square brackets.

X

OF DWARVES AND MEN

This long essay has no title, but on a covering page my father wrote:

> An extensive commentary and history of the interrelation of the
> languages in *The Silmarillion* and *The Lord of the Rings*, arising
> from consideration of the Book of Mazarbul, but attempting
> to clarify and where necessary to correct or explain the references
> to such matters scattered in *The Lord of the Rings*, especially in
> Appendix F and in Faramir's talk in LR II.

'Faramir's talk' is a reference to the conclusion of the chapter *The
Window on the West* in *The Two Towers*. To a rough synopsis of the
essay he gave the title *Dwarves and Men*, which I have adopted.

The text was begun in manuscript, but after three and a half pages
becomes typescript for the remainder of its length (28 pages in all). It
was written on printed papers supplied by Allen and Unwin, of which
the latest date is September 1969. A portion of the work was printed
in *Unfinished Tales*, Part Four, Section 1, *The Drúedain*, but otherwise
little use of it was made in that book. Unhappily the first page of the
text is lost (and was already missing when I received my father's
papers), and takes up in the middle of a sentence in a passage discussing knowledge of the Common Speech.

In relation to the first part of the essay, which is concerned with the
Longbeard Dwarves, I have thought that it would be useful to print
first what is said concerning the language of the Dwarves in the two
chief antecedent sources. The following is found in the chapter on the
Dwarves in the *Quenta Silmarillion* as revised and enlarged in 1951
(XI.205, §6):

> The father-tongue of the Dwarves Aulë himself devised for them,
> and their languages have thus no kinship with those of the Quendi.
> The Dwarves do not gladly teach their tongue to those of alien race;
> and in use they have made it harsh and intricate, so that of those few
> whom they have received in full friendship fewer still have learned
> it well. But they themselves learn swiftly other tongues, and in con-
> verse they use as they may the speech of Elves and Men with whom
> they deal. Yet in secret they use their own speech only, and that (it
> is said) is slow to change; so that even their realms and houses that
> have been long and far sundered may to this day well understand
> one another. In ancient days the Naugrim dwelt in many mountains

of Middle-earth, and there they met mortal Men (they say) long ere the Eldar knew them; whence it comes that of the tongues of the Easterlings many show kinship with Dwarf-speech rather than with the speeches of the Elves.

The second passage is from Appendix F, *Dwarves* (with which cf. the original version, p. 35, §15).

> But in the Third Age close friendship still was found in many places between Men and Dwarves; and it was according to the nature of the Dwarves that, travelling and labouring and trading about the lands, as they did after the destruction of their ancient mansions, they should use the languages of men among whom they dwelt. Yet in secret (a secret which, unlike the Elves, they did not willingly unlock, even to their friends) they used their own strange tongue, changed little by the years; for it had become a tongue of lore rather than a cradle-speech, and they tended it and guarded it as a treasure of the past. Few of other race have succeeded in learning it. In this history it appears only in such place-names as Gimli revealed to his companions; and in the battle-cry which he uttered in the siege of the Hornburg. That at least was not secret, and had been heard on many a field since the world was young. *Baruk Khazâd! Khazâd ai-mênu!* 'Axes of the Dwarves! The Dwarves are upon you!'
> Gimli's own name, however, and the names of all his kin, are of Northern (Mannish) origin. Their own secret and 'inner' names, their true names, the Dwarves have never revealed to any one of alien race. Not even on their tombs do they inscribe them.

Here follows the text of the essay which I have called *Of Dwarves and Men*.

... only in talking to others of different race and tongue, the divergence could be great, and intercommunication imperfect.[1] But this was not always the case: it depended on the history of the peoples concerned and their relations to the Númenórean kingdoms. For instance, among the Rohirrim there can have been very few who did not understand the Common Speech, and most must have been able to speak it fairly well. The royal house, and no doubt many other families, spoke (and wrote) it correctly and familiarly. It was in fact King Théoden's native language: he was born in Gondor, and his father Thengel had used the Common Speech in his own home even after his return to Rohan.[2] The Eldar used it with the care and skill that they applied to all linguistic matters, and being longeval and retentive in memory they tended indeed, especially when speaking formally or on important matters, to use a somewhat archaic language.[3]

The Dwarves were in many ways a special case. They had an ancient language of their own which they prized highly; and even when, as among the Longbeard Dwarves of the West, it had ceased to be their native tongue and had become a 'book-language', it was carefully preserved and taught to all their children at an early age. It thus served as a *lingua franca* between all Dwarves of all kinds; but it was also a written language used in all important histories and lore, and in recording any matters not intended to be read by other people. This Khuzdul (as they called it), partly because of their native secretiveness, and partly because of its inherent difficulty,[4] was seldom learned by those of other race.

The Dwarves were not, however, skilled linguists – in most matters they were unadaptable – and spoke with a marked 'dwarvish' accent. Also they had never invented any form of alphabetic writing.[5] They quickly, however, recognized the usefulness of the Elvish systems, when they at last became sufficiently friendly with any of the Eldar to learn them. This occurred mainly in the close association of Eregion and Moria in the Second Age. Now in Eregion not only the Fëanorian Script, which had long become a mode of writing generally used (with various adaptations) among all 'lettered' peoples in contact with the Númenórean settlements,[6] but also the ancient 'runic' alphabet of Daeron elaborated [> used] by the Sindar was known and used. This was, no doubt, due to the influence of Celebrimbor, a Sinda who claimed descent from Daeron.[7] Nonetheless even in Eregion the Runes were mainly a 'matter of lore' and were seldom used for informal matters. They, however, caught the fancy of the Dwarves; for while the Dwarves still lived in populous mansions of their own, such as Moria in particular, and went on journeys only to visit their own kin, they had little intercourse with other peoples except immediate neighbours, and needed writing very little; though they were fond of inscriptions, of all kinds, cut in stone. For such purposes the Runes were convenient, being originally devised for them.

The Longbeard Dwarves therefore adopted the Runes, and modified them for their own uses (especially the expression of Khuzdul); and they adhered to them even far into the Third Age, when they were forgotten by others except the loremasters of Elves and Men. Indeed it was generally supposed by the unlearned that they had been invented by the Dwarves, and they were widely known as 'dwarf-letters'.[8]

Here we are concerned only with the Common Speech. Now

the Common Speech, when written at all, had from its beginning been expressed in the Fëanorian Script.[9] Only occasionally
and in inscriptions not written with pen or brush did some of
the Elves of Sindarin descent use the Runes of Daeron, and their
spelling was then dependent on the already established usages
of the Fëanorian Script. The Dwarves had originally learned the
Common Speech by ear as best they could, and had no occasion
to write it; but in the Third Age they had been obliged in the
course of trade and other dealings with Men and Elves to learn
to read the Common Speech as written, and many had found it
convenient to learn to write it according to the then general
customs of the West. But this they only did in dealings with
other peoples. For their own purposes they (as has been said)
preferred the Runes and adhered to them.

Therefore in such documents as the Book of Mazarbul – not
'secret' but intended primarily for Dwarves, and probably
intended later to provide material for chronicles[10] – they used
the Runes. But the spelling was mixed and irregular. In general
and by intention it was a transcription of the current spelling
of the Common Speech into Runic terms; but this was often
'incorrect', owing to haste and the imperfect knowledge of
the Dwarves; and it was also mingled with numerous cases of
words spelt phonetically (according to the pronunciation of the
Dwarves) – for instance, letters that had in the colloquial pronunciation of the late Third Age ceased to have any function
were sometimes omitted.[11]

In preparing an example of the Book of Mazarbul, and
making three torn and partly illegible pages,[12] I followed the
general principle followed throughout: the Common Speech
was to be represented as English of today, literary or colloquial
as the case demanded. Consequently the text was cast into
English spelt as at present, but modified as it might be by writers
in haste whose familiarity with the written form was imperfect,
and who were also (on the first and third pages) transliterating
the English into a different alphabet – one that did not for
instance employ any letter in more than one distinct value,
so that the distribution of English k, c — c, s was reduced to
k — s; while the use of the letters for s and z was variable
since English uses s frequently as = z. In addition, since documents of this kind nearly always show uses of letters or shapes
that are peculiar and rarely or never found elsewhere, a few
such features are also introduced: as the signs for the English

vowel pairs *ea*, *oa*, *ou* (irrespective of their sounds).

This is all very well, and perhaps gives some idea of the kind of text Gandalf was trying to read in great haste in the Chamber of Mazarbul. It also accords with the general treatment of the languages in *The Lord of the Rings*: only the actual words and names of the period that are in Elvish languages are preserved in what is supposed to have been their real form.[13] Also, this treatment was imposed by the fact that, though the actual Common Speech was sketched in structure and phonetic elements, and a number of words invented, it was quite impossible to translate even such short extracts into its real contemporary form, if they were visibly represented. But it is of course in fact an erroneous extension of the general linguistic treatment. It is one thing to represent all the dialogue of the story in varying forms of English: this must be supposed to be done by 'translation' – from memory of unrecorded sounds, or from documents lost or not printed, whether this is stated or not, whenever it is done in any narrative dealing with past times or foreign lands. But it is quite another thing to provide *visible* facsimiles or representations of writings or carvings supposed to be of the date of the events in the narrative.[14]

The true parallel in such a case is the glimpse of Quenya given in Galadriel's Farewell – either in a transcription into our alphabet (to make the style of the language more easily appreciated) or in the contemporary script (as in *The Road Goes Ever On*) – followed by a translation. Since, as noted, the provision of a contemporary text in the actual Common Speech was not possible, the only proper procedure was to provide a translation into English of the legible words of the pages hastily examined by Gandalf.[15] This was done in the text; and short of a construction of the actual Common Speech sufficient to allow the text to be in its contemporary form, all that can legitimately be done.

A special difficulty is presented by the inscription on Balin's tomb. This is effective in its place: giving an idea of the style of the Runes when incised with more care for a solemn purpose, and providing a glimpse of a strange tongue; though all that is really necessary for the tale is the six lines on I.334[16] (with the translation of the inscription in bigger and bolder lettering). The actual representation of the inscription has however landed in some absurdities.[17]

The use in the inscription of the older and more 'correct'

values and shapes of the *Angerthas*, and not the later 'usage of Erebor', is not absurd (though possibly an unnecessary elaboration); it is in accord with the history of the Runes as sketched in the Appendix E. The older Runes would be used for such a purpose, since they were used in Moria before the flight of the Dwarves, and would appear in other inscriptions of like kind – and Balin was claiming to be the descendant and successor of the former Lords of Moria. The use of the Dwarf-tongue (Khuzdul) is possible in so short an inscription, since this tongue has been sketched in some detail of structure, if with a very small vocabulary. But the names *Balin* and *Fundin* are in such a context absurd. The Dwarves, as is stated in III.411,[18] had names in their own language; these they only used among themselves (on solemn occasions) and kept strictly secret from other peoples, and therefore never spelt them out in writing or inscriptions meant for or likely to be seen by strangers. In times or places where they had dealings, in trade or friendship, with their neighbours, they adopted 'outer names' for convenience.[19] These names were in form generally suited to the structure of the Common Speech [> the structure of the language from which they were derived]. Very frequently they had recognizable meanings in that language, or were names current in it; sometimes they were names [> current in it, being names] used by neighbouring Men among whom they dwelt, and were derived from the local Mannish language in which they might have a still known meaning, though this was not often the case [*this phrase struck out*].[20] Whether the adopted names that had meanings were selected because these meanings had some relation to their secret 'inner' names cannot be determined. The adopted names could be and sometimes were changed – usually in consequence of some event, such as the migration of either the Dwarves or their friends that separated them.

The case of the Dwarves of Moria was an example of adoption of names from Mannish languages of the North, not from the Common Speech.[21] It might have been better in that case to have given them in their actual forms. But in carrying out the theory (necessary for the lessening of the load of invention of names in different styles of language), that names derived from the Mannish tongues and dialects of the West historically related to the Common Speech should be represented by names found (or made of elements found in) languages related to English, the Dwarvish names were taken from Norse: since the

Mannish language from which they were adopted was closely
related to the more southerly language from which was derived
the language of Rohan (represented as Old English, because of
its greater archaism in form as compared with those elements in
the Common Speech derived from the languages of the same
kinship). In consequence such names as *Balin*, etc. would not
have appeared in any contemporary inscription using actual
Khuzdul.[22]

Relations of the Longbeard Dwarves and Men[23]

In the Dwarvish traditions of the Third Age the names of the
places where each of the Seven Ancestors had 'awakened' were
remembered; but only two of them were known to Elves and
Men of the West: the most westerly, the awakening place of the
ancestors of the Firebeards and the Broadbeams; and that of the
ancestor of the Longbeards,[24] the eldest in making and awakening. The first had been in the north of the Ered Lindon, the great
eastern wall of Beleriand, of which the Blue Mountains of the
Second and later ages were the remnant; the second had been
Mount Gundabad (in origin a Khuzdul name), which was therefore revered by the Dwarves, and its occupation in the Third
Age by the Orks of Sauron was one of the chief reasons for their
great hatred of the Orks.[25] The other two places were eastward,
at distances as great or greater than that between the Blue
Mountains and Gundabad: the arising of the Ironfists and Stiffbeards, and that of the Blacklocks and Stonefoots. Though
these four points were far sundered the Dwarves of different
kindreds were in communication, and in the early ages often
held assemblies of delegates at Mount Gundabad. In times of
great need even the most distant would send help to any of their
people; as was the case in the great War against the Orks (Third
Age 2793 to 2799). Though they were loth to migrate and make
permanent dwellings or 'mansions' far from their original
homes, except under great pressure from enemies or after some
catastrophe such as the ruin of Beleriand, they were great and
hardy travellers and skilled road-makers; also, all the kindreds
shared a common language.[26]

But in far distant days the Dwarves were secretive [*struck
out*: – and none more so than the Longbeards –] and had few
dealings with the Elves. In the West at the end of the First
Age the dealings of the Dwarves of the Ered Lindon with King
Thingol ended in disaster and the ruin of Doriath, the memory

of which still poisoned the relations of Elves and Dwarves in after ages. At that time the migrations of Men from the East and South had brought advance-guards into Beleriand; but they were not in great numbers, though further east in Eriador and Rhovanion (especially in the northern parts) their kindred must already have occupied much of the land. There dealings between Men and the Longbeards must soon have begun. For the Longbeards, though the proudest of the seven kindreds, were also the wisest and the most farseeing. Men held them in awe and were eager to learn from them; and the Longbeards were very willing to use Men for their own purposes. Thus there grew up in those regions the economy, later characteristic of the dealings of Dwarves and Men (including Hobbits): Men became the chief providers of food, as herdsmen, shepherds, and land-tillers, which the Dwarves exchanged for work as builders, roadmakers, miners, and the makers of things of craft, from useful tools to weapons and arms and many other things of great cost and skill. To the great profit of the Dwarves. Not only to be reckoned in hours of labour, though in early times the Dwarves must have obtained goods that were the product of greater and longer toil than the things or services that they gave in exchange – before Men became wiser and developed skills of their own. The chief advantage to them was their freedom to proceed unhindered with their own work and to refine their arts, especially in metallurgy, to the marvellous skill which these reached before the decline and dwindling of the Khazâd.

This system developed slowly, and it was long before the Longbeards felt any need to learn the language of their neighbours, still less to adopt names by which they could be known individually to 'outsiders'. This process began not in barter and trade, but in war; for the Longbeards had spread southward down the Vales of Anduin and had made their chief 'mansion' and stronghold at Moria; and also eastward to the Iron Hills, where the mines were their chief source of iron-ore. They regarded the Iron Hills, the Ered Mithrin, and the east dales of the Misty Mountains as their own land. But they were under attack from the Orks of Morgoth. During the War of the Jewels and the Siege of Angband, when Morgoth needed all his strength, these attacks ceased; but when Morgoth fell and Angband was destroyed hosts of the Orks fled eastwards seeking homes. They were now masterless and without any general leadership, but they were well-armed and very numerous, cruel,

savage, and reckless in assault. In the battles that followed the
Dwarves were outnumbered, and though they were the most
redoubtable warriors of all the Speaking Peoples they were glad
to make alliance with Men.[27]

The Men with whom they were thus associated were for the
most part akin in race and language with the tall and mostly
fair-haired people of the 'House of Hador', the most renowned
and numerous of the Edain, who were allied with the Eldar in
the War of the Jewels. These Men, it seems, had come westward
until faced by the Great Greenwood, and then had divided:
some reaching the Anduin and passing thence northward up the
Vales; some passing between the north-eaves of the Wood and
the Ered Mithrin. Only a small part of this people, already very
numerous and divided into many tribes, had then passed on into
Eriador and so come at last to Beleriand. They were brave and
loyal folk, truehearted, haters of Morgoth and his servants; and
at first had regarded the Dwarves askance, fearing that they
were under the Shadow (as they said).[28] But they were glad of
the alliance, for they were more vulnerable to the attacks of the
Orks: they dwelt largely in scattered homesteads and villages,
and if they drew together into small townships they were poorly
defended, at best by dikes and wooden fences. Also they were
lightly armed, chiefly with bows, for they had little metal and
the few smiths among them had no great skill. These things the
Dwarves amended in return for one great service that Men
could offer. They were tamers of beasts and had learned the
mastery of horses, and many were skilled and fearless riders.[29]
These would often ride far afield as scouts and keep watch on
movements of their enemies; and if the Orks dared to assemble
in the open for some great raid, they would gather great force
of horsed archers to surround them and destroy them. In these
ways the Alliance of Dwarves and Men in the North came early
in the Second Age to command great strength, swift in attack
and valiant and well-protected in defence, and there grew up in
that region between Dwarves and Men respect and esteem, and
sometimes warm friendship.

It was at that time, when the Dwarves were associated with
Men both in war and in the ordering of the lands that they had
secured,[30] that the Longbeards adopted the speech of Men for
communication with them. They were not unwilling to teach
their own tongue to Men with whom they had special friendship, but Men found it difficult and were slow to learn more

than isolated words, many of which they adapted and took into their own language. But on one point the Longbeards were as rigidly secretive as all other Dwarves. For reasons which neither Elves nor Men ever fully understood they would not reveal any personal names to people of other kin,[31] nor later when they had acquired the arts of writing allow them ever to be carved or written. They therefore took names by which they could be known to their allies in Mannish forms.[32] This custom endured among the Longbeards into the Fourth Age and beyond the view of these histories. It would appear that when speaking to Men with whom they had close friendship, and would speak together of the histories and memories of their peoples, they also gave similar names to Dwarves remembered in their annals long before the meeting of Dwarves and Men. But of these ancient times only one name was in the Third Age preserved: *Durin*, the name they gave to the prime ancestor of the Longbeards and by which he was known to Elves and Men. (It appears to have been simply a word for 'king' in the language of the Men of the North of the Second Age.)[33] The names of the Longbeards otherwise are not known in lists going back before the ruin of Moria (Khazad-dûm), Third Age 1980; but they are all of the same kind, sc. in a long 'dead' Mannish language.

This can only be explained by supposing that these names from the early Second Age had been adopted by the Dwarves, and preserved with as little change as their own language, and continued to be given (and often repeated) for something like four thousand years or more since the Alliance was destroyed by the power of Sauron! In this way they soon became to later Men specially Dwarvish names;[34] and the Longbeards acquired a vocabulary of traditional names peculiar to themselves, while still keeping their true 'inner' names completely secret.

Very great changes came to pass as the Second Age proceeded. The first ships of the Númenóreans appeared off the coasts of Middle-earth about Second Age 600, but no rumour of this portent reached the distant North. At the same time, however, Sauron came out of hiding and revealed himself in fair form. For long he paid little heed to Dwarves or Men and endeavoured to win the friendship and trust of the Eldar. But slowly he reverted again to the allegiance of Morgoth and began to seek power by force, marshalling again and directing the Orks and other evil things of the First Age, and secretly building his great fortress in the mountain-girt land in the South that was afterwards known as Mordor. The Second Age had reached only the middle of its course (c. Second Age 1695) when he invaded Eriador and destroyed Eregion, a small realm established by the Eldar migrating from the ruin of Beleriand that had formed an alliance also with the Longbeards of Moria. This marked the end of the Alliance of the Longbeards with Men of the North. For though Moria remained impregnable for many centuries, the Orks reinforced and commanded by servants of Sauron invaded the mountains again. Gundabad was re-taken, the Ered Mithrin infested and the communication between Moria and the Iron Hills for a time cut off. The Men of the Alliance were involved in war not only with Orks but with alien Men of evil sort. For Sauron had acquired dominion over many savage tribes in the East (of old corrupted by Morgoth), and he now urged them to seek land and booty in the West. When the storm passed,[35] the Men of the old Alliance were diminished and scattered, and those that lingered on in their old regions were impoverished, and lived mostly in caves or in the borders of the Forest.

The Elvish loremasters held that in the matter of language the changes in speech (as in all the ways of their lives) of the Speaking Peoples were far slower in the Elder Days than they later became. The tongue of the Eldar changed mainly by design; that of the Dwarves resisted change by their own will; the many languages of Men changed heedlessly in the swift passing of their generations. All things changed in Arda, even in the Blessed Realm of the Valar; but there the change was so slow that it could not be observed (save maybe by the Valar) in great ages of time. The change in the language of the Eldar would thus have been halted in Valinor;[36] but in their early days the Eldar continued to enlarge and refine their language, and to change it, even in structure and sounds. Such change, however, to remain uniform required that the speakers should remain in communication. Thus it came about that the languages of the Eldar that remained in Middle-earth diverged from the language of the High Eldar of Valinor so greatly that neither could be understood by speakers of the other; for they had been separated for a great age of time, during which even the Sindarin, the best preserved of those in Middle-earth, had been subject to the heedless changes of passing years, changes which the Teleri were far less concerned to restrain or to direct by design than the Ñoldor.

II

The Atani and their Languages[37]

Men entered Beleriand late in the First Age. Those with whom we are here concerned and of whose languages some records later were preserved belonged mostly to three peoples, differing in speech and in race, but known in common to the Eldar as the *Atani* (Sindarin *Edain*).[38] These *Atani* were the vanguard of far larger hosts of the same kinds moving westwards. When the First Age ended and Beleriand was destroyed, and most of the Atani who survived had passed over sea to Númenor, their laggard kindred were either in Eriador, some settled, some still wandering, or else had never passed the Misty Mountains and were scattered in the lands between the Iron Hills and the Sea of Rhûn eastward and the Great Forest, in the borders of which, northward and eastward, many were already settled.

The Atani and their kin were the descendants of peoples who in the Dark Ages had resisted Morgoth or had renounced him, and had wandered ever westward from their homes far away in the East seeking the Great Sea, of which distant rumour had reached them. They did not know that Morgoth himself had left Middle-earth;[39] for they were ever at war with the vile things that he had bred, and especially with Men who had made him their God and believed that they could render him no more pleasing service than to destroy the 'renegades' with every kind of cruelty. It was in the North of Middle-earth, it would seem, that the 'renegades' survived in sufficient numbers to maintain their independence as brave and hardy peoples; but of their past they preserved only legends, and their oral histories reached no further back than a few generations of Men.

When their vanguards at last reached Beleriand and the Western Shores they were dismayed. For they could go no further, but they had not found peace, only lands engaged in war with Morgoth himself, who had fled back to Middle-earth. 'Through ages forgotten,' they said, 'we have wandered, seeking to escape from the Dominions of the Dark Lord and his Shadow, only to find him here before us.'[40] But being people both brave and desperate they at once became allies of the Eldar, and they were instructed by them and became ennobled and advanced in knowledge and in arts. In the final years of the War of the Jewels they provided many of the most valiant warriors and captains in the armies of the Elvish kings.

The Atani were three peoples, independent in organisation and leadership, each of which differed in speech and also in form and bodily features from the others – though all of them showed traces of mingling in the past with Men of other kinds. These peoples the Eldar named the Folk of Bëor, the Folk of Hador, and the Folk of Haleth, after the names of the chieftains who commanded them when they first came to Beleriand.[41] The Folk of Bëor were the first Men to enter Beleriand – they were met in the dales of East Beleriand by King Finrod the Friend of Men, for they had found a way over the Mountains. They were a small people, having no more, it is said, than two thousand full-grown men; and they were poor and ill-equipped, but they were inured to hardship and toilsome journeys carrying great loads, for they had no beasts of burden. Not long after the first of the three hosts of the Folk of Hador came up from southward, and two others of much the same strength followed before the fall of the year. They were a more numerous people; each host was as great as all the Folk of Bëor, and they were better armed and equipped; also they possessed many horses, and some asses and small flocks of sheep and goats. They had crossed Eriador and reached the eastern feet of the Mountains (Ered Lindon) a year or more ahead of all others, but had not attempted to find any passes, and had turned away seeking a road round the Mountains, which, as their horsed scouts reported, grew ever lower as they went southwards. Some years later, when the other folk were settled, the third folk of the Atani entered Beleriand.[42] They were probably more numerous than the Folk of Bëor, but no certain count of them was ever made; for they came secretly in small parties and hid in the woods of Ossiriand where the Elves showed them no friendship. Moreover they had strife among themselves, and Morgoth, now aware of the coming of hostile Men into Beleriand, sent his servants to afflict them. Those who eventually moved westward and entered into friendship and alliance with the Eldar were called the Folk of Haleth, for Haleth was the name of their chieftainess who led them to the woods north of Doriath where they were permitted to dwell.

The Folk of Hador were ever the greatest in numbers of the Atani, and in renown (save only Beren son of Barahir descendant of Bëor). For the most part they were tall people, with flaxen or golden hair and blue-grey eyes, but there were not a few among them that had dark hair, though all were fair-skinned.[43]

Nonetheless they were akin to the Folk of Bëor, as was shown by their speech. It needed no lore of tongues to perceive that their languages were closely related, for although they could understand one another only with difficulty they had very many words in common. The Elvish loremasters[44] were of opinion that both languages were descended from one that had diverged (owing to some division of the people who had spoken it) in the course of, maybe, a thousand years of the slower change in the First Age.[45] Though the time might well have been less, and change quickened by a mingling of peoples; for the language of Hador was apparently less changed and more uniform in style, whereas the language of Bëor contained many elements that were alien in character. This contrast in speech was probably connected with the observable physical differences between the two peoples. There were fair-haired men and women among the Folk of Bëor, but most of them had brown hair (going usually with brown eyes), and many were less fair in skin, some indeed being swarthy. Men as tall as the Folk of Hador were rare among them, and most were broader and more heavy in build.[46] In association with the Eldar, especially with the followers of King Finrod, they became as enhanced in arts and manners as the Folk of Hador, but if these surpassed them in swiftness of mind and body, in daring and noble generosity,[47] the Folk of Bëor were more steadfast in endurance of hardship and sorrow, slow to tears or to laughter; their fortitude needed no hope to sustain it. But these differences of body and mind became less marked as their short generations passed, for the two peoples became much mingled by intermarriage and by the disasters of the War.[48]

The Folk of Haleth were strangers to the other Atani, speaking an alien language; and though later united with them in alliance with the Eldar, they remained a people apart. Among themselves they adhered to their own language, and though of necessity they learned Sindarin for communication with the Eldar and the other Atani, many spoke it haltingly, and some of those who seldom went beyond the borders of their own woods did not use it at all.[49] They did not willingly adopt new things or customs, and retained many practices that seemed strange to the Eldar and the other Atani, with whom they had few dealings except in war. Nonetheless they were esteemed as loyal allies and redoubtable warriors, though the companies that they sent to battle beyond their borders were small. For they were and

remained to their end a small people, chiefly concerned to protect their own woodlands, and they excelled in forest warfare.
Indeed for long even those Orks specially trained for this dared
not set foot near their borders. One of the strange practices
spoken of was that many of their warriors were women, though
few of these went abroad to fight in the great battles. This
custom was evidently ancient;[50] for their chieftainess Haleth
had been a renowned amazon with a picked bodyguard of
women.

> At this point a heading is pencilled on the typescript: III *The
> Drúedain (Púkel-men)*; after this there are no further divisions with
> sub-titles inserted. Together with the concluding paragraph of
> section II printed above, the account of the Drúedain that now
> follows is given in *Unfinished Tales*, pp. 377–82, concluding with
> the story called *The Faithful Stone*; and there is no need to repeat
> this here.[51] At the end of the story is a passage contrasting Drûgs
> and Hobbits, which since it was given in curtailed form in *Un-
> finished Tales* (p. 382) is printed here in full; the present text then
> continues to the end, or rather abandonment, of the essay.

This long account of the Drúedain has been given, because it
throws some light on the Wild Men still surviving at the time of
the War of the Ring in the eastern end of the White Mountains,
and on Merry's recognition of them as living forms of the carved
Púkel-men of Dun Harrow. The presence of members of the
same race among the Edain in Beleriand thus makes another
backward link between *The Lord of the Rings* and *The Silmarillion*, and allows the introduction of characters somewhat
similar to the Hobbits of *The Lord of the Rings* into some of the
legends of the First Age (e.g. the old retainer (Sadog) of Húrin
in the legend of Túrin).[52]

The Drûgs or Púkel-men are not however to be confused with
or thought of as a mere variant on the hobbit theme. They were
quite different in physical shape and appearance. Their average
height (four feet) was only reached by exceptional hobbits; they
were of heavier and stronger build; and their facial features
were unlovely (judged by general human standards). Physically
they shared the hairlessness of the lower face; but while the
head-hair of the hobbits was abundant (but close and curly),
the Drûgs had only sparse and lank hair on their heads and
none at all on their legs and feet. In character and temperament
they were at times merry and gay, like hobbits, but they had a

grimmer side to their nature and could be sardonic and ruthless; and they had or were credited with strange or magical powers. (The tales, such as 'The Faithful Stone', that speak of their transferring part of their 'powers' to their artefacts, remind one in miniature of Sauron's transference of power to the foundation of the Barad-dûr and to the Ruling Ring.)[53] Also the Drûgs were a frugal folk, and ate sparingly even in times of peace and plenty, and drank nothing but water. In some ways they resembled rather the Dwarves: in build and stature and endurance (though not in hair); in their skill in carving stone; in the grim side of their character; and in 'strange powers'. Though the 'magic' skills with which the Dwarves were credited were quite different; also the Dwarves were much grimmer; and they were long-lived, whereas the Drûgs were short-lived compared with other kinds of Men.

The Drûgs that are met in the tales of the First Age – cohabiting with the Folk of Haleth, who were a woodland people – were content to live in tents or shelters lightly built round the trunks of large trees, for they were a hardy race. In their former homes, according to their own tales, they had used caves in the mountains, but mainly as store-houses only occupied as dwellings and sleeping-places in severe weather. They had similar refuges in Beleriand to which all but the most hardy retreated in times of storm and bitter weather; but these places were guarded and not even their closest friends among the Folk of Haleth were welcomed there.

Hobbits on the other hand were in nearly all respects normal Men, but of very short stature. They were called 'halflings'; but this refers to the normal height of men of Númenórean descent and of the Eldar (especially those of Ñoldorin descent), which appears to have been about seven of our feet.[54] Their height at the periods concerned was usually more than three feet for men, though very few ever exceeded three foot six; women seldom exceeded three feet. They were not as numerous or variable as ordinary Men, but evidently more numerous and adaptable to different modes of life and habitat than the Drûgs, and when they are first encountered in the histories already showed divergences in colouring, stature, and build, and in their ways of life and preferences for different types of country to dwell in (see the Prologue to *The Lord of the Rings*, p. 12). In their unrecorded past they must have been a primitive, indeed 'savage' people,[55] but when we meet them they had (in varying degrees) acquired many arts and customs by contact with Men, and to a less extent with Dwarves and Elves. With Men of normal stature they recognized their close kinship, whereas Dwarves or Elves, whether friendly or hostile, were aliens, with whom their relations were uneasy and clouded by fear.[56] Bilbo's statement (*The Lord of the Rings* I.162)[57] that the cohabitation of Big Folk and Little Folk in one settlement at Bree was peculiar and nowhere else to be found was probably true in his time (the end of the Third Age);[58] but it would seem that actually Hobbits had liked to live with or near to Big Folk of friendly kind, who with their greater strength protected them from many dangers and enemies and other hostile Men, and received in exchange many services. For it is remarkable that the western Hobbits preserved no trace or memory of any language of their own. The language they spoke when they entered Eriador was evidently adopted from the Men of the Vales of Anduin (related to the Atani, / in particular to those of the House of Bëor [> of the Houses of Hador and of Bëor]); and after their adoption of the Common Speech they retained many words of that origin. This indicates a close association with Big Folk; though the rapid adoption of the Common Speech in Eriador[59] shows Hobbits to have been specially adaptable in this respect. As does also the divergence of the Stoors, who had associated with Men of different sort before they came to the Shire.

The vague tradition preserved by the Hobbits of the Shire was that they had dwelt once in lands by a Great River, but long ago had left them, and found their way through or round high mountains, when they no longer felt at ease in their homes because of the multiplication of the Big Folk and of a shadow of fear that had fallen on the Forest. This evidently reflects the troubles of Gondor in the earlier part of the Third Age. The increase in Men was not the normal increase of those with whom they had lived in friendship, but the steady increase of invaders from the East, further south held in check by Gondor, but in the North beyond the bounds of the Kingdom harassing the older 'Atanic' inhabitants, and even in places occupying the Forest and coming through it into the Anduin valley. But the shadow of which the tradition spoke was not solely due to human invasion. Plainly the Hobbits had sensed, even before the Wizards and the Eldar had become fully aware of it, the awakening of Sauron and his occupation of Dol Guldur.[60]

On the relations of the different kinds of Men in Eriador and Rhovanion to the Atani and other Men met in the legends of the First Age and the War of the Jewels see *The Lord of the Rings* II.286–7 [in the chapter *The Window on the West*]. There Faramir gives a brief account of the contemporary classification in Gondor of Men into three kinds: High Men, or Númenóreans (of more or less pure descent); Middle Men; and Men of Darkness. The Men of Darkness was a general term applied to all those who were hostile to the Kingdoms, and who were (or appeared in Gondor to be) moved by something more than human greed for conquest and plunder, a fanatical hatred of the High Men and their allies as enemies of their gods. The term took no account of differences of race or culture or language. With regard to Middle Men Faramir spoke mainly of the Rohirrim, the only people of this sort well-known in Gondor in his time, and attributed to them actual direct descent from the Folk of Hador in the First Age. This was a general belief in Gondor at that time,[61] and was held to explain (to the comfort of Númenórean pride) the surrender of so large a part of the Kingdom to the people of Eorl.

The term Middle Men, however, was of ancient origin. It was devised in the Second Age by the Númenóreans when they began to establish havens and settlements on the western shores of Middle-earth. It arose among the settlers in the North (between Pelargir and the Gulf of Lune), in the time of Ar-Adûnakhôr; for the settlers in this region had refused to join in the rebellion against the Valar, and were strengthened by many exiles of the Faithful who fled from persecution by him and the later Kings of Númenor. It was therefore modelled on the classification by the Atani of the Elves: the High Elves (or Elves of Light) were the Ñoldor who returned in exile out of the Far West; the Middle Elves were the Sindar, who though near kin of the High Elves had remained in Middle-earth and never seen the light of Aman; and the Dark Elves were those who had never journeyed to the Western Shores and did not desire to see Aman. This was not the same as the classifications made by the Elves, which are not here concerned, except to note that 'Dark Elves' or 'Elves of Darkness' was used by them, but in no way implied any evil, or subordination to Morgoth; it referred only to ignorance of the 'light of Aman' and included the Sindar. Those who had never made the journey to the West Shores were called 'the Refusers' (*Avari*). It is doubtful if any of the Avari ever reached

Beleriand[62] or were actually known to the Númenóreans.

In the days of the earlier settlements of Númenor there were many Men of different kinds in Eriador and Rhovanion; but for the most part they dwelt far from the coasts. The regions of Forlindon and Harlindon were inhabited by Elves and were the chief part of Gil-galad's kingdom, which extended, north of the Gulf of Lune, to include the lands east of the Blue Mountains and west of the River Lune as far as the inflow of the Little Lune.[63] (Beyond that was Dwarf territory.)[64] South of the Lune it had no clear bounds, but the Tower Hills (as they were later called) were maintained as an outpost.[65] The Minhiriath and the western half of Enedhwaith between the Greyflood and the Isen were still covered with dense forest.[66] The shores of the Bay of Belfalas were still mainly desolate, except for a haven and small settlement of Elves at the mouth of the confluence of Morthond and Ringló.[67] But it was long before the Númenórean settlers about the Mouths of Anduin ventured north of their great haven at Pelargir and made contact with Men who dwelt in the valleys on either side of the White Mountains. Their term Middle Men was thus originally applied to Men of Eriador, the most westerly of Mankind in the Second Age and known to the Elves of Gil-galad's realm.[68] At that time there were many men in Eriador, mainly, it would seem, in origin kin of the Folk of Bëor, though some were kin of the Folk of Hador. They dwelt about Lake Evendim, in the North Downs and the Weather Hills, and in the lands between as far as the Brandywine, west of which they often wandered though they did not dwell there. They were friendly with the Elves, though they held them in awe and close friendships between them were rare. Also they feared the Sea and would not look upon it. (No doubt rumours of its terror and the destruction of the Land beyond the Mountains (Beleriand) had reached them, and some of their ancestors may indeed have been fugitives from the Atani who did not leave Middle-earth but fled eastward.)

Thus it came about that the Númenórean term Middle Men was confused in its application. Its chief test was friendliness towards the West (to Elves and to Númenóreans), but it was actually applied usually only to Men whose stature and looks were similar to those of the Númenóreans, although this most important distinction of 'friendliness' was not historically confined to peoples of one racial kind. It was a mark of all kinds of Men who were descendants of those who had abjured the

Shadow of Morgoth and his servants and wandered westward to escape it – and certainly included both the races of small stature, Drûgs and Hobbits. Also it must be said that 'unfriendliness' to Númenóreans and their allies was not always due to the Shadow, but in later days to the actions of the Númenóreans themselves. Thus many of the forest-dwellers of the shorelands south of the Ered Luin, especially in Minhiriath, were as later historians recognized the kin of the Folk of Haleth; but they became bitter enemies of the Númenóreans, because of their ruthless treatment and their devastation of the forests,[69] and this hatred remained unappeased in their descendants, causing them to join with any enemies of Númenor. In the Third Age their survivors were the people known in Rohan as the Dunlendings.

There was also the matter of language. It was six hundred years after the departure of the survivors of the Atani oversea to Númenor that a ship came first to Middle-earth again out of the West and passed up the Gulf of Lune.[70]

The story that follows, recounting the meeting of the Númenórean mariners with twelve Men of Eriador on the Tower Hills, their mutual recognition of an ancient kinship, and their discovery that their languages though profoundly changed were of common origin, has been given in *Unfinished Tales*, pp. 213–14.[71] Following the conclusion of that extract (ending with the words 'they found that they shared very many words still clearly recognizable, and others that could be understood with attention, and they were able to converse haltingly about simple matters') the essay continues as follows.

Thus it came about that a kinship in language, even if this was only recognizable after close acquaintance, was felt by the Númenóreans to be one of the marks of 'Middle-men'.[72]

The loremasters of later days held that the languages of Men in Middle-earth, at any rate those of the 'unshadowed' Men, had changed less swiftly before the end of the Second Age and the change of the world in the Downfall of Númenor. Whereas in Númenor owing to the longevity of the Atani it had changed far more slowly still. At the first meeting of the Shipmen and the Men of western Eriador it was only six hundred years since the Atani went oversea, and the Adûnaic that they spoke can hardly have changed at all; but it was a thousand years or more since the Atani who reached Beleriand had parted from their kin. Yet even now in a more changeful world languages that have been separated for fifteen hundred years and longer may be recognized as akin by those unlearned in the history of tongues.

As the long years passed the situation changed. The ancient Adûnaic of Númenor became worn down by time – and by neglect. For owing to the disastrous history of Númenor it was no longer held in honour by the 'Faithful' who controlled all the Shorelands from Lune to Pelargir. For the Elvish tongues were proscribed by the rebel Kings, and Adûnaic alone was permitted to be used, and many of the ancient books in Quenya or in Sindarin were destroyed. The Faithful, therefore, used Sindarin, and in that tongue devised all names of places that they gave anew in Middle-earth.[73] Adûnaic was abandoned to unheeded change and corruption as the language of daily life, and the only tongue of the unlettered. All men of high lineage and all those who were taught to read and write used Sindarin, even as a daily tongue among themselves. In some families, it is said, Sindarin became the native tongue, and the vulgar tongue of Adûnaic origin was only learned casually as it was needed.[74] The Sindarin was not however taught to aliens, both because it was held a mark of Númenórean descent and because it proved difficult to acquire – far more so than the 'vulgar tongue'. Thus it came about that as the Númenórean settlements increased in power and extent and made contact with Men of Middle-earth (many of whom came under Númenórean rule and swelled their population) the 'vulgar tongue' began to spread far and wide as a *lingua franca* among peoples of many different kinds. This process began in the end of the Second Age, but became of general importance mainly after the Downfall and the establishment of the 'Realms in Exile' in Arnor and Gondor. These kingdoms penetrated far into Middle-earth, and their kings were recognized beyond their borders as overlords. Thus in the North and West all the lands between the Ered Luin and the Greyflood and Hoarwell[75] became regions of Númenórean influence in which the 'vulgar tongue' became widely current. In the South and East Mordor remained impenetrable; but though the extent of Gondor was thus impeded it was more populous and powerful than Arnor. The bounds of the ancient kingdom contained all those lands marked in maps of the end of the Third Age as Gondor, Anórien, Ithilien, South Ithilien, and Rohan (formerly called Calenardhon) west of the Entwash.[76] On its extension at the height of its power, between the reigns of Hyarmendacil I and Rómendacil II (Third Age 1015 to 1366) see *The Lord of the Rings* Appendix A p.325.[77] The wide lands between Anduin and the Sea of Rhûn were however never effectively settled or occupied, and the only true north boundary of the Kingdom east of Anduin was formed by the Emyn Muil and the marshes south and east of them. Númenórean influence however went far beyond even these extended bounds, passing up the Vales of Anduin to its sources, and reaching the lands east of the Forest, between the River Celon[78] (Running) and the River Carnen (Redwater).

Within the original bounds of the Kingdoms the 'vulgar speech' soon became the current speech, and eventually the native language of nearly all the inhabitants of whatever origin, and incomers who were allowed to settle within the bounds adopted it. Its speakers generally called it Westron (actually *Adûni*, and in Sindarin *Annúnaid*). But it spread far beyond the bounds of the Kingdoms – at first in dealings with 'the peoples of the Kingdoms', and later as a 'Common Speech' convenient for intercourse between peoples who retained numerous tongues of their own. Thus Elves and Dwarves used it in dealings with one another and with Men.

The text ends here abruptly (without a full stop after the last word, though this may not be significant), halfway down a page.

NOTES

1   A notable case is that of the conversation between Ghân chieftain of the Wild Men and Théoden. Probably few if any of the Wild Men other than Ghân used the Common Speech at all, and he had only a limited vocabulary of words used according to the habits of his native speech.

2   The Kings and their descendants after Thengel also knew the Sindarin tongue – the language of nobles in Gondor. [Cf. Appendix A (II), in the list of the Kings of the Mark, on Thengel's sojourn in Gondor. It is said there that after his return to Rohan 'the speech of Gondor was used in his house, and not all men thought that good.']

3   The effect on contemporary speakers of the Common Speech of Gondor being comparable to that which we should feel if a foreigner, both learned and a skilled linguist, were when being courteous or dealing with high matters to use fluently an English of say about 1600 A.D., but adapted to our present pronunciation.

4   Structurally and grammatically it differed widely from all other

languages of the West at that time; though it had some features in common with Adûnaic, the ancient 'native' language of Númenor. This gave rise to the theory (a probable one) that in the unrecorded past some of the languages of Men – including the language of the dominant element in the Atani from which Adûnaic was derived – had been influenced by Khuzdul.

5 They had, it is said, a complex pictographic or ideographic writing or carving of their own. But this they kept resolutely secret.

6 Including their enemies such as Sauron, and his higher servants who were in fact partly of Númenórean origin.

7 [Like Gil-galad, Celebrimbor was a figure first appearing in *The Lord of the Rings* whose origin my father changed again and again. The earliest statement on the subject is found in the post-*Lord of the Rings* text *Concerning Galadriel and Celeborn*, where it is said (cf. *Unfinished Tales* p. 235):

> Galadriel and Celeborn had in their company a Noldorin craftsman called Celebrimbor. He was of Noldorin origin, and one of the survivors of Gondolin, where he had been one of Turgon's greatest artificers – but he had thus acquired some taint of pride and an almost 'dwarvish' obsession with crafts.

He reappears as a jewel-smith of Gondolin in the text *The Elessar* (see *Unfinished Tales* pp. 248 ff.); but against the passage in *Concerning Galadriel and Celeborn* just cited my father noted that it would be better to 'make him a descendant of Fëanor'. Thus in the Second Edition (1966) of *The Lord of the Rings*, at the end of the prefatory remarks to the Tale of Years of the Second Age, he added the sentence: 'Celebrimbor was lord of Eregion and the greatest of their craftsmen; he was descended from Fëanor.'

On one of his copies of *The Return of the King* he underlined the name *Fëanor* in this sentence, and wrote the following two notes on the opposite page (the opening of the first of these means, I think: 'What then was his parentage? He must have been descended from one of Fëanor's sons, about whose progeny nothing has been told').

> How could he be? Fëanor's only descendants were his seven sons, six of whom reached Beleriand. So far nothing has been said of their wives and children. It seems probable that *Celebrinbaur* (silverfisted, > *Celebrimbor*) was son of Curufin, but though inheriting his skills he was an Elf of wholly different temper (his mother had refused to take part in the rebellion of Fëanor and remained in Aman with the people of Finarphin). During their dwelling in Nargothrond as refugees he had grown to love Finrod and ^ his wife, and was aghast

at the behaviour of his father and would not go with him. He later became a great friend of Celeborn and Galadriel.

The second note reads:

Maedros the eldest appears to have been unwedded, also the two youngest (twins, of whom one was by evil mischance burned with the ships); Celegorm also, since he plotted to take Lúthien as his wife. But Curufin, dearest to his father and chief inheritor of his father's skills, was wedded, and had a son who came with him into exile, though his wife (unnamed) did not. Others who were wedded were Maelor, Caranthir.

On the form *Maelor* for *Maglor* see X.182, §41. The reference in the first of these notes to the wife of Finrod Felagund is notable, since long before, in the *Grey Annals*, the story had emerged that Felagund had no wife, and that 'she whom he had loved was Amárië of the Vanyar, and she was not permitted to go with him into exile'. That story had in fact been abandoned, or forgotten, but it would return: see the note on Gil-galad, p. 350.

These notes on Celebrimbor son of Curufin were the basis of the passages introduced editorially in the published *Silmarillion*, p. 176 (see V.300–1), and in *Of the Rings of Power, ibid.* p. 286. But in late writing (1968 or later) on the subject of Eldarin words for 'hand' my father said this:

Common Eldarin had a base KWAR 'press together, squeeze, wring'. A derivative was *kwāra : Quenya *quár*, Telerin *pār*, Sindarin *paur*. This may be translated 'fist', though its chief use was in reference to the tightly closed hand as in using an implement or a craft-tool rather than to the 'fist' as used in punching. Cf. the name *Celebrin-baur* > *Celebrimbor*. This was a Sindarized form of Telerin *Telperimpar* (Quenya *Tyelpinquar*). It was a frequent name among the Teleri, who in addition to navigation and ship-building were also renowned as silver-smiths. The famous Celebrimbor, heroic defender of Eregion in the Second Age war against Sauron, was a Teler, one of the three Teleri who accompanied Celeborn into exile. He was a great silver-smith, and went to Eregion attracted by the rumours of the marvellous metal found in Moria, Moria-silver, to which he gave the name *mithril*. In the working of this he became a rival of the Dwarves, or rather an equal, for there was great friendship between the Dwarves of Moria and Cele-brimbor, and they shared their skills and craft-secrets. In the same way *Tegilbor* was used for one skilled in calligraphy (*tegil* was a Sindarized form of Quenya *tekil* 'pen', not known to the Sindar until the coming of the Noldor).

When my father wrote this he ignored the addition to Appen-dix B in the Second Edition, stating that Celebrimbor 'was

descended from Fëanor'; no doubt he had forgotten that that
theory had appeared in print, for had he remembered it he would
undoubtedly have felt bound by it. – On the statement that
Celebrimbor was 'one of the three Teleri who accompanied
Celeborn into exile' see *Unfinished Tales*, pp. 231–3.

Yet here in the present essay, from much the same time as that
on Eldarin words for 'hand' just cited, a radically different
account of Celebrimbor's origin is given: 'a Sinda who claimed
descent from Daeron'.]

8   They did not, however, appear in the inscriptions on the West
Gate of Moria. The Dwarves said that it was in courtesy to the
Elves that the Fëanorian letters were used on that gate, since it
opened into their country and was chiefly used by them. But
the East Gates, which perished in the war against the Orks, had
opened upon the wide world, and were less friendly. They had
borne Runic inscriptions in several tongues: spells of prohibition
and exclusion in Khuzdul, and commands that all should depart
who had not the leave of the Lord of Moria written in Quenya,
Sindarin, the Common Speech, the languages of Rohan and of
Dale and Dunland.

[In the margin against the paragraph in the text at this point
my father pencilled:

> N.B. It is actually said by Elrond in *The Hobbit* that the Runes
> were *invented* by the Dwarves and written with silver pens.
> Elrond was half-elven and a master of lore and history. So
> either we must tolerate this discrepancy or modify the history
> of the Runes, making the actual *Angerthas Moria* largely an
> affair of Dwarvish invention.

In notes associated with this essay he is seen pondering the latter
course, considering the possibility that it was in fact the Longbeard Dwarves who were the original begetters of the Runes; and
that it was from them that Daeron derived the idea, but since
the first Runes were not well organised (and differed from one
mansion of the Dwarves to another) he ordered them in a logical
system.

But of course in Appendix E (II) he had stated very explicitly
the origin of the Runes: 'The Cirth were devised first in Beleriand
by the Sindar'. It was Daeron of Doriath who developed the
'richest and most ordered form' of the Cirth, the Alphabet of
Daeron, and its use in Eregion led to its adoption by the Dwarves
of Moria, whence its name *Angerthas Moria*. Thus the inconsistency, if inconsistency there was, could scarcely be removed;
but in fact there was none. It was the 'moon-runes' that Elrond
declared (at the end of the chapter *A Short Rest*) to have been
invented by the Dwarves and written by them with silver pens,
not the Runes as an alphabetic form – as my father at length

noted with relief. I mention all this as an illustration of his intense concern to avoid discrepancy and inconsistency, even though in this case his anxiety was unfounded. – For an earlier account of the origin of the Runes see VII.452–5.]

9   [At this point the text in manuscript ends, and the typescript takes up.]

10   As things went ill in Moria and hope even of escaping with their lives faded the last pages of the Book can only have been written in the hope that the Book might be later found by friends, and inform them of the fate of Balin and his rash expedition to Moria – as indeed happened.

11   Cases were the reduction of double (long) consonants to single ones medially between vowels, or the alteration of consonants in certain combinations. Both are exemplified in the Third Age colloquial *tunas* 'guard', i.e. a body of men acting as guards. This was a derivative of the stem TUD 'watch, guard' + *nas* 'people': an organized group or gathering of people for some function. But *tudnas*, though it was often retained in 'correct' spelling, had been changed to *tunnas* and usually was so spelt: *tunas* which occurred in the first line of the preserved three pages was 'incorrect' and represented the colloquial. (Incidentally this *nas* is probably an example of the numerous loanwords from Elvish that were found in Adûnaic already and were increased in the Common Speech of the Kingdoms. It is probably < Quenya *nossë* or Sindarin *nos*, 'kindred, family'. The short *o* of Elvish became *a* in such borrowed words.)

12   [The three pages were reproduced in *Pictures by J. R. R. Tolkien*, 1979, no.23 (second edition, 1992, no.24).]

13   Exceptions are a few words in a debased form of the Black Speech; a few place-names or personal names (not interpreted); the warcry of the Dwarves. Also a few place-names supposed to be of forgotten origin or meaning; and one or two personal names of the same kind (see Appendix F, p. 407).

14   The sherd of Amenartas was in Greek (provided by Andrew Lang) of the period from which it was supposed to have survived, not in English spelt as well as might be in Greek letters. [For the sherd of Amenartas see H. Rider Haggard, *She*, chapter 3.]

15   The first song of Galadriel is treated in this way: it is given only in translation (as is all the rest of her speech in dialogue). Because in this case a verse translation was attempted, to represent as far as possible the metrical devices of the original – a considered composition no doubt made long before the coming of Frodo and independent of the arrival in Lórien of the One Ring. Whereas the Farewell was addressed direct to Frodo, and was an extempore outpouring in free rhythmic style, reflecting the overwhelming increase in her regret and longing, and her personal despair

after she had survived the terrible temptation. It was translated accurately. The rendering of the older song must be presumed to have been much freer to enable metrical features to be represented. (In the event it proved that it was Galadriel's abnegation of pride and trust in her own powers, and her absolute refusal of any unlawful enhancement of them, that provided the ship to bear her back to her home.) [Cf. the passage in a letter from my father of 1967 cited in *Unfinished Tales*, p. 229; *Letters* no.297, at end.]

16 [This refers to the last six lines (which include the interpretation of the inscription on the tomb) of the chapter *A Journey in the Dark*, beginning '"These are Daeron's Runes, such as were used of old in Moria," said Gandalf', which in the three-volume hardback edition of *The Lord of the Rings* alone appear on that page.]

17 Possibly observed by the more linguistically and historically minded; though I have received no comments on them.

18 [This refers to the end of Appendix F, I ('Gimli's own name ...'), cited above, p. 296.]

19 In later times, when their own Khuzdûl had become only a learned language, and the Dwarves had adopted the Common Speech or a local language of Men, they naturally used these 'outer' names also for all colloquial purposes. [*Khuzdûl* is in this case spelt with a circumflex accent on the second vowel.]

20 [At the same time as the alterations shown were made to the text of this passage my father wrote in the margin: 'But see on this below – they were derived from a long lost Mannish language in the North.' See pp. 303–4, and note 23 below.]

21 The references (in Appendix A [beginning of III, *Durin's Folk*]) to the legends of the origin of the Dwarves of the kin known as Longbeards (Khuzdul *Sigin-tarâg*, translated by Quenya *Andafangar*, Sindarin *Anfangrim*) and their renowned later 'mansions' in Khazad-dûm (Moria) are too brief to make the linguistic situation clear. The 'deeps of time' do not refer (of course) to geological time – of which only the Eldar had legends, derived and transmuted from such information as their loremasters had received from the Valar. They refer to legends of the Ages of Awakening and the arising of the Speaking Peoples: first the Elves, second the Dwarves (as they claimed), and third Men. Unlike Elves and Men the Dwarves appear in the legends to have arisen in the North of Middle-earth. [This note continued as follows, but the continuation was subsequently struck out.] The most westerly point, the place of the birth or awakening of the ancestor of the Longbeards, was in the traditions of the Third Age a valley in the Ered Mithrin. But this was in far distant days. It was long before the migrations of Men from the East reached the North-western regions. And it was long again before the

Dwarves – of whom the Longbeards appear to have been the most secretive and least concerned to have dealings with Elves or Men – still felt any need to learn any languages of their neighbours, still less to take names by which they could be known to 'outsiders'.

22   [My father's point was that *Balin* and *Fundin* are actual Old Norse names used as 'translations' for the purpose of *The Lord of the Rings*. What he should have done in a visual representation of the tomb-inscription was to use, not of course their 'inner' names in Khuzdul, but their *real* 'outer' names which in the text of *The Lord of the Rings* are represented by *Balin* and *Fundin*.]

23   [It seems that it was when my father reached this point in the essay that he made the alterations to the text on p. 300 with the marginal observation given in note 20, and struck out the latter part of note 21.]

24   He alone had no companions; cf. 'he slept alone' (III.352). [The reference is to the beginning of Appendix A, III. The passage in the text is difficult to interpret. My father refers here to four places of awakening of the Seven Ancestors of the Dwarves: those of 'the ancestors of the Firebeards and the Broadbeams', 'the ancestor of the Longbeards', 'the Ironfists and Stiffbeards', and 'the Blacklocks and Stonefoots'. (None of these names of the other six kindreds of the Dwarves has ever been given before. Since the ancestors of the Firebeards and the Broadbeams awoke in the Ered Lindon, these kindreds must be presumed to be the Dwarves of Nogrod and Belegost.) It seems that he was here referring to Durin's having 'slept alone' in contrast to the other kindreds, whose Fathers were laid to sleep in pairs. If this is so, it is a different conception from that cited in XI.213, where Ilúvatar 'commanded Aulë to lay the fathers of the Dwarves severally in deep places, each with his mate, save Durin the eldest who had none.' On the subject of the 'mates' of the Fathers of the Dwarves see XI.211–13. – In the margin of the typescript my father wrote later (against the present note): 'He wandered widely after awakening: his people were Dwarves that joined him from other kindreds west and east'; and at the head of the page he suggested that the legend of the Making of the Dwarves should be altered (indeed very radically altered) to a form in which other Dwarves were laid to sleep near to the Fathers.]

25   [In the rejected conclusion of note 21 the place of the awakening of the ancestor of the Longbeards was 'a valley in the Ered Mithrin' (the Grey Mountains in the far North). There has of course been no previous reference to this ancient significance of Mount Gundabad. That mountain originally appeared in the chapter *The Clouds Burst* in *The Hobbit*, where it is told that the

Goblins 'marched and gathered by hill and valley, going ever by tunnel or under dark, until around and beneath the great mountain Gundabad of the North, where was their capital, a vast host was assembled'; and it is shown on the map of Wilderland in *The Hobbit* as a great isolated mass at the northern end of the Misty Mountains where the Grey Mountains drew towards them. In *The Lord of the Rings*, Appendix A (III), Gundabad appears in the account of the War of the Dwarves and Orcs late in the Third Age, where the Dwarves 'assailed and sacked one by one all the strongholds of the Orcs that they could [find] from Gundabad to the Gladden' (the word 'find' was erroneously dropped in the Second Edition).]

26 According to their legends their begetter, Aulë the Vala, had made this for them and had taught it to the Seven Fathers before they were laid to sleep until the time for their awakening should come. After their awakening this language (as all languages and all other things in Arda) changed in time, and divergently in the mansions that were far-sundered. But the change was so slow and the divergence so small that even in the Third Age converse between all Dwarves in their own tongue was easy. As they said, the change in Khuzdul as compared with the tongue of the Elves, and still more with those of Men, was 'like the weathering of hard rock compared with the melting of snow.'

27 The Dwarves multiplied slowly; but Men in prosperity and peace more swiftly than even the Elves.

28 For they had met some far to the East who were of evil mind. [This was a later pencilled note. On the previous page of the typescript my father wrote at the same time, without indication of its reference to the text but perhaps arising from the mention (p. 301) of the awakening of the eastern kindreds of the Dwarves: 'Alas, it seems probable that (as Men did later) the Dwarves of the far eastern mansions (and some of the nearer ones?) came under the Shadow of Morgoth and turned to evil.']

29 No Dwarf would ever mount a horse willingly, nor did any ever harbour animals, not even dogs.

30 For a time. The Númenóreans had not yet appeared on the shores of Middle-earth, and the foundations of the Barad-dûr had not yet been built. It was a brief period in the dark annals of the Second Age, yet for many lives of Men the Longbeards controlled the Ered Mithrin, Erebor, and the Iron Hills, and all the east side of the Misty Mountains as far as the confines of Lórien; while the Men of the North dwelt in all the adjacent lands as far south as the Great Dwarf Road that cut through the Forest (the Old Forest Road was its ruinous remains in the Third Age) and then went North-east to the Iron Hills. [As with so much else in this account, the origin of the Old Forest Road in 'the Great Dwarf

Road', which after traversing Greenwood the Great led to the Iron Hills, has never been met before.]

31   Only the personal names of individuals. The name of their race, and the names of their families, and of their mansions, they did not conceal.

32   Either actual Mannish names current among the Northern Men, or names made in the same ways out of elements in the Mannish tongue, or names of no meaning that were simply made of the sounds used by Men put together in ways natural to their speech.

33   [My father might seem to write here as if *Durin* was the 'real' Mannish name of the Father of the Longbeards; but of course it is a name derived from Old Norse, and thus a 'translation'.]

34   Somewhat similar to the way in which the 'runes' of Elvish origin were widely regarded by Men in the Third Age as a Dwarvish mode of writing.

35   Sauron was defeated by the Númenóreans and driven back into Mordor, and for long troubled the West no more, while secretly extending his dominions eastward.

36   Though such changes and divergence as had already occurred before they left Middle-earth would have endured – such as the divergence of the speech of the Teleri from that of the Ñoldor.

37   [This and the subsequent section-heading, together with their numbers, were pencilled in later. The title of section I is lost with the loss of the first page of the essay.]

38   The name is said to have been derived from *atan* 'man, human being as distinct from creatures', a word used by that kindred which the Eldar first encountered in Beleriand. This was borrowed and adapted to Quenya and Sindarin; but later when Men of other kinds became known to the Eldar it became limited to Men of the Three Peoples who had become allies of the Eldar in Beleriand.

[A typewritten draft for the page of the essay on which this second section begins is preserved (though without the section-heading or number, see note 37): in this draft the present note begins in the same way, but diverges after the words 'adapted to Quenya and Sindarin' thus:

It was however associated by the Eldar with their own word *atar (adar)* 'father' and often translated 'Fathers of Men', though this title, in full *atanatar*, properly belonged only to the leaders and chieftains of the peoples at the time of their entry into Beleriand. In Sindarin *adan* was still often used for 'man', especially in names of races with a preceding prefix, as in *Dún-adan*, plural *Dúnedain*, 'Men of the West', Númenóreans; *Drû-edain* 'Wild-men'.

The statement here that *Atani* was derived from a word in the

Bëorian language, *atan* 'man', contradicts what was said in the
chapter *Of the Coming of Men into the West* that was added to
the *Quenta Silmarillion*, XI.219, footnote: '*Atani* was the name
given to Men in Valinor, in the lore that told of their coming;
according to the Eldar it signified "Second", for the kindred of
Men was the second of the Children of Ilúvatar'; cf. *Quendi and
Eldar*, XI.386, where essentially the same is said (the devising of
the name *Atani* is there ascribed to the Ñoldor in Valinor).]

39 [This refers to Morgoth's captivity in Aman. See X.423, note 3.]
40 [Cf. the words of Andreth, X.310, and of Bereg and Amlach,
    XI.220, §18).]
41 [Haleth was not the name of the chieftain who commanded the
    Folk of Haleth when they first came to Beleriand: see XI.221–2
    and the genealogical tree, XI.237. But this is probably not sig-
    nificant, in view of what is said at the end of the paragraph: these
    people 'were called the Folk of Haleth, for Haleth was the name
    of their chieftainess who led them to the woods north of Doriath
    where they were permitted to dwell.' On the other hand, the
    statement that Hador was the name of the chieftain who led
    the Folk of Hador into Beleriand seems to ignore that greatly
    enlarged and altered history that had entered in the chapter *Of
    the Coming of Men into the West* (cf. note 38), according to
    which it was Marach who led that people over the Mountains,
    and Hador himself, though he gave his name to the people, was
    a descendant of Marach in the fourth generation (see XI.218–19
    and the genealogical tree, XI.234). In that work the division of
    the Folk of Hador into three hosts, referred to a little later in the
    present paragraph, does not appear – indeed it was said (XI.218,
    §10) that Bëor told Felagund that 'they are a numerous people,
    and yet keep together and move slowly, being all ruled by one
    chieftain whom they call Marach.']
42 [In other accounts the Folk of Haleth were the second kindred of
    the Edain to enter Beleriand, not the last; thus in QS §127
    (V.275), when Haleth was still Haleth the Hunter and had not
    been transformed into the Lady Haleth, 'After Bëor came Haleth
    father of Hundor, and again somewhat later came Hador the
    Goldenhaired', and in *Of the Coming of Men into the West* §13
    (XI.218) 'First came the Haladin ... The next year, however,
    Marach led his people over the Mountains'. In that text (§10)
    Bëor told Felagund that the people of Marach 'were before us in
    the westward march, but we passed them', and there is no sug-
    gestion of the story told here that they reached Eredlindon first of
    all the Edain, but that 'seeking a road round the Mountains' they
    'came up from southward' into Beleriand. – Of internal strife
    among the Folk of Haleth, referred to a few lines later in this
    paragraph, there has been no previous mention.]

43   No doubt this was due to mingling with Men of other kind in the past; and it was noted that the dark hair ran in families that had more skill and interest in crafts and lore.

44   With a knowledge of the language of the Folk of Bëor that was later lost, save for a few names of persons and places, and some words or phrases preserved in legends. One of the common words was *atan*. [With the last sentence cf. note 38.]

45   [With this is perhaps to be compared what my father wrote elsewhere at this time (p. 373, note 13) concerning the long period during which the 'Bëorians' and the 'Hadorians' became separated in the course of their westward migration and dwelt on opposite sides of a great inland sea.]

46   Beren the Renowned had hair of a golden brown and grey eyes; he was taller than most of his kin, but he was broad-shouldered and very strong in his limbs.

47   The Eldar said, and recalled in the songs they still sang in later days, that they could not easily be distinguished from the Eldar – not while their youth lasted, the swift fading of which was to the Eldar a grief and a mystery.

48   [With this account of the Folk of Bëor and the Folk of Hador may be compared the description that my father wrote many years before in the *Quenta Silmarillion*, V.276, §130.]

49   [On the alteration of the relationship between the three languages of the Atani, whereby that of the Folk of Haleth replaced that of the Folk of Hador as the tongue isolated from the others, see p. 368 and note 4.]

50   Not due to their special situation in Beleriand, and maybe rather a cause of their small numbers than its result. They increased in numbers far more slowly than the other Atani, hardly more than was sufficient to replace the wastage of war; yet many of their women (who were fewer than the men) remained unwed.

51   [Apart from some slight and largely unnecessary modifications to the original text (in no case altering the sense) there are a few points to mention about that printed in *Unfinished Tales*. (1) The spelling *Ork(s)* was changed to *Orc(s)*, and that of the river *Taiglin* to *Teiglin* (see XI.228, 309–10). (2) A passage about the liking of the Drûgs for edible fungus was omitted in view of my father's pencilled note beside it: 'Delete all this about funguses. Too like Hobbits' (a reference of course to Frodo and Farmer Maggot's mushrooms). This followed the account of the knowledge of the Drûgs concerning plants, and reads:

> To the astonishment of Elves and other Men they ate funguses with pleasure, many of which looked to others ugly and dangerous; some kinds which they specially liked they caused to grow near their dwellings. The Eldar did not eat these things. The Folk of Haleth, taught by the Drúedain, made

some use of them at need; and if they were guests they ate what was provided in courtesy, and without fear. The other Atani eschewed them, save in great hunger when astray in the wild, for few among them had the knowledge to distinguish the wholesome from the bad, and the less wise called them ork-plants and supposed them to have been cursed and blighted by Morgoth.]

52 [See *Unfinished Tales*, p. 386, note 8. Elsewhere Húrin's serving-man is named *Sador*, not *Sadog*.]

53 [This sentence is cited in *Unfinished Tales*, p. 387, note 11.]

54 See the discussion of lineal measurements and their equation with our measures in the legend of *The Disaster of the Gladden Fields*. [This discussion (which, with the work itself, belongs to the very late period – 1968 or later) is found in *Unfinished Tales*, pp. 285 ff., where a note on the stature of Hobbits is also given.]

55 In the original sense of 'savage'; they were by nature of gentle disposition, neither cruel nor vindictive.

56 Of different kinds: Dwarves they found of uncertain temper and dangerous if displeased; Elves they viewed with awe, and avoided. Even in the Shire in the Third Age, where Elves were more often to be met than in other regions where Hobbits dwelt or had dwelt, most of the Shire-folk would have no dealings with them. 'They wander in Middle-earth,' they said, 'but their minds and hearts are not there.'

57 ['Nowhere else in the world was this peculiar (but excellent) arrangement to be found': opening of the chapter *At the Sign of the Prancing Pony*. This observation is here attributed to Bilbo as the ultimate author of the Red Book of Westmarch.]

58 Indeed it is probable that only at Bree and in the Shire did any communities of Hobbits survive at that time west of the Misty Mountains. Nothing is known of the situation in lands further east, from which the Hobbits must have migrated in unrecorded ages.

59 When they entered Eriador (early in the second century of the Third Age) Men were still numerous there, both Númenóreans and other Men related to the Atani, beside remnants of Men of evil kinds, hostile to the Kings. But the Common Speech (of Númenórean origin) was in general use there, even after the decay of the North Kingdom. In Bilbo's time great areas of Eriador were empty of Men. The desolation had begun in the Great Plague (soon after the Hobbits' occupation of the Shire), and was hastened by the final fall and disappearance of the North Kingdom. In the Plague it would seem that the only Hobbit communities to survive were those in the far North-west at Bree and in the Shire. [The opening sentence of this note, placing the entry of the Hobbits into Eriador 'early in the second century of the

Third Age', is plainly a casual error: presumably my father intended 'millennium' for 'century' (in Appendix B the date of the coming of the Harfoots is given under Third Age 1050, and that of the Fallohides and the Stoors under 1150).]

60   The invasions were no doubt also in great part due to Sauron; for the 'Easterlings' were mostly Men of cruel and evil kind, descendants of those who had served and worshipped Sauron before his overthrow at the end of the Second Age.

61   Though the native traditions of the Rohirrim preserved no memories of the ancient war in Beleriand, they accepted the belief, which did much to strengthen their friendship with Gondor and their unbroken loyalty to the Oath of Eorl and Cirion. [In relation to this note and to the passage in the text to which it refers my father wrote in the margin of the typescript:

It may have been actually true of those Men in Middle-earth whom the returning Númenóreans first met (see below); but other Men of the North resembling them in features and temper can only have been akin as descending from peoples of which the Atani had been the vanguard.]

62   [In *Quendi and Eldar* (XI.377) there is a reference to Avari 'who had crept in small and secret groups into Beleriand from the South', and to rare cases of an Avar 'who joined with or was admitted among the Sindar'; while in that essay Eöl of Nan Elmoth was an Avar (XI.409 and note 33).]

63   [The Little Lune was first marked on the third and last of my father's general maps of the West of Middle-earth (that on which my original map published with *The Lord of the Rings* was closely based), but this appears to be the first time that it has been named.]

64   [With this statement that the region beyond the inflow of the Little Lune was 'Dwarf territory' cf. Appendix A (I, iii), where it is told that Arvedui, the last king of Arthedain, 'hid in the tunnels of the old dwarf-mines near the far end of the Mountains'.]

65   Gil-galad's people were mainly Ñoldorin; though in the Second Age the Elves of Harlindon were mainly Sindarin, and the region was a fief under the rule of Celeborn. [In the prefatory note to the annals of the Second Age in Appendix B it is said: 'In Lindon south of the Lune dwelt for a time Celeborn, kinsman of Thingol'; see *Unfinished Tales* p. 233 and note 2, where the present note is referred to.]

66   [See *Unfinished Tales*, pp. 262–3 (extract from a late essay on the names of the rivers and beacon-hills of Gondor). – The name was typed *Enedwaith* with the *h* added subsequently, but later in this essay (note 76) the form typed is *Enedhwaith*; so also in that on river-names just mentioned, although in the extracts given in

Unfinished Tales I printed *Enedwaith* for agreement with published texts.]

67 This according to the traditions of Dol Amroth had been established by seafaring Sindar from the west havens of Beleriand who fled in three small ships when the power of Morgoth overwhelmed the Eldar and the Atani; but it was later increased by adventurers of the Silvan Elves seeking for the Sea who came down the Anduin. The Silvan Elves were Middle Elves according to the Númenórean classification, though unknown to the Atani until later days: for they were like the Sindar Teleri, but were laggards in the hindmost companies who had never crossed the Misty Mountains and established small realms on either side of the Vales of Anduin. (Of these Lórien and the realm of Thranduil in Mirkwood were survivors in the Third Age.) But they were never wholly free of an unquiet and a yearning for the Sea which at times drove some of them to wander from their homes. [On this haven (Edhellond) see *Unfinished Tales*, pp. 246–7 and note 18 on p. 255.]

68 The first sailings of the Númenóreans to Middle-earth were to the lands of Gil-galad, with whom their great mariner Aldarion made an alliance.

69 As the power of Númenor became more and more occupied with great navies, for which their own land could not supply sufficient timber without ruin, their felling of trees and transportation of wood to their shipyards in Númenor or on the coast of Middle-earth (especially at Lond Daer, the Great Harbour at the mouth of the Greyflood) became reckless. [See *Unfinished Tales*, p. 262, on the tree-felling of the Númenóreans in Minhiriath and Enedhwaith. Of the kinship of the forest-dwellers of those regions with the People of Haleth there is no suggestion elsewhere (see also note 72 below). With the following sentence in the text, 'In the Third Age their survivors were the people known in Rohan as the Dunlendings' cf. *Unfinished Tales*, p. 263: 'From Enedwaith they [the native people fleeing from the Númenóreans] took refuge in the eastern mountains where afterwards was Dunland'.]

70 [This was the voyage of Vëantur the Númenórean, grandfather of Aldarion the Mariner: see *Unfinished Tales*, pp. 171, 174–5.]

71 [At the words in the text printed in *Unfinished Tales* 'as if addressing friends and kinsmen after a long parting' there is a note in the essay which I did not include:

The Atani had learned the Sindarin tongue in Beleriand and most of them, especially the high men and the learned, had spoken it familiarly, even among themselves: but always as a learned language, taught in early childhood; their native language remained the Adûnaic, the Mannish tongue of the Folk of Hador (except in some districts of the west of the Isle where the rustic folk used a Bëorian dialect). Thus the Sindarin they used had remained unchanged through many lives of Men.

With this cf. *Unfinished Tales*, p. 215 note 19. I do not know how the mention here of 'a Bëorian dialect' surviving in the west of Númenor is to be related to the total loss of the language of the Folk of Bëor referred to in note 44; see also p. 368 and note 5.]

72   This may have been one of the reasons why the Númenóreans failed to recognize the Forest-folk of Minhiriath as 'kinsmen', and confused them with Men of the Shadow; for as has been noted the native language of the Folk of Haleth was not related to the language of the Folks of Hador and Bëor.

73   And those that they adopted from older inhabitants they usually altered to fit the Sindarin style. Their names of persons also were nearly all of Sindarin form, save a few which had descended from the legends of the Atani in the First Age.

74   It thus became naturally somewhat corrupted from the true Sindarin of the Elves, but this was hindered by the fact that Sindarin was held in high esteem and was taught in the schools, according to forms and grammatical structure of ancient days.

75   The Elf-realm became diminished in the wars against Sauron, and by the establishment of Imladris, and it no longer extended east of the Ered Luin.

76   The Enedhwaith (or Central Wilderness) was shared by the North and South Kingdoms, but was never settled by Númenóreans owing to the hostility of the Gwathuirim (Dunlendings), except in the fortified town and haven about the great bridge over the Greyflood at Tharbad. [The name *Gwathuirim* of the Dunlendings has not occurred before.]

77   [It was said in Appendix A (I, iv) that at the height of its power the realm of Gondor 'extended north to Celebrant', and a long note in the essay at this point, beginning 'But for "Celebrant" read "Field of Celebrant"', is an exposition of the significance of the latter name (*Parth Celebrant*). This note is given in *Unfinished Tales*, p. 260.]

78   [The River Running is named *Celduin* in Appendix A, III (RK p. 353). *Celon* was the river that in the First Age rose in the Hill of Himring and flowed past Nan Elmoth to join the Aros; and since *Celduin* as the name of the River Running appears in the very late text *Cirion and Eorl* (*Unfinished Tales* p. 289) *Celon* here is presumably no more than a casual confusion of the names.]

XI

THE SHIBBOLETH OF FËANOR

With an excursus on the name of
the descendants of Finwë

In all my father's last writings linguistic history was closely inter-
twined with the history of persons and of peoples, and much that he
recounted can be seen to have arisen in the search for explanations of
linguistic facts or anomalies. The most remarkable example of this is
the following essay, arising from his consideration of a problem of historical phonology, which records how the difference in pronunciation
of a single consonantal element in Quenya played a significant part in
the strife of the Noldorin princes in Valinor. It has no title, but I have
called it *The Shibboleth of Fëanor*, since my father himself used that
word in the course of the essay (p. 336).

Like *Of Dwarves and Men*, it was written (composed in typescript
throughout) on paper supplied by Allen and Unwin, in this case
mostly copies of a publication note of February 1968; and as in that
essay there are very many notes interpolated into the body of the text
in the process of composition. Appended to it is a lengthy excursus
(half as long again as the essay from which it arose) on the names of
Finwë's descendants, and this I give also; but from both *The Shibboleth of Fëanor* proper and from this excursus I have excluded a number of notes, some of them lengthy, of a technical phonological nature.
The work was not finished, for my father did not reach, as was his
intention, discussion of the names of the Sons of Fëanor; but such
draft material as there is for this part is given at the end of the text.
All numbered notes, both my father's and mine, are collected on pp.
356 ff.

This work was scarcely used in *Unfinished Tales* except for a
passage concerning Galadriel, which is here repeated in its original
context; but elements were used in the published *Silmarillion*.

The Shibboleth of Fëanor

The case of the Quenya change of þ to s[1]

The history of the Eldar is now fixed and the adoption of
Sindarin by the Exiled Ñoldor cannot be altered. Since Sindarin
made great use of *þ*, the change *þ* > *s* must have occurred in
Ñoldorin Quenya in Valinor before the rebellion and exile of
the Ñoldor, though not necessarily long before it (in Valinorian

reckoning of time). The change cannot therefore be explained as a development (that is a sound-substitution of s for an un-familiar þ) in Quenya of the Third Age: either due to the Elves themselves, since they were familiar with þ; or to such people as the Númenórean scholars in Gondor, since þ occurred in the Common Speech, and also in the Sindarin which was still used as a spoken language among the upper classes, especially in Minas Tirith.

The use by Galadriel, as reported in *The Lord of the Rings*, must therefore be normal. It is not however an obstacle to the use of þ in representing the classical book-Quenya, pre-Exilic or post-Exilic, in grammars, dictionaries or transcripts. It is in fact desirable, since the older þ was always kept distinct in writing from original s. This in Exilic conditions, which made necessary the writing down anew from memory of many of the pre-Exilic works of lore and song,[2] implies a continuing memory of the sound þ, and the places in which it had previously occurred; also probably a dislike of the change to s in the colloquial Quenya on the part of the scholars. It is in any case impossible to believe that any of the Ñoldor ever became unfamiliar with the sound þ as such. In Valinor they dwelt between the Vanyar (Ingwi) and the Teleri (Lindar),[3] with whom they were in com-munication and sometimes intermarried. The Vanyar spoke virtually the same language (Quenya) and retained þ in daily use; the Teleri spoke a closely related language still largely intel-ligible to the Ñoldor,[4] and it also used þ. The Ñoldor were, even compared with other Eldar, talented linguists, and if þ did not occur in the language that they learned in childhood – which could only be the case with the youngest generations of those who set out from Aman – they would have had no difficulty in acquiring it.

The change þ > s must therefore have been a conscious and deliberate change agreed to and accepted by a majority of the Ñoldor, however initiated, after the separation of their dwellings from the Vanyar. It must have occurred after the birth of Míriel, but (probably) before the birth of Fëanor. The special connexion of these two persons with the change and its later history needs some consideration.

The change was a general one, based primarily on phonetic 'taste' and theory, but it had not yet become universal. It was attacked by the loremasters,[5] who pointed out that the damage this merging would do in confusing stems and their derivatives that had been distinct in sound and sense had not yet been sufficiently considered. The chief of the linguistic loremasters at that time was Fëanor. He insisted that *þ* was the true pronunciation for all who cared for or fully understood their language. But in addition to linguistic taste and wisdom he had other motives. He was the eldest of Finwë's sons and the only child of his first wife Míriel. She was a Ñoldorin Elda of slender and graceful form, and of gentle disposition, though as was later discovered in matters far more grave, she could show an ultimate obstinacy that counsel or command would only make more obdurate. She had a beautiful voice and a delicate and clear enunciation, though she spoke swiftly and took pride in this skill. Her chief talent, however, was a marvellous dexterity of hand. This she employed in embroidery, which though achieved in what even the Eldar thought a speed of haste was finer and more intricate than any that had before been seen. She was therefore called *Perindë* (Needlewoman) – a name which she had indeed already been given as a 'mother-name'.[6] She adhered to the pronunciation *þ* (it had still been usual in her childhood), and she desired that all her kin should adhere to it also, at the least in the pronunciation of her name.

Fëanor loved his mother dearly, though except in obstinacy their characters were widely different. He was not gentle. He was proud and hot-tempered, and opposition to his will he met not with the quiet steadfastness of his mother but with fierce resentment. He was restless in mind and body, though like Míriel he could become wholly absorbed in works of the finest skill of hand; but he left many things unfinished. Fëanáro was his mother-name, which Míriel gave him in recognition of his impetuous character (it meant 'spirit of fire'). While she lived she did much with gentle counsel to soften and restrain him.[7] Her death was a lasting grief to Fëanor, and both directly and by its further consequences a main cause of his later disastrous influence on the history of the Ñoldor.

The death of Míriel Þerindë – death of an 'immortal' Elda in the deathless land of Aman – was a matter of grave anxiety to the Valar, the first presage of the Shadow that was to fall on Valinor. The matter of Finwë and Míriel and the judgement that the Valar after long debate finally delivered upon it is elsewhere told.[8] Only those points that may explain the conduct of Fëanor are here recalled. Míriel's death was of free will: she forsook her body and her *fëa* went to the Halls of Waiting, while her body lay as if asleep in a garden. She said that she was weary in body and spirit and desired peace. The cause of her weariness she believed to be the bearing of Fëanor, great in mind and body beyond the measure of the Eldar. Her weariness she had endured until he was full grown, but she could endure it no longer.

The Valar and all the Eldar were grieved by the sorrow of Finwë, but not dismayed: all things could be healed in Aman, and when they were rested her *fëa* and its body could be re-united and return to the joy of life in the Blessed Realm. But Míriel was reluctant, and to all the pleas of her husband and her kin that were reported to her, and to the solemn counsels of the Valar, she would say no more than 'not yet'. Each time that she was approached she became more fixed in her determination, until at last she would listen no more, saying only: 'I desire peace. Leave me in peace here! I will not return. That is my will.'

So the Valar were faced by the one thing that they could neither change nor heal: the free will of one of the Children of Eru, which it was unlawful for them to coerce – and in such a case useless, since force could not achieve its purpose. And after some years they were faced by another grave perplexity. When it became clear at last that Míriel would never of her own will return to life in the body within any span of time that could give him hope, Finwë's sorrow became embittered. He forsook his long vigils by her sleeping body and sought to take up his own life again; but he wandered far and wide in loneliness and found no joy in anything that he did.

There was a fair lady of the Vanyar, Indis of the House of Ingwë. She had loved Finwë in her heart, ever since the days when the Vanyar and the Ñoldor lived close together. In one of his wanderings Finwë met her again upon the inner slopes of Oiolossë, the Mountain of Manwë and Varda; and her face was lit by the golden light of Laurelin that was shining in the plain of Ezellohar below.[9] In that hour Finwë perceived in her eyes the love that had before been hidden from him. So it came to pass that Finwë and Indis desired to be wedded, and Finwë sought the counsel of the Valar.

The long debate that they held on the matter may be passed over briefly. They were obliged to choose between two courses: condemning Finwë to bereavement of a wife for ever, or allowing one of the Eldar to take a second wife. The former seemed a cruel injustice, and contrary to the nature of the Eldar. The second they had thought unlawful, and some still held to that opinion.[10] The end of the Debate was that the marriage of Finwë and Indis was sanctioned. It was judged that Finwë's bereavement was unjust, and by persisting in her refusal to return Míriel had forfeited all rights that she had in the case; for either she was now capable of accepting the healing of her body by the Valar, or else her *fëa* was mortally sick and beyond their power, and she was indeed 'dead', no longer capable of becoming again a living member of the kindred of the Eldar.

'So she must remain until the end of the world. For from the moment that Finwë and Indis are joined in marriage all future change and choice will be taken from her and she will never again be permitted to take bodily shape. Her present body will swiftly wither and pass away, and the Valar will not restore it. For none of the Eldar may have two wives both alive in the world.' These were the words of Manwë, and an answer to the doubts that some had felt. For it was known to all the Valar that they alone had the power to heal or restore the body for the re-housing of a *fëa* that should in the later chances of the world be deprived; but that to Manwë also was given the right to refuse the return of the *fëa*.

During the time of his sorrow Finwë had little comfort from Fëanor. For a while he also had kept vigil by his mother's body, but soon he became wholly absorbed again in his own works and devices. When the matter of Finwë and Indis arose he was disturbed, and filled with anger and resentment; though it is not recorded that he attended the Debate or paid heed to the reasons given for the judgement, or to its terms except in one point: that Míriel was condemned to remain for ever discarnate, so that he could never again visit her or speak with her, unless he himself should die.[11] This grieved him, and he grudged the happiness of Finwë and Indis, and was unfriendly to their children, even before they were born.

How this ill will grew and festered in the years that followed is the main matter of the first part of *The Silmarillion*: the Darkening of Valinor. Into the strife and confusion of loyalties in that time this seemingly trivial matter, the change of *þ* to *s*, was caught up to its embitterment, and to lasting detriment to the Quenya tongue. Had peace been maintained there can be no doubt that the advice of Fëanor, with which all the other loremasters privately or openly agreed, would have prevailed. But an opinion in which he was certainly right was rejected because of the follies and evil deeds into which he was later led. He made it a personal matter: he and his sons adhered to þ, and they demanded that all those who were sincere in their support should do the same. Therefore those who resented his arrogance, and still more those whose support later turned to hatred, rejected his shibboleth.

Indis was a Vanya, and it might be thought that she would in this point at least have pleased Fëanor, since the Vanyar adhered to þ. Nonetheless Indis adopted s. Not as Fëanor believed in belittlement of Míriel, but in loyalty to Finwë. For after the rejection of his prayers by Míriel Finwë accepted the change (which had now become almost universal among his people), although in deference to Míriel he had adhered to þ while she lived. Therefore Indis said: 'I have joined the people of the Ñoldor, and I will speak as they do.' So it came about that to Fëanor the rejection of þ became a symbol of the rejection of Míriel, and of himself, her son, as the chief of the Ñoldor next to Finwë. This, as his pride grew and his mood darkened, he thought was a 'plot' of the Valar, inspired by fear of his powers, to oust him and give the leadership of the Ñoldor to those more servile. So Fëanor would call himself 'Son of the Perindë', and when his sons in their childhood asked why their kin in the house of Finwë used s for þ he answered: 'Take no heed! We speak as is right, and as King Finwë himself did before he was led astray. We are his heirs by right and the elder house. Let them sá-sí, if they can speak no better.'

There can thus be no doubt that the majority of the Exiles used s for þ in their daily speech; for in the event (after Morgoth had contrived the murder of Finwë) Fëanor was deprived of the leadership, and the greater part of the Ñoldor who forsook Valinor marched under the command of Fingolfin, the eldest son of Indis. Fingolfin was his father's son, tall, dark, and proud, as were most of the Ñoldor, and in the end in spite of the enmity between him and Fëanor he joined with full will in the rebellion and the exile, though he continued to claim the kingship of all the Ñoldor.

The case of Galadriel and her brother Finrod is somewhat different.[12] They were the children of Finarfin, Indis' second son. He was of his mother's kind in mind and body, having the golden hair of the Vanyar, their noble and gentle temper, and their love of the Valar. As well as he could he kept aloof from the strife of his brothers and their estrangement from the Valar, and he often sought peace among the Teleri, whose language he learned. He wedded Eärwen, the daughter of King Olwë, and his children were thus the kin of King Elwë Þindikollo[13] (in Sindarin Elu Thingol) of Doriath in Beleriand, for he was the brother of Olwë; and this kinship influenced their decision to join in the Exile, and proved of great importance later in Beleriand. Finrod was like his father in his fair face and golden hair, and also in noble and generous heart, though he had the high courage of the Ñoldor and in his youth their eagerness and unrest; and he had also from his Telerin mother a love of the sea and dreams of far lands that he had never seen. Galadriel was the greatest of the Ñoldor, except Fëanor maybe, though she was wiser than he, and her wisdom increased with the long years.

Her mother-name was Nerwen 'man-maiden', and she grew to be tall beyond the measure even of the women of the Ñoldor; she was strong of body, mind, and will, a match for both the loremasters and the athletes of the Eldar in the days of their youth. Even among the Eldar she was accounted beautiful, and her hair was held a marvel unmatched. It was golden like the hair of her father and her foremother Indis, but richer and more radiant, for its gold was touched by some memory of the star-like silver of her mother; and the Eldar said that the light of the Two Trees, Laurelin and Telperion, had been snared in her tresses. Many thought that this saying first gave to Fëanor the thought of imprisoning and blending the light of the Trees that later took shape in his hands as the Silmarils. For Fëanor beheld the hair of Galadriel with wonder and delight. He begged three times for a tress, but Galadriel would not give him even one hair. These two kinsfolk, the greatest of the Eldar of Valinor,[14] were unfriends for ever.

Galadriel was born in the bliss of Valinor, but it was not long, in the reckoning of the Blessed Realm, before that was dimmed; and thereafter she had no peace within. For in that testing time amid the strife of the Ñoldor she was drawn this way and that. She was proud, strong, and self-willed, as were all the descendants of Finwë save Finarfin; and like her brother Finrod, of all her kin the nearest to her heart, she had dreams of far lands and dominions that might be her own to order as she would without tutelage. Yet deeper still there dwelt in her the noble and generous spirit (*órë*) of the Vanyar, and a reverence for the Valar that she could not forget. From her earliest years she had a marvellous gift of insight into the minds of others, but judged them with mercy and understanding, and she withheld her good will from none save only Fëanor. In him she perceived a darkness that she hated and feared, though she did not perceive that the shadow of the same evil had fallen upon the minds of all the Ñoldor, and upon her own.

So it came to pass that when the light of Valinor failed, for ever as the Ñoldor thought, she joined the rebellion against the Valar who commanded them to stay; and once she had set foot upon that road of exile, she would not relent, but rejected the last message of the Valar, and came under the Doom of Mandos. Even after the merciless assault upon the Teleri and the rape of their ships, though she fought fiercely against Fëanor in defence of her mother's kin, she did not turn back. Her pride was unwilling to return, a defeated suppliant for pardon; but now she burned with desire to follow Fëanor with her anger to whatever lands he might come, and to thwart him in all ways that she could. Pride still moved her when, at the end of the Elder Days after the final overthrow of Morgoth, she refused the pardon of the Valar for all who had fought against him, and remained in Middle-earth. It was not until two long ages more had passed, when at last all that she had desired in her youth came to her hand, the Ring of Power and the dominion of Middle-earth of which she had dreamed, that her wisdom was full grown and she rejected it, and passing the last test departed from Middle-earth for ever.

The change to *s* had become general among the Ñoldor long before the birth of Galadriel and no doubt was familiar to her. Her father Finarfin, however, loved the Vanyar (his mother's people) and the Teleri, and in his house *þ* was used, Finarfin being moved by Fëanor neither one way or the other but doing as he wished. It is clear nonetheless that opposition to Fëanor soon became a dominant motive with Galadriel, while her pride did not take the form of wishing to be different from her own people. So while she knew well the history of their tongue and all the reasons of the loremasters, she certainly used *s* in her own daily speech. Her Lament – spoken before she knew of the pardon (and indeed honour) that the Valar gave her – harks back to the days of her youth in Valinor and to the darkness of the years of Exile while the Blessed Realm was closed to all the

Ñoldor in Middle-earth. Whatever she may have done later, when Fëanor and all his sons had perished, and Quenya was a language of lore known and used only by the dwindling remnant of the High Elves (of Ñoldorin descent), she would in this song certainly have used s.

The s was certainly used in Beleriand by nearly all the Ñoldor.[15] And it was in this form (though with knowledge of its history and the difference in spelling) that Quenya was handed on to the loremasters of the Atani, so that in Middle-earth it lingered on among the learned, and a source of high and noble names in Rivendell and in Gondor into the Fourth Age.

The essay is followed by three 'notes'. Note 1 is a substantial development of the words in the essay (p. 332) 'The change was ... based primarily on phonetic "taste" and theory', which is here omitted. Note 2, given below, is an account of Elvish name-giving that differs in some important respects from the earlier and far more complex account in Laws and Customs among the Eldar, X.214–17. Note 3 is the long account of the names of Finwë's descendants.

Note on Mother-names

The Eldar in Valinor had as a rule two names, or essi. The first-given was the father-name, received at birth. It usually recalled the father's name, resembling it in sense or form; sometimes it was simply the father's name, to which some distinguishing prefix in the case of a son might be added later when the child was full-grown. The mother-name was given later, often some years later, by the mother; but sometimes it was given soon after birth. For the mothers of the Eldar were gifted with deep insight into their children's characters and abilities, and many had also the gift of prophetic foresight.

In addition any of the Eldar might acquire an epessë ('after-name'), not necessarily given by their own kin, a nickname – mostly given as a title of admiration or honour. Later some among the exiles gave themselves names, as disguises or in reference to their own deeds and personal history: such names were called kilmessi 'self-names' (literally names of personal choice).[16]

The 'true names' remained the first two, but in later song and history any of the four might become the name generally used and recognized. The true names were not however forgotten by the scribes and loremasters or the poets, and they might often be introduced without comment. To this difficulty – as it proved to those who in later days tried to use and adapt Elvish traditions of the First Age as a background to the legends of their own heroes of that time and their descendants[17] – was added the alteration of the Quenya names of the Ñoldor, after their settlement in Beleriand and adoption of the Sindarin tongue.

The names of Finwë's descendants

Few of the oldest names of the Eldar are recorded, except those of the four leaders of the hosts on the Great Journey: *Ingwë* of the Vanyar; *Finwë* of the Ñoldor; and the brothers *Elwë* and *Olwë* of the Teleri. It is not certain that these names had any 'meaning', that is any intentional reference to or connexion with other stems already existing in primitive Eldarin; in any case they must have been formed far back in the history of Elvish speech. They consist each of a stem (*ing-*, *fin-*, *el-*, *ol-*) followed by a 'suffix' *-wë*. The suffix appears frequently in other Quenya names of the First Age, such as *Voronwë*, generally but not exclusively masculine.[18] This the loremasters explained as being not in origin a suffix, though it survived in Quenya only as a final element in names, but an old word for 'person', derivative of a stem EWE. This took as a second element in a compound the form *wë*; but as an independent word *ewë*, preserved in Telerin as *evë* 'a person, somebody (unnamed)'. In Old Quenya it survived in the form *eo* (< *ew* + the pronominal suffix -ŏ 'a person, somebody'), later replaced by *námo*; also in the Old Quenya adjective *wéra*, Quenya *véra* 'personal, private, own'.

The first elements were often later explained as related to Quenya *inga* 'top, highest point' used adjectivally as a prefix, as in *ingaran* 'high-king', *ingor* 'summit of a mountain'; to Common Eldarin PHIN 'hair', as in Quenya *finë* 'a hair', *findë* 'hair, especially of the head', *finda* 'having hair, -haired'; and to the stem *el*, *elen* 'star'. Of these the most probable is the relation to *inga*; for the Vanyar were regarded, and regarded themselves, as the leaders and principal kindred of the Eldar, as they were the eldest; and they called themselves the *Ingwer* – in fact their king's proper title was *Ingwë Ingweron* 'chief of the chieftains'. The others are doubtful. All the Eldar had beautiful hair (and were especially attracted by hair of exceptional loveliness), but the Ñoldor were not specially remarkable in this respect, and there is no reference to Finwë as having had hair of exceptional length, abundance, or beauty beyond the measure of his people.[19] There is nothing known to connect Elwë more closely with the stars than all the other Eldar; and the name seems invented to go as a pair with Olwë, for which no 'meaning' was suggested. OL as a simple stem seems not to have occurred in Eldarin, though it appears in certain 'extended' stems, such as *olos/r* 'dream', *olob* 'branch' (Quenya *olba*); neither of which seems to be old enough, even if suitable in sense, to have any connexion with the name of the Ciriáran (mariner king) of the Teleri of Valinor.[20]

It must be realized that the names of the Eldar were not necessarily 'meaningful', though composed to fit the style and structure of their spoken languages; and that even when made or partly made of stems with a meaning these were not necessarily combined according to the normal modes of composition observed in ordinary words. Also that when the Eldar arrived in Aman and settled there they had already a long history behind them, and had developed customs to which they adhered, and also their languages had been elaborated and changed and were very different from their primitive speech as it was before the coming of Oromë. But since they were immortal or more properly said 'indefinitely longeval' many of the oldest Eldar had names devised long before, which had been unchanged except in the accommodation of their sounds to the changes observed in their language as compared with Primitive Eldarin.

This accommodation was mainly of the 'unheeded' kind: that is, personal names being used in daily speech followed the changes in that speech – though these were recognized and observed. The changes from the Quenya names of the Ñoldor to Sindarin forms when they settled in Beleriand in Middle-earth were on the other hand artificial and deliberate. They were made by the Ñoldor themselves. This was done because of the sensitiveness of the Eldar to languages and their styles. They felt it absurd and distasteful to call living persons who spoke Sindarin in daily life by names in quite a different linguistic mode.[21]

The Ñoldor of course fully understood the style and mode of Sindarin, though their learning of this difficult language was swift; but they did not necessarily understand the detail of its relation to Quenya. At first, except in the few words which the great changes in the Sindarin form of Telerin in Middle-earth had left unaltered or plainly similar, none of them understood or were yet interested in the linguistic history. It was at this early period that the translation of most of their Quenya names took place. In consequence these translations, though fitted entirely to Sindarin in form and style, were often inaccurate: that is, they did not always precisely correspond in sense; nor were the equated elements always actually the nearest Sindarin forms of the Quenya elements – sometimes they were not historically related at all, though they were more or less similar in sound.

It was, however, certainly the contact with Sindarin and the enlargement of their experience of linguistic change (especially the much swifter and more uncontrolled shifts observable in Middle-earth) that stimulated the studies of the linguistic loremasters, and it was in Beleriand that theories concerning Primitive Eldarin and the interrelation of its known descendants were developed. In this Fëanor played little part, except in so far as his own work and theories before the Exile had laid the foundations upon which his successors built. He himself perished too early in the war against Morgoth, largely because of his recklessness, to do more than note the differences between the dialects of North Sindarin (which was the only one he had time to learn) and the Western.[22]

The learning of the loremasters was available to all who were interested; but as the hopeless war dragged on, and after its earlier and deceptive successes passed through defeats and disasters to utter ruin of the Elvish realms, fewer and fewer of the Eldar had opportunity for 'lore' of any kind. An account of the years of the Siege of Angband in chronicle form would seem to leave neither place nor time for any of the arts of peace; but the years were long, and in fact there were intervals as long as many lives of Men and secure places long defended in which the High Eldar in exile laboured to recover what they could of the beauty and wisdom of their former home. All peace and all strongholds were at last destroyed by Morgoth; but if any wonder how any lore and treasure was preserved from ruin, it may be answered: of the treasure little was preserved, and the loss of things of beauty great and small is incalculable; but the lore of the Eldar did not depend on perishable records, being stored in the vast houses of their minds.[23] When the Eldar made records in written form, even those that to us would seem voluminous, they did only summarise, as it were, for the use of others whose lore was maybe in other fields of knowledge,[24] matters which were kept for ever undimmed in intricate detail in their minds.

Here are some of the chief names of Finwë and his descendants.

1. *Finwë* for whom no other names are recorded except his title *Ñoldóran* 'King of the Ñoldor'. His first wife was *Míriel* (first name) *Þerindë* (mother-name). The names of her kin are not recorded. Her names were not translated. His second wife was *Indis*, which means 'great or valiant woman'. No other names are recorded. She is said to have been the daughter of King Ingwë's sister.

2. The only child of Míriel was afterwards usually called *Fëanor*. His first name was *Finwë (minya)*, afterwards enlarged when his talents developed to *Kurufinwë*. His mother-name was in Quenya, as given by Míriel, *Fëanáro* 'spirit of fire'. *Fëanor* is the form nearly always used in histories and legends, but is as it stands only half Sindarized: the genuine Sindarin form was *Faenor*; the form *Fëanor* (the ë is only a device of transcription, not needed in the original) probably arose through scribal confusion, especially in documents written in Quenya, in which *ea* was frequent but *ae* did not normally occur.[25]

3. Finwë had four children by Indis: a daughter *Findis*, a son, a daughter *Írimë*, and a son.[26] *Findis* was made by combining the names of her parents. Little is said of her in *The Silmarillion*. She did not go into exile, but went with her mother after the slaying of Finwë and they abode among the Vanyar in grief until such time as it seemed good to Manwë to restore Finwë to life.[27] His second daughter was named *Írien*[28] and her mother-name was *Lalwendë* (laughing maiden). By this name, or in shortened form *Lalwen*, she was generally known. She went into exile with her brother Fingolfin, who was most dear to her of all her kin; but her name was not changed, since *Lalwen* fitted the style of Sindarin well enough.[29]

To his sons Finwë gave his own name as he had done to Fëanor. This maybe was done to assert their claim to be his legitimate sons, equal in that respect to his eldest child *Kurufinwë Fayanáro*, but there was no intention of arousing discord among the brothers, since nothing in the judgement of the Valar in any way impaired Fëanor's position and rights as his eldest son. Nothing indeed was ever done to impair them, except by Fëanor himself; and in spite of all that later happened his eldest son remained nearest to Finwë's heart.

As with Fëanor, Finwë later added prefixes to their name: the elder he called Ñolofinwë, and the younger Arafinwë. Ñolo was the stem of words referring to wisdom,[30] and Ara, ar- a prefixed form of the stem Ara- 'noble'. Fëanor felt aggrieved both by the use of his father's name for his two younger brothers, and again by the prefixes that were added; for his pride was growing and clouding his reason: he thought himself not only the greatest master of Kurwë (which was true) but also of Ñolmë (which was not true, save in matters of language), and certainly the noblest of the children of Finwë (which might have proved true, if he had not become the proudest and most arrogant).

The Ñoldor in exile as a rule chose one only of their names to be given a Sindarin shape; this was the name, usually, which each preferred (for various reasons), though the ease of 'translation' and its fitting into Sindarin style was also considered.

On Fëanor, Faenor see above. Ñolofinwë (one of the first to be changed) was given the form Fingolfin, that is Finwë Ñolofinwë was given a Sindarin style in sounds, and combined in one name. A most unusual procedure, and not imitated in any other name.[31] It was not a translation. The element Quenya ñolo- was merely given its equivalent Sindarin form gol. Finwë was simply reduced to fin in both places; thus was produced a name very much in Sindarin style but without meaning in that language. (If Finwë had been treated as a word of this form would have been, had it occurred anciently in Sindarin, it would have been Finu – but in the Northern dialect Fim, as in Curufim.)[32] Fingolfin had prefixed the name Finwë to Ñolofinwë before the Exiles reached Middle-earth. This was in pursuance of his claim to be the chieftain of all the Ñoldor after the death of Finwë, and so enraged Fëanor[33] that it was no doubt one of the reasons for his treachery in abandoning Fingolfin and stealing away with all the ships. The prefixion in the case of Finarfin was made by Finrod only after the death of Fingolfin in single combat with Morgoth. The Ñoldor then became divided into separate kingships under Fingon son of Fingolfin, Turgon his younger brother, Maedros son of Fëanor, and Finrod son of Arfin; and the following of Finrod had become the greatest.

4.   The children of Fingolfin. Fingolfin's wife Anairë refused to leave Aman, largely because of her friendship with Eärwen wife of Arafinwë (though she was a Ñoldo and not one of the Teleri).

But all her children went with their father: *Findekáno*, *Turukáno*, *Arakáno*, and *Írissë* his daughter and third child; she was under the protection of Turukáno who loved her dearly, and of *Elenwë* his wife.[34] Findekáno had no wife or child;[35] neither had Arakáno.

These names were probably father-names, though *Arakáno* had been the mother-name of Fingolfin. *Káno* meant in Quenya 'commander', usually as the title of a lesser chief, especially one acting as the deputy of one higher in rank.[36] The Sindarizing of these names as *Fingon* and *Turgon* shows knowledge of the sound-changes distinguishing Sindarin from Telerin, but disregards meaning. If these names had actually been ancient Sindarin names they would at the time of the coming of the Exiles have taken the forms *Fingon* and *Turgon*, but they would not have had their Quenya meanings, if interpretable at all. Possibly they would have conveyed 'Hair-shout' and 'Master-shout' [see note 36]. But this did not matter much since old Sindarin names had by that time frequently become obscured by sound-changes and were taken as names and not analysed. With regard to *Findekáno* / *Fingon* it may be noted that the first element was certainly Quenya *findë* 'hair' – a tress or plait of hair[37] (cf. *findessë* a head of hair, a person's hair as a whole), but this is not conclusive proof that the name *Finwë* was or was thought to be derived from this stem. It would have been sufficient for Fingolfin to give to his eldest son a name beginning with *fin-* as an 'echo' of the ancestral name, and if this was also specially applicable it would have been approved as a good invention. In the case of Fingon it was suitable; he wore his long dark hair in great plaits braided with gold.

Arakáno was the tallest of the brothers and the most impetuous, but his name was never changed to Sindarin form, for he perished in the first battle of Fingolfin's host with the Orks, the Battle of the Lammoth (but the Sindarin form *Argon* was often later given as a name by Ñoldor and Sindar in memory of his valour).[38]

Írissë who went ever with the people of Turgon was called *Íreth*,[39] by substitution of Sindarin *-eth* (< *-ittā*) frequent in feminine names for Quenya *-issë*. Elenwë her mother had no Sindarin name, for she never reached Beleriand. She perished in the crossing of the Ice; and Turgon was thereafter unappeasable in his enmity for Fëanor and his sons. He had himself come near to death in the bitter waters when he attempted to save her and his daughter *Itaril*, whom the breaking of treacherous ice had cast into the cruel sea. Itaril he saved;[40] but the body of Elenwë was covered in fallen ice.

Itaril, or in longer form *Itarillë*, was the only child in the third generation from Finwë to go with the exiles, save only Arothir son of Angrod brother of Finrod.[41] Both have renown in the legends of the *Silmarillion*; but Itaril had a great destiny, for she was the mother of Ardamir Eärendil. Her name in Sindarin form was *Idril*, but this also was only an alteration of form, for neither of the Quenya stems that the name contains were found in Sindarin.[42]

5. The children of Finarfin. These were named: *Findaráto Ingoldo*; *Angaráto*; *Aikanáro*; and *Nerwendë Artanis*, sur-named *Alatáriel*. The wife of *Angaráto* was named *Eldalótë*, and his son *Artaher*. The most renowned of these were the first and the fourth (the only daughter), and only of these two are the mother-names remembered. The names of Sindarin form by which they were usually called in later song and legend were *Finrod*, *Angrod* (with wife *Eðellos* and son *Arothir*), *Aegnor*, and *Galadriel*.

The names *Findaráto* and *Angaráto* were Telerin in form (for Finarfin spoke the language of his wife's people); and they proved easy to render into Sindarin in form and sense, because of the close relationship of the Telerin of Aman to the language of their kin, the Sindar of Beleriand, in spite of the great changes that it had undergone in Middle-earth. (*Artafindë* and *Artanga* would have been their more natural Quenya forms, *arta-* the equivalent of *aráta-* preceding, as in *Artanis* and *Artaher*.)[43] The order of the elements in compounds, especially personal names, remained fairly free in all three Eldarin languages; but Quenya preferred the (older) order in which adjectival stems preceded, while in Telerin and Sindarin the adjectival elements often were placed second, especially in later-formed names, according to the usual placing of adjectives in the ordinary speech of those languages. In names however that ended in old words referring to status, rank, profession, race or kindred and so on the adjec-tival element still in Sindarin, following ancient models, might be placed first. Quenya *Artaher* (stem *artahér-*) 'noble lord' was correctly Sindarized as *Arothir*.

Eðellos translated *Eldalótë* according to sense: 'Elven-flower'. *Angaráto* became naturally *Angrod*. It is probable that both brothers first received the name *Aráto*, later differentiated.

The *Find-* in *Findaráto* referred to hair, but in this case to the golden hair of this family derived from Indis. The *Ang-* in *Angaráto* was from Common Eldarin *angā* 'iron' (Quenya, Telerin *anga*, Sindarin *ang*). Angrod early developed hands of great strength and received the *epessë Angamaitë* 'iron-handed', so that *ang-* was used by Finarfin as a differentiating prefix.

Aikanáro was called by his father *Ambaráto*. The Sindarin form of this would have been *Amrod*; but to distinguish this from *Angrod*, and also because he preferred it, he used his mother-name[44] (which was however given in Quenya and not Telerin form). *Aika-nār-* meant 'fell fire'. It was in part a 'prophetic' name; for he was renowned as one of the most valiant of the warriors, greatly feared by the Orks: in wrath or battle the light of his eyes was like flame, though otherwise he was a generous and noble spirit. But in early youth the fiery light could be observed; while his hair was notable: golden like his brothers and sister, but strong and stiff, rising upon his head like flames. The Sindarin form *Aegnor* that he adopted was however not true Sindarin. There was no Sindarin adjective corresponding to Quenya *aika* 'fell, terrible, dire', though *aeg* would have been its form if it had occurred.[45]

Galadriel was chosen by Artanis ('noble woman') to be her Sindarin name; for it was the most beautiful of her names, and, though as an *epessë*, had been given to her by her lover, Teleporno of the Teleri, whom she wedded later in Beleriand.[46] As he gave it in Telerin form it was *Alatāriel(lë)*. The Quenyarized form appears as *Altariel*, though its true form would have been *Ñaltariel*. It was euphoniously and correctly rendered in Sindarin *Galadriel*. The name was derived from the Common Eldarin stem ÑAL 'shine by reflection'; **ñalatā* 'radiance, glittering reflection' (from jewels, glass or polished metals, or water) > Quenya *ñalta*, Telerin *alata*, Sindarin *galad*, + the Common Eldarin stem RIG 'twine, wreathe', **rīgā* 'wreath, garland'; Quenya, Telerin *ría*, Sindarin *rî*, Quenya, Telerin *riellë*, *-ríel* 'a maiden crowned with a festival garland'. The whole, = 'maiden crowned with a garland of bright radiance', was given in reference to Galadriel's hair. *Galad* occurs also in the *epessë* of Ereinion ('scion of kings') by which he was chiefly remembered in legend, *Gil-galad* 'star of radiance': he was the last king of the Eldar in Middle-earth, and the last male descendant of Finwë[47] except Elrond the Half-elven. The *epessë* was given to him because his helm and mail, and his shield overlaid with silver and set with a device of white stars, shone from afar like a star in sunlight or moonlight and could be seen by Elvish eyes at a great distance if he stood upon a height.

There were other descendants of Finwë remembered in legend who may be noted here, though their names were given in Sindarin or in Quenya at later times when Sindarin was the daily language of the Noldor, and they do not offer the problems of translation or more formal adjustment which are presented by the Quenya names given before the Exile.

Itarildë (Idril)[48] daughter of Turgon was the mother of Eärendil; but his father was a Man of the Atani, of the House of Hador: Tuor son of Huor.[49] Eärendil was thus the second of the Pereldar (Half-elven),[50] the elder being Dior, son of Beren and Lúthien Tinúviel daughter of King Elu Thingol. His names were, however, given in Quenya; for Turgon after his foundation of the secret city of Gondolin had re-established Quenya as the daily speech of his household. Eärendil had this name as father-name, and as mother-name he was called *Ardamírë*. In this case both names were 'prophetic'. Tuor in his long journey by the west shores of Beleriand, after his escape from captivity, had been visited by the great Vala Ulmo in person, and Ulmo had directed him to seek for Gondolin, foretelling that if he found it he would there beget a son ever afterwards renowned as a mariner.[51] Improbable as this seemed to Tuor, since neither the Atani nor the Noldor had any love of the sea or of ships, he named his son in Quenya 'sea-lover'. More purely prophetic was the name *Ardamírë* 'Jewel of the World'; for Itarildë could not foresee in her waking mind the strange fate that brought at last the Silmaril into the possession of Eärendil, and enabled his ship to pass through all the shadows and perils by which Aman was at that time defended from any approach from Middle-earth. These names were not given Sindarin forms in legend,[52] though Sindarin writers sometimes explained that they meant *mír n'Arðon* and *Seron Aearon*. By the marriage of Eärendil to Elwing daughter of Dior son of Beren the lines of the Pereldar (Pereðil) were united. Elros and Elrond were the sons of Eärendil. Elros became the first king of Númenor (with the Quenya title *Tar-Minyatur*, 'high first-ruler'). Elrond was received into the company and life-span of the Eldar, and became esquire and banner-bearer of Ereinion Gil-galad. When in later days he wedded Celebrían, daughter of Galadriel and Celeborn, the two lines of descent from Finwë, from Fingolfin and Finarfin, were united and continued in Arwen their daughter.[53]

The names *Elros* and *Elrond*, the last of the descendants of Finwë born in the Elder Days, were formed to recall the name of their mother *Elwing*. The meaning of *wing* is uncertain, since it occurs in no other personal name, nor in the records of either Sindarin or Quenya. Some of the loremasters, remembering that after their return to a second life Beren and Lúthien dwelt in Ossiriand,[54] and that there Dior dwelt after the fall of Doriath among the Green Elves of that forest country, have supposed that *wing* is a word of the tongue of the Green Elves; but little was preserved of that tongue after the destruction of Beleriand, and the interpretation of *wing* as meaning 'foam, spume, spindrift' as of water blown by the wind, or falling steeply over rocks, is but a likely guess. It is supported, however, by the fact that Ossiriand was a land cloven by seven rivers (as its name signifies), and that these fell steeply and very swift from the Mountains of Ered Lindon. Beside one great waterfall, called in Sindarin *Lanthir Lamath* ('waterfall of echoing voices'), Dior had his house. Moreover the name *Elros* (in Quenya form *Elerossë*) means 'star foam', sc. starlit foam.[55]

The numbered notes to the preceding text are given on pp. 356 ff., but the following editorial notes on Gil-galad and Felagund are most conveniently placed here.

The parentage of Gil-galad

My father originally supposed that Gil-galad was the son of Felagund King of Nargothrond. This is probably first found in a revision to the text FN II of *The Fall of Númenor* (V.33); but it remained his belief until after the completion of *The Lord of the Rings*, as is seen from the major early text of the Tale of Years (p. 173), and from *Of the Rings of Power*, where in the published text (*The Silmarillion* p. 286) *Fingon* is an editorial alteration of *Felagund*. In additions of uncertain date made to the *Quenta Silmarillion* (XI.242) it is told that Felagund sent away his wife and his son Gil-galad from Nargothrond to the Havens of the Falas for their safety. It is to be noted also that in the text of the Tale of Years just referred to not only was Gil-galad the son of Felagund but Galadriel was Gil-galad's sister (and so Felagund's daughter): see pp. 174 and 185 note 10.

It emerged, however, in the *Grey Annals* of 1951 (XI.44, §108) that Felagund had no wife, for the Vanya Amárië whom he loved had not been permitted to leave Aman.

Here something must be said of Orodreth, son of Finarfin and brother of Felagund, who became the second King of Nargothrond (for intimations of the decline in importance of Orodreth in earlier phases of the *legendarium* see III.91, 246, V.239; also *Unfinished Tales* p. 255 note 20). In the genealogical tables of the descendants of Finwë, which can be dated to 1959 but which my father was still using and altering when he wrote the excursus to *The Shibboleth of Fëanor* (see note 26), the curious history of Orodreth can be traced. Put as concisely as possible, Finrod (Felagund) was first given a son named *Artanáro Rhodothir* (so contradicting the story in the *Grey Annals* that he had no wife) the second King of Nargothrond, and father of Finduilas. Thus 'Orodreth' was now moved down a generation, becoming Finrod's son rather than his brother. In the next stage my father (recalling, apparently, the story in the *Grey Annals*) noted that Finrod 'had no child (he left his wife in Aman)', and moved Artanáro Rhodothir to become, still in the same generation, the son of Finrod's brother Angrod (who with Aegnor held the heights of Dorthonion and was slain in the Battle of Sudden Flame).

The name of Angrod's son (still retaining the identity of 'Orodreth') was then changed from *Artanáro* to *Artaresto*. In an isolated note found with the genealogies, scribbled at great speed but nonetheless dated, August 1965, my father suggested that the best solution to the problem of Gil-galad's parentage was to find him in 'the son of Orodreth', who is here given the Quenya name of *Artaresto*, and continued:

> Finrod left his wife in Valinor and had no children in exile. Angrod's son was Artaresto, who was beloved by Finrod and escaped when Angrod was slain, and dwelt with Finrod. Finrod made him his 'steward' and he succeeded him in Nargothrond. His Sindarin name was *Rodreth* (altered to *Orodreth* because of his love of the mountains .. .. His children were Finduilas and Artanáro = Rodnor later called Gil-galad. (Their mother was a Sindarin lady of the North. She called her son Gil-galad.) Rodnor Gil-galad escaped and eventually came to Sirion's Mouth and was King of the Ñoldor there.

The words that I cannot read contain apparently a preposition and a proper name, and this latter could be *Faroth* (the High Faroth west of the river Narog). – In the last of the genealogical tables *Artanáro (Rodnor) called Gil-galad* appears, with the note that 'he escaped and dwelt at Sirion's Mouth'. The only further change was the rejection of the name *Artaresto* and its replacement by *Artaher*, Sindarin *Arothir*; and thus in the excursus (note 23) Arothir [Orodreth] is named as Finrod's 'kinsman and steward', and (note 47) Gil-galad is 'the son of Arothir, nephew of Finrod'. The final genealogy was:

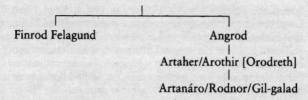

Finrod Felagund   Angrod
                                                      |
                                      Artaher/Arothir [Orodreth]
                                                      |
                                      Artanáro/Rodnor/Gil-galad

Since Finduilas remained without correction in the last of the genealogies as the daughter of Arothir, she became the sister of Gil-galad.

There can be no doubt that this was my father's last word on the subject; but nothing of this late and radically altered conception ever touched the existing narratives, and it was obviously impossible to introduce it into the published *Silmarillion*. It would nonetheless have been very much better to have left Gil-galad's parentage obscure.

I should mention also that in the published text of *Aldarion and Erendis* (*Unfinished Tales* p. 199) the letter of Gil-galad to Tar-Meneldur opens 'Ereinion Gil-galad son of Fingon', but the original has 'Finellach Gil-galad of the House of Finarfin' (where *Finellach* was changed from *Finhenlach*, and that from *Finlachen*). For the name *Ereinion* see p. 347 and note 47. So also in the text of *A Description of the Island of Númenor* (*Unfinished Tales* p. 168) I printed 'King Gil-galad of Lindon' where the original has 'King Finellach Gil-galad of Lindon'; I retained however the words 'his kinswoman Galadriel', since Fingon and Galadriel were first cousins. There is no trace among the many notes and suggestions written onto the genealogical tables of a proposed descent of Gil-galad from Finarfin; but in any case *Aldarion and Erendis* and the closely related *Description of Númenor* preceded by some time (I would now be inclined to date them to about 1960) the making of Gil-galad into the grandson of Angrod, with the name Artanáro Rodnor, which first appears as a new decision in the note of August 1965 given above. Much closer analysis of the admittedly extremely complex material than I had made twenty years ago makes it clear that Gil-galad as the son of Fingon (see XI.56, 243) was an ephemeral idea.

The Dwarvish origin of the name Felagund

Among the notes accompanying the Elvish genealogies and dated December 1959 (see note 26) the following should be recorded. I have mentioned (XI.179) that against the name *Felagund* in the chapter *Of the Siege of Angband* in the *Quenta Silmarillion* (where it was said that 'the Gnomes of the North, at first in jest, called him ... Felagund, or "lord of caverns"') my father noted on the late typescript: 'This was in fact a Dwarfish name; for Nargothrond was first made by Dwarves as is later recounted.' The statement in the 1959 notes is as follows:

The name *Felagund* was of Dwarvish origin. Finrod had help of Dwarves in extending the underground fortress of Nargothrond. It is supposed originally to have been a hall of the Petty-dwarves (*Nibinnogs*), but the Great Dwarves despised these, and had no compunction in ousting them – hence Mîm's special hatred for the Elves – especially for great reward. Finrod had brought more treasure out of Túna than any of the other princes.

Felagund: Dwarvish √*felek* hew rock, *felak* a tool like a broad-bladed chisel, or small axe-head without haft, for cutting stone; to use this tool. √*gunud* equivalent of Eldarin *s-rot*:[56] *gundu* underground hall. *felakgundu*, *felaggundu* 'cave-hewer'. This name was given because of Finrod's skill in lighter stone-carving. He cut many of the adornments of the pillars and walls in Nargothrond. He was proud of the name. But it was often by others Eldarized into *Felagon*, as if it had the same ending (*-kānō*) as in *Fingon*, *Turgon*; and the first element was associated with Sindarin *fael* 'fair-minded, just, generous', Quenya *faila* (? from √*phaya* 'spirit', adjectival formation meaning 'having a good *fëa*, or a dominant *fëa*').

This note is the basis of the brief statement in the index to the published *Silmarillion*, entry *Felagund*.

The names of the Sons of Fëanor with the legend of the fate of Amrod

My father did not fulfil his intention to give in the 'excursus' an account of the names of the Sons of Fëanor (see note 32), but some pages of initial drafting are extant. The text begins legibly in ink, but at the end of the list of 'mother-names' changes to ball-point pen, and the legend of Amrod and Amras would be too illegible to reproduce had not my father gone over it and glossed the worst parts more clearly. There are many experimental etymological notes on the Eldarin words referring to red colour and copper, and on the names of the twin brothers, which are here omitted. In the first list I have added the Sindarin names for clarity.

(1) [Maedros] *Nelyafinwë* 'Finwë third' in succession.[57]
     (Nelyo)

(2) [Maglor] *Kanafinwë* 'strong-voiced or ?commanding'.
     (Káno)[58]

(3) [Celegorm] *Turkafinwë* 'strong, powerful (in body)'.
     (Turko)

(4) [Curufin] *Kurufinwë* Fëanor's own name; given to this, his favourite son, because he alone showed in some degree the same temper and talents. He also resembled Fëanor very much in face. *(Kurvo)*

(5) [Caranthir] *Morifinwë* 'dark' – he was black-haired as his grandfather. *(Moryo)*

(6) [Amrod] *Pityafinwë* 'Little Finwë'. *(Pityo)*[59]

(7) [Amras] *Telufinwë* 'Last Finwë'. *(Telvo)*[60]

Their 'mother-names' are recorded (though never used in narrative) as:

(1) *Maitimo* 'well-shaped one': he was of beautiful bodily form. But he, and the youngest, inherited the rare red-brown hair of Nerdanel's kin. Her father had the *epessë* of *rusco* 'fox'. So Maitimo had as an *epessë* given by his brothers and other kin *Russandol* 'copper-top'.[61]

(2) *Makalaurë* Of uncertain meaning. Usually interpreted (and said to have been a 'prophetic' mother-name) as 'forging gold'. If so, probably a poetic reference to his skill in harping, the sound of which was 'golden' (*laurë* was a word for golden light or colour, never used for the metal).

(3) *Tyelkormo* 'hasty-riser'. Quenya *tyelka* 'hasty'. Possibly in reference to his quick temper, and his habit of leaping up when suddenly angered.

(4) *Atarinkë* 'little father' – referring to his physical likeness to Fëanor, later found to be also seen in his mind.

(5) *Carnistir* 'red-face' – he was dark (brown) haired, but had the ruddy complexion of his mother.

(6) *Ambarto*[62]

(7) *Ambarussa*

These two names of [the] twins *(i·Wenyn)* were evidently meant to begin similarly. *Ambarussa* 'top-russet' must have referred to hair: the first and last of Nerdanel's children had the reddish hair of her kin. Around the name Ambarto [> Umbarto] – which one might expect to begin with an element of the same sense as (7) – much legend and discussion gathered. The most authentic seems to be thus:

The two twins were both red-haired. Nerdanel gave them both the name *Ambarussa* – for they were much alike and remained so while they lived. When Fëanor begged that their names should at least be different Nerdanel looked strange, and after a while said: 'Then let one be called [*Ambarto* >] *Umbarto*, but which, time will decide.'

Fëanor was disturbed by this ominous name ('Fated'), and changed it to *Ambarto* – or in some versions thought

Nerdanel had said *Ambarto*, using the same first element as in *Ambarussa* (sc. *amba* + Quenya *arta* 'exalted, lofty'). But Nerdanel said: '*Umbarto* I spoke; yet do as you wish. It will make no difference.'

Later, as Fëanor became more and more fell and violent, and rebelled against the Valar, Nerdanel, after long endeavouring to change his mood, became estranged. (Her kin were devoted to Aulë, who counselled her father to take no part in the rebellion. 'It will in the end only lead Fëanor and all your children to death.') She retired to her father's house; but when it became clear that Fëanor and his sons would leave Valinor for ever, she came to him before the host started on its northward march, and begged that Fëanor should leave her the two youngest, the twins, or one at least of them. He replied: 'Were you a true wife, as you had been till cozened by Aulë, you would keep all of them, for you would come with us. If you desert me, you desert also all of our children. For they are determined to go with their father.' Then Nerdanel was angry and she answered: 'You will not keep all of them. One at least will never set foot on Middle-earth.' 'Take your evil omens to the Valar who will delight in them,' said Fëanor. 'I defy them'. So they parted.

Now it is told how Fëanor stole the ships of the Teleri, and breaking faith with Fingolfin and with those faithful to him sailed away in them to Middle-earth, leaving the rest of his host to make their way on foot with great travail and loss. The ships were anchored off the shore, in the Firth of Drengist, and all the host of Fëanor went on land and camped there.

In the night Fëanor, filled with malice, aroused Curufin, and with him and a few of those most close to Fëanor in obedience he went to the ships and set them all aflame; and the dark sky was red as with a terrible dawn. All the camp was roused, and Fëanor returning said: 'Now at least I am certain that no faint-heart or traitor among you will be able to take back even one ship to the succour of Fingolfin and his folk.' But all save few were dismayed, because there were many things still aboard that they had not yet brought ashore, and the ships would have been useful for further journeying. They were still far north and had purposed to sail southward to some better haven.

In the morning the host was mustered, but of Fëanor's seven sons only six were to be found. Then Ambarussa (6) went pale with fear. 'Did you not then rouse Ambarussa my brother (whom you called Ambarto)?' he said. 'He would not come ashore to sleep (he said) in discomfort.' But it is thought (and no doubt Fëanor guessed this also) that it was in the mind of Ambarto to sail his ship back [?afterwards] and rejoin Nerdanel; for he had been much [?shocked][63] by the deed of his father.[64]

'That ship I destroyed first,' said Fëanor (hiding his own dismay). 'Then rightly you gave the name to the youngest of your children,' said Ambarussa, 'and *Umbarto* "the Fated" was its true form. Fell and fey are you become.' And after that no one dared speak again to Fëanor of this matter.[65]

For the mention, in a note on the typescript of the *Annals of Aman*, of the story of the death of one of the twin-brothers in the burning of the ships at Losgar see X.128, §162; and for the account of Nerdanel and her estrangement from Fëanor in late rewriting of the *Quenta Silmarillion* see X.272–3, 279.

The material concerning the names of the twin brothers is confused and confusing, clearly because it was only as my father worked on them that the strange and sinister story emerged. It seems to me very probable that when he gave the mother-names *(6)* *Ambarto* and *(7)* *Ambarussa* it had not yet arisen, nor yet when he began the note that follows the list of the mother-names, saying that 'the first and last of Nerdanel's children had the reddish hair of her kin' – that is Maedros with his nickname *Russandol* and the younger of the twins *Ambarussa* (Amras).

The story first emerged, I think, with the words 'The most authentic seems to be thus: The two twins were both red-haired. Nerdanel gave them both the name *Ambarussa* ...' It was then, no doubt, that my father changed the name *Ambarto* to *Umbarto* in the list and reversed the names of the twin brothers (see note 62), so that *Ambarussa* becomes the elder of the two and *Ambarto/Umbarto* the youngest of Fëanor's children, as he is in the legend told here.

At the head of the first page of this text concerning the names of the Sons of Fëanor my father wrote, when the story was now in being:

All the sons save Curufin preferred their mother-names and were ever afterwards remembered by them. The twins called each other *Ambarussa*. The name *Ambarto/Umbarto* was used by [?no one]. The twins remained alike, but the elder grew darker in hair, and was more dear to his father. After childhood they [?were not to be] confused. ...

Thus in the legend 'Ambarussa (6)' asked Fëanor whether he had not roused 'Ambarussa my brother' before setting fire to the ships.

NOTES

1 [This heading is derived from the opening sentence of the essay, which is in fact 'The case of *þ > s* is more difficult.' I have not been able to discover the reference of this. The typescript is extant as a separate whole, paginated consecutively from A to T.]

2 Few of these can have been carried from Valinor, and fewer still can have survived the journey to Middle-earth; but the memory of the loremasters was prodigious and accurate.

3 [The term *Ingwi* seems not to have been used since the *Lhammas* of the 1930s, where '*Ingwelindar* or *Ingwi*' appears as the name of the house and people of Ingwë, chief among the First Kindred of the Elves (then called the *Lindar*), V.171. For the much later application of the term *Lindar* see XI.381–2.]

4 Without special study. But many of the Noldor could speak Telerin and *vice versa*. There were in fact some borrowings from one to another; of which the most notable was the general use of the Telerin form *telpë* 'silver' for pure Quenya *tyelpë*. [For the substitution of *telpë* see *Unfinished Tales* p. 266.]

5 They continued to deplore it, and were able to insist later that the distinction between older *þ* and *s* should at least always be preserved in writing.

6 [See the Note on Mother-names at the end of the essay, p. 339. It is not stated elsewhere that *Serindë* was Míriel's 'mother-name'.]

7 [It had been said several times in the later *Quenta Silmarillion* texts that *Fëanáro* was a 'name of insight' given to him by Míriel at his birth; moreover in the story of Míriel when it first appeared her spirit passed to Mandos soon after Fëanor was born, and it is expressly said in *Laws and Customs among the Eldar* that he never saw his mother (X.217). The story has now been altogether changed in this aspect: Míriel named him with this name 'in recognition of his impetuous character'; 'while she lived she did much with gentle counsel to soften and restrain him'; and subsequently 'her weariness she had endured until he was full grown, but she could endure it no longer'. After Míriel's 'death' or departure 'for a while he also had kept vigil by his mother's body, but soon he became wholly absorbed again in his own works and devices' (p. 335).]

8 [A full account of other texts bearing on this matter is given in X.205–7, 225–7, 233–71. These texts are substantially earlier than the present essay (see X.300), which is by no means entirely congruent with them.]

9 [Elsewhere *Ezellohar* is the name not of the plain but of the Green Mound on which grew the Two Trees (X.69, etc.); while in *Quendi and Eldar* (XI.399, 401) *Korollairë* is said to be a translation of the Valarin name *Ezellohar*, of which the first element

ezel, *ezella* meant 'green'. But perhaps by 'the plain of Ezello-har' my father meant 'the plain in which stood the mound of Ezellohar'.]

10 Doubting that the test of a few years could show that the will of any one of the Children was fixed immovably; and foreboding that breaking the law would have evil consequences.

11 Death by free will, such as Míriel's, was beyond his thought. Death by violence he thought impossible in Aman; though as is recorded in *The Silmarillion* this proved otherwise.

12 [With a necessary change in the opening sentence, the following passage, as far as 'and passing the last test departed from Middle-earth for ever' on p. 338, was printed in *Unfinished Tales*, pp. 229–31 – since it is of great importance in the history of Galadriel – but with no indication of its context: it seems desirable there-fore to give it again here.]

13 [Elwë's name *Þindikollo* (elsewhere *Sindikollo*, *Sindicollo*) was omitted from the text in *Unfinished Tales*.]

14 Who together with the greatest of all the Eldar, Lúthien Tinúviel, daughter of Elu Thingol, are the chief matter of the legends and histories of the Elves.

15 It is not even certain that all Fëanor's sons continued to use *þ* after his death and the healing of the feud by the renowned deed of Fingon son of Fingolfin in rescuing Maedhros [> Maedros] from the torments of Morgoth.

16 [The wholly different account of 'Chosen Names' in *Laws and Customs among the Eldar* (X.214–15) appears to have been abandoned.]

17 As is seen in *The Silmarillion*. This is not an Eldarin title or work. It is a compilation, probably made in Númenor, which includes (in prose) the four great tales or lays of the heroes of the Atani, of which 'The Children of Húrin' was probably composed already in Beleriand in the First Age, but necessarily is preceded by an account of Fëanor and his making of the Silmarils. All how-ever are 'Mannish' works. [With this cf. X.373 and p. 390, note 17 in this book.]

18 Notably in *Manwë*, the Quenya name of the 'Elder King', the chief of the Valar. This is said to have been of the same age as the names *Ingwë*, etc., and to contain the Valarin element *aman*, *man* 'blessed, holy' learned from Oromë, and of course unconnected with the Eldarin interrogative element *ma*, *man*. [See XI.399.]

19 He had black hair, but brilliant grey-blue eyes.

20 Connexion with Telerin *vola* 'a roller, long wave', which was sometimes made by the Teleri themselves, was not a serious 'etymology' but a kind of pun; for the king's name was not normally *Volwë* (Common Eldarin **wolwë*) but Olwë in Telerin as in Quenya, and *w* was not lost before *o* in Telerin as it was

in Quenya. Also the connexion of the Teleri with sea-faring developed long after the naming of Olwë.

21   It was otherwise in written histories (which were by the Ñoldor in any case mostly composed in Quenya). Also the names of 'foreign persons' who did not dwell in Beleriand and were seldom mentioned in daily speech were usually left unaltered. Thus the names of the Valar which they had devised in Valinor were not as a rule changed, whether they fitted Sindarin style or not. The Sindar knew little of the Valar and had no names for any of them, save Oromë (whom all the Eldar had seen and known); and Manwë and Varda of whose eminence they had been instructed by Oromë; and the Great Enemy whom the Ñoldor called Melkor. For Oromë a name had been made in Primitive Eldarin (recalling the sound of his great horn) of which *Oromë* was the Quenya form, though in Sindarin it had become *Araw*, and by the Sindar he was later more often called *(Aran) Tauron* 'the (king) forester'. Manwë and Varda they knew only by the names 'Elder King' and 'Star-queen': *Aran Einior* and *Elbereth*. Melkor they called *Morgoth* 'the Black Enemy', refusing to use the Sindarin form of *Melkor*: *Belegûr* 'he that arises in might', save (but rarely) in a deliberately altered form *Belegurth* 'Great Death'. These names *Tauron*, *Aran Einior*, *Elbereth*, and *Morgoth* the Ñoldor adopted and used when speaking Sindarin.

   [For the association of the name *Oromë* with that of his great horn see XI.400–1. – The names *Belegûr*, *Belegurth* have been mentioned in the index to the published *Silmarillion*, which here derives from the present note. Very many years before, the name *Belegor* is found as an ephemeral name of Morgoth in *The Lay of the Children of Húrin* (III.21, note 22).]

22   His sons were too occupied in war and feuds to pay attention to such matters, save Maglor who was a poet, and Curufin, his fourth and favourite son to whom he gave his own name; but Curufin was most interested in the alien language of the Dwarves, being the only one of the Ñoldor to win their friendship. It was from him that the loremasters obtained such knowledge as they could of the Khuzdûl.

23   Nor were the 'loremasters' a separate guild of gentle scribes, soon burned by the Orks of Angband upon pyres of books. They were mostly even as Fëanor, the greatest, kings, princes and warriors, such as the valiant captains of Gondolin, or Finrod of Nargothrond and Rodothir [> Arothir] his kinsman and steward. [For Arothir see the note on the parentage of Gil-galad, pp. 349–51.]

24   And as some insurance against their own death. For books were made only in strong places at a time when death in battle was likely to befall any of the Eldar, but it was not yet believed that

Morgoth could ever capture or destroy their fortresses.

25 [In an addition to the *Annals of Aman* Fëanor's first name is given as 'Minyon First-begotten' (X.87); in *Laws and Customs among the Eldar* his first name was *Finwë*, in the second version *Finwion* (X.217 and note 20). For previous references to *Kurufinwë* see the index to Vol.X (*Curufinwë*); and with the mention here of the form *Faenor* cf. X.217, footnote.]

26 [In *The War of the Jewels* I referred to a set of Elvish genealogies with a clear resemblance to those of the Edain given in that book: see XI.229, where I noted that the former are followed by notes expressly relating to them and dated December 1959. These genealogies are almost exclusively concerned with the descendants of Finwë, and are set out in four separate tables, all apparently belonging to much the same time, and showing the same sort of development in stages as is seen in those of the houses of the Edain. At least eight years and probably more divide them from the present 'excursus', whose date is fixed as not earlier than February 1968; but my father clearly had them in front of him when he wrote this, and alterations made to the latest of the four agree with statements made in it. In all these tables there are still three daughters of Finwë and Indis: *Findis*, *Faniel*, and *Írimë* (see X.207, 238, and also X.262, where *Finvain* appears for *Írimë*), and no correction was made. In the excursus *Faniel* has disappeared, and the younger daughter appears both as *Írimë* and *Írien* (see note 28).]

27 If he ever did so. Little has been ever heard in Middle-earth of Aman after the departure of the Ñoldor. Those who returned thither have never come back, since the change of the world. To Númenor in its first days they went often, but small part of the lore and histories of Númenor survived its Downfall. [With the words in the text at this point concerning Indis cf. *Laws and Customs among the Eldar* (X.249 and note 17), where Finwë in Mandos said to Vairë: 'But Indis parted from me without death. I had not seen her for many years, and when the Marrer smote me I was alone. ... Little comfort should I bring her, if I returned.']

28 [It is strange that my father should give the name of the second daughter of Finwë as both *Írimë* and *Írien* within the space of a few lines. Possibly he intended *Írien* at the first occurrence but inadvertently wrote *Írimë*, the name found in all the genealogies (note 26).]

29 But the true equivalent in Sindarin was *Glaðwen* (Common Eldarin stem *g-lada-* > Quenya *lala-*, Telerin *glada*, Sindarin *glað-*).

30 'Wisdom' – but not in the sense 'sagacity, sound judgement (founded on experience and sufficient knowledge)'; 'Knowledge'

would be nearer, or 'Philosophy' in its older applications which included Science. Ñolmë was thus distinct from *Kurwë* 'technical skill and invention', though not necessarily practised by distinct persons. The stem appeared in Quenya (in which it was most used) in forms developed from Common Eldarin ñgol-, ñgōlo-, with or without syllabic ñ: as in *Ñgolodō > Quenya *Noldo* (Telerin *golodo*, Sindarin *goloð*) – the Noldor had been from the earliest times most eminent in and concerned with this kind of 'wisdom'; *ñolmë* a department of wisdom (science etc.); *Ingolë (ñgōlē)* Science/Philosophy as a whole; *ñolmo* a wise person; *ingólemo* one with very great knowledge, a 'wizard'. This last word was however archaic and applied only to great sages of the Eldar in Valinor (such as Rúmil). The wizards of the Third Age – emissaries from the Valar – were called *Istari* 'those who know'.

The form *Ingoldo* may be noted: it is a form of *Ñoldo* with syllabic ñ, and being in full and more dignified form is more or less equivalent to '*the* Ñoldo, one eminent in the kindred'. It was the mother-name of Arafinwë [Finarfin], and like the name *Arakáno* 'high chieftain' that Indis gave to Nolofinwë [Fingolfin] was held to be 'prophetic'. Eärwen gave this name [Ingoldo] to her eldest child Artafindë (Finrod), and by it he was usually called by his brothers and sister who esteemed him and loved him. It was never Sindarized (the form would have been *Angoloð*). The name spread from his kin to many others who held him in honour, especially to Men (the Atani) of whom he was the greatest friend among the Eldar. Thus later it became frequent as a given name in Númenor, and continued to be so in Gondor, though reduced in the Common Speech to *Ingold*. One such Ingold appears in *The Lord of the Rings* as the commander of the guard of the North Gate into the Pelennor of Gondor.

[In earlier texts (see X.265 note 10) the name *Ingoldo* was the mother-name of Ñolofinwë (Fingolfin), 'signifying that he came of both the kin of the Ingar and of the Noldor'; while the mother-name of Arafinwë (Finarfin) was *Ingalaurë* 'for he had the golden hair of his mother's people'. Apart from the first one, the genealogical tables give Fingolfin and Finarfin the mother-names *Arakáno* and *Ingoldo* as here.]

31 Except for *Finarfin* as the name of his younger brother. This was also the only name of a Ñoldo who did not come into exile to receive a Sindarin form. This was because Arafinwë's children had a special position among the exiles, especially in relation to King Thingol of Doriath, their kinsman, and were often referred to collectively by the Sindar as 'the children of Finarfin' or the *Nothrim* [> *Nost*] *Finarfin*, 'the house/family of Finarfin'.

32 [In the text at this point there is a reference forward to discussion of the names of the Sons of Fëanor, but this was not reached

in the typescript before it was abandoned; see pp. 352 ff.]

33 As he said with some justice: 'My brother's claim rests only upon a decree of the Valar; but of what force is that for those who have rejected them and seek to escape from their prison-land?' But Fingolfin answered: 'I have not rejected the Valar, nor their authority in all matters where it is just for them to use it. But if the Eldar were given free choice to leave Middle-earth and go to Aman, and accepted it because of the loveliness and bliss of that land, their free choice to leave it and return to Middle-earth, when it has become dark and desecrated, cannot be taken away. Moreover I have an errand in Middle-earth, the avenging of the blood of my father upon Morgoth, whom the Valar let loose among us. Fëanor seeks first his stolen treasures.'

[It is said in the text at this point that Fingolfin claimed to be 'the chieftain of all the Ñoldor after the death of Finwë', and the same was said in the essay proper (p. 336). All the texts agree that after the banishment of Fëanor from Tirion, and the departure of Finwë with him to Formenos, Fingolfin ruled the Ñoldor in Tirion; and it was said in the *Quenta Silmarillion* (see IV.95, V.235) that afterwards, when the Flight of the Ñoldor began, those of Tirion 'would not now renounce the kingship of Fingolfin'. On the other hand, in the final story of the events leading to the Flight, when Fëanor and Fingolfin had become half-brothers, they were reconciled 'in word' before the throne of Manwë at the fateful festival; and in that reconciliation Fingolfin said to Fëanor: 'Thou shalt lead and I will follow' (see X.197, 287).]

34 [On *Anairë* wife of Fingolfin and *Elenwë* wife of Turgon see XI.323, §12; and on *Arakáno*, Sindarin *Argon*, see note 38.]

35 [In all the genealogical tables Fingon's Quenya name is *Finicáno* except in the last, in which it is *Findicáno* (altered to *Findecáno*). In all the tables he is marked as having a wife, though she is not named; in the first, two children are named, *Ernis* and *Finbor*, *Ernis* subsequently becoming *Erien*, but in the final table they were struck out, with the note that Fingon 'had no child or wife'.]

36 It was a derivative of Common Eldarin KAN 'cry, call aloud', which developed divergent meanings (like 'call' in English or the Germanic stem *hait-*) depending on the purposes for which a loud voice would be used: e.g. to take an oath, make a vow or promise; to announce important news, or messages and orders; to issue orders and commands in person; to 'call for' – to name a thing or person desired, to summons; to call a person by name, to name. Not all of these were found in any one of the later languages (Quenya, Telerin, Sindarin). In Quenya the sense *command* had become the usual one: to issue orders in person, whether by

derived authority or one's own; when applied to things it meant *demand*. In archaic language the older and simplest agental form **kānō > káno* still had the sense 'crier, or herald', and *kanwa* 'an announcement' as well as 'an order' – later *terkáno* (one *through* whom orders or announcements are made) was used for 'herald'. In Telerin *cāno* meant 'herald', and the verb *can-* was mostly used in the sense 'cry aloud, call', but also 'to summons or name a person'. In Sindarin *can-* was used for 'cry out, shout, call', with implications supplied by the context; it never meant either 'order' or 'name'; *caun* (**kānā*) meant 'outcry, clamour', often in plural form *conath* when referring to many voices, and often applied to lamentation (though not as English 'cry' to weeping tears): cf. *naergon* 'woeful lament'.

37   Common Eldarin **phini-* a single hair, **phindē* a tress; Sindarin *fîn; find, finn-*.

38   When the onset of the Orks caught the host at unawares as they marched southwards and the ranks of the Eldar were giving way, he sprang forward and hewed a path through the foes, daunted by his stature and the terrible light of his eyes, till he came to the Ork-captain and felled him. Then though he himself was surrounded and slain, the Orks were dismayed, and the Ñoldor pursued them with slaughter.

[The third son of Fingolfin, Arakáno (Argon), emerged in the course of the making of the genealogies. A pencilled note on the last of the four tables says that he fell in the fighting at Alqualondë; this was struck out, and my father noted that a preferable story was that he perished in the Ice. It is curious that this third son, of whom there had never before been any mention, entered (as it seems) without a story, and the manner of his death was twice changed before the remarkable appearance here of 'the first battle of Fingolfin's host with the Orks, the Battle of the Lammoth', in which he fell. In the account in the *Grey Annals* (XI.30) Fingolfin, after the passage of the Helkaraxë, 'marched from the North unopposed through the fastness of the realm of Morgoth, and he passed over Dor-Daedeloth, and his foes hid beneath the earth'; whereas in the present note his host was attacked in Lammoth 'at unawares as they marched southwards' (see the map, XI.182).]

39   [All the genealogical tables give the name of Fingolfin's daughter as *Írissë (Írith)*; in the last of them *Írith* was changed to *Íreth*, the form found here, but later still both names were struck out and replaced by *(Ar)Feiniel* 'White Lady' (on this see XI.317–18, and 409 with note 34).

There is a strange confusion in this paragraph. Above, my father said that Írissë was 'under the protection of' Turukáno (Turgon) her brother and his wife Elenwë; but here Írissë is the *daughter* of Elenwë who perished in the Ice. This cannot be rectified by the substitution of the correct name (*Anairë* for *Elenwë*, or *Itaril* for *Írissë*, *Íreth*), because he was expressly writing of Elenwë and expressly writing of Írissë.]

40 [Turgon's saving of his daughter Idril Celebrindal from death in the Helkaraxë has not been referred to before.]

41 [Arothir has been named earlier (note 23) as the 'kinsman and steward' of Finrod; see also note 47.]

42 (1) *it* in *itila* 'twinkling, glinting', and *íta* 'a flash', *ita*- verb 'to sparkle'. (2) *ril*- 'brilliant light': cf. *silmaril(lë)*, the name given by Fëanor to his three Jewels. The first was especially applied to the bright lights of the eyes, which were a mark of all the High Eldar who had ever dwelt in Valinor, and at times in later ages reappeared in their descendants among mortal men, whether from Itaril or Lúthien.

43 **arat*- was an extended form of the stem *ara*- 'noble'. The derivative *arātā* was much used as an adjective in Telerin and Sindarin (Telerin *arāta*, Sindarin *arod*). In Quenya it had become specialized, and mainly used in *Aratar* 'the Exalted', the Nine of the chief Valar. It was however still used in noble names.

44 [On p. 346 my father said that of the children of Finarfin the mother-names were remembered only in the cases of Finrod (*Ingoldo*) and Galadriel (*Nerwendë*); he omitted to mention Aikanáro.]

45 Quenya *aika* was derived from a Common Eldarin stem GAYA 'awe, dread'; but the adjectival form **gayakā* from which *aika* descended was not preserved in Telerin or Sindarin. Other derivatives were **gāyā* 'terror, great fear': Telerin *gāia*, Sindarin *goe*, Quenya *áya*. Adjectives formed on this, Telerin *gāialā*, Sindarin *goeol*, replaced Quenya *aika*. In a name of this sort in Sindarin the noun would most naturally have been used, producing *goenaur* > *Goenor*. Also **Gayar*- 'the Terrifier', the name made for the Sea, the vast and terrifying Great Sea of the West, when the Eldar first came to its shores: Quenya *Eär*, *Eären*, Telerin *gaiar*; Sindarin *gaear*, *gae(a)ron*, *Belegaer*. This word is also found in the Quenya name *Eärendil*, the mariner (sea-lover); see p. 348.

The stem acquired in Quenya a specially high and noble sense – except in *eär*, though that was also majestic in its vastness and power; and *aika*, though that was seldom applied to evil things. Thus Quenya *áya* meant rather 'awe' than 'fear', profound reverence and sense of one's own littleness in the presence of things or persons majestic and powerful. The adjective *aira* was the nearest equivalent to 'holy'; and the noun *airë* to 'sanctity'. *Airë* was used by the Eldar as a title of address to the Valar and the greater Máyar. Varda would be addressed as *Airë Tári*. (Cf. Galadriel's Lament, where it is said that the stars trembled at the sound of the holy queen's voice: the prose or normal form of which would have been *tintilar lirinen ómaryo Airë-tário.*) This change, though possible to have occurred (as it has in our 'awe') without extraneous influence, was said by the loremasters to have been partly due to the influence of the Valarin language, in which *ayanu-* was the name of the Spirits of Eru's first creation. [With the last sentence of this note cf. XI.399.]

46   [On the remarkable change whereby Celeborn (Teleporno) became a Telerin Elf of Aman see *Unfinished Tales* pp. 231–3, where the present passage is cited. The etymology of *Galadriel* that follows in the text was used for the account of the name in the Appendix to *The Silmarillion*, entry *kal-*.]

47   He was the son of Arothir, nephew of Finrod. [See the note on the parentage of Gil-galad, pp. 349 ff. – From this work was derived Gil-galad's name *Ereinion* introduced into *The Silmarillion*.]

48   [Earlier (p. 346) the name is *Itarillë*; *Itarildë* appears in the first three genealogical tables, but the fourth has *Itarillë*.]

49   These names were given in the language of that kindred of the Atani (Edain) – but adapted to Sindarin – from which in the main the Adûnaic or native Atanic language of Númenor was descended. Their explanation is not here attempted.

50   [The term *Pereldar* 'Half-eldar' was originally used of the Nandor or Danas (see V.200, 215), but it is here used as is the Sindarin form *Peredhil* in Appendix A (I, i) of Elrond and Elros; cf. *i·Pheredhil* p. 256, *Pereðil* p. 348.]

51   [In the account of Ulmo's words to Tuor on the coast at Vinyamar in the later *Tale of Tuor* the Vala did indeed allude prophetically to Eärendil, but in a manner far more veiled and mysterious: 'But it is not for thy valour only that I send thee, but to bring into the world a hope beyond thy sight, and a light that shall pierce the darkness' (*Unfinished Tales* p. 30).]

52   Forms affected by Sindarin in manuscripts, such as *Aerendil*, *Aerennel*, etc. were casual and accidental.

53   When Aragorn, descended in long line from Elros, wedded Arwen in the third union of Men and Elves, the lines of all the Three Kings of the High Elves (Eldar), Ingwë, Finwë, and Olwë and Elwë were united and alone preserved in Middle-earth. Since Lúthien was the noblest, and the most fair and beautiful, of all the Children of Eru remembered in ancient story, the descendants of that union were called 'the children of Lúthien'. The world has grown old in long years since then, but it may be that their line has not yet ended. (Lúthien was through her mother, Melian, descended also from the Máyar, the people of the Valar, whose being began before the world was made. Melian alone of all those spirits assumed a bodily form, not only as a raiment but as a permanent habitation in form and powers like to the bodies of

the Elves. This she did for love of Elwë; and it was permitted, no doubt because this union had already been foreseen in the beginning of things, and was woven into the *Amarth* of the world, when Eru first conceived the being of his children, Elves and Men, as is told (after the manner and according to the understanding of his children) in that myth that is named The Music of the Ainur.)

[As is said in the text at this point Arwen was descended from Finwë both in the line of Fingolfin (through Elrond) and in the line of Finarfin (through Celebrían); but she was also descended from Elwë (Thingol) through Elrond's mother Elwing, and through Galadriel's mother Eärwen from Olwë of Alqualondë. She was not directly descended from Ingwë, but her fore-mother Indis was (in earlier texts) the sister of Ingwë (X.261–2, etc.), or (in the present work, p. 343) the daughter of his sister. It is hard to know what my father had in mind when he wrote the opening of this note.]

54 Until they died the death of mortal Men, according to the decree of the Valar, and left this world for ever.

55 [Here the typescript stops, not at the foot of a page; and at this point my father wrote:

   Alter this to: *Wing*. This word, which the loremasters explained as meaning 'foam, spindrift', only actually occurs in two names of the Eärendil legend: *Elwing* the name of his wife, and (in Quenya form) *Vingilótë* (translated in Adûnaic as *Rothinzil*) 'Foam-flower', the name of Eärendil's ship. The word is not otherwise known in Quenya or Sindarin – nor in Telerin despite its large vocabulary of sea-words. There was a tradition that the word came from the language of the Green Elves of Ossiriand.]

56 [Elsewhere in these notes the stem *rot*, *s-rot* is given the meaning 'delve underground, excavate, tunnel', whence Quenya *hróta* 'dwelling underground, artificial cave or rockhewn hall', *rotto* 'a small grot or tunnel'.]

57 ['Finwë third': his grandfather was *Finwë*, and his father *Kurufinwë*, first named *Finwë* also (p. 343).]

58 [*Káno*: see note 36.]

59 [The *P* of *Pityafinwë*, but not of the short form *Pityo*, was changed to *N*.]

60 [*Pityafinwë* and *Telufinwë* are bracketed with the words 'Twins   *Gwenyn*'.]

61 [On a separate page written at the same time is a note on the father of Nerdanel (Fëanor's wife);

   Nerdanel's father was an 'Aulendil' [> 'Aulendur'], and became a great smith. He loved copper, and set it above gold.

His name was [space; pencilled later Sarmo?], but he was most widely known as *Urundil* 'copper-lover'. He usually wore a band of copper about his head. His hair was not as dark or black as was that of most of the Ñoldor, but brown, and had glints of coppery-red in it. Of Nerdanel's seven children the oldest, and the twins (a very rare thing among the Eldar) had hair of this kind. The eldest also wore a copper circlet.

A note is appended to *Aulendur*:

'Servant of Aulë': sc. one who was devoted to that Vala. It was applied especially to those persons, or families, among the Ñoldor who actually entered Aulë's service, and who in return received instruction from him.

A second note on this page comments on the name *Urundil*:

√RUN 'red, glowing', most often applied to things like embers, hence adjective *runya*, Sindarin *ruin* ' "fiery" red'. The Eldar had words for some metals, because under Oromë's instruction they had devised weapons against Morgoth's servants especially on the March, but the only ones that appear in all Eldarin languages were iron, copper, gold and silver (ANGA, URUN, MALAT, KYELEP).

Earlier Nerdanel's father, the great smith, had been named *Mahtan* (see X.272, 277), and he was so called in the published *Silmarillion*. For earlier statements concerning the arming of the Eldar on the Great Journey see X.276–7, 281.]

62 [*Ambarto* was changed to *Umbarto*, and the positions of Umbarto and Ambarussa were reversed: see p. 355.]

63 ['shocked' was an uncertain interpretation on my father's part of the illegible word.]

64 [The deed of his father: the treacherous taking of all the Telerian ships for the passage of the Fëanorians to Middle-earth.]

65 [The text ends with brief notes on the 'Sindarizing' of the Quenya names of the Sons of Fëanor, but these are too rapid, elliptical, and illegible to be reproduced. It may be mentioned, however, that Sindarin *Maedros* is explained as containing elements of Nelyafinwë's mother-name *Maitimo* (Common Eldarin *magit-* 'shapely', Sindarin *maed*) and of his *epessë Russandol* (Common Eldarin *russā*, Sindarin *ross*); and also that the Sindarin form of *Ambarussa* (numbered 6, i.e. the elder twin) is here *Amros*, not *Amras*.]

XII

THE PROBLEM OF *ROS*

In his last years my father attached the utmost importance to finding explanations, in historical linguistic terms, of names that went far back in the 'legendarium' (see for example his discussion of the very old names *Isfin* and *Eöl* in XI.317–18, 320), and if such names had appeared in print he felt bound by them, and went to great pains to devise etymologies that were consonant with the now minutely refined historical development of Quenya and Sindarin. Most taxing of all was the case of the name *Elros*, and others associated with it either in form or through connection in the legends; but, equally character-istically, his writings on this matter contain many observations of interest beyond the detail of phonological history: for the linguistic history and the 'legendarium' became less and less separable.

In the long excursus on the names of the descendants of Finwë given in the last chapter he had said (p. 349) that *Elros* and *Elrond* were 'formed to recall the name of their mother *Elwing*', and he had noted that the element *wing* occurs only in that name and in the name of Eärendil's ship *Vingilótë* (p. 365, note 55): he referred to a speculation of loremasters that *wing* was a word of the tongue of the Green-elves of Ossiriand, whose meaning was guessed with some probability to be 'foam, spindrift'. The name *Elros* he stated there without hesitation to mean 'star(lit) foam', in Quenya form *Elerossë* (but earlier, in *Quendi and Eldar* (XI.414), he had said that the meaning was 'star-glitter', while *Elrond* meant 'star-dome', as still in the present essay).

But this was not the last of his speculations on the matter, and there are several typewritten texts that return to the problem (all of them belonging to the same period, 1968 or later, as *The Shibboleth of Fëanor*, but certainly following that work). The most notable of these I give in full. It has no title, but begins with a statement defining the content:

> The best solution of the difficulty presented by the name *Elros*, fixed by mention in *The Lord of the Rings*, and the names of the sons of Fëanor: *Maedros*, the eldest, and *Amros*, now proposed as the name of both the twins (sixth and seventh) – to which a story is attached that it is desirable to retain.

This is a reference to the very rough manuscript text (appended to the list of father-names and mother-names of the Sons of Fëanor) in which the extraordinary story of the twin brothers is told (pp. 353–5); for the form *Amros* (not *Amras*) see p. 366, note 65.

The typescript was made very rapidly (with the usual number of interspersed notes, among them two of great interest), and it has required some editing, of a very minor kind, for the sake of clarity.

The one *-ros* was supposed (at its adoption) in *Elros* to contain a Sindarin stem **ross-* from base ROS 'spray, spindrift' (as scattered by a wind from a fountain, waterfall, or breaking waves).[1] The other is supposed to be a colour word, referring to the red, red-brown hair of the first, sixth, and seventh sons of Fëanor, descending to them from their maternal grandfather, father of Nerdanel, Fëanor's wife, a great craftsman, devoted to the Vala Aulë.

It is difficult to accept these two homophonic elements – of unconnected, indeed unconnectable, meanings – as used in Sindarin, or Sindarized names.[2] It is also unfortunate that the first appears too reminiscent of Latin *rōs* ['dew'] or Greek *drosos*, and the latter too close to well-known modern European 'red' words: as Latin *russus*, Italian *rosso*, English *russet*, *rust*, etc. However, the Elvish languages are inevitably full of such reminiscences, so that this is the lesser difficulty.

Proposed solution. Associate the name *Elros* with that of his mother *Elwing*: both contain final elements that are isolated in the legendary nomenclature (see note on *wing* in the discussion of the Sindarizing of the Ñoldorin heroic names).[3] But instead of deriving them from the Nandorin (or Green-elvish) of Ossiriand, it would be an improvement to derive them from the Mannish tongues: the language of Beren father of Dior; both **ros* and **wing* could thus be removed from Eldarin. The Adûnaic of Númenor was mainly derived from that of the most powerful and numerous people of 'the House of Hador'. This was related to the speech of Bëor's people who first entered Beleriand (probably about as nearly as Ñoldorin Quenya to Telerin of Valinor): communication between the two peoples was possible but imperfect, mainly because of phonetic changes in the Bëorian dialect. The language of the Folk of Haleth, so far as it was later known, appears to have been unrelated (unless in remote origin) and unintelligible to the other two peoples.[4]

The folk of Bëor continued to speak their own tongue among themselves with fair purity, though many Sindarin words were borrowed and adapted by them.[5] This was of course the native tongue of Beren, lineal descendant of Bëor the Old. He spoke Sindarin after a fashion (probably derived from North Sindarin); but his halting and dialectal use of it offended the ears of King Thingol.[6] But it was told in the legend of Beren and Lúthien that Lúthien learned Beren's native tongue during their long journeys together and ever after used it in their speech together. Not long before they came at last back to the borders of Doriath he asked her why she did so, since her own tongue was richer and more beautiful. Then she became silent and her eyes seemed to look far away before she answered: 'Why? Because I must forsake thee, or else forsake my own people and become one of the children of Men. Since I will never forsake thee, I must learn the speech of thy kin, and mine.' Dior their son, it is said, spoke both tongues: his father's, and his mother's, the Sindarin of Doriath. For he said: 'I am the first of the *Pereðil* (Half-elven); but I am also the heir of King Elwë, the *Eluchíl*.'[7]

He gave to his elder son the name *Eluréd*, that is said to have the same significance, but ended in the Bëorian word *rêda* 'heir'; to his second son he gave the name *Elurín*,[8] but his daughter the name *Elwing*. For she was born on a clear night of stars, the light of which glittered in the spray of the waterfall by which his house was built.[9] The word *wing* was Bëorian, meaning fine rain or the spray from fountains and waterfalls blown by a wind; but he joined this to Elvish *el-* 'star' rather than to the Bëorian,[10] because it was more beautiful, and also went with the names of her brothers: the name *Elwë* (Sindarin *Elu*) was believed to be and probably was derived from *el* 'star'.[11]

Eluréd and Elurín, before they came to manhood, were both slain by the sons of Fëanor,[12] in the last and most abominable deed brought about by the curse that the impious oath of Fëanor laid upon them. But Elwing was saved and fled with the Silmaril to the havens of the surviving Eldar at the Mouths of Sirion. There she later wedded Eärendil, and so joined the two Half-elven lines. Her sons she named *Elros* and *Elrond*; and after the manner of her brothers the first ended in a Bëorian word, and the second in an Elvish. *Elros* was indeed close in meaning to her own name: it contained the Bëorian word for 'foam' and the white crest of waves:[13] *rôs*. Its older form [was] *roth* (*róþ*). This was used in Adûnaic songs and legends concerning the coming of the Atani to Númenor in a translation of the name of Eärendil's ship. This they called *Rothinzil*.[14] Also in Númenor their first king was usually given the name *Elroth*. The word *wing(a)* was not known in Adûnaic. It was maybe an invention of the Lesser Folk,[15] for in their steep shores there had been waterfalls, whereas in the wooded land of the Greater Folk that went down in gentle slopes there had been none.

In this way also may be explained the name that Eärendil gave to his ship in which he at last succeeded in passing over the Great Sea. He himself called it *Wingalótë*, which like his own names were Quenya in form; for Quenya was his childhood's speech, since in the house of his mother's father, Turukáno (Turgon), King of Gondolin, that speech was in daily use.[16] But *Vinga-* was not a Quenya word: it was a Quenyarized form of the Bëorian *wing* that appeared in *Elwing* the name of his spouse. The form given to this name in Sindarin was *Gwingloth*, but as said above it was in the Adûnaic of Númenor translated as *Rothinzil*.

In the havens of refuge, when Morgoth's conquest was all but complete, there were several tongues to be heard. Not only the Sindarin, which was chiefly used, but also its Northern dialect; and among the Men of the Atani some still used their Mannish speeches; and of all these Eärendil had some knowledge. It is said that before Manwë he spoke the errand of Elves and Men first in Sindarin, since that might represent all those of the suppliants who had survived the war with Morgoth; but he repeated it in Quenya, since that was the language of the Ñoldor, who alone were under the ban of the Valar; and he added a prayer in the Mannish tongues of Hador and Bëor,[17] pleading that they were not under the ban, and had aided the Eldar only in their war against Morgoth, the enemy of the Valar. For the Atani had not rebelled against the Valar; they had rejected Morgoth and fled Westward seeking the Valar as the representatives of the One. This plea Manwë accepted, and one voice alone spoke aloud the doubt that was in the hearts of all the Valar. Mandos said: 'Nonetheless they are descendants of Men, who rejected the One himself. That is an evil seed that may grow again. For even if we under Eru have the power to return to Middle-earth and cast out Morgoth from the Kingdom of Arda, we cannot destroy all the evil that he has sown, nor seek out all his servants – unless we ravaged the whole of the Kingdom and made an end of all life therein; and that we may not do.'

The names *Elros* and *Elrond* that Elwing gave to her sons were held prophetic, as many mother-names among the Eldar.[18]

For after the Last Battle and the overthrow of Morgoth, when the Valar gave to Elros and Elrond a choice to belong either to the kin of the Eldar or to the kin of Men, it was Elros who voyaged over sea to Númenor following the star of Eärendil; whereas Elrond remained among the Elves and carried on the lineage of King Elwë.[19] Now *Elrond* was a word for the firmament, the starry dome as it appeared like a roof to Arda; and it was given by Elwing in memory of the great Hall of the Throne of Elwë in the midst of his stronghold of Menegroth that was called the *Menelrond*,[20] because by the arts and aid of Melian its high arched roof had been adorned with silver and gems set in the order and figures of the stars in the great Dome of Valmar[21] in Aman, whence Melian came.

But alas! This explanation fell foul of a small fact that my father had missed; and it was fatal. He noted on the text that 'most of this fails', because of the name *Cair Andros* (a Sindarin name, as were virtually all the place-names of Gondor), the island in the Anduin north of Minas Tirith, of which it had been said in Appendix A (RK p. 335, footnote) that it 'means "Ship of Long-foam"; for the isle was shaped like a great ship, with a high prow pointing north, against which the white foam of Anduin broke on sharp rocks.' So he was forced to accept that the element *-ros* in *Elros* must be the same as that in *Cair Andros*, the word must be Eldarin, not Atanic (Bëorian), and there could be no historical relationship between it and the Númenórean Adûnaic *Rothinzil*.[22]

Evidently following this is another note, from which it emerges that he still held to the view that the word *wing* ('spray, spindrift') was of Bëorian origin; and while noting that the name Wingalótë [> Wingelótë] of Eärendil's ship had not appeared in print, he observed that it 'must be retained, since it is connected with the name *Elwing*, and is in intention formed to resemble and "explain" the name of Wade's ship Guingelot.'[23] On *Guingelot* and *Wingelot* see my discussion in III.142–4 (in which I overlooked this remarkable statement). Concerning *wing* he said again that Eärendil named his ship in Quenya form, since that language had been his childhood speech, and that he intended its meaning to be 'Foam-flower'; but he adopted the element *wing* from the name of Elwing his wife. That name was given to her by her father Dior, who knew the Bëorian tongue (cf. p. 369).[24]

NOTES

1 [Cf. the *Etymologies*, V.384, stem ROS[1], 'distil, drip': Quenya *rossë* 'fine rain, dew', Noldorin *rhoss* 'rain', seen also in *Celebros*

'Silver-rain' (when *Celebros* was the name of the waterfall rather than the stream, XI.151).]

2   [Added in the margin: 'Though *Maedros* is now so long established that it would be difficult to alter'. In a later note, however, my father declared that he would change *Maedros* to *Maedron*.]

3   [See p. 365, note 55.]

4   This was the reason, in addition to their admiration of the Eldar, why the chieftains, elders, and wise men and women of the Atani learned Sindarin. The Halethian language was already failing before Túrin's time, and finally perished after Húrin in his wrath destroyed the small land and people. [Cf. *Of Dwarves and Men*, pp. 307–8 and note 49. In the chapter *Of the Coming of Men into the West* added to the *Quenta Silmarillion* Felagund learned from Bëor that the Haladin (the Folk of Haleth) 'speak the same tongue as we', whereas the People of Marach (the 'Hadorians') were 'of a different speech' (XI.218, §10). This was changed in the published *Silmarillion*: see XI.226. – With what is said here of the decline of the 'Halethian' language cf. *The Wanderings of Húrin* (XI.283 and note 41): 'the old tongue of the Folk which was now out of daily use'.]

5   Not necessarily confined to names of things that had not before [been] known. In the nomenclature of later generations assimilation to the Eldarin modes, and the use of some elements frequent in Eldarin names, can be observed. [It has been stated many times that the 'Bëorians' forsook their own language in Beleriand: see V.275 (footnote), XI.202, 217 (first footnote), 226; *Unfinished Tales* p. 215, note 19.]

6   He [Thingol] had small love for the Northern Sindar who had in regions near to Angband come under the dominion of Morgoth, and were accused of sometimes entering his service and providing him with spies. The Sindarin used by the Sons of Fëanor also was of the Northern dialect; and they were hated in Doriath.

7   [*Eluchíl* (Thingol's Heir): see XI.350.]

8   'Remembrance of Elu': containing Sindarin *rîn* from Common Eldarin *rēnē* < base REN 'recall, have in mind'. [These names *Eluréd* and *Elurín* replace *Eldún* and *Elrún* (originally *Elboron* and *Elbereth*); and the story that Dior's sons were twins had been abandoned (see XI.300, 349–50). From this passage and note were derived the names in the published *Silmarillion* and the statements in the index concerning them.]

9   [Cf. *The Shibboleth of Fëanor*, p. 349: 'Beside one great waterfall, called in Sindarin *Lanthir Lamath* ("waterfall of echoing voices"), Dior had his house.' From these passages the reference in the published *Silmarillion* (p. 235) was derived.]

10 Which is not recorded, but was probably similar to the Adûnaic *azar*. [In *The Notion Club Papers*, IX.305, the Adûnaic name of

Eärendil, *Azrubêl*, was said to be 'made of *azar* "sea" and the stem *bel*- (*azra*, IX.431).]

11 [This opinion is referred to in *The Shibboleth of Fëanor* (pp. 340–1), but regarded as improbable.]

12 [The original story was that Dior's sons 'were slain by the evil men of Maidros' host' (see IV.307). Subsequently they were 'taken captive by the evil men of Maidros' following, and they were left to starve in the woods' (V.142); in a version of the Tale of Years the perpetrators were 'the cruel servants of Celegorn' (XI.351).]

13 The Atani had never seen the Great Sea before they came at last to Beleriand; but according to their own legends and histories the Folk of Hador had long dwelt during their westward migration by the shores of a sea too wide to see across; it had no tides, but was visited by great storms. It was not until they had developed a craft of boat-building that the people afterwards known as the Folk of Hador discovered that a part of their host from whom they had become separated had reached the same sea before them, and dwelt at the feet of the high hills to the south-west, whereas they [the Folk of Hador] lived in the north-east, in the woods that there came near to the shores. They were thus some two hundred miles apart, going by water; and they did not often meet and exchange tidings. Their tongues had already diverged, with the swiftness of the speeches of Men in the 'Unwritten Days', and continued to do so; though they remained friends of acknowledged kinship, bound by their hatred and fear of the Dark Lord (Morgoth), against whom they had rebelled. Nonetheless they did not know that the Lesser Folk had fled from the threat of the Servants of the Dark and gone on westward, while they had lain hidden in their woods, and so under their leader Bëor reached Beleriand at last many years before they did.

[There has of course never been any previous trace or hint of this story of the long sojourn of the 'Bëorians' and the 'Hadorians' ('the People of Marach', a name not mentioned in this essay, see p. 325, note 41) by the shores of a great inland sea. In this account of their dwellings my father first wrote 'south-east' and 'north-west', changing them at once; and the particularity of this suggests that he had a specific geographical image in mind. This must surely be the Sea of Rhûn, where (features going back to the First Map to *The Lord of the Rings*, VII.305) there are hills on the south-western side and a forest coming down to the north-eastern shores; moreover the distance of two hundred miles across the sea agrees with the map. – It is said here that the 'Bëorians' reached Beleriand 'many years' before the 'Hadorians'. According to the later *Quenta Silmarillion* chapter *Of the Coming of Men into the West* Felagund met Bëor in Ossiriand in

310, and the People of Marach came over the Blue Mountains in 313 (XI.218, §13 and commentary). In *Of Dwarves and Men* (p. 307) 'the first of the three hosts of the Folk of Hador' came into Beleriand 'not long after' the Folk of Bëor, having in fact reached the eastern foothills of the Ered Lindon first of all the kindreds of the Edain. In that text there is mention of an opinion that a long period of separation between the two peoples would account for the divergence of their languages from an original common tongue (p. 308 and note 45).]

14   [The name *Rothinzil* 'Flower of the Foam' appeared in *The Drowning of Anadûnê*, IX.360 (*Rôthinzil*).]

15   ['The Lesser Folk': the People of Bëor. This sentence refers to the content of note 13.]

16   Though for most of its people it had become a language of books, and as the other Ñoldor they used Sindarin in daily speech. In this way there arose several blended forms, belonging strictly to neither language. Indeed, the name of the great city of Turgon by which it was best known in legend, *Gondolin(d)*, is an example. It was given by Turgon in Quenya *Ondolindë*, but generally its people turned it towards Sindarin, in which Eldarin **gon*, **gondo* 'stone, rock' had retained the *g-* lost in Quenya. [See XI.201.]

17   The language of the Folk of Haleth was not used, for they had perished and would not rise again. Nor would their tongue be heard again, unless the prophecy of Andreth the Wise-woman should prove true, that Túrin in the Last Battle should return from the Dead, and before he left the Circles of the World for ever should challenge the Great Dragon of Morgoth, Ancalagon the Black, and deal him the death-stroke.

[This remarkable saying has long roots, extending back to the prophecy at the end of the old *Tale of Turambar* (II.115–16), where it was told that the Gods of Death (Fui and Vefántur) would not open their doors to Túrin and Nienóri, that Úrin and Mavwin (Húrin and Morwen) went to Mandos, and that their prayers

> came even to Manwë, and the Gods had mercy on their unhappy fate, so that those twain Túrin and Nienóri entered into Fôs'Almir, the bath of flame, even as Urwendi and her maidens had done in ages past before the first rising of the Sun, and so were all their sorrows and stains washed away, and they dwelt as shining Valar among the blessed ones, and now the love of that brother and sister is very fair; but Turambar indeed shall stand beside Fionwë in the Great Wrack, and Melko and his drakes shall curse the sword of Mormakil.

In the *Sketch of the Mythology* or 'earliest *Silmarillion*' of the

1920s the prophecy with which it ends (IV.40) declares that when Morgoth returns, and 'the last battle of all' is fought,

> Fionwë will fight Morgoth on the plain of Valinor, and the spirit of Túrin shall be beside him; it shall be Túrin who with his black sword will slay Morgoth, and thus the children of Húrin shall be avenged.

The development of this in the *Quenta* (IV.165) tells that in the day of the last battle, on the fields of Valinor,

> Tulkas shall strive with Melko, and on his right shall stand Fionwë and on his left Túrin Turambar, son of Húrin, Conqueror of Fate; and it shall be the black sword of Túrin that deals unto Melko his death and final end; and so shall the children of Húrin and all Men be avenged.

And the final passage of the *Quenta*, concerning the prophecy of the recovery of the Two Trees, ends with the words (*ibid.*):

> But of Men in that day the prophecy speaks not, save of Túrin only, and him it names among the Gods.

These passages reappear in the revised conclusion of the *Quenta* that belongs with the *Quenta Silmarillion* of 1937 (see V.323–4, 333), with two changes: Túrin in the Last Battle is said to be 'coming from the halls of Mandos', and in the final sentence concerning the prophecy 'no Man it names, save Túrin only, and to him a place is given among the sons of the Valar.' In the cursory corrections that my father made much later to this conclusion (see XI.245–7) he changed 'Túrin ... coming from the halls of Mandos' to 'Túrin ... returning from the Doom of Men at the ending of the world', and against the concluding passage (including the reference to Túrin as 'a son of the Valar') he placed a large X.

Another reference is found in the *Annals of Aman* (X.71, 76), where it is said of the constellation Menelmakar (Orion) that it 'was a sign of Túrin Turambar, who should come into the world, and a foreshowing of the Last Battle that shall be at the end of Days.'

In this last reappearance of the mysterious and fluctuating idea the prophecy is put into the mouth of Andreth, the Wise-woman of the House of Bëor: Túrin will 'return from the Dead' before his final departure, and his last deed within the Circles of the World will be the slaying of the Great Dragon, Ancalagon the Black. Andreth prophesies of the Last Battle at the end of the Elder Days (the sense in which the term 'Last Battle' is used shortly afterwards in this text, p. 371); but in all the early texts (the *Quenta*, IV.160; the *Annals of Beleriand*, IV.309, V.144; the *Quenta Silmarillion*, V.329) it was Eärendil who destroyed Ancalagon.]

18   They had no other names that are recorded; for Eärendil was
     nearly always at sea in many fruitless voyages, and both his sons
     were born in his absence.

19   And also that of Turgon; though he preferred that of Elwë, who
     was not under the ban that was laid on the Exiles.

20   *Menelrond*: 'heaven-dome'.

21   [On the Dome of Varda above Valinor see X.385–8.]

22   [Another note among these papers derives the Adûnaic word *roth*
     (as in *Rothinzil*) from a stem RUTH, 'not originally connected
     to foam. Its basic sense was "scar, score, furrow", and yielded
     words for plough and ploughing; when applied to boats it
     referred to their track on water, especially to the curling water at
     the prow (*obroth* "fore-cutting", whereas the wake was called
     nadroth "hind-track", or the smooth *roth*).']

23   [He also said here that though *Rothinzil* had not appeared in
     print he wished to retain it.]

24   [This 'Bëorian' explanation of *wing* seems to have been aban-
     doned also, since what seems to be the latest among these
     discussions my father said that both elements in *Elwing* were
     Sindarin: he proposed an etymology whereby Quenya *wingë*,
     Sindarin *gwing* 'appears to be related' to the Quenya verb *winta*
     'scatter, blow about' (both transitive and intransitive), comparing
     Quenya *lassewinta* as a variant of *lasselanta*, 'leaf-fall, autumn'.]

XIII

LAST WRITINGS

Of Glorfindel, Círdan,
and other matters

There is a small collection of very late manuscripts, preserved together, closely similar in appearance, and all written on the blank sides of publication notices issued by Allen and Unwin. Most of these are copies of the same notice dated 19 January 1970 (used also by my father for his late work on the story of Maeglin, XI.316), but one of these writings was stated by him to be developed from a reply to a correspondent sent on 9 December 1972, and another is dated by him 20 November 1972. I think it very probable that the whole collection belongs to that time, the last year of his life: he died on the second of September, 1973, at the age of eighty-one. There are clear evidences of confusion (as he said at one point, 'my memory is no longer retentive'); but there are elements in them that are of much interest and should be recorded.

Though writing in manuscript he retained his practice of interspersing notes into the body of the text, distinguishing them by a different (italic) script. All the numbered notes, authorial and editorial, are collected at the end of the chapter.

GLORFINDEL

In the summer of 1938, when my father was pondering *The Council of Elrond* in *The Lord of the Rings*, he wrote: 'Glorfindel tells of his ancestry in Gondolin' (VI.214). More than thirty years later he took up the question of whether Glorfindel of Gondolin and Glorfindel of Rivendell were indeed one and the same, and this issued in two discussions, together with other brief or fragmentary writings closely associated with them. I will refer to these as '*Glorfindel I*' and '*Glorfindel II*'. The first page of *Glorfindel I* is missing, and the second page begins with the words 'as guards or assistants.' Then follows:

An Elf who had once known Middle-earth and had fought in the long wars against Melkor would be an eminently suitable companion for Gandalf. We could then reasonably suppose that Glorfindel (possibly as one of a small party,[1] more probably as a sole companion) landed with Gandalf–Olórin about Third Age 1000. This supposition would indeed explain the air of special power and sanctity that surrounds Glorfindel – note how the Witch-king flies from him, although all others (such as King Eärnur) however brave could not induce their horses to face him (Appendix A (I, iv), RK p. 331). For according to accounts (quite independent of this case) elsewhere given of Elvish nature, and their relations with the Valar, when Glorfindel was slain his spirit would then go to Mandos and be judged, and then would remain in the Halls of Waiting until Manwë granted him release. The Elves were destined to be by nature 'immortal', within the unknown limits of the life of the Earth as a habitable realm, and their disembodiment was a grievous thing. It was the duty, therefore, of the Valar to restore them, if they were slain, to incarnate life, if they desired it – unless for some grave (and rare) reason: such as deeds of great evil, or any works of malice of which they remained obdurately unrepentant. When they were re-embodied they could remain in Valinor, or return to Middle-earth if their home had been there. We can therefore reasonably suppose that Glorfindel, after the purging or forgiveness of his part in the rebellion of the Ñoldor, was released from Mandos and became himself again, but remained in the Blessed Realm – for Gondolin was destroyed and all or most of his kin had perished. We can thus understand why he seems so powerful a figure and almost 'angelic'. For he had returned to the primitive innocence of the First-born, and had then lived among those Elves who had never rebelled, and in the companionship of the Maiar[2] for ages: from the last years of the First Age, through the Second Age, to the end of the first millennium of the Third Age: before he returned to Middle-earth.[3] It is indeed probable that he had in Valinor already become a friend and follower of Olórin. Even in the brief glimpses of him given in *The Lord of the Rings* he appears as specially concerned for Gandalf, and was one (the most powerful, it would seem) of those sent out from Rivendell when the disquieting news reached Elrond that Gandalf had never re-appeared to guide or protect the Ring-bearer.

The second essay, *Glorfindel II*, is a text of five manuscript pages which undoubtedly followed the first at no long interval; but a slip of paper on which my father hastily set down some thoughts on the matter presumably came between them, since he said here that while Glorfindel might have come with Gandalf, 'it seems far more likely that he was sent in the crisis of the Second Age, when Sauron invaded Eriador, to assist Elrond, and that though not (yet) mentioned in the annals recording Sauron's defeat he played a notable and heroic part in the war.' At the end of this note he wrote the words 'Númenórean ship', presumably indicating how Glorfindel might have crossed the Great Sea.

This name is in fact derived from the earliest work on the mythology: *The Fall of Gondolin*, composed in 1916–17, in which the Elvish language that ultimately became that of the type called Sindarin was in a primitive and unorganized form, and its relation with the High-elven type (itself very primitive) was still haphazard. It was intended to mean 'Golden-tressed',[4] and was the name given to the heroic 'Gnome' (Ñoldo), a chieftain of Gondolin, who in the pass of Cristhorn ('Eagle-cleft') fought with a Balrog [> Demon], whom he slew at the cost of his own life.

Its use in *The Lord of the Rings* is one of the cases of the somewhat random use of the names found in the older legends, now referred to as *The Silmarillion*, which escaped reconsideration in the final published form of *The Lord of the Rings*. This is unfortunate, since the name is now difficult to fit into Sindarin, and cannot possibly be Quenyarin. Also in the now organized mythology, difficulty is presented by the things recorded of Glorfindel in *The Lord of the Rings*, if Glorfindel of Gondolin is supposed to be the same person as Glorfindel of Rivendell.

As for the former: he was slain in the Fall of Gondolin at the end of the First Age, and if a chieftain of that city must have been a Ñoldo, one of the Elf-lords in the host of King Turukáno (Turgon); at any rate when *The Fall of Gondolin* was written he was certainly thought to be so. But the Ñoldor in Beleriand were exiles from Valinor, having rebelled against the authority of Manwë supreme head of the Valar, and Turgon was one of the most determined and unrepentant supporters of Fëanor's rebellion.[5] There is no escape from this. Gondolin is in *The Silmarillion* said to have been built and occupied by a people of almost entirely Ñoldorin origin.[6] It might be possible, though inconsistent, to suppose that Glorfindel was a prince of Sindarin origin who had joined the host of Turgon, but this would entirely contradict what is said of Glorfindel in Rivendell in *The Lord of the Rings*: most notably in *The Fellowship of the Ring*, p. 235, where he is said to have been one of the 'lords of the Eldar from beyond the furthest seas ... who have dwelt in the Blessed Realm.' The Sindar had never left Middle-earth.

This difficulty, far more serious than the linguistic one, may be considered first. At any rate what at first sight may seem the simplest solution must be abandoned: sc. that we have merely a reduplication of names, and that Glorfindel of Gondolin and Glorfindel of Rivendell were different persons. This repetition of so striking a name, though possible, would not be credible.[7] No other major character in the Elvish legends as reported in *The Silmarillion* and *The Lord of the Rings* has a name borne by another Elvish person of importance. Also it may be found that acceptance of the identity of Glorfindel of old and of the Third Age will actually explain what is said of him and improve the story.

When Glorfindel of Gondolin was slain his spirit would according to the laws established by the One be obliged at once to return to the land of the Valar. Then he would go to Mandos and be judged, and would then remain in the 'Halls of Waiting' until Manwë granted him release. Elves were destined to be 'immortal', that is not to die within the unknown limits decreed by the One, which at the most could be until the end of the life of the Earth as a habitable realm. Their death – by any injury to their bodies so severe that it could not be healed – and the disembodiment of their spirits was an 'unnatural' and grievous matter. It was therefore the duty of the Valar, by command of the One, to restore them to incarnate life, if they desired it. But this 'restoration' could be delayed[8] by Manwë, if the *fëa* while alive had done evil deeds and refused to repent of them, or still harboured any malice against any other person among the living.

Now Glorfindel of Gondolin was one of the exiled Ñoldor, rebels against the authority of Manwë, and they were all under a ban imposed by him: they could not return in bodily form to the Blessed Realm. Manwë, however, was not bound by his own ordinances, and being still the supreme ruler of the Kingdom of Arda could set them aside, when he saw fit. From what is said of Glorfindel in *The Silmarillion* and *The Lord of the Rings* it is evident that he was an Elda of high and noble spirit: and it can be assumed that, though he left Valinor in the host of Turgon, and so incurred the ban, he did so reluctantly because of kinship with Turgon and allegiance to him, and had no part in the kinslaying of Alqualondë.[9]

More important: Glorfindel had sacrificed his life in defending the fugitives from the wreck of Gondolin against a Demon out of Thangorodrim,[10] and so enabling Tuor and Idril daughter of Turgon and their child Eärendil to escape, and seek refuge at the Mouths of Sirion. Though he cannot have known the importance of this (and would have defended them even had they been fugitives of any rank), this deed was of vital importance to the designs of the Valar.[11] It is therefore entirely in keeping with the general design of *The Silmarillion* to describe the subsequent history of Glorfindel thus. After his purging of any guilt that he had incurred in the rebellion, he was released from Mandos, and Manwë restored him.[12] He then became again a living incarnate person, but was permitted to dwell in the Blessed Realm; for he had regained the primitive innocence and grace of the Eldar. For long years he remained in Valinor, in reunion with the Eldar who had not rebelled, and in the companionship of the Maiar. To these he had now become almost an equal, for though he was an incarnate (to whom a bodily form not made or chosen by himself was necessary) his spiritual power had been greatly enhanced by his self-sacrifice. At some time, probably early in his sojourn in Valinor, he became a follower, and a friend, of Olórin (Gandalf), who as is said in *The Silmarillion* had an especial love and concern for the Children of Eru.[13] That Olórin, as was possible for one of the Maiar, had already visited Middle-earth and had become acquainted not only with the Sindarin Elves and others deeper in Middle-earth, but also with Men, is likely, but nothing is [> has yet been] said of this.

Glorfindel remained in the Blessed Realm, no doubt at first by his own choice: Gondolin was destroyed, and all his kin had perished, and were still in the Halls of Waiting unapproachable by the living. But his long sojourn during the last years of the First Age, and at least far into the Second Age, no doubt was also in accord with the wishes and designs of Manwë.

When did Glorfindel return to Middle-earth? This must probably have occurred *before* the end of the Second Age, and the 'Change of the World' and the Drowning of Númenor, after which no living embodied creature, 'humane' or of lesser kinds, could return from the Blessed Realm which had been 'removed from the Circles of the World'. This was according to a general ordinance proceeding from Eru Himself; and though, until the end of the Third Age, when Eru decreed that the Dominion of Men must begin, Manwë could be supposed to have received the permission of Eru to make an exception in his case, and to have devised some means for the transportation of Glorfindel to Middle-earth, this is improbable and would make Glorfindel of greater power and importance than seems fitting.

We may then best suppose that Glorfindel returned during the Second Age, before the 'shadow' fell on Númenor, and while the Númenóreans were welcomed by the Eldar as powerful allies. His return must have been for the purpose of strengthening Gil-galad and Elrond, when the growing evil of the intentions of Sauron were at last perceived by them. It might, therefore, have been as early as Second Age 1200, when Sauron came in person to Lindon, and attempted to deceive Gil-galad, but was rejected and dismissed.[14] But it may have been, perhaps more probably, as late as c.1600, the Year of Dread, when Barad-dûr was completed and the One Ring forged, and Celebrimbor at last became aware of the trap into which he had fallen. For in 1200, though he was filled with anxiety, Gil-galad still felt strong and able to treat Sauron with contempt.[15] Also at that time his Númenórean allies were beginning to make strong permanent havens for their great ships, and also many of them had actually begun to dwell there permanently. In 1600 it became clear to all the leaders of Elves and Men (and Dwarves) that war was inevitable against Sauron, now unmasked as a new Dark Lord. They therefore began to prepare for his assault; and no doubt urgent messages and prayers asking for help were received in Númenor (and in Valinor).[16]

The text ends here, with no indication that it was unfinished, although the 'linguistic difficulty' referred to on p. 379 was not taken up.

Written at the same time as the 'Glorfindel' texts is a discussion of the question of Elvish reincarnation. It is in two versions, one a very rough draft (partly written in fact on the manuscript of Glorfindel I) for the other. This text is not included here,[17] except in its concluding part, which concerns the Dwarves' belief in the rebirth or reappearance of their Fathers, most notably Durin. I give this passage in the form that it has in the original draft. It was written at a speed (with punctuation omitted, and variant forms of phrases jostling one another) that the printed form that follows does not at all convey; but it is a record of emerging thought on a matter concerning which very little is to be found in all my father's writings.

It is possible that this false notion[18] was in some ways connected with the various strange ideas which both Elves and Men had concerning the Dwarves, which were indeed largely derived by them from the Dwarves themselves. For the Dwarves asserted that the spirits of the Seven Fathers of their races were from time to time reborn in their kindreds. This was notably the case in the race of the Longbeards whose ultimate forefather was called Durin, a name which was taken at intervals by one of his descendants, but by no others but those in a direct line of descent from Durin I. Durin I, eldest of the Fathers, 'awoke' far back in the First Age (it is supposed, soon after the awakening of Men), but in the Second Age several other Durins had appeared as Kings of the Longbeards (Anfangrim). In the Third Age Durin VI was slain by a Balrog in 1980. It was prophesied (by the Dwarves), when Dáin Ironfoot took the kingship in Third Age 2941 (after the Battle of Five Armies), that in his direct line there would one day appear a Durin VII – but he would be the last.[19] Of these Durins the Dwarves reported that they retained memory of their former lives as Kings, as real, and yet naturally as incomplete, as if they had been consecutive years of life in one person.[20]

How this could come to pass the Elves did not know; nor would the Dwarves tell them much more of the matter.[21] But the Elves of Valinor knew of a strange tale of Dwarvish origins, which the Ñoldor brought to Middle-earth, and asserted that they had learned it from Aulë himself. This will be found among the many minor matters included in notes or appendices to *The Silmarillion*, and is not here told in full. For the present point it is sufficient to recall that the immediate author of the Dwarvish race was the Vala Aulë.[22]

Here there is a brief version of the legend of the Making of the Dwarves, which I omit; my father wrote on the text: 'Not a place for telling the story of Aulë and the Dwarves.'[23] The conclusion then follows:

The Dwarves add that at that time Aulë gained them also this privilege that distinguished them from Elves and Men: that the spirit of each of the Fathers (such as Durin) should, at the end of the long span of life allotted to Dwarves, fall asleep, but then lie in a tomb of his own body,[24] at rest, and there its weariness and any hurts that had befallen it should be amended. Then after long years he should arise and take up his kingship again.[25]

The second version is very much briefer, and on the question of the 'rebirth' of the Fathers says only: '... the reappearance, at long intervals, of the person of one of the Dwarf-fathers, in the lines of their kings – e.g. especially Durin – is not when examined probably one of rebirth, but of the preservation of the *body* of a former King Durin (say) to which at intervals his spirit would return. But the relations of the Dwarves to the Valar and especially to the Vala Aulë are (as it seems) quite different from those of Elves and Men.'

THE FIVE WIZARDS

Another brief discussion, headed 'Note on the landing of the Five Wizards and their functions and operations', arose from my father's consideration of the matter of Glorfindel, as is seen from the opening words: 'Was in fact Glorfindel one of them?' He observed that he was 'evidently never supposed to be when *The Lord of the Rings* was written', adding that there is no possibility that some of them were Eldar 'of the highest order of power', rather than Maiar. The text then continues with the passage given in *Unfinished Tales*, p. 394, beginning 'We must assume that they were all Maiar ...'; but after the words with which that citation ends ('... chosen by the Valar with this in mind') there stands only 'Saruman the most powerful', and then it breaks off, unfinished. Beside these last words is a pencilled note: 'Radagast a name of Mannish (Anduin vale) origin – but not now clearly interpretable' (see *Unfinished Tales* p. 390 and note 4).

On the reverse of the page are some notes which I described in *Unfinished Tales* as uninterpretable, but which with longer scrutiny I have been largely able to make out. One of them reads as follows:

No names are recorded for the two wizards. They were never seen or known in lands west of Mordor. The wizards did not come at the same time. Possibly Saruman, Gandalf, Radagast did, but more likely Saruman the chief (and already over mindful of this) came first and alone. Probably Gandalf and Radagast came together, though this has not yet been said. ... (what is most probable) ... Glorfindel also met Gandalf at the Havens. The other two are only known to (have) exist(ed) [*sic*] by Saruman, Gandalf, and Radagast, and Saruman in his wrath mentioning five was letting out a piece of private information.

The reference of the last sentence is to Saruman's violent retort to Gandalf at the door of Orthanc, in which he spoke of 'the rods of the Five Wizards' (*The Two Towers* p. 188). Another note is even rougher and more difficult:

The 'other two' came much earlier, at the same time probably as Glorfindel, when matters became very dangerous in the Second Age.[26] Glorfindel was sent to aid Elrond and was (though not yet said) pre-eminent in the war in Eriador.[27] But the other two Istari were sent for a different purpose. Morinehtar and

Rómestámo.[28] Darkness-slayer and East-helper. Their task was to circumvent Sauron: to bring help to the few tribes of Men that had rebelled from Melkor-worship, to stir up rebellion ... and after his first fall to search out his hiding (in which they failed) and to cause [?dissension and disarray] among the dark East ...   They must have had very great influence on the history of the Second Age and Third Age in weakening and disarraying the forces of East ...   who would both in the Second Age and Third Age otherwise have ... outnumbered the West.

At the words in the citation from this text in *Unfinished Tales* (p. 394) 'Of the other two nothing is said in published work save the reference to the Five Wizards in the altercation between Gandalf and Saruman' my father wrote: 'A note made on their names and functions seems now lost, but except for the names their general history and effect on the history of the Third Age is clear.' Conceivably he was thinking of the sketched-out narrative of the choosing of the Istari at a council of the Valar (*Unfinished Tales* p. 393), in which the Two Wizards (or 'the Blue Wizards', *Ithryn Luin*) were named Alatar and Pallando.

CÍRDAN

This brief manuscript is also associated with the discussion of Glorfindel: rough drafting for it is found on the verso of one of the pages of the text *Glorfindel II*.

This is the Sindarin for 'Shipwright',[29] and describes his later functions in the history of the First Three Ages; but his 'proper' name, sc. his original name among the Teleri, to whom he belonged, is never used.[30] He is said in the Annals of the Third Age (c.1000) to have seen further and deeper into the future than anyone else in Middle-earth.[31] This does not include the Istari (who came from Valinor), but must include even Elrond, Galadriel, and Celeborn.

Círdan was a Telerin Elf, one of the highest of those who were not transported to Valinor but became known as the Sindar, the Grey-elves;[32] he was akin to Olwë, one of the two kings of the Teleri, and lord of those who departed over the Great Sea. He was thus also akin to Elwë,[33] Olwë's elder brother, acknowledged as high-king of all the Teleri in Beleriand, even after he withdrew to the guarded realm of Doriath. But Círdan and his people remained in many ways distinct from the rest of the Sindar. They retained the old name Teleri (in later Sindarin[34] form *Telir*, or *Telerrim*) and remained in many ways a separate folk, speaking even in later days a more archaic language.[35] The Ñoldor called them the *Falmari*, 'wave-folk', and the other Sindar *Falathrim* 'people of the foaming shore'.[36]

It was during the long waiting of the Teleri for the return of the floating isle, upon which the Vanyar and Ñoldor had been transported over the Great Sea, that Círdan had turned his thoughts and skill to the making of ships, for he and all the other Teleri became impatient. Nonetheless it is said that for love of his kin and allegiance Círdan was the leader of those who sought longest for Elwë when he was lost and did not come to the shores to depart from Middle-earth. Thus he forfeited the fulfilment of his greatest desire: to see the Blessed Realm and find again there Olwë and his own nearest kin. Alas, he did not reach the shores until nearly all the Teleri of Olwë's following had departed.

Then, it is said, he stood forlorn looking out to sea, and it was night, but far away he could see a glimmer of light upon Eressëa ere it vanished into the West. Then he cried aloud: 'I will follow that light, alone if none will come with me, for the ship that I have been building is now almost ready.' But even as he said this he received in his heart a message, which he knew to come from the Valar, though in his mind it was remembered as a voice speaking in his own tongue. And the voice warned him not to attempt this peril; for his strength and skill would not be able to build any ship able to dare the winds and waves of the Great Sea for many long years yet. 'Abide now that time, for when it comes then will your work be of utmost worth, and it will be remembered in song for many ages after.' 'I obey,' Círdan answered, and then it seemed to him that he saw (in a vision maybe) a shape like a white boat, shining above him, that sailed west through the air, and as it dwindled in the distance it looked like a star of so great a brilliance that it cast a shadow of Círdan upon the strand where he stood.

As we now perceive, this was a foretelling of the ship[37] which after apprenticeship to Círdan, and ever with his advice and help, Eärendil built, and in which at last he reached the shores of Valinor. From that night onwards Círdan received a foresight touching all matters of importance, beyond the measure of all other Elves upon Middle-earth.

This text is remarkable in that on the one hand nothing is said of the history and importance of Círdan as it appears elsewhere, while on the other hand almost everything that is told here is unique. In the *Grey Annals* it was said (XI.8, §14):

> Ossë therefore persuaded many to remain in Beleriand, and when King Olwë and his host were embarked upon the isle and passed over the Sea they abode still by the shore; and Ossë returned to them, and continued in friendship with them. And he taught to them the craft of shipbuilding and of sailing; and they became a folk of mariners, the first in Middle-earth ...

But of Ossë there is now no mention; shipbuilding on the coasts of Beleriand is said to have begun in the long years during which the Teleri awaited Ulmo's return, and is indeed spoken of (see note 29) as the further evolution of a craft already developed among the Teleri during the Great Journey.

Other features of this account that appear nowhere else (in addition of course to the story of Círdan's desire to cross the Sea to Valinor, and his vision of the white ship passing westward through the night above him) are that the Teleri delayed long on the shores of the Sea of Rhûn on the Great Journey (note 29; cf. p. 373, note 13); that Círdan was the leader of those who sought for Elwë Thingol, his kinsman; and that Eärendil was 'apprenticed' to Círdan, who aided him in the building of Vingilot.

NOTES

1   It may be noted that *Galdor* is another name of similar sort and period of origin, but he appears as a messenger from Círdan and is called Galdor of the Havens. *Galdor* also appeared in *The Fall of Gondolin*, but the name is of a more simple and usual form [than *Glorfindel*] and might be repeated. But unless he is said in *The Fall of Gondolin* to have been slain, he can reasonably be supposed to be the same person, one of the Ñoldor who escaped from the siege and destruction, but fled west to the Havens, and not southwards to the mouths of Sirion, as did most of the remnant of the people of Gondolin together with Tuor, Idril, and Eärendil. He is represented in *The Council of Elrond* as less powerful and much less wise than Glorfindel; and so evidently had not returned to Valinor, and been purged, and reincarnated.

[See note 3. – The words 'the name [Galdor] is of a more simple and usual form [than Glorfindel] and might be repeated' show that on the lost first page my father had discussed (as he would do in the following text) the possibility that there were two distinct persons named Glorfindel, and had concluded that it was too improbable to be entertained. – 'But unless he is said in *The Fall of Gondolin* to have been slain': my father would probably have been hard put to it to lay his hand on *The Fall of Gondolin*, and without consulting it he could not say for certain what had been Galdor's fate (this, I take it, is his meaning). In fact, Galdor was not slain, but led the fugitives over the pass of Cristhorn while Glorfindel came up at the rear (II.191–2), and in the 'Name-list to *The Fall of Gondolin*' (II.215) it is said that he went to Sirion's mouth, and that 'he dwelleth yet in Tol Eressëa'. He was the lord of the people of the Tree in Gondolin, and of him it was said in the old tale that he 'was held the most valiant of all the Gondothlim save Turgon alone' (II.173).]

2 That angelic order to which Gandalf originally belonged: lesser in power and authority than the Valar, but of the same nature: members of the first order of created rational beings, who if they appeared in visible forms ('humane' or of other kind) were self-incarnated, or given their forms by the Valar [*added later:* and who could move/travel simply by an act of will when not arrayed in a body – which they could assume when they reached the places that ... *(illegible)*.]

3 Galdor in contrast, even in the brief glimpses we have in the Council, is seen clearly as an inferior person, and much less wise. He, whether he appears in *The Silmarillion* or not, must be either (as his name suggests) a Sindarin Elf who had never left Middle-earth and seen the Blessed Realm, or one of the Ñoldor who had been exiled for rebellion, and had also remained in Middle-earth, and had not, or not yet, accepted the pardon of the Valar and returned to the home prepared for them in the West, in reward for their valour against Melkor. [The view of Galdor expressed in this note and in note 1 seems hardly justified by the report of his contributions to the Council of Elrond; and if he were indeed Galdor of Gondolin he had had long ages in which to acquire wisdom in the hard world of Middle-earth. But there is no reason to suppose that when my father wrote the chapter *The Council of Elrond* he associated Galdor of the Havens with Galdor of Gondolin.]

4 [For the original etymology of *Glorfindel*, and the etymological connections of the elements of the name, see II.341.]

5 [In the *Annals of Aman* (X.112, §135) it is told that following the Oath of the Fëanorians 'Fingolfin, and his son Turgon, therefore spoke against Fëanor, and fierce words awoke'; but later (X.118, §156), when it is told that even after the utterance of the Prophecy of the North 'all Fingolfin's folk went forward still', it is said that 'Fingon and Turgon were bold and fiery of heart and loath to abandon any task to which they had put their hands until the bitter end, if bitter it must be.']

6 [The original conception that Gondolin was peopled entirely by Ñoldor was changed in many alterations to the text of the *Grey*

Annals (see the Index to *The War of the Jewels*, entry *Gondolin*, references under 'population'): it is stated indeed (XI.45, §113) that when Turgon sent all his people forth from Nivrost to Gondolin they constituted 'a third part of the Noldor of Fingolfin's House, and *a yet greater host of the Sindar*'. The statement here that Gondolin was 'occupied by a people of almost entirely Ñoldorin origin' obviously runs entirely counter to that conception.]

7 [In the margin of the page my father asked subsequently: 'Why not?' The question seems to be answered, however, in the following sentence of the text – where the emphasis is of course on the word 'Elvish': 'no other major character in the *Elvish* legends … has a name borne by another *Elvish* person of importance.' It would indeed have been open to him to change the name of Glorfindel of Gondolin, who had appeared in no published writing, but he did not mention this possibility.]

8 Or in gravest cases (such as that of Fëanor) withheld and referred to the One.

9 Though he [Glorfindel] is not yet named in the unrevised part of *The Silmarillion* treating of this matter, it is recorded that many of the Noldor of Turgon's following were in fact grieved by the decision of their king, and dreaded that evil would soon result from it. In the Third Host, that of Finarfin, so many were of this mind that when Finarfin heard the final doom of Mandos and repented, the greater part of that host returned to Valinor. Yet Finrod son of Finarfin, noblest of all the Ñoldor in the tales of Beleriand, also went away, for Turgon had been elected supreme lord of the Ñoldorin hosts.

[In the *Annals of Aman* (X.113, §138) there was no suggestion that Finrod (= Finarfin) led a separate 'Third Host': 'Thus at the last the Noldor set forth divided in two hosts. Fëanor and his following were in the van; but the greater host came behind under Fingolfin'; and the same was said in the *Quenta Silmarillion* (V.235, §68, not changed later). But this note carries an extreme departure from the tradition, in the entire omission of Fingolfin. This has in fact been encountered before, in my father's very late work – of this same period – on the story of Maeglin, where relationships are distorted on account of a defective genealogy making Turgon the son of Finwë (XI.327); but here, in a central story of *The Silmarillion*, Turgon is called 'king', and 'supreme lord of the Ñoldorin hosts', and Fingolfin disappears. Of course it is not to be thought that my father actually intended such a catastrophic disruption of the narrative structure as this would bring about; and it is reassuring to see that in a reference elsewhere in these papers Fingolfin reappears.]

10   [In the margin, and written at the same time as the text, my
     father noted: 'The duel of Glorfindel and the Demon may need
     revision.']

11   This is one of the main matters of *The Silmarillion* and need not
     here be explained. But in that part of *The Silmarillion* as so far
     composed it should not be left to appear that Ulmo, chiefly
     concerned in the coming of Tuor to Gondolin, in any way acted
     contrary to the Ban, against Manwë or without his knowledge.
     [My father perhaps had in mind Ulmo's words to Tuor on the
     shore at Vinyamar, *Unfinished Tales* p. 29.]

12   This implies that Glorfindel was natively an Elda of great bodily
     and spiritual stature, a noble character, and that his guilt had
     been small: sc. that he owed allegiance to Turgon and loved his
     own kindred, and these were his only reasons for remaining with
     them, although he was grieved by their obstinacy, and feared the
     doom of Mandos.

13   [Cf. the *Valaquenta* (*The Silmarillion*, p. 31): 'In later days he was
     the friend of all the Children of Ilúvatar, and took pity on their
     sorrows ...']

14   No doubt because Gil-galad had by then discovered that Sauron
     was busy in Eregion, but had secretly begun the making of a
     stronghold in Mordor. (Maybe already an Elvish name for that
     region, because of its volcano Orodruin and its eruptions – which
     were not made by Sauron but were a relic of the devastating
     works of Melkor in the long First Age.) [See note 15.]

15   [This passage concerning Gil-galad and Sauron in the year 1200
     of the Second Age, with the express statement that 'Sauron came
     in person to Lindon', seems to conflict with what is said in *Of the
     Rings of Power* (*The Silmarillion* p. 287), that 'Only to Lindon
     he did not come, for Gil-galad and Elrond doubted him and his
     fair-seeming', and would not admit him to the land.]

16   For the Valar were open to the hearing of the prayers of those in
     Middle-earth, as ever before, save only that in the dark days of
     the Ban they would listen to one prayer only from the Ñoldor: a
     repentant prayer pleading for pardon.

17   [My father here discussed again the idea that Elvish reincarnation
     might be achieved by 'rebirth' as a child, and rejected it as em-
     phatically as he had done in the discussion called 'Reincarnation
     of Elves', X.363–4; here as there the physical and psychological
     difficulties were addressed. He wrote here that the idea 'must be
     abandoned, or at least noted as a false notion, e.g. probably of
     Mannish origin, since nearly all the matter of *The Silmarillion* is
     contained in myths and legends that have passed through Men's
     hands and minds, and are (in many points) plainly influenced by
     contact and confusion with the myths, theories, and legends of
     Men' (cf. p. 357, note 17).

My discussion of this matter in X.364 must be corrected. I said there that the idea that the 'houseless' *fëa* was enabled to rebuild its *hröa* from its memory became my father's 'firm and stable view of the matter', 'as appears from very late writing on the subject of the reincarnation of Glorfindel of Gondolin'. This is erroneous. This last discussion of Elvish reincarnation refers only to the 'restoration' or 'reconstitution' of the former body by the Valar, and makes no mention of the idea that it could be achieved by the 'houseless *fëa*' operating of itself.]

18 [The 'false notion' is that of Elvish rebirth as a child: see note 17.]

19 ['Durin VII & Last' is shown in the genealogical table in Appendix A, III as a descendant of Dáin Ironfoot. Nothing is said of him in that Appendix; but see p. 278 in this book.]

20 Yet it is said that their memories were clearer and fuller of the far-off days.

21 That the Elves ever came to know so much (though only at a time when the vigour of both their races was declining) is thought to be due to the strange and unique friendship which arose between Gimli and Legolas. Indeed most of the references to Dwarvish history in Elvish records are marked with 'so said Legolas'.

22 Who was sometimes called *Návatar*, and the Dwarves *Aulëonnar* 'children of Aulë'.

23 [This brief version ends with these remarkable words: 'But Eru did not give them the immortality of the Elves, but lives longer than Men. "They shall be the third children and more like Men, the second." ']

24 The flesh of Dwarves is reported to have been far slower to decay or become corrupted than that of Men. (Elvish bodies robbed of their spirit quickly disintegrated and vanished.)

25 [A note at the end of the text without indication for its insertion reads:] What effect would this have on the succession? Probably this 'return' would only occur when by some chance or other the reigning king had no son. The Dwarves were very unprolific and this no doubt happened fairly often.

26 [These notes go with the text *Glorfindel II*, when my father had determined that Glorfindel came to Middle-earth in the Second Age, probably about the year 1600 (p. 382).]

27 [With this reference to Glorfindel's part in the war in Eriador cf. the note cited on pp. 378–9.]

28 [Elsewhere on this page this name is written *Róme(n)star*.]

29 Before ever they came to Beleriand the Teleri had developed a craft of boat-making; first as rafts, and soon as light boats with paddles made in imitation of the water-birds upon the lakes near their first homes, and later on the Great Journey in crossing rivers, or especially during their long tarrying on the shores of the 'Sea of Rhûn', where their ships became larger and stronger. But

in all this work Círdan had ever been the foremost and most inventive and skilful. [On the significance of the Sea of Rhûn in the context of the Great Journey see XI.173–4.]

30 Pengoloð alone mentions a tradition among the Sindar of Doriath that it was in archaic form *Nōwē*, the original meaning of which was uncertain, as was that of Olwë. [On the meaning of *Olwë* see p. 341 and note 20.]

31 [Cf. Appendix B (head-note to the Third Age): 'For Círdan saw further and deeper than any other in Middle-earth' (said in the context of his surrender of Narya, the Ring of Fire, to Mithrandir). The statement here that this is said 'in the Annals of the Third Age (c.1000)' is puzzling, but is presumably to be related to the words in the same passage of Appendix B 'When maybe a thousand years had passed ... the *Istari* or Wizards appeared in Middle-earth.']

32 A Quenya name given by the exiled Ñoldor, and primarily applied to the folk of Doriath, people of Elwë Grey-cloak.

33 [That Círdan was a kinsman of Elwë is mentioned in *Quendi and Eldar* (XI.384 and note 15).]

34 This is used as a general term for the Telerian dialect of Eldarin as it became in the changes of long years in Beleriand, though it was not entirely uniform in its development.

35 [Cf. *Quendi and Eldar*, XI.380: 'The *Eglain* became a people somewhat apart from the inland Elves, and at the time of the coming of the Exiles their language was in many ways different.' (The *Eglain* are the people of Círdan.)]

36 [For *Falathrim* see *Quendi and Eldar*, XI.378; and with *Falmari* cf. X.163, §27: 'The Sea-elves therefore they became in Valinor, the Falmari, for they made music beside the breaking waves.']

37 *Vingilótë*, 'Sprayflower'. [Beside 'Spray' my father subsequently wrote 'Foam', and noted also: '*wingë*, Sindarin *gwing*, is properly a flying spume or spindrift blown off wavetops': see p. 376, note 24.]

PART THREE

TEACHINGS OF
PENGOLOÐ

XIV

DANGWETH PENGOLOÐ

This work, example and record of the instruction of Ælfwine the Mariner by Pengoloð the Wise of Gondolin, exists in two forms: the first ('**A**') a good clear text with (apart from one major exception, see note 6) very few changes made either in the act of writing or subsequently, and the second ('**B**') a superb illuminated manuscript of which the first page is reproduced as the frontispiece of this book. This latter, together with the brief text *Of Lembas*, was enclosed in a newspaper of 5 January 1960, on which my father wrote: 'Two items from the lore of Pengoloð', and also '*Danbeth* to question. How/Why did Elvish language change? Origin of *Lembas*.' On a cardboard folder enclosing the newspaper he wrote: 'Pengoloð items. §*Manen lambë Quendion ahyanë* How did the language of Elves change? §*Mana i·coimas Eldaron* What is the "*coimas*" of the Eldar?'

Above the *gw* of *Dangweth* on the illuminated manuscript he lightly pencilled *b*; but on an isolated scrap of paper found with the two texts are some jottings of which the following are clear: 'Keep *Dangweth* "answer" separate from *-beth* = *peth* "word"'; '√*gweth* "report, give account of, inform of things unknown or wished to be known"'; and '*Ndangwetha* S[indarin] *Dangweth*'.

The *Dangweth Pengoloð* cannot be earlier than 1951, while from the date of the newspaper (on which the two texts are referred to) it cannot be later than the end of 1959. I would be inclined to place it earlier rather than later in the decade; possibly the second manuscript B is to be associated with the fine manuscript pages of the Tale of Years of the First Age (see X.49), one of which is reproduced as the frontispiece to *Morgoth's Ring*.

Version B follows A very closely indeed for the most part (which is probably an indication of their closeness in time): a scattering of very minor changes (small shifts in word-order and occasional alterations in vocabulary), with a very few more significant differences (see the notes at the end of the text). That it was a work of importance to my father is evident from his writing it again in a manuscript of such elegance; and an aspect of his thought here, in respect of the conscious introduction of change by the Eldar on the basis of an understanding of the phonological structure of their language in its entirety, would reappear years later in *The Shibboleth of Fëanor* (see p. 332 and note 3 to the present essay).

The text that follows is of course that of Version B, with alteration of a few points of punctuation for greater clarity.

Dangweth Pengoloð
the
Answer
of
Pengolod
to Aelfwine who asked him how came
it that the tongues of the Elves changed
and were sundered

Now you question me, Ælfwine, concerning the tongues of the Elves, saying that you wonder much to discover that they are many, akin indeed and yet unalike; for seeing that they die not and their memories reach back into ages long past, you understand not why all the race of the Quendi have not maintained the language that they had of old in common still one and the same in all their kindreds. But behold! Ælfwine, within Eä all things change, even the Valar; for in Eä we perceive the unfolding of a History in the unfolding: as a man may read a great book, and when it is full-read it is rounded and complete in his mind, according to his measure. Then at last he perceives that some fair thing that long endured: as some mountain or river of renown, some realm, or some great city; or else some mighty being, as a king, or maker, or a woman of beauty and majesty, or even one, maybe, of the Lords of the West: that each of these is, if at all, all that is said of them from the beginning even to the end. From the spring in the mountains to the mouths of the sea, all is Sirion; and from its first upwelling even to its passing away when the land was broken in the great battle, that also is Sirion, and nothing less. Though we, who are set to behold the great History, reading line by line, may speak of the river changing as it flows and grows broad, or dying as it is spilled or devoured by the sea. Yea, even from his first coming into Eä from the side of Ilúvatar, and from the young lord of the Valar in the white wrath of his battle with Melkor unto the silent king of years uncounted that sits upon the vanished heights of Oiolosse and watches but speaks no more: all that is he whom we call Manwë.

Now, verily, a great tree may outlive many a Man, and may remember the seed from which it came ere all the Men that now walk the earth were yet unborn, but the rind upon which you lay your hand, and the leaves which overshadow you, are not as that seed was, nor as the dry wood shall be that decays into the mould or passes in flame. And other trees there are that stand about, each different in growth and in shape, according to the chances of their lives, though all be akin, offspring of one yet older tree and sprung therefore from a single seed of long ago.[1] Immortal, within Eä, are the Eldar, but since even as Men they dwell in forms that come of Eä, they are no more changeless than the great trees, neither in the forms that they inhabit, nor in the things that they desire or achieve by means of those forms. Wherefore should they not then change in speech, of which one part is made with tongues and received by ears?

It hath been said by some among our loremasters that, as for Men, their elders teach to their children their speech and then soon depart, so that their voices are heard no more, and the children have no reminder of the tongue of their youth, save their own cloudy memories: wherefore in each brief generation of Men change may be swift and unrestrained. But this matter seemeth to me less simple. Weak indeed may be the memories of Men, but I say to you, Ælfwine, that even were your memory of your own being as clear as that of the wisest of the Eldar, still within the short span of your life your speech would change, and were you to live on with the life of the Elves it would change more, until looking back you would perceive that in your youth you spake an alien tongue.

For Men change both their old words for new, and their former manner of speaking for another manner, in their own lifetimes, and not only in the first learning of speech; and this change comes above all from the very changefulness of Eä; or if you will, from the nature of speech, which is fully living only when it is born, but when the union of the thought and the sound is fallen into old custom, and the two are no longer perceived apart, then already the word is dying and joyless,[2] the sound awaiting some new thought, and the thought eager for some new-patterned raiment of sound.

But to the changefulness of Eä, to weariness of the un-changed, to the renewing of the union: to these three, which are one, the Eldar also are subject in their degree. In this, however, they differ from Men, that they are ever more aware of the words that they speak. As a silversmith may remain more aware than others of the tools and vessels that he uses daily at his table, or a weaver of the texture of his garments. Yet this makes rather for change among the Eldar than for steadfastness; for the Eldar being skilled and eager in art will readily make things new, both for delight to look on, or to hear, or to feel, or for daily use: be it in vessels or raiment or in speech.

A man may indeed change his spoon or his cup at his will, and need ask none to advise him or to follow his choice. It is other indeed with words or the modes and devices of speech. Let him bethink him of a new word, be it to his heart howsoever fresh and fair, it will avail him little in converse, until other men are of like mind or will receive his invention. But among the Eldar there are many quick ears and subtle minds to hear and appraise such inventions, and though many be the patterns and devices so made that prove in the end only pleasing to a few, or to one alone, many others are welcomed and pass swiftly from mouth to mouth, with laughter or delight or with solemn thought – as maybe a new jest or new-found saying of wisdom will pass among men of brighter wit. For to the Eldar the making of speech is the oldest of the arts and the most beloved.

Wherefore, Ælfwine, I say to you: whereas the change that goes long unperceived, as the growth of a tree, was indeed slow of old in Aman ere the Rising of the Moon, and even in Middle-earth under the Sleep of Yavanna slower far than it is now among Men, yet among the Eldar this steadfastness was offset by the changes that come of will and design: many of which indeed differ little in outward seeming from those of unwitting growth. Thus the Eldar would alter the sounds of their speech at whiles to other sounds that seemed to them more pleasant, or were at the least unstaled. But this they would not do at haphazard. For the Eldar know their tongue, not word by word only, but as a whole: they know even as they speak not only of what sounds is that word woven which they are uttering, but of what sounds and sound-patterns is their whole speech at one time composed.[*3] Therefore none among the Eldar would change the sounds of some one word alone, but would rather change some one sound throughout the structure of his speech; nor would he bring into one word only some sound or union of sounds that had not before been present, but would replace

_____

*And these are for the most part few in number, for the Eldar being skilled in craft are not wasteful nor prodigal to small purpose, admiring in a tongue rather the skilled and harmonious use of a few well-balanced sounds than profusion ill-ordered.

some former sound by the new sound in all words that contained it – or if not in all, then in a number selected according to their shapes and other elements, as he is guided by some new pattern that he has in mind. Even as a weaver might change a thread from red to blue, either throughout his web, or in such parts thereof as were suitable to the new pattern, but not randomly here and there nor only in one corner.[4]

And lo! Ælfwine, these changes differ little from like changes that come in the speeches of Men with the passing of time. Now as for the Eldar we know that such things were done of old by choice, full-wittingly, and the names of those who made new words or first moved great changes are yet often remembered. For which reason the Eldar do not believe that in truth the changes in the tongues of Men are wholly unwitting; for how so, say they, comes the order and harmony that oft is seen in such changes? or the skill both in the devices that are replaced and the new that follow them? And some answer that the minds of Men are half asleep: by which they mean not that the part whereof Men are unaware and can give no account slumbers, but the other part. Others perceiving that in nothing do Men, and namely those of the West,[5] so nearly resemble the Eldar as in speech, answer that the teaching which Men had of the Elves in their youth works on still as a seed in the dark. But in all this maybe they err, Ælfwine, for despite all their lore least of all things do they know the minds of Men or understand them.[6]

And to speak of memory, Ælfwine: with regard to the Elves – for I know not how it is with Men – that which we call the *coirëa quenya*, the living speech, is the language wherethrough we think and imagine; for it is to our thought as the body to our spirit, growing and changing together in all the days of our being.[7] Into that language therefore we render at once whatsoever we recall out of the past that we heard or said ourselves. If a Man remembers some thing that he said in childhood, doth he recall the accents of childhood that he used in that moment long ago? I know not. But certainly we of the Quendi do not so. We may know indeed how children not yet accomplished in speech, and how the 'fullspoken', as we say, spake at times long ago, but that is a thing apart from the images of life-memory, and is a matter of lore. For we have much lore concerning the languages of old, whether stored in the mind or in writings; but we hear not ourselves speak again in the past save with the language that clothes our thought in the present. Verily, it may chance that in the past we spake with strangers in an alien tongue, and remember what was then said, but not the tongue that was used. Out of the past indeed we may recall the sounds of an alien speech as we may other sounds: the song of birds or the murmur of water; but that is but in some cry or brief phrase. For if the speech were long or the matter subtle then we clothe it in the living language of our present thought, and if we would now relate it as it was spoken, we must render it anew, as it were a book, into that other tongue – if it is preserved still in learned lore. And even so, it is the alien voices that we hear using words in our memory, seldom ourselves – or to speak of myself, never. It is true indeed that the Eldar readily learn to use other tongues skilfully, and are slow to forget any that they have learned, but these remain as they were learned, as were they written in the unchanging pages of a book;*[8] whereas the *coirëa quenya*, the language of thought, grows and lives within, and each new stage overlies those that went before, as the acorn and the sapling are hidden in the tree.

Wherefore, Ælfwine, if thou wilt consider well all that I have said to thee at this time, not only what is plainly expressed, but also what is therein to be discovered by thought, thou wilt now understand that, albeit more wittingly, albeit more slowly, the tongues of the Quendi change in a manner like to the changes of mortal tongues. And that if one of the Eldar survives maybe the chances of fifty thousand of your years, then the speech of his childhood will be sundered from the speech of his present, as maybe the speech of some city or kingdom of Men will be sundered in the days of its majesty from the tongue of those that founded it of old.

In this last point also our kindreds are alike. Greater as is the skill of the Quendi to mould things to their will and delight, and to overcome the chances of Eä, yet they are not as the Valar, and with regard to the might of the World and its fate, they are but weak and small. Therefore to them also severance is severance, and friends and kin far away are far away. Not even the Seeing

---

* Save only in the strange event of the learning by one whole people of an alien speech, that thereafter they take into living and daily use, which will then change and grow with them, but their own former tongue pass away or become but a matter of lore. This has happened only once in the history of the Eldalië, when the Exiles took up the speech of Beleriand, the Sindarin tongue, and the Noldorin was preserved among them as a language of lore.

Stones of the craftsmen of old could wholly unite those that were sundered, and they and the masters that could make them were few. Therefore change, witting or unwitting, was not even long ages ago shared, nor did it proceed alike save among those that met often and had converse in labour and in mirth. Thus, swifter or slower, yet ever inescapably, the far-sundered kindreds of the Quendi were sundered also in speech: the Avari from the Eldar; and the Teleri from the other Eldar; and the Sindar, who abode in Middle-earth, from the Teleri that came at last unto Aman; and the Exiles of the Noldor from those that remained in the land of the Valar. And so still it goes in Middle-earth.

Yet long since, Ælfwine, the fashion of the World was changed; and we that dwell now in the Ancient West are removed from the circles of the World, and in memory is the greater part of our being: so that now we preserve rather than make anew. Wherefore, though even in Aman – beyond the circles of Arda, yet still with Eä – change goes ever on, until the End, be it slow beyond perceiving save in ages of time, nonetheless here at last in Eressëa our tongues are steadfast; and here over a wide sea of years we speak now still little otherwise than we did – and those also that perished – in the wars of Beleriand, when the Sun was young.

Sin Quente Quendingoldo
Elendilenna

NOTES

1 The end of this sentence, from 'offspring of one yet older tree', is not found in version A.

2 'dying or dead' A.

3 In the note to *The Shibboleth of Fëanor* which I have omitted (p. 339) my father wrote:

> The Eldar had an instinctive grasp of the structure and sound-system of their speech as a whole, and this was increased by instruction; for in a sense all Eldarin languages were 'invented' languages, art-forms, not only inherited but also material engaging the active interest of their users and challenging awarely their own taste and inventiveness. This aspect was evidently still prominent in Valinor; though in Middle-earth it had waned, and the development of Sindarin had become, long before the arrival of the Ñoldorin exiles, mainly the product of unheeded change like the tongues of Men.

4   Version A has here a footnote omitted in B:

Thus it was that when the name *Banyai* of old was changed to *Vanyar* this was done only because the sound *b* was changed to *v* throughout the language (save in certain sequences) – and this change, it is recorded, began among the Vanyar; whereas for the showing of many the new device of *r* was brought in and used in all words of a certain shape – and this, it is said, was begun among the Noldor.

5   *namely* is used here in the original but long lost sense of the word, 'especially, above all'. The phrase is absent in A, which reads simply: 'Or some answer that the teaching ...'

6   Here version A, as originally written, moves at once to the concluding paragraphs of the *Dangweth*, from 'But in this point at least our kindreds are alike ...' (p. 400) to its ending in the words 'we speak now still little otherwise than they did who fought in Beleriand when the Sun was young.' These paragraphs were struck out, and all the intervening matter (from 'And to speak of memory, Ælfwine ...') introduced, before they were reached again, somewhat changed in expression but not in content, and now virtually identical to the form in version B.

7   This sentence, from 'for it is to our thought ...', is absent in A.

8   The footnote here is absent in A.

XV

OF LEMBAS

For the association of this brief work, extant in a single manuscript, with the *Dangweth Pengoloð* see p. 395. It is a finely written text of two pages, in style like that of the fine manuscript of the *Dangweth* which it accompanies, but not of the same quality, and on thin paper. My father introduced some illumination at its beginning in red ball-point pen, and with the same pen wrote at the head of the first page, above the title *Of Lembas*: '*Mana i·coimas in·Eldaron?*' *maquente Elendil* (the same question as appears on the cardboard folder enclosing the two texts, p. 395). At the same time he added quotation marks at the beginning and end of the text, showing that it is the answer of Pengoloð to Ælfwine's question, 'What is the *coimas* of the Eldar?' It seems possible that these additions in ball-point pen were added later, to make the text into a companion piece to the *Dangweth*; but there is in any case no evidence for date, beyond the limits of 1951 and 1959 (p. 395).

Of Lembas

'This food the Eldar alone knew how to make. It was made for the comfort of those who had need to go upon a long journey in the wild, or of the hurt whose life was in peril. Only these were permitted to use it. The Eldar did not give it to Men, save only to a few whom they loved, if they were in great need.*

The Eldar say that they first received this food from the Valar in the beginning of their days in the Great Journey. For it was made of a kind of corn which Yavanna brought forth in the fields of Aman, and some she sent to them by the hand of Oromë for their succour upon the long march.

---

* This was not done out of greed or jealousy, although at no time in Middle-earth was there great store of this food; but because the Eldar had been commanded to keep this gift in their own power, and not to make it common to the dwellers in mortal lands. For it is said that, if mortals eat often of this bread, they become weary of their mortality, desiring to abide among the Elves, and longing for the fields of Aman, to which they cannot come.

Since it came from Yavanna, the queen, or the highest among the elven-women of any people, great or small, had the keeping and gift of the *lembas*, for which reason she was called *massánie* or *besain*: the Lady, or breadgiver.[1]

Now this corn had in it the strong life of Aman, which it could impart to those who had the need and right to use the bread. If it was sown at any season, save in frost, it soon sprouted and grew swiftly, though it did not thrive in the shadow of plants of Middle-earth and would not endure winds that came out of the North while Morgoth dwelt there. Else it needed only a little sunlight to ripen; for it took swiftly and multiplied all the vigour of any light that fell on it.

The Eldar grew it in guarded lands and sunlit glades; and they gathered its great golden ears, each one, by hand, and set no blade of metal to it. The white haulm was drawn from the earth in like manner, and woven into corn-leeps[2] for the storing of the grain: no worm or gnawing beast would touch that gleaming straw, and rot and mould and other evils of Middle-earth did not assail it.

From the ear to the wafer none were permitted to handle this grain, save those elven-women who were called *Yavannildi* (or by the Sindar the *Ivonwin*),[3] the maidens of Yavanna; and the art of the making of the *lembas*, which they learned of the Valar, was a secret among them, and so ever has remained.'

Lembas is the Sindarin name, and comes from the older form *lenn-mbass* 'journey-bread'. In Quenya it was most often named *coimas* which is 'life-bread'.[4]

Quente Quengoldo.

NOTES

1   In the story of Túrin it is said of Melian's gift of *lembas* to Beleg the Bowman (*The Silmarillion* p. 202) that it was 'wrapped in leaves of silver, and the threads that bound it were sealed at the knots with the seal of the Queen, a wafer of white wax shaped as a single flower of Telperion; for according to the customs of the Eldalië the keeping and giving of *lembas* belonged to the Queen alone. In nothing did Melian show greater favour to Túrin than in this gift; for the Eldar had never before allowed Men to use this waybread, and seldom did so again.'

With '*massánie* or *besain*' cf. the entry in the *Etymologies*, V.372, stem MBAS 'knead': Quenya *masta*, Noldorin *bast*, 'bread'; also the words *lembas*, *coimas*, explained at the end of the present text as 'journey-bread' and 'life-bread'. Above the *ain* of *besain* is faintly pencilled *oneth*. sc. *besoneth*.

In using the word *Lady* here my father no doubt had an eye to its origin in Old English *hlǽf-dīġe*, of which the first element is *hlāf* (modern English *loaf*) with changed vowel, and the second a derivative of the stem *dīg-* 'knead' (to which *dough* is ultimately related); cf. *lord* from *hlāf-weard* 'bread-keeper'.

2 *haulm*: the stalks of cultivated plants left when the ears or pods have been gathered; *corn-leeps*: *leep (leap)* is an old dialect word for a basket (Old English *lēap*).

3 *Ivonwin*: the Noldorin (i.e. later Sindarin) form *Ivann* for *Yavanna* appears in the *Etymologies*, V.399, stem YAB 'fruit'.

4 This was written at the same time as the rest of the manuscript, but set in as printed, and was excluded from the quotation marks added later to the body of the text. The words *Quente Quengoldo* ('Thus spoke Pengoloð') also belong to the time of writing.

PART FOUR

UNFINISHED TALES

XVI

THE NEW SHADOW

This story, or fragment of a story, is now published for the first time, though its existence has long been known.[1] The textual history is not complicated, but there is a surprising amount of it.

There is, first, a collection of material in manuscript, beginning with two sides of a page carrying the original opening of the story: this goes no further than the recollection of the young man (here called Egalmoth)[2] of the rebuke and lecture that he received from Borlas[3] when caught by him stealing apples from his orchard as a boy. There is then a text, which I will call 'A', written in rapid but clear script, and this extends as far as the story ever went (here also the young man's name is Egalmoth). This was followed by a typescript in top copy and carbon 'B', which follows A pretty closely and ends at the same point: there are a great many small changes in expression, but nothing that alters the narrative in even minor ways (the young man, however, now bears the name Arthael). There is also an amanuensis typescript derived from B, without independent value.[4]

Finally, there is another typescript, 'C', also with carbon copy, which extends only to the point in the story where the young man – here named Saelon[5] – leaves Borlas in his garden 'searching back in his mind to discover how this strange and alarming conversation had begun' (p. 416). This text C treats B much as B treats A: altering the expression (fairly radically in places), but in no way altering the story, or giving to it new bearings.

It seems strange that my father should have made no less than three versions, each showing very careful attention to improvement of the text in detail, when the story had proceeded for so short a distance. The evidence of the typewriters used suggests, however, that C was made very substantially later. The machine on which B was typed was the one he used in the 1950s before the acquisition of that referred to in X.300, while the italic script of A could with some probability be ascribed to that time; but the typewriter used for C was his last.[6]

In his *Biography* (p. 228) Humphrey Carpenter stated that in 1965 my father 'found a typescript of "The New Shadow", a sequel to *The Lord of the Rings* which he had begun a long time ago but had abandoned after a few pages. ... He sat up till four a.m. reading it and thinking about it.' I do not know the source of this statement; but further evidence is provided by a used envelope, postmarked

8 January 1968, on the back of which my father scribbled a passage concerning Borlas, developing further the account of his circumstances at the time of the opening of the story (see note 14). This is certain evidence that he was still concerned with *The New Shadow* as late as 1968; and since the passage roughed out here would follow on from the point reached in the typescript C (see note 14) it seems very likely that C dates from that time.

Such as the evidence is, then, the original work (represented by the manuscript A and the typescript B) derives from the 1950s. In a letter of 13 May 1964 (*Letters* no.256) he wrote:

> I did begin a story placed about 100 years after the Downfall [of Sauron], but it proved both sinister and depressing. Since we are dealing with *Men* it is inevitable that we should be concerned with the most regrettable feature of their nature: their quick satiety with good. So that the people of Gondor in times of peace, justice and prosperity, would become discontented and restless – while the dynasts descended from Aragorn would become just kings and governors – like Denethor or worse. I found that even so early there was an outcrop of revolutionary plots, about a centre of secret Satanistic religion; while Gondorian boys were playing at being Orcs and going round doing damage. I could have written a 'thriller' about the plot and its discovery and overthrow – but it would be just that. Not worth doing.

From the evidence given above, however, it is seen that his interest in the story was subsequently reawakened, and even reached the point of making a new (though incomplete) version of what he had written of it years before. But in 1972, fifteen months before his death, he wrote to his friend Douglas Carter (*Letters* no.338):

> I have written nothing beyond the first few years of the Fourth Age. (Except the beginning of a tale supposed to refer to the end of the reign of Eldarion about 100 years after the death of Aragorn. Then I of course discovered that the King's Peace would contain no tales worth recounting; and his wars would have little interest after the overthrow of Sauron; but that almost certainly a restlessness would appear about then, owing to the (it seems) inevitable boredom of Men with the good: there would be secret societies practising dark cults, and 'orc-cults' among adolescents.)

To form the text that now follows I print C so far as it goes, with the sinister young man given the name Saelon; and from that point I give the text of B, changing the name from Arthael in B to Saelon.

THE NEW SHADOW

This tale begins in the days of Eldarion, son of that Elessar of whom the histories have much to tell. One hundred and five years had passed since the fall of the Dark Tower,[7] and the story of that time was little heeded now by most of the people of Gondor, though a few were still living who could remember the War of the Ring as a shadow upon their early childhood. One of these was old Borlas of Pen-arduin. He was the younger son of Beregond, the first Captain of the Guard of Prince Faramir, who had removed with his lord from the City to the Emyn Arnen.[8]

'Deep indeed run the roots of Evil,' said Borlas, 'and the black sap is strong in them. That tree will never be slain. Let men hew it as often as they may, it will thrust up shoots again as soon as they turn aside. Not even at the Feast of Felling should the axe be hung up on the wall!'

'Plainly you think you are speaking wise words,' said Saelon. 'I guess that by the gloom in your voice, and by the nodding of your head. But what is this all about? Your life seems fair enough still, for an aged man that does not now go far abroad. Where have you found a shoot of your dark tree growing? In your own garden?'

Borlas looked up, and as he glanced keenly at Saelon he wondered suddenly if this young man, usually gay and often half mocking, had more in his mind than appeared in his face. Borlas had not intended to open his heart to him, but being burdened in thought he had spoken aloud, more to himself than his companion. Saelon did not return his glance. He was humming softly, while he trimmed a whistle of green willow with a sharp nail-knife.

The two were sitting in an arbour near the steep eastern shore of Anduin where it flowed about the feet of the hills of Arnen. They were indeed in Borlas's garden and his small grey-stone house could be seen through the trees above them on the hill-slope facing west. Borlas looked at the river, and at the trees in their June leaves, and then far off to the towers of the City under the glow of late afternoon. 'No, not in my garden,' he said thoughtfully.

'Then why are you so troubled?' asked Saelon. 'If a man has a fair garden with strong walls, then he has as much as any man can govern for his own pleasure.' He paused. 'As long as he keeps the strength of life in him,' he added. 'When that fails, why trouble about any lesser ill? For then he must soon leave his garden at last, and others must look to the weeds.'

Borlas sighed, but he did not answer, and Saelon went on: 'But there are of course some who will not be content, and to their life's end they trouble their hearts about their neighbours, and the City, and the Realm, and all the wide world. You are one of them, Master Borlas, and have ever been so, since I first knew you as a boy that you caught in your orchard. Even then you were not content to let ill alone: to deter me with a beating, or to strengthen your fences. No. You were grieved and wanted to improve me. You had me into your house and talked to me.

'I remember it well. "Orcs' work," you said many times. "Stealing good fruit, well, I suppose that is no worse than boys' work, if they are hungry, or their fathers are too easy. But pulling down unripe apples to break or cast away! That is Orcs' work. How did you come to do such a thing, lad?"

'*Orcs' work!* I was angered by that, Master Borlas, and too proud to answer, though it was in my heart to say in child's words: "If it was wrong for a boy to steal an apple to eat, then it is wrong to steal one to play with. But not more wrong. Don't speak to me of Orcs' work, or I may show you some!"

'It was a mistake, Master Borlas. For I had heard tales of the Orcs and their doings, but I had not been interested till then. You turned my mind to them. I grew out of petty thefts (my father was not too easy), but I did not forget the Orcs. I began to feel hatred and think of the sweetness of revenge. We played at Orcs, I and my friends, and sometimes I thought: "Shall I gather my band and go and cut down his trees? Then he will think that the Orcs have really returned." But that was a long time ago,' Saelon ended with a smile.

Borlas was startled. He was now receiving confidences, not giving them. And there was something disquieting in the young man's tone, something that made him wonder whether deep down, as deep as the roots of the dark trees, the childish resentment did not still linger. Yes, even in the heart of Saelon, the friend of his own son, and the young man who had in the last few years shown him much kindness in his loneliness.[9] At any rate he resolved to say no more of his own thoughts to him.

'Alas!' he said, 'we all make mistakes. I do not claim wisdom, young man, except maybe the little that one may glean with the passing of the years. From which I know well enough the sad truth that those who mean well may do more harm than those who let things be. I am sorry now for what I said, if it roused hate in your heart. Though I still think that it was just:

untimely maybe, and yet true. Surely even a boy must understand that fruit is fruit, and does not reach its full being until it
is ripe; so that to misuse it unripe is to do worse than just to rob
the man that has tended it: it robs the world, hinders a good
thing from fulfilment. Those who do so join forces with all that
is amiss, with the blights and the cankers and the ill winds. And
that was the way of Orcs.'

'And is the way of Men too,' said Saelon. 'No! I do not mean
of wild men only, or those who grew "under the Shadow", as
they say. I mean all Men. I would not misuse green fruit now,
but only because I have no longer any use for unripe apples,
not for your lofty reasons, Master Borlas. Indeed I think your
reasons as unsound as an apple that has been too long in store.
To trees all Men are Orcs. Do Men consider the fulfilment of
the life-story of a tree before they cut it down? For whatever
purpose: to have its room for tilth, to use its flesh as timber or
as fuel, or merely to open the view? If trees were the judges,
would they set Men above Orcs, or indeed above the cankers
and blights? What more right, they might ask, have Men to feed
on their juices than blights?'

'A man,' said Borlas, 'who tends a tree and guards it from
blights and many other enemies does not act like an Orc or a
canker. If he eats its fruit, he does it no injury. It produces fruit
more abundantly than it needs for its own purpose: the continuing of its kind.'

'Let him eat the fruit then, or play with it,' said Saelon. 'But I
spoke of slaying: hewing and burning; and by what right men
do such things to trees.'

'You did not. You spoke of the judgement of trees in these
matters. But trees are not judges. The children of the One are
the masters. My judgement as one of them you know already.
The evils of the world were not at first in the great Theme, but
entered with the discords of Melkor. Men did not come with
these discords; they entered afterwards as a new thing direct
from Eru, the One, and therefore they are called His children,
and all that was in the Theme they have, for their own good,
the right to use – rightly, without pride or wantonness, but with
reverence.[10]

'If the smallest child of a woodman feels the cold of winter,
the proudest tree is not wronged, if it is bidden to surrender its
flesh to warm the child with fire. But the child must not mar
the tree in play or spite, rip its bark or break its branches. And

the good husbandman will use first, if he can, dead wood or an old tree; he will not fell a young tree and leave it to rot, for no better reason than his pleasure in axe-play. That is orkish.

'But it is even as I said: the roots of Evil lie deep, and from far off comes the poison that works in us, so that many do these things – at times, and become then indeed like the servants of Melkor. But the Orcs did these things at all times; they did harm with delight to all things that could suffer it, and they were restrained only by lack of power, not by either prudence or mercy. But we have spoken enough of this.'

'Why!' said Saelon. 'We have hardly begun. It was not of your orchard, nor your apples, nor of me, that you were thinking when you spoke of the re-arising of the dark tree. What you were thinking of, Master Borlas, I can guess nonetheless. I have eyes and ears, and other senses, Master.' His voice sank low and could scarcely be heard above the murmur of a sudden chill wind in the leaves, as the sun sank behind Mindolluin. 'You have heard then the name?' With hardly more than breath he formed it. 'Of Herumor?'[11]

Borlas looked at him with amazement and fear. His mouth made tremulous motions of speech, but no sound came from it.

'I see that you have,' said Saelon. 'And you seem astonished to learn that I have heard it also. But you are not more astonished than I was to see that this name has reached you. For, as I say, I have keen eyes and ears, but yours are now dim even for daily use, and the matter has been kept as secret as cunning could contrive.'

'Whose cunning?' said Borlas, suddenly and fiercely. The sight of his eyes might be dim, but they blazed now with anger.

'Why, those who have heard the call of the name, of course,' answered Saelon unperturbed. 'They are not many yet, to set against all the people of Gondor, but the number is growing. Not all are content since the Great King died, and fewer now are afraid.'

'So I have guessed,' said Borlas, 'and it is that thought that chills the warmth of summer in my heart. For a man may have a garden with strong walls, Saelon, and yet find no peace or content there. There are some enemies that such walls will not keep out; for his garden is only part of a guarded realm after all. It is to the walls of the realm that he must look for his real defence. But what is the call? What would they do?' he cried, laying his hand on the young man's knee.

'I will ask you a question first before I answer yours,' said Saelon; and now he looked searchingly at the old man. 'How have you, who sit here in the Emyn Arnen and seldom go now even to the City – how have you heard the whispers of this name?'

Borlas looked down on the ground and clasped his hands between his knees. For some time he did not answer. At last he looked up again; his face had hardened and his eyes were more wary. 'I will not answer that, Saelon,' he said. 'Not until I have asked you yet another question. First tell me,' he said slowly, 'are you one of those who have listened to the call?'

A strange smile flickered about the young man's mouth. 'Attack is the best defence,' he answered, 'or so the Captains tell us; but when both sides use this counsel there is a clash of battle. So I will counter you. I will not answer you, Master Borlas, until you tell me: are you one of those who have listened, or no?'

'How can you think it?' cried Borlas.

'And how can *you* think it?' asked Saelon.

'As for me,' said Borlas, 'do not all my words give you the answer?'

'But as for me, you would say,' said Saelon, 'my words might make me doubtful? Because I defended a small boy who threw unripe apples at his playmates from the name of Orc? Or because I spoke of the suffering of trees at the hands of men? Master Borlas, it is unwise to judge a man's heart from words spoken in an argument without respect for your opinions. They may be meant to disturb you. Pert maybe, but possibly better than a mere echo.[12] I do not doubt that many of those we spoke of would use words as solemn as yours, and speak reverently of the Great Theme and such things – in your presence. Well, who shall answer first?'

'The younger it would have been in the courtesy of old,' said Borlas; 'or between men counted as equals, the one who was first asked. You are both.'

Saelon smiled. 'Very well,' he said. 'Let me see: the first question that you asked unanswered was: *what is the call, what would they do?* Can you find no answer in the past for all your age and lore? I am young and less learned. Still, if you really wish to know, I could perhaps make the whispers clearer to you.'

He stood up. The sun had set behind the mountains; shadows were deepening. The western wall of Borlas's house on the hill-side was yellow in the afterglow, but the river below was dark. He looked up at the sky, and then away down the Anduin. 'It is a fair evening still,' he said, 'but the wind has shifted eastward. There will be clouds over the moon tonight.'

'Well, what of it?' said Borlas, shivering a little as the air chilled. 'Unless you mean only to warn an old man to hasten indoors and keep his bones from aching.' He rose and turned to the path towards his house, thinking that the young man meant to say no more; but Saelon stepped up beside him and laid a hand on his arm.

'I warn you rather to clothe yourself warmly after nightfall,' he said. 'That is, if you wish to learn more; for if you do, you will come with me on a journey tonight. I will meet you at your eastern gate behind your house; or at least I shall pass that way as soon as it is full dark, and you shall come or not as you will. I shall be clad in black, and anyone who goes with me must be clad alike. Farewell now, Master Borlas! Take counsel with yourself while the light lasts.'

With that Saelon bowed and turned away, going along another path that ran near the edge of the steep shore, away northward to the house of his father.[13] He disappeared round a bend while his last words were still echoing in Borlas's ears.

For some while after Saelon had gone Borlas stood still, covering his eyes and resting his brow against the cool bark of a tree beside the path. As he stood he searched back in his mind to discover how this strange and alarming conversation had begun. What he would do after nightfall he did not yet consider.

He had not been in good spirits since the spring, though well enough in body for his age, which burdened him less than his loneliness.[14] Since his son, Berelach,[15] had gone away again in April – he was in the Ships, and now lived mostly near Pelargir where his duty was – Saelon had been most attentive, whenever he was at home. He went much about the lands of late. Borlas was not sure of his business, though he understood that, among other interests, he dealt in timber. He brought news from all over the kingdom to his old friend. Or to his friend's old father; for Berelach had been his constant companion at one time, though they seemed seldom to meet nowadays.

'Yes, that was it,' Borlas said to himself. 'I spoke to Saelon of Pelargir, quoting Berelach. There has been some small disquiet down at the Ethir: a few shipmen have disappeared, and also a small vessel of the Fleet. Nothing much, according to Berelach.

' "Peace makes things slack," he said, I remember, in the voice of an under-officer. "Well, they went off on some ploy of their own, I suppose – friends in one of the western havens, perhaps – without leave and without a pilot, and they were drowned. It serves them right. We get too few real sailors these days. Fish are more profitable. But at least all know that the west coasts are not safe for the unskilled."

'That was all. But I spoke of it to Saelon, and asked if he had heard anything of it away south. "Yes," he said, "I did. Few were satisfied with the official view. The men were not unskilled; they were sons of fishermen. And there have been no storms off the coasts for a long time." '

As he heard Saelon say this, suddenly Borlas had remembered the other rumours, the rumours that Othrondir[16] had spoken of. It was he who had used the word 'canker'. And then half to himself Borlas had spoken aloud about the Dark Tree.

He uncovered his eyes and fondled the shapely trunk of the tree that he had leaned on, looking up at its shadowy leaves against the clear fading sky. A star glinted through the branches. Softly he spoke again, as if to the tree.

'Well, what is to be done now? Clearly Saelon is in it. But is it clear? There was the sound of mockery in his words, and scorn of the ordered life of Men. He would not answer a straight question. The black clothes! And yet – why invite me to go with him? Not to convert old Borlas! Useless. Useless to try: no one would hope to win over a man who remembered the Evil of old, however far off. Useless if one succeeded: old Borlas is of no use any longer as a tool for any hand. Saelon might be trying to play the spy, seeking to find out what lies behind the whispers. Black might be a disguise, or an aid to stealth by night. But again, what could I do to help on any secret or dangerous errand? I should be better out of the way.'

With that a cold thought touched Borlas's heart. Put out of the way – was that it? He was to be lured to some place where he could disappear, like the Shipmen? The invitation to go with Saelon had been given only after he had been startled into revealing that he knew of the whispers – had even heard the name. And he had declared his hostility.

This thought decided Borlas, and he knew that he was resolved now to stand robed in black at the gate in the first dark of night. He was challenged, and he would accept. He smote his palm against the tree. 'I am not a dotard yet, Neldor,' he said; 'but death is not so far off that I shall lose many good years, if I lose the throw.'

He straightened his back and lifted his head, and walked away up the path, slowly but steadily. The thought crossed his mind even as he stepped over the threshold: 'Perhaps I have been preserved so long for this purpose: that one should still live, hale in mind, who remembers what went before the Great Peace. Scent has a long memory. I think I could still smell the old Evil, and know it for what it is.'

The door under the porch was open; but the house behind was darkling. There seemed none of the accustomed sounds of evening, only a soft silence, a dead silence. He entered, wondering a little. He called, but there was no answer. He halted in the narrow passage that ran through the house, and it seemed that he was wrapped in a blackness: not a glimmer of twilight of the world outside remained there. Suddenly he smelt it, or so it seemed, though it came as it were from within outwards to the sense: he smelt the old Evil and knew it for what it was.

Here, both in A and B, *The New Shadow* ends, and it will never be known what Borlas found in his dark and silent house, nor what part Saelon was playing and what his intentions were. There would be no tales worth the telling in the days of the King's Peace, my father said; and he disparaged the story that he had begun: 'I could have written a "thriller" about the plot and its discovery and overthrow – but it would be just that. Not worth doing.' It would nonetheless have been a very remarkable 'thriller', and one may well view its early abandonment with regret. But it may be that his reason for abandoning it was not only this – or perhaps rather that in saying this he was expressing a deeper conviction: that the vast structure of story, in many forms, that he had raised came to its true end in the Downfall of Sauron. As he wrote (*Morgoth's Ring* p. 404): 'Sauron was a problem that Men had to deal with finally: the first of the many concentrations of Evil into definite power-points that they would have to combat, *as it was also the last of those in "mythological" personalized (but non-human) form.*'

NOTES

1 It has also been read publicly, by myself (Sheldonian Theatre, Oxford, 18 August 1992). At that time, not having studied the papers with sufficient care, I was under the impression that text B was the latest, and it was this that I read – the young man's name being therefore Arthael.

2   In the original draft of the opening of the story (preceding A) the name was first written *Álmoth*, but changed immediately to Egalmoth. The original *Egalmoth* was the lord of the people of the Heavenly Arch in Gondolin; it was also the name of the eighteenth Ruling Steward of Gondor.

3   *Borlas* was the name of the eldest son of Bór the Easterling, later changed to *Borlad* (XI.240); he was slain in the Battle of Unnumbered Tears, faithful to the Eldar.

4   The first page of this was typed on the machine that my father first used about the end of 1958 (X.300), and the remainder on the previous one (that used for text B).

5   The name *Saelon* is found in drafting for the *Athrabeth Finrod ah Andreth* as a name of the wise-woman Andreth of the Edain, who debated with Finrod; in the final text this became *Saelind*, translated 'Wise-heart' (X.305, 351–2).

6   This is the machine on which the very late 'historical-etymological' essays were typed, and which I use to this day.

7   A puzzling question is raised by this dating, concerning the historical period in which the story is set. In the opening paragraph the original draft (preceding A) has:

> It was in the days of Eldarion, son of that Elessar of whom ancient histories have much to tell, that this strange thing occurred. It was indeed less than one hundred and twenty years since the fall of the Dark Tower ...

The first complete text, the manuscript A, has: 'Nearly one hundred and ten years had passed since the fall of the Dark Tower', and this is repeated in B. My father typed the opening page of the late text C in two closely similar forms, and in the first of these he retained the reading of A and B, but in the second (printed here) he wrote 'One hundred and five years'. In the letter of 1964 cited on p. 410 he said 'about 100 years after the Downfall', and in that of 1972 (*ibid.*) 'about 100 years after the death of Aragorn'. We thus have, in chronological order of their appearance, the following dates after the fall of the Dark Tower:

> less than 120 years (original opening of the story);
> nearly 110 years (A and B);
> about 100 years (letter of 1964);
> nearly 110 years (first copy of the opening page of C, c.1968);
> 105 years (second copy of the opening page of C).

The fall of the Dark Tower took place in the year 3019 of the Third Age, and that Age was held to have been concluded at the end of 3021; thus the dates from the fall of the Tower (in the same order, and making them for brevity definite rather than approximate) are Fourth Age 118, 108, 98, 108, 103. Thus every date given in the texts (and that in the letter of 1964) places the story *before* the death of Aragorn – which took place in Fourth Age

120 = Shire Reckoning 1541 (Appendix B, at end); yet every one of the texts refers it to the days of his son Eldarion.

The solution of this must lie in the fact that in the First Edition of *The Lord of the Rings* (*ibid.*) Aragorn's death was placed twenty years earlier, in Shire Reckoning 1521, i.e. Fourth Age 100. The date given in the letter of 1964 ('about 100 years after the Downfall') is indeed too early even according to the dating of the First Edition, but that is readily explained as being a rough approximation appropriate in the context. More puzzling are the dates given in the two versions of the first page of the late text C, which do not agree with the date of Aragorn's death in the Second Edition (1966). The first of these ('nearly 110 years') can be explained as merely taking up the reading of text B, which my father was following; but in the second version he evidently gave thought to the date, for he changed it to '105 years': that is, Fourth Age 103. I am at a loss to explain this.

In the letter of 1972 he gave a much later date, placing the story in about Fourth Age 220 (and giving to Eldarion a reign of at least 100 years).

8   See *The Return of the King* (chapter *The Steward and the King*), p. 247.

9   Both A and B have 'sons' for 'son', and they do not have the words 'in his loneliness'. With the latter difference cf. the last sentence of the C text and its difference from B (note 14).

10 This passage in the argument was expressed rather differently in B (which was following A almost exactly):

'A man,' said Borlas, 'who tends a tree and guards it from blights, and eats its fruit – which it produces more abundantly than its mere life-need; not that eating the fruit need destroy the seed – does not act like a canker, nor like an Orc.

'But as for the cankers, I wonder. They live, it might be said, and yet their life is death. I do not believe that they were part of the Music of the Ainur, unless in the discords of Melkor. And so with Orcs.'

'And what of Men?' said Arthael.

'Why do you ask?' said Borlas. 'You know, surely, what is taught? They were not at first in the Great Music, but they did not enter with the discords of Melkor: they came from Ilúvatar himself, and therefore they are called the Children of God. And all that is in the Music they have a right to use – rightly: which is with reverence, not with pride or wantonness.'

11 The name *Herumor* is found in *Of the Rings of Power and the Third Age* (*The Silmarillion* p. 293) as that of a renegade Númenórean who became powerful among the Haradrim in the time before the war of the Last Alliance.

12 B (exactly repeating A) has here: 'No, Master Borlas, in such a matter one cannot judge words by the shape they are spoken in.'

13 A has here 'his father Duilin'. This, like Egalmoth, is another name from the story of Gondolin: Duilin was the leader of the people of the Swallow, who fell from the battlements when 'smitten by a fiery bolt of the Balrogs' (II.178). It was also the original name of the father of Flinding, later Gwindor, of Nargothrond (II.79, etc.): Duilin > Fuilin > Guilin.

14 At this point C comes to an end, at the foot of a page. B has here: 'He had not been in good health since the spring; old age was gaining upon him' (see note 9). From here onwards, as noted earlier, I follow text B, changing the name Arthael to Saelon. – The passage written on an envelope postmarked 8 January 1968, referred to on pp. 409–10, would follow from this point in C; it reads (the last phrases being very difficult to make out):

> For he lived now with only two old servants, retired from the Prince's guard, in which he himself had once held office. Long ago his daughter had married and now lived in distant parts of the realm, and then ten years ago his wife had died. Time had softened his grief, while Berelach [his son] was still near home. He was his youngest child and only son, and was in the King's ships; for several years he had been stationed at the Harlond within easy reach by water, and spent much time with his father. But it was three years now since he had been given a high command, and was often long at sea, and when on land duty still held him at Pelargir far away. His visits had been few and brief. Saelon, who formerly came only when Berelach [? ... been his old friend] was with Borlas, but had been most attentive when he was in Emyn Arnen. Always in to talk or bring news, or [?run] any service he could

For the site of 'the quays and landings of the Harlond' see *The Return of the King* (chapter *Minas Tirith*), p. 22.

15 Borlas is described at the beginning of the story as the younger son of Beregond, and he was thus the brother of Bergil son of Beregond who was Pippin's companion in Minas Tirith. In A Borlas gave the name *Bergil* to his own son (preceded by *Berthil*).

16 For *Othrondir* A has *Othrondor*.

XVII

TAL-ELMAR

The tale of Tal-Elmar, so far as it went, is preserved in a folded paper, bearing dates in 1968, on which my father wrote the following hasty note:

Tal-Elmar

Beginnings of a tale that sees the Númenóreans from the point of view of the Wild Men. It was begun without much consideration of geography (or the situation as envisaged in The Lord of the Rings). But either it must remain as a separate tale only vaguely linked with the developed Lord of the Rings history, or – and I think so – it must recount the coming of the Númenóreans (Elf-friends) *before the Downfall*, and represent their choice of permanent havens. So the geography must be made to fit that of the mouths of Anduin and the Langstrand.

But that was written thirteen years after he had abandoned the story, and there is no sign that he returned to it in his last years. Brief as it is, and (as it seems) uncertain of direction, such a departure from all other narrative themes within the compass of Middle-earth will form perhaps a fitting conclusion to this History.

The text is in two parts. The first is a typescript of six sides that breaks off in the middle of a sentence (p. 432); but the first part of this is extant also in a rejected page, part typescript and part manuscript (see note 5). Beyond this point the entire story is in the first stage of composition. The second part is a manuscript on which my father wrote 'Continuation of Tal-Elmar' and the date January 1955; there is no indication of how long a time elapsed between the two parts, but I believe that the typescript belongs also to the 1950s. It is remarkable that he should have been working on it during the time of extreme pressure between the publication of *The Two Towers* and that of *The Return of the King*. This manuscript takes up the story from the point where it was left in the typescript, but does not complete the unfinished sentence; it becomes progressively more difficult, and in one section is at the very limit of legibility, with some words uninterpretable. Towards the end the narrative breaks up into experimental passages and questionings. With a few exceptions I do not record corrections to the text and give only the later reading; and in one or two cases I have altered inconsistent uses of 'thou' and 'you'.

In the days of the Dark Kings, when a man could still walk dry-shod from the Rising of the Sun to the Sea of its setting, there lived in the fenced town of his people in the green hills of Agar an old man, by name Hazad Longbeard.[1] Two prides he had: in the number of his sons (seventeen in all), and in the length of his beard (five feet without stretching); but his joy in his beard was the greater. For it remained with him, and was soft, and ruly to his hand, whereas his sons for the most part were gone from him, and those that remained, or came ever nigh, were neither gentle nor ruly. They were indeed much as Hazad himself had been in the days of his youth: broad, swarthy, short, tough, harsh-tongued, heavy-handed, and quick to violence.

Save one only, and he was the youngest. Tal-elmar Hazad his father named him. He was yet but eighteen years of age, and lived with his father, and the two of his brothers next elder. He was tall, and white-skinned, and there was a light in his grey eyes that would flash to fire, if he were wroth; and though that happened seldom, and never without great cause, it was a thing to remember and be ware of. Those who had seen that fire called him Flint-eye, and respected him, whether they loved him or no. For Tal-elmar might seem, among that swart sturdy folk, slender-built and lacking in the strength of leg and neck that they praised, but a man that strove with him soon found him strong beyond guess, and sudden and swift, hard to grapple and harder to elude.

A fair voice he had, which made even the rough tongue of that people more sweet to hear, but he spoke not over much; and he would stand often aloof, when others were chattering, with a look on his face that men read rightly as pride, yet it was not the pride of a master, but rather the pride of one of alien race, whom fate has cast away among an ignoble people, and there bound him in servitude. For indeed Tal-elmar laboured hard and at menial tasks, being but the youngest son of an old man, who had little wealth left save his beard and a repute for wisdom. But strange to say (in that town) he served his father willingly, and loved him, more than all his brothers in one, and more than was the wont of any sons in that land. Indeed it was most often on his father's behalf that the flint-flash was seen in his eyes.

For Tal-elmar had a strange belief (whence it came was a wonder) that the old should be treated kindly and with courtesy, and should be suffered to live out their life-days in such ease as they could. 'If ye must gainsay them,' he said, 'let it be done with respect; for they have seen many years, and many times, maybe, have they faced the evils which we come to untried. And grudge not their food and their room, for they have laboured longer than have ye, and do but receive now, belatedly, part of the payment that is due to them.' Such plain folly had no effect on the manners of his people, but it was law in his house; and it was now two years since either of his brothers had dared to break it.[2]

Hazad loved this youngest son dearly, in return for his love, yet even more for another cause which he kept in his heart: that his face and his voice reminded him of another that he long had missed. For Hazad also had been the youngest son of his mother, and she died in his boyhood; and she was not of their people. Such was the tale that he had overheard, not openly spoken indeed, for it was held no credit to the house: she came of the strange folk, hateful and proud, of which there was rumour in the west-lands, coming out of the East, it was said. Fair, tall, and flint-eyed they were, with bright weapons made by demons in the fiery hills. Slowly they were thrusting towards the shores of the Sea, driving before them the ancient dwellers in the lands.

Not without resistance. There were wars on the east-marches, and since the older folk were yet numerous, the in-comers would at times suffer great loss and be flung back. Indeed little had been heard of them in the Hills of Agar, far to the west, for more than a man's life, since that great battle of which songs were yet sung. In the valley of Ishmalog it had been fought, the wise in lore told, and there a great host of the Fell folk had been ambushed in a narrow place and slaughtered in heaps. And in that day many captives were taken; for this had been no affray on the borders, or fight with advance guards: a whole people of the Fell Folk had been on the move, with their wains and their cattle and their women.

Now Buldar, father of Hazad, had been in the army of the North King[3] that went to the muster of Ishmalog,[4] and he brought back from the war as booty a wound, and a sword, and a woman. And she was fortunate; for the fate of the captives was short and cruel, but Buldar took her as his wife. For she was beautiful, and having looked on her he desired no woman of his own folk. He was a man of wealth and power in those days, and did as he would, scorning the scorn of his neighbours. But when his wife, Elmar, had learned at length enough of the speech of her new kin, she said to Buldar on a day: 'I have much to thank thee for, lord; but think not ever to get my love so. For thou hast torn me from my own people, and from him that I loved and from the child that I bore him. For them ever shall I yearn and grieve, and give love to none else. Never again shall I be glad, while I am held captive among a strange folk that I deem base and unlovely.'

'So be it,' said Buldar. 'But it is not to be thought that I should let thee go free. For thou art precious in my sight. And consider well: vain is it to seek to escape from me. Long is the way to the remnant of thy folk, if any still live; and thou wouldst not go far from the Hills of Agar ere thou met death, or a life far worse than shall be thine in my house. Base and unlovely thou namest us. Truly, maybe. Yet true is it also that thy folk are cruel, and lawless, and the friends of demons. Thieves are they. For our lands are ours from of old, which they would wrest from us with their bitter blades. White skins and bright eyes are no warrant for such deeds.'

'Are they not?' said she. 'Then neither are thick legs and wide shoulders. Or by what means did ye gain these lands that ye boast of? Are there not, as I hear men say, wild folk in the caves of the mountains, who once roamed here free, ere ye swart folk came hither and hunted them like wolves? But I spoke not of rights, but of sorrow and love. If here I must dwell, then dwell I must, as one whose body is in this place at thy will, but my thought far elsewhere. And this vengeance I will have, that while my body is kept here in exile, the lot of all this folk shall worsen, and thine most; but when my body goes to the alien earth, and my thought is free of it, then in thy kin one shall arise who is mine alone. And with his arising shall come the end of thy people and the downfall of your king.'

Thereafter Elmar said no more on this matter; and she was indeed a woman of few words while her life lasted, save only to her children. To them she spoke much when none were by, and she sang to them many songs in a strange fair tongue; but they heeded her not, or soon forgot. Save only Hazad, the youngest; and though he was, as were all her children, unlike her in body, he was nearer to her in heart. The songs and the strange tongue he too forgot, when he grew up, but his mother he never forgot; and he took a wife late, for no woman of his own folk seemed desirable to him that knew what beauty in a woman might be.[5]

Not that many were his for the wooing, for, even as Elmar had spoken, the people of Agar had waned with the years, what with ill weathers and with pests, and most of all were Buldar and his sons afflicted; and they had become poor, and other kindreds had taken their power from them. But Hazad knew naught of the foreboding of his mother, and in her memory loved Tal-elmar, and had so named him at birth.

And it chanced on a morning of spring that when his other sons went out to labour Hazad kept Tal-elmar at his side, and they walked forth together and sat upon the green hill-top above the town of their people; and they looked out south and west to where they could see far away the great bight of the Sea that drove in on the land, and it was shimmering like grey glass. And the eyes of Hazad were growing dim with age, but Tal-elmar's were keen, and he saw as he thought three strange birds upon the water, white in the sun, and they were drifting with the west wind towards the land; and he wondered that they sat upon the sea and did not fly.

'I see three strange birds upon the water, father,' he said. 'They are unlike any that I have seen before.'

'Keen may be thine eyes in youth, my son,' said Hazad, 'but birds on the water thou canst not see. Three leagues away are the nearest shores of the Sea from where we sit. The sun dazzles thee, or some dream is on thee.'

'Nay, the sun is behind me,' said Tal-elmar. 'I see what I see. And if they be not birds, what are they? Very great must they be, greater than the Swans of Gorbelgod,[6] of which legends tell. And lo! I see now another that comes behind, but less clearly, for its wings are black.'

Then Hazad was troubled. 'A dream is on thee, as I said, my son,' he answered; 'but an ill dream. Is not life here hard enough, that when spring is come and winter is over at last thou must bring a vision out of the black past?'

'Thou forgettest, father,' said Tal-elmar, 'that I am thy youngest son, and whereas thou has taught much lore to the dull ears of my brethren, to me thou hast given less of thy store. I know nothing of what is in thy mind.'

'Dost thou not?' said Hazad, striking his brow as he stared out towards the Sea. 'Yes, mayhap it is a long while since I spoke of it; it is but the shadow of a dream in the back of my thought. Three folk we hold as enemies. The wild men of the mountains and the woods; but these only those who stray alone need fear.

The Fell Folk of the East; but they are yet far away, and they are my mother's people, though, I doubt not, they would not honour the kinship, if they came here with their swords. And the High Men of the Sea. These indeed we may dread as Death. For Death they worship and slay men cruelly in honour of the Dark. Out of the Sea they came, and if they ever had any land of their own, ere they came to the west-shores, we know not where it may be. Black tales come to us out of the coast-lands, north and south, where they have now long time established their dark fortresses and their tombs. But hither they have not come since my father's days, and then only to raid and catch men and depart. Now this was the manner of their coming. They came in boats, but not such as some of our folk use that dwell nigh the great rivers or the lakes, for ferrying or fishing. Greater than great houses are the ships of the Go-hilleg, and they bear store of men and goods, and yet are wafted by the winds; for the Sea-men spread great cloths like wings to catch the airs, and bind them to tall poles like trees of the forest. Thus they will come to the shore, where there is shelter, or as nigh as they may; and then they will send forth smaller boats laden with goods, and strange things both beautiful and useful such as our folk covet. These they will sell to us for small price, or give as gifts, feigning friendship, and pity for our need; and they will dwell a while, and spy out the land and the numbers of the folk, and then go. And if they do not return, men should be thankful. For if they come again it is in other guise. In greater numbers they come then: two ships or more together, stuffed with men and not goods, and ever one of the accursed ships hath black wings. For that is the Ship of the Dark, and in it they bear away evil booty, captives packed like beasts, the fairest women and children, or young men unblemished, and that is their end. Some say that they are eaten for meat; and others that they are slain with torment on the black stones in the worship of the Dark. Both maybe are true. The foul wings of the Sea-men have not been seen in these waters for many a year; but remembering the shadow of fear in the past I cried out, and cry again: is not our life hard enough without the vision of a black wing upon the shining sea?'

'Hard enough, indeed,' said Tal-elmar, 'yet not so hard that I would leave it yet. Come! If what you tell is good sooth we should run to the town and warn men, and make ready for flight or for defence.'

'I come,' said Hazad. 'But be not astonished, if men laugh at me for a dotard. They believe little that has not happened in their own days. And have a care, dear son! I am in little danger, save to starve in a town empty of all but the crazed and the aged. But thee the Dark Ship would take among the first. Put thyself not forward in any rash counsel of battle.'

'We will see,' answered Tal-elmar. 'But thou art my chief care in this town, where I have and give little love. I will not willingly part from thy side. Yet this is the town of my folk, and our home, and those who can are bound to defend it, I deem.'

So Hazad and his son went down the hill-side, and it was noon; and in the town were few people, but crones and children, for all the able-bodied were abroad in the fields, busy with the hard toil of spring. There was no watch, for the Hills of Agar were far from hostile borders where the power of the Fourth King⁷ ended. The town-master sat by the door of his house in the sun, dozing or idly watching the small birds that gathered scraps of food from the dry beaten mud of the open place in the midst of the houses.

'Hail! Master of Agar!' said Hazad, and bowed low; but the master, a fat man with eyes like a lizard, blinked at him, and did not return his greeting.

'Sit hail, Master! And long may you sit so!' said Tal-elmar, and there was a glint in his eye. 'We should not disturb your thought, or your sleep, but there are tidings that, maybe, you should heed. There is no watch kept, but we chanced to be on the hill-top, and we saw the sea far off, and there – birds of ill omen on the water.'

'Ships of the Go-hilleg,' said Hazad, 'with great wind-cloths. Three white – and one black.'

The master yawned. 'As for thee, blear-eyed carl,' he said, 'thou couldst not tell the sea itself from a cloud. And as for this idle lad, what knows he of boats or wind-cloths, or all the rest, save from thy crazed teaching? Go to the travelling knappers⁸ with thy crone-tales of Go-hilleg, and trouble me not with such folly. I have other matters of more weight to ponder.'

Hazad swallowed his wrath, for the Master was powerful and loved him not; but Tal-elmar's anger was cold. 'The thoughts of one so great must needs be weighty,' said he softly, 'yet I know not what thought of more weight could break his repose than the care of his own carcase. He will be a master without people, or a bag of bones on the hillside, if he scorns the wisdom of Hazad son of Buldar. Blear eyes may see more than those lidded with sleep.'

The fat face of Mogru the Master grew dark, and his eyes were blood-shot with rage. He hated Tal-elmar, yet never before had the youth given him cause, save that he showed no fear in his presence. Now he should pay for that and his new-found insolence. Mogru clapped his hands, but even as he did so he remembered that there were none within call that would dare to grapple with the youth, nay, not three together; and at the same time he caught the glint of Tal-elmar's eye. He blanched, and the words that he had been about to speak, 'Slave's son and your brat', died on his lips. 'Hazad uBuldar, Tal-elmar uHazad, of this town, speak not so with the master of your folk,' he said. 'A watch is set, though ye who have not the ruling of the town in hand may know it not. I would wait till I have word from the watchers, whom I trust, that anything ill-boding has been seen. But if ye be anxious, then go summon the men from the fields.'

Tal-elmar observed him closely as he spoke and he read his thought clearly. 'Now I must hope that my father errs not,' he said in his heart, 'for less peril will battle bring me than the hate of Mogru from this day forth. A watch! Yea, but only to spy on the goings and comings of the townsfolk. And the moment I go forth to the field, a runner will go to fetch his servants and club-bearers. An ill turn have I done to my father in this hour. Well! He who begins with the hoe should wield it to the row's end.' He spoke therefore still in wrath and scorn. 'Go you to the knappers yourself,' he said, 'for you are wont to use these sly folk, and heed their tales when they suit you. But my father you shall not mock while I stand by. It may well be that we are in peril. Therefore you shall come now with us to the hill-top, and look with your own eyes. And if you see there aught to warrant it, you shall summon the men to the Moot-hill. I will be your messenger.'

And Mogru also through the slits of his eyelids watched the face of Tal-elmar as he spoke, and guessed that he was in no danger of violence if he gave way for this time. But his heart was filled with venom; and it irked him also not a little to toil up the hill. Slowly he rose.

'I will come,' he said. 'But if my time and toil be wasted, I shall not forgive it. Aid my steps, young man; for my servants are in the fields.' And he took the arm of Tal-elmar and leaned heavily upon him.

'My father is the elder,' said Tal-elmar; 'and the way is but short. Let the Master lead, and we will follow. Here is your staff!' And he released himself from the grasp of Mogru, and gave him his staff which stood by the door of his house; and taking the arm of his father he waited until the Master set out. Sidelong and black was the glance of the lizard-eye, but the gleam of the eye of Tal-elmar that it caught stung like a goad. It was long since the fat legs of Mogru had made such speed from house to gate; and longer since they had heaved his belly up the slippery hill-sward beyond the dike. He was blown, and panting like an old dog, when they came to the top.

Then again Tal-elmar looked out; but the high and distant sea was now empty, and he stood silent. Mogru wiped the sweat from his eyes and followed his gaze.

'For what reason, I ask, have ye forced the Master of the town from his house, and brought him hither?' he snarled. 'The sea lies where it lay, and empty. What mean ye?'

'Have patience and look closer,' said Tal-elmar. Away to the west highlands blocked the view of all but the distant sea; but rising to the broad cap of the Golden Hill they fell suddenly away, and in a deep cleft a glimpse could be seen of the great inlet and the waters near its north shore. 'Time has passed since we were here before, and the wind is strong,' said Tal-elmar. 'They have come nearer.' He pointed. 'There you will see their wings, or their wind-cloths, call them what you will. But what is your counsel? And was it not a matter that the Master should see with his own eyes?'

Mogru stared, and he panted, now with fear as much as for the labour of walking uphill, for bluster as he might he had heard many dark tales of the Go-hilleg from old women in his youth. But his heart was cunning, and black with anger. Sidelong he looked first at Hazad, and then at his son; and he licked his lips, but he let not his smile be seen.

'You begged to be my messenger,' he said, 'and so shalt thou be. Go now swiftly and summon the men to the Moot-hill! But that will not end thy errand,' he added, as Tal-elmar made ready to run. 'Straight from the fields thou shalt go with all speed to the Strand. For there the ships, if ships they be, will halt, most likely, and set men ashore. Tidings thou must win there, and spy out well what is afoot. Come not back at all, unless it is with news that will help our counsels. Go and spare thyself not! I command thee. It is time of peril to the town.'

Hazad seemed about to speak in protest; but he bowed his head, and said naught, knowing it vain. Tal-elmar stood one moment, eyeing Mogru, as one might a snake in the path. But he saw well that the Master's cunning had been greater than his. He had made his own trap, and Mogru had used it. He had declared a time of peril to the town, and he had the right to command any service. It was death to disobey him. And even if Tal-elmar had not named himself as messenger (desiring to prevent any secret word being passed to servants of the Master), all would say that the choice was just. A scout should be sent, and who better than a strong bold youth, swift on his feet? But there was malice, black malice, in the errand nonetheless. The defender of Hazad would be gone. There was no hope in his brothers: strong louts, but with no heart for defiance, save of their old father. And it was likely enough that he would not return. The peril was great.

Once more Tal-elmar looked at the Master, and then at his father, and then his glance passed to Mogru's staff. The flint-flash was in his eyes, and in his heart the desire to kill. Mogru saw it and quailed.

'Go, go!' he shouted. 'I have commanded thee. Thou art quicker to cry wolf than to start on the hunt. Go at once!'

'Go, my son!' said Hazad. 'Do not defy the Master. Not where he has the right. For then thou defiest all the town, beyond thy power. And were I the Master, I would choose thee, dear though thou be; for thou hast more heart and luck than any of this folk. But come again, and let not the Dark Ship have thee. Be not over-bold! For better would be ill tidings brought by thee living than the Sea-men without herald.'

Tal-elmar bowed and made the sign of submission, to his father and not to the Master, and strode away two paces. And then he turned. 'Listen, Mogru, whom a base folk in their folly have named their master,' he cried. 'Maybe I shall return, against thy hope. My father I leave in thy care. If I come, be it with word of peace, or with a foe on my heel, then thy master-ship will be at an end, and thy life also, if I find that he has suffered any evil or dishonour that thou couldst prevent. Thy knife-men and club-bearers will not help thee. I will wring thy fat neck with my bare hands, if needs be; or I will hunt thee through the wilds to the black pools.' Then a new thought struck him, and he strode back to the Master, and laid hands on his staff.

Mogru cringed, and flung up a fat arm, as if to ward off a blow. 'Thou art mad today,' he croaked. 'Do me no violence, or thou wilt pay for it with death. Heardest thou not the words of thy father?'

'I heard, and I obey,' said Tal-elmar. 'But first errand is to the men, and there is need now of haste. Little honour have I among them, for they know well thy scorn of us. What heed will they pay, if the Slave's bastards, as thou namest us when I am not by, comes⁹ crying the summons to the Moot-hill in thy name without token. Thy staff will serve. It is well known. Nay, I will not beat thee with it yet!'

With that he wrested the staff from Mogru's hand and sped down the hill, his heart yet too hot with wrath to take thought for what lay before him. But when he had declared the summons to the startled men in the acres on the south slopes and had flung down the staff among them, bidding them hasten, he ran to the hill's foot, and out over the long grass-meads, and so came to the first thin straggle of the woods. Dark they lay before him in the valley between Agar and the downs by the shore.

It was still morning, and more than an hour ere the noon, but when he came under the trees he halted and took thought, and knew that he was shaken with fear. Seldom had he wandered far from the hills of his home, and never alone, nor deep into the wood. For all his folk dreaded the forest¹⁰

Here the typescript text breaks off, not at the foot of a page, and the manuscript 'Continuation of Tal-Elmar' (as the name is now written) begins (see p. 422).

It was swift for the eye to travel to the shore, but slow for feet; and the distance was greater than it seemed. The wood was dark and unwholesome, for there were stagnant waters between the hills of Agar and the hills of the shoreland; and many snakes lived there. It was silent too, for though it was spring few birds built there or even alighted as they sped on to the cleaner land by the sea. There dwelt in the wood also dark spirits that hated men, or so ran the tales of the people. Of snake and swamp and wood-demon Tal-Elmar thought as he stood within the shadow; but it needed short thought to come to the conclusion that all three were less peril than to return, with lying excuse or with none, to the town and its master.

So, helped a little perhaps by his pride, he went on. And the thought came to him under the shadow as he sought for a way through swamp and thicket: What do I know, or any of my people, even my father, of these Go-hilleg of the winged boats? It might well be that I who am a stranger in my own people should find them more pleasing than Mogru and all others like him.

With this thought growing in him, so that at length he felt rather as a man who goes to greet friends and kinsmen than as one who creeps out to spy on dangerous foes, he passed unhurt through the shadow-wood, and came to the shore-hills, and began to climb. One hill he chose, because bushes clambered up its slope and it was crowned with a dense knot of low trees. To this cover he came, and creeping to the further brink he looked down. It had taken him long, for his way had been slow, and now the sun had fallen from noon and was going down away on his right towards the Sea. He was hungry, but this he hardly heeded, for he was used to hunger, and could endure toil day-long without eating when he must. The hill was low, but ran down steeply to the water. Before its feet were green lands end-ing in gravels, beyond which the waters of the estuary gleamed in the westering sun. Out in the midst of the stream beyond the shoals three great ships – though Tal-Elmar had no such word in his language to name them with – were lying motionless. They were anchored and the sails down. Of the fourth, the black ship, there was no sign. But on the green near the shingles there were tents, and small boats drawn up near. Tall men were standing or walking among them. Away on the 'big boats' Tal-Elmar could see [?others] on watch; every now and then he caught a flash as some weapon or arms moved in the sun. He trembled, for the tales of the 'blades' of the Cruel Men were familiar to his childhood.

Tal-Elmar looked long, and slowly it came to him how hope-less was his mission. He might look until daylight failed, but he could not count accurately enough for any use the number of men there were; nor could he discover their purpose or their plans. Even if he had either the courage or the fortune to come past their guards he could do nothing useful, for he would not understand a word of their language.

He remembered suddenly – another of Mogru's schemes to be rid of him, as he now saw, though at the time he had thought it an honour – how only a year ago, when the waning town of Agar was threatened by marauders from the village of Udul far inland,[11] all men feared that an assault would come, for Agar was a drier, healthier, and more defensible site (or so its towns-men believed). Then Tal-Elmar had been chosen to go and spy out the land of Udul, as 'being young, bold, and better versed in the country round'. So said Mogru, truly enough, for the towns-folk of Agar were timid and seldom went far afield, never daring to be caught by dark outside their homes. Whereas Tal-Elmar often, if he had chance and no labour called (or if it did, some-times), would walk far afield, and though (being so taught from babyhood) he feared the dark, he had more than once been benighted far from the town, and was even known to go out to the watch-hill alone under the stars.

But to creep into the unfriendly fields of Udul by night was another and far worse thing. Yet he had dared to do it. And he had come so close to one of the huts of watchmen that he could hear the men inside speaking – in vain. He could not understand the purport of their speech. The tones seemed mournful and full of fear [12] (as men's voices were at night in the world as he knew it), and a few words he seemed to recognize, but not enough for understanding. And yet the Udul-folk were their near neigh-bours – indeed though Tal-Elmar and his people had forgotten it, as they had forgotten so much, their near kin, part of the same people in past and better years. What hope then was there that he would recognize any single word, or even interpret rightly the tones, of the tongue of men alien from his own since the beginning of the world? Alien from his own? My own? But they are not my people. Only my father. And again he had that strange feeling, coming from where he knew not to this young lad, born and bred in a decaying half-savage people: the feeling that he was not going to meet aliens but kinsmen from afar and friends.

And yet he was also a boy of his village. He was afraid, and it was long before he moved. At last he looked up. The sun on his right was now going down. Between two tree-stems he caught a glimpse of the sea, as the great round fire, red with the light sea-mist, sank level with his eye, and the water was kindled to fiery gold.

He had seen the sun sink into the sea before, yet never before had he seen it so. He knew in a flash (as if it came from that fire itself) that he had seen it so, [? he was called,][13] that it meant something more than the approach of the 'King's time', the dark.[14] He rose and as if led or driven walked openly down the hill and across the long sward to the shingles and the tents.

Could he have seen himself he would have been struck with
wonder no less than those who saw him now from the shore.
His naked skin – for he wore only a loin-cloth, and little cloak
of … fur cast back and caught by a thong to his shoulder –
glowed golden in the [? sunset] light, his fair hair too was
kindled, and his step was light and free.

'Look!' cried one of the watchmen to his companion. 'Do you
see what I see? Is it not one of the Eldar of the woods that comes
to speak with us?'

'I see indeed,' said the other, 'but if not some phantom from
the edge of the [? coming] dark [? in this land accursed] it
cannot be one of the Fair. We are far to the south, and none
dwell here. Would indeed we were [? north away near to (the)
Havens].'

'Who knows all the ways of the Eldar?' said the watchman.
'Silence now! He approaches. Let him speak first.'

So they stood still, and made no sign as Tal-Elmar drew near.
When he was some twenty paces away his fear returned, and he
halted, letting his arms fall before him and opening his palms
outwards to the strangers in a gesture which all men could
understand.

Then, as they did not move, nor put hand to any weapon so
far as he could see, he took courage again and spoke, saying:
'Hail, Men of the sea and the wings! Why do you come here? Is
it in peace? I am Tal-Elmar uHazad of the folk of Agar. Who are
you?'

His voice was clear and fair, but the language that he used
was but a form of the half-savage language of the Men of the
Dark, as the Shipmen called them. The watchman stirred.
'Elda!' he said. 'The Eldar do not use such a tongue.' He called
aloud, and at once men tumbled out of the tents. He himself
drew forth a sword, while his companion put arrow to bow-
string. Before Tal-Elmar had time even to feel terror, still less to
turn and run – happily, for he knew nothing of bows and would
have fallen long before he was out of bowshot – he was surrounded by armed men. They seized him, but not with harsh
handling, when they found he was weaponless and submissive,
and led him to a tent where sat one in authority.

Tal-Elmar feels the language to be *known* and only veiled
from him.

The captain says Tal-Elmar must be of Númenórean race,
or of the people akin to them. He must be kindly treated. He

guesses that he had been made captive as a babe, or born of captives. 'He is trying to escape to us,' he says.

'A pity he remembers nothing of the language.' 'He will learn.' 'Maybe, but after a long time. If he spoke it now, he could tell us much that would speed our errand and lessen our peril.'

They make Tal-Elmar at last understand their desire to know how many men dwell near; are they friendly, are they like he is?

The object of the Númenóreans is to occupy this land, and in alliance with the 'Cruels' of the North to drive out the Dark People and make a settlement to threaten the King. (Or is this while Sauron is absent in Númenor?)

The place is on estuary of Isen? or Morthond.

Tal-Elmar could count and understand high numbers, though his language was defective.

Or does he understand Númenórean? [*Added subsequently:* Eldarin – these were Elf-friends.] He said when he heard the men speak to one another: 'This is strange for you speak the language of my long dreams. Yet surely now I stand in my own land and do not sleep?' Then they were astonished and said: 'Why did you not speak so to us before? You spoke like the people of the Dark who are our enemies, being servants of our Enemy.' And Tal-Elmar answered: 'Because this tongue has only returned to my mind hearing you speak it; and because how should I have known that you would understand the language of my dreams? You are not like those who spoke in my dreams. Nay, a little like; but they were brighter and more beautiful.'

Then the men were still more astonished, and said: 'It seems that you have spoken with the Eldar, whether awake or in vision.'

'Who are the Eldar?' said Tal-Elmar. 'That name I did not hear in my dream.'

'If you come with us you may perhaps see them.'

Then suddenly fear and the memory of old tales came upon Tal-Elmar again, and he quailed. 'What would you do to me?' he cried. 'Would you lure me to the black-winged boat and give me to the Dark?'

'You or your kin at least belong already to the Dark,' they answered. 'But why do you speak so of the black sails? The black sails are to us a sign of honour, for they are the fair night before the coming of the Enemy, and upon the black are set the silver stars of Elbereth. The black sails of our captain have passed further up the water.'

Still Tal-Elmar was afraid because he was not yet able to imagine black as anything but the symbol of the night of fear. But he looked as boldly as he could and answered: 'Not all my kind. We fear the Dark, but we do not love it nor serve it. At least so do some of us. So does my father. And him I love. I would not be torn from him not even to see the Eldar.'

'Alas!' they said. 'Your time of dwelling in these hills is come to an end. Here the men of the West have resolved to make their homes, and the folk of the dark must depart – or be slain.'

Tal-Elmar offers himself as a hostage.

There is no more. At the foot of the page my father wrote 'Tal-Elmar' twice, and his own name twice; and also 'Tal-Elmar in Rhovannion', 'Wilderland', 'Anduin the Great River', 'Sea of Rhûn', and 'Ettenmoors'.

NOTES

1　In the rejected version of the opening section of the text the story begins: 'In the days of the Great Kings when a man could still walk dryshod from Rome to York (not that those cities were yet built or thought of) there lived in the town of his people in the hills of Agar an old man, by name *Tal-argan* Longbeard', and Tal-argan remained the name without correction in the rejected page. The second version retained 'the Great Kings', the change to 'the Dark Kings' being made later on.

2　This paragraph was later placed within square brackets.

3　Both versions had 'the Fourth King', changed on the second to 'the North King' at the same time as 'the Great Kings' was changed to 'the Dark Kings' (note 1).

4　In the rejected version the father of Tal-argan (Hazad) was named *Tal-Bulda*, and the place of the battle was the valley of *Rishmalog*.

5　At this point the rejected first page ends, and the text becomes primary composition. A pencilled note at the head of the replacement page proposes that Buldar father of Hazad should be cut out, and that it should be Hazad himself who wedded the foreign woman Elmar (who is unnamed in the rejected version).

6　The name typed was *Dur nor-Belgoth*, corrected to *Gorbelgod*.

7　'the Fourth King' was not corrected here: see note 3.

8　*knappers*: a 'knapper' was one who broke stones or flints. This word replaced 'tinkers', here and at its occurrence a little later.

9　I have left the text here as it stands.

10 A marginal note here says that Tal-elmar had 'no weapon but a casting-stone in a pouch'.

11 The text as written had 'far inland, and all men feared', corrected to 'far inland. All men feared'. I have altered the text to provide a complete sentence, but my father (who was here writing at great speed) doubtless did not intend this, and would have rewritten the passage had he ever returned to it.

12 In the margin my father wrote that the village of Udul was dying of a pestilence, and the marauders were in fact seeking food in desperation.

13 The conclusion of the text is in places in excruciatingly difficult handwriting, and the words I have given as 'he was called' are doubtful: but I can see no other interpretation of them.

14 Against the words on p. 434 'never daring to be caught by dark outside their homes' my father wrote: 'Dark is "the time of the King".' As is seen from a passage on p. 436, the King is Sauron.

INDEX

The very great number of names occurring in this book, and the frequency of reference in many cases, would require an index much larger than those of the previous volumes if the same pattern were followed; and I have therefore reduced it by omitting three categories of names. Each of these is concentrated in a small part of the book, and in the case of the second and third it seems to me that, even apart from considerations of overall length, the utility of detailing alphabetically such complex material is very doubtful.

(1) *Hobbit names*. The number of names of individual Hobbits, including all the recorded changes, is so large (about 370) that I have restricted the references to the entry *Hobbit-families*. Here all the family-names are listed, with references to every page (including all the geneaological tables) where the name of the family, or of any member of the family, occurs. Exceptions to this are Bilbo and Frodo Baggins, Sam Gamgee, Meriadoc Brandybuck, and Peregrin Took, who are entered separately in the index on account of the large number of references to them.

(2) *The Calendars*. All page-references for the names of the *months* and the *days of the week* in the different languages are collected under those entries. Under *Calendars* are listed the entries in the index concerning the matter of Chapter IV, and references to the Elvish names and terms are given under *Calendars* and *Seasons*.

(3) *The Common Speech*. References are given under *Common Speech* and *Hobbit families* to all pages where 'true' names (supposed to underlie the 'translated' names) appear, these being only exceptionally included in the index.

The entries *Second Age*, *Third Age*, *Fourth Age* and *Shire-reckoning* do not include simple references to dates. Some names spelt with initial C in *The Lord of the Rings* will be found under *K*: *Calimehtar*, *Calimmacil*, *Calmacil*, *Castamir*, *Cemendur*, *Cirith Ungol*, *Ciryaher* (*Ciryahir*), *Ciryandil*.

J R R Tolkien

The History of Middle-earth
Volume 1
The Book of Lost Tales 1

Edited by Christopher Tolkien

The Book of Lost Tales stands at the beginning of the entire conception of Middle-earth and Valinor, for the *Tales* were the first form of the myths and legends that came to be called *The Silmarillion*. Embedded in English legend and English association, they are set in the narrative frame of a great westward voyage over the Ocean by a mariner named Eriol (or Ælfwine) to Tol Eressëa, the Lonely Isle, where Elves dwelt; from them he learned their true history, the *Lost Tales of Elfinesse*. In the Tales are found the earliest accounts and original ideas of Gods and Elves, Dwarves, Balrogs and Orcs; of the Silmarils and the Two Trees of Valinor; of Nargothrond and Gondolin; of the geography and cosmology of the invented world.

'In these Lost Tales we have the scholar joyously gambolling in the thickets of his imagination ... a Commentary and Notes greatly enrich the quest.' THE DAILY TELEGRAPH

'Affords us an almost over the shoulder view into the evolving creative process and genius of J R R Tolkien in a new, exciting aspect ... the superb, sensitive and extremely helpful commentary and editing done by Christopher Tolkien makes all this possible' MYTHLORE

ISBN 978 0 261 10222 4

J R R Tolkien

The History of Middle-earth
Volume 2
The Book of Lost Tales 2

Edited by Christopher Tolkien

This second part of *The Book of Lost Tales* includes the tales of Beren and Lúthien, Túrin and the Dragon, and the only full narratives of the Necklace of the Dwarves and the Fall of Gondolin. Each tale is followed by a commentary in the form of a short essay, together with the texts of associated poems, and contains extensive information on names and vocabulary in the earliest Elvish languages.

'Christopher Tolkien shows himself to be his father's son, delving into the question of Elvish genealogies ... he gives the reader histories of each of the character's names as it evolved in the course of Tolkien's revisions ... Tolkien devotees will rejoice'   THE NEW YORK TIMES BOOK REVIEW

'The *Tales* will be appreciated by those who have read *The Silmarillion* and wish to examine how Tolkien improved his story and style from their original form, and how eventually *The Lord of the Rings* came to stand independently with only a few hints from the early mythology'   BRITISH BOOK NEWS

ISBN 978 0 261 10214 9

J R R Tolkien

The History of Middle-earth
Volume 3
The Lays of Beleriand

Edited by Christopher Tolkien

This, the third volume of *The History of Middle-earth*, gives us a privileged insight into the creation of the mythology of Middle-earth, through the alliterative verse tales of two of the most crucial stories in Tolkien's world – those of Túrin and Lúthien. The first of the poems is the unpublished *Lay of the Children of Húrin*, narrating on a grand scale the tragedy of Túrin Turambar. The second is the moving *Lay of Leithian*, the chief source of the tale of Beren and Lúthien in *The Silmarillion*, telling of the Quest of the Silmaril and the encounter with Morgoth in his subterranean fortress.

Accompanying the poems are commentaries on the evolution of the history of the Elder Days. Also included is the notable criticism of *The Lay of Leithian* by C S Lewis, who read the poem in 1929.

'A worthy addition to *The History of Middle-earth*'

MALLORN

'Anyone loving the original books will want to study this one'

DAILY MAIL

ISBN 978 0 261 10226 2

J R R Tolkien

The History of Middle-earth
Volume 4
The Shaping of Middle-earth

Edited by Christopher Tolkien

In this fourth volume of *The History of Middle-earth*, the shaping of the chronological and geographical structure of the legends of Middle-earth and Valinor is spread before us.

We are introduced to the hitherto unknown *Ambarkanta* or 'Shape of the World', the only account ever given of the nature of the imagined Universe, accompanied by maps and diagrams of the world before and after the cataclysms of The War of the Gods and the Downfall of Númenor. The first map of Beleriand is also reproduced and discussed.

In *The Annals of Valinor* and *The Annals of Beleriand* we are shown how the chronology of the First Age was moulded; and the tale is told of Aelfwine, the Englishman who voyaged into the True West and came to Tol Eressea, the Lonely Isle, where he learned the ancient history of Elves and Men.

Also included are the original 'Silmarillion' of 1926, and the *Quenta Noldorinwa* of 1930 – the only version of the myths and legends of the First Age that J R R Tolkien completed to their end.

'Illustrates the development, depth and richness of J R R Tolkien's personal mythology'   VECTOR

ISBN 978 0 261 10218 7

J R R Tolkien

The History of Middle-earth
Volume 5
The Lost Road
and other writings

Edited by Christopher Tolkien

At the end of 1937, J R R Tolkien reluctantly set aside his work on the myths and heroic legends of Valinor and Middle-earth and began *The Lord of the Rings*.

This fifth volume of *The History of Middle-earth* completes the examination of his writing up to that time. Later forms of *The Annals of Valinor* and *The Annals of Beleriand* had been composed, *The Silmarillion* was nearing completion in a greatly amplified form, and a new Map had been made. The legend of the Downfall of Númenor had entered the work, including those central ideas: the World Made Round and the Straight Path into the vanished West. Closely associated with this was the abandoned 'time-travel' story *The Lost Road*, linking the world of Númenor and Middle-earth with the legends of many other times and peoples.

Also included in this volume is *The Lhammas*, an essay on the complex languages and dialects of Middle-earth, and an 'etymological dictionary' containing an extensive account of Elvish vocabularies.

ISBN 978 0 261 10225 5

J R R Tolkien

The History of Middle-earth
Volume 6
The Return of
the Shadow

Edited by Christopher Tolkien

The Return of the Shadow is the first part of the history of the creation of *The Lord of the Rings*, a fascinating study of Tolkien's great masterpiece, from its inception to the end of the first volume, *The Fellowship of the Ring*.

In *The Return of the Shadow* (the abandoned title of the first part of *The Lord of the Rings*) we see how Bilbo's 'magic' ring evolved into the supremely dangerous Ruling Ring of the Dark Lord; and the precise, and astonishingly unforeseen, moment when a Black Rider first rode into the Shire. The character of the hobbit called Trotter (afterwards Strider or Aragorn) is developed, though his true identity seems to be an insoluble problem. Frodo's companions undergo many changes of name and personality; and other major figures appear in unfamiliar guises: a sinister Treebeard, in league with the Enemy, and a ferocious, malevolent Farmer Maggot.

The book comes complete with reproductions of the first maps and facsimile pages from the earliest manuscripts.

ISBN 978 0 261 10224 8

J R R Tolkien

The History of Middle-earth
Volume 7
The Treason of Isengard

Edited by Christopher Tolkien

The Treason of Isengard continues the account of the creation of
The Lord of the Rings started in the earlier volume, *The Return of
the Shadow.*

It traces the great expansion of the tale into new lands and new
peoples south and east of the Misty Mountains: the emergence
of Lothlórien, of Ents, of the Riders of Rohan, and of Saruman
the White in the fortress of Isengard.

In brief outlines and pencilled drafts dashed down on scraps of
paper are seen the first entry of Galadriel, the earliest ideas of
the history of Gondor, and the original meeting of Aragorn and
Éowyn, its significance destined to be wholly transformed.

The book also contains a full account of the original map which
was to be the basis of the emerging geography of Middle-earth;
and an appendix examines the Runic alphabets, with illustrations
of the forms and an analysis of the Runes used in the Book of
Mazarbul found beside Balin's tomb in Moria.

ISBN 978 0 261 10220 0

J R R Tolkien

The History of Middle-earth
Volume 8
The War of the Ring

Edited by Christopher Tolkien

The War of the Ring takes up the story of *The Lord of the Rings* with the Battle of Helm's Deep and the drowning of Isengard by the Ents, continues with the journey of Frodo, Sam and Gollum to the Pass of Cirith Ungol, describes the war in Gondor, and ends with the parley between Gandalf and the ambassador of the Dark Lord before the Black Gate of Mordor. Unforeseen developments that would become central to the narrative are seen at the moment of their emergence: the palantír bursting into fragments on the stairs of Orthanc, its nature as unknown to the author as to those who saw it fall, or the entry of Faramir into the story ('I am sure I did not invent him, I did not even want him, though I like him, but there he came walking through the woods of Ithilien').

The book is illustrated with plans and drawings of the changing conceptions of Orthanc, Dunharrow, Minas Tirith and the tunnels of Shelob's Lair

ISBN 978 0 261 10223 1

J R R Tolkien

The History of Middle-earth
Volume 9
Sauron Defeated

Edited by Christopher Tolkien

In the first section of *Sauron Defeated* Christopher Tolkien completes his fascinating study of *The Lord of the Rings*. Beginning with Sam's rescue of Frodo from the Tower of Cirith Ungol, and giving a very different account of the Scouring of the Shire, this section ends with versions of the hitherto unpublished Epilogue, in which, years after the departure of Bilbo and Frodo from the Grey Havens, Sam attempts to answer his children's questions.

The second section is an edition of *The Notion Club Papers*, now published for the first time. These mysterious papers, discovered in the early years of the twenty-first century, report the discussions of an Oxford club in the years 1986-7, in which, after a number of topics, the centre of interest turns to the legends of Atlantis, the strange communications received by other members of the club from the past, and the violent irruption of the legend into the North-west of Europe. Closely associated with the *Papers* is a new version of the *Drowning of Anadûnê*, which constitutes the third part of the book. At this time the language of the Men of the West, *Adûnaic*, was first devised, and the book concludes with an account of its structure provided by Arundel Lowdham, a member of the Notion Club, who learned it in his dreams.

ISBN 978 0 261 10305 4

J R R Tolkien

The History of Middle-earth
Volume 10
Morgoth's Ring

Edited by Christopher Tolkien

In *Morgoth's Ring*, the first of two companion volumes, Christopher Tolkien describes and documents the later history of *The Silmarillion*, from the time when his father turned again to 'the Matter of the Elder Days' after *The Lord of the Rings* was at last achieved. The text of the Annals of Aman, the 'Blessed Land' in the far West, is given in full; while in writings hitherto unknown is seen the nature of the problems that J R R Tolkien explored in his later years, as new and radical ideas, portending upheaval in the old narratives, emerged at the heart of the mythology, and as the destinies of Men and Elves, mortals and immortals, became of central significance, together with a vastly enlarged perception of the evil of Melkor, the Shadow upon Arda.

The second part of this history of the later *Silmarillion* is concerned with developments in the legends of Beleriand after the completion of *The Lord of the Rings*.

ISBN 978 0 261 10300 9

J R R Tolkien

The History of Middle-earth
Volume 11
The War of the Jewels

Edited by Christopher Tolkien

In *The War of the Jewels* Christopher Tolkien takes up his account
of the later history of *The Silmarillion* from the point where it
was left in *Morgoth's Ring*. The story now returns to Middle-
earth, and the ruinous conflict of the High Elves and the Men
who were their allies with the power of the Dark Lord. With
the publication in this book of all J R R Tolkien's later narrative
writing concerned with the last centuries of the First Age, the
long history of *The Silmarillion*, from its beginning in *The Book
of Lost Tales*, is completed; and the enigmatic state of the work at
his death can be understood.

The book contains the full text of the *Grey Annals*, the primary
record of *The War of the Jewels*, and a major story of Middle-earth
now published for the first time: the tale of the disaster that
overtook the forest people of Brethil when Húrin the Steadfast
came among them after his release from long years of captivity
in Angband, the fortress of Morgoth.

ISBN 978 0 261 10324 5